Explore New Zealand and a world of love through these three novels by Gloria Bevan, all from Harlequin's Romance Library

Beyond the Ranges... However shabby and isolated the store was, Lesley owned it now. And she meant to keep it, despite Stuart Carrington's plans for the property—which didn't include her. She'd never admit defeat to that arrogant and supremely self-confident man! (#1459)

Vineyard in a Valley... Suddenly Tracy found herself wanting to stay in New Zealand to change her image. Her beautiful headstrong cousin had vanished after jilting Cliff Crane. Now Tracy was left to sort out matters as best she could with Cliff's difficult domineering brother, Stephen. (#1608)

The Frost and the Fire... Liz's dream of a riding center for disabled children finally seemed possible, so she promptly purchased some land in Auckland. One problem remained: Peter Farraday, Liz's new neighbor, a man who wanted the land for himself. But falling in love with Peter didn't make Liz any less determined.... (#1682)

**Another collection
of Romance favorites...
by a best-selling Harlequin author!**

In the pages of this specially selected anthology are three delightfully absorbing Romances—all by an author whose vast readership all over the world has shown her to be an outstanding favorite.

For those of you who are missing these love stories from your Harlequin library shelf, or who wish to collect great romance fiction by favorite authors, these Harlequin Romance anthologies are for you.

We're sure you'll enjoy each of the engrossing and heartwarming stories contained within. They're treasures from our library... and we know they'll become treasured additions to yours!

The first anthology of 3 Harlequin Romances by

Gloria Bevan

Harlequin Books

TORONTO • LONDON • LOS ANGELES • AMSTERDAM
SYDNEY • HAMBURG • PARIS • STOCKHOLM • ATHENS • TOKYO

Harlequin Romance anthology 61

Copyright © 1977 by Harlequin Enterprises Limited. Philippine copyright 1982.
Australian copyright 1982. All rights reserved. Except for use in any review, the
reproduction or utilization of this work in whole or in part in any form by any
electronic, mechanical or other means, now known or hereafter invented,
including xerography, photocopying and recording, or in any information storage or
retrieval system, is forbidden without the permission of the publisher, Harlequin
Enterprises Limited, 225 Duncan Mill Road, Don Mills, Ontario, Canada M3B 3K9.

All the characters in this book have no existence outside the imagination of the
author and have no relation whatsoever to anyone bearing the same name or
names. They are not even distantly inspired by any individual known or unknown to
the author, and all the incidents are pure invention.

These books by Gloria Bevan were originally published as follows:

BEYOND THE RANGES
Copyright © 1970 by Gloria Bevan
First published in 1970 by Mills & Boon Limited
Harlequin edition (#1459) published January 1971

VINEYARD IN A VALLEY
Copyright © 1972 by Gloria Bevan
First published in 1972 by Mills & Boon Limited
Harlequin edition (#1608) published July 1972

THE FROST AND THE FIRE
Copyright © 1973 by Gloria Bevan
First published in 1973 by Mills & Boon Limited
Harlequin edition (#1682) published May 1973

Cover Photography © Tom Mareschal/The Image Bank
of Canada

ISBN 0-373-20061-7

First edition published as Harlequin Omnibus in June 1977

Second printing June 1982

The Harlequin trademarks, consisting of the words HARLEQUIN ROMANCES
and the portrayal of a Harlequin, are trademarks of Harlequin Enterprises Limited;
the portrayal of a Harlequin is registered in the United States Patent and
Trademark Office and in the Canada Trade Marks Office.

Printed in Canada

Contents

Beyond the Ranges 9

Vineyard in a Valley 221

The Frost and the Fire 405

Beyond the Ranges

Lesley's heart sank when she first saw the store. So this was her legacy—a run-down building in the wilds of New Zealand forest country! But it was hers, and somehow she had to make the business succeed.

The fact that Stuart Carrington wanted her to sell out only added to her determination. She'd never sell to that man!

Stuart's response shocked her, though. "I'll wait," he said confidently, "or get it the other way...."

CHAPTER ONE

As SHE RATTLED over the fern-fringed highway, Lesley tried to convince herself that the ominous clanking noises emerging at ever increasing intervals from her decrepit motor scooter were really nothing to be concerned about. The heavy old machine was mobile, wasn't it? And that was all that mattered. All she asked of it was that it carry her safely to her destination in the New Zealand timber woods in the blue distance ahead.

"Want a tow, miss?"

A logging truck, piled high with radiata pine, swept past. The driver, bronzed chest bare, turned to throw a grin toward the small girl mounted on the elderly machine. But Lesley, her scarlet jacket whipping around her slim figure, dark blond hair streaming behind her in the breeze, was intent on the bush-shadowed roadway and failed to catch the man's appreciative backward glance.

Skirting the waters of a jewellike blue lake that glimmered through a screen of native bush, she took a rise leading toward the somber green of the sea of pine forests clothing the hills above.

A champagne day! Ahead of her, a heat haze danced in the shimmering air above the hot bitumen, and the serrated line of pine plantations she was fast approaching were cut blade sharp against the blue. And the air! Unbelievably fresh and clear, it was spiced with the aromatic tang of the bush. If this was a typical New Zealand day in high summer, she was glad, glad, glad that she'd stood firm on her decision to come out to this country and claim her inheritance—in spite of the elderly solicitor's somewhat discouraging attitude.

Her eyes took in the unfamiliar scenes flashing past: an arm of the lake, where small cabins, probably belonging to trout fishermen, nestled among water willows; a fishing lodge on the lakeshore; a small jetty running out into the water. But all the time her thoughts wandered.

Could it be a mere three weeks since she had returned one night to her London bed-sitter to find an official important-looking document awaiting her? Important! The contents were breathtaking. Indeed, Lesley had read the communication through twice before fully taking in the import of the legal phrases.

> Regret to advise... death of your father, James William Monteith... inherit freehold property situated at Waione, Urewera Country, in the North Island of New Zealand, comprising thirty acres of land, this including a store with living quarters. Also a legacy of £600....

She skipped a number of legally-worded paragraphs that conveyed nothing to her.

> Would be glad to receive your instructions re disposal of the property. If you could kindly call at the above address at your convenience....

Lesley's first reaction to the letter was one of shock. To think that her father had been living out there in New Zealand! If only she'd known she would have tried to obtain his address, got in touch with him. She pushed aside the unwelcome thought that had he so wished he could have communicated with her at any time.

Of her mother, Lesley retained little more than a shadowy recollection of someone tall and kind and fair haired. The aunt who had taken care of Lesley when she was a small child had told her that her parents had gone their separate ways when she was two years old. Her mother, always delicate in health, had died shortly afterward. Many times during those early years when Lesley found herself shuffled from one family connection to another, she would try to picture her father. The only gleam of information she had of him was a rumor that he had been thought to have left the country for Australia some years previously. But none of her mother's relatives had the slightest interest in the whereabouts of James Monteith, and for a long time now Lesley had tried not to think of him. A father who hadn't wanted her, who had never troubled himself to find out how she fared, wasn't really worth pining for.

So the years had drifted uneventfully by. School, high school, followed by a period of training in secretarial work. Then had come employment in a busy London office, where it seemed to Lesley that life was slipping by to the metallic click-clicking of the typewriter keys.

Had she been offered any choice in the matter, she thought rebelliously at times, she would have preferred to work in a more creative field. Something...something.... She didn't quite know what. Not very clever. Not very talented. Not very anything outstanding. She liked to sew and cook—ordinary things like that. But then she was an ordinary sort of person.

The letter from the solicitor, it seemed to her, offered her a way out—even if it led her halfway across the world to a land in the South Pacific of which she knew practically nothing.

Promptly at nine Lesley presented herself in the shadowy edifice of the office of Grey & Beckett.

Mr. Grey—stout, bald, with shrewd blue eyes in a smooth pink-and-white plump face that put Lesley in mind of an overgrown baby—saw her seated opposite him at the massive desk.

"I'm Miss Monteith—Lesley Monteith—"

"Yes, yes, we've been expecting you." The elderly man consulted the papers laid out on the desk. "I understand you have had no contact with your father for a number of years."

"No." Lesley leaned toward him. "You see, I never knew him, not really."

"Hmm...understandable...under the circumstances...." Mr. Grey was skimming a legal document. "In point of fact, our New Zealand office anticipated some difficulty in tracing you."

The dark blue eyes, set at a slight angle in the pale face,

widened in surprise. "But he knew my aunt's address—my mother's family—"

Mr. Grey shook his shiny dome. "It appears that your father was under some misapprehension. Apparently he imagined that you had been legally adopted by strangers shortly after he left the country seventeen years ago."

"And he went on thinking that...all those years." Lesley was speaking her thoughts aloud. In the dim light of the shadowed office Mr. Grey failed to catch the sudden tide of happiness that lighted the features of the girl seated opposite. So that was why her father had made no effort to contact her. He had been fearful of disturbing the even tenor of a new life that had, in point of fact, never existed. All the same, it was good to know.

With a start she brought her mind back to the leisurely measured tones of the elderly man. "I have a letter here from our New Zealand branch office in Wellington. It seems they have a buyer in view—someone living in the district who is willing to purchase the property and store at a reasonable price." He cleared his throat. "More than reasonable, in fact. The prospective buyer is only awaiting the new owner's signature to the documents relating to the sale before taking over the land. And I shouldn't imagine," the smooth tones ran on, "that there would be any difficulty about the terms of the sale."

"Oh, but I couldn't *sell* it!" Lesley burst out. "I've only just got it! And my father—he wanted me to have it! I'm going out there!" she went on in a flurry of excitement. "I made up my mind about it the minute I got your letter! Sell it? Goodness, no!"

Mr. Grey appeared slightly taken aback at Lesley's eager acceptance of her inheritance. "The New Zealand office," he advised ponderously, "recommend immediate sale."

"Bother the New Zealand branch!"

The solicitor disregarded Lesley's involuntary interruption. Or perhaps she thought he hadn't heard her. "They would like you to realize the fact that the district is isolated, situated in the heart of heavy bush country—a most remote locality. No doubt in the ordinary way such a property would be most difficult to sell. I strongly advise you, Miss

Monteith," he warned, "to reconsider your decision. I have no wish to discourage you, but—" he fingered a document on his desk "—this seems scarcely the place for a young girl—" He broke off, eyeing her inquiringly. "I presume it is your intention to go out to New Zealand alone?"

"Oh, yes," Lesley's face was radiant. "But I don't mind that. I haven't any friends who could afford the trip. And besides...." Her voice died away and the unspoken words hung in the air between them. "No one else would want to come away out there with me anyway."

"Precisely." The elderly man put his fingertips together and leaned back in his leather-covered swivel chair. He cleared his throat warningly. "Only fair to let you know the facts. The matter of the financial state of the store, for instance. The turnover appears extremely low, scarcely worth the trouble of keeping the place open—very low indeed."

"Oh, but I can change all that! At least—" she caught his stern glance "—I can try!"

"And why not?" The solicitor suddenly found himself thinking aloud. He gave himself a mental shake. Had he said that? He couldn't imagine what had possessed him to make such a statement. It must be the effect of the unseasonable sunshiny day, almost like spring, and something about this eager-eyed girl with her sensitive mouth and clear excited blue eyes. The thoughts ran irrelevantly through his mind. Not that she was outstandingly pretty: a small girl with a slim, clean-cut figure; a dusting of freckles over a slightly tip-tilted nose; smoky-fair hair drawn back from a generous forehead and tied with a black chiffon scarf. Indeed, there were better lookers right here in his own office. But damn it all, there was something about her. Could be it was that trick she had of gazing directly into his eyes with a rapt attention that was undeniably flattering. Or that curving sensitive mouth. She had spirit, too, no doubt about that! For a crazy moment he found himself wishing that he were twenty years old himself with a small legacy, a stake in a few acres of forest land on the other side of the world. And a chance... a chance....

With a determined swing of his swivel chair he jerked himself back to reality.

"Well, my dear, if I can't manage to dissuade you in your decision not to sell out, all I can do is help. Now about the legacy... I could let you have a check at once, if— you wish it?"

"Oh, *please*!" A random shaft of sunlight slanted across the dingy office furniture, turning Lesley's eyes to a dark sapphire. "If you would? You see, I want to go out to New Zealand by air. It's quicker. And I won't need to wait for a booking. The rest of the money will keep me going until I get the store paying."

If you do, the solicitor intended to reply. To his amazement, however, the words emerged instead in a heartfelt, "Good for you, Miss Monteith! I hope you make a go of it!" Rising to his feet, he stood politely aside as the girl moved toward the open doorway. "You'll keep in touch, I hope. Let me know how things go with you out there in—" just in time he remembered the odd-sounding name, the correct Maori pronunciation of which he could only guess, and substituted "—the forest country."

"Yes, of course. And thank you for your advice, Mr. Grey." The dark blue eyes with their black-fringed lashes looked up at him with that direct gaze. And there was a catch in the light laugh that was quite enchanting. "Even if I didn't follow it!"

A girl like that.... Mr. Grey forgot that he hadn't at first sight considered her particularly attractive. And she was going to bury herself in the wilds of the New Zealand forest country!

With a sigh he seated himself once more at his desk, pressing a buzzer to summon his secretary. He'd have to let the New Zealand branch office know about the girl's decision not to sell. Advise them of her decision to take up the property in person.

LESLEY'S MOOD OF WILD ELATION lasted all the while she gave notice of leaving at the office where she had been employed for the past two years and made a booking with a travel agency for a BOAC flight leaving London for New Zealand in a week's time.

The following few days seemed to take on the impression

of a dream from which she might awaken at any moment. There was exciting shopping to do. Cool summer frocks and shorts and tops to be purchased, all in vivid colors and fashioned in light washable fabrics. And one, just one special frock for dancing—a wild extravagance that in the wilds of the New Zealand timber woods she would probably never have an opportunity of wearing.

"Something special coming up?" The friendly saleswoman was wrapping the silver sheath in protective tissue.

"That's what I'm hoping!" Lesley smiled with sheer happiness. To wear such a frock one would indeed have need of a special occasion. But you never could tell what fate could have in store. Just look at the astonishing events that had come her way during the past week!

Baggage suitable for air travel was her next purchase. Lesley chose fiber suitcases, light and inexpensive, for the air fare combined with the cost of a complete new summer wardrobe had made deep inroads in her legacy. And she must conserve the remainder, even if it meant forfeiting a stay in the exciting stopovers where the airliner was scheduled to touch down during the long flight to New Zealand: Rome—Athens—Singapore—Sydney—Perth.

There were, of course, the necessary formalities to be attended to; letters to be written to friends and relatives. So much to be done; so little time. But at last Lesley found herself seated awaiting takeoff in the luxuriously appointed cabin on the great BOAC VC 10 jet.

There was no one at the airport to see her off. Not that she had expected to glimpse a familiar face among the groups gathered on the tarmac. The few friends she possessed would be at work in the city. And her relatives lived too far away to make a special journey to London merely for the purpose of bidding her farewell.

"Fasten your safety belts, please. Fasten your safety belts...." As the pleasant tones of the air hostess echoed through the cabin, a reddish fair head was suddenly thrust toward Lesley as the girl seated at her side leaned across to wave energetically from the window.

"Sorry—" she threw Lesley an apologetic grin "—but it's aunt! She's just this minute arrived. Late as usual! Seeing she's giving me this trip, bless her kind heart, I'd hate to think she'd missed out altogether on seeing me off."

The other girl continued to wave as the engines of the great plane throbbed into life. Soon they were taxiing along the tarmac toward the runway. Then the giant wings lifted and they were airborne. The groups waiting on the ground below dwindled to dwarflike proportions, then vanished from sight.

"I'm Anna." The other girl sank back in her seat and smiled companionably across at Lesley. "And you're Lesley Monteith—saw your name on your luggage."

Lesley's slanting glance took in a girl older than herself, twenty-eight or so, dressed with a casual elegance: sparrow thin with slightly protruding teeth, a thin alive face and short-cropped hair.

"What's taking you to the other side of the world?" Anna inquired lightly. And in the lively interested gaze Lesley forgot her first impression of plainness. "Business? Or pleasure?"

"Both, actually." Idly Lesley eyed the approaching air hostess, immaculate in her attractive uniform, as she paused to answer a child's inquiry, hand a magazine to a businessman seated opposite. "I've been left some property in New Zealand. In a place I've never even heard of. My... father left it to me." How strange the word "father" sounded on her lips—unfamiliar, yet oddly satisfying, as though at long last she possessed someone, some family, of her own.

"Nice for you." The pale eyes moved toward her, but it was obvious to Lesley that the other girl had little interest in the event that had caused such an upheaval in the even tenor of her own life.

"How about you?" Lesley's inquiry was prompted more by politeness than curiosity. "Have you an interest out in New Zealand, too?"

"You could put it that way." Anna gave a wry smile. "I call it men!"

"Men?" Lesley echoed lamely. "What sort of men?"

"The marrying sort, actually." Her companion laughed on catching sight of Lesley's astonished expression. "Oh, *one* would do! Just to make aunt happy, of course." In spite of the light words a shadow lingered in the pale green eyes.

If it hadn't been so utterly improbable, the thought crossed Lesley's mind, she could almost have imagined that the other girl's sandy eyelids were swollen and reddened with weeping. Certainly she appeared curiously pale and strained. But perhaps she had recently been ill.

"Aunt paid for this trip I'm taking out to New Zealand," Anna was saying. "She's even arranged for me to take coach trips through both Islands when we arrive. New clothes, too! The lot! Not that she can't well afford it, but still.... I think actually she meant it as a sort of consolation prize for me after—" the light tones broke "—after the wedding yesterday. Guess someone must have told her that there are supposed to be three men to every girl out there in Maoriland. And besides, it was probably the most far-off place she could think of—away from everything. Smoke?"

With a jerky movement she extended a cigarette case. Lesley shook her head and the other girl lit a cigarette and inhaled deeply. "I'd have got over it at home somehow I guess—after all, there's always work. Hospital work's my line—occupational therapy—and I love it." Suddenly the low tones were ragged with emotion. "That's where I met Darren. He'd collected a broken arm in a motor smash—" She stopped short and the pale eyes took on a faraway expression. "There's no accounting for love, is there? Darren wasn't any better-looking than other men, or any brainier, or better educated. He was just...Darren. Oh, what's the use? It's over. I've got to get that into my head. It's over...over...Look, I'll show you his picture."

She drew from her shoulder bag a photograph depicting a smiling, fair-haired young man, his arm lying lightly around the shoulders of a girl who, although she appeared much plumper at the time the picture was snapped, was undoubtedly Anna herself.

"But I don't quite get it." Glancing up from the photograph, Lesley chose her words carefully. "If you—if he...."

"But that's the point!" The other girl's smile was a wry grimace. "He married Lois, my young sister! The wedding was yesterday. I just happened to know him first, be the one who introduced them to each other." She gave a high brittle laugh. "Lil' ole Cupid, that's me!" She exhaled a cloud of smoke and regarded Lesley consideringly. "Guess you wouldn't know what it's like, being on the losing end of a love affair?"

Lesley shook her head. "No."

"I didn't think you would! You've got that look about you somehow. Sort of sure of yourself. I bet you've never even been in love! *Really* in love, I mean! Fathoms deep overboard, so that nothing else in the whole world matters—" She stopped short. "It doesn't work, you know, thinking, *It couldn't happen to me. I wouldn't let any man mean so much to me as all that.*

It was so exactly the thought passing through Lesley's mind that she gave a self-conscious laugh. "Well, anyway," she said matter-of-factly, "nothing like that ever has happened to me."

"Not even boyfriends?"

"Heavens, yes! There've been screeds of them." Lesley laughed lightly. "But they didn't mean a thing. Honestly—" the clear blue eyes surveyed the other girl's strained features "—sometimes I can't help wondering what this thing called love is all about."

"Believe me, it's plain hell," the other girl said brokenly. "And I should know! Engaged for three years to Darren, waiting to be married until he completed his engineering studies. And then—" the thin hand holding the cigarette between two fingers trembled "—one holiday I took him home and he and my sister Lois...." She made an expressive gesture. "Just like that! One of those things you read about. Only this was for real! Oh, at first I tried to fool myself, pretended that it was just a passing attraction between them, told myself it wouldn't last. I think they even tried to fight it themselves at the beginning, Lois and Darren. But it wasn't any use. All I could do was release him. I told him everything was over between us, that I didn't care any more. If only," she sighed on a long breath, "it were the truth. I guess I overplayed my part slightly, though. They insisted on my being bridesmaid at their wedding, and that took some doing. But I got through the day somehow.

Beyond the Ranges 19

At least, I suppose I did. Everyone told me afterward that I looked great and the whole thing went off wonderfully. I guess the only one there who wasn't fooled was aunt. She knows me too well. So you see," she went on after a moment as Lesley, searching her mind, could find nothing suitable to say, "I really owe aunt something, wouldn't you say? Nothing less than a six-foot-tall, husky New Zealander! Preferably a wealthy sheep-station owner. But the main thing is the man! It wouldn't matter about love—" the thin lips curved cynically "—that's just a trap anyway." She gave her light brittle laugh and gazed unseeingly toward a drifting shape suspended like a fairy castle in the translucent blueness beneath the great wing. "It couldn't happen, of course. Things like that never do. But wouldn't it be wonderful if it could!"

As the journey proceeded it seemed to Lesley that her flight companion, having unburdened her problems to a stranger, had made up her mind to put aside everything else and devote herself to the enjoyment of the trip, for during the ensuing hours of the long flight Anna made no further mention of the past, but sat smoking incessantly as she read and chatted desultorily with Lesley.

As for Lesley, her enjoyment of the air trip was heightened by the companionship of a girl belonging more or less to her own age group. She was glad to have found someone with whom to discuss the wonders of the places where they touched down on the long flight over the Indian Ocean— magic names that to Lesley had hitherto been no more than brightly colored pictures splashed over a travel folder: "Who'd have thought Singapore would be so hot!" And later: "Oh, look, Anna—Perth coming up! I can see high buildings and a river."

At last, in blazing sunshine, the great VC 10 jet touched down at Auckland's modern airport, and the two girls boarded the blue-and-silver coach that took them through a smooth winding highway bordered with incredibly green paddocks, dotted with grazing sheep and cattle.

Presently the route to the city led through recently constructed housing blocks, where the brightly painted timber bungalows were surrounded with sweeping green lawns and gay flower borders. Soon, however, they were entering an older, more established area, where the gracious timber homes of an earlier era were shaded by tall trees and flowering shrubs. The sweeping lawns facing the highway were brilliant with a profusion of blossoming shrubs and vividly hued creepers: hibiscus, bougainvillea and the great fringed leaves of softly waving banana palms.

All too soon they found themselves joining in the stream of traffic moving toward the city. Lesley gazed entranced at the blue waters of the Waitemata Harbor with its bush-covered Islands of the Gulf.

One day, she promised herself, she'd return to explore the attractions of this colorful seaport city with its endless sandy bays, its bush-filled gullies and red roofs gleaming among lush greenery.

Together the two girls strolled down the slope of Auckland's main street, where wide glass windows displayed an attractive selection of high-fashion summer merchandise. Pink geraniums trailed from hanging baskets high above the pavements and tall tufted cabbage trees fluttered their green fans at the curbside in the harbor breeze. At the foot of Queen Street, overseas liners crowded the wharves and cranes traced their abstract patterns like giant steel giraffes against the skyline.

The two girls entered the wide doors of the South Pacific Hotel, where Anna was booked for a short stay before departing on a sightseeing tour of the North Island. In the foyer, beneath the sightless marble stare of a life-size figure of Captain Cook, the Yorkshireman who had explored the far-flung islands of the South Seas so long ago, Lesley turned toward Anna.

"When you're through with sightseeing," she suggested, "why not come and stay with me at Waione for a week? You've got my address. Who knows—" Lesley flashed her bright smile "—I might even be able to provide you with that hulking big New Zealand sheep farmer you want! From what I can make out, the area's famous for trout fishing, forestry, deer stalking—" she threw Anna a teasing glance "—real 'hunting' territory—that is, if you're still interested by then."

The other girl laughed in turn. "I might just take you up on that!"

"I'll be expecting you, then. Bye!" Lesley turned away and moving out into the brilliant sunshine, made her way through the lunch-hour crowds of coolly attired men and girls in the colorful street.

In the travel agency, however, she encountered more difficulty than she had anticipated in arranging her transport to Waione. "Thing is," the helpful young clerk explained, "it's pretty rugged country down that way. Only two coaches a week and none now until Wednesday." Were her friends expecting her arrival in Waione quite soon?

Leslie didn't take the trouble to explain that she wasn't expected. At least, for a moment she wondered if the London solicitor had informed anyone of her expected arrival. But who was there to tell? The only person who could be in the slightest degree interested in her movements was her father's friend, who had discovered James Monteith's will, and to him she would be merely an unknown girl.

"You could get as far as Rotorua today by coach," the clerk was suggesting. "After that you might be able to connect with something going through the Urewera, if you're lucky! Maybe you could even pick up a lift in a freighter going Waione way, if you don't mind roughing it!"

Well, it was the best she could do.

Rotorua, the clerk informed her, was the center of a spectacular thermal wonderland, so she could spend a pleasurable day or two there taking the many tourist trips in the area with its geysers and boiling mud pools.

But Lesley had but one objective in mind at the moment, and that was to press on toward her destination as quickly as possible.

Nevertheless, on reaching Rotorua she had to admit that had she not been so anxious to proceed, she would have enjoyed a stay in this fascinating thermal area with its pungent sulphurous air. Here the scrolled carved cross timbers of Maori meeting houses gleamed from the roadside; boiling mud pools bubbled in the nearby Maori village and plumes of steam gushed high in the air from the hot pools close by the water-lily ponds and colorful rose gardens of the Government Gardens situated in the heart of the city.

She was fascinated, too, by the souvenir stores with shady verandas and displays of native craftsmanship and local curios, and it was a new experience to stroll along the wide streets that were crowded with overseas tourists, local *pakehas* and well-dressed Maoris.

As she strolled along one of the main thoroughfares Lesley's eye was caught by a motor showroom, filled with new and secondhand vehicles of all descriptions. Now there was an idea! For a brief period in England she'd once owned a motor scooter, and if the distance to Waione weren't too far.... The first thing she must do was to invest in a road map of the district.

"I was wondering," Lesley inquired of the stout, middle-aged woman standing behind the counter of the stationery shop, "how far it is to Waione, in the Urewera Country. Have you a road map?"

Business at the moment was slack, and the two leaned over the map, spread out over the magazines lying on the counter. "You see," Lesley explained, "I've got to get there today."

"Bad luck!" The older woman was sympathetic. "You've just missed a delivery van going down that way. And there's no coach through today."

"I thought—" Lesley was studying the map "—that I might buy a motor scooter and take off myself."

"It's a seventy-mile trip," the woman murmured doubtfully.

Lesley glanced up, her eyes alight with interest. "But that's not far!"

"Not on a smooth straight road maybe, but the uphill stretches slow you down, and the downward grades are awfully steep. Besides, when you turn off the bitumen, the roads are loose metal. And the dust! I know all about it," the older woman added with a friendly smile, "because my niece did exactly the same trip three weeks ago. She was on holiday from university—bought a secondhand motor scooter and took off from here with the intention of touring the district. But when she got as far as Waione she rang through and told me that she'd stay in the bush forever if it meant coming back over those roads again by motor scooter."

But Lesley didn't wish to hear anything that would dampen her enthusiasm for her newly formed plan. "Well, if *she* could do it...." Curiosity, however, got the better of her and she couldn't resist inquiring, after a moment, "What happened?"

"Oh, she came back by coach," the woman replied. "Had the scooter sent back by truck. There it is, out there in the shed." Lesley followed her glance toward a small timber outbuilding, where a battered old machine was propped against a wall. "She asked me to give it a coat of paint to cover up the rust, sell it and get what I could for it."

"Well, then," Lesley cried eagerly, "that solves my problem! Could I...."

"I really couldn't recommend it," the woman demurred with a worried frown. "It was a secondhand job when my niece bought it, plenty of rust on it. And after a run on those metal roads anything could have happened to it—anything!"

"I'll take a chance," Lesley said promptly, and thrust determinedly aside the thought of the niece who had lost her nerve on the journey that she was about to attempt.

"But the roads are so steep," the shop assistant persisted in a troubled tone. "You have no idea what they're like! High divides and ravines and deep gorges. I really don't think—"

But Lesley swept aside the older woman's objections.

"Don't *worry*. You've given me fair warning. And I'm quite happy to give it a go. Look, it's up to me."

"Ye-es, I suppose so...." To Lesley, the woman's next remark was even less encouraging. "And I suppose if it does break down on the way and leave you stranded in the bush, you can always wait and get a lift. Someone's bound to come along sooner or later. There's always the odd tourist—" she brightened perceptibly "—and all those forestry men, deer hunters, opossum trappers—whatever."

Lesley, setting aside the humiliating prospect of being forced to await rescue on a lonely country road by these husky men of the great outdoors, pulled herself together.

It was absurd to think that she couldn't safely travel a distance of a mere seventy-odd miles by motor scooter on a main highway. At the recollection of the reason why the scooter was available at a bargain price, her courage almost failed her, but she thrust the unwelcome thought aside. At this rate she'd never reach Waione, and that was all that mattered at the moment—taking up her inheritance and getting started on the exciting new life that awaited her.

At what seemed to Lesley a ridiculously low figure, the matter of the scooter sale was accomplished, and once again she smothered the niggling inner voice that warned her that she might, she just might, be taking on more than she'd bargained for.

It was a simple matter to arrange for her baggage to be sent on by coach to her destination, and it took only a short time to arrange with the local authorities for a driving license and change of ownership papers. A check at the nearest garage for oil and petrol, a pull of the starter and she was off, spinning along the streets in the hot sunshine, breathing in the strange sulphurous odour of the thermal activity all around her.

And if the old machine was making a strange roaring noise and various parts rattled alarmingly, well, what of it? You could scarcely expect a smoothly running, perfect vehicle at the throwaway price for which she had acquired it!

It was exhilarating to feel the wind rushing past her, and Lesley's spirits soared as she left the lake waters behind and found herself in open country. As she sped along the smooth gray highway she was aware of sloping green paddocks, divided by closely barbed fences and dotted with grazing sheep; of tea-tree loading ramps built alongside the road.

A chartered tourist coach lumbered past her. It was followed by a stock transporter and trailer, tightly packed with sheep. But at least, Lesley thought, approaching a young Maori driver astride his sturdy stock pony, his dogs frisking about him, here was someone whom she was confident of passing on the long winding ascent.

Presently she reached a fork in the road and a signpost

loomed above her: Rainbow Mountain. Lesley's swift sideways glance took in the vividly hued clays in shades ranging from salmon to rose, from white to saffron, of the high volcanic peak rising from the surrounding bush and low scrub. She hadn't yet left the area of the thermal activity behind, judging by the steam rising from around the lower slopes of the mountain.

Then the smooth bitumen swept between the vast undulating sea of pine plantations on either side. Long shadows splashed the roadway, and Lesley found herself riding through a sea of pines. Lightened with the brighter hues of saplings and cut with frequent firebreak clearings, the plantations merged into the distance. The road appeared to go on and on—a gray ribbon stretching toward the horizon.

Lesley decided to slow to a stop. She'd pause for a cigarette and a look around. The disadvantage of driving a vehicle was that one missed so much of the scenery, and this place was worth seeing, definitely! A somber green world sparkled with the clean sharp fragrance of pine needles in the sun.

Pulling off the road, she propped up the scooter and threw herself down on the dried grass edging the highway. Then, pushing her long fair hair behind her ears in a characteristic gesture, she drew out a cigarette. It was pleasant to lie back and look around her, agreeably conscious of the smell of smoke rising from her cigarette and mingling with the resinous tang of the pine-scented air.

As Lesley gazed over the shimmering landscape she reflected that here there seemed nothing but sky and pines. Even the long undeviating road appeared empty of traffic, except for the Maori driver and his dogs, still some distance away. At least.... Idly she eyed the Land Rover that had swept into view and was rapidly approaching her. To her surprise, however, instead of sweeping past the vehicle jerked to a stop and a tall man leaped from the vehicle and came striding purposefully toward her.

She stared up into the man's set face in astonishment as, without a word, he hurried past her, and only then, glancing over her shoulder, did she become aware of the plume of smoke that was rising from the clustered ferns behind her.

As the stranger's workmanlike boots stamped out the licking tongues of flame, Lesley was flooded with an odd feeling of apprehension. Hadn't there been a notice, somewhere back on this long straight road: Extinguish Pipe And Cigarettes. Cigarette! She made to throw it away, but a strong tanned hand jerked it from her grasp. Flinging it to the ground, the stranger proceeded to stamp it into the dried earth with those thick-soled dusty boots.

"Didn't you see *that*?"

Lesley found herself gazing up into the most angry face and steeliest gray eyes she had ever encountered. He was pointing directly over her head, and obediently her eyes rose to the board with its all too clear black lettering: Fire May Cost You Your Life. Be Careful.

"N-no," she stammered, and could have bitten out her tongue as she heard herself add, "Not...that one."

"*Any* one! You must have seen *some* of the fire warnings along the route!"

He stood glaring down at her: a tall man with soft dark hair, blazing gray eyes and a formidable jaw; wide shouldered, narrow hipped, sparsely built, with an air of contained vitality and tensed energy. It showed in the light gray eyes—or did they only appear light against the deeply bronzed skin? The thoughts raced through her mind. A man who in other circumstances—*any* other circumstances—she might have found attractive, if only for his dark and forceful good looks.

"Don't you know," he demanded with barely contained anger, "that there's a lookout post up there on the summit of Rainbow Mountain and every one of the peaks around here—" a muscular bronzed arm embraced the distant hills in an extensive gesture "—with fire watchers whose job it is to report on smoke signals like this! Lucky for you," he added tersely, "that it wasn't the ranger who happened along, instead of me!"

Lucky! Lesley opened her mouth, then closed it again without speaking. Any other man, she was certain, would have been easier to deal with than this one.

"If you're talking about that fire that you've just stamped out," she said at last with heightened color, "I didn't even

Beyond the Ranges

know it was there! Oh, I smelled smoke, of course, but I thought...." Under the impact of that direct gray stare, her voice trailed away. It sounded so lame an excuse. And he had the evidence of his own eyes—that wretched cigarette! She should have taken note of the highway warnings in respect of the ever present dangers of fire in the forest area. But all the same, she thought indignantly, it wasn't she who was responsible for the fire in the dried fern of the roadside.

"In this heat, you could have had the whole place blazing within an hour!"

So he didn't believe her. He still thought that she was the cause of the leaping flames. He would!

Well, I didn't! But she didn't quite find the courage to say the words aloud. It was no use arguing with him. He simply ignored her protests. He'd made up his mind that she was the culprit, and that was that.

He threw her a piercing look from beneath beetling black brows as he jerked a dark head toward the motor scooter. "Trouble?"

"Oh, no!" Lesley said, thankful to escape the subject of fire. "She's going fine. I just stopped here for a look at the view, and a cig—" She stopped short.

To avoid having to meet that accusing stare once again, she made a pretense of retying the laces of her dark blue sneakers. If all the forestry workers in this district proved to be as belligerent as this one, she didn't know how she was going to cope.

"Well, don't next time!" The stranger put a bronzed hand to his forehead in a salute that Lesley was to find increasingly familiar during the next few months. Then he turned on his heel and without another word slid behind the wheel of the Land Rover and roared away.

And good riddance, Lesley told herself, staring after the vehicle as it sped along the pine-shaded highway. Odd, though, how his cultured voice didn't match his rough working garb. But even the heavy serviceable slacks, open-necked cotton shirt, and thick-soled boots seemed in no way to detract from his lean virile appearance. Bad tempered, overbearing, masterful—and yet a man one couldn't easily forget. She only wished she could, Lesley thought, mounting her red motor scooter and giving a vicious pull at the starter.

But the unexpected encounter had shaken her more than she cared to admit, and as she took the long road cutting through the vast plantations, she asked herself how she could possibly have overlooked the significance of the warning forest protection notices erected at frequent intervals along the route. She was aghast at the thought of the flickering flames that could so easily by now have grown to a ravaging sheet of fire, crackling through the timber-covered slopes. All the same, he might have shown some politeness toward her in the matter, instead of brushing aside her protestations of innocence, disbelieving her explanation, glowering at her as though she had already set the entire timber woods alight.

A few miles farther along the road, the green expanse of pine-clad slopes gave way to fenced farmlands and sheep-threaded hills. Presently Lesley found herself approaching a small settlement with its modern housing block of gaily painted timber homes and a new attractive shopping area surrounded by parking bays. A name above a store caught her eye. So that was Murupara township!

How pleasant the trip was proving to be, she mused, and how unexpectedly easy. But even as the thought came to her, she left the small township behind, and the smooth gray bitumen of the highway gave place to a rough, winding metal road.

A water tanker lumbered past, and for a moment Lesley was blinded by the cloud of fine yellow dust rising around her. As it cleared she endeavored to steer her machine in the dusty imprints of the tire tracks. But a timber truck, piled high with gigantic logs, swept up beside her, showering her with flying stones and crowding her toward the road edge with its dangerously loose metal. Lesley skidded, then righted herself, lurched over a boulder and went on.

And now as the highway narrowed, climbing endlessly toward the blue peaks that merged into the distance, Lesley began to realize just why the previous owner of her battered vehicle had decided to make this a one-way trip.

Thrown mercilessly from side to side, half blinded with

Beyond the Ranges

dust, she jolted on over the bush-covered ridges, where she could see only a short distance of the road ahead as it looped around the mountains. The gritty taste of dust on her lips, she plunged down into a shadowed valley, passing a Maori meeting house with its carved crossed barge board and grotesque figurehead.

Then once again she was climbing, swinging around the hairpin bends as the road wound upward to meet a wisp of cloud on the skyline, up and up. Presently a road sign swung into view: To Mount Tarapounamu (Mountain of a Thousand Peaks).

A thousand! Lesley blinked the fine dust from her eyes. Somewhere in the green depths of the dense native forest surrounding her she caught the tinkle of an unseen waterfall. A bellbird's glorious chime of notes echoed from the red flowers of a rata tree at the roadside. Lesley zig-zagged down the narrow road toward a small one-way bridge over a stream. And there amid the wooded peaks, in what seemed to her to be a spot hundreds of miles from the nearest civilization, her motor scooter suddenly lost power and with a final ominous clank, spluttered to a stop.

Just at first she wasn't unduly concerned. She could do with a rest from driving. Indeed, she felt as though every bone in her body had been attacked with a very hard, very efficient hammer. The pungent crystal-clear fragrance of the bush was a delight, and there was even a miniature waterfall trickling down between the ferns on a bushy bank. As well as she could, Lesley washed her heated face, then let the cool water trickle over her hands. She'd mislaid her hand mirror, but no matter. On this dusty journey attempts at renewing her makeup were useless. And, anyway, somewhere along the route she'd got past caring about her appearance. She dried face and hands on a small towel from her overnight bag strapped to the carrier of the scooter, then settled down in the long grass at the roadside to await rescue. After all, there had been no lack of traffic on this nightmare stretch of mountainous highway, even if it had consisted in the main of logging trucks, stock transporters and, of all things, a beer tanker!

But the shadows were lengthening, and as the minutes

dragged by Lesley was struck by a frightening thought. Supposing no further traffic passed this way? Perhaps the truck drivers had now all returned from their day's work in the forest. Darkness would come early here in the depths of the silent forest. What if she were forced to spend the night on the lonely highway in this isolated area, alone?

And now the minutes seemed weighted, so slowly did they go by. To make matters worse, she had forgotten to wind her watch and she had no idea of the time. The bellbird's chime of notes echoed once again, but now, amid the somber silence of the bush, the fluted call sounded indescribably lonely and desolate. Then she heard it! At last! For, straining her ears, she caught the faint but unmistakable sound of an approaching vehicle. Stepping into the metal of the roadway, she watched expectantly as a Land Rover swung around a bend, hurtled down the steep grade and jerked to a stop beside her.

Oh, *no*! One glance toward the man leaning from the open vehicle was sufficient to make Lesley wish frantically that it had been any other vehicle rather than this particular one that had happened along.

The tall dark man unfolded his long length from the Land Rover and stepped toward her. "Not *you* again!" The amused glint in the gray eyes was even more infuriating to Lesley than the lecture that she had been forced to endure from the lips of this stranger.

"Yes, it's me!" she said crossly. "I'm sorry to be such a nuisance, but my scooter's let me down."

"Let's see what the trouble is." The skeptical look he sent her before turning toward the machine left Lesley with the distinct impression that there could be nothing of a mechanical nature wrong with the motor scooter. The fault would almost certainly prove to lie in her inexpert handling of it.

She was almost relieved when after a brief inspection and a few unsuccessful pulls at the starter, the heavy old machine remained silent.

"Shot!" the stranger announced briefly, adding, at Lesley's puzzled expression, "Finished! It's a miracle you got this far. Looks like a few vital parts have rattled off somewhere between here and there." He shot her one of the accusing stares that Lesley was fast coming to dread. "Didn't you have a checkup before you took off on this trip?"

Flustered and uneasy, Lesley shook her head. "No. You see, I only bought it today—in Rotorua. I—" She broke off as she caught the man's gray-eyed, incredulous look.

"*Bought* it? In Rotorua? That?" He aimed an idle kick at the immobile old machine and swung around to pinpoint her with that direct uncompromising look. "What sort of firm would sell you a beat up old junk heap like that?"

"It wasn't a firm," Lesley broke in unhappily, conscious of the man's disapproving glance. "It was...a friend. She didn't know—she'd only used it once," Lesley went on breathlessly. "She sold it to me in good faith—"

"Some friend!" There he was, disbelieving her once again! If anyone else came along the road at this moment, she'd stop them and beg them for a lift. She'd show this arrogant male that she wasn't entirely dependent on his mercy. She didn't have to stand here and listen to his scathing comments. She'd— But a furtive glance over the man's broad shoulder only confirmed her dreary suspicion that the road would be empty of traffic. It was.

"It was awfully cheap," Lesley protested weakly. "And I didn't know then about the roads. At least, someone tried to tell me, but I—" Oh, blast, she told herself furiously. Why was she bothering to make excuses to this hateful stranger, with his infuriating knack of somehow always contriving to put her in the wrong?

The man propped the machine against the trunk of a massive kauri tree and swung around to eye her inquiringly. "How far were you aiming to get today?"

"How far?" It took her a moment to realize that he evidently mistook her for a student, touring the district by motor scooter. Well, that was all right with her. All she wanted was to reach Waione without further delay. The means weren't important, although she wished that she weren't forced to be dependent on this formidable stranger, of all folk, for transport. Aloud she said, "I thought...Waione."

"Good! That's no problem. I'm on my way there right

now!" Striding toward the Land Rover with its tattered side curtains and dust-covered wheels, he flung open the door on the passenger side. "Jump in!"

Lesley hesitated. The dark blue eyes, clear and candid as a child's, swept anxiously up to the man's face. "But what about my scooter?"

"She'll be right, mate!" With this cryptic utterance he closed the door, went around to the driver's side and slid behind the wheel. "I'll send one of the boys back for it with the truck," he added carelessly as he let in the clutch and the vehicle moved off. "They can drop it in to the nearest garage, get her fixed—if that's possible! You sure bought trouble when you bought that! For my money I'd say you could toss it in the nearest ditch."

With an effort of will, Lesley bit back the angry words that trembled on her lips. "Send it to the garage, please," she said stiffly.

As they swept along the rough road and the man slowed to take a blind bend, Lesley wondered who "the boys" could be. She made the mental observation that if *he* sent them to collect the old machine, the job would be as good as done. He had the air of a man accustomed to organizing, to giving orders—the man in command. Except, of course, where she herself was concerned.

Lesley watched a hawk skim down from a cloudless sky toward the lifeless body of an opossum sprawled on the roadway.

The four-wheel-drive vehicle took the winding curves with ease and they made good time, speeding up the wooded peaks where Lesley, glancing back, could glimpse only a fragment of the winding road, far, far below. They plunged down into a shadowed valley, passing a picnic ground, a small clearing beside a trout stream, where a tent gleamed beside a caravan on the grassy patch of cleared ground. Great kauri trees lined the road, the straight trunks piercing the blue, as they sped upward once again, and dust-coated flax brushed the vehicle with its long spears as they went on.

Once they passed a lookout with its notice: Walking Track. Nine Miles. Lesley mused how pleasant it would be on such a hot day as this to wander along the marked track in the green shade of the great forest giants. Gazing over the bush-clad ridges, she was content to enjoy the newness and novelty of her surroundings. She was fascinated by this wild and untamed splendor, where the panorama unfolded before her of range upon range, a green sea of native forest sweeping westward from the Pacific and stretching to the horizon.

Her companion, for his part, seemed intent on the road. At least he made little effort at conversation, and Lesley wondered if he were still feeling annoyance at being forced to transport the silly girl who hadn't even the sense to read a warning notice in clear letters that was placed directly over her head, nor the foresight to check the roadworthiness of a motor vehicle before setting out on a hazardous journey over mountainous roads.

Having had her attention drawn to road signs in no uncertain terms, she now found herself taking particular note of them. There was one flashing by at her side:

> Urewera National Park
> Native Forest
> 2,420 Feet.

Urewera! Then she must be nearing her destination.

"Waione coming up!" The man's voice broke into her thoughts.

"Oh." She peered forward, taking in the small settlement ahead with its cluster of brightly painted timber houses set against a backdrop of bush-clad hills. Blue smoke drifted up from the chimneys and hung in the still air below the high wooded peaks.

"Put you down at the store," her companion was saying. "Okay?"

"Oh yes, *please.*" A quiver of excitement ran along her nerves. *Her* store. For there could surely be only one such building in this tiny township, where the only folk in sight were a group of Maori women, chatting over the dividing fence between their neat and attractive homes, and a small boy, the soles of his bare feet clearly toughened to the hardness of leather, who was happily chasing a cattle dog along the rough metal of the road.

Lesley was unaware that her hands were clasped tensely together as the Land Rover moved along the dusty track and pulled up alongside a rough timber building with peeling white paint work.

She blinked. It wasn't possible! For where was the neat little shop with its sparkling windows and attractive display of foodstuffs and household wares? Where the acres of cleared green land she'd expected to find here?

What she saw was a shabby building set against a hill clothed in dense native bush. The paint work was flaked off in patches, so that she could barely decipher the faded red lettering above the veranda: Monteith's General Store.

Swiftly her glance ran over the premises. "Living quarters at the back," the solicitor had informed her. Living quarters! Those small boxlike rooms, evidently added to the store as an afterthought. Her gaze moved over the surround of white concrete at the entrance toward the glass windows on either side of the open entrance door of the small timber dwelling. She took in a collection of rifles and hunting knives that lay together with a tangle of leather sandals of all sizes on the timber floor. In the opposite window, a woman's cotton frock, bleached in patches from the effect of the brilliant sunshine pouring through the unprotected glass, hung dejectedly by one shoulder from a twisted wire hanger.

A huge Alsatian dog lay asleep beside the entrance, and inside Lesley caught a glimpse of long, half-empty shelves running the length of the room. As she watched, a woman's figure moved past the opening. Lesley could imagine the interior of the place only too well.

That solicitor in London—that Mr. Grey—he had tried to tell her something of the truth, but deliberately blinding herself to his warning, she had clung stubbornly to her own dream picture. And now....

"But this can't be it!" Torn between tears and laughter, she scarcely realized that she was giving voice to her thoughts. "Not this shabby old place!"

"Watch it!" The man at her side made no move to get

out of the vehicle but sat eyeing the small decrepit building, one bronzed, well-shaped hand resting lightly on the steering wheel. "You're speaking of my property—I hope."

"Yours?" Lesley stared across at him in bewilderment.

"That's right! I'm taking over any day now. Monty was one of the best," he went on reflectively. "Too bad he bought it in that pileup with a logging truck down in the ravine. Days later I came across his will among his papers in the back room. Only by chance, actually. Seems the place is left to the only relative he had in the world. Funny he never mentioned him before, but then Monty never was one to give away much about his affairs. Seems this bloke hangs out in London. City type. Shouldn't be any problem there about his wanting to sell out at a good price." He sent her a lopsided grin. "Can you see a bloke like this Leslie Monteith character showing up out here in the outback and coping with an outfit like that?"

The jerk of his dark head indicated a decrepit truck now pulling up beside them. Lesley followed his gaze toward the cluster of sporting dogs and piled rifles in the rear of the vehicle. As she watched, three powerfully built Maori hunters, wearing peaked caps, black bush shirts and tough working slacks, hunting knives in holsters at their belts, climbed out of the truck and sauntered across the road.

"Hiya, boss!"

"Good day!"

The man at her side grinned and raised a lean tanned hand in friendly salutation. Then the group moved toward the store, stepping noiselessly over the strip of concrete in rubber-soled hunting boots.

"Oh, I don't know—" Lesley endeavored to subdue the quirk of her lips "—maybe he could, given time."

"You reckon?" He shot her a skeptical glance. "Well, here's hoping he won't take the trouble! I may as well tell you—" the soft deep tones were alive with enthusiasm "—I've got a thing about this place! Had it on my mind for years. But it never seemed possible to get the project off the ground—not until this chance came up."

The man's eyes narrowed. "The way I figure it, Monty's place is the perfect answer for the survival camp I'm planning to set up here—a sort of bushcraft school, if you get what I mean? Buying land anywhere in this area is right out of the question. Most of it belongs to the Maoris and it's just about impossible to get hold of. I've got a few thousand acres myself just over the hill there. Nine hundred acres of it in beef, cattle and sheep; the rest is still covered in native bush and I've let it out in milling rights. But this—" the man's eager glance swept over the shabby building and moved upward to the bush-covered rise behind "—this is ideal for my purposes, bang in the center of the forest country yet right on the main road. The bush is second-growth timber—no use for milling, but just right for a camp. There's even a stream running through it. About the right amount of land, too. I've got it all figured out."

Have you indeed? Lesley brought her thoughts back to the man's vibrant tones.

"I'll leave the old store, renew the walls, strengthen the timbers, maybe slap on a new roof. Then up goes a community hall, library, gymnasium, washrooms, kitchen. I'm counting on bunkrooms and huts to accommodate about thirty kids. You know yourself how little those city kids ever know of the real outback. Never get a chance to see it, even, let alone survive in rugged conditions. It's not good enough. I want them all to have a chance, and if they want to take it, this is the place! There are wild pigs and deer and opossums here by the hundred, rare blue mountain duck by the river...."

Clearly, Lesley thought, he had forgotten all about her. All he wanted was an audience to whom he could expound his precious plans and theories. She brought her mind back to the man's animated tones.

"The camp would be available to school parties under strict surveillance—that goes without saying. There'd be training officers from the forestry service—they're with me all the way in this. The kids could learn bushcraft, biology, whatever, right here on the premises! The girls— Well, they could get cracking on how to prepare meals. None of the fancy stuff. Good basic things like porridge, curry and rice, stews, Maori bread. Then they could get familiar with the forest, learn first aid.

"The boys could be taught safe firearm handling, fire fighting, river crossing, bushcraft, opossum shooting. Go bush! The Mountain Safety Council was pretty keen on the idea, too, when I put it to them. They see it as a campaign to lower the national death toll from accidental shooting, drowning, camping, exploring. It's something that's badly needed—especially for city kids. What I want to do is get 'em out in the wind and rain and sun. Let 'em earn the right to become Children of the Mist—" He broke off on catching Lesley's puzzled expression. "Never heard of the Tuhoi tribe of the mighty Ureweras? That's the name they gave themselves, the first inhabitants here, long before the white man came. No wonder they thought of themselves as children of the mist, up here in the rain forests of the mountains."

But Lesley was scarcely listening. Once again she had trouble concealing her inner amusement. Why, he was so keen to buy the land— *her* land—that he couldn't stop talking of it; outlining his plans for the future. One only had to catch the note of enthusiasm lacing the man's low tones to know that he was desperately anxious to acquire the property. It meant a lot to him. If he only knew that it was she, the "Leslie Monteith character," who had the power to sell or to retain her inheritance, just as she decided. Well, he might as well understand right now that his survival camp idea was an impossible dream—at any rate, as far as her land was concerned.

"All I'm waiting for now," the man was saying, "is the signature to the bill of sale from this Leslie bloke in London, so here's hoping he won't take long in making up his mind. Once I get the green light from him, I'm away." He swung toward her with an apologetic grin. "Sorry, I get carried away when I start on this survival camp scheme. Mustn't hold you up any longer, Miss...."

As he hesitated, Lesley drew a deep breath. This, she thought triumphantly, will wipe that stupid grin from his face. After all, he had already put her in an embarrassing position today. He hadn't even given her a chance to explain her innocence in the matter of the flames licking along the sun-dried fern. He had simply assumed that she was responsible for the fire. True, he had given her a lift over the ranges, but it was no more than any passing motorist would have done—courtesy of the road. She could scarcely imagine that the "damsel in distress" angle would cut much ice with him. She still smarted under the impact of those stern eyes and accusing stare.

"*Monteith!*" she said, clearly and distinctly. She looked directly into the gray eyes, blissfully unaware of two grease spots streaked down her sun-reddened cheeks; of smoky-blond hair sprayed out in little damp tendrils from her heated forehead. But even to reap the full benefit of her revenge on this formidable stranger, she couldn't seem to sustain that deep intent gaze. And to her dismay her voice emerged in a nervous squeak, "*L-Lesley* Monteith!"

CHAPTER TWO

"GOOD GRIEF!" He was regarding her intently, and this time, Lesley thought with a thrust of satisfaction, it was the man's turn to look surprised. One thing was for sure. She had scattered to the four winds his plans concerning making use of the property for some sort of bush survival camp.

"Lesley!" A grin tugged at the corners of the chiseled well-shaped lips. "Well, what d'you know!" He stared at her incredulously. "And you've come all that way—"

"And you," she broke in nervously, "you're the man who made the offer for the place?"

"Right." He continued to eye her narrowly. "Carrington's the name—Stuart Carrington. Bit of a shock, hmm, all this?" He glanced in the direction of the dilapidated building, where at the moment the group of Maori hunters were emerging from the opening. Passing the Land Rover, they grinned, white teeth flashing in copper faces, before crossing the stony road and climbing back into the waiting truck.

"Not to worry, though," the man was saying lightly, "I can take it off your hands any old time you like. Just say the word." The deep soft tones took on a warm inflection. "I've been dreaming up this bushcraft camp project for years. Tried to sell Monty the idea once or twice, but he wasn't having it on. Guess he'd got used to living in the old place and couldn't stir himself to make a move. Said he was too old to sell up and make new plans."

"And was he?"

"Heck, no! On the right side of fifty. He could have put his hand to half a dozen different sort of jobs. He was like that, handy with his hands—" He broke off. "But I guess you know all this."

"Please go on," Lesley said in a low voice. "I didn't

know him at all. Not really. He and my mother parted when I was a child, so...."

He slanted her a quick glance. "Like that, was it? He was a good sort, old Monty, dependable sort of bloke. A darn sight too good-hearted for his own good, though, and simply no head whatever for business...." He studied her dispassionately: the generous sweep of brow, the wide mouth, the blue eyes tilted at a slight angle. "You're like him."

Lesley was uncertain as to whether the observation referred to her appearance or her business acumen. But remembering the old motor scooter lying immobile in the depths of the bush, she played for safety and said hastily, "You mean, he allowed store customers too much credit?"

"Did he ever! Old Monty collected more bad debts than you'd believe possible in such a small district. Anyone could put a sob story over on him."

Lesley, conscious of the stern lines of the man's face, reflected that at least Stuart Carrington would never err on the side of sentimentality. She had a feeling that his quick perceptive look missed nothing; that he was a shrewd judge of character—except where she herself was concerned, of course. Anyway, her thoughts flew off at a tangent, how could anyone help his own character? A tape rolled back and the voice of a former flat mate echoed once again in her mind: "You'll simply have to be more firm, Lesley. You've just *got* to! You've already lent that girl who used to work at the office far too much, and she's never paid you back a penny! What if she hasn't found a job yet? She has a perfectly good home and parents she can go back to for a while if she wants to. Will you never learn?"

Well.... The soft lines of Lesley's mouth tightened. This was the day she changed! Right here. This minute. She'd make a success of running this business no matter what difficulties stood in her way, or how hard she was forced to work. She'd succeed where her father had failed. All at once it seemed desperately important that she should prove to this overbearing stranger with the clean-cut features and soft voice that Lesley Monteith could make a go of the venture. Even if she weren't a man!

"Well, anyway," Lesley said loyally, eyeing the snowy

concrete surrounding the shabby premises, "at least my father was industrious, judging by the new concrete."

"Makes all the difference," her companion agreed calmly. "Put it down myself last week."

"You...you...." Her eyes swept up to meet the man's amused grin.

"Let's say I was a bit previous—just a bit, though." His bright stare challenged her. "You've got to make a start somewhere, and when the community hall goes up it'll keep the place dry. With a spot of luck," the eager tones ran on, "the camp should be ready for the first lot of kids to move in before the end of summer."

"But—aren't you forgetting something?" Lesley put in as the man paused.

His inquiring glance was unnerving, but she forced herself to go on. "I don't want to sell the place."

"No?" Amusement flickered in the cool gray eyes. "Not just at this minute, maybe. But you will."

"Why will I?" she challenged him with spirit. "After all," she added, stung to sudden anger, "I wouldn't have come all this way if I wasn't serious about it. Anyway," she flung at him, "I'll tell you this much: I'm going to give it a go!"

"You look a trifle small and feminine—" a slightly softer expression gleamed in the twinkling gray eyes "—and rather young to take it all on single-handed."

"I'm not all that young," Lesley protested heatedly. "I'm twenty!"

"That's about what I thought." His mocking expression was maddening. "Had any experience in that sort of game?"

Lesley hesitated, her fleeting upward glance taking in the masculine figure, lean and hard and brown; the deeply tanned throat; the muscular arms suntanned to a deep shade of copper. How could you explain to this bronzed New Zealander that you had once for a brief time assisted a friend in her exclusive little boutique in Chelsea? Chances were that he wouldn't even know what a boutique was. No doubt all he was familiar with was his own little remote corner of the world, where he appeared to regard himself as some sort of reigning monarch.

"A little," she murmured, adding quickly, "and anyway, I can learn."

The lurking amusement in the man's gaze deepened to an indulgent grin. "Oh sure, sure. You can try it out! Give you a month—two at the outside! But the offer'll still stand," he added carelessly, "so you've nothing to worry about. You can't lose too much in that time."

"I won't lose at all!" Never in her life had Lesley felt so roused and indignant about anything. The hot color flooded her cheeks. To think that she had come halfway across the world and this—this arrogant stranger took it upon himself to interfere in her affairs and forecast her future! Worse, he was regarding her with the indulgent amusement of an adult watching a child playing at some infantile game, not even taking her words seriously. But just let him wait! One month, he'd said! She'd show him!

But before she could bring to mind a sufficiently crushing retort, the man had leaped to the ground, and moving around the vehicle, held open the passenger door.

"Come on in," he invited, adding with the gentle irony that so infuriated her, "Make yourself at home!"

Together they strolled over the snowy expanse of courtyard. The Alsatian, ears pricked, rose to his feet and ambled forward to meet Lesley. She glanced up at the tall man at her side. "Was he...."

The man nodded. "That's Prince, your dad's dog. Yours now."

As if understanding the meaning of the words, the huge Alsatian came to stand beside Lesley, raising friendly eyes to her face as she stooped to lay a hand on the thick mustard-and-black coat.

As she glanced toward the interior, Lesley wasn't surprised to find it no more prepossessing than the dreary outside appearance of the country store. The long shelves were sparsely stocked with foodstuffs and household items. A stack of discolored faded cardboard containers had the appearance of having lain undisturbed for many months. There appeared, however, to be a plentiful supply of cigarettes and pipe tobacco. Probably, Lesley reflected, these were the bestselling commodities. But she could see no sign of a deep-freeze cabinet. In this heat—

At that moment a woman entered the room from a side door, and Lesley, coming from the brilliant sunshine outside, had difficulty for a moment in focusing her gaze. Then she took in a tall, broad-shouldered woman, middle-aged, with bright brown eyes, cropped gray hair and a tanned healthy skin innocent of makeup. She was dressed in a crisp lilac-colored nylon smock and wore rubber thongs on her bare tanned feet. Lesley, in that first brief glance, took her to be an exceptionally clean, no-nonsense type of woman, one who would speak her mind in no uncertain terms. And never had cause to alter that first opinion.

"Stuart!" The older woman dropped an armful of boxes to the floor and stared in surprise at the two standing in the open doorway.

"How are you, Mrs. Mac?" The man leaned a bronzed elbow on the worn counter and regarded her with his tantalizing grin. "Got a surprise for you!" Once again Lesley realized that the accents were those of a well-educated man. Here in this wild solitude? How odd.

"Someone here who wants to meet you," Stuart was saying. "Guess who?"

The woman's round brown eyes studied Lesley consideringly: slim, little-girl figure in dark blue trews and scarlet jacket, the long fall of shiny fair hair, a spattering of freckles over the small nose, and those eyes....

"She reminds me of someone," the woman murmured at last in a puzzled tone, "but for the life of me, I can't think who it is. Come on Stuart, don't be so aggravating. Tell me!"

"I'm Lesley, Monty's daughter," Lesley put in, and couldn't resist a smile as she met the older woman's dumbfounded look.

"But—" the brown eyes widened in startled disbelief "—Leslie's a boy."

"Oh, come, Mrs. Mac," Stuart said chidingly, "where are your eyes?" For a second the man's amused glance lingered on the creamy English complexion, reddened now with sun and windburn from the journey, the dark blue eyes with their glimmer of laughter.

Lesley, encountering that look, saw as if for the first time the strong brown face, the deep indentation in the chin. And the eyes.... It was the eyes with their swiftly changing expression that held you, stayed with you.

Oddly affected by that instant of awareness, she wrenched her glance away. But in that fragment of time something had happened. Something.... It was as if she were coming back from a long distance, and deep in her mind a small voice whispered, this is the moment you'll remember all your life long. This second, when it all started.

Ridiculous! With an effort of will she forced her attention back to the older woman's matter-of-fact tones. "I'm Janet MacPhail, my dear, but everyone calls me Mrs. Mac. I worked for your dad for quite a number of years. You know—housekeeping and looking after the store most days." A faint color crept up beneath the tan of the smooth unlined cheeks. "If only Monty had told us about you! But he never did. And when we discovered about you from his papers— Well, it was only a name."

Only a name. Lesley was conscious of an odd little pang of hurt. But she thrust it determinedly aside.

"You haven't just arrived in the country?" Mrs. Mac inquired curiously.

Lesley nodded "This morning, by air. It seems ages ago now. I took the coach from Auckland to Rotorua, and then—"

"But—" the older woman's bewildered glance moved toward the man "—where did Stuart—"

"Pick me up? On the road," Lesley explained, laughing. "He really did! My motor scooter packed up, miles back in the bush, and he happened to come along at the right moment."

"Motor scooter? My goodness!" Mrs. Mac stared at her incredulously. "You *were* brave, taking on these roads on a scooter! But come along," she added briskly, "you must feel like a shower and a change of clothing after that dusty trip. Stuart, did you bring in Lesley's bag?"

"It's all right," Lesley said quickly, "my luggage is coming on later by the road services bus, but I've brought an overnight bag with me."

Mrs. Mac regarded the small zipped bag slung over Lesley's shoulder doubtfully. "Don't tell me you've got a change of clothes in *that*!"

"The trouble with you, Mrs. Mac," the man put in easily, "is that you're way out-of-date. Ever heard of miniskirts?"

He was right, of course. Lesley was conscious of an inexplicable prick of annoyance. He would be! Ignoring the man's remark, she turned toward the older woman. "That shower sounds wonderful!"

"Come along, then. I'll show you to your room. Stuart—" she turned in the doorway "—you'll stay to tea? It's almost ready."

"Thanks, Mrs. Mac—if you don't mind my zooming away right afterward." He was putting a light to his cigarette.

Lesley, thankful to escape the man's watchful presence, followed the older woman into a narrow passage. On one side she caught a glimpse of a small kitchen with faded cream-painted walls, an electric range, refrigerator cabinet. A stainless-steel bench gleamed below a high stack of cupboards. An opening led into a small living room, spotlessly clean and neatly furnished with a worn oak dining suite, deep, shabby, cretonne-covered chairs, a TV set. Deerskin rugs lay on the polished timber of the floor and crisp blue-and-red patterned curtains billowed from the open windows.

But Lesley's attention was caught by a framed photograph hanging above the mantel, and stepping into the room, she paused to glance up into the twinkling eyes of the pleasant-faced, middle-aged man whose features bore an unmistakable resemblance to her own.

"This was your dad's room." Lesley crossed the passage and followed the older woman into a small square bedroom, where a utility chest of drawers stood beneath a hanging circular mirror. Small deerskin rugs were scattered on the pine timber of the floor and the single bed was covered with a cherry-colored spread.

"I've put all Monty's things away," Mrs. Mac murmured, and Lesley wondered briefly what the room had been like a few weeks ago. Probably at that time it had been filled with the pungent odor of pipe smoke. There'd have been books and magazines stacked on the low table; photographs on the bureau, perhaps.

"Bathroom's at the end of the passage," Mrs. Mac was saying in her brisk tones. "Come along and have tea when you're ready. I'll just go and put the coffee on to perk."

"Thank you—" Lesley stopped short on catching sight of her mirrored reflection. Could it be only this morning that she had left Auckland, feeling fresh and neat and, she had fondly imagined, suitably attired to meet any eventuality? But she hadn't counted on riding a motor scooter over the rugged mountainous terrain. And now, streaks of grease that her cold-water wash had failed to dislodge smeared her cheeks. Her face was burned to a deep unbecoming scarlet. And her hair! She jerked at a small twig and a shower of pine needles fell from the long fair strands.

Snatching up her toilet bag, she made her way toward the bathroom, passing a second bedroom along the passage. At the end of the hall she caught a glimpse of a lean-to room, evidently a wash-house with ironing bench, stainless-steel tub and an electric washing machine.

The bathroom, with its gay primrose-colored plastic hand basin and bath and curtained shower recess, proved surprisingly attractive. And Lesley was forced to admit that the living quarters were far more comfortable than she had anticipated, judging by the outside appearance of the premises. Her first task would be to renovate the discolored paint work. Soft pastel shades would make all the difference, and the faded wallpaper in living room and bedroom could well do with a coat of paint.

Meanwhile the shower was cool and refreshing. After a change of underclothing she slipped into a crisp dark blue frock, sleeveless and miniskirted with a froth of white lace at the neckline, white textured stockings, navy blue sandals. In spite of the dust in her hair, vigorous brushing brought back the golden tints. And it was amazing what could be achieved with skilful makeup when it came to toning down a too flamboyant complexion. At least now she felt delightfully fresh and clean and ready for anything—even if "anything" meant being forced to hold her own in an argument with an infuriating stranger, name of Stuart Carrington, who couldn't or wouldn't accept no as an answer!

The meal, set out on a snowy cloth on the worn table in the small room opening off the kitchen, was a pleasant one. Lesley enjoyed the tender cold lamb and crisp and colorful salad. Mrs. MacPhail's crusty golden scones were a delight. The coffee was hot and strong, and the breeze blowing through the wide open windows was refreshingly cool on her burning cheeks.

As the meal progressed she realized just how much of a shock her appearance here today must be to the two who had evidently made up their minds that the property would pass within a short time into the hands of the masterful man who had already made such extensive plans. Well, she told herself stubbornly, she, too, had plans, and it would take more than Stuart Carrington's ridicule to cause her to abandon them.

She wouldn't have minded so much had it not been for the man's blank assumption that she would prove quite unable to cope with the new responsibilities she had taken on. For to her chagrin, both he and Mrs. MacPhail calmly discussed the proposed plans for the bush survival camp just as though she had no say whatever in the matter. Not that she could blame the older woman. Mrs. MacPhail was unaware of Lesley's decision to stay here in Waione, but Stuart Carrington knew very well. And it would do him not the slightest good to deliberately ignore her decision. As he'd soon find out.

Her opportunity came when the older woman's round brown eyes turned inquiringly in Lesley's direction. "And what do you think of this camp project of Stuart's, Lesley?"

All at once the food seemed to stick in her throat. She fixed her gaze on Mrs. MacPhail in an effort to avoid the glance of the man seated opposite. "Actually, the question doesn't arise." With an effort she tried to still the tremor in her low tones. "I was telling Mr. Carrington before we came inside—I thought he understood—that I've decided to carry on here with the store myself...."

Her voice trailed away, and in the somewhat disquieting silence Lesley sensed the older woman's stunned disapproval. "I've got to work somewhere," she pressed on jerkily, "so it may as well be here! And if my father could earn a living from the store—"

"Oh, but he didn't!" Mrs. MacPhail hastened to correct her. "Not really. He used the place more or less as living quarters. Monty used to say that so long as the shop brought in sufficient to cover my housekeeping wages and a little extra, that suited him. He didn't depend on it for a living. Heavens, no! He ran a delivery truck. It was a total wreck after the smash. There was no insurance on it, and he—" At the remembrance of her employer's accidental death, the decisive tones broke.

"I see." Lesley stared down into her coffee cup. No doubt Stuart was eyeing her with his triumphant grin. But her quick upward glance surprised an expression remarkably akin to pity in the gray eyes. The next moment it had vanished, and she told herself that she must have been crazy ever to have imagined such a human emotion in connection with him. No doubt, she thought bitterly, now that she was aware of the true state of her father's finances he was waiting for her to humbly beg him to make good his offer of purchase. And for that, Mr. Stuart Carrington, you'll wait a long time!

She buttered the scone on her plate. But her appetite had unaccountably vanished. It was all *his* fault! He had goaded her into attempting what now appeared to be an impossible task. But immediately she chided herself for her lack of courage. It was clear from the meager supplies of stock, the uncared-for surroundings, that her father had little interest in the business. With her, it would be different. She'd succeed. She just *had* to!

A bell shrilled through the room, and Mrs. MacPhail excused herself from the table and hurried away.

"Your father was stubborn, too," the man remarked pleasly. He reached toward the tall chrome jug. "More coffee?"

"Stubborn?" Lesley's blue eyes blazed with sudden anger. "Is that what you call it? How about you? You... you...." Her voice choked and to her horror she felt the prick of tears behind her eyelids.

She tried to blink away the moisture. "One of these days," she said huskily, "you'll have to admit that—that—"

But this hateful male creature, far from being impressed,

merely fished a snowy man-size handkerchief from the pocket of his thin cotton shirt and held it toward her. "Blow!" he commanded, as though she were a distraught two-year-old, adding airily, "Don't bother returning it. I can always buy another one—at the store." Calmly he pushed the steaming coffee cup toward her. "I don't know what you're worrying about. I'm not—"

"But you—but you—" Lesley was too surprised to choose her words carefully. "You still want the place, don't you?"

"Want it?" The gray eyes with their vivid look held her own. "I'm going to have it! Like I said. Get things running by the end of summer."

"But," Lesley stammered in bewilderment, "if I won't sell...."

"You will." He sounded almost carelessly offhand, and infuriatingly confident.

"How do you mean?"

"Oh, nothing." He grinned and poured himself a second cup of coffee. "Just that if all else fails I can always have a go at getting it the other way— Cigarette? Calms the nerves."

What did he mean, Lesley thought wildly, by "the other way?" Through the wild tumult of her senses she glimpsed an unfathomable expression in the man's eyes, and somehow...somehow she couldn't bring herself to frame the question that trembled on her lips.

So instead she took a cigarette, waited while the man set a lighter to it. Then, inhaling deeply, she managed to get herself under some control. She couldn't understand herself, giving way like this. It was just that everything was so strange, so utterly different from what she'd imagined she'd find here, and in some odd way it was this man Stuart who dominated the scene—even herself. He spoke so quietly in that soft voice. And yet....

"Things'll look different in the morning," he offered casually. "Why not come out with me and have a look around at some of the forest country? You mightn't be here very long—better take it in while you're in the district."

"Mightn't be...." Oh, he was simply impossible! "I don't know." Wildly she cast about in her mind, seeking an excuse that would serve to keep her at the house. "I'd planned," she said at last, "to have a look over the account books tomorrow morning. Just to see how things are financially, you know?"

Against her will she found her gaze enmeshed in that gray probing stare. "You know damn well how things are! And if you don't believe me, have a word with Mrs. Mac. She ran through the stocktaking with me last month. She's got the whole thing taped. Well, if you'll excuse me...." Pushing back the chair, he rose to his long length. "Got to get cracking. Pick you up at ten. Okay?"

Suddenly Lesley felt tired and dispirited, weary of fighting verbal battles with this arrogant stranger. After all, she might as well go with him. It was less trouble than arguing the matter. She became aware that he was still awaiting her reply.

"If you like," she murmured carelessly.

But it seemed that being omniscient rendered one impervious both to insults and downright indifference. For the stranger merely nodded, crushing out his cigarette in a gleaming opalescent paua shell lying on the sideboard. "Right, that's fixed, then. Well, if you'll excuse me...." He turned, throwing a challenging grin over his shoulder. "See you!" The next moment he was gone.

As the sound of the departing Land Rover died away in the distance, Lesley sat on at the table. She felt strung up, excited, and very much alone.

"Stuart had to rush away." Mrs. MacPhail had come back into the room. "He had an appointment with a mill owner fifty miles farther along the road—had to see about cutting rights for his timber." She bent toward the table, but Lesley put out a detaining hand. "Sit down for a moment, please," she begged, "and we can fix the dishes later, together. Care for a cigarette?"

"Not for me, thanks," Mrs. Mac replied in her definite tones. "But you go right ahead. Smoke doesn't bother me any, not after all those years of Monty's pipe. Well, just for a few minutes, then." She dropped to a chair. "If I can, that is. That bell in the store! It nearly drives me up the wall! Stuart tells me I should shut the doors at six and call it a day. But I wouldn't do that—not in this isolated spot!"

"Stuart. Does he," Lesley inquired diffidently, "live near here?"

Beyond the Ranges

The older woman nodded. "Just over the hill." She waved a hand toward the window, where a towering bush-clad mountain was a dark mass against the rose-and-apricot tints of a spectacular sunset. "Actually he owns more land than any other private property owner around these parts. I guess over in the States they'd term his place a ranch. Not that the farm's all that extensive, but he's got thousands of acres in heavy bush. He lets out the cutting rights for the timber. Got a big new brick home up there now, too. When he took over the property, Stuart had the old family homestead pulled down and a new one built in its place. I guess," she murmured thoughtfully, "he hoped it might take Kathy's mind off the tragedy."

"Oh?" Lesley glanced up curiously. "What was that?"

"It happened over a year ago," Mrs. MacPhail explained on a long sigh. "Kathy's Stuart's sister. She's older than he, a widow with a little stepdaughter called Debbie. Kathy married a chap named Victor Carson—a widower he was then, with one little girl. Victor was a lawyer practicing in Wellington, but when he married Kathy Carrington they decided they'd take over the property here. Old Mr. Carrington had died a short time before and there was a manager in charge. There were just the two, Stuart and Kathy, in the Carrington family, and Stuart was dead keen on social studies and welfare work. He was in London at the time, completing his final examinations in that line, when he got word of Victor's accident."

"What happened?" Lesley asked as the older woman paused.

Mrs. MacPhail shrugged, spreading large work-worn hands in an expressive gesture. "Something that never should have happened. Wouldn't have, either, if only Victor Carson had known the first thing about the dangers of tramping in the Urewera Country. He forgot his insurance, and that can be fatal."

"Insurance?"

"Food, extra clothing—he hadn't a clue about all that. He hadn't been in the district a month when he decided to take Debbie away in the bush on a weekend camping trip. It was too bad that Kathy was called away from home that weekend or she would have put him in the picture. As it was, off he went into a remote area without a guide—didn't even follow the unwritten law around these parts of always letting someone know where you're bound for when you start out on a tramping trip. It was winter time, cold and wet. But Victor went off into the heavy bush without even a change of clothing for either himself or Debbie. I guess he'd never even heard of hypothermia; that's the killer around here."

Lesley's eyes widened. "What...."

"Exposure's another name for it," Mrs. MacPhail explained grimly. "Caught out in the open in wind and wet and cold, you can die in a single night."

"Die?"

"That's what happened. They took a wrong track. Debbie fell head first over a cliff, and her father tried to climb down to get to her where she was trapped on a narrow ledge. It wasn't until the beginning of the second night that the search parties finally caught up with them, and by that time it was too late! Victor had tumbled to the foot of the cliff and was dead from injuries and exposure when they found him. Debbie—well, she's only just getting on her feet again after months in hospital with spinal injuries.

"When Stuart got the news he caught the first available plane back to New Zealand, tossed in all his ideas about a career in welfare services and took over the family property instead. He'd been brought up here, mind you, so he knew all about the running of it. Actually, he's in a big way. The Big Boss, they call him around these parts!"

The Big Boss. Lesley's eyes were thoughtful. So that explained the man's high-handed attitude and domineering ways!

Mrs. MacPhail's strident tones broke into her musing. "I suppose that if Kathy'd been a city girl, she'd have sold up right then and there, after the accident. But she happens to be crazy about country life—wins all the show-jumping ribbons at the local gymkhanas. So having Stuart take over the place solved her problem. And then, of course, Tim's there, too, a lot of the time."

"Tim?" Lesley inquired. "He's another Carrington?"

"That's right," Mrs. MacPhail nodded. "Not that you'd ever know he was a cousin of Stuart's. Tim's so different. He just doesn't worry over a thing—not that he needs to. It beats me," she went on in a thoughtful tone, "how Stuart can have such patience with him. Maybe it's a sort of family obligation. Stuart sets him up in one thing after another, and none of them lasts with Tim. He's what you'd call one of those arty types," Mrs. Mac explained with obvious disapproval. "First it was painting pictures. He was training for art teaching at the high schools until he left in the second term. Said he couldn't stick the routine. Then it was pottery. Stuart paid the earth for a kiln to be set up for him at the house, but that didn't last long, either. Then just a while ago there was the job that Stuart got for him at the timber company office in Taupo. That didn't last more than two days! Never done an honest day's work in his life," Mrs. Mac snorted, "and doesn't want to, I shouldn't wonder! Maybe Stuart is taken in by what he says about not being unsuccessful—it's just that he hasn't yet found the right art form! That's what *he* says! What Tim needs," Mrs. Mac observed flatly, "is a wife to prod him along, give him something to work for! Not one of those airy-fairy types of girl that he goes around with. Someone with a bit of common sense. A girl with her wits about her who'd give him a push along in the right direction! The sort of girl that would make up his mind for him, make him do something that would bring in some money. Oh, he's got a little capital of his own, of course. And what with having Stuart's place as a handy base.... Not," she admitted reluctantly, "that he isn't rather nice—to talk to, I mean. He's got a way with him." As if regretting the moment of weakness she added quickly, "But what's the use of that— There's that bell again!" She turned and hurried into the store.

"You can see now," she said on her return, "why you need a couple of folk around this place."

"That's what I wanted to talk to you about." Lesley was unaware of the appeal shadowing her blue eyes as she glanced toward Mrs. MacPhail. "Do you think you'd care to stay on here with me? Just as you did... before?" She knew nothing of the business arrangements entered into between this woman and her father, beyond what Mrs. MacPhail had told her. She hurried on in a nervous flurry of words. "I thought... under the same arrangements—your wages, I mean. That is," she finished uncertainly, "if it suits you that way?"

"Suits me just fine, my dear!" Mrs. MacPhail beamed with approval. "I'm a widow, you see, and I was wondering what I was going to do when Stuart took over. Not that I haven't got two daughters in Wellington, but I like to be independent, and now that you can do with a spot of help I'll be only too pleased to stay on. I'm not around all the time," she explained. "Take the odd nursing case in the district, and if a woman's suddenly rushed to hospital or someone needs household help urgently, I lend a hand. But most times I'm right here at the store. And I daresay you could do with someone to show you the ropes, what with prices and ordering and everything—" She broke off, eyeing Lesley inquiringly. "You're quite sure you want me, though? Stuart says you'll only be here for a month at the outside. Just while you have a look around, see the district."

"Oh, he did?" Lesley's voice was dangerously quiet.

"That's what he *thought*," Mrs. MacPhail amended hastily, as two danger signals flared in Lesley's cheeks.

"*He* doesn't know everything," Lesley muttered, half to herself.

The older woman gave an indulgent laugh. "You don't like him, do you? Funny, you know," she added thoughtfully, "because your dad thought the world of him."

"Well, *I* don't!" But Mrs. Mac, hurrying away at the urgent summons of the bell in the adjoining room, failed to catch the low words.

"Ever done any shop work?" she asked, when once again she joined Lesley in the dining room.

"None to speak of, but I can learn! And if you could stay here with me, that would be wonderful!" Lesley was flooded with a great tide of relief. She wouldn't, after all, find herself alone in this unfamiliar men's world, struggling with unexpected problems that were looming larger with every hour.

"But it's no use your expecting to make a fortune out of the place," Mrs. MacPhail's uncompromising tones jerked Lesley back to reality. "Not the way it is."

"Oh, I know! I know!" Lesley leaned forward eagerly. "But I thought if I could brighten the place up, make it look more attractive—get more stock: clothing, shirts for the men, maybe frocks for the women. You know? That sort of thing."

"It'll cost you a pretty penny," the older woman prophesied darkly. "And it's taking a risk, putting money into this place. There isn't the population here, really, to make it worthwhile. Most folks run into Murupara once a week to get their supplies. It's a change of scene for them. And there's everything they need there—even a modern supermarket, though it's just a mill town in the middle of nowhere. If you ask me," she said flatly, "you'd be throwing your money away. And unless you've got some extra cash to play around with...."

Lesley shook her head. "But I haven't! I've only what's left of the money my dad left me."

Mrs. MacPhail eyed her with amazement. "Well, for goodness' sake, then! Why on earth don't you let Stuart take the place off your hands? It's not as though he isn't offering a fair price, more than fair—"

"No!" Lesley surprised herself at the vehemence of her tone. "I made up my mind to keep on here when I first heard about all this," she went on in a milder tone, "and that's the way it's going to be."

"Well, I must say that suits me fine. And anyway," Mrs. Mac glanced toward Lesley, taking in the deep blue eyes, black lashed, the deceptive look of fragility, "it won't make much odds. You'll never last long here."

Not you, too, Lesley thought in dismay. And she had imagined that in the older woman she had found an ally.

Aloud she protested, "Oh, Mrs. Mac! You're as bad as that Carrington man! And I thought you were on my side!"

Mrs. MacPhail laughed heartily. "You've taken me up all wrong, honey. What I was trying to tell you was that the Urewera is man's country. And there are precious few women living anywhere around. 'Specially young ones! Oh, there's the odd daughter belonging to a farmer or mill owner. But as soon as they're through primary school here they're sent away to town to high school and colleges. And they never come back, except maybe for something special that's going on at home. Girls around this district are mighty scarce. Bachelors are two a penny! *And* starved for a pretty face."

"How come then," Lesley teased, "if the position's as desperate as all that, that *you* haven't married again?"

To Lesley's surprise, for she had imagined that nothing could disturb the older woman's air of brisk efficiency, Mrs. Mac looked oddly embarrassed, and Lesley regretted having made the light personal observation.

"Happen," Mrs. Mac said at last in her definite tones, "that some folk know when they're well off!" She turned away, but not before Lesley had caught the faint color that stained the tanned cheeks. "And maybe I like my independence." She began stacking cups and saucers with a clatter that made Lesley fear for the safety of the china. "Not that I haven't had my chances, you understand? But if the one you fancy never thinks about you—not like that. Not the way you want him to." Her eyes went to the smiling face of the man's portrait hanging above the mantel. Then, with a sigh, Mrs. Mac began gathering together a stack of plates. "Anyway," she said briskly after a moment, "it's not *me* that we're talking about! I'll tell you this much, though. In Waione anyone with your looks could take their pick of husband material any old time. Except for Stuart, of course," she added as an afterthought.

"Oh?" Lesley discovered that for some ridiculous reason she was holding her breath expectantly. She hated herself for her curiosity, but she couldn't seem to control it. "Isn't he free? Or doesn't he care for girls' company?"

"Free?" Mrs. MacPhail gave the matter some thought. "If you mean is he still single, at twenty-eight, the answer's yes. Women always fall for him, but he doesn't ever seem to get involved. Maybe," she said reflectively, "it's because he's so wrapped up in his work. And then of course there's always Judith."

"Judith?"

"Judith Roth. And it's not for the want of trying," the older woman went on significantly, "that she hasn't been Mrs. Stuart Carrington long before this. She's a year older than he is— Oh, she tells everyone that she's years younger, but I happen to have been a friend of her mother's and I know the date she was born. Judith's a great friend of Kathy's—or pretends to be. I'd say that the liking is all on Kathy's side. They were school friends and Kathy still thinks Judith's wonderful, has her to stay at the house almost every weekend. And unless I miss my guess, it suits Judith very well indeed to be there with Stuart. Not that she isn't attractive," the older woman admitted reluctantly, "if you happen to like that skinny type, all mouth and false eyelashes—like those models in the fashion magazines, only more so." She added after a moment, "I can't see *her* having any part in Stuart's bush survival camp that he's so wrapped up in. He's brought her around here once or twice, showed her the layout of the scheme, drawn diagrams on bits of paper. Anyone could see she was bored to tears with the whole business, although she pretended to him that she was wildly interested in it all. And as to living here in this remote spot— But of course she wouldn't let on to him that she wouldn't even consider it. At least, not until after they were married."

"I shouldn't imagine," Lesley was speaking her thoughts aloud, "that a man like that would let anyone fool him."

"Now don't you be too sure! He's so keen on his camp project that if she pretended enough— Mind you, I can understand why the bush survival training scheme means so much to him. After what happened to Victor and Debbie...."

Lesley nodded. "I got the impression," she agreed, "that he wouldn't give up the idea of the camp being built here easily."

"Give it up?" Mrs. Mac stared back at Lesley blankly. "He'll never do that! He'll get this property, one way or another! You'll see! Now don't look like that, my dear—" For Lesley's mobile face, which mirrored each passing emotion, had fallen despairingly. "By that time you won't be caring about the store one way or the other. You'll have much more important things to think about. See what I mean?" Her gaze went past Lesley to the store beyond. Her powerful accents rose. "Hey there, Wayne, come on in! There's someone here I want you to meet!"

Lesley, glancing up expectantly, saw a young man of medium height, thin and wiry, with tousled fair hair, a boyish smile. The light blue eyes lighted with interest at the sight of the girl seated at the table.

"Wayne, this is Monty's daughter, Lesley."

"Nice to meet you." The warm tones lent meaning to the conventional words. Then the young man's puzzled gaze moved toward the older woman. "Did you say Monty's daughter? Never knew he had one!"

"None of us did," Mrs. Mac answered in her loud cheerful accents. "But here she is, all the way from London! And she says she's going to carry on at the store."

The young man eyed her with interest. "Good for you! If I can help at all...." He regarded her with eager blue eyes. "Got the old jalopy parked outside. Any place you want to go, just say the word! I'm at the forestry headquarters just along the road—got some free time this weekend, too. Maybe you'd like a run into Murupara, have a look around?"

"Well, maybe, one of these days," Lesley temporized, taken by surprise. She wondered if Mrs. Mac's pronouncement re the bachelor element of Waione was indeed the truth. There was no doubt that this friendly young man with the candid gaze and beaming smile was only too anxious to be of assistance to her—a rather different attitude from the treatment accorded her by Stuart Carrington.

"I guess meeting you put everything else out of my mind," Wayne was saying, "including the cigarettes I made the trip for." He turned away with a lingering glance. "Don't forget, if you want some transport...."

Lesley smiled in return. "Thank you."

All the time she helped Mrs. Mac deal with the neglected dinner dishes, Lesley's thoughts dwelt on the kindness and warmth of the greeting accorded her by the tousled-haired young man. At least he didn't regard her as some sort of moron. Like— With a prick of irritation she realized that once again her thoughts had strayed in the direction of Stuart Carrington. Stuart, who was free, and yet not free. Who apparently liked girls, but not her. Not stupid clots who set fire to pine forests and rode motor scooters with parts that rattled off at the most inconvenient moments.

It was late when at last Mrs. Mac closed the doors of the store. And presently, account books spread out over the sun-bleached surface of the varnished table, she and Lesley discussed the financial position of the business, which transpired to be very much as Mrs. Mac had already informed Lesley.

Long after she got into bed, Lesley lay wakeful and overexcited, trying to sort out the events and impressions of the long day. At long intervals the lights of passing vehicles flashed their fitful beams across the windows. She caught the cry of a night owl. A dog barked. Occasionally she heard the tramp of men's feet on the nearby roadway, followed by a burst of masculine laughter, or the soft melodious syllables of the Maori tongue. Then once again the intense stillness of the bush settled over the dark landscape.

She was just drifting off to sleep when a thunderous scratching and banging echoed from the corrugated iron roof overhead. Lesley jerked herself upright in startled alarm.

"You awake, Lesley?" An even louder knocking came from the dividing wall between the two bedrooms. "'Possums up on the roof!" shrieked Mrs. Mac in her powerful accents. "Won't hurt you! Forgot to warn you about them. Go back to sleep!"

Sleep! Lesley slid down again, pulling over her the single sheet that was sufficient covering on such a warm night. She lay staring into the darkness, thinking...thinking... She'd come halfway across the world, and where had it brought her? It had brought her to a shabby cottage in a bush clearing, where 'possums lightheartedly chased one another over the roof—*her* roof—under cover of darkness.

It had also brought her to Stuart Carrington, a man who had for her nothing but contempt, yet who had practically forced her into promising to go out with him on the morrow. And the worst part of it all was—she turned her pillow, thumping it angrily—that for some utterly inexplicable reason, she couldn't seem to stop herself from thinking of him!

CHAPTER THREE

IT WAS AMAZING, Lesley mused, lying in bed on the following morning, how discouragements and frustrations melted away in the mellow light of the sunshine slanting across her pillow. Especially when one was awakened from deep refreshing sleep by the liquid call on two notes of a tui perched somewhere in the high trees at the rear of the dwelling. Right now the problems that had loomed so menacingly last night seemed no more than exciting challenges to be met and conquered.

She'd be glad, though, when her baggage arrived by the road services bus today from Rotorua. Then at last she'd be able to unpack her suitcases, and maybe with familiar belongings around her, her gay new frocks swinging from their hangers in the empty wardrobe, she'd feel a little less like a passing traveler putting up for a day or two at the Waione General Store.

Meantime, her dark blue trews would have to serve. She shook them vigorously to remove the dust of the roads, pulled a soft white cotton sweater over her head. Scarcely a high-fashion outfit, but it would have to do.

After a light breakfast, Lesley helped Mrs. MacPhail to clear away and attend to the usual household chores. Then she wandered out the back door and down the steps. She had washed her hair and now it hung clean and burnished, blowing loosely around her shoulders. On the grass below she paused, held by the loveliness of her surroundings. The towering peaks rising above were wreathed in drifting mist; the forest trees a dark fretted outline against the pearl, shading to a misty azure, of the morning sky. Conscious of a breathless quality in the crystal-clear atmosphere, she wandered on down a winding path toward the orchard below, pleasantly aware of the dew-drenched grass beneath her bare feet.

Someone—probably that unknown father of hers—had cultivated a garden here, for runner beans hung in profusion from a high framework. There were long rows of crisp lettuce and peas, and scarlet tomatoes, frosted with dew, gleamed from plants staked in neat rows.

She moved on toward the orchard, where high trees were studded with purplish plums. Peach trees bent low with their load of downy, golden yellow fruit. There were apples, nectarines, green and glossy. Nectarines! If only they were ripe! Thick leafy bushes were covered in a profusion of smooth bluish green fruit. Grapevines, hung with bunches of green grapes, twisted along a low boundary fence, and a derelict timber shed was hidden by a curtain of thickly growing vine with shiny green leaves. Tentatively Lesley reached up to touch one of the unfamiliar green fruit that was suspended like a small oval balloon from the lush greenery.

"Never come across passion fruit before?" Lesley glanced over her shoulder straight into Stuart Carrington's smiling bronzed face. Stuart, with the glint in his eyes that was so exasperating and somehow disturbing. And that ridiculous name for a fruit! Surely it couldn't be true! But real or not she refused to be drawn into a discussion on the matter.

Confused, she said, "No, I haven't."

The morning breeze tossed the long fall of dark blond hair around her shoulders as she turned away from that deep, intent gaze. "Can you eat them?"

He nodded. "Sure you can. But you'd be darned sorry afterward! They're a dark purple color when they're ripe. And that won't be till March. Pity."

Nettled, she rushed to the attack. "You mean, I won't be here then to sample them?"

He grinned, a hateful, superior male grin. "I didn't say that."

Damn him! He was deliberately taunting her, and like a fool she rose to the bait every time. Clearly he gained a measure of satisfaction from her instant reaction, and that, too, was infuriating.

At that moment she became aware of the faint insistent shrilling of the bell from inside the store, and thankful for the timely interruption, she turned and made to hurry away. "I'd better fly! Mrs. MacPhail doesn't seem to be around."

He raised satirical black brows. "Know how much to charge for a packet of fags? Or a plug of pipe tobacco? It's dollars and cents here, don't forget."

Lesley paused uncertainly. Once again he had the edge on her. "No, I don't," she admitted unhappily. "Not really," and registered a silent vow that he wouldn't again catch her out in that direction.

"Let 'em wait," Stuart advised carelessly. "You're coming with me. Remember?"

She nodded. "I'll just go and say goodbye to Mrs. Mac-Phail."

When she strolled toward the front door, he was waiting for her, a tall erect figure wearing a gray turtleneck sweater, faded linen shorts, light knee-length socks and deerskin moccasins. She had to admit that he appeared cool and casual and devastatingly attractive. That was, of course, if you didn't know him!

Together they strolled across the concrete surround toward the dusty Land Rover with its heavy steel grille protecting the radiator.

"Thought I'd take you to have a look at Lake Waika-reiti," the man suggested, holding open the door of the vehicle. "It's quite a sight—a lake within a lake. An easy track—only a couple of miles through the bush each way. How are you on tramping?"

"I don't mind." Even if she hadn't been fond of walking, Lesley told herself, she wouldn't have admitted the fact, not to him. "I'd like—" She broke off, as the Alsatian dog scrambled in at the open doorway and pushing roughly past her, settled himself in the back seat.

"He'll be okay," Stuart went around to the other side of the vehicle. "Monty used to take him in the truck wherever he went. Guess he's missing all that."

And him, Lesley thought.

The man climbed in at her side, lifting a hand in greeting

as a battered truck drew up at their side. The Maori driver, leaning from the open cab, grinned with a flash of white teeth.

"Tena Koa!"

"Tena Koa," Stuart called across in return. "Meaning—" he flashed a smile toward Lesley as he put the vehicle in gear and they turned in to the rough metal road "—good day. How are you?"

"Oh!" But Lesley was eyeing a fenced clearing in the thick native bush covering the hill at the back of the store. "What was the idea of the enclosure up there?"

"That?" The man's careless glance swept upward. "Monty kept a couple of young deer there, until they got too big to be pets anymore. Their mothers had been shot and the hunters brought them back one day from the forest."

"Shot?"

"Necessary up this way." The man slowed to take a bend and the overhanging tree ferns, coated with dust, swished past the windows. "The government forestry service is all out to preserve the native forest. Know something? There are trees here that grow nowhere else in the world, so it's a case of a real extermination program—get rid of the deer and opossum before they demolish the forest! The forestry boys are all out on the job. Hunting safaris help to keep the numbers down; so does poisoned bait dropped from aircraft. Professional hunters are sent out to remote areas with orders to destroy as many animals as possible. A pretty rugged life, that. The huts are supplied with food, cooking billies, camp ovens, open fires for cooking. They bake their own bread. And those helicopters you see buzzing around are on the job supplying food, building materials, whatever. Quite an advance on hunting a few years ago when servicing was done on foot with food on back packs—stores dropped by parachute. They certainly started something when they introduced the red deer to these forests. Now they can't get rid of them!"

Lesley felt a rush of sympathy for the deer and opossum, hunted on all sides. But a sideways glance at the man's stern profile impelled her to crush down the hot protestations that rose to her lips, for to argue the matter would merely afford Stuart Carrington a further opportunity to point out how little she knew of the country, or the real facts of the matter. Stupidly softhearted about animals, just like her father. That would be her!

But in spite of everything her spirits lifted. The air was so invigorating, and in the clear bright sunshine, amid the scenic grandeur of the surroundings, how could anyone feel anything else but happy? Not even the nearness of the aggravating argumentative man at her side could spoil it. It was too lovely a day.

She said, "I was wondering... have you heard anything about the scooter yet?"

The man braked at a narrow one-way bridge, waiting while a logging truck roared toward them. "Sure. The boys took it in last night. I had a word with the garage bloke first thing and it's like I said. Putting it right would let you in for a lot more than the thing's worth, throwing good money after bad! Forget it!"

"I see," Lesley said in a small voice. For a moment the bright sunlight dimmed and she could almost hear the man's unspoken comment: "The family failing—no money sense."

But she forgot her annoyance as they swept past a mission school in a valley, a tiny post office, a farmhouse where sweeping green lawns were studded with flowering shrubs: pink hibiscus and the scarlet stars of poinsettias. Then they were moving into a steep track winding up the bush-covered hills, where the mist still lingered in the valleys.

A transporter carrying a single massive log from the forest swept past them. Then they were zig-zagging down the track toward a bush-filled valley. At the foot of the slope Stuart brought the vehicle to a stop. He turned toward Lesley. "May as well take in the falls." He climbed out from behind the wheel and went to open the passenger door. "There's an old bridle track through the bush."

For some reason she couldn't define Lesley avoided his outstretched hand and leaped lightly down onto the metal road.

Then they were strolling over the sun-dried grass, turning into a narrow winding path, where the air was pungent with the damp, earthy smell of the bush and sunlight filtered down through the green lace of softly waving punga fronds and high forest trees.

Presently they emerged from the green gloom of the track into the sudden warmth of glittering sunshine, and Lesley, glancing around, caught her breath in trepidation. For a short distance ahead loomed a formidable swing bridge. Why, it must be a hundred feet in length! A foot bridge, the anchored framework rose from smooth gray rocks; the rope sides were suspended above the tossing waters of a turbulent river.

It was absurd. It was silly and childish. Hadn't she told herself so a thousand times in the past? But it made no difference. She simply couldn't help herself. Since childhood she'd been bedeviled by a morbid fear of heights. Even more terrifying was the prospect of being forced to balance unsteadily above height, which was precisely what faced her in the crossing of this long, nightmare suspension bridge.

The forestry notice erected on the rock face overlooking the foaming water below did nothing to ease her sick feeling of apprehension: You Cross This Bridge at Your Own Risk. And like a background to her terror, the Auckland travel clerk's words echoed in her mind: "... most rugged part of the North Island." Why, oh, why, she wondered desperately, with a choice of all New Zealand in which to live, had her father decided to make his home among the wild ravines and rushing rivers of the Urewera country?

But it seemed that for her there was no escape. They had almost reached the framework rising from the great rocks. And Lesley was only half aware of what the man beside her was saying. She'd simply *have* to conquer her fear. For wasn't there something even more important to her at the moment? And that was that Stuart Carrington shouldn't have the satisfaction of knowing that she was a chickenhearted coward. In addition, of course, to being a softhearted, unbusinesslike little idiot—or so he thought.

"You go first," she said with an assumption of nonchalance. But it was no use. She might have known it was a hopeless chance. He was standing aside, waiting for her. Waiting.... Lesley, with a tremendous effort of will, forced herself to take a step onto the swinging bridge and there she froze, the victim of some unassailable mental block. She couldn't move. Not even to prove herself to this satirical and watching stranger.

"Scared? It's nothing! Come on, I'll give you a hand."

"But that's just what I don't want." Through the dizzy sensation of vertigo she didn't know whether she had spoken the words aloud or not.

"Come on, there's nothing to it." She felt a firm clasp around her shoulders, and then he was guiding her across what seemed to her to be an endless expanse of moving structure where sea and rock face swam in a dizzy kaleidoscope, and she was trembling uncontrollably.

At last she felt her feet touch on the smooth rock face at the opposite side of the river and, shuddering, glanced down the sheer cliff to the rushing waters below.

"It's worth it all; you'll see in a minute," her companion said in his soft tones. "Just up this path...." He put out a hand to help her up the overgrown track winding between bush and low shrub. But she shook her head and made her way upward until she reached the summit of the rise.

There below her, tumbling from green fern and flax, thundered the falls, breathlessly enchanting in their bush setting, the white spray cascaded down three levels of smooth rock to dash in a cloud of spray to the river sixty feet below.

Lesley wiped the damp spray from her face and turned an enraptured face toward the man standing at her side. "You're right, you know. It was worth it all."

"Even the bridge?"

She met the man's teasing glance and her gaze fell. "Even the bridge."

But presently, as they turned back and approached the metal framework, Lesley's nerves once again got the better of her.

If only it hadn't been him to whom she was forced to turn for help. But she simply had to depend on him if she

Beyond the Ranges

didn't wish to remain in this remote area beside the river forever.

But there was something about being dependent on him... something in his touch, impersonal probably to him. But not to her. Oh, definitely not to her! Indeed, since reaching Waione something entirely unprecedented seemed to have happened to her. Everything she thought and did and planned seemed somehow connected with this man. Apparently that was the effect that friction with a determined opponent had on you—made you strangely excited and aware—and definitely not wishful to lean on him on the long swinging confines of the narrow footbridge.

"You okay?" Stuart was saying as she paused, one hand resting on the framework.

She would conquer this weakness. She *must*. "Yes, of course." Lesley took a deep breath and took a few faltering steps. Don't look down—that was the trick. Look up... ahead... anywhere but at the turbulent waters below. She was just congratulating herself on a victory over an inherent weakness, when Prince came bounding along behind her, and as the bridge rocked and swayed under her feet with a sickening motion, Lesley stood rooted in the old fear over which she had no control. Wildly she clutched at the steel rope of the railing as the structure swayed beneath her feet.

"Take it easy!"

Blindly she clutched at the hand outstretched toward her, but to her chagrin she found herself rooted to the spot, mesmerized by the glimpse of swirling waters visible through the open timber slats beneath her feet.

"Look up and you'll be right." Gently, step by step, Stuart propelled her forward, and Lesley forced herself shakily on, humiliatingly aware of the Alsatian dog trotting with surefooted confidence a short distance ahead.

It was over at last. Somehow, with Stuart's help, she managed to gain the sanctuary of the rocks on the other side of the river. She drew a great breath of relief and freed herself from the man's grasp. It was the trembling of her limbs that betrayed her still. Betrayed... what? Why, fear, of course. Fear of what? The open slats. What else? She couldn't bear to look down at them. And that frightening swaying motion in midair, like a ship plowing through heavy seas. Of course that's all it was.

"No bridge at Waikareiti." Stuart's reassuring tones broke into her thoughts. "Just an easy walking track through the beech forest."

"You're... sure?" She was still breathing unevenly.

"It's a promise!"

Together they strolled over the grass toward the bush track, and Lesley, when they reached the Land Rover, climbed inside with a feeling of relief. A moment later the Alsatian tumbled in after her and scrambled into the rear of the vehicle.

Up in the ridges mist and drifting cloud still clung to the dark side of the mountains, and the air was heady as wine. Overhanging tea tree and blowing flax edged the winding road, and punga ferns, their drooping fronds still beaded with dew, brushed the Land Rover as they swept past. There was little traffic on the highway. Once they passed a tractor that disappeared in a cloud of dust behind them, and on the long rise ahead Lesley discerned a transporter and trailer, packed with sheep.

Presently the man pulled up beside a clearing, and a signpost flashed up to meet Lesley's gaze: Lake Waikareiti Track.

Stuart got out and slammed the door behind him. "It's a step or two to get there, but it's worth the effort. Quite a place—you'll see."

Almost at once they were entering the green gloom of the beech forest, where the path wound between towering, thickly growing trees and led through dense undergrowth and gullies of fern and wild fuchsia. The hushed stillness, the great columns of the forest giants rising smooth and untapering into the blue, gave Lesley an impression of being in some vast Gothic cathedral. As they moved farther into the depths of the beech forest, supplejack trailed its thick black ropes over high rockfaces, and the fluttering notes of a native bush pigeon echoed somewhere in the branches high overhead. Lesley, pausing to glance upward, caught a flash of iridescent blue-and-green plumage.

"Easy to see old man 'possum's been here." Stuart was

eyeing the freshly broken twigs and branches lying across the narrow path. "He gnaws the bark off the trees; deer go for the undergrowth. And wild pigs like to root around in the earth and fern—like so. If you want to see native timbers, this is your chance! Kauri, matai, totara, tawa...." He was indicating to Lesley the varieties of forest trees. "See that bole up there on the rimu?"

"No. Where?"

"Thataway." He was close—too close for her peace of mind—pointing to an encroaching feathery-leaved tree. Lesley could scarcely see it for the odd pounding in her ears, but she made a pretense of looking in the direction he was indicating. Over the odd tumult in her senses she caught the low tones. "That's a rata. One of these days it will form a massive trunk and end up by strangling the rimu. Would you believe it?"

Lesley thought she would believe anything today. For some ridiculous reason she was swept by a surge of careless happiness. There was just no accounting for it. With an effort she brought her mind back to what Stuart was saying.

He was striding along at her side, footsteps silent on the black, damp leaf mold underfoot. "You have to hand it to those Tuhoi tribesmen—you know, those Children of the Mist that I was telling you about. This is a pretty rigorous place and they led a Spartan sort of life. All they had to depend on for food was what they could get in the forest: fern, root, bitter bread, tawa berries, with the odd bird from the bush they managed to snare a few eels from the lake. Clothing was no problem. They depended on the flax." He gestured toward the spearlike leaves of the bushes growing thickly beside the winding track.

"Clothing?" Lesley glanced in surprise at the stiff green razorlike leaves. "It looks awfully sharp."

"Not on your life! Not when it was woven into sleeping mats and skirts and cloaks— Hey, we're almost there!"

The next moment they turned a bend in the track and Lesley stopped abruptly, catching her breath at the scene before her. "Oh look."

Ahead of her gleamed the lake, island studded, where bush grew down to the water's edge. It was all so remote, utterly still, so that the limpid depths reflected each leaf and fern frond as clearly as a mirror.

At that moment Prince bounded ahead, and leaping up onto a smooth rock at the lake edge, began lapping greedily at the crystal-clear water. Lesley, as she moved toward the lakeshore with Stuart, was utterly intrigued. For this was something—this pale aquamarine gleaming amid a green setting of thickly growing native bush, where tree ferns trailed in water so clear that she could g :pse a gleaming rainbow trout lying motionless as it basked in the filtered sunlight on the clean white sand beneath.

As she gazed around her, once again Lesley was struck by the intense stillness. It was as if the pace were under a spell. A dinghy was drawn up beside the lake. A tramper's cabin by the shore was the only sign of habitation. Standing on tiptoe to peer through the window, she discerned an open fireplace ready laid for the convenience of the next tramper who paused here before continuing through the blazed trails of the limitless forest areas.

Together she and Stuart explored the path edging the island-dotted lake. Rising from the water was a small island, where on the summit gleamed yet another lake. Lesley had a feeling of enchantment, as though they two were remote from everyday living, in a world of their own. Once again she was pierced by that wild inexplicable happiness.

"Time for smoko!"

Lesley glanced at the man bewilderedly. "But...the trees...."

"Different here from the pine forest. It's okay, as long as you don't leave any lighted butts around."

They dropped down on the grass by the lakeside. In the still air the blue smoke rose companionably between them, and Lesley turned impulsively toward him. "Tell me about my father," she begged. "Oh, I know what you said, about him being goodhearted, capable, all that," she ran on quickly, "but that's not enough for me. What was he like really?"

He threw her a dispassionate glance and Lesley endeavored in vain to stem the tide of color she knew was creeping up into her cheeks.

"Like you, I guess." His voice was laconic. "Square chin, freckles."

"Truly? Like me? To look at, you mean?" Lesley glanced across at him, clear blue eyes alight with interest. "That's what I thought, when I saw that photograph of him at the house." She clasped her hands around her knees and sat dreaming.

The diffused light slanting through the tall branches overhead gave a gentle warmth. Above in the trees she heard the harsh cry of a kaka, and shielding her eyes against the gentle sunlight, she spied the gray green sheen of a native parrot as it alighted in the branches of a giant red beech.

"Other ways, too," Stuart was saying, and she caught the twitch of the firmly cut mouth above the deeply cleft chin. "Once he'd set his mind on something, nothing short of an earthquake would shift him."

"Oh!" She glanced away to escape the battery of those keenly observant gray eyes. So they were back to that again! In the pleasure of the outing, the novelty of her surroundings, she'd forgotten everything else. And now.... Unconsciously she sighed. Well, here we go again! Aloud she said, "You mean, about the store? Selling it?"

"How did you guess?" The soft tones, so surprisingly cultured for a man of the outback, were ironic.

Lesley inhaled deeply. She was thankful for her cigarette; it gave her time to think. One thing was for sure—he wanted the store badly. He'd set his heart on obtaining it. And in a way she could understand his feelings. That intended bushcraft school in which he was so caught up was, after all, just another branch of the welfare and social work that he'd been forced to give up when he'd taken on the running of the family property in Waione. If only it wasn't *her* land that he'd settled on as the ideal site for his project! Maybe, though, if she explained all that the place meant to her, he'd understand, accept her decision and drop the subject, once and for all. Well, she could but try.

"Mr. Carrington...." She stared at the cigarette held lightly between her fingers.

He sent her a significant look. "Stuart's the name."

"Stuart, then." She took a deep breath, wondering how

best to frame the words. "About the property—the store. You do understand why I want to hold on to it, make a go of it? I guess," she hesitated, "it's because I've never really had anything of my own up till now. Anything important, that is to say."

"Anything? Or anyone?"

The low voice was careless, offhand. And yet somehow Lesley sensed an undeniable impact in the man's tones. She laughed nervously. "I don't know what you mean."

Leaning back on one elbow, he eyed her narrowly, the smoke from his cigarette curling lazily upward. "Oh, yes, you do!"

"If you're asking," she said in a low tone, "have I ever been in love with anyone, the answer's no."

"Don't be too sure. There's always a first time."

She couldn't meet his gaze. "What do you mean?"

"Nothing! Skip it!"

Hastily she reverted to the subject of property. It seemed safer. "About the store...."

He was eyeing her once again with that hateful glint of amusement. "Forget it. I've waited this long. What's a few more weeks?"

"You still think—" She broke off in exasperation. Oh, he was insufferable! It served her right for having expected her explanation to draw some friendly polite response from him. She might have known it would be like this, after yesterday! But she'd been trapped into false hopes by his impersonal friendliness. Indeed, once or twice she'd come perilously close to liking him— She brought herself up sharply. Hadn't Mrs. Mac warned her that women just couldn't resist him? Well, she'd show him that this was one woman who hadn't fallen a victim to his virile good looks and arrogant manner. She too could act offhandedly. She'd beat him at his own game!

"You know something?" She forced her voice to a light inconsequential note. "Could be you'll wait a long time. You might even get tired of waiting."

He raised black brows and grinned. That hateful derisive grin. "Longer than a month? I shouldn't think so."

Beyond the Ranges

"But what if you do?" she persisted, and then wished she hadn't pursued the subject, for he was fixing her with something in his gaze. Something.... At the man's intent stare she was forced to drop her eyes. She stubbed out her cigarette on the damp leaf mold. Anything to break that mood of dangerous intimacy.

"Like I said," he drawled, his voice as lazy, as soft as ever, "I'd get it just the same. The other way."

Lesley's thoughts were racing wildly. He'd said that yesterday.

"What...other way?"

For a moment there was silence. A tiny flame flickered in the gray eyes, and for no reason at all, Lesley's heart was beating a suffocating tattoo.

"You don't believe me?"

But she had gone too far now to retreat. "Not really."

"If you really want to know...." Before she could make her escape he had moved close, and she felt the strong impact of his lips that seemed to carry her into a wild and rapturous moment. For a second she was caught in a wave of high elation. The gentle sunshine splintered into a dizzying radiance. Then at last she came back to reality and tried to wrench herself away.

He released her gently. "You did ask me, you know."

With an odd sense of hurt, she turned away. So that was what he thought! He imagined he merely had to make love to her and he'd be able to bend her to his will. That she'd immediately fall in love with him, just like all the others—and she so very nearly had! No use denying it. But she told herself that forewarned was forearmed. She'd take care from now on. Never, never again would she allow herself to fall into the trap he had just sprung.

"Yes." She swallowed and pushed the hair back behind her ears in a characteristic gesture, "now I know." Springing to her feet, she glanced back over her shoulder. "Time to go?"

"If you wish." He appeared entirely unperturbed as he joined her on the mossy track. And why not? He hadn't felt the breath of the scorching fire that could so easily sweep one beyond the commonsense dictates of the mind. As for herself, she'd take care not to expose herself to that danger again!

"The Maoris," the man was saying, just as though nothing had happened between them, "had some quaint ideas about the forest. The Children of the Mist believed implicitly in their myths, traced their ancestry back to known time. And according to them, the trees of the forest were the children of Tane, the god of forests. Every tree had its own spirit, and they went to no end of trouble to appease them. The forest was a dangerous place—not that it still isn't a dangerous place."

Look who's talking, Lesley commented silently.

He went on explaining Maori lore, indicating the various types of native bush, pointing out the tawari tree with its graceful foliage and clusters of white flowers. But Lesley heard him as though she were in a dream. All she wanted now was to escape from the presence of this stranger who had in so short a space of time turned her world upside down, and who had for her some crazy magnetism. For of course that was all it could be—and being taken unawares, betrayed by the remote and breathtaking loveliness of her surroundings.

The winding track with its dark leaf mold underfoot and earthy fragrance now seemed endless, but at last they emerged into the sunshine and soon were climbing back into the sturdy dust-coated Land Rover.

Stuart started the engine, then turned toward Lesley, a question in his gray eyes. "Had enough? I could take you on to Waikaremoana, the big lake—the Sea of Rippling Waters, the Maoris call it. Okay, then, another time." For Lesley was shaking her head. He put the Land Rover into gear and they turned into the metal road and headed for the ridges ahead.

As they twisted over the precipitous hills where the sun glistened on tree ferns, light against the somber backdrop of the bush, Lesley was silent. Stuart, too, seemed lost in his thoughts. There was more traffic on the route now, and the odd driver who swept past them lifted a hand toward Stuart in friendly salutation. The Maori workmen employed in the

Beyond the Ranges

construction gangs along the roads also appeared well acquainted with him. Muscular, powerful men, bare to the waist, they glanced toward the driver of the Land Rover with a friendly gesture and a broad grin.

A man's man, Lesley mused. The Big Boss of the district. But not so far as she herself was concerned. To her he was distracting and disturbing, a man against whom she had to be ever on her guard. Almost you could say he was her enemy. Or was it—deep down a small voice asked—her own traitorous heart against which she had to be on guard? Nonsense! She forced her attention back to the highway, telling herself as they took a steep incline toward a familiar one-way bridge over a stream, that she was glad the journey was almost over and they were nearing Waione.

"Thanks for the trip," she murmured as the Land Rover pulled up in a cloud of dust outside the entrance to the country store.

"Enjoy it?"

Lesley glanced evasively away. "Some of it."

"Look," he swung toward her, hands resting lightly on the steering wheel, "I'm sorry about that swing bridge—I'd no idea. Living up here in the back of beyond you're inclined to forget that that sort of lark isn't for everyone. Tell you what—" he sent her a bright disarming smile "—how about a spot of civilization to make up? I've got to run into Taupo tonight. We could take in a thermal hotel there, have a dip in the mineral pools. That is—" he glanced at her keenly "—if you're interested?"

Lesley wrenched her gaze from the bright magnetism of the man's gaze. "Thanks, but—" she contrived a smile and forced her voice to a light careless note "—I'd rather not—tonight." She added with a deliberate vagueness, "Another time, maybe."

"Okay," he grinned. Then, swinging his long legs from beneath the wheel, he slammed the door behind him and went around to the other side of the vehicle. "I'll remind you of that. Well, see you!" He seated himself once more behind the steering wheel.

The fact that she'd declined his invitation to go to Taupo with him didn't matter to him one way or another, Lesley thought with an odd little pang of regret. Why should it? No doubt he had merely asked her as part of his deliberate campaign to influence her to his way of thinking. Well, it wouldn't work!

CHAPTER FOUR

LESLEY WAS SEATED on the back steps, reveling in the hot sunshine, when she caught a flash of green moving up the winding road. A moment later the squeal of brakes sounded from somewhere near at hand as the road services bus pulled up outside the door.

Hurrying inside, Lesley ran toward the open doorway, colliding somewhere in the region of the waist of the massive dark-bearded man who seemed to fill the opening. With a muttered "Sorry," she pushed past him, intent on the waiting coach outside. A handful of passengers were gazing idly through the dust-smeared windows.

The driver, young and sandy haired, was tossing down a green canvas mail bag before climbing back into the vehicle.

"My bags!" Lesley gasped.

"It's okay, miss," the young man turned to throw a grin over a white-clad shoulder. "Dropped them just now. Someone took them inside—big bloke with a black beard."

"Oh, thank you." Lesley turned to meet the smiling gaze of the heavily built young man, who was holding a bag in each hand as though they were no more than feather light. The next moment the surprised glance of the dark eyes changed to a puzzled frown. He pushed his straw sun hat to the back of his head. "Guess there's some mix-up," he murmured in slow, rich tones. "This gear is for Monty's boy—some clobber he's sent on ahead, by the look of it."

"No, no." Lesley burst into laughter at the expression of bewilderment on the dark bearded face. "They're mine! Sorry to give you all such a shock, but I happen to be Lesley—Monty's *girl*! I don't know," she finished on a confused breath, "why everyone here had made up their minds beforehand that I was a boy!"

"Oh, don't apologize." The great liquid eyes fixed on

Lesley's face were warmly appreciative. "We can sure take any amount of shocks like that. But—" he still looked a trifle bewildered "—you mean to say you've come all the way...."

Lesley's lips twitched in amusement. "That's right. Only it was only a few days in a VC 10, actually."

The big man continued to stare at her. "From the Old Country."

"Where?" Lesley stared at him inquiringly.

"England, that is to say. My dad always used to call it the Old Country, and I sort of inherited it from him. Well, what do you know? Must have given Mrs. Mac the shock of her life when you stepped off the bus."

"It did, rather," Lesley admitted. "But she's got used to me now. Anyway, thanks for bringing in my bags."

The big man turned away. "Aw, forget it. Where do you want 'em? I'll stow them away."

As the stranger followed her into the living room, Mrs. Mac came into view. She glanced from one to the other. "Hello, Ross, how are things? You two met? Ross, this is Lesley—Ross Conway. He pilots one of the 'copters for the forestry service up here, when the weather's fine. Well, now that you're here—" it was clear from Mrs. Mac's beaming face that the bearded helicopter pilot was a special favorite with the older woman "—why not have a meal with us—" She stopped short. "Wait a minute, I thought you were away up north. Aren't you still on holiday?"

For a moment the big man looked taken aback. "That's right, until next week. Guess I just couldn't keep away from the old place. Thought I'd take a look up here and see how things were getting along without me." As the man finished speaking his gaze flickered toward Lesley. "Got to zoom into Taupo a bit later on today. How about if you both come along, too? Just for the run."

"Sorry, Ross." Mrs. Mac shook her straight silver locks. "Can't make it today, I'm afraid. Why don't you ask Lesley?"

"Think it would do me any good?"

Lesley's glance slanted up to meet the man's smiling gaze. "You could try, and find out."

"Here goes, then." From his height he stooped toward her. "Care to come for a run, Miss Monteith? Taupo's quite a place: hot springs bubbling up in the sand at the water's edge; boating, trout fishing, mineral baths—the lot. Coming from England, chances are you've never come across a lake quite that size."

Or men who lose so little time in arranging a date, Lesley thought. Well, why not? The men in this district were rugged outdoor types, accustomed to masculine company. Their ways of approach were direct and uncomplicated. Except for that maddening Stuart, who was as devious and underhand and thoroughly despicable—why, he'd use *any* means to further his own ends! He'd even admitted as much, darn him! But she wouldn't allow herself to dwell on him—and immediately broke the resolution as the thought came unbidden: it would serve him right if she did accept the invitation! Why not go to Taupo with this big dark man? He was open and friendly, quite honest about being attracted to a new girl in the district. Besides, what better way to erase that other face, stern and satirical, from her mind than to busy herself with other matters? Better still. Make certain that her time was occupied with someone else. Someone more considerate, more straightforward. And anyway, she told herself, she had to go to the township in order to arrange for supplies for the store, didn't she?

"Thank you. But there are strings to it," Lesley stipulated smilingly. "I'd like to have a look around the town, get some more stores for the shop. Since my ... father—" she stumbled over the unfamiliar word "—died, the stocks seem to have got awfully low. Is this—how do you say it, Tau-po—a big place?"

"Big enough! And you can get the stuff sent through by freighter to Waione. No problem." He eyed her inquiringly. "You planning to carry on with running the place here?" He paused a moment. "I got the idea—didn't anyone pass on the word to you about Carrington wanting to make an offer for the property?"

Lesley's soft lips tightened. "Oh, yes, I know all about it. He told me himself. But I let him know—" how easy it was to be brave and assertive now that she was out of range of those merciless, all-observant gray eyes "—that the idea was out, definitely—that I'd decided to stay on here myself."

"That must have rocked him!" He exchanged a significant glance with Mrs. Mac. "Did you let her in on how things are here?"

The older woman paused in her task of unpacking a carton of cigarettes that had just arrived by the bus. She chuckled gently. "It's all right, Ross, she knows. I explained to Lesley how it is, that there's no fortune to be made here. But she's still determined to carry on. So...."

But Lesley was fast becoming impatient with the subject of her inability to pull the business together and place it on a more financial footing. It seemed to her that everyone she met in Waione was doing their utmost to discourage her, and she was rapidly becoming tired of it!

"About Taupo..." she said cheerfully. "I'll make out some lists of stock we need this afternoon. What time are you setting off?"

"Any old time that suits you," Ross said. "How about later—fourish?"

"I'll be ready," Lesley promised smilingly, "now that I've got something to wear!"

She moved toward the bulging suitcases. But he was there before her, carrying the bags into the bedroom and tossing them on the cherry-colored spread. "Be seeing you at four, then." The dark eyes twinkled merrily. "I sure am glad that 'Lesley' wasn't a boy!"

Lesley watched through the window as Ross Conway strode along the metal in the direction of the timbered huts that were the government forestry service's single men's quarters situated a little farther along the road. A massive figure—she wouldn't be surprised—a gentle, kindly giant withal.

That afternoon, with Mrs. Mac's assistance, Lesley made out lists of the foodstuffs and assorted goods needed to fill the depleted shelves in the store. The task took a long time, for it seemed to Lesley that any suggestion of hers that failed to come under the heading of the barest household necessity was firmly frowned upon by her helper. The older woman made no secret of her disapproval of Lesley's firm decision to stock up on a variety of toilet preparations and summer clothing for both men and women.

"You're mad," she announced bluntly. With a critical flick of her ball-point, she ran her eyes swiftly down the list of figures. "Have you any idea of what all this is going to cost? You'll never get your money back, you know! Not in a hundred years!"

"Well, anyway—" Lesley stuck stubbornly to her decision "—at least I'm going to give it a go!" It was bad enough to be browbeaten by that hateful interfering Stuart Carrington. She was determined not to be intimidated also by Mrs. Mac, no matter how well meant the advice! What's more, she thought rebelliously, she'd a good mind to order a deep-freeze cabinet as well, while she was on the job! In this summer heat it was practically a necessity. It was quite ridiculous—all this argument. After all, it was her own money, wasn't it?

When the dark giant called to take her out, she was ready. She'd swept her hair back from her face, tying it at the nape of her neck with a narrow black ribbon, and in a simple primrose-colored shift, yellow thonged sandals on her feet, she felt cool and comfortable.

As her escort turned to speak to Mrs. Mac, Lesley studied him covertly: magnificent shoulders, steady brown eyes, a slow smile.

Then they were strolling toward the long red car waiting at the entrance, and Mrs. Mac was waving them goodbye. "No need to hurry back," she called in her strident tones. "Take your time! I can manage here."

The big man grinned and raised a huge brown hand. "I just might take you up on that!"

"And don't let Lesley spend all her money!" was Mrs. Mac's parting shot as the dust-coated, late-model car swung around in the narrow road and gathered speed.

"You aimin' to stock up the old place?" Skillfully the man guided the vehicle around a sharp bend in the bush-fringed road. "Guess Monty wasn't all that interested in the business side of the store."

"I know, I know." Lesley turned toward him with eager

interest. Here at last was someone who was prepared to listen to her plans, instead of dashing cold water on everything she suggested. "I thought," she explained, "that if I could get more stock—you know, toiletries, summer clothing that folks would want to buy. And sort of brighten everything up, make the windows attractive."

The man nodded, his gaze fixed on a fragment of winding road that curved into the bush ahead. "Might work at that. You couldn't tell without giving it a go."

"That's just what I've been telling Mrs. Mac! So I thought, when we get to Taupo, I'd order all the things I want. That is," she hesitated, "if it's a big enough place."

"Big? That depends on what you happen to be comparing it with. And seeing you come from London— But you'll be able to see for yourself pretty soon."

Lesley relaxed in the comfort of the well-sprung seat, conscious of the invigorating mountain air, the fresh breeze, spiced with the tang of the bush, that tossed her hair around her shoulders. Idly she listened to her companion's slow considering voice as he pointed out the various landmarks of the district through which they were passing.

"That's Te Whaiti—see those ridges running around the hill at the back of the settlement?" Lesley peered forward, taking in the grass-covered indentations. "They're the remains of the old Maori fortifications. And that's a Maori meeting house."

Lesley turned her head to glance back toward the ornamental carving of the crossed barge boards that she had noticed on her way to Waione. Could it have been only two days ago?

Soon the big car was swaying around the hairpin bends of the winding road, and she glimpsed ahead the undulating sea of pines.

"Kaingaroa pine forest," the big dark man was saying in his rich measured tones. "They tell me it's the largest man-made forest in the world!" As they followed the road cutting between the somber green expanse, he gestured to a tower high above. "Bloke up there in the lookout tower's on duty night and day, keeping an eye open for fires—the big danger around these parts."

"Yes...." But Lesley's thoughts strayed. Fire—and Stuart Carrington. Somehow the two were irrevocably linked in her mind. Linked in some fashion with danger. It wasn't as though she was afraid of the Big Boss. He had no jurisdiction over her. But deep in her mind a small voice whispered, *No? Supposing he's lit a fire already? A secret flame.* Ridiculous! He was disturbing, arrogant, infuriating. How could she help but be affected by someone so aggravatingly sure of himself? And if maybe a small traitorous flame flickered somewhere deep in her heart, well what of it? It was merely a lively antagonism. Nothing that she couldn't extinguish at will. Why on earth was she thinking of Stuart Carrington all the time? Determinedly she wrenched her thoughts away, gazing unseeingly over the vast sea of pine plantations. In the distance, a grader was cutting a firebreak through the trees. But it was no use. A board loomed up in front of her eyes: Fire May Cost You Your Life. Be Careful! Careful!

They swept out into open country, moving past cabbage trees that tossed their shaggy heads in the wind, and isolated mailboxes nailed to the trunks of tall trees at farm gateposts. Then they were approaching Rainbow Mountain, where drifts of steam rose from the fern and tea trees of the colored slopes.

"It's a pretty active thermal area from now on," Ross told her. "In one of the craters of Rainbow Mountain, right by the highway, there's a warm green lake. And there's a freshwater lake opposite."

But Lesley reflected that she was no longer surprised at anything in this incredible thermal area, where for the next few miles vapor wreaths curled upward from hot springs hidden by dense manuka on either side of the roadway. And the white pumice scattered over the countryside was the result of erupting volcanoes, some of which were still not extinct, thousands of years previously.

Now Lesley was viewing unfamiliar country. She glanced ahead toward a low sprawling timbered building with blue iron roofing, the sweeping green lawns dotted with flowering hibiscus shrubs. Surrounding the attractive grounds was a velvety golf course.

Ross followed her gaze toward the luxurious building. "Wairakei Hotel—hear that roaring?"

Lesley laughed. "I couldn't miss it!"

"That's the humming of the geothermal bores at the power station," Ross explained in his deliberate slow tones. "Quite a tourist spot, Wairakei." He gestured toward a plume of steam rising above the pines. "Down in Geyser Valley you can take your pick of steaming mud pools, boiling water terraces, formations, whatever, and the Karapiti blowhole! Pow! At night, with the lighting, it beats any fireworks display! All that steam, pouring through the earth's crust, is really something. Say—" he turned eagerly toward her "—why don't you let me take you one night? Why not today? We could have dinner at the tourist hotel, get our tickets and go on from there."

But Lesley shook her head. "Love to. But I don't think I'd better stop for sightseeing today." She smiled. "I'm a working girl—or supposed to be. Remember? And I've got simply oodles of stuff to buy today."

"Right. We'll just stop for a glance at Huka Falls from the lookout." They sped down between the waving toa-toas that tossed their creamy plumes on either side of the highway, and Ross drew up at a clearing in the bush.

"Come on over the bridge." As they strolled down the rise, Lesley suffered a moment of apprehension as she eyed the swing bridge spanning the torrent of rushing waters below. But the next minute she realized her fears were groundless. This was an entirely different proposition from the forestry bridge that she had crossed, "at her peril", with Stuart Carrington. Lesley approached the solidly built structure with its firm handrails happily, pausing to gaze down at the terrific volume and force of the water as it dashed through the rocky ravine above the falls. On the other side she found herself in a tea-tree bush. The wind whispering in the tall pines overhead mingled with the roar of the water cascading in a shower of blue, churned to white foam, that flowed on between the bush-covered banks.

Leslie slipped her camera from its case. The scene was so sparkling. Cabbage trees pierced a sky of electric blue. Everywhere was color and movement—a scene so fresh and clear that it seemed to her that each leaf and twig glittered in the sunshine.

Afterward they strolled up the rise to the lookout and took the smooth bitumen highway once more, and now Lesley caught her first glimpse of the great inland sea that was Lake Taupo. Presently they swept up beside the water and her eager glance took in the inky-blue water with its white-capped wavelets slapping on the sand. Above were pine-clad hills and beyond, clearly etched against the blue, rose the snow-capped peak of the great volcanic mountain, Ruapehu.

The water was dotted with the gaily colored sails of yachts and keelers, canoes and catamarans, and the wind blowing off the lake was cool and fresh. The murmuring in the tall pines above mingled with the sound of the little waves breaking on the shore.

"Like it?"

"Do I?" Leslie lifted an enraptured face toward the man towering above her. "It's so colorful!" Her roving glance took in the depths of the blues and greens in the tossing water and moved toward the white pumice roads that snaked over the hills around her. Around the lakeshore she glimpsed restaurants and motels; gay, new, attractive timber buildings, brightly painted and shaded by flowering bushes and blossoming trees. And could those really be nectarine, peach and loquat trees that were growing wild along the lakeshore?

"I like this too—this entrance." She strolled over the bitumen toward the high crossed timbers with their intricate scrolled Maori carving. The structure rose above the backdrop of white-capped waves, the supporting timbers hidden at the base by native bronze flax, blowing in the wind.

Lesley gazed up at the carved Maori figures with their three-fingered hands, and the grotesque overlarge faces cocked to one side stared back at her from iridescent blue green eyes.

The man followed her glance. "Paua shell—Eyes of the Gods, the Maoris call it. Well, let's go, shall we? Take a look around the town."

They skirted the marina with its tangled network of masts and spars. The varied craft ranged from light kayak canoes, dinghies, and "paper-tigers," the small, fast-moving catamarans that Lesley could see scudding across the blue water, to cruisers and luxuriously appointed fishing craft. Then they drove up the wide colorful streets, where it seemed to Lesley that each store was new and gaily painted, the wide glass show windows filled with attractively displayed merchandise.

Especially was she drawn to the craft shops that featured such a wealth and variety of locally made handcrafts and souvenirs. Here were deerskin-suede garments and bags, handspun yarn, fluffy sheepskin rugs dyed in glowing shades. But it was the authentic Maori carvings and jewelery, fashioned from local stone and greenstone and the glittering paua shell, the work of native craftsmen, that fascinated her most of all.

"You like that, don't you?" Ross was watching Lesley as she fingered a silver chain from which fell a gray stone medallion decorated with a motif: a rough impression of a boat, such as might have been executed, Lesley mused, puzzled, by a very small child.

"Copy of an early rock painting," Ross explained, glancing down over her shoulder at the painted stone. "Someone came across them by accident not long ago. They were daubed in clay on the walls of a river cave. They're as old as time. A bit of luck, finding them, actually, especially as the bulldozers were due to move in and demolish the caves any day. Look, let me—"

"Oh, no! *Please*...." Lesley hung the medallion back among the tangle of silver chains on a high peg.

"But you've got to have something, some sort of souvenir to mark your first visit here."

It was clear to Lesley that it would be useless to protest further. The kindly giant was determined to purchase the stone medallion, and already the sales lady was hovering near, eyeing the man with speculative eyes.

"Okay, then, if you insist."

"Good as done!" The medallion was packed in a tiny box, which Lesley slipped in her bag. Then she made a purchase on her own account, one of the attractive kits woven from dried flax by local Maori women.

Swinging the kit from her hand, she strolled with Ross up the wide sunshiny street with its modern tourist facilities and sprinkling of overseas visitors.

In the spacious, modern, well-appointed grocery store, Lesley found shopping to be an easy matter. She simply handed her list of requirements to a helpful store assistant. The young man in a white apron ran his eye swiftly down the page. "Can do. You'll want this lot sent up to Waione by freighter? Should be there by the middle of the week. Hold it." He glanced toward Lesley inquiringly. "You haven't got any frozen lines on the order. Did you mean to include any?"

"Yes—no—that is...." Lesley stood irresolute. "I haven't a deep-freeze in the store yet. I wonder...."

Ross, meeting her contemplative glance, shrugged broad shoulders. "It's up to you, I guess. It's a hang of a lot of money to lay out."

"You could pay it off in easy installments," the assistant intervened persuasively. "In small monthly payments, you'd scarcely notice it."

"No, I wouldn't do that." Suddenly she made her decision. Even though it would deplete her small capital to a dangerously low figure, she'd risk it. After all, it was an investment! Lesley took out her checkbook and the matter was soon completed.

"Good-oh! And now you'll want it filled? It can all go together on the freighter."

"That's the idea." Happily, Lesley, with Ross's help, spent some time in choosing the various frozen foodstuffs.

"Not too much in the frozen vegetable line," Ross cautioned. "The mill folk in Waione grow their own greens and tomatoes mostly."

"They might like some out of season ones for a change," Lesley suggested. "We'll take lots of frozen novelties for the children, and swags of the fabulous ice cream you have in this country."

"Should be good," the man agreed. "It's a dairy country with real cream, and plenty of it!"

Lesley went on ordering the supply of frozen stock, pushing away the little pang of apprehension as the figures mounted. But it was done now. She had made her decision, even if she had little of her capital left. Only sufficient really for paint and wallpaper materials and— Oh, dear! She'd forgotten to allow for the purchase of the clothing!

Ross must have caught her anxious expression.

"Running low in cash?"

She nodded. "But not to worry." She smiled gaily up at him. "It's an investment."

"That's the way to look at it, honey!"

He took her arm, relieving her of the flax basket that bulged with luscious peaches and Pacific Island bananas, which Lesley had been unable to resist in the fruit shop next door, and they wandered out into the sunshiny street.

But she was lucky, for the paint shop over the road featured a sale of wallpaper materials and she had little difficulty in choosing quick-drying paint in soft pastel shades and rolls of thick attractive paper in neutral tones.

"It's already pasted," the assistant in the shop assured her. "Anyone could lay it."

"Anyone? Even me?"

"I'll give you a hand if you like," Ross offered obligingly.

"It doesn't seem right somehow—" Lesley smiled up into the bearded dark face as they moved out of the wide doorway "—a helicopter pilot laying wallpaper."

He grinned. "Might come in handy one of these days, with a bit of luck."

Lesley wondered at the sudden bleak look in the great brown eyes.

But the next moment she stood entranced, pausing to gaze at the beautifully draped display window filled with dress fabrics of all shades and patterns. Here were materials that varied from crystal-beaded crimplenes to the gayest of Hawaiian beach cottons.

Lesley, spying a pile of specially marked down prints, stared at the price tag incredulously. At that ridiculously low figure she could afford to buy lengths of gay crisp cottons and run them up herself into simple house frocks and colorful Hawaiian-style shirts. For who could resist these psychedelic swirls and spots and abstract patterns in their dazzling shades?

A selection of patterns were displayed on a shelf, and Lesley chose three simple styles—loose, well-cut shifts for the women, and for the menfolk, a short-sleeved, open-necked style of shirt.

Ross had left her to collect the car and was waiting for her when she emerged into the blaze of late afternoon sunshine. "Wow!" He eyed the bulky packages in surprise. "You been buying the shop out?"

Lesley smiled. "Just about. I've never seen such bargains in materials, or such a selection of colors."

As the long car cruised up the street, her thoughts were busy. She was thinking ahead... planning.

There was an elderly Singer sewing machine stashed away in the hall cupboard in the house. No doubt it belonged to Mrs. Mac. But Lesley was sure the older woman wouldn't mind her making use of it. She could run up these cheap garments, add on a little for expenses and profit and step up her earnings quite a lot. She was certain of it!

As they moved along a ridge looking over the lake below, she told Ross of her plans. "I'll make a half a dozen shifts and shirts for a start, just to see how they go."

"Good for you, Lesley!"

They motored down the slopes and soon were taking a smooth wide bitumen road that skirted the shore; passing the brightly painted motels with their blossoming trees and flowering shrubs that studded the lush green grass sweeping down to the restless waters of the lake.

"Got an idea," Ross was saying, glancing down at the watch encircling his tanned wrist. "You're not in a hurry to get back?"

Lesley shook her head. "Not really."

"Well, then, let's whoop it up a bit! Take in dinner at the De Brett! It's a place I know—thermal hotel a mile or so out of town. They put on a spot of dancing Saturday nights."

Lesley hesitated. She had already refused Stuart Carrington's carelessly extended suggestion to visit the thermal town with him tonight. What if she happened to run into him this evening? So what? She'd be glad if he did see her here—with her escort. That would show him how little he counted in her scheme of things. Prove to him that his kiss—that kiss of expediency—had meant no more to her than it had to him.

"Why not?" She smiled up into the bearded, good-natured face.

Ross swung the car around and they took a rise, climbing higher as they swept through the attractive streets with their gay timber homes, sweeping lawns and profusion of flower gardens. At length the car turned into a wide driveway to draw up beside the wide timber verandas of an old white two-storeyed building with blue iron roofing and sloping green lawns. Stepping out of the car, Lesley was immediately conscious of the exhilarating freshness of the alpine air. Eagerly she glanced around her, held by the fabulous scenic panorama of lake and snow-capped mountains.

"Let's rent some swimsuits and try out the pool," Ross suggested.

Lesley assented smilingly, waiting while the man got swimsuits and towels from the white-painted store at the summit of the winding path.

Together she and Ross wandered down a curving path leading to the thermal valley below, and once again Lesley was conscious of the novelty of the scene.

For beyond the steep, flower-encrusted banks of the winding track she glimpsed a deep valley where landscaped mineral pools fitted naturally into the peaceful beauty of their surroundings. The volcanic soil beneath had been tapped in hot open-air mineral pools and spout baths. Nearby glimmered the waters of a large, heated freshwater swimming pool, where the attractive stonework surround was gay with brightly hued tables and striped beach umbrellas.

Lesley, wearing a black swimsuit, was waiting for Ross when he emerged from the dressing shed and came striding toward her, a big man in brief swimming trunks. And once again she was struck by his magnificent physique.

Then they were plunging together into the soft waters of

a heated mineral pool. And a little while later they strolled over the incredible emerald grass to dive into the crystal-clear depth of a great freshwater pool.

Presently they pulled themselves up onto the stone platform and watched the moving scene around them. It seemed to Lesley, idly taking in the plumes of steam rising from the grounds around her, that the luxurious pools in their native bush setting had the impression of a fairyland.

"Smoke?" She waited while the man lighted her cigarette, then leaned back, watching the smoke as it curled lazily upward to mingle with wisps of steam drifting against the somber green banks of tea tree and fern.

"You know something?" She roused herself from a relaxed feeling that was no doubt due to the properties contained in the soft, heated mineral water. Ross was sprawled on his stomach, his face turned away, his voice muffled. "I haven't brought a girl here since Vicky."

"Oh?" Lesley sat up and moving to the edge of the platform dangled her toes in the crystal-clear water of the pool. Intuitively she sensed a depth of feeling underlining the man's casually worded confidence. "And who," she asked lightly, "was Vicky?"

"'Was' is right!" Lesley caught the bitter note of pain that tinged the deep rich tones. "Well, I may as well tell you...." Ross flung the damp hair back from his eyes and dropping down on the wet tiles beside Lesley, sent her a self-conscious look. "Vicky— Well, I'm pretty keen about that girl. Even got around to thinking about house-building plans, a lounge suite, washing machine—all that. But she—" He broke off on a long sigh.

"Guess it just doesn't work out," he went on after a moment, "having a girl living at the other end of the island. Might as well be at the other side of the world for all I see of her. I guess that's how things got snarled up."

Lesley drew on her cigarette. "What sort of things?"

"Oh, you know, gossip." He shrugged massive, deeply tanned shoulders. "Like this last bust up. I had a few days off work, went up to stay with her and her folks up North. They've got a beach place—bach—in the Bay of Islands. We got on fine, Vicky and I, had a whale of a time—until she got to talking to a guy from the forestry outfit in Rotorua and collected some garbled version of my taking out some girl down here. Oh, it's not the first time we've had this sort of thing out. Trouble with Vicky is that she just won't take my word for it, that there's no one else who matters a damn with me."

"What's she like?" Lesley inquired.

"Like?" The big man searched for words. "Kinda cute. Little, cheeky-looking, sort of... red hair. Maybe that accounts for it. If only," he said on a long sigh, "she wasn't so darned suspicious!"

"Sure you didn't give her reason?" Lesley sent him a teasing smile.

"I swear I didn't." The man's voice was strained. He sat up, regarding Lesley with troubled brown eyes. "That's the heck of it! There was just nothing to it! Oh, a night out, dinner at Brents at Rotorua, a show afterward. But nothing more than that! Damn it all, I hardly know the girl! She was staying with friends for the weekend, up Waione way. Yet Vicky insists on treating it all as a major production."

"But didn't you tell her how it was really? Explain?"

"You just try," Ross said, "explaining things to Vicky! Boy, you don't know her! When she decides to throw a jealous fit she really goes to town! We had one big bust up. Now she won't have anything more to do with me, so she says," he finished gloomily. After a moment the deep tones went on. "Boy, what a holiday! That's why I came back early. Gee—" he glanced away self-consciously "—I don't know why I'm boring you with my life story."

But Lesley broke in crisply, "You'll just have to do something to make her understand. How about a love letter?"

He shook his dark head despondently. "Had a shot at that after our last flare-up, but Vicky sent them all back to me unopened."

"Well then," Lesley suggested, "what about the phone?"

"She doesn't answer the phone," Ross answered moodily, "if she knows that it's me at the other end. 'Long-distance call from Waione' gives her fair warning. If only," he sighed despairingly, "I could see her again, put things right with her! That's why I took this 'copter job. I thought it would give me a chance to see her more often. But I guess it didn't work out like that. And now it seems it's too late."

"Too late?"

The big man nodded. "I rang through to her home town the minute I got back today. Her mother told me she'd taken off by air for Sydney on a working holiday. She's no idea for how long."

"But," Lesley inquired, "you've got Vicky's address in Australia?"

"For what it's worth. If only—" Lesley caught the low muttered words "—I could get her out of my mind." A little shamefacedly the big man added hastily, "we've been going around together for quite a while now. And just when I got to thinking that everything was going along fine...."

"Don't worry." Lesley slipped down into the water. Clinging to the edge of the pool, she smiled up into the heavy, bearded face. "Something'll happen to put things right, you'll see. And if it doesn't... well, you'll just have to do something about it."

"Such as?" The man regarded her with pain-filled dark eyes.

"Don't know yet, but I'll think of something!" As she floated on her back, hair streaming in the water and face upturned to the rays of the westering sun, Lesley's expression was thoughtful. How could it be that merely falling in love with someone could bring such anguish of mind to a man? Or, for that matter, to a woman? For a second the despairing face of Anna, the girl who had shared her plane seat on the journey from London, flashed across the mental screen of her mind. The other girl's voice, ragged with emotion, echoed once again in her ears: "Guess you wouldn't know... you've never been in love."

And I don't want to be—ever, Lesley told herself, if that's all there is to it. Nothing but anguish and longing and torment.

Suddenly, for no reason at all, Stuart Carrington's face flashed into her mind. Stuart, with his disturbing smile, a mocking expression lighting the alive gray eyes. Just as though he were challenging her, laughing at her. He was always laughing at her. Although why on earth she should think of him at this moment....

She thrust the thought aside, and throwing a call over her shoulder to Ross: "Race you to the end," began to cleave the water with her clean strokes, making for the opposite end of the pool.

Presently they left the pool and side by side, their damp towels swinging from their hands, they strolled up the steep winding path, where the rocky walls were encrusted with ice plants and flowering creepers. Lesley was conscious of a delicious sensation of relaxation.

In the foyer of the hotel, with its hospitable atmosphere and wide windows overlooking the lake, she paused to look at the life-size carving of a local paramount Maori chief. And later, seated in the spacious dining room with its luxury and comfort and international cuisine, Lesley reflected that life in the outback of New Zealand, if not what she had expected, was nevertheless proving... well, interesting.

The next moment she had reason to change her mind. The waiter had set before her a bowl of oheroa soup, and as Lesley took up her spoon she caught sight of the group being escorted past the table where she was seated with Ross. The tall man in the rear was, of course, Stuart Carrington! In white turtleneck sweater, slacks, a blue reefer jacket, he appeared as infuriatingly sure of himself as ever. *And* as quick to notice her! For his swift glance had already picked her out from the crowd of diners. He would! At Stuart's knowledgeable grin she sent him a tentative smile, then quickly dropped her glance. Her mind in a turmoil, she found herself wishing that Ross had escorted her to another dining room in the town—any other one rather than the De Brett! Now she regretted having remained in Taupo tonight, after refusing Stuart Carrington's invitation to come here. That was, if you could regard his offhanded remark as an invitation to dine out.

But she couldn't resist a swift glance toward the party who were approaching the table where she and Ross were seated. One woman was short and plump, with a round dimpled face and curly chestnut-colored hair. She appeared to laugh a great deal. The other.... Unconsciously Lesley sighed. Judith, undoubtedly. The extremely tall brunette, jet black hair dressed high in a complicated chignon, swept past the table in a flutter of black chiffon, leaving Lesley with an acute awareness of her own crumpled cotton dress. No wonder that all heads turned in the direction of the arresting-looking couple, Judith with her air of confidence and catlike walk, her tall escort with his indefinable air of distinction.

As Stuart saw the dark girl seated, she glanced up at him, the wide thin lips parted in a glittering smile. Swiftly Lesley's glance moved toward the remaining man in the group. He was short and slight, with a light brown mustache and a sprouting brown beard. Tim, Lesley mused. The one who "didn't conform." At least not according to Mrs. Mac's rigid and uncompromising standards. Actually—Lesley took in the slight figure in the tired suede jacket, corduroys, desert boots—he looked rather nice. At that moment the young man's glance flickered in her direction, and hastily she looked away, bringing her mind back to her escort.

As the meal progressed through the unfamiliar seafoods and main courses, served with delectable local wines, Lesley assured herself that the nearby presence of the party from Waione didn't matter to her in the least. Certainly none of the group would be interested in her.

But she was not to escape so easily. For when the leisurely meal had ended and a few couples moved toward the small expanse of dance floor, Lesley became aware of a tall figure approaching the table. And her heart beat a wild tattoo. If he should ask her to dance with him....

"Hi, Lesley! How are things, Ross?" Pausing beside them, Stuart jerked a dark head toward the group seated at a table at the end of the room. "How about joining us? Kathy's keen to meet Lesley, so...."

For a moment Ross hesitated, and Lesley prayed that he would make some excuse to avoid the proposed encounter. But the next moment he was rising to his feet. "Okay, if you like. Coming, Lesley?" And because she had no choice in the matter, she preceded the two men over the carpeted floor as they threaded their way between the tables.

"My sister, Kathy," Stuart said as they reached the other party, "Lesley Monteith." Lesley nodded and smiled toward the plump young woman with the welcoming smile and the gray eyes that were so like, yet so unlike, her brother's. Stuart's eyes without their satirical gleam.

"And Judith—Judith Roth."

As Lesley glanced up to meet the twisted condescending smile of the wide thin lips, the thought whirled through her mind that Judith's makeup and grooming were flawless. But why was the other girl looking at her with that condescending discomfiting scrutiny? For the glance that was raking her relentlessly from head to foot brought the hot color to Lesley's cheeks.

"Cousin Tim," Stuart was saying in his soft tones. With an effort Lesley wrenched her confused mind free. The slight young man with the amiable smile was younger, she realized now, than she had considered him at first glance. The drooping mustache lent him rather a dashing appearance, until one noticed the slightly receding chin, the small nondescript features.

Stuart was pulling out a chair for her and she sank down, disquietingly conscious of the simplicity of her short frock—of hair still damp from her swim in the pool in the thermal valley below.

Then she realized that Judith was leaning across the table toward her, the pale thin lips twisted in a travesty of a smile. "So you're the little girl," she said in the deep throaty tones that nevertheless seemed to carry with devastating clearness, "who Stuart picked up in the bush."

Just as though, Lesley thought hotly, she was a stray kitten whom the man had rescued! Or could it be merely her own fevered foolish imagination that lent the light remark such wounding significance? Perhaps. For everyone was laughing good naturedly. But the next moment, meeting the triumphant gleam in the other girl's wide dark eyes, Lesley knew that her first instinctive impression had been correct. The barbed shaft had been deliberately aimed to wound.

Lesley forced herself to make light conversation with the rest of the party, but all the time her thoughts spun in wild confusion. Somehow she'd have to make her escape. From the dark girl with the glittering two-edged smile that hid a malicious gleam in her outsize brown eyes. And from Stuart. Oh, especially from Stuart! What if he should ask her to dance, she thought in panic. She didn't want to dance with him. She couldn't! Come on, admit it, jeered the small inner voice that took no toll of time or place. You don't want to risk it, do you?

Risk what?

Why, the effect of his nearness. You're afraid.

All right, then, I'm afraid. But only because she could well imagine how he'd remind her, in no uncertain terms, of having refused his invitation to bring her here today, only to visit the thermal area with someone else. It would be just like him to ask her to dance so that he could have an opportunity to lecture her in private. He'd take a devilish delight in tormenting her. She knew he would. Run, Lesley—while you can!

Under cover of the gay chatter and laughter she whispered to the man at her side, "Ross, would you mind if we left now for home?"

"Whatever you say, honey." The gentle giant smiled down at her.

Thank heaven for Ross! "You won't mind," Lesley heard her own voice, surprisingly normal in tone, as she turned toward Kathy Carrington, "if Ross and I run away now? I've been shopping. Honestly, I've nearly bought the shops out this afternoon. I can't wait to get back to unpack everything."

"But of course." Kathy glanced up with her pleasant heartwarming smile. "You must come over and visit us up at the house. We've scarcely seen you yet." She appealed to the dark girl seated opposite. "Have we, Judith?"

The other girl made no reply other than a cool stare and Kathy's warm tones rushed on, "Stuart's told us so much about you."

Stuart. She could imagine!

Lesley forced a smile to her lips and said, yes, she'd certainly come and visit the house sometime. It had been nice meeting them all. The last thing she noticed was the expression of mild astonishment on the face of Stuart's cousin, Tim, as she walked away with Ross. At Stuart she didn't look at all.

"You didn't mind," Lesley asked anxiously as she settled herself in the long red car standing in the parking lot, "our rushing away so soon?"

"Whatever you say's okay with me, Lesley." The deep measured tones were soothing to Lesley's taut nerves. "You just relax, honey. Take it easy. Guess that hot mineral bath'll be having an effect pretty soon. You'll sleep tonight, and that's for sure!"

Lesley nodded, thankful that he'd accepted so unthinkingly the abrupt departure from the dining room. It was absurd to have this panicky feeling that she must escape from Stuart Carrington at all costs. Never again, she vowed, would she put herself in a situation of being forced to run away. For that was what it amounted to. But running away from what? She dodged the answer to that question.

CHAPTER FIVE

THE FOLLOWING DAY found Lesley throwing all her energies into her self-appointed task of dressmaking. It was better, she found, to keep herself frantically occupied with other things. Otherwise her thoughts strayed inevitably in the direction of Stuart Carrington. It wasn't as if he meant anything to her, one way or the other. He was merely using her to achieve his own ends. The only thing in which he was interested was his precious bushcraft project, and some inner sense warned her that she'd best not let herself forget it!

Business in the store this morning happened to be slack. The early-morning rush of customers, when men employed by the local timber mill called in on their way to the forest to procure cigarettes, tea, biscuits, had already been dealt with. And now, while Mrs. Mac went out the back door with the intention of weeding the garden, Lesley set up the electric sewing machine on the worn table.

Soon, mats pushed aside, she was kneeling on the floor, surrounded by lengths of colorful dress materials, and a short time later she was slicing around the edges of the printed paper patterns, marking the darts in readiness for machining.

Absorbed in her work, she hadn't realized it was lunchtime until Mrs. Mac came into the dining room and began to lay cups and saucers on the other end of the big old table.

Lesley got to her feet, proudly holding up a pinned shift frock. "Think they'll go for this style?" She shook out the violet blue folds of the garment. "Drip-dry—no ironing! And the patterns are awfully easy to follow. These *should* sell."

Mrs. Mac eyed the garment disapprovingly. "Not around here, they won't! You're wasting your time with those," she said bluntly. "They're far too small."

"But," Lesley faltered, "I got up to women's size in patterns."

Mrs. Mac threw her a direct glance. "Have you ever taken a good long look at some of the Maori women around here who come into the store? The ones with large families, I mean. They're the ones who do the buying! Not the young girls. They go into the towns for a choice of styles. But the ones you're catering for—all they're wanting is something cool and bright and comfortable. You should have started with women's size, instead of finishing with it." She banged down a butter dish. "And 'finish' it is! Haven't you ever noticed the size of the Maori matrons around the village? They're not exactly your fitting."

"Ye-es, I see what you mean." Lesley's newly found confidence was rapidly oozing away. With a sinking heart she brought to mind the generous proportions of the majority of the Maori women of her acquaintance, the regular customers at the store. A friendly, laughing, good-natured group, no doubt of that, but on the average, frankly stout! Some—there was no avoiding it—were downright plump! Why hadn't she realized it before?

"I'll take this white-and-yellow spot off your hands for myself, if you like," Mrs. Mac offered by way of consolation. "But likely that'll be the only one you'll ever sell."

And she'd cut out every single one! Lesley surveyed the pile of garments, pinned in readiness for machine stitching, with dismay. But there was nothing she could do in the matter, except to complete them and hope for the best.

All through the afternoon the gentle humming of the electric sewing machine filled the room, as Lesley swiftly seamed the notched edges together. But her enthusiasm in the work had vanished. All she wanted now was to get the task completed as soon as possible.

In the end, after countless interruptions, it took her a further two days of head-bent, concentrated toil before the last frock was finished. But when the garments were given a final press with the iron, she couldn't resist a sense of pride in her achievement. The gay shirts and shifts had almost a professional appearance, and even Mrs. Mac's grudging qualifying statement that "the sewing looked nice" couldn't entirely spoil Lesley's pleasure in her handiwork.

"I'll hang them up by the doorway," she said, slipping the frocks onto hangers, "where they can be seen." She pulled an empty packing case toward her and mounted it to reach up to a nail above her head. "Maybe someone the right size will come along."

"And maybe they won't," Mrs. Mac muttered grimly. But Lesley was regarding with pride the gay ripple of scarlets and orange and kingfisher blue that moved gently in the breeze at the opening.

And indeed within half an hour a customer requested two shifts—a vividly patterned scarlet and a clear yellow. Lesley, observing with new eyes the ample proportions of the smiling Maori matron, hesitated before lifting the garments from the nail. "Are you sure—wouldn't you like to try them on first? Just to make sure they fit?"

The Maori woman shook her long, black, wavy hair from side to side. "She'll be right." It seemed to Lesley that the inevitable Kiwi phrase was used to cover almost any eventuality.

"You see," the Maori woman explained in her soft musical tones, "I want them for my girl, Belinda. She works in Murapara—comes home for the weekends. She get a surprise when she sees these, eh, *choa*? Maybe she wear one to the *hangi*?" The broad, good-natured face broke into a friendly chuckle.

"Oh, that's different." With a sigh of relief Lesley folded the glowing shifts, watching as Mrs. Wahonga placed them in her woven flax kit and went out of the shop, her brown feet in rubber thongs silent on the floor, her small dark-eyed children following her out into the sunshine.

VERY SOON Lesley found that she was becoming accustomed to the smiling Maoris with their calm unhurried gait and unfailing sense of humor.

She understood now that a *hangi* was a native feast. And she was no longer curious when she witnessed *te hongi*, the traditional Maori greeting where hand clasped hands and noses touched briefly in the ancient salutation. "You don't see the *te hongi* much nowadays," Mrs. Mac told Lesley, "except in remote places like the Ureweras."

But it was the Maori children who were a constant fascination to Lesley. Intelligent and endearing with their smooth dark skins, their limpid brown eyes were quick to sparkle with mischief or widen with a sudden onslaught of shyness. Lesley made certain that she was in the store at the time when the Maori children returned to their homes from the small mission school in the bush-lined valley, small laughing folk with school bags slung over their shoulders.

Swiftly Lesley had made herself conversant with the various prices of foodstuffs and cigarettes. Unconsciously now she found herself thinking in terms of the currency of the country in place of the familiar pounds, shillings and pence.

The urgent summons of the shop bell would bring her hurrying into the store, a small slight figure wearing one of the brilliantly colored frocks with a cool scooped neckline that she'd brought with her from London, her feet tanned in their gold thongs. And there was no disguising the extra spattering of freckles across her nose that she'd collected since coming here, in spite of working indoors for the greater part of the time.

She never knew what the day would bring forth in the way of customers, for to her surprise an amazing variety of travelers paused at the store in the clearing in the wilderness: overseas tourists motoring through the country in hired cars, engaged in exploring the outback; campers and holidaymakers; travelers passing through on their way to the peace and comfort of the Tourist Hotel overlooking the deep blue waters of Lake Waikaremoana, fifty miles farther along the winding road. Lesley, giving the strangers the lyrical Maori translation, The Sea of Rippling Waters, would suppress a secret smile as she realized how recent was her own knowledge of the customs and language of the country.

She met, too, geologists and scientists engaged in a study of the geothermal area and the vast government forestry projects situated in the half million acres of forest land.

Once it was a voice in friendly American accents that

"Hmm," the older woman commented dourly, "times I've eaten there, they put on a lot better meal than I could rustle up."

"Anyway," Lesley said hastily, "I'm sure it will work out all right."

Mrs. Mac gave an audible sniff. "That remains to be seen! You can't," she added suspiciously, "have much money left."

Oh, dear, Lesley thought, the question she'd been avoiding! "No, I haven't," she admitted, and began sorting boxes and parcels stacked in heaps on the newly painted counter.

"That's the lot, miss." The freighter driver tossed the last carton onto the littered counter. He glanced over the welter of packages and piles of groceries that were jumbled with tobacco and toiletries. "Guess you're pretty well stocked up with that lot. You name it, you've got it!"

"That's right," Lesley agreed. But beneath her bright smile her heart faltered. This mountain of stock represented almost every cent she possessed. She'd invested her entire capital in the store against the advice of folk who lived here, and knew the district. Now she had to make a success of things, or at the very least, break even. That way Stuart Carrington wouldn't be able to jeer at her, to regard her with that hateful "I told you so" gleam in the depths of his gray eyes.

Thrusting the disheartening thoughts aside, she began to attack the teetering pile of unopened packages.

Luckily, as far as customers were concerned it was a quiet day, and by early afternoon, helped by the indefatigable but silently disapproving Mrs. Mac, the store was once again in order. Lesley knew a feeling of pride at sight of the shining deep-freeze cabinet, its frosty white interior stocked to the brim with frozen foods. The shelves that lined the walls were closely packed with new and attractively packaged foodstuffs.

Then suddenly the store was no longer quiet. The children returning to their homes from the mission school in the valley seemed to know, as if by some telepathic magic, that there were frozen goodies at "Monty's," as the store was still called. Soon a seemingly endless stream of customers peered over the top of the counter, diminutive hands clutching coins, small brown faces intent on their choice of purchase.

At length, just when Lesley was about to take advantage of the lull for a cool shower and change of clothing, she heard the slither of tires on metal as an unfamiliar white Jaguar drew up outside.

The next minute a short plump woman with curly chestnut hair appeared in the opening, her deeply tanned arms dark against the stark whiteness of her crisp sheath frock.

"Hi, there, Lesley! Remember me? Kathy, Stuart's sister?" She smiled with warm friendliness and the eyes so like Stuart's in color crinkled at the corners.

"I've been meaning to call ever since I met you last week." Kathy ran on in her bright tones, "You know—in Taupo. But the days just fly! And then, with Tim coming back to stay, and the doctor calling to check up on Debbie's progress every now and again—not that I didn't expect to see the doctor. But Tim— Well, not so soon. Not quite! I really thought that Stuart had got him fixed up with a town job he'd like this time. I mean to say, a salesman's job is so *easy*! Trouble was they *would* put him on to selling men's clothing. And Tim's simply not interested! I mean, you only have to look at what he wears himself! He just doesn't care! Those ghastly torn old jeans that he won't let me mend and that dreary old black sweater, all unraveled around the ribbing. And bare feet all the time! Then there's Debbie, always wanting me around. She's been laid up for so long I haven't the heart to go off and leave her any more than I can help! Stuart says I spoil her, but—" across the counter the candid gray eyes appealed to Lesley "—you know what brothers are!"

Lesley didn't. She did know, though, what Stuart Carrington was like, only too well. She'd just hate to be his sister, or anyone else belonging to him.... She brought her thoughts up with a jerk and tried to follow the torrent of words.

"Thing is," Kathy was saying, "we want you to come

over to the house—bring Mrs. Mac, too, if you can. But don't worry if she's tied up. I know how hard she is to shift. I've just about given up asking her. After all," Kathy said with her warm smile, "we're neighbors, sort of. Stuart said to be sure and ask you to come. He said he'll call for you. Tomorrow afternoon, then?"

Lesley's thoughts whirled. Stuart! So that was the source of the invitation! Oh, she might have known that the Big Boss wouldn't give up his campaign so easily. She was certain now that Stuart had engineered the invitation. No doubt he was planning to change her mind with some further "gentle persuasion." She wouldn't put it past him. She wouldn't put anything past him, she thought heatedly, that would serve to further his own ends.

Nevertheless, there was no gainsaying the sincerity of the twinkling gray eyes with their long black lashes, which were the single point of similarity she could discern between the Carrington brother and sister.

"I don't know." She hesitated. "I'm awfully busy at the moment—"

"Oh, come on," Kathy's voice held a genuine note of entreaty. "No one's all that busy, not in Waione on a Saturday afternoon! We'd love to have you! Debbie, that's my daughter—step, actually, but I always forget to tell folks that—is looking forward so much to seeing you. She's had to rest up for months with back trouble. But she's coming along fine now, just about on her feet again. But she's so *restless*! Half the time I simply don't know how to keep her amused. Honestly, you'd be doing me a real favor if you'd come over and see her. Besides, we want you."

We? Speak for yourself, Kathy Carrington. Stuart had but one reason for seeking her company, and she knew only too well what that was. Aloud she said slowly, "When you put it like that, I'd love to."

"Wonderful!" Kathy swung the gold chain of her white handbag from a tanned hand. "We'll see you tomorrow, then. Stuart'll call for you. No trouble— Heavens, I've got to fly! Judith's waiting for me out in the car and I said I wouldn't be long. Bye now!"

She was gone, and Lesley, stepping toward the opening, was in time to see Kathy take her place behind the steering wheel of the dust-smeared white Jaguar. Another woman was seated at her side, and as the car moved away Lesley caught a fleeting glimpse of a high black chignon above an exquisitely made-up face with thin lips and a classical profile. Owllike sunglasses obscured Judith's dark eyes.

Slowly Lesley turned away and began to add up a long line of figures. But somehow she felt unsettled. She couldn't concentrate. It must be that she was overtired. She'd leave everything else and go and tidy up.

Tonight, she promised herself, she must set her hair in an upswept, more sophisticated style, go over her wardrobe to make sure everything was in perfect order, muster her resources. For she had an uneasy suspicion that for that visit tomorrow she'd have need of every ounce of confidence she could summon up, now that she was committed to meet her enemy once again. And on his own ground!

IN THE MORNING, however, she had no time to dwell on personal matters in the sudden influx of Maori customers who crowded the tiny store.

It wasn't long before Lesley discovered the reason for her sudden rush of trade. It seemed that the Maori families of the district were preparing a celebration in the traditional style. A *hangi* that was to be held in a nearby grassy paddock, where pork and vegetables—golden pumpkin, the sweet, purple-skinned kumera that Lesley had already come to enjoy—were cooked by steam in the ground in the ancient native fashion. The delicacies, Lesley was told, were wrapped in leaves and then lowered in flax baskets into pits lined with hot rocks and covered with a wet sack. Some hours later, the food, steamed to perfection, was lifted out in baskets from the earthen pits.

But Lesley found that in addition to the customary *hangi*, many *pakeha* items such as sweets, soft drinks and ice cream were in demand at the local roadside store, for added enjoyment at the traditional native feast. Soon her hair was clinging in little damp tendrils to her forehead as, flushed with the exertion of serving so many customers in fast succession, she hurried between the counter and the long freezer standing against the back wall. Swiftly she wrapped parcels, spooned ice cream into cones, added up lists of foodstuffs.

Then all at once the intense activity was over, and as the last customers drifted away, Lesley hurried to take a shower, then change into the short frock of coarsely woven natural-colored linen that she had laid out on the bed in readiness for her visit to the Carrington home today. With a vague impression at the back of her mind that maybe if she appeared older, more sophisticated, Stuart Carrington would take her more seriously, she gathered the long silky hair in both hands and twisted it into a bun high at the back of her head. She was slipping her bare feet into thonged brown leather sandals when she heard the sound of an approaching Land Rover in the distance.

Swiftly she said goodbye to Mrs. Mac and hurried out through the empty shop. A moment later she found herself looking up at the man who was strolling toward her with his long-legged stride across the sunlit concrete, gazing into those disturbingly attractive features that for some utterly inexplicable reason invaded her waking thoughts and nightly dreams.

"All ready to go?"

She nodded. Then, as the man's gaze went past her toward the shining interior of the store, she couldn't resist the words that, against all caution, rose impulsively to her lips.

"Well, what do you think of it?"

Too late she caught the skeptical expression that lighted the lean dark face; noticed the lift of the thick brows.

"Quite a change... all that nice shiny paint work. Do-it-yourself job?"

"Of course." In vain she endeavored to subdue the note of pride in her voice. "Mrs. Mac helped a lot with it, though."

"Did she now?" The mobile lips twitched. "Bet she didn't go along with you when it came to buying all this." His sweeping glance took in the neatly stocked shelves with their varied sections of packaged foodstuffs.

"We-ell...."

"Or that?" He was eyeing the long freezer taking up almost the entire length of the back wall.

"It isn't Mrs. Mac's concern," Lesley said stiffly, and added silently, *Or yours*!

Why did he have to spoil everything? Even though he didn't say so in so many words it was obvious that for reasons of his own he was trying to discourage her as usual.

"I suppose," she said huskily, "you think it's not worthwhile my going to all this trouble—" hastily she tried to cover her slip of the tongue "—*financially*, that is to say."

Suddenly, unexpectedly, he grinned. The heartwarming disarming grin that despite all her annoyance, succeeded in drawing a reluctant responsive smile from her own lips. "That's what I thought you meant! What else? Let's go!" He waved a hand around the store with its freshly painted counters and neatly arranged shelves. "Looks like you could do with a day off duty after all this activity."

"I didn't mind. It was 'fun work.'" The man pushed aside the cluster of vividly hued cotton shifts and Hawaiian shirts moving gently in the breeze at the opening, and together they went out into a world that quite suddenly seemed to Lesley to be filled with an extraspecial brand of sunlight, shimmering and golden.

When they reached the Land Rover, Prince was already waiting expectantly at the side of the vehicle. But Lesley waved the dog aside. "Not today, feller! You're on duty tonight! Mrs. Mac's going to be all by herself."

As if understanding the words, the big Alsatian trotted back to the doorway. Dropping down on the coir doormat, he lay, his head resting on his front paws, ears pricked and eyes observant. "Just as though," Lesley remarked to Stuart with a laugh, "he really is keeping guard over the place."

She slid into the passenger seat and Stuart closed the door of the Land Rover and climbed behind the wheel. As he threw the vehicle into gear Lesley stole a glance at the strong profile. She approved the open-throated cotton shirt, the walk shorts and knee-length socks, the outfit that appeared to be standard masculine summer garb in this country.

"Funny to think," he observed as the four-wheel-drive

vehicle swept along the bush-shaded roadway, "that this area has scarcely changed since the days before the *pakeha* arrived here. See those tracks around the hillside?" He waved a lean muscular brown arm, indicating the winding indentations that threaded a nearby rise.

Leslie nodded.

"Old Maori fortifications! Just about every hill around here was a fortress once, a stockade. Great fighters, those old Tuhoi tribesmen! It was just too bad for the ones who lost the battle! They were all taken as slaves. When the white man came there was quite a trade in them—ten slaves to a musket at first. Later on the price dropped to a slave a musket—" He broke off, glancing across at Lesley with a swift inquiring look. "Am I boring you?"

"Of course not!"

"Looks like you've got yourself a Maori souvenir already." His sideways glance was fixed on the stone medallion with its ancient scarlet motif, swinging from a cord around Lesley's slender neck. "Maori cave drawing, that red canoe."

"I know." Lesley fingered the cool stone. "Ross told me it was when he gave it to me."

"Ross, eh?" He slackened speed to allow a lumbering sheep trailer to cross the narrow one-way bridge ahead. "Been seeing a lot of him?"

Such soft tones, and yet somehow Lesley sensed an impact beneath the casual words. Nettled, she heard herself say quickly, "No, I haven't!" and once again she reminded herself that she was under no obligation to account to Stuart Carrington regarding her movements.

"It was nothing really," she went on, wondering why on earth she was bothering to explain the friendship between her and Ross. But having begun, she had perforce to continue. "Just that I had to go into town to get—well, you saw what I got there! Ross was good enough to give me a lift into Taupo...." She broke off in confusion, remembering that Stuart had extended the same offer. An offer that she'd declined. "It...got late," she finished in a low flurry of words, "and we just...stayed on."

"So I gathered." He seemed about to say something

more, Lesley thought. But whatever it was, he must have thought better of it.

The next minute he swung the vehicle sharply toward a side turning, and soon they were rattling over a cattle stop, following the winding twin paths that spiraled up the sun-dried grass of the hillside and led toward a sprawling brick house on the crest above.

"Whanga-riri." Lesley had learned to give the soft Maori syllables their separate pronunciation. She turned her head to glance over her shoulder at the rough board nailed to a tree trunk by the roadside. "Is that it? The name of your property?"

"That's right." His eyes were fixed on the dusty white pumice tracks ahead. "Place of the Sun."

"I might have guessed that one." And indeed, it fulfilled its name, she mused, her eyes on the homestead above. Set against a vast backdrop of somber timber-covered slopes, the cleared hillside lay in the sunshine. Beyond the surrounding shelterbelt of tall native trees Lesley glimpsed sweeping lawns, studded with brightly flowering shrubs and trees. Some of these Lesley had come to recognize by name. The high branches of a flame tree were indeed aflame with blood-red blossoms. Suva Queen hibiscus shrubs glowed with a profusion of great, wide-open pink cups, and along the length of the patio poinsettias tangled their scarlet stars among tall greenery.

Stuart brought the Land Rover to a stop below the steps of the wide tiled terrace, and soon they were strolling into the coolness of the patio with its heavy overhead beams, scattered tubs of climbing tropical and native plants and low coolie chairs.

"Hi, there, Debbie!" Stuart guided Lesley toward a small figure curled up on a long bamboo couch, a girl of about eight with a pale little face and short, straight light brown hair. The child's hazel eyes were alight with interest as her glance moved from the man to Lesley, fresh and attractive in her short simple frock.

"This is Lesley, Debbie." Lightly the man ruffled the child's nondescript fine hair.

"I know," Debbie said shyly. "Mummy told me." She

lifted clear considering eyes to Lesley's glowing face and dark sapphire eyes. "She's awfully pretty, isn't she?"

"You think so, too, kitten?" With one of the swift movements to which she was becoming accustomed, Stuart swung toward Lesley, and she prayed that he hadn't noticed the pink that had risen in her cheeks. "Debbie's had to take things easy for a bit. Another month, though, and she'll be as good as new!"

"I've been in bed for nearly a year," the thin little girl announced with pride. "I was there longest of anyone in the children's ward of the hospital."

"I'll go and track Kathy down." Stuart had turned away and was moving with his long strides toward a hallway. "She's been looking forward to having you. Now you've arrived she's taken off outside some place. Typical!"

As he vanished through a doorway Lesley seated herself on a low bamboo chair beside the child resting on the couch.

"I had an accident," Debbie confided with vast importance. "Daddy didn't know about camping trips or he wouldn't have taken me along; that's what Uncle Stuart says."

Stuart again! Lesley was conscious of a prick of irritation. Why was it that they all deferred to his opinion?

But this discerning child had evidently interpreted Lesley's fleeting expression of dissent.

"And Uncle Stuart," Debbie announced with supreme confidence, "knows everything! 'Specially about camping in the bush. But it wasn't daddy's fault he got lost 'cause he'd always lived in town. And there's no bush there, is there? We took my sleeping bag and we were out there for *two* whole nights," Debbie chattered on, "only we couldn't use the sleeping bags after all, 'cause on the way I slipped over a cliff and I got hooked up on a bit of rock, halfway down. I was scared stiff!" At the memory the child's eyes widened. "But daddy wasn't scared. He came down after me. And then he fell—boom, boom, boom, way down to the bottom. There were dogs and search parties and *everyone* was out looking for us. But they couldn't find us that night, or the next night, either. Then some trampers found us, only I don't 'member much about that. Daddy was sick and he died and I have to rest until my busted back gets mended, only it's nearly better now. And do you know what? The doctor says I can walk around by Christmas! And when I'm better Uncle Stuart's going to teach me all about bushcraft. You know? How to look after yourself if you get lost. Then I won't be scared of the bush anymore." The high childish treble ran on. "He's going to start a school at the old store so that all the city kids can come and learn, too—"

"Hello, there!" Kathy Carrington came hurrying into the shaded patio. She wore jodhpurs and riding boots, a simple white cotton blouse, and above her flushed cheeks the short curly chestnut hair was unruly.

"So sorry I wasn't here to welcome you." The breathless tones were tinged with genuine regret as she took Lesley's hand in a warm eager clasp. "Heaven knows what you must think of me! But it's this new thoroughbred I've just bought! I was giving her a tryout over the jumps down in the horse paddock and lost all count of time. I was watching for the Land Rover to arrive, too. Never mind; I can see Debbie's been entertaining you. And here's someone you've met before," she added, turning toward the tall feminine figure standing in the doorway. "My friend Judith; you met her at Taupo, remember?"

Lesley's gaze swept up to meet the cool appraising glance of the girl who stood in a model's stance, long legs apart, one hand resting on a slim hip. Incredibly thin, she wore her violet slack suit with verve and a careless elegance. Like a fashion model, Lesley thought swiftly, taking in the older girl's arresting appearance. Maybe she was a model: blue black hair dressed in a complicated chignon, smooth pale skin. The only flaws Lesley could discern were the sneering downward curves of the wide, too thin lips and the tiny lines that fanned from the corners of the great dark eyes. Probably they were due to the hot summers of the area. Or—Mrs. Mac's description of Judith Roth returned to mind: "Older than she lets on." But for the rest—unconsciously Lesley sighed—a ravishing brunette, and very much aware of the power of her own special brand of beauty.

Beyond the Ranges

"What did you say your name was?" Judith inquired carelessly in her deep throaty tones. "I've forgotten. Lucie, wasn't it—Lynn? Something like that."

"Lesley." She was thinking, as if the other girl didn't have sufficient in her favor, without that cherry-soft, intimate-sounding voice!

"Oh, yes, I remember now." Judith seated herself on a low black coolie chair, crossed her long legs and let her gaze flicker over Lesley with deliberate amusement. "We haven't seen you since Taupo." Lazily she lit a cigarette and slowly exhaled. "What have you been doing with yourself? Staging any more rescue attempts? I'd better warn you, though; I wouldn't think that Stuart would fall for the idea a second time. Rather amusing, though, wasn't it? Or maybe it was just the way he described it."

Lesley swallowed unhappily. All the pleasure of the warm welcome extended to her a few minutes previously drained away. It wasn't Judith's words exactly, but an underlying meaning, something deep and spiteful. She was pierced by a mental picture of the two: the beautiful assured woman and Stuart Carrington, laughing together over the incident. Probably, she thought miserably, that was the manner in which they customarily referred to her—the little girl he found on the road!

Lesley was well aware that a devastating sense of honesty rendered her anything but competent at countering swift and deadly verbal barbs. She had no aptitude for clever repartee—come to that, for repartee of any description. Invariably a sparkling reply would come to her mind long after the opportunity to make use of it was past.

A chill wind blew over her spirit, and she shrank back in her seat. All at once she felt a stranger here, alone and defenseless. An old sense of inferiority, buried deep and stemming from the long ago days of an unsettled childhood, rose to the surface and flooded her with a surge of loneliness. She thought in panic: I'm stranded here in this wild bush country among strangers! I've spent my inheritance—burned my boats! I should never have come here. And now it's too late. What have I done?

"Well, I think it was just the luckiest thing—" Kathy's

kindly cheerful tones jerked Lesley back to the present "—Stuart coming across you just then! Why you might have been there for hours! And so much more comfortable, riding with him, than having to be crushed in the cab of one of the timber trucks beside one of those *huge* Maori drivers!" She gave her high trill of laughter.

Lesley rallied, pulling her scattered wits together. Steady. The sister seems kind—really kind. And the child, Debbie. No subterfuge there.

"Hi, there!" A slight young man came strolling toward the patio from the bright sunshine outside. Barefooted, his sloppy dark sweater hung loosely over faded blue denim shorts. He had, Lesley thought in that one brief glance, an indolent air, a lazy smile. But what if he did have rather a weak face? At least, she reflected with a rush of gratitude, *he* wasn't looking at her as though she were something that had been picked up on the road! On the contrary.

"Gee—" he dropped lightly to the floor beside Lesley's bamboo chair "—it's good to see someone young and beautiful around the place!"

"I like that!" Judith pouted her thin lips in a provocative smile.

"Someone *new*, that is to say." Tim fished a hunting knife from the scabbard of his belt, and reaching toward a piece of totara timber lying beneath a chair, began idly whittling at the wood.

In the general wave of laughter, Kathy, with a murmur about bringing coffee, slipped away. She was back in a few minutes, carrying a tray of steaming pottery beakers. And presently, while Tim pulled himself upright to hand around coffee, Stuart returned to join the group relaxing in the filtered sunlight of the long terrace.

If only she weren't so absurdly *aware* of him, Lesley thought—even at this moment, when he wasn't even thinking of her, merely straddling a chair and silently smoking. He only had to enter a room and he drew her gaze like a magnet. Was it because of that kiss, an incident that he'd already forgotten? Why couldn't she, too, forget? With an effort she brought her mind back to the present, trying to concentrate on Kathy's light friendly tones.

"Lesley, you'll be able to tell Judith all about the latest in fashions over there. She's a model, you know, with her own fashion boutique in Rotorua."

Of course, Lesley mused. How could anyone so perfectly proportioned for the wearing of fashion garments be anything else?

"*Really*, Kathy!" Judith's dark penciled brows rose in a pretense of modesty.

"Well, it's true!" Kathy's gray eyes dwelt with pride on her friend's classical features. "And it's not a bit of use your pretending it's not—being modest and all that. Anyone has only to take one look at you to know that you're one of the top models in the country."

"You're prejudiced, Kathy. And anyway...." Languidly Judith spread her exquisitely manicured hands, ablaze with jeweled rings, in an expressive gesture, and Lesley's thoughts went uncomfortably to the appearance of her own hands. She'd scarcely given them a thought since arriving at Waione. And now...tanned, marred with tiny cuts and disfigured with scars from recent burns; roughened with cooking chores and painting and dishwashing.... Hastily she thrust them out of sight. But you couldn't run a store and retain silky-smooth hands, like Judith's. What was the other girl saying now in her deep soft tones?

"I wouldn't imagine—" the condescending glance swept over Lesley, taking in the slight figure, the slim neck, the almost childishly simple short-short frock "—that Lesley would be much help in that direction."

"Not really," Lesley stammered uncomfortably. "I was a typist in London."

"I thought so," Judith said with immense self-satisfaction.

Once again Lesley was conscious of feeling out of her depth. The cool silky tones had placed her in the position of an outsider in this closely knit group, alone and unwanted.

"Well, I think she looks great!" Tim's lazy masculine tones acted as a balm to Lesley's taut nerves. The man's glance went to her sandaled feet, the toenails gleaming with pink iridescent varnish. "All over. Learn about fashion? Heck, anyone who can wear a miniskirt like that doesn't need to learn. She *knows*—all that matters, anyhow! But then—" his warm smile brought Lesley's failing spirits up with a rush "—I always did go for blondes!"

Thank heaven for Tim, Lesley thought swiftly. So gay, lighthearted, and blessedly easy to talk to.

"Don't let Judith rock you." Tim perched on a high stool opposite Lesley, and as she met the twinkling blue eyes she realized that he hadn't missed the significance of her own heightened color and tremulous smile. "She's just spoiled," Tim said. "Wicked example of what winning a local beauty contest can do to a nice girl."

Judith's magnificent dark eyes flashed as she sent the man a challenging glance.

"Don't forget *you* helped to vote me in!"

"I didn't know then that it would go straight to that charming little head of yours!"

He turned his face with its stubble of brown beard toward Lesley. "You certainly go in for contrasts, Lesley! From the bright lights of Piccadilly to the mountain vastness of the Ureweras! I was over in London—" the light tones were nostalgic "—this time last year. Man, do I miss it! Bet you do, too! Come on, admit it."

Lesley hesitated, glancing across at the indolent smiling face. She was thinking that she was grateful to this slight young man. Even if Tim Carrington were all that Mrs. Mac had said of him—shiftless, undependable, with little sense of responsibility—at least he was human and approachable. Not like Stuart, standing over by the window, smoking, not saying a word. But no doubt he was taking everything in, deriving a measure of enjoyment from her discomfiture.

With a start she brought her mind back to Tim's interested gaze. "I haven't had much chance to look around this part of the world yet," she said. "I haven't been here long. And up till now I've been so—" she broke off, aware that Stuart had come to stand silently, and no doubt jeeringly, at her side "—busy."

"We'll have to do something about that," Tim said promptly. "You've done Rotorua, of course?"

Lesley said, "Not really. I just passed through there on the way to Waione." She smiled across at him. "But I'd love to see it—properly, I mean. It all looked so utterly different from any other place I've ever seen."

"'Different' is an understatement," Tim assured her, "when it comes to Geyserland."

"My teacher told me," Debbie's piping tones cut in, "that it's New Zealand's top tourist town. My teacher said—"

"Okay, okay," Tim waved the child to silence, "we know all about that! What we're trying to get through to you—" he grinned toward Lesley "—is that it claims to be one of the most spectacular areas on earth. And you haven't seen it!"

Lesley smiled down at him. "Have I missed so much?"

He threw her a significant glance. "Well, I ask you! Where else will you find a geyser gently blowing its top outside the town hall? Or a golf course where you can tee off between steaming fumeroles?"

"What's a fumerole, Uncle Tim?"

"Silence, infant! I'm on a New Zealand promotion campaign speech. Where was I? Oh, yes, a town whose contours are always changing because of subterranean movements. You know something, Lesley? Home owners in Rotorua cook their meals with underground steam, bang in their own backyards."

Lesley sent him an incredulous glance. "No!"

"Fact. Isn't that right, Stuart?"

Stuart's gray eyes narrowed as he surveyed Lesley through a screen of cigarette smoke. "I'll prove it to you if you like. Why not take a run over today and you can see for yourself?"

"That's an idea," Tim agreed with enthusiasm. "At least...." He broke off, glancing inquiringly toward Kathy.

But Kathy shook her curly head. "I've been there hundreds of times. If you wouldn't mind, Lesley, I'll stay here with Debbie. I'm expecting the doctor to call sometime today to give her a checkup. Honestly—" as Lesley made to protest "—I don't mind a scrap! Not seen Rotorua yet? Heavens, you mustn't miss the trip."

"I just never tire of it," Judith added in her deep tones. "To me it's eternally fascinating, no matter how many times one goes there."

"But you said—" Debbie stared at the tall girl in wide-eyed amazement "—that you loathed it! You said you *hated* that horrid sulphury smell—"

"That's settled, then," Stuart broke in. "We'll take off after lunch—the four of us. Excuse me, folks. I've got to take a look at the pump down in the gully...."

Almost at once Lesley realized that Kathy Carrington's entire interests lay with her family, her home, her horses. In that order. Without domestic help she managed the big brick house on the hill, tending the flower borders and blossoming shrubs that seemed to Lesley to grow so much taller and lustier than their counterparts back home in England.

The delectable luncheon, attractively set out on the long mahogany table, was a delight both to eye and palate. Delicious spaghetti Bolognaise was followed by chilled boysenberries served with rich dairy cream.

Lesley was enjoying the meal until, glancing across the table, she met Debbie's eye fixed on her with a speculative expression. Lesley had an apprehensive feeling that the child's next remark might well prove embarrassing. It was.

For the next moment the shrill childish treble pierced with devastating clearness, the low murmur around the Colonial-style table. "Are you the girl from the store?" Debbie inquired of Lesley.

"That's right." Lesley endeavored to sound nonchalant, hoping against hope that the question she dreaded wouldn't be the outcome of this direct attack.

"Oh." Debbie digested this information. "Then you must be Monty's daughter?"

"Right again." Lesley's bright smile concealed her inner agitation. She had a dreadful suspicion of the direction in which Debbie's mind was working. "Did you ever see the baby deer that he used to keep at the store?" she inquired brightly.

But it was of no use. Ignoring the conversational lure, the child continued to regard Lesley with a puzzled stare. "But if the store's yours," she asked perplexedly, "then how come Uncle Stuart...."

Wildly Lesley searched her mind for a reply that would satisfy this persistent child with her shrewd mind and piercing voice. In desperation she lifted her eyes to Stuart's intent glance.

"I guess that's my problem, kitten," the man said in his deceptively soft tones. "We'll have to work that one out, won't we?"

"How?" Debbie demanded.

"Oh," Stuart murmured, "I guess she'll sell it to me, one of these days." The note of nonchalant confidence in the man's tones had the effect of making Lesley forget everything else—even the sudden hush that had fallen around her. Impulsively the hot denial rose to her lips.

"No!"

Debbie's bewildered glance moved from Stuart to Lesley. The next minute, however, the child's pale face brightened and she clapped her hands excitedly. "I know!" she cried triumphantly. "Uncle Stuart, you can mar—"

"Debbie! Look what you've done!" Unexpectedly it was Judith who saved the situation. She was pulling her chair free from the stream of milk that was dripping from an overturned glass over the table mats and trickling down to the carpet.

Outraged, Debbie turned an innocent face toward the tall dark girl at her side. "I didn't do it! I did *not*! I wasn't touching it even!"

"It doesn't matter," Kathy put in swiftly. "Accidents happen, just like that! I'll fetch a cloth to mop it up— Oh, but your suit, Judith! I didn't realize...." She stared in dismay at the wet patch staining the immaculately pressed violet linen slacks.

"What's a spot of milk?" Judith said lightly. "I can change into something else anyway—that's the best of having a spare wardrobe here."

"That's the spirit," Tim said. "No use being a model if you don't carry half a dozen changes of clothing around with you."

With a great sigh of relief Lesley realized that the subject of the sale of the store was forgotten. It was odd—the thought flashed through her mind—that Judith had taken the incident of a ruined garment so good-naturedly. With that tight, thin-lipped mouth, one would have imagined— But maybe she had misjudged the older girl.

CHAPTER SIX

AFTER LESLEY HAD HELPED KATHY to clear away the luncheon dishes there was time for only a brief stroll around the grounds surrounding the homestead before leaving on the trip to Rotorua.

Lesley glanced up at the giant hibiscus bushes with their paperlike pink blossoms, admired the purple velvet petals of the spreading lasiandra shrub and reached out an exploratory hand—"just to make sure it's real," she said, smiling to Kathy—toward the exotic bird of paradise plant with its standing tangerine, violet and rose pink bloom, which in form and coloring bore such an uncanny resemblance to a vividly hued parrot.

When they rounded the corner of the house, the white Jaguar that Lesley had seen standing outside the store on the previous day was waiting below the patio.

As if by right Judith seated herself in the front seat, leaving Lesley and Tim to share the rear compartment. Not that she minded, Lesley told herself, turning to wave toward Kathy and Debbie as the car moved down the winding driveway. Much wiser for her to keep as far away as possible from the tall figure behind the driving wheel—if she wanted to keep a clear head!

Anyway, she mused a little later as the car took the long pull over the ranges, Tim was proving himself an unexpectedly entertaining companion with a surprising fund of knowledge concerning legends of the district.

"How come you know so much about it all?" Lesley asked. "Somehow I'd have imagined you to be more at home in the city than out here in the bush country."

For a moment Tim looked a trifle self-conscious. "You'd be surprised! Frankly, I didn't know a thing about all this—not until a few months ago. It's the native trees that I'm interested in. The rest of the gen I've picked up here and there—a sort of fringe benefit."

"The trees?" Lesley looked across at him with a puzzled glance. "You mean you're in government forestry? Milling? Something like that?"

"Good grief, no!" He gave his light laugh. "I've never gone for that Tarzan, he-man stuff, and I'd like to keep it that way! I go more for the artistic touch, you know? At the moment I'm keen on wood sculpture—the odd bird or Maori canoe. Kind of abstract effect. Maori carving, too. I tried my hand at painting for a while—oils and watercolors. Even had a crack at work in oils on a black velvet backdrop. Very dramatic, that medium, if you can bring it off. Unfortunately, I couldn't!"

"I see." Lesley was only half listening. Judith was keeping up an animated conversation with Stuart. The whirring of the tires on the metal combined with the dull thudding of stones thrown up at frequent intervals against the undercarriage of the vehicle deadened the sound of the words. But Lesley was aware of the low intimate murmur of Judith's voice punctuated by her frequent throaty laugh.

She brought her mind back to the man seated at her side.

"It just wasn't my line," Tim was saying. "So then I had a bash at acting. But there's no future in that line—not in this country. That's why I took off overseas, to try my luck in London. But let's face it, I just didn't have what it takes, and it didn't take me long to find that out over there! So then I tried office work for a time—a very short time. Soon gave that away—eh, Stuart?"

The man behind the steering wheel turned a strong, profile. "What's that?"

"That office job you jacked up for me, the one I turned in—place that drove me up the wall."

"You didn't give it a chance," Stuart told him. "Another month and you'd have been right—"

"Come off it, Stu. You know as well as I do that I'm a total flop when it comes to figures. It's so deadly boring. Like I said—" he swung toward Lesley "—I've tried 'em all—nearly all, anyhow. Old Stuart's been pretty generous on the financial side of things. Now I'm back where I started, right here in old Waione for a spell! I'll tell you something, though. This Maori carving lark, it grabs you! I never knew until I began to swot it up that each one of those darned swirls and spirals has got a definite meaning! I took a few lessons from an old Maori carver in Rotorua—they're pretty rare these days—and he put me on the right track. Honestly, it gets you— Well, my life story, to date."

Lesley threw him a teasing glance. "Haven't you left out a lot—all the interesting bits?"

"Life story, I said, not love story. I ask you—" he sent her a wide-eyed stare "—how could I keep a wife on Maori carving, which I wouldn't be lucky enough to sell anyhow, even if I wanted to?"

"Oh, I don't know," Lesley demurred. "Couldn't you keep it as a hobby, get a job with regular pay?"

"No, thanks," Tim said hurriedly. "I'm not like Stuart, you know," he went on after a moment, "all carried away with ideas about saving lives and all that. He's got a thing about his bush camp—" Tim broke off, eyeing her inquiringly. "You didn't seem madly keen about selling out to him, though."

"I can't," Lesley said quickly. "It's all I've got, that property. I've put every cent of my capital into it. Now I have to make it pay. I've just *got* to!"

Tim shrugged his thin shoulders. "Old Stuart'll probably make it all up to you," he murmured, "without the hard labor. The cash without the slog! Well, why not? Makes sense to me."

"But I don't want it that way," Lesley protested.

"It's up to you," Tim said carelessly. "But for myself, there'd be no problem! I'd take the cash and call it a day! Work's a drag any way you look at it. Then for me it would be back to London and the bright lights! Hey, we're at the Rainbow Mountain turnoff already! What d'you know? Just goes to show what a spot of the right company can do."

Lesley glanced out of the open window toward the colored clays gleaming through the bush and tea tree clad slopes of the mountain. A helicopter hovered overhead, and she wondered if Ross were the pilot. His hand on the controls, his mind seeking a way in which to win back a girl who was also probably eating her heart out over a stupid misunderstanding that could have been so easily resolved, if only they had both been able to talk over their differences. Come to think of it, she'd promised Ross that she'd show him a way out of his difficulties. Poor Ross, he was so confident that her feminine viewpoint would solve his problem for him. And she'd promised to do just that! Well, maybe she'd think up a plan by the time she met him again.

But she forgot the kindly dark giant as they swept along the smooth gray bitumen of the highway toward the thermal city ahead. Soon they were spinning along the wide pleasant streets, and once again Lesley was conscious of the sulphurous fumes in the air. The rest of the party didn't seem to notice, but then they were no doubt well accustomed to the strange odor that pervaded the area.

Now she could see, to her amazement, boiling mud pools bubbling at the edge of the road, a wisp of steam rising from the nearby grassy verge.

Stuart swung his gaze upward and his eyes met Lesley's glance in the small overhead mirror. "Where would you like to go first?"

Before she could make a reply, however, Judith's husky tones cut in. "Oh, do let's have a run around the Blue and Green Lakes, Stuart! I simply adore the colors in them."

But once again the man's eyes sought the mirror. "Lesley?"

"It's all new to me."

"She'll have to see Whaka first," Tim put in. "No tourist ever goes to Rotorua without taking in Whaka first of all."

"I'm not a tourist," Lesley disclaimed, "but if you mean that wonderful thermal area just ahead of us, I'd love to go there."

"That's it!" Tim said. "That's Whakarewarewa."

Lesley pushed the small tendrils of hair, damp with the heat, back from her forehead as she leaned forward to view the native reserve. The next moment Stuart braked to a stop at the Memorial Archway of the native village with its ornamental gateway of carved images. Lesley, gazing toward the narrow paths that wove and criss-crossed through the tea tree at the edge of the boiling, bubbling mud pools, was glad to see that Stuart was engaging the services of a Maori guide to show them around the volcanic craters.

The smiling young woman, wearing her traditional flax skirt and woven bodice, led the party toward a carved meeting house, and as they stood beneath the vast crossed portals carved in the intricate scroll designs with which Lesley was fast becoming familiar, the guide explained in her musical tones the legend of ancient Maori mythology, when the bush was peopled by supernatural beings. Lesley, walking over the dried grass in the cool dim interior of the high structure, had for a moment an odd sensation. It was as if she had slipped back in time into another civilization.

Soon, however, they were strolling along the winding path toward a completely fortified modern *pa*. "Just to show," the Maori girl told them in her pleasant tones, "the idea of the Maori village system as it was before the coming of the *pakeha*." They wandered past the various thatched huts, all with their carved barge boards and entrances, while the guide indicated the "sleeping huts," the ones in which food was prepared and the *pakata*, perched high on tea tree stilts, used for the storage of food.

Standing a little apart from the cluster of huts was the special whare belonging to the *tohunga*, with his supposedly supernatural powers of life and death over the tribe.

"You're just in time to see the geyser 'play,'" the guide told them smilingly. "Pohuto plays every few hours— Look, there she goes!" As she spoke a great plume of steam gushed upward, and as the geyser continued to play, rising high against the blue, Lesley stared upward in amazement.

"Just look at her!" Judith's jeering tones jarred Lesley back to reality. "Struck dumb. Little Lesley in Wonderland!"

Lesley forced a smile to stiff lips. "Well, who wouldn't be?" she returned lightly. But deep in her heart, the hurt bewildered feeling persisted. Why had the other girl come on the trip, she wondered with a sudden flare of anger, if she only wanted to needle her? Although Judith had professed that she never tired of the thermal activity, it was clear that she was bored to distraction by geyser and boiling mud pools alike. Was that why she spent the time in deliberately taunting Lesley? Just for something to do? What other reason could there possibly be? Lesley no longer thought the other girl's beauty breathtaking. She was cruel and horrible and deliberately hurtful—a fact that neither of the men appeared to perceive. Right from the beginning Judith had taken an unreasoning dislike to her. But why? There was no explanation that she could think of.

Lesley forced herself to follow the Maori guide's lilting voice as she led them through the Maori Arts and Crafts Institute, explaining the crafts and culture of her race.

It was all incredible and awe inspiring: the snowy silica terraces, the hot springs, the weird manifestations that were both eerie and enchanting. But at last they took a winding path through scrub and tea tree that skirted boiling mud pools and brought them back to the entrance gates.

Stuart glanced down at his wristwatch. "Just time to take in Fairy Springs."

A little later he brought the car to a stop on the main highway, and Lesley found that Fairy Springs did indeed deserve the name. Concealed in a bower of fern and native bush was a cold, crystal-clear pool with water so clear that the light reflection gave the water a hue of fascinating blue. Cruising among the springs, a multitude of sleek rainbow trout swam effortlessly against the current, and a short walk along a pathway through native trees and punga palms brought the party to a bank at the edge of a stream, where, to Lesley's delight, the huge specimens of rainbow trout "rose" to take bread from her fingers.

It was later, as they sat over coffee and cigarettes at Brent's, an attractive hotel situated among lush greenery in the heart of the city, that Stuart brought up the subject of attending a Maori concert that evening.

Tim leaned toward Judith. "Look, we've seen this concert so many times we could just about join in the choruses ourselves. How about if we take off and do a show instead? Stuart can look after Lesley. It's all new to her."

Oh, no, Lesley wanted to cry. Stay, please! For some unaccountable reason she didn't want to be alone with Stuart Carrington. Not ever again. The next moment she chided herself. How crazy could you get, for heaven's sake? It was only a concert. Even the Big Boss could scarcely pressure her on a business matter amid such surroundings.

"Okay, then." Judith's lips twisted in a pettish downward curve, and Lesley had a suspicion that the other girl had agreed to Tim's suggestion only because she saw no way to circumvent it.

All at once she became aware of Stuart's speculative glance fixed on her face, heard his voice, so soft, indifferent almost. It was all very well for him! "Well, what do you say, Lesley?"

It must be something about the way he said her name. It *must* be. For she was overcome by such a cloud of confusion that all she could do was to nod her head and try to look as though she didn't care, hide the terrible admission that the thought of the evening ahead with Stuart Carrington in this strange and colorful city filled her with a wild elation. A feeling utterly unfamiliar swept over her, something wild and exciting—and quite beyond her control.

A little later Stuart drove the car through a main street, pulling up outside the neon signs of a theater. A silent, tight-lipped Judith, followed by Tim, got out of the vehicle, and Stuart arranged to pick the other two up after the performance.

As the big white car cruised along the wide street, where street lights glowed against the blue haze of early evening, Lesley gazed ahead toward a lighted hall bearing a notice: Tonight: Maori Concert Party.

Stuart guided her up the steps toward the open doorway, where a crowd was already threading its way inside, and once again Lesley felt that throb of excitement.

From her place in the long crowded hall, she glanced curiously at the many Maori men and women seated close by, well-dressed, well-spoken, with skins little deeper in tint than those of the suntanned *pakehas* seated around them. Then the stage lights dimmed, the curtains parted and the scene was one of Maori figures in swaying flax skirts as the naturally lyrical voices rose in perfect harmony. Arms outstretched, mobile hands quivering, they moved to the rhythm of the action which told of the great carved fleet of canoes that had found their way over the trackless waters of the Pacific to these far-flung islands in the South Seas.

Fascinated by the movement and melody, Lesley turned an eager face toward the man at her side. As her gaze rested on the clear-cut profile, the soft dark hair, she thought that tonight Stuart looked different, more human. Somehow she couldn't tear her glance away. Too late she caught his quick sideways look. Not so different after all. Not with that mocking glint in his gray eyes!

Hastily, in confusion, she looked back toward the stage, where the men of the concert party, with their magnificent physique and smooth dark skins, had stepped forward. The next moment, as if by some magic, they were transformed into fearsome warriors of another age. Their tongues protruded in fierce grimace, spears were raised threateningly, as with stamping movements of the *peruperu* and wild glaring eyes, they roared out the ancient war *haka*.

The wild war chant ended, and soon the women and girls appeared on stage, dark hair flying over bare brown shoulders, the traditional jade figurine of a *tiki*—a tiny crouched greenstone figure—swinging from a cord around each neck. They moved in time to the swing and tap of the tiny raupo balls on their long flax strings. The only musical accompaniment was the song of the leader of the dance, as swaying hips and supple wrists kept time with the soft flick-flack of the twirling *pois*.

A masculine voice, tinged with an American accent, drifted past Lesley. "They sure are naturally gifted singers. The Maori guide was telling me all about it. No musical training, nothing written down, just these songs, handed down from one generation to the next—a sort of record, you know? But they can sing so it can break your heart. Listen to this love song and you'll see what I mean."

A young Maori girl stood alone, spotlighted against the dark backdrop of the stage. Slim and graceful, she wore the traditional costume of flax bodice woven in the conventional black, white and red *taniko* pattern; a flax skirt, woven headband. A hush fell over the crowded hall as the soft Maori syllables fell on the air. Then the haunting melody died away into a pool of silence and a thunder of applause broke out. Above the clamor Lesley was aware of a man rising to his feet. The next moment a pleasant American voice called toward the stage, "Say, we'd sure appreciate hearing that sung in English. Could you...."

The Maori girl smiled in assent, tossing the long black hair back from her shoulders. "Of course!"

High and sweet, the haunting tones echoed in Lesley's ears with a strange poignancy.

> "Over the hills
>   Your voice calls
> Asking
>   What is it
> You want of me
>   The voice... of love...."

Lesley was still under the spell of color and movement and melody as she moved with Stuart in the throng that was surging out of the hall into the cool crisp darkness of the night sky, ablaze with stars.

Tim and Judith were already waiting when the car pulled up outside the brightly lighted theater. Lesley, through the haze of happiness that enveloped her, was vaguely aware that the other two seemed quiet and uncommunicative, as though they had quarreled. Or maybe they were bored with each other's company.

Stuart escorted the party to a small, dimly lit coffeehouse and a little later they returned to the car. It seemed to Lesley that, once again seated in the car beside Stuart, the other girl came to radiant life. As they moved through the lighted streets and out into the stillness of the quiet country roads Judith chatted gaily in a low tone that deliberately excluded the two seated behind her.

"Enjoy it?" Lesley became aware of Tim's light pleasant tones.

"Did I ever!" It was as though she were still under a spell. "It was something— Oh, I just can't describe it! I've never seen anything like it." She smiled across at him companionably. "And that goes for the whole day."

But it seemed that Judith, for all her laughter and chatter, had evidently caught the remark, for the other girl raised her voice tauntingly. "Just listen to her, Stuart! I told you she was Lesley in Wonderland—or would you say, Lesley in Geyserland!"

It could have been a careless friendly comment. It *could*. But Lesley, sensitive always to criticism and ridicule, sensed the jeering note in the light words. All at once the sense of enchantment died away, leaving her feeling young and inexperienced and gauche, a silly youngster carried away by unfamiliar tourist sights. *I'm stupid to allow her to affect me so, to let her spoil everything*, she told herself. But it was of no use. The feeling of hurt persisted.

"Quite a place," Tim was saying in his relaxed manner. "Sorry, Judith, we never did make your Blue and Green Lakes! And as for you, Lesley, you haven't even started on the sightseeing tours yet. You'll have to take in a weekend there sometime, to cover all the trips."

"I guess...." Lesley roused herself to some degree of animation. "I noticed a tourist bus," she went on, "carrying passengers from one of the cruise ships that are in port in Auckland just for one day. How could they possibly see it all and get back by midnight?"

"They don't! But they pack in what they can of the main sights in the time. Tell me, what did you think of the London night spots? Know many of them?"

"Not really." Lesley shook her head. She seemed, she mused, to have led a most dull and uneventful life in London. But when one worked for a living and every penny counted—well, it wasn't exactly the sort of existence that made for gracious living. Not the kind that Tim was referring to, anyway.

Judith's dark head was very close to Stuart's shoulder, and somehow Lesley couldn't focus her attention on anything else. What *was* the matter with her tonight?

"When I was over there...." Vaguely she was aware of Tim's voice as he went on to speak of the merits and attractions of various cabarets and shows on the other side of the world.

The powerful car ate up the miles and the darkness swallowed up the landmarks, and as they rattled over a cattle-stop, Lesley realized, with a little shock of surprise, that they were once more on Stuart Carrington's land.

But she hadn't counted on the drive home alone with him, she thought with a feeling of panic, as the man drew up at the doorway and the other two passengers climbed out.

Stuart turned toward Lesley inquiringly. "Coming in for a while?"

She shook her head. "Thank you, but I'd better get back. Mrs. Mac's at the store by herself."

"At least come in the front and keep me company," Stuart said, "or I'll feel like a taxi-driver!"

Lesley laughed and came around to the front seat, turning to wave at the two who stood watching at the foot of the wide steps.

"Bye. Tell Kathy I had a lovely time today and I'll ring her in the morning."

For a second car lights beamed an arc over the pathway, pinpointing Tim's smiling face and Judith's tense and angry features. Then the big car was hurtling down the pumice tracks, pale in the star shine. As the vehicle swung into the metal road below, Lesley was aware of the intense stillness of the country, broken only by the occasional cough of a sheep on the hills or the mournful "More-pork" of the native owl perched somewhere in the dense bush surrounding them. Small white moths, caught in the glare of the headlights, blundered against the windscreen.

If only Stuart would say something, Lesley thought wildly, instead of whistling a tune under his breath. *That* tune! Strange that the Big Boss was familiar with a Maori love song. But he had probably forgotten, had he ever known, the haunting words that still tugged at her heart.

> Asking
>   What is it
> You want of me?
>   The voice... of love.

Love! She caught herself up sharply. What had love to do with an agreement of sale? It was hate that she felt for Stuart Carrington! Definitely. And as for him, of course he was only pretending—that she knew. And yet... and yet....

Stuart reached out his hand to touch a switch and soon the soft beat of dance music pulsed around them.

It was as if, Lesley mused dreamily, the dim light from the dashboard wrapped them in a world of their own—enclosed, intimate and subtly potent.

One more bend and they'd be in sight of the store. Lesley found herself wishing that the journey could go on forever.

"It's been a fantastic day." She roused herself from the sense of deep happiness, soothing yet exciting, that was enveloping her senses. "Thanks to you."

"My pleasure." She caught a glint of the gray eyes turned toward her for a moment. She was conscious of a strange feeling, a sense of heightened awareness that was half pleasure, half pain, and her heart began a slow heavy hammering. She heard his low controlled tone as from a distance.

"Mind if I say something?"

"No, of course not." But she did mind, terribly. Her heart dropped like a heavy weight and she jerked herself upright on a long sigh. Wait for it. Here it comes—the property! Always the property! Oh, she might have known. What a fool she'd been to have been deceived by the fact that Stuart hadn't mentioned the matter all day. He'd been merely biding his time, she reflected bitterly, waiting until the scene was set and they were alone. And she had so very nearly fallen into the trap. There was something about him—useless to deny it any longer—some masculine magnetism against which she must be ever on her guard. Hadn't Mrs. Mac warned her, that first day she'd arrived here, that "women were crazy about him"? But she wasn't "women." She was Lesley Monteith, who was going it alone, in spite of the tactics this man might use in an attempt to make her change her mind. Or could it be *because of him* that she was determined to see the thing through?

She braced herself and waited, glad now that they were almost in sight of the store. Only a minute or so now....

"I wanted to have a word with you about Ross," Stuart said.

"Ross?" Taken by surprise, Lesley stared at him, her

lips parted in amazement. "Whatever has Ross to do with me?"

"Nothing, I hope."

Really, she thought hotly, it was too much! First of all he'd interfered in the matter of her inheritance. Now she was no doubt in for a lecture regarding her choice of friends. But Ross, of all men? What could Stuart possibly have against such a friendly uncomplicated type?

"Well, then," she asked bewilderedly, "what *is* all this about? What's the matter with Ross?"

"Not a thing." He changed gear to take the narrow bend, and overhanging tea-tree branches scraped past the windows. "Good bloke, old Ross, one of the best. Conscientious as they come." He turned toward her for a moment, his eyes dark with an expression she couldn't interpret. "But he's not for you, little one! Didn't anyone ever tell you—" He broke off. "What the devil...." His tone sharpened as he peered into the darkness ahead. "Smoke! Smell it?"

"Yes, I can!" Into Lesley's mind flashed a terrifying possibility. Fire at the store! But it couldn't be! Not with Mrs. Mac right there on the premises. She was always late in going to bed. She would have noticed it.

As Stuart accelerated and the car hurtled up the dark roadway, Lesley leaned tensely forward. The next moment a shower of sparks rose and hung for a moment against the darkness, and her heart gave a great lurch. Wildly she clutched at Stuart's arm. "Hurry! It's the store, I know it is! And Mrs. Mac...."

To Lesley the minutes until the vehicle lurched to a stop seemed endless. Then she stared in horror and dismay at smoke rising from the blackened timbers of the side wall. As she leaped from the car and hurried forward toward the store she was vaguely aware of dark forms silhouetted against the light pouring from the opening of the fire-damaged building. A small boy wearing short striped pajamas was leaping up and down as he called excitedly, "Here's Miss Monteith! Here she is now!"

"Wait here while I take a look around." She scarcely

heard Stuart throw the words over his shoulder. Then he was striding past her. Lesley's mind was possessed by one overpowering fear. Swiftly she turned, her anxious gaze flickering over the shadowy groups. Then she ran blindly forward, unaware of her own voice crying on a high cracked note, "Mrs. Mac, Mrs. Mac, where are you?"

"She's okay." Lesley stood still, breathing hard. She tried to focus her gaze in the gloom as she recognized Ross's deep soothing tones. "Don't worry—" he was at her side, water dripping from his clothing "—we've just about got it licked! Old Prince gave the alarm and one of the Maori boys was passing and hot footed along to me."

But Lesley was staring up at him with dilated eyes. "Mrs. Mac?"

"It's okay, I tell you. She wasn't here. No one was. Seems there was an emergency—some woman up country having a baby—panic stations, husband raced down and picked up Mrs. Mac just after you left the place."

Lesley let out her breath on a long shuddering sigh. "Prince? You said he gave the alarm? He's not—"

"Not on your life," Ross answered reassuringly. "There he is—right over there." Dimly Lesley discerned a dark patch that at that moment detached itself from the surrounding shadows as the big Alsatian ambled toward her. "Too bad we had to break in." Only now did Lesley realize that the front door was shattered, exposing a jagged gaping hole. "I knew there was a fire extinguisher inside if I could only get in."

Slowly Lesley felt her nerves relax. Now she was aware of the acrid smell of charred wood. In the dim glow from the windows of the lighted rooms she realized that Ross's bearded face was streaked with soot and smoke, his cotton shirt clinging wetly to his chest. Slowly she brought her mind back to the measured tones.

"Not that it was much use after all. But it helped. After that—" he flung the wet hair back from his eyes "—it was a case of all hands to the buckets and water tanks! Sorry about the damage. I guess the stock's had it, except for a few cartons we managed to shove out of the way. If only I'd known ten minutes earlier when it first started." Grimly his gaze went beyond the gaping charred timbers propping up what remained of the wall, to the smoke-blackened interior of the store. Lesley saw with dismay that the entire stock appeared to be ruined. Tins and packaged foodstuffs that had escaped damage by heat and smoke were rendered useless by the water still dripping from the blackened shelving.

"The deep-freeze!" Lesley hadn't realized that she'd spoken her thoughts aloud until she became aware of his cheerful "Not to worry. We pushed it out into the passage. Could be it's as good as new."

As good as new, Lesley thought despairingly. It *is* new. That is to say, it was!

"It's not too bad." She became aware that Stuart was at her side, his glance raking the blackened timbers of the damaged wall. He swung toward the bearded figure. "You did a darned good job, Ross."

The big man grinned deprecatingly. "Had a lot of help. The boys from the forestry quarters turned out, and we had the flames beaten in no time! They all went back home when things quietened down. But I thought I'd stick around for a while, just to make sure everything was all right, and wait for Lesley."

"I've had a good look around," Stuart reported, "and the rest of the place is okay. Front door's a mess, but that can be replaced easily enough. Otherwise, the damage seems to be all in one room—the store. The stock's had it, but insurance'll take care of that. And the same goes for a new wall."

"But—" Lesley raised a chalk-white face; her voice came slowly "—I haven't got any—insurance, I mean."

"What!" Stuart's quick surprised stare pierced her. "You mean you didn't get extra cover when you went in for all the stock? What about the deep-freeze?"

Lesley shook her head.

He stared at her incredulously. "But Monty must have had some cover."

"He didn't, you know." Lesley turned away from the man's accusing stare. After a minute she added in a low tone, "Mrs. Mac told me, when I first came here, that he was always intending to get around to fixing it up. But somehow he...never did. And I haven't given it a thought—until now."

Her voice trailed disconsolately away. What lunatic hope had impelled her to imagine that she could succeed in this new venture when everything seemed to conspire against her! She turned aside to hide the tears welling in her eyes.

"Forget about it." Ross's big hand closed around her fingers in a comforting squeeze. "Well, I guess," he said awkwardly, "that's about all I can do right now. I'll be over to give you a hand with things first thing in the morning."

"Thank you. You've been wonderful." Lesley's voice broke as he strode into the darkness.

Everyone had gone, Lesley realized suddenly, as the last straggler was swallowed up in the gloom of the bush-fringed roadway. She stared dazedly at the store, open to the mercy of wind and weather, unprotected from the ravages of marauding opossums living in the surrounding bush.

"No use trying to do anything in the clearing-up line tonight," Stuart said gently. "Why not," he suggested, "let me take you back to the house? Just for the night, then. Kathy would—"

"No!" Lesley broke in. "I'll stay here! The rest of the place is just the same." She scarcely realized what she was saying. In one cruel stroke of fate she had lost all that she'd put into the place—even before she'd had a chance to prove her ability to make it a paying concern. Now it was too late. She wrenched her distraught mind back to the man at her side. What was he saying? Something about the paint going up in flames. The paint that was to have been used in the renovation of the remainder of the dwelling. Now it was lost. Everything was lost—including the last of her bank balance. But what an unexpected stroke of luck—the thought came unbidden—for Stuart Carrington!

All at once frustration and shock and disappointment culminated in a burst of anger against the man standing at her side. In some obscure way she connected all her losses with him. Instead of offering some slight comfort, all he had done was to make her feel even more inept than ever by pointing out in no uncertain terms her lack of forethought in neglecting to arrange for fire cover on the property.

Suddenly her control snapped and tears gathered behind her eyelids. She blinked them away furiously. "I suppose you think I deserve to lose it all?" Her voice choked.

But this hateful man merely remarked coolly, "It's not all that bad. The deep-freeze seems to be all right, in spite of the heat. Bad luck about the stock damage, but apart from that I'd say you've been lucky! Anyhow," he pointed out with unfeeling comfort, "the old place could do with some new timber; those shelves badly wanted renewing. And the ceiling was crying out for paint."

"But," she heard herself say dazedly, "you—you wanted to pull it down."

He didn't appear to have heard her. "All it needs is a new wall, a spot of floor covering, some counters and shelves—and you're away and in business again."

"All?" Lesley's eyes were bright with anger. "Don't you see? It's not like that at all! I've spent almost every cent of money I've got on paint and—and things! And now," she said huskily, "there's nothing left. And I can't get it fixed up again because I just can't afford to. I suppose," she faltered in a small hopeless voice, "you're glad! It's what you wanted, isn't it? You must be relieved that it's happened!"

"Don't be a little idiot! Look...." He put out a hand toward her, but she pretended not to see it.

Stuart's lips were tightly compressed. "Lesley...."

But once having started, she couldn't seem to stop, as all the frustrations and tensions and shock of the night swept over her. "I suppose I should be glad that the rest of the place isn't burned out. At least I've got somewhere to sleep. Well—" she turned dejectedly away "—good night." Like a polite child, she added belatedly, "And thanks again for the trip."

To her surprise, however, he made no reply, but simply remained standing, eyeing her in that intent discomfiting way of his.

"Aren't you going?" she stammered uneasily.

"Sure." He was standing perfectly still hands thrust in his pockets, the lean dark face in shadow. "The minute I

Beyond the Ranges

see your bedroom light go off, and I know you're not still wandering around here."

"Oh, all *right*, then!" If that was the only way in which to rid herself of him, she might as well do as he advised. For after all there was nothing she could do to help matters tonight. The damage was done.

Without another word Lesley stepped over the streaming floor, picking her way between the piled cardboard cartons that littered the narrow passage, and turned the handle of the door leading into her bedroom. Here, except for the lingering smell of smoke, everything was normal. All at once she realized that her legs were trembling and she felt oddly weak. But she'd have to get into bed, otherwise *that man* would wait and wait outside. Hurriedly she threw off her clothes, crawled into bed and switched off the bedside lamp.

She lay, eyes open, staring into the darkness, listening for the sound of a departing car.

How pleased Stuart must be, she told herself, as a tear trickled down her cheek, to think that victory had come his way so effortlessly. And so soon! Why, the two months that he'd mockingly allowed her here weren't yet up! So he wouldn't have to wait even that long. She had no money to replace the losses. She had no option now but to sell. Oddly, the thing that disturbed her most of all was being forced to admit to that hateful, overbearing know-all Stuart that he'd been right all along. In spite of all her efforts she hadn't been able to make good her grand plans and promises. Uncontrolled, the tears spilled onto the pillow.

But in spite of everything, she must have fallen asleep, for when she opened her eyes sunlight was slanting through the open window. She'd been too distraught to remember to draw the curtains last night. Maybe if she shut out the brightness she'd be able to go back to sleep. She moved to the window, then stood transfixed, staring unbelievingly at the man who was strolling along the path below: a tall athletic figure with an easy stride, a cigarette in his mouth, a jacket tossed carelessly over one shoulder.

"Stuart!" She was so surprised she called his name before she could stop to think. And then like a dark cloud it all flooded back to mind: the fire, the loss, the damage.

Stuart paused and his searching gaze swept over Lesley, taking in the pallor of her face, the swollen eyelids.

"Been crying?"

"A bit."

He looked as fresh and alive, Lesley found herself thinking, as though he'd slept for hours. "Have you been here all night?" she asked involuntarily.

He tossed the cigarette butt down on the pathway, stamping it into the soft pumice with his heavy-soled boot. "What was left of it."

Her thoughts whirled in confusion. Had he remained here with the idea of protecting her, alone in the fire-damaged open dwelling? It seemed scarcely possible, knowing him. And yet.... She didn't know what to think.

"You didn't need to, you know." And then, with the directness that had in the past involved her in so many later moments of regret, "Why did you?"

"Why?" He grinned up at her, that maddening sardonic grin that he very well knew infuriated her beyond words. "Just thought I'd stick around." He was eyeing her closely, and all at once Lesley was aware of tousled hair and cotton short pajamas. "You could say," he drawled in that soft offhanded voice, "that I was just... keeping an eye on my property!"

"Oh!" Lesley pulled the window shut with an angry bang. So that was it! He had the nerve already—*already*—to speak of the store in terms of "his property." And to think that she had actually imagined—well, anyway, the thought had crossed her mind, that he might, he just might have stayed here through the night with some idea of protecting her. *As if he would!*

As the noise of the car engine died away in the still air she reflected that it was useless now to try to return to sleep. She'd only lie there awake, regretting. Why had she given way to that childishly angry outburst? With a heavy sigh she reflected that she never used to be so quick-tempered before coming here. But now it seemed that, especially where Stuart was concerned, she had changed into an entirely different person. Emotional, easily hurt, swiftly roused to anger or.... Hastily she wrenched her thoughts away. But it was all *his* fault—goading her like that! All the same she wished she hadn't been quite so rude. Regrets... regrets....

She dressed swiftly in scarlet shorts and a white cotton sweater. Then, moving silently on bare feet into the kitchen, she made herself a beaker of black coffee and took it with her into the store. Dispiritedly she stared around her. Pale sunlight, slanting through the openings in the charred timbers, revealed the muddy floor, wet damaged stock and blackened counters. Half-burned labels peeled from smoke-darkened tinned foods, and fragments of charred paper floated in the early-morning breeze. Hours, probably days, of arduous cleaning up lay ahead. All the stock would have to be sorted, the damaged goods disposed of. Some of the tinned foods had lost their labels and she wasn't even aware of the contents.

She raised heavy eyes to the front entrance, where the soaked and singed cotton frocks clung together in a dejected cluster. In a sudden spurt of anger she snatched them down. The charred fabric disintegrated in her hands, and she stared down at the frocks with a dull feeling of hopelessness. Why pretend any longer? The garments would probably never have sold anyway. They were too small a fitting. She should have known the frocks weren't worth the labor of making up.

She should have known a lot of things. She might as well face it—that horrible superior Stuart Carrington was right! She had proved herself utterly inexperienced and unbusinesslike. She'd been altogether far too sure of herself, and now look where it had got her! Precisely to the point where he could regard her with his mocking triumphant grin. Although why she was concerning herself with Stuart Carrington in the midst of this holocaust.... She put down her beaker—the coffee was cold now anyway—and began gathering together armfuls of blackened tins and wet foodstuffs and stacking them in a heap on the grass outside.

She was still there two hours later, when an old truck drew up outside and Mrs. Mac leaped down from the vehicle and came hurrying toward her.

"Lesley!" The older woman's brown eyes were sympathetic and concerned. "I've just heard the news." Glancing toward the shop, she took in the broken timbers of the wall, the damaged foodstuffs, the charred fragments of paper floating in the smoke-tinged air. "What wretched bad luck! If only I hadn't been called away! A difficult labor it was, too! I was up all night. And then, just when everything was over, the trained nurse turned up. Seems she'd had a breakdown in her Mini and had had to wait in the forge for hours until someone turned up. It's awfully isolated up there." She stared around her in dismay. "If only I'd been here!"

"It doesn't matter." Listlessly Lesley stooped to lift a charred carton from a low shelf, noticing with a wry lift of her lips that the box was labeled: "Smoked Fillets."

Mrs. Mac was jerking up fragments of water-soaked linoleum and tossing the soggy pieces onto the heap outside. "Who gave the alarm?" she asked curiously.

Lesley raised a dazed pale face. "Prince—good old Prince. Someone investigated and went to tell Ross, and he was wonderful, rushed along with some of the men from the forestry units and they—" She turned away as the telephone shrilled from the hallway. Listlessly she picked up the receiver. "Hello?"

A deep male voice answered. "That you, Lesley?"

"Oh, it's you! Hi, Ross."

"Say, I'm sorry about this. I was just leaving to come over to help clear up over there. And what do you know? Darned emergency job turned up—just had a ring from the boss. Someone's gone off on sick leave, and I've got to take over—a crayfish job down in the Chatham Islands. And that means a week away at least! Of all the rotten luck! But I'll be back."

"It's all right, Ross."

Something in her apathetic tone must have got through to him, Lesley realized, for he inquired anxiously, "You all right, Lesley?"

She forced a hearty note into her voice. "Of course, I am! Never better!"

"That's the ticket! Keep it up! Just don't worry about a thing," he went on encouragingly. "You'll make out. Gotta go. Goodbye!" As Lesley put down the receiver her eyes were dark and thoughtful.

Make out? The only way in which she could do that at the present time was with the help of a king-sized very special miracle.

THE MIRACLE HAPPENED ALONG within an hour.

Mrs. Mac was asleep at the time, having at last agreed to Lesley's plea that the older woman take a much needed rest. And Lesley was kneeling on the sodden floor, pulling out a soaked carton of rice from a low cupboard, when she heard a vehicle draw up outside.

I'm not exactly open for business, she thought ruefully, glancing over her shoulder at the open truck at the entrance. As she went out to throw a cardboard box atop the mounting pyramid of damaged foodstuffs on the grass, she reflected drearily that passing travelers would be unaware of changed circumstances at the roadside store until they came in sight of the building.

Almost at once, however, it became clear to her that the three young men who climbed out of the shabby truck hadn't arrived with the idea of purchasing anything.

"Morning, miss!" A well-built, open-faced, fair young man sent her a friendly grin from a deeply tanned face. "You Miss Monteith?"

"Yes, that's me." Lesley gazed in bewilderment at the bronzed young faces. All three men wore khaki shorts and faded drill shirts. Carpenter's hammers were tucked in their belts.

"Came to fix up the fire damage at the store," the fair young man, who appeared to be the foreman in charge of the gang, was saying. "Okay if we get started right away?"

"Yes—no—wait!" Lesley said dazedly. "There must be some mistake," she went on diffidently, trying to collect her wits. "I didn't order any repairs to be done. I—" She stopped short. No need to admit the truth, that she simply couldn't afford to have the necessary repair work attended to.

"Don't know anything about that, miss, but we've got orders to fix it up after the fire, and that's good enough for me!" He was staring around him, assessing the extent of the damage. The other two men had returned to the truck. One was drawing lengths of sawn timber from the tray. The other carried an extension ladder.

"Priority job," the young man in charge of the work said. "So we dropped everything else and zipped up here first thing—"

Lesley blinked. "You said," she remarked slowly, "that you had orders to come here. Orders from who?"

The fair young man answered without hesitation. "The boss. Burke & Marks is the name, building contractors. The headquarters are at Murapara. Well, let's get cracking. Afraid we're going to make a bit of noise bashing the place into shape again."

"Noise?" Lesley's thoughts were in confusion. "I don't mind how much noise you make. But I'm sure there's some mistake. I didn't—"

"No mistake, miss. I checked before I left!" The firm tones were quite definite. "Operation Monteith, that's our project for the next day or two—clearing-up operations first, then replacing the damaged wall with new timber, painting and floorcovering. It'll be as good as new in no time!" His gaze moved from the great pile of debris lying on the scorched grass to Lesley's pale face, streaked with ash; the charred fragments of paper clinging in the long fall of fair hair. "You didn't really think you could carry on here, with the place in this state, all by yourself?"

"No, not carry on," Lesley said in a tremulous tone. "Give up."

But the brisk young man did not appear to catch the low words. He was moving toward the damaged store. "How about the deep-freeze? Touch of smoke won't hurt, as long as it's still doing its job! Seems okay by the look of it. Hey, Bill, give me a hand to shift this freezer outside, will you?"

Lesley's mind was in a tumult. Ross! It must surely be Ross who had ordered the work to be carried out. Wouldn't it be just like the kindly good-natured giant to make such a gesture? Although how he could afford the expense.... Her thoughts whirled. She'd have to pay him back, somehow. From what he had told her, Ross intended to restore the damaged timbers of the store himself, had he been available. But seeing he'd been unexpectedly called away from the district, he'd evidently delegated the repair work to a building firm. She didn't quite see how she could do anything but allow the enthusiastic gang of workmen to carry out their instructions.

WHEN LATER IN THE MORNING Mrs. Mac, looking remarkably refreshed, appeared in the doorway, she assumed that Lesley had ordered the repair work. And it was easier, Lesley decided swiftly, to allow the older woman to think along those lines rather than for Lesley to attempt to explain a situation that she was far from understanding herself, and about which she felt a vague sense of disquietude.

Within the following three days the workmen had replaced the damaged timbers of the store, repaired the entrance door and put up a new ceiling. Then with the all-round ability of men living in out-of-the-way areas, they proceeded to paint the interior and exterior of the store premises with quick-drying paint and lay new floor coverings where needed.

When the work was complete, Lesley, despite her misgivings at the cost of the renovations, couldn't help a feeling of pleasure at the transformation of the old building.

On stacking the remaining foodstuffs on the shelves, she found that a surprising amount of stock was still intact, and thank heaven the deep-freeze cabinet had escaped any damage. But the cost of the repairs would be way beyond her slender resources. And somehow she must pay Ross back for all this. As she stood staring around her with unseeing eyes, a thought whizzed into her mind. How many times had she answered enquiries from passing travelers as to whether they could find any sort of refreshment in the area? Well, why not? It was a service that was in demand, and she had the necessary room. The big store could easily accommodate two tables and the necessary chairs. One set would be sufficient for a start. And seeing she was here in any case.... Close on the idea came another. While she was about it, why not, in addition to light refreshments, supply takeaways? Sandwiches, filled rolls, hamburgers, even pies—

both the meat and fruit variety—she could manage to provide. There should be a ready sale for such fare among the hunters and forestry workers passing along the winding road. Even the children bound for the little mission school in the valley would no doubt buy filled rolls for their lunches.

With Lesley, to have a brainwave was to act on it immediately. Within a short time she was engaged in pulling a small table through the narrow door of an outside shed. She had placed it in the store and was setting chairs around it when Mrs. Mac entered the room. Swiftly Lesley outlined her latest money-making scheme.

"It'll leave us mighty short of seating in the house," Mrs. Mac observed dourly.

"No matter," Lesley said brightly, "We can get some more chairs later, when business improves."

"All the same, I think you might have something with that 'light refreshment' notion." For once, Lesley thought, Mrs. Mac was enthusiastic about a new venture of Lesley's. "Scones and Devonshire cream! Folks would really go for that! Much more attractive when you're hot and dusty and stopping off on a long motor trip than just everyday cakes and biscuits. We can always rustle up some sandwiches if anyone orders them."

"Scones and cream it is!"

Mrs. Mac's unexpected approval of her scheme gave Lesley fresh impetus. That day found her busier than she had been since her arrival at Waione. The new glass display case she had ordered from Taupo before the fire had, after some delay, arrived by freighter. And soon, with *Edmonds' Cookery Book*, the manual that appeared to be a standard work on the subject, propped up on the table in front of her, Lesley was measuring out flour and sugar in readiness for her first attempt at scone making.

The initial batch emerged from the oven a rocklike failure, and even though Mrs. Mac assured Lesley that any traveler who had progressed over the rugged terrain as far as Monty's store would be far too boneshaken and weary to care overmuch regarding the matter of baking perfection, still Lesley wanted her efforts to be at least eatable. And before long,

Beyond the Ranges

with the aid of a few pertinent hints from the older woman in connection with the eccentricities of the elderly electric range, she achieved a moderate amount of success. Indeed, she was thankful during that first day of her new venture that she had doubled the quantities of ingredients listed in the scone recipe, for at intervals throughout the day tourists and travelers continued to pull up beneath the rough board bearing the notice: Teas and Takeaways, which Lesley had executed in large black eye-catching letters and nailed above the doorway.

That night, in spite of aching muscles, she dropped into bed with a feeling of hopefulness.

It was hard exhausting work, she realized during the days that followed, but the thing was the venture was proving profitable. She had been forced to order increasingly larger quantities of flour and other baking ingredients. The hours spent over the electric range in the summer heat were long and arduous. But at least she had the satisfaction of knowing that her plan was working out. She was making sufficient money to pay expenses and show a profit. The main part of the summer season lay ahead, and if things continued on in the way they had started.... *He* had once called her stubborn. Well, she'd be just that! She made up her mind to stay on here; work as hard as she could. And who knew, she might yet pull through and surmount her financial difficulties!

Even though it meant rising at the crack of dawn, when Lesley was still only half awake, she would wander out into the kitchen and sleepily switch on the oven of the electric range.

Right from the start she had made sure that the scones she served were always freshly baked, sandwiches and hamburgers prepared only a short time in advance of the early-morning rush of customers. Yet everything must be in readiness when the first of the mill workers, with a grin and a greeting, strolled into the store on the roadside, or a truck with radio communication paused outside while the driver made his purchases before continuing on to his day's work in the green sea of pine forests a few miles distant.

At the end of the week Ross strolled into the shop, and as

she took in the man's surprised expression Lesley knew that she had been mistaken in thinking that it was Ross who had ordered the recent renovations to the store. He couldn't have appeared so astonished had he known anything of the matter.

"How are you, Lesley?" He leaned over the counter, a dark, heavily built man with placid dark eyes. "Well—" his gaze moved over the attractive interior "—this is really something! Professional job, by the look of things! Quick work! I didn't think you'd be in business again so soon!"

"You didn't?" she echoed lamely. She was endeavoring to draw together her scattered senses. If not Ross who had ordered the repair work, then who? With an effort she brought her mind back to the rich slow tones. "I'd planned to have a bash at that wall myself. But seeing you've got it done—a good job, too." His gaze roved approvingly over the freshly painted walls. "You were lucky to get someone on the job right away. And what's this Teas And Takeaways caper? Something new?"

She nodded, relieved that he had dropped the subject of the recent renovations. "Just an idea I had. Luckily it seems to be paying off. I've just made the scones, so I can guarantee they're fresh. Why don't you try them out?"

"Good idea" The big man moved toward the table, and Lesley went into the kitchen. A few moments later she set down a tray on the plastic tablecloth. Seating herself opposite him, she poured a steaming cup of tea and pushed it toward him. "How did you get on at—where was it you went to—the Chathams?"

"Thanks. Wow, did you really make those?" He eyed the crumbly, golden-topped scones and helped himself to a generous serving of cream and jam. "Oh, it was fine. There's a huge factory over there in the Chatham Islands packing crayfish tails for air freighting over to the American market. Seemed a long week, though. I kept hoping there'd be some mail from Australia, from Vicky, waiting for me when I got back." He sent her a self-conscious look. "But no luck."

Over the rim of her teacup Lesley threw him a teasing look. "You really go for that girl, don't you, Ross?"

He nodded, stirring his coffee. "Don't ask me why! It

beats me! She's jealous and quick-tempered as the devil—doesn't believe a word I say. But I guess," he said heavily, "that it's just one of those things. I keep wondering," the anxious dark eyes lifted to meet Lesley's smiling gaze. "Oh, hell," he muttered brokenly, "how can I get it through to Vicky that I'm nuts about her? Make her believe that I'm not off with some other girl the moment I'm out of her sight?"

"You'll just have to keep on writing to her and telling her that you love her—that no one else counts," Lesley said promptly. "Even if she doesn't answer. She—" She stopped short, tracing a finger abstractedly along the garish flowers of the plastic table cloth. "Tell me—" she raised clear blue eyes to the man's bearded face "—you said that you and Vicky have been going together for quite a while. How long? One year—two?"

He nodded. "Two years almost to the day."

"That's quite a time. I wonder...." Lesley's tone was thoughtful. After a moment she asked, "And Vicky is how old?"

"How *old*?" Ross stared at her in surprise. "Twenty-four, same as me. But I don't get it."

"I've just had a thought," Lesley said slowly. "It could be that she's wildly jealous about you because she's not sure of you."

"Not sure? But I've told her how I feel about her a thousand times!"

Lesley looked directly up into the shy bearded face; met the concern in the great dark eyes. "I know, I know. But did you ever say right out that you wanted to settle down—get married?"

"Well...." He hesitated. "How could I? At first I didn't think there was a chance in the wide world for me, and afterward I was saving, flat out. I wanted to have something to offer a girl before I asked her to marry me, enough to start a home together. And then," he went on morosely, "just when I had everything jacked up to ask the big question, when I went north on holiday a while ago, we had that blazing set-to."

"I see. Well, if you really want my advice," Lesley said,

"here it is! If I were you I'd buy a ring—a gorgeous sparkling engagement ring! Don't wait until you see Vicky again. Don't wait for anything! Send it by post to Australia if you have to! Somehow I think it'll solve your problem. No girl could possibly mistake the meaning of that!"

Unbidden, another voice jeered deep in her mind. Good old Aunt Lesley! Arranging everyone else's love affairs. No trouble, as long as it's someone else's problem!

She thrust the thought aside and brought her mind back to the man seated opposite.

"You reckon?" A gleam of hope flickered in the depths of the man's dark eyes. "You really think it might work?" Without waiting for an answer, he went on in a thoughtful tone, "It's an idea. I'll think about it. Tell you what, though—if I decide to give it a go, will you give me a hand? You know, help me to choose a ring? You'll have some clues about the sort of setting Vicky'd like. And you know what—" taking Lesley's small hand in his huge brown paw, the man studied the slim fingers "—your hands are just about the same size as Vicky's."

"But not half so presentable, that's for sure," Lesley remarked ruefully, conscious of skin roughened by endless dishwashing and scarred with unsightly burns.

"It's a promise, then?" Still holding her hand, Ross eyed her imploringly. "You'll come into town with me, if I need you?"

"Of course, I will! We'll find a beauty—one Vicky just won't be able to resist! I—" She broke off with a glance toward the open doorway. Stuart Carrington stood in the entrance, a silent observer of the little scene that he no doubt took to be a romantic moment between the two leaning so closely over the small table. Evidently, Lesley thought, he had merely paused at the store during the course of his duties, for he was wearing a dusty khaki shirt and faded khaki drill shorts. But the eyes—the eyes were the same as ever, Lesley noticed—cold and hard, like chips of gray ice, and there was a sardonic twist to the man's curving lips that made her snatch her hand away from Ross's grasp. To her chagrin she could feel the color creeping up her tanned cheeks.

"Hello, Lesley." Stuart strode across the shining new linoleum. "Hi, Ross!" Then, coming to stand beside the table, he pinned the other man with a formidable stare. "How's Vicky?" he inquired, and Lesley formed an impression that the conversational words were underlined with deliberate meaning.

Ross paused for a moment uncertainly. Then: "Oh, she's fine," he answered with assumed heartiness. "That is—" he gave a twisted smile "—she was the last time I saw her, when I was up north on holiday a week or two ago."

"Heard on the grapevine that you'd been away up there," Stuart remarked in his deceptively soft accents. "I thought you and Vicky might have got around to naming the day—be looking for married quarters, hmm?"

Ross, obviously ill at ease, muttered an unintelligible reply, but Lesley was furious. *I'm beginning to understand you, Mr. Stuart Carrington*, she thought with anger. Misinterpreting the significance of the little scene he'd witnessed, he'd taken it upon himself to interfere—as usual. He was deliberately making it clear to her—darn him—that Ross wasn't free, that he was in love with someone else. Doubtless he was taking a malicious pleasure in giving her what he imagined to be an unexpected blow. If only he knew the real reason why Ross sought her out!

But it appeared that Ross, too, had had quite enough of Stuart Carrington's interference in his private affairs. Rising to his feet, the big man gazed down at Lesley. "Got to get along. I'll keep in touch."

Lesley nodded. "Thanks for calling. Goodbye now!"

As Ross sauntered from the room, she turned toward Stuart. She had no wish to meet those cool gray eyes, but there was no alternative. "Won't you sit down?"

He cocked a bushy eyebrow at her. "*Stuart, please.*"

"Stuart, then." Suddenly she was confused. What was it about this man that caused him to have this disturbing effect on her?

He jerked a dark head toward the sign at the entrance. "'Teas and Takeaways'—that's a new one on me!"

"Me, too. I just thought," Lesley said breathlessly, "I'd try it out! So many folks keep asking if there's a restaurant anywhere along the road from here to there that I decided I'd give it a try."

"Not a bad idea. Do all the baking yourself?"

She nodded, following his gaze toward the glass-topped fittings filled with pyramids of temptingly crisp scones and freshly filled rolls and hamburgers.

"Well, what d'you know!" A half smile tugged at the curving lips, tender yet decisive, which seemed to Lesley not to match the stern lines of the man's face. "I have to hand it to you, Lesley—" there was a quizzical expression in the gray eyes "—you do *try*!"

"Try?" Despite all her resolutions to remain calm and poised his first shaft entirely shattered her composure. She flung him a sparkling glance from dark blue eyes. "I've more to do than I can cope with! If it wasn't for Mrs. Mac, I just couldn't manage."

"Things'll ease up when school breaks up in a week or two." He spoke absently. He was moving around the room with his long easy stride, his quick searching glance running over the new timbers, the freshly painted ceiling.

"I suppose...." Lesley's thoughts were running wild. What must he be thinking of all these renovations? She had told him that she had no capital left. And now he hadn't inquired further into her financial position or how she'd managed to afford the repair work. Probably he took it for granted that she had succeeded in raising a loan from the bank. Maybe if she didn't bring up the subject he'd naturally assume this to be the explanation of the extensive repairs.

It was unthinkable that he should learn the truth. For she was well aware that to confess her ignorance in the matter would merely serve to confirm the low opinion he already held regarding her crashing ignorance when it came to business affairs.

The shrill summons of the telephone broke into her thoughts and, excusing herself, she fled thankfully toward the instrument in the hall. She picked up the receiver and an operator inquired "Monteith? Long-distance call for you from Wellington."

Wellington? But she knew no one in that city.

"That you, Lesley?" Anna's clear light tones came floating over the wire, as clearly as though the other girl stood at Lesley's elbow. "How's everything?"

"Fine — now."

"That's good. Listen. Is it all right if I come down to Waione for a few days between trips? I'm stuck here with an elderly friend of aunt's and I can't take much more of it. Honestly! If you don't happen to be all wrapped up in Persian cats or bridge parties, you've had it! Anything would be better — even your timberlands! The afternoon bus on Friday, then? You're *sure* it's all right?"

"Love to see you," Lesley answered warmly. "Ask the bus driver to put you off at Monty's. He'll know—"

"Sorry," a strange voice cut in, "but your time is up!" A faint "Goodbye" echoed over the wire.

As she went back into the store Lesley became aware that Stuart was still there, waiting. He was eyeing her inquiringly, and once again she wondered why it was that he was so interested in her affairs.

"That was my friend, Anna," Lesley said. "At least, I only met her on the plane coming out from London. She's coming here to stay for a few days."

Stuart's intent look was unnerving, but he only remarked with an enigmatic smile. "She sure was lucky. Good timing!"

What did he mean, Lesley wondered. That it was lucky that Anna had timed her arrival when the place was once again habitable for guests? Or was he implying that Lesley's time here was running out? He seemed to take a perverse delight in tormenting her on that score. Well, he might as well know right now that she had changed her mind about letting the store pass from her hands. *That* would serve to wipe the self-gratified grin from his face!

"If you mean it's lucky she didn't come later, when I wouldn't be here," she flung at him, the words running into one another in wild confusion, "I—I've changed my mind! I'm staying on, after all."

"Good for you!" To her surprise, he didn't appear unduly perturbed. She couldn't understand it.

"You know something," he drawled, "when you push

your hair behind your ears that way it does things to me—puts everything out of my mind, including what I called to tell you. It's Kathy. She sent a message that she wants you to come over. Says she scarcely got a chance to have a word with you the other day, what with your getting spirited off to Rotorua all afternoon. So how about coming over on Saturday?"

Lesley hesitated. An inner voice warned her that she would be well advised wherever possible to avoid further contact with the master of Whangariri. There was something about him, some indefinable quality that was infinitely disturbing to her peace of mind. When she was with him she was strangely happy. A wild elation seemed to take possession of— her. And then, afterward she remembered who he was, and the reason why it was that he sought her out. Even this invitation— Did it really emanate from Kathy? Could be it was merely another one of his ways of getting around her? Especially now when, far from appealing to him to take the property off her hands, she'd let him know that she intended to go ahead, just as she'd planned.

"I'm sorry," she heard her own voice, too jerky and too fast, "but you can see how it is around here. I'm awfully busy. The shop—"

"Get Mrs. Mac to take over."

"I couldn't do that!"

"Why not?"

Once again, as she met his level gaze, the curious magnetism that this man seemed to exert over her wrought its magic. She struggled against its insidious power.

"And anyway," she was running on wildly, "I've got this friend coming to stay. Anna—the one I was telling you about, who rang just now."

He grinned, the heartstopping smile that weakened all her defenses and turned her resolve to nothing. "Bring her along with you. Pick you both up on Saturday. Okay?"

Lesley, flustered and at a loss for words, realized that, once again, without apparent effort on his part, Stuart had contrived to gain his objective, regardless of her protests.

Suddenly a wave of anger surged over her, sweeping away all her previous resolutions that never again would she

Beyond the Ranges 155

allow herself to argue with this man. That way, she knew, lay almost certain defeat.

But now a devil of contrariness took over. She'd *make* him take notice of her! And goodness, she knew just how to provoke him! She'd crack that cool complacency—or else!

"You don't mind, then, about my staying on here. I mean...." At something in his bland inquiring gaze she faltered and wished she hadn't introduced the subject.

"Mind?" His eyes had taken on the expression she hated most of all, a blank and expressionless stare. "Why should I?"

"But—but what about your bushcraft school? You're not worried about that?"

"Heck, no—" the soft tones were carelessly confident "—I've got that all jacked up."

She dropped her eyes before his bright gaze. It was as if his thoughts weren't on the matter of the store at all, but engaged with something much more personal—herself, for instance.

"You mean—" Lesley was having difficulty in concentrating "—that you've decided on what you want?"

He was silent for a moment, regarding her with an odd smiling look. "I guess you could put it that way."

"Well," Lesley said, still avoiding his gaze, "it isn't any use, you know."

"Why not?" His lazy grin challenged her.

She began placing the teacups in a heap on the tray. Anything was safer than being forced to meet that mocking gaze. "You gave me a month to make a go of things here," she reminded him. "Two at the outside. Remember? Well, time's almost up, and I'm still here."

"I know. I've extended it."

"You've... extended it?" she echoed bewilderedly. "Whatever do you mean?"

"Got a plan—a better one."

With a rush of emotion Lesley recollected the man's earlier plan, and the outcome. "Well, one thing," she said hastily, "you never give up!"

The silence lasted so long that she was aware of a dangerous intimacy. "Anyway—" nervously she found herself rushing into speech "—what—sort of plan did you have in mind?"

He was still regarding her with that odd half smile. "I'll tell you—later." Something warm and intent in his gaze sent her pulses hammering.

Lesley was well aware that she was adrift on a current that could sweep her away into dangerously unknown waters, but she no longer cared. Straightening, she looked directly into his face. "Go on, then." But at something in Stuart's expression, she faltered. "T-try me!"

In the moment of silence Lesley wondered faintly, over the thudding of her heart, if this time she had gone too far. For his eyes had blazed into sudden life. A feeling of powerlessness swept over her so that now she couldn't wrench her gaze away. There was a glitter of excitement in the gray eyes that sent an unexpected tingle through her—like ice, or fire.

The next moment the light in the man's eyes vanished, leaving them cool and hard again, and much too observant. His voice was as soft, as nonchalant as ever. "I'll take you up on that one of these days. Right now it's too soon. I've got to be sure." His meaningful grin as he rose to his feet did nothing to ease Lesley's spinning senses. "Remind me to tell you about it sometime!"

He was gone. And in the sudden stillness Lesley gained an odd impression that something of vital importance to her had been said—if only she knew Stuart Carrington well enough to interpret it!

Ridiculous! She pushed the absurd thought away.

CHAPTER SEVEN

LESLEY HADN'T REALIZED how much she had missed the feminine company of her own age group until the moment when she glimpsed Anna's thin plain face and short reddish hair thrust through the open window of the dust-smeared coach.

A few moments later Anna, trim and neat in her impeccable coffee-colored traveling suit, dropped lightly down from the high step of the vehicle to the metal roadway below. The driver tossed the luxuriously appointed cream travel bags belonging to his single passenger for Waione down on to the concrete. They were followed by a green canvas mailbag.

"Lesley! Am I glad to see you!"

A warm hug, then the two girls each picked up a travel bag and crossed the strip of white concrete together.

"What a gorgeous hound!" Anna paused to drop a friendly pat on the thick black-and-tan coat. "Is he yours?"

Lesley nodded. "I inherited him—along with the rest. Come along inside."

As they moved toward the open doorway Anna glanced curiously around her. "You certainly are in the outback—and then some! It's the stillness that gets me! I never knew there was such utter intense quietness anywhere—" She broke off, eyeing the sign above her head. "'Teas and Takeaways!' My goodness, what next? You don't do all that yourself?"

"No, I've got a helper, a good one, too. Come along and meet her."

Mrs. Mac gave a friendly nod as Lesley made the introduction, and a little later the two girls moved along the hallway toward Lesley's small bedroom.

"You'll have to share, I'm afraid," she told Anna apologetically, "but I found a camp stretcher out in the shed and that'll do me." Throwing the travel bag down on the cherry-colored spread, she smiled across at the other girl. Anna's pale skin on face, neck and arms appeared to have acquired an extra dusting of freckles during the past weeks. "You look as though you've had lots of sun."

"Look who's talking!" Anna's frank scrutiny ran over Lesley, taking in the air of vitality and health evident in the glowing face; the eyes so startlingly blue against the golden tan of her face. "You look different," Anna said slowly, "more alive somehow... like someone else. I guess," she smiled, "it's this open-air life. Country living must suit you."

"Actually," Lesley murmured lightly, "I haven't had time to know whether it does or not."

"You know something?" Anna's teasing voice ran on. "Looking at you, I'd almost say that you were in love."

"Love?" Lesley laughed the suggestion away. "There's no one around here to be in love with!"

Anna took a comb from her travel bag and began to run it through the short-cropped, reddish-fair hair. "How are you liking it away out here anyway?" she inquired, her eyes fixed on her mirrored reflection above the worn rimu bureau: a thin freckled-faced girl with a wide mouth, slightly protruding teeth and an air of casual elegance. "How's life been treating you? What's been happening?"

Lesley considered. "Quite a lot! We had some excitement the week before you rang to say you were coming to Waione—a fire! The whole of one wall of the store went up in flames—whoosh! Just like that! But luckily it was put out before—"

"Bad luck!" Anna swung around from the mirror and regarded Lesley with her laughing, green-eyed gaze. "But that's not quite what I'm getting at. How about romance? Love affairs? Anyone interesting?"

Lesley shook her head. "Definitely not."

The other girl sent her an incredulous look. "With all these rugged bushmen types queuing up at the store?"

"Oh, there are plenty of men around," Lesley agreed with a smile. "They're in and out of the shop all the time, wanting cigarettes, pipe tobacco, all that stuff. But there's only one guy that I've got to know at all, and that's Ross. Poor Ross," she laughed on a half note, "he's got quite a problem. He's parted from the girl he's crazy about, and he's depending on me to come up with some feminine advice as to how he can win her back. But apart from Ross, I haven't met anyone. At least—" she turned away "—only Stuart Carrington."

Something in her voice, some odd emphasis on the man's name must have given her away, for Anna paused in the act of unzipping her travel bag to glance up inquiringly.

"Why?" she inquired idly. "What's wrong with him?"

"Oh, nothing," Lesley said slowly. "According to what you hear, he's the Big Boss around the district."

"Married? He's got to be married?"

"No." For some reason she couldn't define Lesley had no wish to discuss Stuart Carrington. She wouldn't be surprised if he hadn't engineered the invitation to his home tomorrow for the sole purpose of trying to persuade her to change her mind about selling out. Or maybe—on a pretense of opening the wardrobe door she turned away to hide the sudden color that mounted in her cheeks—he had ideas of employing the tactics that he'd tried out on the last occasion when she'd been out with him. If so, if he were planning anything like that—her thoughts whirled in confusion—it wouldn't work. Not this time. Not now that she was forewarned.

"Well, go on," Anna's impatient tones broke into her tumultuous thoughts. "What's he like? You don't mean...." She stopped short. "Not the man I heard some girls discussing coming over the ranges today in the bus? Wait a minute...tick, tick, tick...I remember now! Carrington! That was the name! They said he was a wealthy young bachelor, the sort of guy that women just can't resist!"

"Don't you believe it," Lesley muttered. Then, aware of the other girl's expression of surprise, she added hastily, "Oh, the 'wealthy' part's true enough. He owns endless acres of property—about five thousand acres of bushland not far from here."

"Five thousand!" Anna was obviously impressed.

"That's what I call a landowner in a big way!" After a moment she asked curiously, "But that's not what I meant. What's he like? I mean... good-looking?"

"Yes," the word came reluctantly. "Very."

"No strings?"

Lesley hesitated. "Well, there's a girl. Judith's her name. She spends a lot of time at the house. She's a friend of his sister Kathy, and Mrs. Mac says—"

"I can guess," Anna broke in dryly, "what Mrs. Mac says. What I can't make out," she went on with a puzzled glance toward Lesley's downcast face, "is why you're so unenthusiastic about the man. Wealthy, good-looking, unattached—my goodness, what more could you want?"

"I can't stand him!" All at once Lesley's feelings, so long suppressed, flooded to the surface of her mind. "He's the one man who infuriates me!" The depth of feeling in her low tone surprised herself. "He's dominating and interfering and—oh, altogether impossible!"

"For heaven's sake!" Anna turned to eye her in astonishment. "What's he ever done to you?"

"It's not what he's done—" Lesley's low voice throbbed with intensity "—it's what he's trying to do! He wants to make the place into some sort of bushcraft school." She went on in a rush of words. "He tried to buy it from me when I first arrived, and he won't—he simply refused to believe me when I tell him that I don't want to sell out, that I'm determined to make a go of it here." Aware that Anna was eyeing her with a puzzled expression, she swept on hotly. "Well, you wouldn't like it, either! He treats me as though I were a child, a stupid inexperienced child! He's given me a time limit—a couple of months—" Lesley's soft lips were compressed "—at the outside. He thinks by then I'll have given in and agreed to sell him the place! You see," she went on in a burst of confidence, "it's difficult to buy land around here. Mostly it belongs to the Maoris—to the different members of the tribe—a sort of trust. But the store is different. It happens to be private property. It's right on the main road, too, just what he wants! He thought he had everything fixed up to take over when my dad died, and then I turned up, out of the blue! And do you know what?" she added indignantly. "He thought I was a boy!"

Anna burst into a ripple of laughter. "So that's it!" After a moment she sobered. "Don't hate him too much, my pet."

Lesley stared at her, a perplexed expression lighting her eyes. "What do you mean?"

"Nothing. Forget it. One thing's for sure, he's certainly got under your skin! Oh, well," Anna said with her careless smile, "that leaves the field clear for me! Although, if he's half as disagreeable as you say—"

"He's worse—a thousand times worse," Lesley assured her vehemently.

Anna shook out the folds from a blue-and-white striped overblouse. "Oh, well," she offered mildly, riffling through the neatly folded garments in search of matching shorts, "you don't have to see a lot of him, I take it?"

"But that's just it." Lesley avoided the other girl's questioning eyes. "He's a neighbor— Well, as neighbors go, around these parts. I've promised that we'll both go over to his place tomorrow. Whangariri, it's called. It means The Place of the Sun. He's calling for us."

Aware of the other girl's surprised expression, she burst out indignantly, "Oh, I didn't *want* to go there! But his sister asked me up there and she was so insistent that I couldn't very well refuse. She's rather a pet, Kathy. I like her a lot. I tried to wriggle out of the invitation by telling her that you were coming to stay, but they only told me to bring you along, too."

"Sounds interesting. Who else," Anna inquired, "lives up at this—what did you say it was called—Place of the Sun?"

"There's a little girl," Lesley explained, "Debbie her name is. Her father was killed in a tramping accident two years ago. Debbie was hurt at the same time. She has some sort of spinal trouble through a fall over a cliff in the bush, but she's almost well again now. She still has to rest a lot. I guess that's one of the reasons why Kathy welcomes visitors to the house. It means there's someone fresh for Debbie to meet."

Anna nodded. "I see. Is that all?"

"Not quite. There's Stuart's cousin, Tim."

"Oh!" Anna glanced up with interest. "Where does he fit in?"

"He doesn't, actually," Lesley answered thoughtfully. After a moment she went on, "He's a Carrington, too, but utterly different from the rest of the family—artistic type. I gather he's staying down here at the homestead between jobs. Seems he hasn't yet found his niche in life and keeps trying out different art forms. Right now it happens to be Maori carving and wood sculpture. He uses the native timbers that he finds in the bush here."

"*Really!*" Anna was regarding her, wide-eyed. All at once Lesley remembered that the other girl earned her living as an occupational therapist and would naturally be interested in Tim's hobbies. .

"Tell me more," Anna begged.

"That's about all, except for the two boys who work on the station," Lesley said, "but I didn't see them the time I was there. Judith—I told you about her. She spends a lot of time at the house."

"This gets more interesting every minute!" Anna lifted an orange sheath from her travel bag and slipping it on a hanger, opened the door of the long, old-fashioned wardrobe.

"Sorry," Lesley said, "but I've grabbed half the space before you got here."

But Anna's mind was still engaged with the subject of the Carringtons.

"I can't wait to go to this sun-house place." She shook out the folds of a boldly printed minifrock. "I don't know. In this country there are supposed to be three males to every girl. But if that's the truth, which I very much doubt, I'd just like to know where they're hiding. The surplus males, I mean! I know I didn't see a sign of them on my travels up north, but the scenery was fantastic."

"Come and tell me about it," Lesley suggested, "while I show you around."

Soon they were strolling down the narrow path at the rear of the dwelling, moving over the long dried grass between the high trees, where the branches bent low with loads of ripening fruit.

Lesley reached up to pick two luscious yellow peaches and listened attentively as Anna, munching the juicy fruit appreciatively, described the various towns and historical places she had visited during her recent tour of the Northland. At frequent intervals the colorful narrative was interrupted by the imperative ringing of the bell in the store, but when Lesley returned to the orchard Anna took up the account at the point where she had broken off.

It would be good to have a friend here with her at Waione, Lesley mused later in the day, someone of her own age group to talk to. Besides, Anna's gay chatter dispelled, even if only temporarily, a lurking worry that had niggled at the back of Lesley's mind ever since the repair work to the store had been completed, for as yet she had received no account from the building firm concerned, and as the days went by she asked herself if it was possible that no bill would be forthcoming? That someone else had settled the account? She decided now that she would wait no longer. Tomorrow she would inquire from the contractors in Murapara and find out the truth of the matter. Either there had been some mistake or....

Fortunately Lesley remembered the name of the building firm mentioned by the workmen. She found the name in the telephone book without difficulty and early on the following morning, while Anna was still asleep, she put through a call. A moment later a crisp masculine voice answered her.

"Lesley Monteith speaking," Lesley said. "You did some repair work for me at the store in Waione a while ago."

"That's right."

"I was wondering," Lesley inquired, "about the account. I don't seem to have received it yet."

"Hold on a minute, miss. I'll check."

The man was absent for only a minute or so. "Not to worry," he said cheerfully. "Account's all square, paid up the day after the job was finished."

"Paid up?" Lesley echoed. "I wonder.... Could you tell me, please, the name of the person who signed the check?"

"Sure. Hold on." There was a brief pause. Then: "Here

we are—signature's Stuart Carrington's. Everyone knows Stuart. Nothing to worry about."

Nothing to worry about! As Lesley replaced the receiver, the thoughts whizzed through her mind.

That Stuart again! The nerve of him! So confident was he that she'd soon have left the district, so sure of his power to change her mind about selling out that he'd actually spent money on renewing the blackened timbers. No wonder he hadn't told her what he'd done! No doubt he was counting on her remaining in ignorance as to who had given the order for the repairs to be carried out.

What was it that he'd said, that day of her arrival here? He'd been discussing the strip of newly laid concrete at the store entrance. "A bit previous" was the way he'd put it. No doubt he regarded the repairs in the same light. Necessary for the sake of his property, or what he mistakenly regarded would be his property in the near future. As for her, she simply didn't count in his scheme of things! He never doubted for a moment but that he would take over from her within a few weeks. True the time he'd allowed her wasn't yet up. She was still here—even if only just. But it was a hollow victory, she reflected despairingly, as the full implication of the situation swept over her. She was hopelessly indebted to that arrogant, all-sufficient, all-powerful Stuart Carrington! How long would it take for her to pay back to him the amount of all people! For a brief period she'd imagined that she had the edge on him. And now how pleased and triumphant he must be feeling. But then— a deep sigh escaped her—when did he ever feel any other way?

"Anything the matter?" Pajama-clad, her thin fine hair in blue plastic rollers, Anna pattered on bare feet into the room. "I heard the phone."

"No, no, of course not." Lesley forced a smile, wrenching her mind back to the present.

"Couldn't be, on a day like this!" Anna moved toward the window and kneeling on the low seat, parted the curtains to peer out into the incredible freshness of a summer morning where every leaf and branch seemed burnished in the sunshine. "Mmm—" appreciatively she breathed in the air, crystal clear and fresh with the fragrance of the bush "—smells wonderful! This is the day we're taking off for the Carringtons', isn't it?"

"That's right." It was Mrs. Mac, entering the room at that moment with a breakfast tray, who answered. "And don't let Lesley talk you out of going! She thinks she's leaving me with a lot of work, but that's nonsense! Here you are, Anna." She placed a glass of chilled grapefruit juice on the table. "Lesley and I've breakfasted ages ago."

"But I'll have coffee with you just the same," Lesley said with a smile, pulling her chair up to the table.

"You'll like Kathy Carrington." Mrs. Mac turned toward Anna. "Just about kills you with kindness when you go to her place. But that little girl of hers.... It'll be a good thing for her when she gets back to school, instead of being at home—thoroughly spoiled. She gets far too much of her own way! I told Kathy so, too, last time I saw her, but she said it was because of the child having been sick for so long. I know what I'd say to her impertinence!" Mrs. Mac emphasized her point by jamming slices of toast down into the silver-plated toast rack with a heavy hand.

"Does she have any sort of schooling at home?" Anna inquired.

"Supposed to have," the older woman answered. "But Debbie says she hates doing correspondence lessons. If Kathy tries to insist, Debbie immediately manufactures a headache, or some such nonsense. If she were my child...." Mrs. Mac's voice was grim. "And as for that Tim...."

Anna glanced inquiringly up from the toast she was buttering.

"All those years at University.... Why, he must be all of twenty-seven, and hasn't got around yet to earning his living—not seriously. And those paintings of his! Last time I was up at the house he showed me one of them, said it was abstract art. A woman—so *he* said! If that's his idea of what a woman looks like!"

"If you ask me—" Mrs. Mac lifted the coffeepot "—it's about time that Tim forgot about all those foolish fancies of his about remaking the world and got started on doing a bit in that line on his own account. It's just lucky for him that he happens to have a relative like Stuart who lends him money and puts up with him around the place. That is, when Tim can't find anything better to do, or anywhere else to go. Did Lesley tell you about the setup there? About the accident?"

"No. What was that?"

The conversation between the other two women faded from Lesley's consciousness as, staring abstractedly out of the window, she lost herself in another world. In the technicolored daydream she had miraculously grown several inches taller and checkbook in hand, was in the act of greeting Stuart Carrington. "If you'll just give me the amount of the repairs to *my property*," she was murmuring with hauteur and careless disdain, "I'll write you out a check!" *That* would make him think twice before he took it on himself again to—

"Coffee getting cold!" Mrs. Mac's piercing tones cut across the dream.

Lesley came back to the present with a guilty start. "I—didn't see it was there."

Mrs. Mac regarded her suspiciously. "What *is* the matter with you today, Lesley?"

"Nothing... nothing." Hastily she took a sip of the liquid, envying Anna her lighthearted chatter and expression of excited anticipation. But then Anna didn't have her problems. Other ones perhaps, but not anything so pressing—or disturbing. At least the other girl's problem wasn't tall and dark and so vital and—yes, attractive—that there was no forgetting him. Not for a moment!

CHAPTER EIGHT

WHEN LATER IN THE DAY the Land Rover drew up at the store and Stuart leaped out of the vehicle, Lesley saw at a glance that he had left work on the sheep station to pick her and Anna up. In khaki shorts and shirt and heavy work boots, there was a red rim around his bronzed forehead as he removed the wide-brimmed sunhat and came strolling toward her.

"Hello, Lesley!"

"Stuart!" For the first time she used the name unconsciously. Then she stopped short, the carefully prepared speeches with which she'd planned to greet him vanishing from her mind like mist on the ridges in the warmth of early-morning sunshine. For how could she possibly remember anything when he was regarding her with that warm special look in his gray eyes? Her thoughts raced in confusion. Maybe he approved of the sea-green color she was wearing. Maybe....

Lesley was unaware that a random shaft of sunlight, slanting through the open window, caught the swinging fall of satiny fair hair, or that the short frock, falling softly from its high bodice, looked cool and fresh, and infinitely becoming.

The next moment she became aware that Anna had come into the room and was eyeing Stuart with an expression of mingled interest and delighted surprise. It was then that a strange thing happened to Lesley. It was as if her heart flipped then settled again, leaving her with an odd desolate little ache.

"My friend Anna." She heard her own voice, determinedly light and bright "—the one I met on the plane coming over, remember? Stuart Carrington."

The man's intent look swept over the alert freckled face as he took Anna's fingers in a firm clasp. "Kathy's expecting you, and Debbie's all excited—just about counting the hours until you get there! Strangers are quite an event around these parts, you know. I'd better get you over right away. Mrs. Mac going to cope here?"

"She certainly is!" The older woman came hurrying toward them. "I want them to go off and enjoy themselves," she told Stuart in her definite no-nonsense manner. "Lesley's been working hours over the hot stove already today. She can do with a bit of fun!"

Fun! Lesley all but cried the word aloud. A day spent in the enforced company of Stuart Carrington! Especially now that she knew that it was he who had secretly footed that repair bill. Of all the mean, underhand things to do. But maybe, she told herself hopefully, she wouldn't be compelled to be alone with him today. He was wearing working clothes, and a glance through the window showed her that he was towing a trailer crowded with sheep dogs.

"Had to take the dogs to the vet," Stuart explained a little later as he went around to the driver's side of the vehicle and threw the Land Rover into gear. He turned toward Anna. "Your first trip up this way?"

"And last, probably." Anna's gaze was fixed on a fragment of road that disappeared into the bush ahead. "Frankly," she murmured laughingly, "I've never come across roads like this! And I've toured a few hundred miles in the last few weeks! I admit they warned me in the travel office before I set off that the Urewera country was pretty rugged territory, but I didn't really believe it! Not until yesterday! What gets me, though, is Lesley! Making the trip all by herself and not saying a word about it."

"You can't go by Lesley." Stuart's gaze was fixed on the winding curves ahead, where overhanging bush threw long shadows over the metaled roadway. "She's game for anything!"

And just what, Lesley wondered, did he mean by that?

"I mean to say—" the man threw her a teasing sideways grin "—any girl who takes on these roads on a beat-up old motor scooter—"

Her spirits fell with a plop! So that was it! Once again he was finding amusement in taunting her, in reminding her of her foolhardiness, her utter ignorance when it came to the understanding of anything of a mechanical nature.

"Lesley! You didn't!" Anna swung around and regarded Lesley incredulously. "Not up here?" She stopped short. "What on earth happened?"

"Nothing," Lesley muttered unhappily. "Just... well, some parts fell off the thing and it broke down in the bush...." Her voice trailed away.

"Well, go on!" Anna urged impatiently. "What happened then? Someone come along and rescue you? Knight-of-the-road sort of thing?"

"Actually, yes," Lesley admitted reluctantly. "Stuart."

"*Stuart!* Well, for goodness' sake.... You must have been relieved to see him! I hope," she said laughingly, "that you were sufficiently grateful to him."

Grateful! If Anna only knew how infuriating he could be! But of course if the other girl knew what he was really like, she wouldn't be playing into Stuart's hands in this way.

At that moment Lesley caught Stuart's derisive sideways look. Stung, she couldn't resist the retort that rose to her lips.

"*Was* I grateful?"

He grinned. "Not enough! I guess you owe me something at that. One of these days I'll remind you."

Hurriedly she made to change the subject. "You'd never believe, Anna, the legends there are about this place. Up here in the hills in the thick bush," she was rushing on breathlessly, "the Maori people who lived here—they used to call themselves Children of the Mist."

"Couldn't blame them for that," the man remarked. Branches of tea tree scraped against the vehicle as he swung around a hairpin bend. "Most of the year there's mist hanging over the tops of the ridges. It's a dominant symbol in the Ureweras. The local Maoris trace their descent from a symbolic union of Te Maunga—that's their name for the high mountain you passed on the way here yesterday, Anna—and Hine-Pokohu-Rangi, the Mist Maid."

He went on to explain something of the history of the area, pointing out the ridges surrounding them. On every knoll could be seen the earthworks and fortifications built by the old-time Maori around his *pa*. Soon they were rattling over a cattlestop, passing a tea tree loading ramp at the roadside, and Lesley, glancing up at the name of Stuart's property, thought how odd were these men of the New Zealand outback. They drove late-model cars that were invariably coated in dust; owned vast tracts of land marked only by means of a rough board nailed to a tree. And who, seeing Stuart in his worn khaki shirt and shorts, working alongside the men whom he employed, would dream that he was the owner of all this?

As they mounted the wide steps leading up to the shadowed patio, the child seated on a bamboo lounge leaned eagerly forward. "Mum!" she called loudly. "They're here!"

The next moment Kathy came hurrying toward them, her high tinkling laugh falling incessantly as, chatting merrily, she welcomed both girls into the house.

Seeing no sign of Judith, Lesley felt a lessening of some inner tension.

Tim, whose sprouting brown beard appeared to have made progress since Lesley's last visit to Whangariri, appeared delighted to meet her once again. A slight figure in the inevitable sloppy sweater and shabby denim shorts, he greeted Anna with his own relaxed brand of charm and dropped down to the polished floor beside her chair.

"Want to see my bride book?" Debbie inquired eagerly of Lesley. Delving behind her, the small girl produced from beneath a scarlet cushion a large and much handled scrapbook.

Lesley looked slightly startled. "Of course."

"She's got this thing about brides," Kathy explained apologetically. "I keep hoping she'll grow out of it, but she only seems to get worse. She cuts the pictures out of newspapers and magazines and sticks them into scrapbooks. To date this is the fifth! When she gets back to school next year I guess she'll have more to think about. And I don't suppose," she finished doubtfully, "that it does her any harm!"

"See!" the child flicked over the pages, and politely Lesley surveyed the smiling faces with their varied frocks and glittering head ornaments.

"Look at this one." Debbie pointed toward a miniskirted young bride accompanied by a long-haired groom. "This is a mod one. I give them all places, and this one has first place of all!" She broke off. "I wish I could see a real bride," the child murmured wistfully. "I've never been to a wedding, not even one. Stuart says I can come to his if I wait long enough, but I think he's only fooling."

Lesley felt her gaze drawn to the man who was standing a short distance away, and found to her discomfiture that he was eyeing her, an unfathomable expression lighting the gray eyes. The next moment he ground out his cigarette. "Sorry, folks, got to get cracking! The creek's drying up fast down in the gully—looks like I'll have to blast a new watering hole over in the back paddocks. Be free later on today, though. How about a look around the place then?" His quick vibrant glance included both Anna and Lesley. "See you!"

His long-legged stride took him swiftly down the patio steps and out toward a cluster of barns a short distance away. Lesley, glancing through the opening, watched him mount a red tractor, and soon he was moving across a grassy rise and out of sight.

With an effort she brought her mind back to Debbie, who was still apparently engrossed in her favorite topic of conversation.

"An' when I ask Judith when she's going to have a wedding, she just laughs and says she'll let me know. *Nobody*," Debbie complained bitterly, "*ever* gets married around this place."

"Don't look at me," Tim protested hastily as the small girl's gaze moved accusingly in his direction. "Who'd want a guy like me?"

"*I would*," Debbie said stoutly, adding after a moment's deep consideration, "I *like* beards!"

"Okay, then," Tim said, "I'll wait for you to grow up. But you'll have to hurry up and get mobile again. Can't have a bride who does nothing but sit around on the patio all day and never does a thing about the housekeeping!"

"Oh, dear," Kathy sighed, "you can't imagine how sick I am of brides! Even dogs and horses don't count with Debbie! I just wish I could get her interested in something else—*anything* else."

Something plucked at Lesley's mind and she turned toward Anna. "Didn't you tell me that you're a trained occupational therapist?"

"That's right," Anna agreed. "But I'm sure Debbie would have had folks in that line helping her when she was in hospital, showing her what a lot of fun it can be making things."

The child's lips closed mutinously and she became extremely busy with her scrapbook. "Stupid old clown dolls," she muttered sulkily.

"Is that the only thing you made?" Anna inquired.

"I didn't want to make anything. They made me," Debbie answered resentfully. Under her breath she added, "Silly old clown dolls!"

"She only had a few visits from the occupational therapist in hospital," Kathy put in. "Since then she's been recovering at home with regular checkups with the local doctor."

"Well, if you wanted me to," Anna suggested carefully, "I could show you lots of things you could make—much better than clowns."

Debbie regarded her suspiciously. "What sort of things?"

Anna considered. "Let's see. Well, you've got oodles of sheep wool here—this is a sheep station, isn't it? You could make wonderful things with scraps of sheepskin. When the skins are dyed the colors are simply beautiful: tangerines and emeralds and blues. I've seen them in the shops in other parts of the country, gorgeous fluffy scuffs and purses and bags and big fat slippers. There's no end to what you can make." As the child looked faintly interested, Anna continued, "And then there's leather. With all the deerhide around here you can really go to town. Even if you don't want them yourself," Anna suggested, "there's Christmas coming up soon. How'd you like to get going and make your own gifts, all ready for Christmas Day?"

Debbie regarded her doubtfully for a moment. Then: "Would you show me how?"

"Of course I would," Anna promised. "I've taught lots of children—and grown-ups, too—how to make things like that."

"All right, then," the child agreed slowly, "if you help me?"

"It's a promise."

"But that's marvelous—your being an occupational therapist, I mean." Kathy regarded Anna with eager interest. "Tell me, have you ever done any wool spinning? You see," she explained before the other girl could answer, "I'm trying to teach myself. With all this sheep's wool around the place, I thought I should. So I've been saving wool from the black sheep on the run for ages, bought a spinning wheel and an instruction book. But I don't know—I just can't seem to master it. There's something I'm doing wrong. If only I had someone to start me off I know I'd be away in no time."

"I've tried my hand at it a few times," said Anna. We should be able to work something out between us. Why don't you bring out your fleece? And the wheel? We can have a go at it together."

When the Land Rover pulled up below the patio that afternoon Kathy glanced up, an expression of dismay clouding her cheerful rounded face. "Don't tell me it's that late already! It can't be!" And then, as Stuart came into the room, "You simply can't drag Anna away, Stuart! I'm just getting the hang of it! And if you take her away now...." She appealed to the girl at her side. "*You* tell him you don't want to go any place at the moment."

Anna showed her prominent teeth in a wide smile. "It's nice to be needed." she said.

"Right." The man's glance took in the two women bent in concentration over the spinning wheel. His glance went to Lesley. "It'll have to be Lesley, then!"

As Lesley met the man's smiling gaze, the thought ran through her mind that he didn't look at all as though he were being forced to make do with her. Rather he appeared inordinately pleased with himself, as though the outing would give him an opportunity— She brought herself up short. An opportunity for what? To make her change her mind about the store sale? As if she would!

But she forgot everything else as the Land Rover took off and they swept through a gate and along the wide pumice path that led past the shearing sheds; the huts that were the shearers' quarters. Lesley noticed a cluster of farm machinery; sheep dogs secured by their long chains to their kennels. Soon they were passing paddocks, where sturdy stock ponies and riding hacks grazed, and then they were swinging down a sun-dried grassy slope.

"Hold on!" said Stuart, and they plunged down the incline. Lesley, laughing, rocked from side to side of the vehicle, her hair tossing around her shoulders and veiling her face. Around them the black-polled Angus steers wheeled and raced away in panic to pause at a safe distance, following the progress of the Land Rover with great curious eyes.

At the foot of the incline they turned into a narrow bush track. The heavy grille of the Land Rover swept aside overhanging branches on either side as, lurching over half-hidden tree roots and brushed by sweeping fronds of giant tree ferns, they moved into a gully filled with cabbage trees and native ferns. All around them rose the damp aromatic smell of the bush. Filtered sunlight pierced the lush green undergrowth and the wind rushed through the open sides of the Land Rover. To Lesley it all added up to an exciting and novel experience.

"This is an old mill road," Stuart was saying. "They're all over the place in this area. A lot of the trails are overgrown now, but the trampers still use them."

Lesley peered ahead to where the tracks radiated through the thickly growing trees.

"What I can't make out—" she was gazing around her at the surrounding hills with their dense mantle of native bush, sparked with the lighter green of umbrellalike pungas "—is where you keep all the sheep."

"Here and there, over the hills," Stuart answered carelessly. "Have to muster them for shearing next week."

Lesley swung sideways to avoid the long fronds of a giant tree fern sweeping past her. "Where are we going?" But it didn't really matter, she reflected. It was sufficient to be here in this unfamiliar twilight world, where even though the sun blazed high overhead, long shadows met and merged across the narrow track.

"We'll take a look at the mill." The man's gaze was fixed on a creek gleaming through the bushes. "If we don't get rain soon," he observed, "that's going to dry up. See where the deer have come down to drink...." He gestured toward the imprints of hoofs plainly visible in the dried mud at the water's edge.

But Lesley's apprehensive gaze was fixed on a makeshift bridge they were fast approaching. If only he didn't realize how she felt about moving over the two rough planks extending over the creek below!

But of course it was useless to even try to conceal her foreboding from that swift observant gaze. She might have known!

"Not to worry," he said. "Takes the weight of tractors on the way to the mill every day."

"But," Lesley asked faintly, endeavoring to make a mental calculation of the distance between the open planks, "what happens if you don't gauge the exact distance for the Land-Rover wheels? Make a mistake?"

"You don't!" Stuart answered dryly. And anyway, Lesley thought, as the four-wheel-drive vehicle moved unerringly over the rough planks a few moments later, she need not have concerned herself.

As they followed the overgrown track, Stuart pointed out the forest giants surrounding them. "Some of the finest timber in the world here," he said. "Swags of beech, rata, miro. See that?" He gestured toward the feathery foliage of a seventy-foot-high tree. "Rimu—great for house building. And that fellow—he's a kauri, king of the bush!" Lesley followed with her eyes the straight trunk that rose untapering into the blue far above. "Nothing to beat that for boatbuilding!"

Then, quite suddenly, they swept out of the filtered green gloom and emerged into a clearing. At the side of the road Lesley glimpsed battered trucks, machinery, tractors; caught the high-pitched whine of a chain saw.

"I've got a contractor cutting five hundred acres down here," Stuart explained as they approached the timber mill. "Over the hill I'm selling the trees on a royalty basis—so much for a hundred feet. Let's see how they're getting along."

As they drew up alongside the mill, Maori faces, gleaming with sweat, glanced with a friendly grin toward the man and girl who were climbing out of the dusty Land Rover.

"Hiya, Stuart!"

"Good day, boss!"

"How's things? Stick around, billy's on the boil!"

Lesley caught the flicker of flames beneath a blackened billy suspended by a tea-tree stick over the fire. While Stuart paused to discuss the cutting of timber with a powerful-looking bearded man in a black bush shirt, sturdy slacks and heavy boots, Lesley picked her way around a pile of sawdust. She watched, fascinated, the flash of an ax raised by a muscular arm. The next moment the ax flashed down to trim the posts free of splinters. Then, her ears filled with the racket of chain saws' biting teeth slicing through the white marrow of a tall tree, she turned to watch the great logs being fed into the machines.

Presently a tractor swung into view along a narrow bush track, and soon bushmen with their rope-scarred hands began dragging out the logs with wire rope. Chains rattled as the logs towed downhill were unhooked and flung onto the stack.

"Tea-oh!" At the shattering yell, accompanied by an unmistakable gesture of a raised enamel mug from the bushman tending the billy, the clamor of saws and machinery stopped abruptly. The next minute workmen began converging toward the flickering flames. While she sipped the strong dark brew in her mug, Lesley covertly eyed the working gang whom Stuart had just made known to her by name. Whether *pakeha* or Maori, she mused, the men of the timber gang shared one attribute in common, and that was the well-developed muscles rippling beneath their black bush shirts.

"Jim Neaves, Lesley." The shy, middle-aged foreman of the gang, who had just come to join the group, put out a work-calloused hand toward Lesley. "How're you making out with the cut, Jim?" Stuart inquired.

"Not bad. We'll have this area cut out in a week or two if the weather holds."

Suddenly an explosive sound echoed and reverberated around them, making Lesley jump. "What was *that*?" she asked fearfully, and realized the next moment that she was gripping Stuart's arm in a compulsive clutch.

"Just blasting," the man explained in his soft voice, and hastily Lesley pulled her hand away. Why was it, she asked herself helplessly, that in moments of emergency she turned unconsciously to Stuart, just as though it were the most natural thing in the world? Why *him*? Why not the smiling Maori bushman standing on her other side? Or kindly, gentle-spoken Jim Neaves? It was just something she couldn't understand. *Or wouldn't*, the annoying small voice jeered in her mind.

"Splitting a big one," Stuart was saying for her benefit. "Idea is to bore a hole down and insert blasting powder. Had enough tea? Right! We'll push off, then, There's a patch of timber farther on that I want to take a look at. Feel like hiking up the hill to have a look?" His gaze went to Lesley's tanned feet in their fragile scuffs. "How are you on climbing?"

"All right." Resolutely she crushed down the thought of the filmy frock that couldn't be more unsuitable for scrambling up rugged slopes, her summery white footwear. But her frock would just have to take care of itself. She wasn't going to have him thinking she was afraid of rough terrain, along with a lot of other unfamiliar things "down under." And one advantage about the New Zealand bush, she consoled herself, it was strong and tough. You could depend on its help when it came to hauling yourself upward and onward.

Back in the Land Rover, they took one of the network of tracks radiating through the trees, and Lesley gazed curiously around her. A crawler tractor was hauling a tree through the overhead branches. Lesley caught the swishing and drag as the steel ropes pulled the great tree toward the mill.

A little farther along the track a gang of bushmen with straining stomach muscles heaved at the poles that start the trees as they dragged great hooks and lengths of wire rope and clipped on the wire strops. Lesley caught the sound as the tree pushed its way through the top branches and then crashed to the ferny ground.

As they went on she could see where the timber workers had depleted the native bush.

"We don't cut them all out," Stuart told her, "but some of this is second growth—needs taking out." He raised a hand in a friendly salute toward a passing tractor driver.

Lesley turned back to watch a bushman, his ax raised high in a muscular arm, before the ax came flashing deep into the wood.

It seemed to her that they were moving ever deeper into the heart of the bush. But at length the milling road ended abruptly and Stuart turned toward Lesley with a smile. "This is where we push our way through. I'll go first."

They climbed out of the Land Rover and Stuart strode toward what appeared to Lesley to be a vertical cliff with low bush growing on the steep slope. "I might as well be a mountain climber," Lesley thought ruefully as she glanced up, up, up toward the grassy summit so far above. She would much prefer to stay here in the gully, where the wind sighed in the high branches above like the sound of distant surf.

"There's a trail blazed here for the trampers, but it's fairly overgrown." Stuart pushed aside tea tree and undergrowth. He took the first few feet up the steep slope, then paused to swing around and extend a lean bronzed hand. "Come on, I'll help you."

"I can manage," Lesley said stiffly. Clutching a small bush, she swung herself upward, deliberately avoiding his outstretched hand. She didn't want his help, or anything to do with him. Especially—oh, especially, must she avoid his touch! So she scrambled on, hot and breathless. She didn't dare to glance downward because of an uneasy suspicion that to do so would be to freeze right where she was. Nor could she glance up the sheer slope because if she did she might fear that she'd never make the summit, and wouldn't *that* be a triumph for the man climbing a few feet above her!

Grasping at low ferns and tufts of bushes, she made slow progress. But at length, face flushed, bare legs scratched and filmy frock torn by the thorny clutch of an encroaching bushlawyer vine, she neared the summit. Once again she ignored the man's hand, outstretched to help her over the last rise, and in a final undignified effort, she scrambled up onto the grassy knoll above.

After the arduous climb, the track winding down the mountain seemed no more than a pleasant stroll.

At length Stuart paused, surveying the opposite slopes, where the smooth boles rose straight toward the blue. Lesley came to stand at his side. She was breathless now, hot damp tendrils of hair clinging to her flushed forehead. She glanced up toward Stuart as he looked out over the endless blue peaks that stretched, ridge after ridge, to the horizon — tall, wide-shouldered, lean-hipped — a man of the land, a man whom she might have liked a lot, had things been different between them.

"I'll take a look farther down the slope," Stuart was saying. "Why don't you wait here and cool off?"

"Right." Lesley dropped down to the ferny undergrowth, pleasantly conscious of the wind, cool and fresh, caressing her flushed face and tossing her long hair around her shoulders. It was utterly still, the only sound the chorus of cicadas piping their summer song in the long sun-dried grass around her.

Clasping her hands around her bare, suntanned knees, she gazed at the panorama spread out before her. From this height she could see a long way away. On a green expanse at the foot of far bush-clad slopes she glimpsed small white dots that were sheep in fenced paddocks, the dwarflike figures of two boundary riders inspecting the fences. So she'd seen some of Stuart's sheep at last! Farther away a ribbon of white roadway threaded the hills and a small boxlike building gleamed through a screen of tall trees.

The store! It was as if a lowering gray cloud had come down over her spirit, blotting out all the lighthearted pleasure in the sunshiny day.

"Like I thought—needs a spot of thinning out." She realized that Stuart was dropping down at her side, a lean virile figure with dark hair blowing back from his forehead in the wind. He threw a searching glance toward Lesley's averted face. "Anything wrong?"

"No." Nervously she plucked at a small fern growing at her feet. "Only—" she turned to face him, eyes dark with feeling "—*you*, really!" and could have taken the words back as she caught the flame that leaped in the man's gray eyes.

Wildly she stammered, "You—you just take it for granted that I ... won't stay. Even at your home.... Kathy, everyone—they all think that place is going to be yours pretty soon."

"And you," he inquired in that deceptively soft tone, "don't agree?"

"No, I don't!" A wave of color ran up beneath the apricot tan of her cheeks. She could have struck him! He was so obviously reveling in his prospective victory. "I'm not going to give up so easily! You'll see!"

"Will I?" He was leaning back lazily on one elbow, laughing at her again. Oh, she hated him! Hated him!

She swung around to face him, blue eyes stormy, voice trembling with indignation. "And the fire—it was *you* who had the place all repaired." She tried to speak accusingly, but somehow her courage oozed away. She raised puzzled eyes to the man's face. "Why did you do it?"

He grinned disarmingly. "Would you believe me if I told you it was because you're so darned game?"

For no reason she found herself trembling. Just in time she caught herself up. Remember, he's only pretending. It's all a trick, a calculated scheme to charm her into changing her mind. Summoning all her willpower, she said, "No, I wouldn't! Not when I know you were planning to renew it anyway for yourself! How much," she inquired, very low, "do I owe you?"

"Can't remember at the moment." Stuart's voice was careless. "I'll let you know." She was conscious that he was eyeing her narrowly.

"I'll pay it back," Lesley asserted, "every cent of it!"

and somewhat spoiled the effect of the brave speech by adding uncertainly, "But goodness knows when that will be. It will take me ages."

"Not to worry," Stuart said. "I don't mind waiting *for what I want!*"

The expression in his eyes lent the words an odd significance. Lesley struggled against the enervating haze that threatened to engulf her. Wildly she fought her way clear of the golden web, the strands of which were drawing her away from her stern resolutions. She wanted to move away from him, but to do so would be to admit something she'd rather not face up to. Over the heavy beat of her heart she said breathlessly, "What makes you so certain that you'll get your own way, about the store?"

"I told you, I've got a plan! And this one," he went on confidently in that quiet voice that seemed to have some strange impact on her today, making her feel confused and uncertain, conscious only of his nearness, "you won't be able to resist!"

She tried to focus her whirling thoughts. If he imagined he could change her mind by raising the offer.... He actually believed that he had only to step up the purchase price — the Big Boss, the landowner whose property extended all around her. "If you're thinking of offering me more money...."

He was regarding her with that maddening half smile, his eyes never leaving her face. "Not money."

The thoughts whizzed madly through Lesley's mind. If not money that he had in mind, then what....

"You said," she murmured unsteadily, "that you had a plan."

His eyes challenged her. "That's right."

"If it's anything like the other one," Lesley whispered, looking anywhere but in the direction of his gaze, "it didn't work before. What makes you so sure that it will this time?"

"Let's just say," Stuart murmured in his relaxed way, "that I happen to have inside information. Besides—" his gaze, resting on her face, softened, darkened "—I usually get what I want in the end!"

Commonplace enough words. And yet something in the man's low tones sent Lesley's traitorous senses spinning wildly. There was the feeling... the feeling.... A heady excitement took possession of her. She knew that she'd have to escape, now, this minute! Or—

"Look...." He moved closer, throwing a bronzed arm around her shoulders. But conscious of that strong awareness, Lesley sprang wildly to her feet. She bent to dust the white pumice dust from her legs with fingers that trembled. "Let's go, shall we?"

Stuart sent her a glance that she couldn't interpret, but there was no doubt regarding the tense taut look around his mouth. "If you wish."

He got to his feet. And as they moved in silence back toward the steep incline Lesley reflected bleakly that at least she had brought things out into the open. She'd got through to him that she, too, could be determined; could fight to retain her own property—even if it was only a tiny country store surrounded by thirty acres of wild bush country in the middle of nowhere. She'd make him understand that it was useless trying to make her change her mind—*that way*!

Somehow, though, she felt no sense of satisfaction in the victory, only a dreary sense of letdown. It must surely be the effect of the arduous climb beneath the merciless rays of the afternoon sun that was making her feel all at once so tired and dispirited.

Hot and breathless, she hurried along the narrow sheep trail, bare legs stained with the dark smears of paspalum seeds and scuffs gritty with dust to the touch of her feet. But to request Stuart to slow his pace would be to admit defeat. Besides, there was something stern and forbidding about the set straight line of his lips.

As she followed him down the steep incline she had a suspicion that he was deliberately slowing his pace to suit her halting progress as, slithering, sliding, clinging fast to low-growing scrub, she made her way step-by-step down the slope. She was still some distance from the foot of the bushy cliff when she made the error of glancing below her, and immediately the landscape tilted and blurred in a sickening whirl as vertigo overcame her.

Vaguely she was aware of Stuart glancing up toward her. "You all right, Lesley?"

"Yes, of course." But even as she answered, she was aware of a sound of whirring in her ears, louder...louder. She took a step forward, stumbled as her heel caught in an exposed tree root, then felt herself pitching forward, clutching desperately at fern and scrub in her headlong rush. It all happened so quickly. One moment she had lost her footing and was flying through the air, the next she felt herself caught up. Lithe and strong, Stuart was holding her as effortlessly as though she were a child, and secure in the strength of those strong arms, she lay passive though her heart was racing, as the man picked his way down the steep slope. A few moments later he leaped down to the carpet of ferns growing below.

The lean brown face was close, and for a crazy second she was limp in his arms, caught in a wild ecstasy she was powerless to combat. Something stronger than herself made her cling to him, trembling. Then his arms tightened around her as his lips sought hers and some strange enchantment held her a willing captive.

Gently he slid her to the ground, and Lesley tried in vain to focus her whirling senses. All her sensible resolutions—and fate had literally thrown her into his arms! She hadn't counted on this!

"I don't know what came over me...." Her voice was barely audible as she bent to retrieve her fallen scuff. "It was the height—looking down, like the suspension bridge."

"You'll get used to it." With a little shock of surprise she realized that for once, there was no mockery in his gaze.

What did he mean, she wondered with a sudden clutch of the heart. Was it just an idle remark or.... As she made her way along the narrow winding track, where the man waited to push aside the great trailing ropes of black supplejack from her way, she puzzled over the matter.

Was he admitting defeat? Perhaps, then, his kiss hadn't been just a way of gaining her confidence. For no reason at all, once again she was swept by that surge of wild, unthinking happiness.

"The Land Rover's just over the rise," Stuart was saying.

"Yes." Lesley was still shaken by an emotion she couldn't define. She was deep in a sense of elation as the vehicle lumbered along the rough mill road, throwing her against the man at the wheel. For a moment his arm swept around her to steady her, and her heart began its crazy thud-thud. She jerked herself back to her own side of the seat. To allow herself to feel like this was madness. She mustn't give way to this dangerous magic, not if she wanted to keep her senses—and her business head. She had a suspicion that nothing would achieve the latter, but at least she must stick by her decision. A red light flashed in her mind. *Careful*, Lesley. Most likely this was all part of his plan to soften her up. And then, at the right moment, a moment like this, say.... She *had* to break the spell.

Jerkily she said, "With all these acres, surely you could make your bush camp here?"

He shook a dark head. "Not so easy. Nearly all this lot is covered in millable timber—not the ideal spot by a long way. Hey, look over there!"

As Lesley followed the direction of his gaze, she caught a glimpse of antlers gleaming through the fronds of tall tree ferns. The next moment, however, the shy brown eyes had vanished and only a swaying frond among the lush green undergrowth betrayed the spot where the deer had stood.

To Lesley it was clear that Stuart had already forgotten the kiss that to her had been so disturbing. Well, why not? To him she was nothing more than a silly stubborn girl who didn't mean a thing to him, except as a stumbling block to his plans. A block that he was determined to remove, by one means or another!

His sudden sideways grin sent her defenses crumbling, and determinedly she fixed her gaze on the twisting trail ahead. For she knew that to meet his gaze today was to invite disaster; send her thoughts spinning dangerously. When he looked at her with that warm glance she had the crazy feeling that everything was different between them, that they were friends instead of enemies. More than friends....

They rattled over the rough planks that spanned the creek below. But now Lesley forgot to be apprehensive. To think.... Her cheeks flamed at the recollection of the events of the last half hour, and she crouched over in her seat in an endeavor to be as far away as possible from Stuart. He probably imagined that he had merely to make love to her and she'd be wax in his hands. The Big Boss—on his own ground! She had planned to defeat him, but once again he had the edge on her. But only because he was enigmatic and horrible and impossible to understand. Smiling and friendly one moment, inscrutable and forbidding the next. But, then, he could of course afford to behave in any way he chose.

They jolted up the slope toward the rambling brick house on the rise, and a few minutes later Stuart brought the Land Rover to a stop beside the long line of scarlet poinsettias, which fringed the entrance steps.

As she stepped into the checkered sunlight of the patio she became aware, with a start of surprise, of Judith, seated in a low bucket chair, watching her. It was almost as though the other girl had been waiting for her and Stuart to arrive back at the house.

Why was it, she wondered uneasily, that she was so conscious of the older girl? It was absurd the way in which she allowed Judith to affect her. Judith, in her impeccable dark blue trouser suit, a flicker of amusement lighting her dark eyes.

"For goodness' sake—" the throaty tones broke into Lesley's thoughts "—whatever has Stuart been doing to you? Dragging you through the undergrowth by your hair?"

All at once Lesley was discomfitedly aware of her bedraggled frock and wind-tangled hair. In her wild scramble down the steep incline, one scuff had broken away from the sole and she hadn't even noticed—until now.

"You should let me design you some suitable gear for tramping," Judith suggested with her poison-arrow smile. "I don't suppose you had a clue about the sort of place you were coming to, out here. But then," she finished idly, "it's scarcely worthwhile, is it? You won't be staying long at the store, from what Stuart told me."

All at once Lesley felt exasperated by this girl's barbed

remarks and cruel smile. And Stuart! How dared he answer for her! Just because he had made up his mind that she wouldn't be staying. It seemed, she thought crossly, that everyone here decided what she should do in advance, and she was sick of it!

So she drew herself up, torn frock and broken footwear and all. She said quietly, "I don't know how you got that idea, because it's all wrong. Of course I'm staying here. I never dreamed of anything else."

Clearly Judith was startled by Lesley's frank avowal.

"Oh, yes," Lesley went on, blue eyes alive with interest in her subject. Perhaps Judith was endeavoring to be friendly. Maybe she'd misjudged the other girl, misinterpreted her remarks.

"Frankly," she smiled her friendly smile, "before I got here, I did expect things to be different. You know? More modern." The dark eyes were eyeing her attentively. "And then when I found out about everything it was a bit of a shock—at first. But all the same I'm going to carry on. At least, give it a go."

"Smart of you." The deep tones were tinged with malice. "No harm in trying—if the stakes are high enough."

Lesley flinched as from a physical blow. Ordinary enough words, and yet beneath them she sensed a deeper significance, a note of warning.

What was Judith trying to imply? Surely she couldn't be referring to Stuart? Why, it was unthinkable that the other girl should imagine that Lesley was staying here, not for her own financial interest, but to capture those "higher stakes," which if Mrs. Mac were to be believed, Judith had attempted so long and so unsuccessfully to gain for herself.

"I told Stuart," Lesley said in a low voice, "that I wasn't going to sell."

"Why on earth not?" There was a tenseness in Judith's expression. "He's offered a good price, hasn't he?"

"Oh, yes, it isn't that! It's just that I like it here. I want to make a go of it," Lesley said lamely. How stupid her explanation must seem, saying she wanted to stay here and manage a country store. How could a girl like Judith understand the vital importance of a few dollars' profit? Or even, for that matter, a few hundred?

"I take it—" a cold smile curved the translucent pink lips "—that Stuart's still hopeful of making you change your mind?"

"Oh, yes! He...." Lesley stopped in confusion. There was something in the other girl's watchful expression that she didn't understand. Anyway, she didn't have to confide her affairs to Judith.

"So that's it!" the other girl said on a long breath of relief. "I *thought* there must be a reason."

"A reason?" Lesley stared back at her in perplexity. "What do you mean?"

"Nothing. Only let me give you a word of advice, little Lesley! It doesn't always pay to take what people say too seriously. I mean to say, folks often have a reason for being nice to you, seeking you out. Ever thought that a man like Stuart—"

But Lesley had heard enough. Even though the mocking words merely served to confirm her own suspicions, she didn't have to endure such treatment from Judith. She turned, narrowly avoiding colliding with Tim, who was entering the room.

"I was just telling Lesley," Judith said smoothly, "that I'll have to design her some suitable clobber for tramping around in the bush."

"She looks okay to me." A smile lighted Tim's rounded features. "Why don't you come into the workshop? Quite a scene of activity. You'd never believe it." Taking Lesley's arm, he guided her through the open French doors and into the spacious lounge room with its white carpet and long floor-to-ceiling windows framing a view of the bush-clad hills.

"Come and see!" Debbie, her knees tucked beneath her on a low seat, called to Lesley excitedly. "Anna's showing me how to make the most fab things! I'll show you."

Lesley picked her way between the scraps of fluffy sheepskin and newspaper cuttings that littered the floor. Anna, kneeling on the carpet, was slicing around an outline penciled on a sheet of newspaper. Kathy was busily engaged in sorting through a massive print drawstring bag filled with scraps of leather and pieces of sheepskin.

"I'm going to make you all Christmas presents this year— *myself*," Debbie chattered with animation. "Anna's going to show me how. We're going to join scraps together to make a tea cosy for Aunt Susan. And see this...." She waved a paper pattern shape in Lesley's direction. "Bet you wouldn't think that was a pattern for a leather moccasin, would you? But it is! I'm going to make them for mum." She turned a small anxious face toward Kathy. "You don't mind knowing what I'm giving you, do you, mum?"

Kathy shook her head, her radiant face expressing the delight she felt in the child's suddenly aroused interest.

"An' I'm going to make coin purses out of sheepskin for you and Judith, Lesley, with a zip an' everything," Debbie cried excitedly, "an' a car-seat cover for Stuart. You can have one, too, Tim, if you like, or I might make you some moccasins. I'll see."

"Whoops," said Tim. "I've always yearned for a car-seat cover. I'll put it away for my car—when I get one!"

But the child was far too absorbed in her new project to listen. "An' I'm going to make them all before Christmas," she announced, "for everyone."

"I'll have to send away to town for a punch, some special needles and cutters," Anna told her. She swung around toward Lesley, tossing an armful of sheepskin pieces in her direction. "Like to sort out the biggest scraps into matching shades for us."

Obligingly Lesley seated herself beside the small girl and began to place the long fluffy tonings into piles according to their shadings: Off-white, cream, beige, dark brown.

It was amazing, she mused, as she continued with her task, how much at home here Anna appeared to be. This was an Anna far removed from the heartbroken girl Lesley had met on the plane leaving that London airport. Absorbed in the work she loved, confident, filled with an infectious enthusiasm, Anna was drafting a man's moccasin pattern for Debbie, turning to answer a query Kathy had made concerning the spinning wheel, flashing a swift retort toward Tim. Almost she seemed to be one of the family. Whereas she herself....

Absently Lesley ran her fingers down the smooth lines of an abstract wood sculpture of a seabird which stood on a low table at her side.

"Like it?" She became aware of Tim watching her, a gleam of interest lighting the pale blue eyes.

"Like it?" she echoed. "Why, it's one of the most beautiful pieces of wood sculpture I've come across! Something about the lines...the smoothness.... I've seen a lot of this sort of art work, but nothing to equal this—" She broke off as a sudden thought struck her. "This isn't your work? I remember you told me, in the car going to Rotorua, that you were interested in this type of thing. But surely this—"

Tim waved a deprecating hand. "One of my efforts, actually. Totara from the bush around here. And that reminds me, I must go and get some more. It's great to work with, ideal for this type of thing."

"You don't mean to say—" Anna had risen from the floor and had come to stand beside them "—that you've actually carved this yourself out of totara timber from the bush?" The freckled fingers caressed the flowing lines suggestive of a graceful seabird. She glanced across at Tim. "A heron, isn't it?"

He nodded carelessly, but there was a gratified light in the light blue eyes nevertheless. "All my own work."

"Just this one?" Anna's pale eyes glanced around the room. "But you must have done others—lots of them—before you got to this stage! Let me see them, please, Tim?"

"We-ell, if you insist. But I warn you," he said, "it's on your own head. Only a hobby—passes the time."

He left the room, to return in a few moments holding a cardboard carton. Soon he was arranging on a low table a varied assortment of sculptured wood shapes: the curving lines of a dolphin, a leaping swordfish, a tiny packhorse, a deer and an exquisitely carved miniature model of a Maori canoe.

Anna picked them up, one after another. "You market them, of course?"

"What?" Tim fixed her with a stern glance. "Are you asking me to prostitute my art?"

"You're crazy," Anna told him in her forthright manner. "You should be selling all you can produce."

"And how much," Tim asked with a grin, "do I produce?"

It was Kathy who answered. "Very little," she admitted. "But that's not to say you couldn't do lots more, if you wanted to. Anna," Kathy appealed to the girl who was examining with interest the small Maori canoe, "couldn't you persuade him? It's in your line, after all. Get him to concentrate on this instead of all the other things he tries out."

"I doubt," said Anna, smiling up into the small features and laughing blue eyes, "if I'd have much influence. But I might at that, if I thought I had a chance."

"I'm always open to suggestion," said Tim. "Stick around."

"I'll see what I can do." As Lesley took in the other girl's determined expression she had a swift thought that Tim's lighthearted challenge could well involve him in quite a lot more opposition than he anticipated at the moment.

"You know something?" Anna was saying thoughtfully. "I've had a look around the art shops all over the north, and they're crying out, they tell me, for souvenir stuff— good stuff, I mean, like this. Honestly! You could make a good living. If you cared to, you could even start up in business—employ other carvers, work it up into something big! Those Maori scroll designs aren't often attempted by Europeans, from what I hear. You could make quite a name for yourself."

Tim eyed her with his lazy grin. "Why?"

Anna's hesitation was only momentary. "Don't you want to make money? Real money, I mean?"

"Frankly, no," Tim murmured. "Why tie yourself down to one line of action," he said carelessly, "when there are so many other things that might prove just as entertaining?"

"But not so profitable."

"Who," Tim inquired with his peculiarly sweet smile, "cares about profits?"

"What about marriage, then?" Anna countered. "Your wife might."

"I wouldn't know." Tim shrugged a slim shoulder. "Girlfriends are more in my line." He flashed Anna a significant laughing glance. "The compliant kind are the ones I go for! Anyhow, like I said, why tie yourself down?"

"I still don't believe it," Anna persisted. "I'm warning you, I'm going to go into Taupo in a day or two to pick up needles and a leather punch, and I'm going to take in some of your work and see what the souvenir shop offers for it."

"Help yourself," Tim said carelessly. "But you'll be in for a disappointment. My stuff isn't all that special, and even if it were, I'm not the energetic type."

"You could be," Anna challenged him, "with a bit of encouragement."

But Tim merely continued to regard her with his amiable smile. "It would take more than that! You'd have your work cut out, Anna, to get me going on the production line."

Anna showed her prominent teeth in a wide confident smile. "Don't forget," she reminded him, "that I'm in the business. Remember?"

"Too bad," Tim grinned, "that I'm not one of your walking wounded!"

"Isn't it?" Anna agreed. "Then you'd *have* to listen to me."

"Anna," Debbie interrupted plaintively, "you haven't finished cutting out my moccasin pattern."

"Neither I have. Where was I?" Picking up the scissors, Anna proceeded to snip around the penciled outline.

Tim, watching her, regarded the flimsy shape with distaste. "Just my luck," he remarked moodily, "to cop the moccasins."

"You might be surprised," Anna told him with a swift reproving glance.

Lesley was scarcely aware of the amicable wrangling voices. As she glanced around the room she reflected that she didn't belong here. She was the outsider. Even Anna, who had only just arrived, seemed immediately to fit in, to be needed, whereas she herself wasn't needed by anyone.

Not really. And as to Stuart.... She wrenched her thoughts away. Better forget about Stuart.

It was just, she mused forlornly, that they were all so accomplished, so clever. Even Tim. All except herself. *All that I can make*, she reflected ruefully, *are pies and hamburgers.* She raised her eyes to meet Tim's smiling gaze.

"I like you when you do that," he observed.

"Do what?" she asked, bewildered.

"Push your hair back from your ears like that."

"Oh." Stuart had said that, too—lightly, teasingly. *Must she remember everything Stuart had ever said to her?* Was it all that important? Somehow she couldn't answer that query.

It was late when at last the record player died into silence, and Lesley, with a murmur of having to get an early start in the morning, rose to her feet.

Tonight she was thankful that she had Anna for company on the drive back to the small dwelling on the main highway. Arrogant and self-assertive and overconfident though he might be, there was something definitely disturbing about Stuart Carrington. At least there was to her. Something against which she seemed to have no defense—except flight. Something that numbed all her carefully prepared speeches. Anna's gay chatter would dispel those dangerous silences when her stupid heart began to beat faster and, nervous and confused, she found herself saying things that were better left unsaid.

The two girls leaned from the car, waving in answer to the chorus of "Goodbyes." Then Anna leaned back in the seat.

"Debbie's a bright little thing," she remarked to Stuart. "Is she really getting better?"

Lesley's gaze went to the strong profile illuminated by the dim light of the dashboard. If only he wasn't so disturbingly, devastatingly good-looking. It wasn't fair!

"Doc says," Stuart was saying as they rattled over the cattlestop and swept up the rough track, silvered in the moonlight, "that she'll be mobile again by Christmas—and that's only a couple of weeks away! Says there'll be no aftereffects, either. Everything healed up." He turned his head toward Anna, and hurriedly Lesley tore her gaze away.

"Looks like she's going to be pretty busy meantime—just what she needs, some activity to keep her busy. Judith tried her hand at amusing her. She's a fair reader—done a bit in the amateur acting line." She *would*, Lesley thought uncharitably, and brought her mind back to the deep soft tones. "What the kid wants, though, is something she can get her teeth into. And that's where we're going to find you pretty necessary around these parts, unless I miss my guess." He smiled across at Anna. "A bit of luck, your happening to be in the right game."

They chatted together, leaving Lesley feeling strangely young and forlorn and somehow left out. Why was it that Anna could chat with Stuart so effortlessly, so unselfconsciously? But then, she mused, the other girl had no reason to feel otherwise. *She* wasn't indebted to him. Besides, where Anna was concerned Stuart had no hidden motives. He had no need to argue or cajole her.

The store was in darkness when they reached it, a pale blue against the dim outline of bush-covered hills. The two girls tiptoed inside, moving quietly so as not to awaken Mrs. Mac.

When they reached the bedroom Anna's eyes went immediately to a blue aerogram lying on the bureau. "Mail for you from England!" she cried excitedly.

"Yes, I know." Lesley's voice was indifferent.

"But—" Anna looked at her in amazement "—aren't you going to read it?"

"Of course." Lesley put a fingernail beneath the sealed edge, her eyes skimming over the sprawling handwriting of the girl who had once been her workmate. As she'd expected, there was just the usual office gossip. Somehow the news no longer seemed important or even interesting. It was as if this were the reality—this remote clearing in the bush half a world away. It was very strange.

Anna slipped into cool shortie pajamas and began to put up her thin hair in rollers. "That Tim—" her eyes were on her mirrored reflection as she lifted thin arms "—he's got quite a gift, if only I could get him to realize it! What's he been doing with himself all these years?"

"Drifting around, so Mrs. Mac says." Lesley emerged

from the short striped cotton nightdress she had pulled over her head. "Her idea is that he needs someone—some girl, that is—to take him in hand, make him settle down to work." She threw Anna a teasing glance. "Like to take on the job?"

Anna burst out laughing, but the next moment her face sobered. "I've a jolly good mind to try, if he'll let me. Bags the stretcher tonight." She climbed into the low camp bed and pulled up the sheet. Her pale eyes dwelt abstractedly on Lesley, brushing out her swinging fair hair.

"Judith," Anna murmured reflectively, "is awfully keen to move in permanently to that sun house up on the hill, wouldn't you say? In a way," she went on without waiting for Lesley to comment, "you can't blame her. He's awfully attractive."

Lesley held the hairbrush poised in her hand. Her heart, for no reason at all, was behaving strangely. "You mean Stuart? You know something, Anna? You're getting to sound just like Mrs. Mac!"

But Anna wasn't listening. "And Debbie... quite a pet, don't you think? Stuart's right, though. The child does need something to keep her busy. Evidently she's been cooped up in the house for months and months with nothing much to do—no one of her own age to talk to. Did she tell you about her bride's book?"

"Did she ever?" Lesley groaned. "She insisted on showing me every single picture in it. You'd be doing a public duty if you'd get her to switch her interest to handcrafts."

"Oh, I don't know, it's only natural, I suppose. I'm going to dress a bride doll for her for a Christmas gift. Talking of brides—" hands crossed behind her head, Anna lay back on the pillows, thinking aloud "—could be," she murmured, "that Debbie might have a real live wedding in the family one of these days. It's just struck me! Stuart. He's made to order! The exact pattern of the New Zealand sheep farmer you promised to provide for me when we were talking about husband material on the plane out. Remember? Stuart Carrington just about fills the bill, wouldn't you say? Big landowner, devastatingly good-looking in that bronzed tough sort of way. Just the right age for me, too. Wouldn't it be funny if...."

As Anna's voice died thoughtfully away, Lesley felt a swift stab of the heart. The other girl was talking nonsense, of course. Absurd for her to feel this heavy sense of pain and foreboding.

"I just can't understand why you don't like him." She brought her mind back to Anna's musing tones. "Not that I'm complaining. Do you know what?" she ran on as Lesley made no comment. "I just might be spending quite some time around these parts. Stuart asked me tonight if I'd like to come over to his place and stay for a while. I take it the idea is for me to help out with Debbie—sort of keep her amused. That is, when the week's stay with you is over."

Lesley felt ashamed of the cloud of jealousy that without warning descended over her spirit, blotting out everything except this hot searing emotion. Never would she have believed herself capable of feeling like this. And toward Anna! Anna, who was her friend.

"Are you... going?" She forced the words through dry lips.

Fortunately, however, the other girl was too engrossed in her own affairs to notice Lesley's agitation. "Am I? With a good-looking guy like that around the place? You've got to be joking! That's why," Anna went on lightly, "I'm so glad that you're not the slightest bit interested. I mean, I'd hate to be the 'other girl' around here!"

"Don't worry," said Lesley, and switched off the bedside lamp so that Anna couldn't see the shock the words had given her. For a long time she lay, eyes wide open, staring into the darkness, listening to the small noises of the night.

She told herself that she was crazy to feel this shame-making jealousy simply because of Anna's careless words. Even if by some chance it should happen that the other girl should become attracted to the man who appeared to dominate the small forest community, well what of it? Good luck to her! Only why did it hurt so much?

CHAPTER NINE

ANNA SPENT THE FOLLOWING DAY helping Lesley and Mrs. Mac in the shop. "It's fun," the older girl told Lesley. "Such a change from hospital work or just being a tourist!" It would be fun for her, too, Lesley reflected ruefully, if only there weren't always this feeling of urgency. She must show profits quickly so that she could begin to pay back to Stuart Carrington the money she owed him.

In the late afternoon Anna was called to the telephone and a moment later she hurried into the store, where Lesley was busy arranging stacks of tinned tropical fruits in the show window.

"It's Stuart," said Anna, and Lesley, in her swift sideways turn, narrowly avoided knocking over the precariously arranged pyramid that she was in the act of building. "Oh, does he want me?"

Anna shook her head. "He wants to know if I can go over there for a few days, stay at the house. It seems the Maori shearing gang have just arrived—two trucks complete with shearers, wives, families, dogs—whatever. Everyone at the house is flat out with shearers and meals and they want to know if I can go over there and keep Debbie amused for a few days." She glanced inquiringly toward Lesley.

"Do you want to go?" Lesley asked.

"I wouldn't mind," Anna said consideringly, "but it seems so awful, rushing away from the store almost as soon as I've got here."

"No, it's not," Lesley assured her. "I'm tied up here anyway. Besides, the Carringtons might be able to take you around a bit while you're there, once the shearing's over."

"That's what Stuart said." Why was it, Lesley wondered that she felt this queer pain, like a knife piercing her heart, slowly...slowly?

She jerked her thoughts back to Anna's voice. "Heavens, I almost forgot! He's holding the line! He wants to take me for a tour all around the district on Friday, Stuart says I can do all my shopping at the craft shops at Taupo at the same time. He said to ask you if you'd care to come along, too."

All at once Lesley was annoyed. She said quickly, "Sorry, I can't make it, I'm afraid. But you go, Anna."

The other girl hesitated. "If you're sure you don't mind?"

"Don't be silly!"

As Anna ran back to the telephone she paused to throw over her shoulder, "He's sending one of the boys to pick me up in an hour! An hour! And my hair's in a mess! Heavens, what'll I do? My frock—can I borrow the iron?"

"Help yourself."

"You're sure you don't want to come with us?"

Lesley shook her head because she couldn't speak without betraying the silly choking feeling in her throat. She was imagining what it would be like to be whizzing along the road in the early-morning sunshine into the sparkling thermal town on the edges of the blue lake waters—with Stuart. But sharing the journey with Anna, starry-eyed like this, would be no fun at all, especially with this pain in her heart, like a dark shadow, spoiling everything.

Lesley went back to stacking the tins of fruit, but her enthusiasm in the activity had waned. The display window that she envisaged as looking outstandingly attractive appeared little different from other country stores she'd come across during her journey to Waione. The trouble was that she couldn't seem to concentrate on the window anymore. It was all because of Stuart Carrington and his casually extended invitation! She wished that Ross would come along, so that she could show him that she wasn't dependent on *his* transport to enjoy a day away from the store.

And it's just when you're in moods like this, she told herself the next moment, that fate takes a hand in things.

For outside a familiar late-model car was drawing up at the entrance, and soon Ross's massive figure appeared in the entrance.

Picking her way carefully around the precariously stacked foodstuffs, Lesley straightened and leaped lightly down from the display window. She smiled up into the steady dark eyes.

"How are you, Ross?"

"Fine! Just got back from a stint down south. I thought you might care to have a run around. I've got a day's leave due on Friday. We could zip over to Taupo, or take a run into Rotorua if you like. Whatever you say."

"Taupo'd be wonderful!" Some devil of contrariness impelled Lesley to answer without hesitation. If the Carringtons were going there that same day, Stuart might happen to run into her. And maybe, seeing her with someone else, especially with Ross—she remembered his unwarranted interference in the matter of the bearded 'copter pilot—he'd realize that those odd lapses of excitement she betrayed when she was with Stuart meant nothing. Nothing at all.

If he could make love to her—she corrected herself carefully—*pretend* to make love to her.... Oh, not in so many words perhaps. But it was there. Oh, it was there all right! And then demonstrate so obviously his preference for Anna's company, she'd show him that to Lesley Monteith he was merely a business adversary. And he'd better believe it!

Not that it would make a great difference to Ross whether she went with him on his free day or not. She seemed to be a natural for the role of confidant when it came to other folks' love affairs, she thought wryly. First Anna, and now Ross.

"Hey, Lesley, come back!" With a start she became aware that the big man was snapping his fingers before her face.

"Sorry," she smiled contritely. "I was miles away."

"You're telling me! I just wondered if you'd packed a swimsuit in your luggage."

Lesley nodded. "And a bikini!"

"Good girl! Bring along the bikini and we'll have a dip in the lake."

"That sounds like fun!"

A small Maori boy ran into the shop and Ross turned away with a parting smile. "See you Friday, then. Two o'clock?"

It was nice, she reflected as the child departed with his lollipop, to be invited for an afternoon's outing, instead of having the suggestion thrown at one as an obvious afterthought. She only hoped she did meet Stuart when in Taupo. It would prove to him—and herself—that in her scheme of things he didn't count. Not one little bit!

Somehow the week seemed endless. The hectic rush of activity had slackened off, and now with time on her hands she found herself wishing she had more to do to keep herself occupied. Then she wouldn't think endlessly about the big brick house on the hill, and what was happening there.

One thing of which she was sure, though, and that was that Anna was thoroughly enjoying her stay with her newly acquired friends. Nightly the other girl phoned through to Lesley, her voice gay and animated, ringing with excitement.

They'd been having a hectic time, all of them, but being at Whangariri at shearing time was an experience she wouldn't have missed for anything! Debbie was catching on to the handcrafts like wildfire! Walking a lot now, too—just around the house, so far, but still.... She'd persuaded the child to take more exercise, and Kathy was delighted in her mastery in the skill of spinning the wools she'd collected while at the sheep station. Because of the terrific amount of extra work in the house, she'd had to put her hobby aside for a day or two. But the shearing would soon be over, and then Stuart had promised to take Anna on a trip to Lake Waikaremoana—a wonderful place that he'd told her of, not far distant.

"How's Tim?" Lesley found herself asking. She voiced the inquiry more because she wished to stem Anna's chatter regarding herself and Stuart than out of any real curiosity concerning the slight young man with his lighthearted attitude to life.

"You'd never guess!" Anna exulted. "Yesterday Kathy insisted that I borrow the car, so I popped Debbie in, too, and off we went to Rotorua, with samples of Tim's wood sculptures and Maori carvings stacked in a big box on the back seat. The souvenir shop that I took them to didn't want to let them go. They were thrilled! Said they'd take all he could do. So I'm going to hound him into making a few just to keep them happy until he gets into his stride—has a regular output."

"That's what *she* thinks!" A light masculine voice reached Lesley's ears. "Take no notice. It's only my production manager talking...."

Very faintly Lesley caught the sound of scuffling. Then laughing voices echoed over the wire.

"Bet you anything you like...."

"Right! You're on!"

Anna sounded so happy, Lesley thought wistfully, almost as though she were one of the family.... She pulled herself up sharply. But that meant....

She scarcely took in the other girl's excited tones. "Stuart says... Stuart told me...." And then: "Sorry, I've got to fly! It's Stuart—he wants me."

Lesley replaced the receiver with an unconscious sigh. Once again the dark wings of jealousy beat over her spirit.

On Friday Ross arrived promptly, and Lesley took her place in the long car, obviously cleaned and polished for the occasion.

Prince ambled to the roadway to see them off, and as the vehicle swung around, then took the shadow-splashed roadway, Lesley found that she was enjoying the blissful sensation of idleness; the touch of— the wind, fresh and cool on her face as she leaned back in her seat. Of course, it would have been quite different had it been Stuart who'd been taking her into town today. Exciting? Dangerous? Unpredictable? Maybe, but anyway *different*. With Ross there were no peaks and valleys. She knew exactly where she stood with Ross. Whereas with him—

"Care to have a look at the government pine plantations?"

"Oh, yes!" She'd care for anything that would serve to

take her mind from endlessly reverting to Stuart Carrington.

They swept along the curves of the winding bush-fringed highway, and even when the big man threw his arm companionably around her shoulders Lesley made no move to shrug it away, as she would have done with Stuart. There she went again—Stuart. It meant nothing, of course. Just two young people out on a blue-and-gold day that was made to order for touring the country. It was just a pity that Stuart Carrington's white Jaguar had to fly past them at that moment. She heard a wild tooting of a horn, caught a flashing glimpse of smiling waving passengers, and something else— a flash of recognition in the lean bronzed face of the driver. But where was her feeling of triumph? It was what she'd wanted, wasn't it? To show him she couldn't care less for him or his invitation! But somehow the sunshine seemed to have dimmed a little, and all at once she found herself wishing that she hadn't made her point quite so clearly. Absurd to feel this lingering sense of regret.

Except for an occasional dust-coated logging truck, they met little traffic on the road. At length, however, they swept on to smooth bitumen and soon they were turning into the long straight road cutting through the center of a vast green sea, fragrant with the resinous tang of pine needles.

As they moved on through the constant twilight of the pines, Ross pointed out to Lesley the radiata pine, fast growing and mature in forty years, the Douglas fir, growing straight and unforked. Farther on he indicated the cleared firebreaks; the lookout posts raised high above the exotic forest. They passed an area where felling was taking place, swept on to another block acrid with the smell of smoke rising from the debris that was being burned off in a clearing. Then they emerged once again into full sunlight and Lesley, gazing ahead, glimpsed the great inland sea that was Lake Taupo, guarded by its sentinel of the mountain.

It wasn't until she and Ross were seated in a small restaurant overlooking the rippling blue silk of the lake waters, where myriad yachts with their multicolored sails flew along in the stiff breeze, that Lesley broached the question that had trembled on her tongue throughout the journey.

"Ross, I was wondering—how are things with you and Vicky? Have you heard from her—from Australia?"

The big man shook his head. "But I'm not giving up that easily!" Leaning across the table, he spilled out the thoughts that lurked behind the somber dark eyes. "I had to see you! After what you said the other day I got to thinking things over." Absently he twirled a fork in his big fingers. "You know what, Lesley? I reckon you've got something—I mean that idea of yours for me to send Vicky an engagement ring. I've been going over things she said to me, different times, and they sort of add up. Could be you're right! Vicky could have got to thinking that I wasn't on the level, just stringing her along all this time. I didn't put her in the picture as to why I was saving so hard. I guess," he murmured thoughtfully, "it's different for a girl. She can't come right out with it and say what's on her mind."

Lesley agreed that Ross had a point there.

"Look—" Ross's heavy expression lifted "—how about if you give me a hand to choose a ring today? The shop's just along the road."

"That's easy." Lesley smiled across into the earnest bearded face. "Tell me something," she said lightly, "did Vicky ever mention any particular preference? I mean, did she care for any special stone?"

"Wait a minute!" Ross said. "I remember now! She told me once—gee, that was soon after we met—that if ever she had a choice she'd never look at anything else but a diamond solitaire engagement ring. Dammit all—" he stared moodily down at his coffee cup "—why didn't I guess then what she was getting at?" He shook the thought away. "But I've got her Sydney address right here in my shirt pocket. We'll go get the ring and, I'll post it away today while we're handy to a post office. Then— Well, then I'll keep my fingers crossed."

They strolled up the colorful street with its new and attractive stores, sparkling with attractive merchandise. The wide glass show windows displayed a varied assortment of goods: deerskin jackets, trout-fishing rods, a seemingly endless variety of feathered flies, marine engines, canoes and boating accessories. There were, too, all types of camping gear, hunting knives, rifles.

Lesley found the jewelery store consisted of two large showrooms. One one side the long glass shelves glittered with an assortment of rings, watches, silverware and clocks, while the opposite glass display window was given over to Maori carvings and artifacts, local gem-stone jewelery and native souvenirs and ornaments fashioned from greenstone and paua, the shimmering opalescent shell found along the coasts.

"This is the one!" Without hesitation Lesley selected a ring from the velvet-lined case the attendant had laid out on the glass counter for her inspection. From a wide gold band a single diamond gleamed in its high setting. Lesley slipped the ring on her finger and held up her hand to examine the scintillating jewel. "It fits, too."

She never knew what impulse impelled her to look over her shoulder, to meet the startled stare of the tall man who had just entered the store. For a long moment their glances held. Surely, Lesley thought swiftly, she must have imagined the man's stricken look, the expression of shock and dismay evident in the bronzed face. The next moment his expression changed, hardened. Without a word he swung on his heel, and striding out of the doorway, mingled with the crowd moving leisurely along the wide sunlit street.

Lesley was left with a sense of desolation, like the first faint stirring of deeper pain yet to come. It was as though something were very wrong. Something.... She couldn't pinpoint it. Vaguely as from a distance she became aware of Ross's deep deliberate tones. "That's the one! I'll take it! Have to take a chance on the fitting, but it should be all right!"

"But—" the young salesman eyed the big man in astonishment "—the ring fits perfectly."

With an effort Lesley brought her thoughts back to the present. Why, she hadn't even troubled to inquire the price of the diamond solitaire on its wide gold band that she'd selected without hesitation. But the cost, it transpired, came well within Ross's price range. Not that the man would have cared, Lesley reflected, what amount within reason he was asked to pay today.

Come to think of it, she'd paid quite a price herself for her gesture of independence! There was something in the way Stuart had regarded her—almost as though he'd suffered an unexpected blow. She told herself that it didn't matter that he had probably put a totally mistaken construction on the little scene. Who could blame him? But she'd put the matter right, of course she would, when she saw him again. But could she? She could scarcely betray Ross's confidence. It was his affair, after all.

All through the afternoon, while she and Ross motored out to a sheltered sandy bay fringed with bush and fern, swam and laughed and splashed in the limpid lake water, Lesley's gray mood persisted, and although she made a pretense of gaiety, she couldn't seem to shake it off.

The cool breeze that had sprung up, slapping the little wavelets up on the sand, seemed to blow through her heart, as though it were the end of summer, instead of just the beginning. She forced the ridiculous impression away. There was no reason to feel like this unless.... All at once she found herself wishing that she could see Stuart again today. Perhaps he was still here, somewhere in the town. Later in the afternoon, motoring with Ross through the wide smooth streets, Lesley eyed the strolling holiday groups, coolly and attractively clad in light summer clothing, hoping to catch a glimpse of a distinctively tall male figure among the throng.

She waited in the car while Ross went into the post office and sent off the small jeweler's box, together with the letter he had already written, by airmail to Australia, but still she could see no sign of Stuart, or indeed of any of the party from Waione. Not that it mattered, she told herself. For even if she had seen Stuart once again, how could she possibly explain an incident like that, without betraying Ross's secret? Anyway, she mused drearily, the Big Boss probably wouldn't believe her!

On the winding drive homeward Ross dwelt hopefully on the outcome of the plan that Lesley had suggested. Already it seemed he was looking forward to a new life with the girl he loved. But although she tried to concentrate on the deep tones, Lesley's mind wandered, for something else, so shattering that she didn't want to face up to it, niggled at the back of her mind.

She minded—she minded dreadfully that Stuart had been a witness to the little scene in the jewelery shop, because.... At last she took the matter to its bitter conclusion. She was in love with him! She loved the lean brown hardness of him, the swiftly changing expressions in the vibrant face. Nothing else seemed real to her now. Nothing mattered except being with him, hearing the soft voice that made such an impact on her heart.

And he despised her. He thought of her with goodnatured contempt, regarded her as a child who was making a pretense of being a businesswoman, playing at life. Well, wasn't she? And all the time it had been for real! It served her right! In a world of men she had to fall in love with Stuart Carrington! She'd thought she'd hated him, and all the time it had been some kind of built-in defense inside herself—against this!

His brief lovemaking, she knew, had been only pretending. Hadn't he warned her on that point right from the beginning? And still, fool that she was, somehow, somewhere along the line, she'd fallen hopelessly, desperately in love with him. How could she know that love could come like that, sort of sneak up on you so that you never even suspected it?

And she was the girl who so short a time ago had said to Anna, during the plane journey from London, that she wouldn't *let* herself get involved. Oh, no, it couldn't happen to *her*! Secure in her narrow little world, she'd been so smug, so superior, all unaware of the hazards and pitfalls that existed in that other untried territory—the country of the heart.

Lost in her thoughts, she scarcely realized that she was nearing the end of her journey, until suddenly a small white building flashed into sight in a clearing, and the car drew up in the shade of the overhanging tree ferns on the narrow roadway.

"Thanks a lot, Lesley." Ross's arm slipped around her shoulders. His light kiss brushed her cheek.

Lesley summoned up a smile. "Good luck!"

"I sure need it!" As she leaped lightly to the ground he put the car into gear. "I'll keep in touch."

CHAPTER TEN

SOMEHOW LESLEY MANAGED to get through the long night, tossing, turning, thinking, remembering. It was a relief when at last the pearly tint that glowed on the horizon deepened presently to streaks of flame fanning across the eastern sky.

Pale and heavy-eyed, she dressed silently, dragging her long hair away from her face and tying it carelessly back with a ribbon. If this were love... this hopeless aching longing that could never be assuaged.... She thought, *How can I get through the days, without seeing him? Without betraying the way I feel?* For despite the almost intolerable longing to be with Stuart to see him, touch him, she must avoid him at all costs. He must never dream that she loved him. That she couldn't endure.

For Lesley the days passed in a daze of unhappiness. Apparently, however, heartache didn't show—or maybe, she reflected dispiritedly, Mrs. Mac was too involved in attending to a sudden rush of customers to notice anything except the matter in hand. Lesley's lack of appetite was put down by the older woman to the increasing heat of the long summer days.

Fortunately, Lesley told herself, she was well accustomed to the routine tasks. When it came to baking scones, spreading hamburgers, setting out food and handling change correctly, her hands and her mind now functioned automatically. Only her heart was undisciplined, and that she could do nothing about!

Hardest of all to endure was the torture of Anna's daily phone call. For it seemed to Lesley that the other girl's conversation was centered always on the master of Whangariri. Shearing was finished at last, but Stuart was out on the station from dawn to dark these days, seeing to the sheep. It seemed they had developed some infection. Unfortunately the outing to Lake Waikaremoana had of necessity to be postponed. Anna hoped not for long; she was counting the days! There was never any mention of a time limit being set to the other girl's visit. Indeed, Anna spoke of the future as though she were staying indefinitely. "Kathy and I," she told Lesley, "are thinking of planting canna lilies all along the drive up to the house. They're no trouble to look after and they'll make a wonderful splash of color next spring!" Anna had scarcely waited for Lesley's comment before sweeping on. "You know all that stuff about falling in love at first sight," she confided in her gay voice, "I never used to believe in it. But now I'm beginning to change my mind— Well, I'm not so sure!"

A heavy weight seemed to be crushing the words in Lesley's throat. She managed at last to say, "You mean—"

But Anna only laughed. "I'll let you know—later. I'll tell you something, though!" Her voice changed, grew thoughtful. "Am I ever glad that I got asked up here to stay at Stuart's home! Funny, a little thing like being a trained therapist, and it can change your life!"

Lesley replaced the receiver over a desolate sense of aloneness.

Well, there was always work as a means of deadening thought; shutting out the picture in her mind of a purposeful strong face, a tall masculine figure. Slowly she made her way into the store, where a wide-shouldered Maori timber worker waited. "You've given me too much change, miss." The smiling tones brought her up with a jerk. "Oh, so I have! I'm sorry."

It was hopeless. She couldn't even concentrate on her work. And concentrate she must if she were ever to repay her debt to Stuart Carrington.

During the following two days when Anna failed to make any communication, Lesley found herself tortured by her imaginings. In vain she tried to subdue the shame-making jealousy that niggled deep in her mind. She told herself that she was thankful that, happily engrossed in each other's company, Anna and Stuart had apparently forgotten her. At least she was spared the other girl's glowing confidences and the exquisite pain of being forced to see Stuart once again. Not, she mused over a deepening sense of regret, that he'd have any interest in her, apart from business. Not after what had happened in Taupo!

When at last Lesley was called to the telephone, she was unprepared for the wild excitement of Anna's breathless tones. "Lesley, I'm warning you! Take hold of something and hold on tight! I've got news for you—the most fantastic news ever! I'm so happy I scarcely know what I'm saying! I'm going to be married! Yes, it's true! Oh, I know it sounds crazy; we've only known each other for three weeks, and I still can't believe it! Honestly! I've heard of these whirlwind romances and never really believed it was possible—not until now!" Rapturously the light voice flowed on. "Don't breathe a word, Lesley! It's all hush-hush until after tomorrow night. There's to be an engagement party and it's to be announced then. But you see, there was a chance of a Sydney trip and we thought we'd make it a honeymoon! To think that all this," Anna exulted, "is actually happening— to *me*! Imagine! This time next month I'll be Mrs. Carrington!"

Mrs. Carrington. The words fell on Lesley's ears like the somber tolling of a distant bell. Through the mists that were clouding her senses she was vaguely aware of the gay excited tones. "I've never been so happy—ever. And to think I ever thought that I was in love with Darren! I didn't even know what love was! You don't, not until you meet up with the real thing. And it was you who brought us both together— Are you still there, Lesley? The shock hasn't been too much for you?"

But she couldn't answer, "Yes, Anna, I'm still here. But the shock is beyond bearing." *So make yourself snap out of this deadly feeling of inertia or shock or whatever it is that's come over you, Lesley. Talk to Anna! Sound happy! You can if you try hard enough.* What was the customary reaction to unexpected news, whether good or bad?

"I simply can't believe it."

Apparently Anna's wild happiness blinded her to any nuance of the voice that was so often betrayed in a telephone conversation.

"I know! I know! Neither can I! Listen, we're planning to be married quite soon! After all, what is there to wait for? And he says he needs me! So I thought—that is, Kathy—I simply can't get to thinking of her as my sister-in-law—" the breathless tones ran on "—wants us to have the wedding at the house. In three weeks' time! Everyone's happy about it, even Judith. She actually wished us luck, and I think she meant it."

Judith. So Lesley had been mistaken in imagining that Judith's interest had been centered on Stuart. But then she'd been mistaken about so many things.

Her dazed mind returned to the radiant voice. "Debbie's crazy with excitement! Yes, you've guessed it! She's to be bridesmaid at the wedding. Funny, isn't it? That makes two of us, a bride and a bridesmaid who'd both just about given up hope! And then the miracle happened right here in Whangariri. Notice how I've got my tongue right round those Maori syllables at last? Stuart says it's a must if I'm going to live here, to be able to pronounce the name of the place! Heavens, where was I? There are so many exciting things happening all at once I can't keep track of them." Lesley's mind, numbed with misery, tried to take in the excited tones.

"Engagement party...tomorrow night...." Lesley had a swift mental picture of Anna, her thin plain face illuminated with an inner radiance, wide lips parted in a smile revealing the protruding teeth, pale green eyes bright with a newly found happiness. What was she saying now? "Wish me luck, Lesley."

"Of course," she whispered, "All the luck in the world."

"And now," Anna said excitedly, "here's where you come into the picture."

"But I—"

"Now don't start refusing before you know what it is! Of course you're coming to the wedding! And the engagement party! Who else, outside the family, would have the first invitation?" Odd snatches, phrases, registered themselves in Lesley's distraught mind: "...promised Kathy I'd fix the floral arrangements for tomorrow night. Kathy's prepared masses of food. Everyone in the district's invited. But about the flowers—Kathy's got these gorgeous big punga bowls hollowed out from the trunks of trees, for flower holders. I've got a fancy to fill them with rata flowers—you know, from the bush. Kathy wants me to settle for poinsettias. They're fine, but I've got this thing about an all New Zealand decor. It would make a fabulous color photograph to send back home, too. Ferns and palms in big clumps everywhere! That dramatic-looking flax with the black seedpods, and rata—that I must have! It's such a flaming flamboyant sort of red! There were some flowers on a tree down in a gully at the back of the store. You pointed them out to me the day I arrived, only they looked fairly high up the tree to pick. Lesley, get someone to zip up and get some for me, will you? I'll call and pick them up tomorrow."

"I'll get them." Her voice sounded almost normal, if without the slightest expression.

"I knew you wouldn't let me down!"

Somehow Lesley managed to answer fairly sensibly. At least she supposed she must have, for Anna's excited tones continued to flow over the wire.

At last she rang off and Lesley, conscious of an odd sensation, a sort of inner chill, went to her room. Could that be her own reflection in the mirror? Even her lips were pale, like someone who has suffered a shock. Silly really, because in a way she'd been expecting it. Not quite so soon perhaps, but still....

Vaguely through the window she was aware of a crowd of laughing tourists who were converging on the store, and all at once she knew that she couldn't face strangers today. In this dazed anguished state of mind she'd disgrace herself, do something silly.

"Mrs. Mac," she called in a strange thick tone, "would you mind looking after the shop for a little while? I'm just going out for a walk before dark."

"A walk?" She was unaware of the troubled expression in the older woman's clear brown eyes. "You're all right, Lesley? There's nothing wrong?"

"Just a headache." Lesley turned away.

"Take an Aspro. In my room...."

But unheeding, like a girl in a trance, Lesley had already

moved blindly away. Her slow steps carried her along the passage and out through the back entrance. Skirting the house, she gained the roadway, unheedful of the rough stones beneath her feet or the cloud of dust rising around her from a car a short distance ahead.

Like a wounded animal seeking sanctuary, she wanted only to hide herself away in the silent green depths until such time as she could regain some mastery of herself.

Something brushed against her and she turned a dazed ashen face. But it was only Prince, loping along at her side. "Come on then, Prince, let's go for a walk...a long, long way."

"Want a lift, lady?" A jeep was slowing down at her side, and a middle-aged man with a kindly smile leaned from the driver's seat.

But dumbly Lesley shook her head. Once, long ago, on a sunshiny day like this, she'd accepted a lift from a stranger, and look where that had taken her. On a long road that had led only to anguish...almost unbearable to...heartache.

A sheep trailer roared along behind her, and instinctively Lesley fled down a narrow path that zigzagged down into the valley below. With a wild urge toward hysteria she realized that there high against the lush greenery of the bush, flamed the scarlet blossoms of the rata, the strange forest tree that, beginning life as a vine, ends by crushing the tree it entwines and growing itself into a high forest tree. She knew all about it because that was what Stuart had told her. Stuart....

It seemed to her fevered imagination that even here, deep in the depths of the bush, she couldn't escape her thoughts. Well, why not, she thought wildly, do the thing properly? Already she'd provided Anna with the man of her dreams. Why not, for good measure, throw in the flaming floral emblem of the other girl's engagement night?

Turning off the track, Lesley pushed aside the thickly growing undergrowth, the encroaching vines and creepers and made her way slowly forward. Heedless of the scratches on her arms and legs, she was conscious of nothing except a dogged determination that she must reach the rata tree and gather the red flowers, no matter how far she had to go, or how high she was forced to climb to pick the blossoms.

It was extraordinary, though, she thought dully, how one's mind tricked one in the bush. The flowering tree, instead of becoming nearer with every step, appeared to be receding. It seemed so close at hand. And yet she just couldn't seem to approach it. Once she tripped heavily over a fallen log, but she picked herself up, staring dazedly at the trickle of blood running down her bare leg.

In her numbed state of mind it was somehow all-important that she reach the rata tree. But it was becoming increasingly difficult. The undergrowth was thicker now, and there were no longer any blazed trails to follow. Vaguely she was aware that the sun had disappeared below the horizon, leaving behind a luminous golden glow. A shaft of sanity penetrated her shocked mind. Darkness fell early in the depths of the bush. Maybe she'd better put off gathering the rata blossoms until tomorrow. What was it the Maoris said? "*Taihoa*: tomorrow will do."

Even as she turned, however, it seemed to her that the gloom deepened. That must explain the reason why she couldn't be certain of the way she'd taken to arrive at this spot. Blundering forward, pushing her way through ferny undergrowth and between the trunks of tall forest trees, at length the fact registered on her dazed mind that she was hopelessly lost

Not that it mattered, she reflected wearily. What did anything matter now? But the next moment, with a swift pang of fear, she changed her mind, for some large unseen object was crashing through the undergrowth, and out of nowhere came the thought of the wild pigs that she knew abounded in the area. What if.... Rigid with terror she stood rooted to the spot. But the next minute Prince came bounding through the tree ferns toward her, and with a surge of relief she dropped a hand to the Alsatian's collar. With Prince at her side she'd be protected from that particular terror of the night. And maybe she'd come across a tramper's hut—if she walked long enough.

She lost count of the hours as she stumbled blindly on, in what direction she couldn't tell. It was easier to make her way when, much later, the moon rose, flooding the dense greenery with silver. When at length a small hut loomed up directly ahead of her, she could scarcely believe it.

Exhausted, she stumbled inside. Her chilled and fumbling fingers found matches, lit the kerosene lamp standing on a rough table. Then she threw herself down on the bunk, and the big Alsatian, as if guarding her, stretched himself out on the floorboards below.

It didn't matter anymore if the tears came. There was no one now to see or care as the great shuddering sobs rended her. At last, however, exhaustion had its way with her and she slept, one hand tucked under her chin, strands of fair hair entangled with sprigs of leaves and fern, veiling her face.

That was when the dream came, the crazy tender dream when Stuart was right there in the hut. She knew it was a dream because he wasn't sardonic anymore. The gray eyes were no longer steel hard but dark with concern. The beloved tones as he called her name were ragged with anxiety. In the dream he bent over her, gathering her into his arms. How could she help but be filled with a deep unutterable sense of content? It was as though, at last, she'd come home.

Only it wasn't a dream, because all at once she could feel beneath her fingers the smooth fabric of a man's Windbreaker. It must surely, she thought shakily, be a trick of the flickering lamplight that lent his face that shadowed drawn look.

"Lesley! You're not hurt?"

"No." The rough tenderness of his arms sent her spirits soaring. "My darling—" his voice was low with feeling, "—I thought I'd never find you! I've been just about out of my mind! Anna...."

Of course—Anna. Lesley drew herself away from the shelter of those strong arms as remembrance came with a rush.

But Stuart put a hand beneath her rounded chin, forcing her to meet his gaze.

"Don't look like that, little one! Anna's fine! She'll be on top of the world again, once she knows you're all right. What's driving her frantic is knowing that she sent you into the bush after those damned rata flowers! She's blaming herself—and the party Kathy's putting on for her and Tim tomorrow night."

Lesley was staring up at him, blue eyes wide and dilated in the lamplight. "You said... *Tim!*" A wave of happiness surged over her. Had he really called her "my darling," or had she dreamed it? Her voice quickened. "Do you mean that—"

"Good grief—" there was an echo of the old impatient Stuart in the quick tones "—didn't she tell you?"

"Yes, she did," Lesley said slowly. The words were out before she could stop them. "But she said she was going to be Mrs. Carrington, and I thought that you...and Anna...."

"You...what?" The swift glance she knew so well flickered incredulously over her face. "Didn't you guess all these weeks—" the warmth and meaning in his warm glance set her trembling "—that I happen to be in love with *you*?"

A hand cupped around her chin, the pressure of his mouth on hers. A heady intoxication, a dizzy rapture, sent her senses spinning.

At last, holding her at arm's length, Stuart gazed directly into Lesley's face. "I didn't think I had a chance. I thought: Give her time and maybe she'll care, if I'm patient.... But hell, I'm not the patient sort! Seeing you tonight, I couldn't wait any longer to tell you. I've loved you since that first moment when I found you in the bush—remember? Tonight, searching the hills for you, I told myself I didn't care a damn who you were in love with! There'd never be another girl as far as I was concerned! And then, when old Ross joined in the search—" He broke off. "You should have seen him! I've never known a quiet bloke get so het up! He'd just got the big news and he couldn't wait to tell you. That's when he opened up to me and I found I'd been way off beam ever since— Well, ever since Taupo. Old Ross was full of a cable he'd just got from Vicky. Told me I'd have to start thinking of wedding presents. He didn't seem to know whether to be happy about himself and Vicky, or worried stiff about you. But forget about Ross."

Once again his arms tightened around her. "Let's talk about us!"

Presently when she could speak once again, Lesley raised her ruffled head from the region of the man's chest. "You know," she said in a muffled tone, "you never did get around to letting me in on your plan. The one that was fail-safe. Remember?" Her eyes, glimmering with sheer radiance, were raised to the man's quizzical glance. Not that it mattered now. It was all just a part of the man whom she loved best in all the world.

"You're right—" Stuart's low tones deepened "—I didn't."

Tenderly she traced with a finger the outlines of the curving mouth that had always seemed to her not to match the stern outlines of the lean tanned face—until now. "You said," she said softly, "to remind you."

"So I did." His expression as he glanced down at her was tender. "Just a few words, actually. I was going to tell you any minute now. Will you marry me, Lesley?"

It was some time later when she smiled up at him, her voice spilling over with a wild sweet happiness. "Funny, you know, but I don't seem to mind a bit now. About turning the store into a bushcraft school, I mean. The old place is getting pretty run-down anyway. Although I don't know," she teased lightly, "about all these strange children we're starting off with—"

He stopped her laughing words with the urgent pressure of his lips against her own. "What makes you think," Stuart inquired softly with a glimmer of his old tantalizing grin, "that they'll all be strangers?"

VINEYARD IN A VALLEY

Vineyard in a Valley

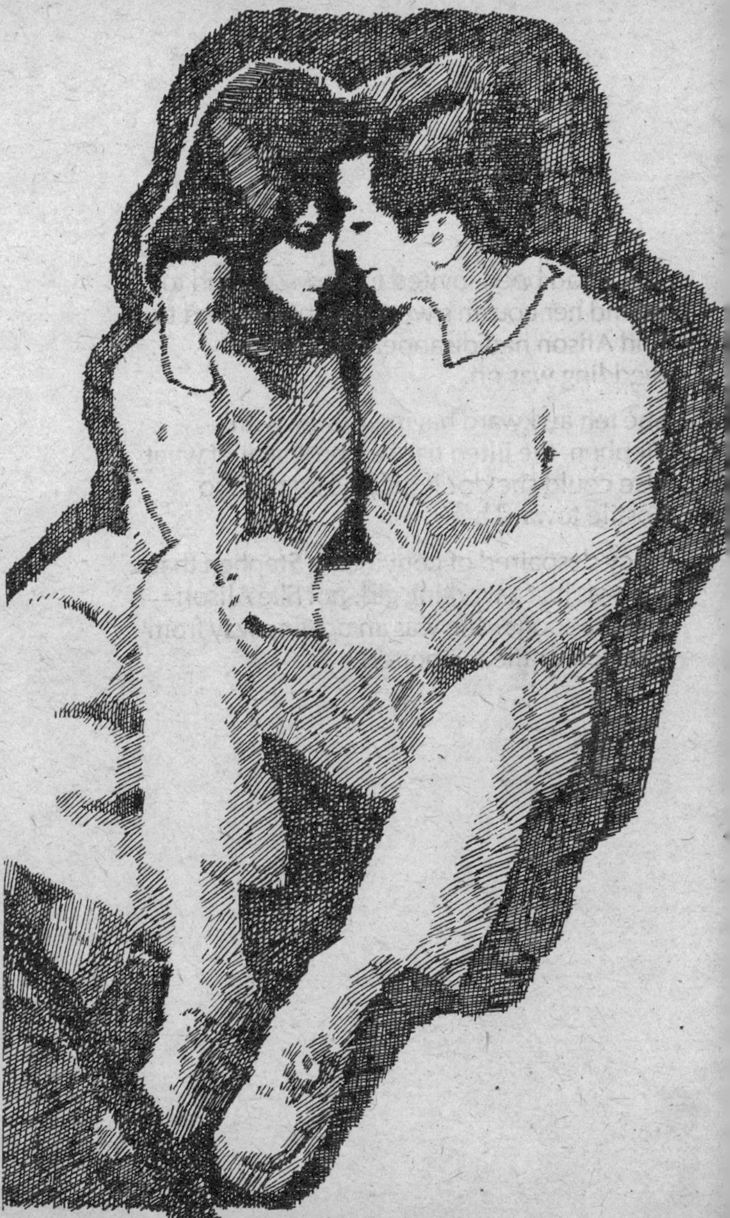

Tracy had been invited to New Zealand to attend her cousin's wedding, but arrived to find Alison had disappeared and the wedding was off.

She felt awkward having to stay with Stephen, the jilted fiancé's brother, yet what else could she do? If only he weren't so hostile toward her!

Tracy despaired of convincing Stephen that she was just a working girl, not like Alison—and the sooner she was an ocean away from Stephen Crane the better!

CHAPTER ONE

HE WAS THE FIRST PERSON to draw Tracy's attention as the *Oriana* berthed at the wharf in Auckland. A dark young man with clear-cut features, crisp black hair and sideburns, he stood alone a little apart from the crowd milling around the long balcony of the overseas terminal building. Not extra tall, broad shouldered, wearing an impeccably cut suit of tropical tan, he was, she mused, undeniably good-looking in a bronzed, scowling sort of way. The next moment, meeting his flinty stare, she knew a fleeting pity for the girl, if it were a girl, for whom he was waiting with that bleak expression of welcome. A little abashed by his cool scrutiny, she wrenched her glance aside, her gaze moving over the sea of faces that lined the railings opposite as she endeavored to distinguish Alison's tall, attention-getting figure among the throng. Then she reminded herself that as yet it was only seven o'clock. Drifts of early morning mist still hung over the hills and spires of this New Zealand seaport city, and when had Alison ever risen early if she could possibly avoid it?

Idly watching the colorful scene taking place all around her, Tracy reflected that she had no regrets about not having married Desmond when he had asked her to do just that a few weeks previously. Now she realized that two years was far too long a period to allow an unsatisfactory love affair to drag its way on. She should have put an end to that unexciting romance long ago. As to this trip out to New Zealand—her sweeping glance moved over the water, sparkling as though sprinkled with handfuls of silver dollars, the bush-clad islands that studded the sheltered harbor—she had no regrets on that score, either, even if it had meant digging deep into her carefully hoarded savings.

She leaned on the ship's rail, a slim girl, medium-tall

with long dark hair swinging and glinting in the sun, a slightly tip-tilted nose with a spattering of freckles, eyes of an unusual shade of sea blue.

Funny to think that it was a color snapshot Alison had enclosed with her letter that had brought her out here to the South Pacific. A small picture, probably taken on an instamatic, depicting Alison with her impudent smile, red hair blowing around her bare tanned shoulders above a low-cut sun dress, against a background of sun-flecked vineyards, and beyond, a vista of distant hills. Sunshine filtering through the grapevines turned Alison's red gold hair to flame, and something, some trick of the light, surely gave Tracy an odd impression of shimmering heat coming right out of the picture. The clarity of the New Zealand atmosphere, perhaps? Or could it be merely in contrast to the weather outside the windows on that particular day when the picture had reached her? A gray winter day with rain falling steadily, making the tiny flat seem even more cramped and cheerless than usual now that her mother was no longer there to share it with her. Clever Alison, to send the sun to plead for her!

Tracy had been surprised to recognize her cousin's sprawling handwriting on the envelope bearing a New Zealand stamp. Why, they hadn't seen each other in years, scarcely at all since school days. Tracy's circumstances were so far removed from those of her more affluent cousin that their paths seldom crossed. From time to time Tracy gleaned fragments of family news. Alison had enrolled at a drama school, but had soon wearied of the study and concentration involved in an acting career. Later her father had set her up in business, a boutique in a fashionable section of the London scene, but that venture, too, had been shortlived. Then, following her father's sudden death from a heart attack a few months previously, Alison had left England on a cruise of the Pacific. And now...this! Alison had written:

Guess what? I've fallen in love! Now don't laugh, Tracy. I know you'll have that little secret smile just the way you used to look at me at school when you didn't quite believe me. It's true! I'm way out here in New Zealand and I've decided to cancel the remainder of the cruise and stay put right here in Auckland. Take a deep breath, Tracy, you'll need it! I'm getting married instead!

Now don't say it! There'll be no second thoughts this time! Besides, don't they say that third time's lucky? His name's Crane and he runs a family vineyard in the western valley here. Great wines they are, too—first-class! The wedding's all arranged for the beginning of February, and here's where *you* come into the picture! Since dad died I haven't a soul of my own when it comes to family, so you've just *got* to come out here and be my bridesmaid.

Tracy could almost hear the soft yet imperious tones.

It's not as if there's anyone in London who'll be missing you....

True enough, Tracy thought. There was only Desmond, and it was unlikely that he would trouble her again, not after the definite way in which she had answered his proposal of marriage just a week previously. She brought her mind back to the letter in her hand.

—And don't worry about fares—my pleasure! That goes for the bridesmaid's gear too! We can have a good splash buying everything you need right here in Auckland at the same exclusive little boutique where I'm having my wedding gown made. Can't tell you the style yet—it's a secret—but I thought a white-and-scarlet wedding, something just a bit different from the usual. Actually, the stores over here happen to be surprisingly up-to-date, so you haven't a thing to worry about.

Now don't let me down, Tracy, because I'm depending on you to be at the wedding. Make it a boat trip if you'd prefer, you've got the time if you start making arrangements right away. Or come by air, but let me know which way you decide to travel so that I can be there to meet you when you arrive. You'll like it out here. See you in New Zealand!

Love, Alison

P.S. When you come (now wasn't that typical of Alison to say not "if" but "when"?) you can stay right here at Valley Vineyards. Lucie said to tell you. Better get an international driving license too—you may need it.

An odd letter, Tracy mused, to receive from a young woman newly engaged to be married. But then, of course, Alison had been in that position on two previous occasions and each time she had broken off arrangements almost at the last moment before the wedding. Maybe all that made a difference. All the same, it seemed strange that there was scarcely a word concerning the man whom her cousin planned to marry in a far-away country. Nothing beyond the bare mention of his name. He didn't even appear in the photograph. But wasn't that characteristic of Alison, who must always be the central figure in any picture. Goodness, she couldn't have known her fiancé for more than a few weeks! It must indeed have been a whirlwind romance. Well, Tracy would meet this unknown man for herself if she went out to New Zealand as Alison suggested. If.... Tracy's soft pink mouth set in a firmer line. One thing for sure, and that was that should she decide to answer the imperious summons, it would be because she wanted to go, not because Alison had ordered her to attend the wedding. What was more, Tracy would pay her own fare and meet the cost of her bridesmaid's outfit, everything!

As if watching an outdated movie, the years rolled back, and for a moment the old feeling of inferiority and poverty and loneliness surged over her. She was a child again, sent away from her beloved mother to attend a fashionable boarding school. The fees would be met by Alison's father, who had insisted on taking the responsibility for Tracy's education along with that of his idolized only child. He owed it to the memory of his brother who had died as a result of injuries in World War II, to treat both girls alike. Only somehow for Tracy things hadn't worked out that way. Not that it was her uncle's fault. He had done his best according to his beliefs and right up to the end had never realized that his attractive, red-haired daughter was anything less than the paragon he had always considered her to be. Tracy was three years younger than her cousin and only gradually had it come to her that beneath Alison's verve and charm was a hard ruthlessness that brooked not the slightest opposition to her wishes. Not for a long time did Tracy come to realize that the monthly allowance spent so carelessly by her cousin had been intended to be shared between both girls.

Well—she jerked herself back to reality—she was no longer a child, helpless and alone. She was Tracy Cadell, twenty years old and perfectly capable of looking after herself, of making her own decisions, whether financially or otherwise. Or was she? *How about this particular decision, Tracy, that you have to handle right now?*

You really need that break away from everything, a small voice in her mind whispered temptingly. *Think of all those months last summer when you nursed your mother through that long last illness. Besides, you've enough in your savings to take care of the return fare to New Zealand, with enough left over to buy that expensive gown and accessories that Alison will expect you to provide for the occasion.*

Nonsense! The cautious part of her mind took over. *Are you crazy? Tossing away all your hard-earned savings in one hit!*

But the small voice had the answer to that. *What odds? It'll be high summer in New Zealand, remember?* That did it! Tracy stole another look at the snapshot. Could a sky *really* be that deep, luminous blue? Well, there was a way to find out for herself. Deep down she'd known all along that she wouldn't be able to resist the lure of that sun-flecked vineyard. One other factor, too, helped to sway her in her decision, a vague half-recognized sense of family loyalty. Not that she and Alison had ever been close, scarcely even friends, but still....

Eagerly her mind ran ahead, thinking, planning. One advantage, she thought ruefully, in having a dreary office job was that you hadn't the least regret about giving in your notice. You could so easily be replaced. She might even decide to stay on in New Zealand throughout the summer, make the trip a working holiday. Hadn't she once read that there was outdoor employment available through the season? Work in the tobacco plantations, hop picking in the south, gathering fruit in the orchards—strawberries, grapes, apricots. She would, however, travel by ship. That way she would gain more return for her fare money, enjoy all the fun and excitement of shipboard life before reaching her destination. Her heart lifted at the thought of the lazy days that lay ahead. She would need a wardrobe to wear on the voyage, but luckily she was handy with a sewing machine and had made a plentiful supply of shorts, blouses and playsuits last summer that she'd scarcely worn. Now she made up her mind to purchase dress patterns and gay materials, run up a dine-and-dance dress suitable for wear on balmy evenings at sea; wash-and-wear garments for poolside lounging.

The wonderful part of it all was that life on board the great ocean liner proved to be every bit as novel and luxurious and exciting as she had envisaged it. Maybe it was partly because of meeting Glenn, a pleasant young man returning from a business trip to England, where he had been buying glassware and crockery for his Auckland firm, that made the voyage so enjoyable. Tall, light blond, he was invariably even tempered, and ever willing to escort Tracy to the various sports and entertainments that seemed never ending.

Now, watching a blue canvas gangway span the narrow stretch of water between wharf and ship, Tracy caught fragments of conversation that drifted past her, but intent on the crowded balcony opposite, she was scarcely aware of the quickening tempo in the clamor of voices. There was a lively atmosphere of excitement as friends greeted one another, hands meeting in warm clasps of welcome over the boundary rail that would separate them until the time when disembarking passengers had descended the stairs and completed necessary customs formalities in the big room below.

The minutes ticked away until half an hour had slipped

Vineyard in a Valley

past and still she could discern no tall, glamorous-looking feminine figure among the throng. Surely at any moment now Alison would come hurrying toward the barrier, calling apologies in her low husky tones for having failed to be on the wharf to welcome Tracy on the *Oriana*'s arrival. Surely she was conspicuous enough herself, she mused, in the loose floral shirt splashed with vivid blues and pinks and violet, that she had purchased so cheaply during the day spent in Suva, the last port of call.

All at once it came to her that Alison had invariably been late for appointments, which was some small consolation. Nevertheless as the minutes slipped past, Tracy couldn't banish a small nagging feeling of anxiety. Many of her fellow passengers had already disembarked. Others who were continuing on the voyage had left the ship in order to board a sight-seeing coach waiting to transport them on a day's excursion to the thermal areas, volcanic wonders and glow-worm grottoes situated in other parts of the country. Once again Tracy's searching glance moved over the scattered groups, hoping to catch sight of a tall girl with masses of reddish-colored hair. Which was silly, she told herself the next moment, for Alison could well have altered her natural hair coloring a dozen times in the interval since the two had last met. *Just as the other girl had changed her mind concerning those two earlier engagements.* Now what in the world had made that thought come into her mind at this particular moment?

"Your friend not shown up yet?" She roused herself to find Glenn at her side, a note of concern in his even tones. Slimly built, he was so tall that she had to look up, up at him, even though the fair head with the smooth blond hair was bent attentively toward her.

She smiled up at him. "Not yet, but I know my cousin. She's always running late! She's that sort of girl!"

A slight frown marked the boyish features. "All the same, I'd like to wait here with you until she does make an appearance."

"Don't be silly!" All at once she realized that the smiling faces in the group across the barrier were friends of his. "You go along with the others, Glenn, I'll be fine—honestly!"

Still he hesitated. "You've got that phone number that I gave you? You'll let me know if your cousin doesn't show up?"

"I will! I will! Don't worry!"

"And you'll keep in touch whatever happens? Promise?"

"Promise!" She flashed the quick smile that lighted up her face. As she lifted a hand in farewell she was thinking, *not that I'll need anyone else when Alison comes along, and she's bound to appear at any moment now.*

But she didn't. Absurd to have this feeling of uneasiness, and yet.... Tracy had been a little disappointed to find no letters from the other girl awaiting her at the various ports of call. Disappointed, then philosophical, for Alison, she knew, never bothered to write letters except when absolutely necessary. Tracy had told herself that the other girl would be waiting on the wharf in Auckland to meet her and there would be time enough then to discuss details of the wedding, including choosing a bridesmaid's dress that Tracy would need to purchase in Auckland during the three weeks that remained before the all-important day. Now she reminded herself that there could be a hundred different explanations for Alison's nonappearance. Anyone could be held up on a motor journey, a traffic jam, perhaps. At seven in the morning? An accident, then? Heaven forbid! But something must have happened to delay the other girl. It was strange and upsetting, just a little. The crowds were thinning rapidly now and a cold wind seemed to blow around her heart as she watched the chattering groups moving away. At this portion of the terminal only one watcher now remained, the black-haired man still standing alone. She noticed now the deep lines scored down on either side of his mouth, the firm set of the curving lips. Tracy thought that despite his outwardly attractive appearance, his expression appeared more grim and forbidding than ever. At that moment, evidently weary of waiting, he turned on his heel and strode away.

"May I have your attention, please?" The booming sound of a loudspeaker cut across her musing. "Will Miss Cadell come to the control office on the passenger floor of

Vineyard in a Valley

the terminal building, please, where someone is waiting to meet her. Will Miss Cadell...."

Cadell! That was her! She hadn't been abandoned here in an unknown country after all. Everything would be all right now. How foolish of her to have been so needlessly concerned. Only, she thought confusedly a few moments later, there must surely be some mistake, for when she reached the office desk where a smiling uniformed girl was seated, there was only one other person in the room, and that was the dark young man with the steely glance.

"Miss Cadell?"

She paused, transfixed, glancing up at him, a shadow of perplexity in her wide eyes.

"Crane's the name," he was saying, still with the cold, unsmiling look. "Stephen Crane."

Crane! Something clicked into place in her brain. Of course! The name that Alison had mentioned as the vineyard owner she was to marry. The thoughts rushed wildly through her mind. No doubt Alison, busy with her approaching wedding, had been unable to meet her and had arranged for her fiancé to come to the wharves in her place.

"And I'm Tracy!" She sent him her wide and friendly smile. "Alison wrote me about you," she ran on in her warm low tones. "She even sent me a picture of herself snapped in your vineyard. Trouble was—" she wrinkled her nose at him "—she forgot to include you in the photo. It was just a background of vines and terraces and sunshine. If only you'd been there, too, I would have recognized you right away." Deliberately disregarding his unresponsive look, she swept brightly on. "Silly, wasn't it? I mean, both of us waiting here all this time, and not knowing—"

"I'd have located you a long time ago—" she was amazed to catch a glint of amusement in his glance "—if I hadn't been given completely misleading information."

She glanced up at him, not understanding. "Misleading?"

"That's right." His expression softened as his cool, assessing glance took in Tracy's slim figure, the young eager face with the high cheekbones and faintly tanned complexion. "I was told that you weren't all that attractive, not so you'd notice it. They were dead wrong!"

Tracy giggled. So he was human after all. "Oh, that would be my cousin Alison! She's such a knockout herself! So tall and sophisticated-looking." Tracy sighed wistfully. "And that gorgeous coloring! Do you know, she did quite a bit of modeling in London. Even at school, she never had freckles even—not like me—"

"You were at school with your cousin?" He cut in so sharply that Tracy blinked. Now why was he eyeing her with that sharply disapproving look, just as though there were something to be ashamed of in the fact that she and Alison had attended the same school?

"Why, yes." She refused to allow herself to be intimidated by him. "You see, her father was my uncle and he—"

But it was clear to Tracy that he was no longer listening. He said coldly, "I thought as much. You have the same way of speaking."

Tracy was disquietingly aware of his flinty look. His own tones, she thought, were cultured and possessed an attractive timbre, or would have had it not been for that cold, hard tone. Why must he say "your cousin"? Why not just "Alison"? Or even "my fiancée"? "Well," she pointed out defensively, "we do happen to be related, so I don't suppose it's all that surprising that we have the same sort of voices."

"I didn't mean that." There was no lightness in his unsmiling tone.

Really, she thought with a prick of annoyance, then what *did* he mean? What was so wrong about her and Alison speaking in the same way? She had half a mind to ask him to explain himself, only he was wearing his closed look again. She simply couldn't understand him—tossing compliments her way at one moment, scowling fiercely at her the next! How could Alison, with her undoubted attraction for men, her gay approach to life, have fallen in love with this strange dark man with his laconic speech and stern expression? *How could she?* The odd part of it all was that he appeared to have taken an unreasoning dislike to Tracy even before their meeting.

Vineyard in a Valley

"I suppose Alison sent you to meet me?" Immediately the words had left her lips she realized how clumsily she had framed the inquiry. For who could imagine any girl, even poised and lovely Alison, being able to *send* this man anywhere? "I mean," she amended carefully, "something happened to stop her coming here this morning to meet the ship?"

He was silent for a moment, an unreadable expression flickering in the gray eyes, but he only said quietly, "That's right. Something happened. Look, we can't talk here. Better get below." He waved a well-shaped bronzed hand in the direction of the stairway. "Get your bags through the customs. After that we can get things sorted out and head for home."

"That will be wonderful!" She couldn't conceal her sense of relief. Back there on the ship she'd had a bad few minutes, wondering what could have happened to delay Alison, but there was nothing after all to worry about.

"Will it?" As she met his quizzical glance a shaft of alarm pierced her, but she thrust it aside. No doubt he was merely seeking to amuse himself at her expense. Probably, she told herself as they strolled out of the office together, Alison had persuaded him to come here against his wishes and he was still feeling resentful; maybe he was regretting the time spent away from his vineyard duties. In a few minutes she left him to enter the customs room, still thronged with passengers from the *Oriana* with their accompanying baggage.

Her modest possessions were soon cleared and in a surprisingly short time she went to join Stephen Crane, who was waiting for her just beyond the connecting doorway. "Come on!" Picking up her travel bags as though they were feather light, he strode in the direction of the elevator. In silence she stood by his side as they ascended to the rooftop parking above. He might *pretend* to look welcoming, just a little, she thought aggrievedly. Not that she expected a speech of welcome, but it was slightly unnerving to be met in an unfamiliar country by this stranger with his cold stare and disapproving expression. For a second something about the grim line of his set jaw faintly disturbed her. All at once she was stung by a frightening suspicion. "There's nothing wrong, is there?" she asked anxiously. But stepping from the lift, moving in the direction of a big gray Holden in the parking lot, he didn't appear to have heard her. Stowing the bags in the back of the vehicle, he slammed the door shut and turned toward her. "Bet you didn't take time out for breakfast this morning?"

She shook her head. "I was so determined not to miss the first sight of the Auckland harbor—"

"Just what I thought! There's a restaurant down below. Come on, you'd better come down with me and we'll get some coffee. You're going to need it."

They moved toward the lift again and soon he was guiding her across the spacious, attractive room, passing the souvenir stalls with their Maori artifacts and native carvings as they moved toward a dining area at the far end of the room. He drew forward a chair from a small table. "Take a seat, Miss Cadell, and I'll bring some coffee from the counter. We've got a lot to talk about—black or white?"

"Black, please." His twisted smile did nothing to ease her growing sense of discomfiture.

He was back at the table in a few minutes, carrying a tray with coffee cups, and she sipped the hot liquid. She even managed an almost-spontaneous smile, which was quite a feat when someone was regarding you in that queer way, almost like...compassion...but that was ridiculous, surely. She was becoming stupidly imaginative. Maybe she shouldn't have skipped breakfast after all. With an effort she rallied herself.

"Now at last we can get acquainted," she said in her friendly manner. Her gay chatter faltered in the face of his abstracted gaze, but she forced herself to go on. "You know something, Mr. Crane? I've never ever been out of England before! All this—" her gaze moved to the glittering waters of the harbor, the luxurious white liner "—not to mention Alison's wedding, staying out here in New Zealand for a while afterward—it all seems just too good to be true!"

"I'm afraid," his tone was unexpectedly gentle, "that it is." He fished in his pocket. "Cigarette?"

Vineyard in a Valley

"Thank you."

He was holding a lighter toward her and as he leaned close she noticed the bleak expression in his eyes. Something was very wrong. She was certain of it now.

"It's Alison, isn't it?" she whispered. "Something's happened? There isn't going to be any wedding?"

"No." The resonant tones were curiously flat. "There isn't going to be any wedding—ever. Look here, Miss Cadell, I'm not much good at this sort of thing. I don't quite know how to put it." She had to strain to catch the low tones, and with a little shock of surprise she realized that he, too, was embarrassed, having difficulty in getting out the words. "The accident happened a couple of weeks after you'd left London. I could have sent you a cable at one of the ports, but I thought I'd let things ride until you arrived here, put you in the picture myself. It couldn't have made any difference to you at that stage of the game."

She waited, holding her breath, thankful that the subdued lighting at the cafeteria away from the bright daylight outside served to hide her horrified expression.

"Thing is—" he flicked the ash from his cigarette into a glass ashtray on the table "—there was this blazing bust up that put a finish to everything. Your cousin's gone! Joined up with a cruise outfit here on a tour of the South Pacific. Right now she'll be somewhere in Tonga, New Caledonia— one of the islands. But the night of the flare-up there was this accident—"

"Accident?" Tracy's tone sharpened in alarm. "What happened?"

He stubbed the ash from his cigarette. "My young brother, Cliff's fault." The low tones were charged with emotion. "He was pretty het up at the time, I guess, went bang through a red traffic light and collected a brand-new station wagon coming the other way. A head-on collision! Both vehicles were complete write-offs. Luckily the other passengers in the wagon weren't seriously hurt, but the guy'll be a fair time in hospital with a knee injury. By some miracle your cousin didn't get a scratch."

"And your brother?" She found she was holding her breath as she waited for the reply.

He drew deeply on his cigarette. "Shock...concussion. He's still in hospital with a broken leg, down on the east coast. Unfortunately—" his voice was grim "—he happens to be a procrastinator, forgot to arrange insurance when he bought the new car. Thing is—" he seemed to be speaking to himself "—he's cleaned out completely, or will be by the time he's settled up the insurance claims and court costs. Not that he had much to play around with after throwing away his savings right and left on—" he stopped short and went on after a moment "—other things."

Something in his closed, unhappy expression made Tracy wonder if he could possibly be blaming Alison for all this. Or did she merely imagine the bitterness in his tone?

"Your brother couldn't afford to lose so much?" she hazarded, but underneath she was thinking that surely a vineyard owner would have some capital.

He must have read her thoughts. "Cliff was on wages, that's all. The capital he had he got through with his mountaineering expeditions. They cost him a packet, and now—" he threw out bronzed, well-shaped hands "—he's cleaned out completely."

And it's all Alison's fault.

She could almost hear the words he left unsaid. Of all the childish, unfair attitudes....Aloud she asked, "How did it happen?"

"We were touring at the time, on our way back from the South Island. Cliff had got this new car and was dead keen for the four of us to tour the country. Alison, Lucie—that's an aunt who keeps house at the Valley—Cliff, myself. On that particular night we were putting up at Gisborne. We couldn't all find accommodation at the same hotel and Cliff was taking Alison back to her lodgings when it happened. It was one of those filthy nights, a summer storm that blew up out of nowhere, with rain pelting down in torrents. On the way, Cliff—well, there'd been this helluva row and he didn't have his mind on driving, that's for sure. Like I said, he just didn't see that red light."

The terse sentences struck her like blows and she set down her coffee cup with a little clatter, vaguely aware that her hand was trembling. So that was the reason why

Vineyard in a Valley

Stephen Crane was acting so strangely. His engagement to his girl broken off so close to the wedding date, his brother injured in a motor smash. She wished, though, that she knew more of the pieces of the puzzle that appeared to be missing. There was so much that he had failed to explain. A blazing quarrel, he had told her, the engagement terminated and then, on that same night, the accident. On top of all that she herself had to arrive from England, an encumbrance to Stephen Crane and his family. An embarrassment, too, reminding him of Alison, forcing him into explanations of matters that obviously he much preferred to forget. What had happened to cause the break between him and her cousin? Well, whatever it was it was clear that he had no intention of taking her into his confidence. As for Tracy there was something that must be said, painful, difficult though it was to put the thought into words.

With quick sympathy her hand went to touch his sleeve. "But how awful for you, just before the wedding... and everything."

His blank expression was as dashing as a shock of cold water thrown in her face. "You don't seem to get it, Miss Cadell. It was my brother, the one who was hurt in the smash, who was to marry your cousin." In a fluid movement he was on his feet. "You've finished your coffee? Shall we go?"

"Go?" she stared bewilderedly up into the set face. "Go where?"

"Back to the house, of course." His tone was impatient. "Where else?"

Slowly she got to her feet, her face drained of color, her eyes shadowed. "But I can't! I mean," she stammered in acute embarrassment, "everything's different now. And there are hotels—"

"Why the hell would you need a hotel?" His incredulous stare jerked her back to reality. "You're coming back to Valley Vineyards with me, Miss Cadell! Lucie would never forgive me if I arrived back home without you!"

He had made it very plain, she thought unhappily, that the invitation stemmed from his aunt and not himself. Without another word she went with him to the parking area on the roof of the building, waiting while he unlocked the car door. He saw her seated, then went around to the driver's side. There wasn't much that she *could* say at the moment, Tracy thought, trying to control her whirling thoughts as they moved through the wharf gates, then turned to merge into the traffic of the main street of the city.

At the pavement edge tall cabbage trees flick-flacked their clustered green spears lazily in the ocean breeze, and from the center of the roadway the great bronze figure of a cloaked Maori chieftain gazed out over the sparkling waters of the harbor. Couples strolled by in the sunshine, the girls wearing vividly colored shifts, the men in crisp white shirts, walk shorts, sandals. It all appeared so normal, yet she felt as though the ground had been cut from under her feet. She must pull herself together, make plans for the future. She gazed with unseeing eyes at the hills around her, where clustered red-roofed houses were surrounded with greenery. There was something about it all that she couldn't understand, and that was the attitude of the man at her side. Why should he be so bitter over the affair that his anger extended to anyone even remotely connected with Alison? Unless, a thought pierced her, he was in love with her himself? Now she came to consider the matter, the explanation fitted perfectly. Indeed, she reflected wryly, it would be more unusual in the circumstances had Stephen Crane proved to be impervious to Alison's peculiar brand of calculated charm. For some reason that she couldn't fathom, she found herself wishing that there were some other explanation for her companion's dark mood. Any other explanation but that one!

The next moment she took hold of herself. What possible difference could it make to her? Forcing herself to concentrate on the present, she gazed toward the wide glass display windows lining each side of the wide thoroughfare. Auckland was certainly an attractive city, she mused, taking in pink geraniums trailing from hanging wrought-iron baskets, bright flower beds in the center of the roadway, the clear, clear blue sky. They swept past a fountain where the breeze was blowing the water onto the pavement, paused at

Vineyard in a Valley

a red traffic light, then took a steep incline that led them into a long street with modern stores and shady verandas. Tracy eyed with interest the big, dark-skinned women with their graceful carriage and flowing black hair, who thronged the street. Smiling, unhurried, they wore their sweeping floral dresses with grace and dignity and one or two of the younger ones had tucked a glowing scarlet or pink hibiscus blossom in their luxuriantly dark tresses. Young mothers had with them appealing little people with lustrous dark eyes, the girls wearing crisp cotton dresses and white socks and shoes, the boys in spotless white shirts and black bow ties.

Tracy was so intrigued that for a moment she forgot Stephen Crane's unfriendly attitude. She turned an eager face toward him. "Those big dark women, so relaxed and smiling, in their long dresses. There are so many of them strolling along the street. Are they Maori women?"

He shook his head, his attention fixed on the road ahead as he skirted a great truck piled high with bales of wool. "Not in this district, though you'll come across plenty of Maori folk all over Auckland. Around this locality they're mostly islanders—"

She glanced up at him with puzzled blue eyes. "You mean they come from the Pacific islands?"

He eyed her briefly and she noticed the lift of his lips. "You happen to be in a South Pacific country yourself right now, Miss Cadell. What would you say if I told you that this little city of Auckland happens to have the largest Polynesian population of any city in the world?"

"Really?" Tracy glanced again toward the dark-skinned women shoppers in their long cotton dresses printed with vividly colored tropical designs of birds and flowers.

"It's true! A part Polynesian population, that's us! And all the better for that. They come here from different islands of the Pacific, mostly from the Cook Islands, Niue, Tokelau, but a lot arrive here from Fiji and Samoa, too."

"But why?"

He shrugged broad shoulders. "There's precious little employment where they come from. Over here in Auckland they can get themselves a job, send part of their wages to their families back home. It must seem a bit strange at first, wouldn't you think, coming straight from a thatched grass hut, a sleeping mat, diet of fish and coconuts and then—instant civilization! But it all goes to make a colorful city! And something else that's a darned lot more important. The Pacific islanders have got something—call it enjoyment of life. To them to sing and dance and laugh comes as naturally as breathing. Take European culture added to that and you could say we've got the best of both worlds."

Tracy nodded. "I know. In Fiji, on the way out here, we were taken to a concert, and the way those natives sang and danced! It was fantastic! You could see they were enjoying every moment of it."

Along the highway the buildings were thinning out. There were many open spaces where, from the ridge, Tracy caught glimpses of hills and valleys, clusters of multicolored roofs and beyond, the blue of distant hills.

"They've got a lot they can show us," Stephen Crane was saying. "Culture, new concepts, a sense of proportion. Much more, actually, than we can offer them."

"But how could that be?" Tracy asked wonderingly. "You have so much here—all the luxuries of modern living." Her gaze moved to a Samoan woman of generous proportions who was making her leisurely way along the pavement, a woven basket of banana palm swinging from a plump hand. Loosely fitting cotton dress, flowing dark hair, bare brown feet in rubber thongs—there was no doubt that the island women appeared cool and comfortable and carefree, but.... Aloud she said, "They seem to have so little. Compared with Europeans, I mean."

"You reckon?" He shot her a swift sideways glance. "They can show us a few things, all the same!" All at once the chill note was back in his low tones. "They've got something that we Europeans seem to have lost somewhere along the way. To the people of the Pacific a little thing like quality of life is highly valued. People are more important than property, if you get what I mean. They know how to laugh and play and enjoy themselves."

Tracy couldn't help thinking that he could well do with

some advice in that direction himself, but immediately she caught herself up. He had good reason for his bitterness.

"I don't blame the islanders for coming here, even if it does mean leaving their tropical home." Her gaze shifted to the green hills around them, clear-cut against the blue in the fresh atmosphere. She laughed lightly. "I've always heard that New Zealand was a pleasant place to live, a very friendly country—" She broke off. Friendly! *Oh, Lord,* she thought, *I hope he won't think I'm getting at him!* She stole a quick glance toward him, caught once again the glimmer of amusement in his eyes, the lifting of the mobile lips, and felt the pink mounting in her cheeks. Well, it was his own fault. He deserved the unintentional rebuke, considering the cool greeting he had accorded her this morning. She said hesitantly, "Where are we going? The Valley Vineyards, you said?"

"That's right. It's a bit out of town—used to be the end of the earth just about before they put the northern motorway through. It's pretty quiet out there, just hills... bush—you'll see. We'll hit the motorway pretty soon now." They were sweeping past the green slopes of a golf course and now the wide road was lined with timber houses, fresh and gay with their pastel tonings. Each home was surrounded by green lawns and colorful with flower beds and blossoming shrubs. Tracy had no idea that there were so many shades of hibiscus blossoms—flame, burgundy, scarlet, salmon, cream. Everywhere was greenery, shrubs, bushes, the graceful foliage of tall evergreens. It was all so pleasant, even more attractive than she had envisaged. If only.... Unconsciously she sighed, then turned her attention to the highway. They were swinging into the wide lines of a smooth asphalt road built on a causeway and in spite of herself her spirits lifted. Everything was so new and different. Even the light seemed to possess a special luminous quality that made colors of the landscape seem deeper, more intense. On either side lapped the waters of the harbor and in an inlet ahead she glimpsed modern ranch-style homes clinging to the cliff edge. Below, pleasure craft varying from kayaks to dinghies, catamarans to keelers rocked at anchor in the sheltered bay. The graceful arc of a bridge spanned the harbor and beyond, guarding the entrance and visible from every angle, rose the almost perfectly symmetrical twin peaks of a volcanic cone.

"What a beautiful harbor," she spoke her thoughts aloud, "so blue and sheltered. It's that sparkle on the water that makes it so lovely."

He nodded. "That's what the Maoris thought when they called it Waitemata—dancing waters. They had quite a knack for naming, those old-time warriors."

She laughed lightly. "Hadn't they! But Auckland, that's not a Maori name, of course?"

"You've got me there! Though the Maoris had their own name for the isthmus. It was known as a contested land—Tamaki-makau-rau—Tamaki of a hundred lovers. You'll see why it was so sought after when you've been around here for a while. It's got a lot going for it, Auckland has—bush, endless sandy beaches, a couple of big harbors, not to mention a subtropical climate, outdoor living." He grinned. "You could say that the Polynesian way of life has rubbed off quite a bit on the rest of us. Might even get into the way of it yourself, if you stick around for a while."

If—but she refused to allow him to spoil things for her. It was true that after what had happened since she'd left London, her stay here would be brief, but for all that she made up her mind that while she was here she would see all that she could of the district, learn something of the culture and way of life of the country.

"That mountain that seems to rise out of the sea—" she couldn't seem to take her mind from the shadowy peak, bush covered, shading to violet where long cloud shadows slanted across the dense vegetation "—doesn't anyone live there?"

"On old Rangi?" For a second his glance moved over the waters of the harbor. "Rangitoto's part of Auckland, the first thing you look for when you come back from a trip overseas. It's quite a place! Don't know if you're interested, but it's the most recently active volcano in the country, and that's saying something in a place that happens to be a city of extinct craters."

"Recent?" Her glance slanted up at him.

"Give and take a few hundred years! Old Rangi's just one big lava rock. Boy, you'll soon find that out if you take a walk over the scoria tracks to the summit. It's a terrific view up there, though, well worth taking on the rough paths! There's a fern grotto on the way up with vegetation that they tell me grows nowhere else in the world."

"Could anyone go up there? I mean, could I—"

"Sure. There's a launch takes off from the wharf steps most days. There are a few baches there—weekend cottages to you—hidden away in the bush. It's only a short spin over to Rangitoto."

Her gaze was still fixed on the misty blue gray slopes. It was the first landmark she had noticed on her arrival in this unknown land. "I'd love to go there one day," she murmured, then immediately regretted the words, for he would think she was asking him to take her to the island. Worse, his silence made it all too clear that he was avoiding the trap. Nevertheless, between them they had managed so far to avoid any personal conversation on the drive to the vineyards, which was something. *He can only be nice to me when he forgets,* she thought unhappily. *Forgets what? That I'm Alison's cousin and deep down I'm just like her, or so he imagines; wealthy, spoiled, demanding. Or could it be that he dislikes me because I'm* not *Alison?* If only she knew the truth of it all!

Presently they left the high-speed lane of the winding motorway to swing into a smooth suburban road lined with gaily painted timber houses set among spacious lawns. As they went on homes became more scattered, giving way to orchard areas where fruit trees, heavily laden, stretched away behind avenues of tall native trees. At roadside entrances Tracy caught glimpses of notice boards:

Fruit for Sale
Peaches, Apples, Pears, Weeny Grapefruit
Melons, Passionfruit.

Ahead a heat haze shimmered on the hot asphalt of the roadway and all around rose what Tracy thought must surely be the smell of summer—a blending of dried grasses, the aromatic perfume of white daisies that raised their tall stems from the grassy roadside, smoke drifting from tea-tree logs smoldering in a nearby paddock.

Then they were sweeping up into hills thickly covered in dense native bush, somber in the shadowed valleys, glinting with lighter green where umbrellalike fronds of pungas were bathed in sunlight. Occasionally she caught the gleam of a brightly painted roof amid surrounding greenery. Then all at once through a gap in the hills she glimpsed a wide harbor, the tranquil depths reflecting bush growing to the water's edge in deep inlets far below.

"So that's Auckland's other harbor? The one you told me about?"

He nodded, his eyes on a sharp bend ahead. "That's the Manukau, and mighty different it is from the Waitemata. It looks peaceful enough today with all those reflections, but don't let it fool you! There's a treacherous bar at the entrance and parts of it are pretty rugged—heavy surf, reefs. All the same, it's got something—"

"You mean it's a sort of challenge?" She couldn't resist the teasing shaft. "Great for fishing, surfing—"

"You've guessed it!" She was surprised to see that he had lost his grim expression. For a moment he looked younger, more carefree, as though, she thought with an odd little pang, they were any couple anywhere, a man taking his girl for a drive on the most perfect of days. Suddenly she was swept by happiness, piercing and sweet, that took her utterly by surprise. *It's this first glimpse of a new country,* she told herself, *where everything is so different, so unexpectedly fresh and lovely. It's always this way, they say, when you travel overseas. There's never anything to equal the first impressions—exciting, stimulating, almost—like falling in love.* She took herself in hand, brought her roving thoughts back to Stephen Crane's vibrant tones.

"The Maoris—"

"I know," she cried, laughing. "You're going to tell me that they thought up exactly the right name for each of the two different coasts? A sort of double-barreled inspiration that fitted perfectly?"

"You guessed it." He swept around a bend obscured by overhanging ferns. "The east coast, where you landed this

Vineyard in a Valley 243

morning, they named that Tai-Tamahine, 'the sea for girls,' but out here on the west coast, that was Tai-Tamatere—"

"I know! 'The sea for men'!"

"You almost got it! 'The manlike ocean,' actually. It took a pretty strong warrior to man the canoes on the dangerous trip. Not many Europeans could handle a craft on this coast in the way those old seafarers did in their curved canoes!"

He turned toward her and something in his swift gaze made her feel confused. There was something definitely disturbing about him, call it a personal magnetism, that made her voice oddly tremulous. "I must admit they had a point there."

She pulled her thoughts together, made her tone light and impersonal. "Have we far to go now?" They were climbing up into the mountains studded with bright roofs where homes were hidden in the bush. From the roadside the boles of giant kauri trees rose straight and tall to pierce the blue and fern and punga trees enclosed them in a world of cool shadows.

"No distance. We'll hit the valley road any minute. There's the signpost—"

"Where? Oh, I see." A faded board nailed to a massive tree trunk and almost entirely hidden by spears of thickly growing flax loomed up before her. She could just make out the weathered black lettering, Valley Vineyards. An arrow pointed in the direction of dense bushland ahead.

Like everything else on this unpredictable day, however, it was the unexpected that happened. They rattled over rickety planks of a one-way bridge spanning a creek below, swung around a hairpin bend, and Tracy found herself on a rise overlooking acres of terraced grapevines. Verdant under the sun, the long avenues of vines with their unbroken masses of black and golden green stretched row after row in the subtropical valley.

"But how funny." She was speaking her thoughts aloud. "All this way up into the hills—mountains they'd call them where I come from—and then, almost at the top of the range, to find a valley—"

"It's quite something, isn't it?" It seemed that at last she had hit on a subject that really interested him. A look of pride crossed the dark face. "You don't expect to see a thing way up here in the bush, then wham! You swing around the bend and it hits you!"

Pulling up to the side of the road, he waited while a truck piled high with crates of wine lumbered past on the narrow track with an inch to spare. From the cab a stockily built man of middle age with furrowed, deeply tanned skin and intensely blue eyes grinned down at them and Stephen raised a hand in a gesture of greeting.

"One of your trucks?" Tracy inquired.

He nodded, reaching toward the steering wheel, but it was clear that his thoughts remained on the sun-splashed valley below. As they came nearer Tracy discerned women pickers, moving along the long avenues of vines as they harvested the grapes. In spite of the heat, it would be not unpleasant work, she mused, out there in the fresh, bush-spiced air, gathering the clustered grapes and filling the wooden boxes. Her gaze moved over the picturesque surroundings. "What a lovely place...hidden among the bush..., and so sheltered by those tall pines and gum trees."

He guided the car along the narrow path. "Guess that's what old Grandfather Crane decided when he arrived in this country from England and started looking around for somewhere to invest his fifty pounds of capital."

"Fifty pounds! That wouldn't go far, even in those days!"

"It didn't! But he had something else that was worth a lot more than money, as things turned out. He had a French wife, one of a family of wine makers for generations back, and it was she who put the idea into his head. They looked around for somewhere to get started and decided that this was it. Folks told them they were crazy. The land wasn't suitable, too poor, they said, only good for gum diggings, and how about the heavy native bush? How were they going to clear that, for a start? They just took no notice, got stuck in, cleared the land, dug out the ground for a cellar. They tried out the different varieties of vines that Grandmother de Thierry had brought out with her from France and in the end found just the right ones that suited the soil. Only half an acre for a start—"

Vineyard in a Valley

"Goodness!" Tracy's gaze moved beyond the cleared valley to a sea of tea tree, the green growth laced with creepers and ropes of black supplejack, fern, flax. "They had no modern machinery in those days. Whatever would they use to clear such heavy bush?"

He grinned. "They had what it took! Guts, plus an ax and a slasher! They burned off the heavy stuff, grubbed out tree roots, cut away undergrowth and fern. Grandmother de Thierry helped, too. That first year they had a little shed on the property and installed two wine vats. The next year they added a lean-to and pulled out an acre of vines. Before long grandfather was crushing the grapes in a backyard cellar in a little kauri-studded handpress he made himself. It was pretty poor stuff they made at the start, but—" once again she caught the note of pride in his tones "—a lot of wine has flowed since those days. They say it takes three generations of wine makers to get results, and if that's true, I guess I qualify."

"And now," she prompted, "you've got a market for it all?"

"Just can't make enough of it."

"So it's easy?"

"Easy?" He threw her a rueful look. "Last year a farmer over on the next hill was spraying his gorse by light aircraft when there was a wind change and our vines copped it. It didn't take much of the poison to put finish to the crop. The year before I'd sent the pickers home, decided to leave the harvest until the next week. That way I figured I'd get not just wine but very good wine. That week we got heavy rain that took the sparkle off the grapes." He shrugged broad shoulders. "It was a calculated risk, of course; it always is. I just happened to lose out that time." He sent her the quick smile that illuminated the dark face. "I'd do the same thing again, too, take a chance on the harvest, maybe, but on the quality of the wine—never. For all the risks it's a game that happens to suit me, the only game I know." There was no mistaking the enthusiasm coloring his tones. "It's only a small place as vineyards go around here, but I'm hoping to make Valley Vineyards a name that stands for something worthwhile in good, matured wines."

"But wouldn't your grandparents find that there was a big difference between grapes grown in France and the same vines grown here in New Zealand?"

"They found out all right, but it didn't stop them pushing ahead. Why should it? Grandmother de Thierry used to say that they had the same father, the sun, but a different mother, the earth. They had the right idea that New Zealand wines should be judged on their own merits, like the rest of the wines from the new world—there's the house, up on the hill."

They swept along a path and all at once they were on a winding drive. Tracy looked eagerly ahead, her glance taking in the sprawling modern timber home standing high on a rise, its wide plate-glass windows overlooking the terraced vineyards. On the flat ground below were garages, a sign, "Office," and steps leading down to a cellar. "Your brother Cliff, was he dedicated to wine making, too?"

"Not really." There was a subtle alteration in his tone. "He wasn't all that wrapped up in the game. To him it was just a job, something to keep him going financially between expeditions. It was the mountains he liked. He was pretty keen on climbing. Working here in the office was just a fill-in. The accident put finish to all that, of course."

Now she was certain of the bitter note in his voice. She could have bitten out her tongue for having introduced the subject of his brother. A mountaineer with leg injuries. It didn't require a super brain to work out who Stephen Crane was holding responsible for that! Just another black mark against Alison and, indirectly, Tracy!

They were approaching the house now. She could see blossoming shrubs that made splashes of color on the lawns, a long flower garden running alongside the path. Then they were pulling up at the entrance and Stephen was opening the car door for her.

"Hello there!" A slender figure came running down the steps toward them. "You're Tracy, aren't you?" Tracy felt the warm grasp of a small age-freckled hand and for the first time since her arrival in New Zealand was aware of a genuine friendliness.

She smiled. "I've heard about you from Alison."

"Oh—Alison." A shadow passed over the soft brown eyes with their carefully penciled brows, but the next moment it had gone. "Yes, of course. I thought you were never coming!" She had a bright smile and a youthful voice. "I've had coffee on the perk for ages. What happened, Steve?" She swung toward Stephen, who was lifting Tracy's luggage from the back of the car. "Couldn't you find her?"

"Not for quite a while. My fault." Over his shoulder he sent Tracy an unexpected grin. "I just didn't know who I was looking for."

"Come along into the house." The slim little woman with a carefully made-up complexion and untidy blond hair led the way up the steps. "Just call me Lucie, Tracy; everyone else does around here!" They passed through a sunny balcony, then moved into a spacious lounge room furnished with comfortable floral, linen-covered chairs. The floor was half-covered by a sheepskin rug evidently in the process of being made, for loose fleeces of all shades were scattered over the polished boards. "Don't take any notice of the mess!" With a teenage-fashion type shoe the older woman kicked an orange-colored sheepskin out of the way and bent to retrieve a pot of carpet glue. "I'm making a big rug to cover this room. Steve says he doesn't want it, but I think he does, and I'm making it anyway. Trouble is, it's getting so big!" Chattering gaily, she guided Tracy along a carpeted hall toward an open doorway. "This is the nicest room, the one Alison had when she was here." Once again Tracy caught the odd inflection when her cousin's name was mentioned, but could you wonder at it, after all the upsets? Oh, dear, she simply couldn't stay here of all places, not after what had happened. "Just put the bags on the bed, will you, Steve?" the older woman was saying.

He put the luggage down, then turned away.

"He's always so *busy*," Lucie said with a sigh. "Never mind, though, at least he didn't bring you back at some ghastly hour this morning before I had time to put my face on. You've no idea what you look like when you're sixty-six, first thing in the morning! I just couldn't bear you to see me like that!"

Privately Tracy thought that the warmth of her welcome here meant infinitely more to her than the most impeccable makeup. What matter that the pale gold hair was at odds with a tanned and wrinkled complexion? Or that the high-fashion little-girl dress was more suited for wear by a seventeen-year-old? Lucie was kind and welcoming and blessedly ordinary, and somehow today these particular qualities counted for quite a lot!

"What a pretty room!" She was glancing around the pale blue walls and ceiling, a violet-tinged bedspread, the floor covered with a luxuriously fluffy white sheepskin rug. At the wide open windows snowy curtains billowed in the breeze, affording a view of rolling hills and bush-clad slopes beyond.

"I'm glad you like it, dear. I copied the color scheme from a furnishing magazine and I made the rug myself. This is the wardrobe." Crossing the room, she slid open a folding concertina-type white door. "Heavens! I'd forgotten that was still there!"

That, Tracy realized at once, was a long white bridal gown exquisitely fashioned from guipure lace. On the shelf above she glimpsed a sculptured headdress and trailing net veil. Looking a trifle flustered, Lucie snatched down the hanger, reached for the headdress and veiling and bundled the trailing gown over her arm.

"Such a waste of money, all this, but it couldn't be helped! It was delivered here by the boutique in Auckland the day we got back from our trip, but of course your cousin ("your cousin" again, Tracy thought uneasily) had gone away from here by then. Here's something else your cousin left behind, or didn't want to take with her!" Lucie was peering into the back of the closet. "May as well leave it there; I don't suppose she'll even miss it. I never knew a girl to have so many expensive outfits." Her brown eyes twinkled across at Tracy. "But that's just jealousy. I expect I'd be just the same if I was her age and had the funds. *And* that perfectly gorgeous complexion that you English girls seem to take for granted. It's the sun over here that's our undoing. It makes you so tanned and dried-up looking. You just can't help it. Not like women of my age over in England. I went there for a trip last year and I did envy them—the oldies, I mean, with their pretty pink and white look. Oh, well, I do love to sunbathe, and you can't have everything!"

"Don't bother taking Alison's things away," Tracy said quietly. "I haven't come to stay, you know. It was just that Stephen—he's your nephew?"

The older woman nodded. "Oh, yes. I'm very proud of him."

Tracy tried not to look too surprised. "It was just that he insisted on my coming here, and of course I wanted to meet you, but I—"

"Let's discuss all that later. Right now you'll want to freshen up. Bathroom's next door, and I'll have coffee ready on the terrace."

"We had coffee in the terminal lounge," Tracy demurred, but Lucie dismissed the matter with a lift of slim shoulders. "That's not the same thing at all. Come along when you're ready, child, and don't argue!"

Tracy flung her a laughing glance. "Just as you say, Lucie!"

"That's better!"

Left alone, Tracy dropped down to the bed and sat motionless, lost in thought. Everyone here seemed reluctant to discuss Alison, but of course that was understandable considering the havoc the other girl had left behind her. If only Alison had left some message for her. A letter, perhaps? Swiftly she leaped to her feet and began opening bureau drawers in swift succession, but there was nothing. She could only hope that Alison would write her a note from the cruise ship explaining what had actually happened to put a finish to all her plans.

In a gleaming lilac washbasin with its chrome fittings, Tracy washed her hands, drying them on a thickly textured mauve towel. Then back in the bedroom she ran a comb through her hair, added a touch of pale pink to her lips. She was making her way along the passage when she paused, arrested by a framed photograph hanging on the wall, a blown-up color print of a party of climbers silhouetted against a sky of blazing blue. Roped in pairs the mountaineers stood braced with ice picks on the slopes of a sheer snow-covered peak. Underneath was a caption:

> Moment of triumph atop Mt. Cook.
> Climbing party led by Cliff Crane.
>
> Crane, who has climbed in Nepal and Peru, is one of the four men who have scaled Mt. Cook's treacherous Caroline Face.

She studied the picture curiously. Cliff... not like his brother, that was for sure, except for the thick dark hair. A man of slighter build with a sensitive face and shy smile. The sort of man, the thought came unbidden, who would provide a ready-made foil for Alison's gay sophistication.

Intent on the photograph, she was unaware that Stephen had come to stand at her side until with a start she turned to find him beside her, his expression grim and forbidding. She forced a smile. "Your brother?"

He nodded. "That's Cliff. Lucie's rattling cups out there like mad. Think you can drink another ration of coffee?"

She turned away. "Glad to." She forbore telling him that she had scarcely been aware of the earlier coffee session. She had been too shocked to realize anything but the significance of what Stephen was telling her. All at once she felt a pang of conscience. "I'm sorry you had to leave your work to go all the way into town to meet me today." His closed look was anything but encouraging, but she hurried on, "I suppose it's a busy time for you in the vineyards just now?"

"It's always a busy time," he said, and followed her out through the wide lounge room to the sun-splashed terrace with its wrought-iron railings.

"Not for me, thanks." He waved aside his aunt's inquiring look. "I've got to get cracking."

"Oh, Steve!" Lucie regarded him with reproachful brown eyes.

"If you'll excuse me—" his cool gaze went to Tracy "—plenty to do outside. See you later."

"Oh, dear," Lucie murmured apologetically as she picked up a coffee percolator and began to pour a stream of brown liquid into pottery mugs, "he isn't always like that, so cross and horrible. It's only since... since...."

"Since Alison, you mean?" Tracy's clear candid gaze went to the older woman.

Lucie sighed. "Yes, that's about it. Did Steve tell you?"

Tracy took the mug and seated herself on a lawn chair in the sunshine. "Well, he did—sort of."

"That's the whole trouble. He doesn't like talking of it. If only he'd discuss it all he'd feel a whole lot better about things."

Tracy helped herself to raw sugar in a pottery jar. "You know something," she said with her engagingly frank smile, "I don't really know yet what actually did happen about Alison... and Cliff. Your nephew told me that there'd been an accident after the engagement was broken off when you were all down south on tour, that Cliff was badly hurt. Only—" her voice died away on a puzzled note "—somehow it all seems so... odd."

"Well, actually that's about it. It all happened so suddenly." She avoided meeting Tracy's gaze and hurried on in a quick, nervous voice. "I never saw Alison again after that last night. She just... took off."

Once again Tracy had a suspicion that something was missing from the bald explanations she had been given, something concerning Alison. Clearly, however, the older woman had no wish to revive the pain and embarrassment of the past few weeks, and Tracy could scarcely pursue the subject. At this rate, she thought with a sigh, she would never know the truth. Stephen? She remembered his grim expression. No help there. It couldn't make the slightest difference to her anyway, whatever the cause of the shattered romance. Yet in some strange way that she couldn't understand, somehow it did matter—awfully.

Aloud she said hesitatingly, "It's just... I mean, I know that Alison rushed off and all that, but I thought she might have left something, some message for me—"

"My goodness!" Lucie ran her fingers through her hair, making it more untidy-looking than ever. "Thank heaven you reminded me! She did! She left a note that I was to give to you and I stuck it in my handbag that morning and never thought of it again. At least, I think I put it in my handbag. If only I could remember! It must be somewhere!" Getting to her feet, she began to riffle through a pile of envelopes on the mantel, then opening the door of a cabinet, she tumbled the papers out on to the floor. "Maybe it's still in my bag." Hurrying from the room, she returned in a few moments carrying a capacious lizard-skin handbag that she proceeded to tip upside down.

A miscellaneous collection of objects fell to the floor. Lipstick, wool labels, fragments of fleece, shells, notebooks, pen—but no letter. "I do hope I haven't lost it," she murmured anxiously to Tracy, who was down on her knees searching through the litter. "But not to worry, dear. It couldn't have been anything that you don't know already, and anyway, it's sure to turn up." Picking up the tangled mass, she jammed it all roughly back into the depths of the handbag. "Things always do sooner or later."

Tracy tried to hide her disappointment. If only Lucie had been a more methodical type of woman! If only she had placed the letter in a safe place. Now probably it was gone forever.

With an effort Lucie brought her mind back to the light tones. "It's got quite a name, Valley Vineyards, as being one of the most picturesque vineyards in the country! No wonder Steve's so proud of it. He's really wrapped up in this place," she confided. "It was his father's first and *his* father's before that. Wine making is all Steve's ever wanted to do. They say that wine makers aren't made, they're born, and that's Steve! By sheer hard work and determination he's brought his wines up to world class! Do you know, just the other day his special sparkling wines were chosen from all the local wines to be served at a special winegrowers' dinner in London. Not bad for such a small place! It is small, you know, compared with the large ones, the well-known vineyards around here that are really big business these days. Steve's is the only one in the district that's owned by someone of non-Dalmatian descent. It's so funny, no one in this country used to care a thing about serving wine at home a few years ago and then suddenly folks have gone crazy over it! Must be something to do with gracious living or something. Anyway, Steve could sell all that he makes, only he happens to be more interested in quality and making a name for Valley Vineyards. Anyone can make an intoxicating beverage from grapes, but there's more to it than that, a sort of mystique somehow. There's a saying around these parts that to make good wine you must love your grapes, and unless you love wine making you should leave it alone. Steve—well, he knows the work and loves it. Not like Cliff."

Tracy glanced up from her mug. "Your nephew said his brother is a mountaineer?"

Lucie's expression of animation faded. "*Was*, dear! He won't be doing any more climbing, but—" her brow cleared "—I always said it was a dangerous game!" She was silent for a moment. "Cliff used to say that was the attraction held for him. Dicing with death, he called it, and yet—" a deep sigh escaped her "—in the end he was hurt in his own car. But that's the way things happen! It just seemed so hard." She went on as if speaking to herself. "The engagement to your cousin finished—he thought the world of Alison—and then the smash-up. All the same, it might have been all for the best, seeing—" She broke off in some confusion. "Have one of these biscuits, dear? I made them myself."

As she took one of the light almond-topped confections, Tracy wondered what it was that the older woman had been about to say. It was clear that she held no brief for Alison, considering her nephew well rid of the girl with whom he had been deeply in love. Why? And Stephen, what were *his* feelings in the matter?

A rifle shot from somewhere close at hand jerked her from her thoughts... and Lucie smiled at Tracy's expression of alarm. "It's only Steve shooting over the heads of the birds to scare them away. They're his main problem out there now the grapes are ripe."

"Oh, is that all?" Tracy relaxed again. "I was wondering, have you been here long?"

"Only a couple of years. Before that I was with my husband on a sheep station farther south. When he died I did think of putting a manager on the place, but in the end I decided to sell out, have a few overseas trips—I just adore travel, don't you—and make Steve's and Cliff's place my home base, as it were. The two of them were here on their own and it seemed a good idea. I thought for a while that Cliff would be moving out, but that's all changed now. Anyway, they seem to like to have me around to see to their meals. What they don't like is my trying to smarten up the place for them! Talk about a bachelor establishment! You should have seen it before I moved in with them—ancient wallpaper, fly-speckled walls, lots of comfort and precious little else!

"How did you like the bathroom color scheme?" she went on. "Lilac and green go well together, I always think. And the bedroom carpet in your room, I made that myself. I was so busy all the time we were on the sheep farm, you've no idea. The days just flew! But all the time I was putting aside the longest and fluffiest of the sheepskins—we used to cure them ourselves. One day I thought, when I have time, I'll make rugs out of all these, and that's just what I'm doing! I've dyed a lot of the pieces myself." She gestured toward the scattered multicolored fleeces. "It's so easy. You just get some hessian, a bottle of carpet glue and you're away! I'm starting with the border first, I thought a Mexican design, all in tawny yellows and russets, then the center filled in with the white fleeces. It's just as well that I enjoy craft work, for I'm sure Stephen won't appreciate all this. He'd probably just as soon have the worn old mats that were on the floor when I came here. All he cares about is the outside layout, and Cliff's as bad in that respect. I must admit, though, the way the grounds are laid out is quite lovely. Mind you," she finished slowly, "I don't think your cousin thought much of it."

"Oh, but she did!" Tracy cried. "She sent me a photograph of it. A gorgeous photo, so clear! You might not believe this, but that snapshot of the vineyards had a lot to do with bringing me all the way out to New Zealand!" She stirred her coffee thoughtfully, groping for the right words. "I didn't want to come here today," she said in a low tone, "be a nuisance to you after... after what happened before. It was just that your nephew said you were expecting me, so I thought...." Her voice trailed unhappily away.

"Of course you had to come," Lucie protested briskly, "and stay here awhile, too. You're very welcome to make this your home for as long as you like!"

"It's awfully kind of you to say that, but—" she raised clear sea-blue eyes "—now that everything's... different... I'll have to make other plans. I thought, though, just for a day or two until I got my bearings?"

"You stay just as long as you wish," Lucie returned warmly. "I'd love to have you."

But it's not your home. She could scarcely say that. All she could do was murmur thank-you and shelve the problem meanwhile. Now that she had no need to hoard her slender resources for expenses connected with a family wedding, she could afford to take some bus tours of the North and South Islands, see something of the scenic attractions of the country.

"You know," Lucie was saying, "you're lucky, Tracy. You've happened to arrive here on the one day when there happens to be something rather special on in the city. I bet you wouldn't even know that Auckland's a hundred years old this year and we're putting on a month of centennial celebrations! That's why tonight there'll be dancing in Queen Street, singing, radio broadcasts, fun. All the young folks will be there—Steve can take you in to see it!"

"Oh, no," Tracy protested hastily, "he'll be busy, I expect. I'm sure he won't want to be bothered piloting me around."

"Who says so?" Tracy glanced up to find him standing in the doorway. He had changed into work garments, a short-sleeved open-weave gray shirt, shorts, sandals. A battered felt Kiwi hat that he held in his hand went spinning across the room to land on a sideboard. "What makes you so sure I won't take you into town tonight?"

The amused glint was back in his eyes. He seemed, she thought with a flash of irritation, to gain an awful lot of amusement from teasing her. Alison's English cousin! He *would* take an opposite stand, probably merely to annoy her.

He was regarding her now with that compelling gaze that for some reason she found so difficult to meet. "You want to see all you can of the country, don't you, while you're here?"

"Oh, I do, I do! But—"

"Well, you won't get a second chance to see Auckland in gala mood like it will be tonight."

Tracy had a feeling that it wouldn't be much fun anyway being partnered to the city by this sardonic man with his unfathomable attitude toward her, but anyway it would be an experience.

"Well, what do you say, Miss Cadell?"

She raised clear blue eyes, smiled gaily. "Love to."

"Right! That's fixed, then. I'll go and take a look at the pickers. If—the weather holds—" he squinted up toward a cloudless sky "—another week should do it."

"It would be dreadful if heavy rain spoiled the crop after all the year's work," Tracy murmured to Lucie as Stephen took his leave.

"Oh, my goodness, yes! Even light rain would take the sparkle off the grapes. But Steve won't *think* of picking them until the grapes are absolutely perfect, not like other growers who take advantage of the weather instead of risking everything! But that's just Steve!"

All afternoon the older woman worked happily on her sheepskin rug and Tracy soon realized that Lucie, absorbed in her task, was undisturbed by such mundane matters as the preparation of meals. It was late when they all sat down to a table overlooking the terraced vineyards. The meal was a simple one, consisting of sliced cold meats, a salad that Tracy had put together because Lucie's hands were sticky with carpet glue that she had difficulty in removing. Slices of honeydew melon, chilled and delicious, served as a dessert, followed by coffee and a selection of local cheeses.

The only other member of the staff, Tracy found, was the truck driver who she had seen on her way to the house. "This is Bill Evans." Stephen made the introduction in his offhand tones. "He's kept busy most of the time with the bottling." As she met the friendly expression in the bright blue eyes, Tracy took an immediate liking to this pleasant, middle-aged man.

"That was tough luck, Miss Cadell," he said in his rich voice as they seated themselves at the table, "coming all this way across the world for a wedding and then finding there wasn't one."

"Well," Tracy admitted, relieved to find someone in the party who was not reluctant to approach the subject of Alison, "it was a bit of a shock."

"Still," Lucie cut in quickly, "she'll get a trip out of it, and in the summer, the best time of all to see the country, too!"

Tracy was speechless with indignation. A trip! Just like that! She'd spent her entire savings on fares and expenses to come here, and they were dismissing the whole thing as carelessly as though she were Alison, with her cousin's freedom from financial concern. How could she make them understand that her own circumstances weren't at all similar? She made one more attempt. "Actually, with me it's different altogether from the way things were with Alison." No one appeared to be listening and her faltering tones died away.

Later, as cigarette smoke rose among the coffee cups, Tracy asked idly, "Who were the women who were picking out in the vineyards today?"

"Oh, they're all local housewives," Lucie said. "The same women come every year in the season, about thirty of them, and they all live somewhere handy."

"They're a good gang." Stephen stubbed out his cigarette. "I'm darned lucky to have them."

"It must be rather fun for them, too," Tracy remarked reflectively, "out there in the open. I've never worked—"

"You wouldn't want to start on that caper!" Once again, she noticed, he was wearing his distant look. "It's hot as blazes! I'll tell you something, Miss Cadell! In my vineyard you wouldn't last the distance, not even one day! It's *work*, real back-breaking sweating physical toil, something you wouldn't even know about."

All at once she was swept by a gust of anger. How dare he! Merely because she and Alison had attended the same school he apparently took it for granted that she was a clueless socialite, untrained, inept when it came to a matter of "real work." She dropped her gaze, fearful that he would catch the angry shine in her eyes. How gratified he would be to realize that he had at last goaded her into furious resentment. She wouldn't give him the satisfaction of knowing how deeply his careless words had penetrated. They were so *untrue*, as he would very soon find out!

"I keep telling you—" in vain she tried to subdue the tremor of indignation in her low tones "—that I'm just a working girl."

His sardonic lift of his lips was more damning than any words. Like Alison, it said, busy with fun work, financed by doting relatives. Playing at work. Playing at life.

"What did you do, Tracy?" Clearly Lucie had noted Tracy's heightened color and was endeavoring to steer the conversation toward less controversial channels. Her gaze went to Tracy's small hands with their smooth skin and gleaming fingertips. "Was it office work?"

She nodded. Well, let him continue to think that she was a worthless socialite whose working career had consisted of a brief fling at finding out how the other half lived. To argue the matter with him merely brought that maddening half smile to his lips, but to prove her point, that would be different! And that was exactly what she intended to do, first thing in the morning. Only she would have to be cunning about her plans. Raising her eyes to his, she asked innocently, "Do you need any more helpers just now?"

"Not at the moment." Clearly he did not connect her inquiry with anything personal, which she supposed was something to be grateful for.

"Oh, but you do, Steve!" His aunt's high sweet tones broke in. "I almost forgot to tell you—Katie rang while you were away at the wharf. She has to go up country to nurse a sick uncle. Said to tell you she was sorry to let you down."

Stephen's face sobered. "One of my best pickers, too. Oh, well, it can't be helped. It's too late now to get hold of anyone else. We'll just have to manage with the others."

Or hire me, Tracy thought jubilantly, but she made the observation silently. She could scarcely wait until morning to put her plan into action. With a start she brought her mind back to the older man's measured tones. "Steve shown you around the place yet?"

"No, but—" Out of a corner of her eye she was aware of Stephen's quizzical glance. "Everyone's busy around here just now," she went on rapidly, "and I'll see it all before I go."

"What's wrong with now?" Stephen rose, pushing back his chair from the table and turning to Tracy. "If you'll excuse us, folks? It won't be dark for a while yet."

Outside the surrounding hills were a dark blur and an amethyst haze lingered over the landscape. They went through the open French windows, crossed the terrace and strolled down the steps. Then they were taking a flight of stairs leading down to a cellar below. He touched a light switch and at once the big room sprang to life. Tracy saw that one end of the area was given over to long shelves stacked with bottles of wine. Below was a curving counter. "This part of it's the shop," Stephen told her.

Tracy looked curiously around her, her gaze roving over the gold and silver medals, the framed certificates of national and international awards that hung on the wall. "But where are the casks?"

"Farther along—Bill's department. I didn't think you'd be interested."

"Oh, but I am!" Moving toward a doorway, she peered into the shadows where against a backdrop of maturing wine she discerned a grape crusher, large vats and smaller wooden barrels, a gleaming stainless-steel clinic and laboratory equipment. "So this is where the wines are fermented?" She put a hand against a great vat of stainless steel. "You're going in for modern equipment now?"

He shook his head. "Only for the whites. The reds need maturing in wood to bring out their full potential."

She glanced around her. "I had no idea—"

"You're learning. As one wine maker around here puts it, the dessert wines, sherry, port, muscatel, are like a strong robust man. They can stand up to almost any onslaught, but the table wine, on the other hand, is a weakling. He has to be protected, fussed over, looked after ever so carefully." He moved toward a desk where a telephone was propped on a pile of account books. "Over here is the office."

"Who does the office work?" Tracy asked, and immediately regretted the careless inquiry, for hadn't he mentioned that his brother....

"No one...now." His tone was curt. "But I'll catch up on it once the picking's over."

He turned and she hurried along at his side as they mounted the concrete steps together. At this rate, she reflected, she would certainly take in the entire vineyard in double-quick time.

"You don't have to, you know," she said breathlessly, quickening her steps to match his long strides as they emerged onto the narrow path.

He stared down at her. "What do you mean?"

"Show me around the place."

"You mean you're like your cousin?" Once again it seemed he had taken her up wrongly. "Not interested?"

"No, no, I didn't mean that! I think it's all awfully interesting. Honestly! It's just...just—" she floundered helplessly "—that you must have other things to do."

He sent her a quizzical glance. "I can put up with it, Miss Cadell—"

"Tracy!" she whispered.

He ignored that. "If you can!"

"Put up with it? I think it's beautiful!" They were passing through a small gateway, coming in sight of a pool surrounded by feathery papyrus grass and tattered banana palms, shadowy in the light that was fast deepening to a velvety blue. She moved toward the pool where a pink plaster flamingo was perched on one leg and a massive russet flower from a banana palm growing nearby hung low over the water.

They strolled on between high hedges to emerge suddenly in sight of a sunken pebble garden where dwarf trees rose from pottery urns and pink geraniums trailed over low walls. "It used to be a tennis court in the old days," Stephen told her. "Now it comes in handy for entertaining. We usually put on something for the pickers at the end of the vintage. They've been working flat out for five weeks now; one more week should see the finish. They seem to want a barbecue-cum-hangi this year—"

"Sounds like fun."

"The hangi?"

"And the picking." They were strolling on toward a rise overlooking the terraced vineyards in the sheltered valley where Tracy had seen the women pickers earlier in the day. The vines stretched away in the fading light, the shelterbelt of silver gums and pines dark shapes in the gathering dusk.

"I doubt if the pickers would agree with you," he said dryly. "It's pretty hard going, what with the heat and the fruit flies and the wasps. But they come back year after year, the same gang of local women. The first day their tongues move faster than their hands, but before long they're getting into their stride. If only we don't get rain this last week—"

"Rain? On a perfect summer night like this?" The velvety blue dusk seemed to enfold them, faint stars pricked the clear dark sky.

He laughed. "You don't know Auckland! We're on a narrow isthmus here, between two big oceans, fair game for all the winds that blow."

"I just can't believe it could change. It's so beautiful, you get the feeling it will go on and on, just like this."

He bent on her his deep compelling gaze. "Don't let it fool you, Tracy!" Why did her perfectly ordinary name sound so different on his lips? "There's a saying around this part of the country—'If you don't like the weather, wait a minute!' That's Auckland—unpredictable."

"Like you!" Some imp of mischief made her say the words. She was leaving in a day or so, so what did it matter what he thought of her? At least he wasn't going to have matters all his own way.

She glanced up to catch once again the twinkle of amusement in his glance. "That's right, like me!"

She laughed her clear young laugh. "Well, anyway, I still think it would be fun working out there with the grapes. If only it wasn't quite so dark I could have a closer look at the vines. I suppose there are ever so many different varieties?"

"Are there ever! These nearer ones—" his gaze swept proudly over the rows and rows of grapes "—are the bread and butter ones that have been all we've needed in the past for the New Zealand wine industry. Now—" he shrugged broad shoulders "—for some reason Kiwis are getting more wine conscious every day. That's why I'm going in for the aristocratic wines, the ones that are going to put this country on the wine makers' map in the future." He reached with pride toward a single vine rising against a low wall. "See this Palomino? Ten years old and last year I took over five hundred pounds of grapes off the vine! My guess is that the newcomers will do just as well as the old varieties!" The ring of enthusiasm in his deep tones sharpened. "You just have to wait a bit longer for the crop, that's all!"

Tracy had an impression that deeply absorbed in his plans for the future of his wine-making industry he had entirely forgotten her existence. In an effort to bring the subject back to her own interests she said lightly, "Maybe it's because I've always been stuck at an office desk that the picking of the grapes appeals to me so much. I've never done any outside work."

All at once he was a stranger again, cold and forbidding. "I scarcely think you'd appreciate the change!"

But she had endured just about enough of being told what she would and wouldn't like. It was clear that he was treating her exactly as though she were Alison—rich, spoiled, capricious, incapable of earning a living. "Oh, but I would!" she argued. They had turned back and in the swiftly falling darkness she couldn't see his expression. "You'd be surprised how much I'd like to try it!" He was silent and she could almost feel his unspoken disapproval. It spurred her on to say brightly, "You did need another helper over there in the vines?"

"I need one all right." Ice crackled in his tone. "But you wouldn't last an hour at the game, let alone a ten-hour day! It's no work for soft city types—needs plenty of arm muscle!"

"I'm not Alison, you know!"

It was a mistake, she realized the next moment, to have mentioned the other girl, for now his tone was more distant than ever. "You're joking, of course?"

"But I'm not! I'm not! I hadn't planned to stay after tomorrow, but if I could have a go at the picking, that would be different!"

"We'll see," he said coolly, "how you feel about it in the morning. Six-thirty's the starting time!"

"Oh, I know how *I*'ll feel about it!" she flung at him. "It's just up to you!" But he didn't appear to be listening and as she hurried along at his side as they approached the lighted house on the rise above, somehow she didn't give much for her chances.

CHAPTER TWO

WHEN THEY REACHED THE HOUSE, Tracy left Stephen in the lounge while she made her way to the kitchen. As she had expected, Lucie and Bill Evans were busy at the sink and Tracy made to take the tea towel from the man's hand. "Women's work!" she smiled.

He looked surprised. "Your cousin never had any ideas in that direction! I didn't have a night off duty all the time she was here."

Not again, Tracy told herself wearily. Why must they all persist in regarding her as nothing more than a carbon copy of Alison? "I don't know about her," she said stiffly, "but I'm helping!"

"Good on you!" Bill said, and relinquished the tea towel.

As the evening progressed Tracy found herself hoping that Stephen had forgotten his offer to escort her into town to view the city centennial celebrations. No doubt he had had quite enough of her enforced company for one day, and she felt exactly the same way about him! They were seated in the lounge, watching a television program, when Lucie's gaze went to the clock on the mantel. "Steve! You'd better get going if you're not going to miss the start of it all! Lawrence and Di rang while you were out in the vineyard just now with Tracy. They said to tell you they'd meet you down by the post office."

"Good! That's what I've been waiting for. How about it, Miss Cadell?" He eyed Tracy with his cool inquiring look. "Still feel like coming along to take a look around?"

She was on the point of refusing the casually extended invitation so obviously made from a sense of politeness, then she had second thoughts on the matter. Why shouldn't she see this unfamiliar city in gala mood? Chances were that she

Vineyard in a Valley

would never again find herself in this part of the world. She wanted to make the most of every minute of her stay, didn't she, even if it meant going with this grim-faced escort who was no doubt hoping she would refuse his offer.

"Oh, I'd love to!" She could discern no change in his expression, which was disappointing, but still she intended to take advantage of the opportunity, even if he didn't speak a single word to her all evening.

The other two came out to the terrace to see them off, waving with the light behind them. As she seated herself in the big gray Holden, Tracy mused that it was an odd way to be taken out for an evening's entertainment, but then everything since her arrival in the country had been strange and hard to fathom. Everything except the vineyard, which was so attractive that she just hoped she'd get her way and be able to stay for a week's grape picking. It would be long enough to prove to the tight-lipped man at her side that in spite of being Alison's cousin she was far from the helpless nit he apparently thought her.

They swept along the winding path and out to the metalled road where there seemed nothing but the dark trees and surrounding hills.

"Penny for them?"

Tracy jumped. "Oh, nothing really. Just...the vineyards...Auckland.... A centenary month, you said?"

"That's right. But don't get the idea that going all gay and lighthearted and dancing in the streets is one of the things that Kiwis do. It's quite a change! There should be crowds there tonight, bands, jazz groups, the lot!"

She decided that he was right when a little later they left the car in a closely packed parking area and made their way through the crowds of young people thronging the main street now closed to traffic. Tracy's gaze went to the Maori men and girls with their smooth bronze skins and attractive features.

A party of laughing Samoan islanders strolled past, the girls wearing the dignified *pulatasi*, black hair elaborately coiled, the men in their brightly patterned shirts. Stephen pointed out various groups from other Pacific islands, the girls in gay loose shifts, rubber thongs on bare brown feet, flaring hibiscus blossoms tucked in flowing dark hair. The men wore cotton shirts vividly patterned in motifs of palm trees and native canoes. Everywhere was sound and music and laughter. For a moment a noisy group sweeping past separated them and Stephen caught her hand. "Come on, I can't afford to lose you already!" Just a clasp of his hand, and yet.... As her fingers curled around his she felt a tingle of excitement. Then all at once music was surging around them and she felt her spirits lift on an unexpected wave of happiness. "When the Saints Come Marching In," thundered the crowd, as the party wove their way through various groups in a street bordered with tufted cabbage trees beneath a sky so brilliant that it seemed to Tracy the stars hung like spangles in the soft dark blue above.

The swinging beat of pop band and traditional jazz provided an intoxicating beat for the crowds that had already entered into the spirit of the carnival. Stephen's gaze searched the milling throng and suddenly a pixie-faced girl with swinging black hair and a bearded fair young man were at their side. "This is Diané, Tracy." Stephen was forced to raise his voice above the throbbing of guitars. "The big guy's her husband, Lawrence." A radio van with a group of commentators on board paused nearby and the small party made its way up the street toward a guitar band playing from a stationary truck.

Soon Tracy was dancing, too, caught up in the rhythmic beat, laughing and chatting with the two strangers. Stephen didn't dance but seemed content to smoke and watch and listen to the various bands. Tracy was surprised when the chimes of the town hall clock rang out the strokes of midnight. Before long the crowds thinned out and at length she moved with the others back toward the parking lot.

"You're Alison's cousin, aren't you?" Diane's candid gaze swept over Tracy's flushed face and shining, excited eyes. "You don't seem a bit like her!"

"Don't I? how do you mean?"

Before the other girl could make a reply Stephen came toward them, car keys rattling in his hand. He grinned toward Lawrence. "Be seeing you two."

"Why don't you come over for dinner one night next week?" Diane suggested warmly. "And don't forget to bring your aunt and Tracy with you. Okay?"

"I'll let you know," Stephen said, and a little of Tracy's lighthearted enjoyment in the gala evening died away.

"We'll hold you to that!" With farewells and laughter, the other two turned away and Tracy went with Stephen toward the waiting car.

She sank down on the upholstery, pulling a face. "My feet... I think practically everyone in Auckland has jumped on them, though I didn't feel a thing at the time!"

He was guiding the vehicle down a steep winding incline of the parking lot, then they were threading their way through a stream of lighted traffic and moving out in the direction of the western suburbs. He was very quiet, she thought sleepily as, huddled in the seat, she leaned back, content to watch the blur of hills pricked by faint lights slide by. It was late when at length they turned into the bush track leading to the vineyards, but as they came in sight of the house Tracy noticed that a light still burned on the terrace.

Stephen slid to a stop in the shadows of an overhanging tree near the house and as he swung around to face her once again she was struck by his dark good looks. Something else struck her at the same moment, an inexplicable sensation of nervousness. "Thanks for taking me in tonight," she said in a quick, high tone. "It was something I would never have seen otherwise. Quite an experience!" She reached toward the door handle, but before she could turn the catch he had laid a detaining hand over her fingers. "Wait! There's something I want to ask you about."

She turned eagerly back to face him. *At last,* she thought, *he's going to talk to me, get things sorted out. Now I'll understand something of what's been puzzling me all day. Why Alison....*

"Yes?" She glanced up at him, but something in the glint in the gray eyes made her swiftly drop her gaze. It was very still, the only sound the fluting note of the cicadas piping their summer song far into the night.

"Just...this!" Raising a hand, he touched her dark hair

where, behind her ear, a pink hibiscus nestled among the black tresses.

"Oh, that," she laughed lightly. "Someone stuck it in my hair when we were dancing. Don't ask me who it was. There was such a crowd around at the time."

"I just wondered," his tones were deceptively careless, "if you know what it means? No, don't touch it, Tracy—" for her hand had flown to her hair "—leave it where it is or you'll spoil everything. The Pacific island girls don't wear flowers in their hair for nothing, you know."

"Don't they?" There was something in his low tone that faintly alerted her, yet she hadn't an idea of what he was getting at. How could a pink hibiscus blossom have any special significance?

"Like me to put you in the picture?" he asked softly.

"Well—" There was something about the deepening of his glance that was doing strange things to her. Her heart was behaving oddly.

"Now if you'd worn that flower tucked behind the other ear," his voice was softly teasing, "that would have meant that you've already found someone you're fond of, like a guy back home in England. True, Tracy?"

She was so taken by surprise she found herself answering without thinking. "Of course not—"

"But when a Pacific island girl wears a hibiscus flower tucked behind her left ear, like you, Tracy...." His low laugh sent her senses spinning in a wild confusion. Somewhere a dim recollection struggled in her mind, but before she could pinpoint it his hand was cupping her small rounded chin and he was turning her face toward him. "You've asked for it, Tracy! Just for your information," he said softly, "it's as good a way as any for a girl to say she's looking for a lover!" Warm and strong, his lips were on her own and for a second she clung to him, swept by a heady excitement. The next moment she wrenched herself free. Now she wanted only escape. He'd made such a *fool* of her! Or was it that she had made a fool of herself? As if he cared whether or not she was emotionally involved with anyone back in England! Wildly she fumbled for the door catch, but he was too quick for her. Swiftly he had leaped from the vehicle and was holding the door open.

"Good *night!*" She was out of the car and running up the steps, away from the influence of that mocking, soft, disturbing voice.

TRACY WAS SO AFRAID that she might oversleep the next day that she tossed and turned restlessly throughout the night. As a precaution against not waking in time to be ready when the other pickers began their day's work, she had left the blinds undrawn, and it was a relief when daylight flooded the room. A glance toward her wristwatch assured her that she would have ample time in which to prepare herself for applying to Stephen Crane for a picking job in his vineyards. Somehow all at once it seemed awfully important to prove one or two things to him. He had been at some pains to point out to her her ignorance in certain matters last night. *Last night!* But she had no wish to dwell on that; hurriedly she wrenched her thoughts aside. Now it would be *her* turn to show him a thing or two! The house was very quiet as she stole into the bathroom and took a quick shower. In the bedroom once again she caught her long hair back with both hands, drawing it severely back from a center part and securing it with a black ribbon. Today she aimed at presenting a workmanlike appearance. A cool dark shift, light comfortable rubber thongs on her feet.

As she moved past the kitchen she glanced inside, noticing dishes piled in the sink. So the two men had already left the house! She hurried down the steps then paused on the pathway below, conscious of the invigorating freshness of the air. In the breathless stillness of early morning the hills were etched sharply against a translucent blue. Moving along the path, she felt a surge of confidence. It was ridiculous of her to have felt so nervous simply because she was applying for temporary employment with Stephen Crane.

Running lightly down the steps, she made her way to the cellars and peered inside, but there was no one there. Probably Stephen had already gone out to the vines to superintend the pickers at their work. The winding path she had taken with him last night was now damp with dew and drops of moisture from overhanging trees brushed against her as she made her way between the greenery on either side. As she came in sight of the sunken garden with its low ornamental hedges she caught sight of Stephen approaching her and sought wildly in her mind for all her carefully prepared speeches. If he dared to say one word to her concerning the love customs of Pacific island females.... Swiftly she took herself in hand. The thing was to make herself *feel* as though that scene last night had never taken place. That way she could act her way successfully through this encounter.

As he neared her, however, his look of amazement was obvious. It was a look, she congratulated herself gleefully, that compensated for an early rising, for it was clear that the last person he expected to meet in his vineyard at six-thirty in the morning was his anything-but-welcome feminine guest.

A little of her newly found confidence oozed away as he paused, facing her with that quietly inquiring glance, but she made her tone light, tried out her gayest smile. "It's me! Your new employee in the grape-picking department! Remember?"

"Oh, yes." His deep tones were guarded, considering. "I remember."

Before he could make any reference to the previous night she said quickly, "Only you didn't really think I'd turn up?"

A lurking amusement touched the corners of his lips. "No, I didn't!"

"I'm serious about this—"

"Don't tell me—" the thick black eyebrows rose sardonically "—that you need the money?"

"Well, I could do with it!" Not that he'd believe her, and yet it happened to be the simple truth.

"Look here, I don't think you know just what you're taking on—"

"Please!" She put all her charm into her winning smile and pleading look. Not that it would cut much ice with him, not with that suspicious look in his eyes, but it was worth a

try. This wasn't at all the way in which she had planned the interview would go. Indeed, it was only the approaching voices of a group of middle-aged women that helped her. He could scarcely stand on the narrow path arguing with a strange girl at this hour of the morning in full view of the pickers. As she had hoped, the advancing party appeared to make up his mind for him.

"Okay," he said reluctantly, "you can give it a go. Guess it'll be something for you to do."

Something to do! So that was his opinion of her. Once again he was judging her by Alison's standards of living, darn him! Furious though she was with him, there was nothing she could do about it but stand meekly at his side and pretend she hadn't heard that last devastating remark.

"This is Miss Cadell, girls," he was saying. "Tracy! She's new to the game, so give her a hand for a start, will you? Fill her in with the main points?"

"Glad to!"

"You bet!"

"Too right!"

Nods and smiling friendly glances were all around her, then the party of middle-aged women continued along the winding path in the direction of the terraced vineyards.

Very clearly and distinctly she said, "May I have a box, please? Like the others?"

"You *are* an eager beaver!"

The germ of amusement in his eyes deepened and she burst out, "It isn't all that funny, my wanting a job!"

"Isn't it? Sorry, Tracy, we always use Christian names on the job. Of course you can have a go at it, if that's what you want?" He sent her a searching glance. "You wouldn't be writing a book, would you? Jobs I have tackled around the world—that sort of stuff?"

"No, I wouldn't! I just want a box and some instructions. What do I do? I mean, what happens when my box is filled? Do I tip it out somewhere or—"

"Here you are, Tracy." He strode toward a stack of crates a short distance away. "Pruning shears?" Taking a pair from a pocket in his drill shorts, he extended them toward her. "I'll be along with the grape bin behind the tractor to collect the grapes when you're ready. That is," he added with his maddening slow grin, "if you're still around by then."

Tracy made a mental vow to last out the week's picking even if it killed her. Aloud she said evenly, "I'll be there. Well—" she was aware that he was still eyeing her with that expression of amused indulgence "—I'd better catch up with the others and get started."

His sardonic voice made her turn back. "Don't you want to know your wages?"

"Oh, yes, I do!" It had been a mistake, she realized now, not to have mentioned the matter of payment before.

"Seventy-nine cents an hour, and you earn every cent of it!" He was cross again. She could see it in the hardening of his smile, the chilly expression in the gray eyes. "But of course that wouldn't mean a thing to you, would it?"

"Yes, it would!" she snapped. "It means a lot—excuse me please!" She hurried past him on the narrow path and continued along the winding path.

In a few minutes she had reached the other pickers moving along the dew-encrusted grass between the long rows of vines. "Hello!" Tracy smiled her wide and friendly smile. "I've come to fill in for Katie, or try to! I only hope I can do as well, but all this—" she waved a hand toward the long avenues where grapes hung heavy, fat and luscious on the vines "—is something new to me! Come to that, just about everything in the country is new to me."

"You're from England?" A buxom fair-haired woman with muscular, deeply tanned arms, regarded Tracy consideringly. "Your accent—"

"That's right. I only arrived here yesterday on the *Oriana*."

There was a silence and all at once Tracy realized why the pleasant sun-tanned faces around her wore puzzled expressions. Although they were too polite to mention the matter, they were no doubt wondering why a new arrival in the country wasn't away sight-seeing, shopping in the city or at the very least, enjoying a rest, instead of rushing into employment. Why was she doing it? Might as well admit that she was going to a lot of trouble merely to get even with a certain aggravating male! But that was a matter between her and the owner of the vineyards.

"What did Stephen say your name was?" a small, sharp-featured dark woman inquired.

"Tracy. Tracy Cadell."

"Cadell!" The eyes of the big fair woman were frankly curious. "Are you the other Miss Cadell's sister? The one who used to stay at the house?"

"No. Just a cousin. You'll have to show me how to go about all this. I haven't a clue."

"Oh, you'll pick it up in no time. There's nothing to it. You'll have aching arms by tonight, though." The fair woman nodded toward the masses of white grapes. "It looks like being a vintage year for the Palominos. It's a lot easier picking before the sun gets too hot, though. You just snip each bunch with the shears—like so...."

The women grouped themselves at intervals between the long rows and Tracy watched them closely, then with great care she snipped a great bunch of fat grapes, bursting with juice. "There! Is that the way you do it?"

"You've got the idea!" In the friendly chorus of voices the strapping blond woman's tones were the most carrying. "Hey, girls, we forgot to tell her the main thing! You've got to make absolutely sure that the bunches you pick are just the best. They have to be glistening and clean and without a single blemish. You know?"

Tracy nodded. Doubtfully she fingered a heavy hanging cluster of grapes. "How about these? I'd better leave them, they've got white dust all over them—unless I brush it off?"

Peals of good-natured merriment echoed around her. "You do that and Stephen won't just send you packing, he'll kill you! It's on all the grapes—"

"But you weren't to know!" A serious-looking older woman took pity on Tracy's bewilderment. "It's really a sort of natural yeast," she explained, "actually a built-in fermenting agent. It acts as a preserver, too. Brush off that white dust and you'll ruin the grape for wine making."

"Oh, I see." Carefully Tracy snipped off the heavy white bunch.

"Leave your box on the side when you've filled it," the woman told her. "Stephen'll be along later to pick them all up with the tractor. He left these Palominos until last so they'd be right at the point of perfection. He's such a perfectionist himself, but I suppose that's how he's built up such a tremendous reputation for first-class wines. Just wait till you try his Valley Rosé! You won't bother to sample any other pink champagne after that!"

As Tracy dropped a luscious bunch into her box she reflected that she was getting awfully tired of listening to Stephen Crane's praises. Almost as tired as she was of having herself continually likened to her cousin. She couldn't understand why in this little wine-making world everyone appeared to look on Stephen Crane as someone special.

Waving aside the fruit flies that hovered in a cloud around her, Tracy got down to her job. She felt that she was awkward in handling the pruning shears and her progress was maddeningly slow in comparison with her workmates, whose boxes were overflowing and waiting to be picked up by the tractor while Tracy's original one was still only a quarter filled.

"Don't worry," came the soft, shy voice of a dark-haired picker a short distance away, "you'll soon get into the way of it!" And indeed before long Tracy found herself becoming accustomed to the unfamiliar work. She filled her first box with grapes, started on a second.

At first it was fun. Morning sunshine filtering through the vines was a delight and her companions were a friendly and entertaining group, even though their endless chatter concerning husbands and families meant nothing to her. There was too a sense of achievement in filling the boxes to overflowing with the pale glistening bunches of grapes, in moving slowly along between the rows with a new and empty crate.

As the sun rose higher, however, she felt her face becoming hot and flushed and already her arms were beginning to ache with the unaccustomed lifting.

She was reaching toward a heavy cluster when she caught sight of the tractor approaching between the long rows of vines. Stephen was engaged in tipping the filled boxes into a foil-lined bin he was towing behind the tractor. Wasps, drunk with juice from the ripe fruit, staggered around the grape bin.

"Oh, Tracy—" She had hoped to avoid being singled out for his attention. Already she had filled a number of the boxes he had just tipped into the bin, so what more did he want? Warily she glanced over her shoulder. "Better get back to the house right away and get Lucie to find you a sun hat." His tone was peremptory, very much employer-to-employee. Too much so for her to accept! She was determined not to allow herself to be browbeaten by him.

"It's all right," she returned carelessly. "I don't need it. The others aren't wearing hats." Indeed she had taken particular notice yesterday that none of the women pickers wore sun hats, so it couldn't be all that important. No doubt he was making a point of it to her because she'd insisted on taking the job against his advice. He just wanted to be officious and bossy!

"The others are used to this climate. You're not!"

She laughed. "I'll be all right." She hoped her careless tone would convey the words she didn't quite have the courage to put into words. *I don't need your advice on every single thing, even my own skin!* "Anyway—" her glance swept upward to the masses of billowing gray cotton-wool clouds overhead "—there isn't any sun now."

"Clouds won't save you." He fixed her with his hatefully stern gaze. "Don't argue, Tracy. Just do as I say. I know what I'm talking about!"

She wrinkled her nose in derision.

"Didn't they put you wise on the ship coming over about the sun's ultraviolet rays getting through cloud out here in the southern hemisphere?"

"Yes, but—"

Fortunately, as she couldn't think up a sufficiently crushing retort, a woman picker at that moment approached Stephen and she was saved from continuing with this ridiculous argument. It was *her* complexion and if she liked to risk getting it all burned up....

As if reading her thoughts he shrugged and climbed back on the tractor. "Pity." But whether he was referring to her stubborn opposition or the manner of her health she neither knew nor cared.

As the morning wore on her face and arms became increasingly and painfully hot, but the discomfort, she told herself, was no doubt due to the unaccustomed outdoor activity. Nevertheless it was with a sense of relief that she followed the other women toward the shade of the towering macrocarpa pines where they had left baskets containing thermos flasks of tea and coffee and packets of sandwiches. Only then did Tracy realize how very thirsty she was.

"You've no tea!" the woman at Tracy's side exclaimed. "Here, have some of mine. I've got this monstrous thermos—"

But already Tracy could see a small figure advancing along the rows of vines in the direction of the women pickers. In a few moments Lucie had joined them. "Good heavens, child—" she put up a hand to wave aside a wasp buzzing around her head "—I didn't know where you'd got to so early in the morning, and then Steve told me you were out here. You're not a magazine writer, are you, dear? I know they often take on unusual work just to get local color."

"No, I'm not," Tracy said shortly. She was conscious of a sudden silence around her. "I wanted the job for myself."

Lucie's small face still wore a puzzled expression and, seeing the flask of tea in her hand, Tracy felt a shaft of regret for not having explained the matter further, but how could she? Lucie simply wouldn't believe her were she to try to tell her that she needed that money. She really did. Not so much, though, as she needed to revenge herself on Stephen Crane. Aloud she murmured, "It was good of you to come down with the tea, though I don't really think," she added with a smile, "that I'd have gone short of a drink."

"Of course you wouldn't, but someone else might. Anyway, you'll be coming up to the house for lunch."

But Tracy had no desire to face her employer at midday. Already she was conscious of the burning discomfort of her face and neck. Besides, she wanted no special favors from him. "If you don't mind, I'll stay here with the others." She eyed the pile of dainty sandwiches Lucie was unwrapping from a dampened napkin. "That'll do for lunch, I guess."

Vineyard in a Valley

The ten-minute break flew by, then once again Tracy took her place in the long avenue of vines. At intervals Stephen drove through with his tractor, collecting the filled boxes, but whenever he was near she carefully turned her head aside. She couldn't bear him to glimpse her burning face, for although the others with their tanned complexions appeared unaffected by the heat, her own cheeks burned painfully and a headache throbbed above her temples. As the afternoon dragged slowly by she felt as though the sun were seeking her out, striking through cloud and vines alike to scorch her already flaming face. That traitorous sun that had beguiled her out to this country in the first place. The worst part of it all was that she was becoming painfully aware that when it came to climatic conditions in his own land, Stephen Crane had been right after all. All the same, she wouldn't admit that she was wrong, nor would she give up. She'd rather endure the burning sensation which, combined with the ache in her arms and shoulders, was becoming harder to endure with every passing moment! And she had to go on picking until five-thirty! It was all *his* fault, she thought bitterly. He had forced her into this position and now she had to go through with it.

"It's always worst on the first day of picking," the soft-voiced dark woman at her side told her. "But what a shame to spoil that lovely complexion!"

Tracy pretended not to hear as she raised her arms once more to the vines overhead.

Around her echoed the chatter of the other women as they moved farther along between the rows of vines. Tracy was scarcely aware of the murmuring voices until mention of her own name jerked her to sudden awareness.

"Don't you love that English voice of hers?"

"Did you notice it, too? And she's pretty enough to take Stephen's mind off the other one!"

First Voice sounded puzzled. "I wasn't here at the beginning of the season. I thought it was his brother Cliff who was engaged to the English girl? Wasn't there a car accident and then the engagement broken off?"

"It would have been broken off in any case." Second Voice seemed sure of her facts, and Tracy found she was unashamedly straining her ears. "Once she met Stephen! I was here a month ago and I saw the whole thing. You could tell how she felt about Stephen just by looking at her when they were together."

"How do you mean?"

"Oh, you know! She hung on his words, and she had that glow about her a woman has when she's really fallen for someone! I thought from the start that a nice simple guy like Cliff wouldn't stand a show with her once she'd met the older brother. She was crazy about him."

"But what about Stephen?" Tracy was holding her breath as she waited for the reply. Yes, *what about Stephen?*

"He—well...." The voices faded as the pickers moved along the leafy aisles out of earshot, leaving Tracy with an odd little ache in her heart, almost like desolation, a queer sense of loss. Last night, out in the translucent darkness, she had told herself that his odd unpredictable attitude toward her was merely an extension of the censure he felt for Alison and all the havoc she had wrought in the life of his brother, but now.... Wearily she pushed back her hair, damp with perspiration, from her forehead and reached once more toward the vines. Would this endless working day never be finished?

The break for afternoon tea revived her a little and afterward she returned to the vineyard with renewed determination. Unfortunately, however, determination made no difference to discomfort and weariness. To make matters worse she had forgotten to wear her wristwatch and she had no idea of the time. At last, just when she had begun to think that knocking-off time would never ever arrive, it did. She bade a brief goodbye to her companions and was turning toward the pathway when she felt a needle-sharp stab of pain. Involuntarily her hand swept down to brush away a large wasp that had chosen that moment to pierce her ankle with its red-hot sting. No one nearby had noticed the incident and she hurried away. What was the antidote against a wasp sting? She couldn't remember; had never needed to know until this moment. To her surprise the flesh surrounding the tiny pinprick was already swelling. She would have to keep the matter to

Vineyard in a Valley

herself, for how delighted Stephen Crane would be at this fresh proof underlining his argument that Tracy Cadell and work in his vineyard just didn't mix! As she moved toward the house, pain like fire swept up her leg, but she told herself that it couldn't be painful like this for long.

But all the time she showered, slipped into a crimson pantsuit that would conceal the strip of bandage around her ankle, plastered makeup thickly over her reddened face, the throbbing pain, far from abating, increased in intensity. The swelling, too, was growing larger with every passing moment. With some vague intention of finding vinegar, or was it baking soda she needed to put on the sting, she went into the kitchen and began searching among the jumbled jars and bottles in the cupboards. Before she could locate either article, however, she heard Lucie's approaching steps and hurriedly left the room.

"Ready for tea, dear?" the older woman inquired brightly. "I got it ready earlier than usual. I thought you'd be pretty tired tonight with the heat and the picking—you might want an early night. How did it go—" she broke off. "Did you want something in the kitchen?"

"No, no, it doesn't matter." It really wasn't worth troubling anyone about, a tiny wasp sting that would probably before long stop paining and swelling.

The evening meal was set out on a table on the terrace, high above the vineyards below. A cool fresh breeze was blowing and Lucie's home-prepared Chinese food looked delicious, yet for some reason Tracy could only pick at her plate.

"Don't you care for chow mein?" Lucie asked with concern. "If only I'd known I could have—"

Conscious of Stephen's penetrating gaze, Tracy crushed back the words that rose unbidden to her lips: *I'm just too tired to eat.* Instead she mumbled something unintelligible that Lucie took to mean an aversion to Chinese cookery.

"Let me boil you an egg?"

"No, no," Tracy protested quickly. "It's just that I'm not... very hungry... somehow." Indeed she was feeling more than strange. Stephen's intent face wavered visibly before her eyes and the throbbing in her head sounded louder than the voices of those seated around her at the table. She opened her mouth to speak, but no sound came. Faces swam dizzily, faded, came back into focus. Then as from a distance she was aware of one voice piercing the mists swirling around her. "Tracy! Tracy!"

She tried to answer, but a terrible feeling of helplessness swept over her. "My... tongue...." She could scarcely get the words out, for her tongue seemed to fill her whole mouth with a frightening choking sensation, almost like drowning. Vaguely she was aware of Stephen rushing to her side, shaking her back to consciousness. "Tracy, listen to me! You didn't get a wasp sting today, did you?"

In her twilight world the answer came subconsciously and she nodded her head.

"Where?"

Dutifully, because it was less bother than arguing, she extended her foot, and as Stephen dropped down beside her she noted in a dreamy way that the swelling on her ankle was so advanced that the material of the crimson pants was pulled tightly over the flesh. In a flash of his pocket knife he had slit the straining fabric and after one glance, a low whistle, he hurried toward the telephone in the hall. "I'll get Doc Milligan over right away!"

"If he's out, get Doctor Milne. Number's on the pad!" Lucie's urgent tones reached her as from somewhere far away. In this world of floating sensation and throbbing pain nothing seemed to matter very much. The next time she was aware of her surroundings, Stephen was saying, "Hell! I can't raise either of them. No matter, I'll run her into hospital...no time to waste! By the look of things any minute now she'll be slipping into a coma."

"No time to waste...no time to waste...." The words beat a refrain in her bemused brain as Stephen stooped to pick her up. Then the overpowering drowsiness that was taking over blotted out everything else. The last thing of which she was conscious was of lying limp in his arms as he carried her down the steps and out to the waiting car on the path below. After that impressions came and went of men in white coats, women's voices, all fading into a mist that was closing in around her. Vaguely she was aware of a word that should mean something significant, but she couldn't pinpoint it. "Coma...coma...she's slipping into a coma."

SHE AWOKE TO FIND HERSELF in a high hospital bed in a sunny room. With surprise she realized she was wearing a white utility nightdress. Even more surprising was a realization that a man was standing looking down at her. Her gaze moved upward to focus on his face. Stephen. She surveyed him with blank astonishment. She couldn't understand it at all. Had there been an accident? Could she have sustained a head injury that had clouded her mind? "What...happened?"

In a dreamy sort of way she was aware that for once his strong face had lost its satirical expression. Indeed, had he been anyone else she would almost have thought that he appeared immeasurably relieved.

"You'll be all right now."

"Yes, but—" She glanced perplexedly up at him, trying to focus her whirling thoughts. "Was there an accident, or what....?"

"You could put it that way." He grinned. "If you could call a wasp an accident."

"Wasp!" She shot into a sitting position, pushing back the long hair from her face. "You don't mean to tell me that one silly little sting—"

"That one little sting happened to strike someone who's allergic to wasp stings!" She was aware of the deepening timbre of his voice. "One of those people who could die in an hour or so without medical attention. You had all the symptoms of serious allergy...swollen tongue, drowsiness, terrific swelling. I've struck it once or twice before in the vineyards with the picking staff. Thing is it affects the lungs. You were in a coma by the time I got you here, even though I shot through red lights all the way in from the Valley, broke all the traffic rules to make it to the casualty department in time. But even so—" he took a long shuddering breath "—it was touch and go, Tracy."

He leaned over her, his voice strangely gentle. "Why didn't you tell me? I'd never have let you come near the vines, not in a thousand years, even if you'd had the medication right there with you every minute!"

"I didn't know," she said simply. Adding with a flash of her old spirit because after all he was still Stephen Crane and would no doubt revert to his all-important, horrible self once she was well again, "And anyway, it wouldn't have stopped me!"

There was a little silence and the way he was eyeing her, the softening of his glance, made her feel suddenly confused.

She raised shadowed eyes in a wan face. "So you ... saved my life?"

"Let's just say—" his bantering tone was very gentle "—that I owed you something, seeing that between the lot of us, Alison, Cliff, myself, we got you into all this."

The magic moment was shattered. Alison. It always came back to her. The way he was looking at her, maybe this was the right moment to ask him something that had been on her mind ever since their meeting.

"I've been thinking ... about Alison...." Her voice died away as she met his look, alert and guarded, eyes chilly as gray ice. It was hopeless, of course, she'd known that from the start, but still she floundered on. "Your aunt," she went on in a low uneven tone, "told me that Alison had left a letter for me, explaining everything, but she can't seem to find it and I wondered—"

"What do you want to know about your cousin?" He was the other Stephen again, she thought with a despairing sigh, his jaw set, expression hard and cold and unyielding.

She hesitated. It was so difficult to put the question into words. "Just ... all sorts of things. I mean, why did Alison change her mind so suddenly ... about your brother?"

"I told you—a flare-up. One of those things! What the heck does it matter? You're the one we're worrying about right now. Doctor says you'll be fine so long as you keep the pills handy with you wherever you are. They told me I could pick you up tomorrow." The sudden smile that so illuminated the dark face flashed out, "Then it's back to the vineyards."

"That's right. I'd only just started on—"

His cool voice cut across her eager tones. "I didn't mean picking out in the vines, Tracy. For you, that's out—definitely!"

There was nothing she could say, for after all, the decision was up to him. She made a final effort to retrieve a situation already out of her control. "I suppose it wouldn't be worthwhile anyway, now that there's only a few days' picking to be done."

"Now you're talking sense!" He flicked a finger lightly against her nose. "I'd better cut along. Let Lucie know you're okay. She'll be pretty relieved to know that you're getting on all right now. Pick you up tomorrow about eleven, they said."

"I'll be ready." All at once she remembered the women gathered in the long avenues of the vineyard, the boxes of grapes lying waiting to be collected by Stephen's tractor. She would have to be a nuisance, causing him to waste precious time on her account—again. Tomorrow would necessitate another trip into town to the hospital far from the western suburbs, in order to bring her back to the house. There seemed no end to the inconvenience she seemed fated to put him to. Before she could say so, however, he had swung around, tossing a grin over his shoulder. "See you!"

Only after he had left the room did she realize that he hadn't really answered her question concerning Alison. Somehow she had a feeling he never would. She might as well get it into her head that interrogating him on the subject was nothing but an embarrassing waste of time. As for herself, her attempts at grape-picking employment had ended in total failure. Indeed, she couldn't have played into his hands more had she tried to do so. Now of course he would be more than ever convinced that she was so like Alison as to make no difference. Inept, inefficient, good for nothing but a gay social existence. Leaning forward, she watched through the window as Stephen went with his easy stride toward the gray Holden in the parking lot below. Dark, intense, unpredictable as they come, with a sudden heart-catching smile, what was it about him that made his opinion of her matter so much?

CHAPTER THREE

THE FOLLOWING MORNING when Stephen arrived at the high modern hospital block he found Tracy waiting in the sunny foyer with its picture windows and trailing greenery. Except for the swelling on her bandaged ankle there was little to show for her emergency dash to the casualty ward.

His penetrating glance raked her face. "Feeling okay now?"

"Of course I am! All this fuss!" She rose from the seat and went with him across the wide room in the direction of the open doorway. "You wouldn't think such a silly little thing as a wasp sting could cause so much bother!"

He grinned down at her. "It wouldn't have with anyone else! But you, Tracy, had to be different!"

"Oh, you admit it, then?" She couldn't resist the opportunity for a quick retort. "That I'm different?" The door swung to behind them and she smiled gaily up at him, a teasing light glimmering in her eyes. "Even from Alison?"

"I didn't say that."

Oh, what was the matter with him, she thought exasperatedly, that the mention of the other girl's name made his jaw tighten and that closed expression cloud his face? Now she had spoiled all the pleasant feeling of strolling together out into the gentle morning sunshine. Unconsciously she sighed. When would she ever learn that with Stephen Crane you didn't mention Alison, that is, not if you wanted to keep the atmosphere light and, on the surface at least, companionable.

In an effort to break the uncomfortable silence that had developed between them she said, "Is that a racecourse opposite?"

He nodded. "That's the trotting grounds. The show grounds are next door and up there—" he waved a tanned hand toward a towering green hill "—is parkland. One Tree Hill, they call it."

Tracy glanced toward the summit where an obelisk pierced the blue. Below sheep grazed over the grassy slopes and wandered down the winding paths. "How funny, all those sheep grazing so near the city!"

"Think so?" They had reached the parking area and he was opening the car door. "Lucie's in a tizzy. She won't take anyone's word for it that you're quite all right now. She's got to see for herself!" Striding around to the other side of the vehicle, he dropped behind the wheel. "Seeing you on the way to a coma last night really got her rattled. I keep telling her that you'll be fine now you've got the tablets—" He broke off, eyeing her closely. "You have got them handy?"

"Right here in my bag!"

"Good! That should make her feel happier. What she can't get over is the fact that without pretty quick medication you could have died—"

At something in the brooding intensity of the dark face a small irrepressible devil in her mind made her say, "Would you have cared?"

The moment the words had left her lips she would have given anything to recall them. Whatever had impelled her to say such a thing, and to *him*, of all men!

"Lucie would!"

Wouldn't you know, she told herself angrily, that he would neatly sidestep the trap. He started the car, put it into gear and they moved along the wide path leading toward the hospital exit. "What gets me is why you had to pick on that particular job to amuse yourself with."

Amuse herself! "But I told you, I had no idea I was allergic to wasp stings!" He sparked in her such a surge of annoyance that her voice rose with indignation. "I've never had such a thing happen to me before!" All at once she realized that her heated denial was proving, no doubt to his satisfaction, just how much his high-handed remarks, his implied criticism of her foolishness, was getting under her skin. Instead of giving way to this argumentative mood into which his remark had plunged her, she supposed she should be showing him some gratitude for his prompt action in, hateful though it was to admit such a thing, having saved her life! "It was good of you," her voice came muffled, "to run me into hospital so quickly."

"My pleasure!" In spite of her rebellious feelings, his sideways grin drew from her a reluctant answering smile.

As they swept along the wide street bordered by suburban timber homes with their greenery and gardens and flowering shrubs, Tracy said diffidently, "I've been thinking—your aunt's been so kind to me, but I—well, I just can't stay on at the vineyards indefinitely." She laughed a little tremulously. "And now that the job's finished—I mean," she amended hurriedly, "it wouldn't be worth my going back to the picking, just for a couple of days—" she pretended not to see his satirical glance "—so I thought I'd better...make some other arrangements."

He was skirting a truck piled high with timber, a red flag fluttering from the end of the long pine planks. "Lucie's counting on you being there for the hangi-cum-barbecue tomorrow night."

Lucie—but not him. He couldn't care less whether or not she remained at the vineyards. At the back of her mind there had niggled a tiny hope that in spite of his initial coolness toward her he might, he just might feel differently toward her now, friendly enough to beg her to stay on at Valley Vineyards. Not that she wanted to stay there at his home indefinitely, just sufficiently long to prove to him how very mistaken were those preconceived notions of his. *Someone* had to show him the truth concerning one Tracy Cadell, and there was no one else to do it.

"Better stick around for a while." Her swift sideways glance could glean nothing from his expression, for his eyes were fixed on the stream of traffic ahead. "She's got a few ideas in that direction that she's going to put to you when you get back—if you're interested. Do you happen to hold a driving license?"

"Yes, I do! An international one. Alison said—"

"And you're not in a mad hurry to get back to England?"

"No, no. I've no special plans...now."

Vineyard in a Valley

She waited for him to elaborate on the suggestion, whatever it was, but intent on the changing traffic lights ahead, he appeared to have lost interest in the subject. They swept along the street where she had first taken notice of the graceful dark Samoan women and other Pacific islanders, then moved out into suburban areas with their sweeping green lawns, an endless variety of flowering hibiscus. Soon they were turning into the busy motorway where the breakwater road was lapped by waters of the harbor.

When they reached the house Lucie had coffee waiting in a pottery jug on the wrought-iron table on the terrace. It seemed to Tracy that Lucie considered coffee to be the answer to most of life's problems and vicissitudes. Bill Evans was there, too, his rugged face smiling a welcome, his rich tones giving real meaning to his strong handclasp. "Good to see you back with us, Tracy!" The odd thing was, she mused, seating herself at the small table overlooking the vineyards below, that she did feel glad to be back here. It must be the genuine warmth of her welcome that was making the place seem all at once like home, ridiculous though it seemed.

As she had expected, Stephen left them almost at once, to change into working gear. Tracy's glance scanned the terraced rows of vines where women pickers were busy. Catching sight of the boxes spaced among the aisles she felt a prick of compunction. No wonder Stephen was in a hurry to get back to the vines with his grape bin and tractor!

"We've been so *worried* about you, child—"

The other two were so obviously relieved to see her back in good health, they were so sympathetic and kindly, that in the end Tracy burst into a bubble of laughter. "Honestly, I'm not sick, you know! I'm perfectly well!"

"*Now,* but heavens," Lucie's soft brown eyes were shadowed with concern, "if Stephen hadn't spotted right away what was wrong you could have died. If only we'd known—"

"If only *I'd* known!" Tracy smiled.

"Anyway," the older woman's light tones held a note of relief, "you'll be all right now for the barbecue and hangi on Saturday night—"

"Yes, I'll stay until then."

"Just until then? But, Tracy—" Lucie put down her coffee mug. "Now look, child, that's not at all what I had in mind. You see, there's something I wanted to have a chat with you about, a little matter of transport. You see," she went on before Tracy could make a reply, "it's so awfully isolated out here in the vineyards. There isn't even a bus service, not a regular one up here in the bush, and I had this marvelous idea. I mean, if you could stay for a month or so, be my driver—"

"And navigator," Bill put in with his wide, good-natured grin. "Be warned, young lady, she'll get you lost quicker than any passenger you ever met up with."

"Poof." Lucie dismissed the warning with an airy wave of a small hand. "Who wouldn't, with all these new motorways and 'no right turns'? No one could possibly keep up with all the changes. As I was saying, if you could just stay on for a while and drive me around the place, Tracy—you've no idea what it would mean to me."

"But," Tracy said bewilderedly, "if you have a car—that dashing little orange Mini that I saw in the garage—"

"Oh, that's not mine, dear." The older woman appeared somewhat flustered. "Mine's a Volkswagen. At the moment it's in a garage in Henderson. A little matter of body repair, and a few other things! But it will be back next week, they promised me. Other drivers are so careless, I always think. They just don't care! Even when you're just driving along slowly and minding your own business, they honk and honk behind you, trying to make you speed up and get out of their way. So rude, I always think. Anyway, I won't be driving my little bus for a while—"

"Three months, wasn't it, that they disqualified you for?" Steve had come out to the terrace, lithe and tanned in khaki shorts, a cool cotton open-necked shirt, leather sandals. He regarded his aunt with a quizzical smile. "And not without good reason."

"Well," Lucie murmured evasively, "I happened to be in a big hurry that day."

"No need to take on a five-ton lorry!" He grinned toward Tracy. "Thing is, she's just had her car put out of action and her license canceled for three months. Has she put it to you about helping her to get mobile again?"

Tracy nodded.

Before she could say any more Lucie's high, eager tones broke in. "You wouldn't have much to do, dear. Just running me into Henderson for shopping and into town to visit friends now and again." On an inspiration she added persuasively, "If you stayed Stephen could take you on some trips to see the country. I mean, you've seen nothing of the place yet."

Stephen! She could imagine. She was disquietingly aware that he was making no effort to influence her decision. Another Miss Cadell, no doubt he was thinking, making trouble, interrupting his work, complicating his life. She jerked her mind back to the matter under discussion. "You wouldn't need to pay me for that," she said slowly, "I'd be very happy to help you out with driving the car. It's just—" She hesitated.

"Just what, dear?" Even without glancing up she was conscious of Stephen's watchful gaze. He was probably hoping she would refuse the offer, which was one reason, she decided, why she was seriously considering accepting it.

Aloud she said, "I couldn't let you pay me for enjoying myself and staying on here. I'd feel—oh, I don't know—as though it wasn't fair to you." An idea that had occurred to her once or twice before returned to her mind. It was worth a try and he could only refuse.

"It would be different—" she avoided glancing in Stephen's direction "—if I could do something else as well, something worthwhile, like taking over the office work downstairs," she went on in a rush. "All that paperwork must be getting a bit behind since—" Her voice faltered.

"Now that's an offer worth thinking about!" To Tracy's relief Bill's hearty tones broke in. "A great idea, wouldn't you say, Steve?"

"It might be—" his tone was guarded "—if Tracy happened to have any real experience—"

"But I have! I have! I keep telling you—" Indignation lent the ring of truth to her fervent tones. "Just give me a trial run and you'll see—"

He sent her a long, considering look. "Fair enough. Come down to the office in the morning and we'll see about it then. As to the driving—"

"Oh, I could easily do that, too!" Her eagerness surprised even herself. She was actually asking to take on dreary office work once again! And with this impossible man as her employer! Why was she doing it? A little matter of revenge on him, actually, for the way in which he had treated her, the false position in which he'd placed her, right from the start, and without the slightest reason! What else?

Lucie's excited voice broke into her thoughts. "I don't suppose you'd have a driving license now?"

"Oh, yes—"

"Good, that's fixed, then!" It was Stephen who answered. "The Mini's in the garage. You may as well make use of it meantime. When the other bus comes back next week you can take over the Mini for your own use. A car's a must if you're staying on here for a while."

"But that's marvelous!" Lucie's brown eyes shone with pleasure. "Maybe we could take a run out to Henderson today? It's no distance and I've run right out of dyes— Oh, all right then," she added as she met her nephew's reproving look. "Sorry Tracy, I keep forgetting you're only just back from hospital. Tomorrow, then?"

Tracy, however, had no intention of allowing Stephen Crane to dictate to her. She had agreed to help out in the matter of driving, but she had made no promises to him. "Today will be fine!" She smiled across at Lucie. "We passed through Henderson township on the way here today. It's quite a place! New shops, wide streets and parking places, modern buildings. I'd like a trip there to look around." But it was useless.

"Tomorrow." He fixed her with a steely gaze. "I promised the doctors I'd see that you took it easy for a day or two, so—"

So what could you do, she thought hotly, but go on chatting about nothing at all, pretending it didn't matter one little bit that she had been forced to obey his hateful instructions. It wasn't until much later in the day when the queer enervating feeling of lassitude overwhelmed her that she was forced to admit that perhaps it was as well that her duties did not begin until tomorrow.

On the following day, however, she felt that she was at last back to normal health and looking forward to the drive to the western township. Someone, probably Stephen, had taken the orange car from the garage and turned on the narrow driveway in readiness for her departure. As she seated herself behind the wheel she was conscious of a pleasurable sense of anticipation, for although she had recently gained her driving license, all her experience had been gained in the instructor's car. This car—she glanced down at the gleaming black upholstery, the gay orange paintwork and matching sheepskin seat covers—hadn't been long out of the showroom. "It's brand-new," she said in wonderment.

"Almost." Lucie had come to seat herself at Tracy's side. She was tying a silk scarf over her golden hair and her small face appeared more puckered and elflike than ever. A gold mesh shopping bag dangled from her hand. "Ever driven a Mini?"

"No, but I'm looking forward to doing just that."

"You'll soon get the feel of it. Now you do the driving, Tracy, and I'll navigate. If we meet anyone on the driveway leading out to the road just pull over to the side and let them pass. Hurray! We're off!"

It was a delight, Tracy found, to be at the wheel of the small car, even if she had to keep a sharp lookout on each bush-concealed bend. But they met only a herd of black steers straggling across the road in the direction of a cleared paddock on the opposite side of the road. Behind them strolled a farmer with his dogs. Pulling to the grassy roadside, Tracy waited until the last of the stragglers made a wild dash through the open gateway.

In spite of her reputation for having little sense of direction, Lucie was at least familiar with the winding tracks that crisscrossed the bush-covered hills and at length the two entered wide suburban streets where timber houses painted in pastel shades were set far back from the highway amid their sweeping lawns. In the flourishing modern settlement with its attractive stores and buildings, Tracy guided the car to a convenient parking lot in the main street. As she strolled with Lucie past the attractive display windows with their fashionable merchandise, she found shopping in the township to be a leisurely and pleasant experience. The young assistants were friendly and helpful and music echoed softly around them as they entered a colorful new shopping mall in search of Lucie's varied requirements. Glimpsing a craft shop with a display of native artifacts and carvings, Tracy left the older woman chatting with a store assistant while she went in search of one of the capacious, light Maori flax bags that she noticed were so popular with other shoppers.

As the softly-spoken Maori girl handed Tracy the woven bag, she smiled shyly. "I saw you parking your car outside a few minutes ago. Don't mind my asking," she went on in her beautifully modulated tones, "but isn't that the car that Miss Cadell used to drive? I've never seen another one around here the same bright shade of orange."

Tracy's clear blue eyes held the Maori girl's lustrous dark gaze. "Did you know her? Miss Cadell?"

"Know her!" The soft laughter rang out. "She was always in here—one of my best customers. She bought oodles of native artifacts, Maori carvings, placemats, bags, greenstone jewelery, just about everything we have in the shop. She said she was getting married, staying on in this country, and wanted the souvenirs to send back to England, but she hasn't been in here for weeks. I thought maybe she's married now and moved away to another town."

"I think she changed her mind about getting married," Tracy said slowly, reluctant to go into the matter of how she came to be driving Alison's car.

"Oh, well," the Maori girl was philosophical, "I guess she could have any man she wanted, a girl like that! She's beautiful, and the way she wears her clothes—a completely different outfit every time she came in here. To dress like that must have cost a fortune! We don't see that high fashion London boutique gear out here, not expensive stuff like that. She was so elegant looking, different somehow from any other girl I ever saw. Everyone in town used to turn around for a second look whenever she walked down the street. Guess they never saw anyone quite like her in the village, a gorgeous English girl like that!"

I'm from England, too. But Tracy made the observation silently. Somehow it wasn't at all the same thing, as she well knew. She brought her mind back to the musical tones.

"And that fabulous little orange Mini! I recognized it the minute I saw it today. I sold her the yellow sheepskin seat covers the first day she drove it into town here." Dark eyes regarded Tracy curiously. "Did you buy the Mini from her?"

"No, no, I just have a loan of it from someone else for the day."

"I see. I just wondered. She told me her fiancé had given it to her as an engagement gift." She stopped short as the hanging bead curtain was pushed aside and a woman customer entered the tastefully decorated room. "There's nothing else I can show you?"

"No." Tracy stared back at the attractive Maori girl with dazed blue eyes. "No, thank you."

Moving from the dim interior of the softly lighted craft shop, she blinked a little in the brilliance of the sunshine falling across the street. Alison's car! Oh, she should have guessed as much right at the beginning. Who else but Alison would own the most conspicuous little car in the district? One facet, though, of what she had just learned struck her as puzzling. On the single occasion when Stephen had discussed with her his brother's affairs—if you could term his terse bald statements a discussion—he had told her that Cliff wasn't a partner in the wine-making business, as Alison had intimated in her letter, but drew wages from occasional employment in the vineyards; that all he earned was immediately swallowed up in the equipment and expenses incurred with his mountaineering expeditions. For a young man in those circumstances a new car seemed a somewhat expensive engagement gift, but then—a sigh escaped her—when it came to Alison, it seemed that nothing was too good. Lucky Alison!

All at once she became aware that from the opposite side of the roadway she was in the act of crossing Lucie was beckoning wildly. The next moment she was brought to a sudden horrified halt as a truck with a squeal of brakes pulled up almost upon her. "Better watch where you're going, miss!" The truck driver's irate expression softened as, grizzled head thrust from the cab opening, he looked down on Tracy's small surprised face, eyes wide with shock.

All the time she was driving back to the vineyards Tracy was busy with her thoughts. She hoped that Lucie would put her abstracted mood down to unfamiliarity with the car she was driving and the winding roads, and indeed the older woman, chatting happily, appeared unaware of Tracy's short replies.

When they reached the house Lucie collected her parcels and hurried up the steps. "I'll put the car away in the garage," Tracy called after her. *And as far as I'm concerned,* she added mentally, *it's going to stay there!* She wasn't going to drive the orange Mini; she couldn't now that she knew who the vehicle belonged to. Guiding the car to the dimness of a long garage, she switched off the motor, picked up her flax bag and was moving toward the door of the garage when a deep familiar voice arrested her.

"Hi! How did you like driving the Mini?" Stephen stood in the shadows. He must have been there all the time, but even shadows, she thought crossly, couldn't conceal the sardonic gleam in his eyes.

She swung around to face him. "It was fine, but—" she was surprised to find her heart beating faster "—why didn't you tell me," she burst out accusingly, "that it was Alison's car?"

"Lucie tell you?" His tone was carefully controlled.

"No, someone else! A girl I met in one of the shops in Henderson. She said—" she avoided his glance "—that your brother gave it to her as an engagement gift."

"That's right!" There was a taut note in his tones that warned her she was treading on dangerous ground, but she was determined to make herself clear.

"But if it belongs to her," she persisted, "why hasn't she done something about it? Sold it ... or something?"

He shrugged. "That's up to her. Guess she'll get around to it one of these days. Meantime," he went on in that maddening laconic tone, "you may as well make use of it, keep the battery up, hmm?"

"No!" The vehemence of her denial surprised herself. All these years, forced to make do with Alison's leftovers and now.... No, she'd rather walk!

"Why not?" He was regarding her narrowly. "She's your cousin, isn't she?"

Useless to attempt to explain to this chilly-eyed stranger that that was precisely the reason why she was refusing his offer. "I just... don't want to have anything to do with it," she said in a low, unsteady voice.

"As you please." To her surprise and relief, he appeared to have abandoned the argument. "Lucie's bus will be back from the body shop in a day or two."

"That's good!" Tracy forced a smile and turned away to make her escape. As she hurried away she marveled at Stephen's inexplicable behavior. Moody, changeable, unpredictable, she simply couldn't understand him.

BEFORE SEEKING OUT STEPHEN in the morning, she glanced over the terraced rows of vines. It was clear that the last day of the harvest was over, for no pickers were to be seen. She made her way down the steps to the underground office and, as she expected, found him there, his dark head bent over the piles of invoices, correspondence and account books lying open on the big desk.

"Morning!" she said brightly. "Want any help?"

For a moment his gaze remained abstracted, then his lips twitched with the old indulgent amusement. "No, thanks, Tracy." He might just as well have completed the sentence, she thought with a quick intake of breath, "Not from you!"

She bit back the angry retort that trembled on her lips and said instead, "You look awfully busy down here. All these papers—"

He threw her an expressive, rueful glance. "Only about six months' backlog to catch up with! Thing is—" he ran a harassed hand through his hair "—where the devil to make a start on sorting it all out?"

"I could help you." He wasn't making it any easier for her, she reflected helplessly, with his "humor-the-child" attitude. "You said you'd talk it over with me today." She raised clear blue eyes to his cool glance. "Remember?"

For a moment he regarded her uncomprehendingly. "Oh, that! I'd forgotten. The typewriter's over there on the other desk. You can play around with it if you like—you'll find paper in the drawer."

Play around with a typewriter. It was too much to take. Frantically busy or not, whether he wished or no, nevertheless she was determined that he was going to hear the truth of her capabilities.

"It wasn't play to me, it was a job!"

"Oh, yes?" Leafing through a toppling pile of receipts, it was clear that he was only half listening. "Got to get some sort of order around the place. Sit down, Tracy." He pulled forward a chair and she dropped down to face him across the litter of papers. "Working, you said? How long?"

She shrugged lightly. "Ever since I left business college in London. I worked for the same firm of importers until I resigned to come out here on this trip to New Zealand. About five years altogether. Not that they'll miss me all that much." The old habit of deprecation against which she had long struggled in vain made her add, "I guess any girl who's trained for it can do shorthand and typing and bookkeeping."

He was so surprised that the match he was holding to her cigarette scorched his finger. "Damn!" He lighted his own, then blew out the tiny flame. "You shouldn't give me shocks like that! You're a working girl, then?" The thick black brows were raised in perplexity, the deep tones thoughtful as he studied her reflectively. "How come, then—"

She smiled ruefully. "How come I went to an expensive school? How come I can afford a trip halfway across the world just to be bridesmaid at a family wedding? That's what I've been trying and trying to tell you all this time! This trip out here," she cried with feeling, "has taken every bit of my savings. Five long years of them!" She went on to explain the circumstances of her education, the drab pennypinching years that had followed.

He listened in silence, his chair tilted back, a sandaled foot propped on the desk, until her low sweet voice died away.

"Well, I'll be—" His considering look, Tracy thought, was heartwarming—very.

She flicked the ash from her cigarette in a glass ashtray balanced on a heavy open ledger. "I *did* try to tell you."

"So you did, but I wouldn't listen! Well, I'm listening now. How are you on an adding machine?"

"Can do!"

"Tremendous! You've got yourself a job, Tracy! Get stuck into these, will you?" The chair legs came down with a crash on the concrete floor as he reached toward a sheaf of invoices. "After that—shorthand, you said? That means we can get rid of a few letters, the urgent ones can go in the post today. They're mostly just inquiries about prices. There's a ball-point pen around somewhere—" He flung open a drawer in the desk. "Here you are, Tracy. Latch onto this! And this!" A noteboook came flying over the litter of papers. "Forget about the invoices, that can wait! Right now we'll get this order off the ground for a start. Ready? Right! Make it to the manager, Hong Kong Imports Ltd.—got it?"

"Yes, *sir!*" Her gay and confident reply evoked no answering response and she realized that he was already absorbed in the details of his task. It was an unfamiliar world to him, she surmised. You only had to look at his worried frown, the dark hair rumpled where he had run his hands through it. Obviously an outdoor type of man, he would be more at ease out in the open among the vines, tending, cultivating, spraying, anything rather than struggling with the irksome paperwork that must be dealt with. With her wide office experience she could help him a lot...if he'd let her.

"Give me that last bit again, will you?"

With a jerk she brought her mind back to the squiggles in her shorthand notebook.

He had dictated half a dozen letters when he paused to regard her consideringly. "Reckon you could run off a few answers to these inquiry ones? Just give them the prices, different varieties in the wines. I'll give you the gist of it and you can do the rest. Right?"

She nodded, following his pointing finger to the printed catalog giving details of red and white wines that he had placed before her.

Making an effort to banish all personal matters from her mind, she settled down to transcribing the letters Stephen had dictated, then went on to compose answers to the inquirers, giving the required information as he had instructed. Soon a pile of neatly typed letters lay beside the heavy elderly typewriter awaiting Stephen's signature.

In the early afternoon he left the office to attend to duties in the vineyard and Tracy, left alone, worked steadily as the hours slipped by. From outside on a high puriri tree she caught the sound of a soft cooing and, glancing upward, glimpsed a flash of iridescent green and blue as a wood pigeon flew past the window. Sunlight slanted across her desk and the breeze blowing in at the open windows was cool and fresh, spiced with the aromatic tang of the surrounding bush.

All at once she was conscious of a deep sense of satisfaction out of all proportion to the circumstances. What was the matter with her? She was back to square one tied down once again to dreary office work. But of course it wasn't just like that. There was no doubt that whatever their personal disagreements, working with Stephen Crane had turned out to be an oddly satisfying experience. At last, at last, he was treating her as a person in her own right. She was doing the only job she knew, and doing it well, for no one could fault the neatly set-out letters and flawless typescript.

She worked all afternoon and at last pulled the cover over the typewriter. Then, stretching both arms above her head, she sat on in the silent office, dreaming. After today they could start afresh, she and Stephen, she mused happily, with no more misunderstandings between them. Now that he realized she wasn't just another Alison, he might even cease to regard her with that wary, guarded expression. Maybe he'd even—she checked herself sharply. Where were her random thoughts leading her? Come to that, why was it so awfully important to her that he should change his earlier opinion of her? She shied away from following the matter to its conclusion. She only knew that she was looking forward to the barbecue tonight.

TRACY FOUND THAT when it came to organizing a social function Lucie proved to be amazingly competent. "Get the chops out of the deep freeze, will you, please, Tracy?" she requested. "I'll make some honey-and-wine sauce to go with them. You'll find coffee up on the shelf—we'll need lots of that. Steve will set up the barbecue later. The wine's his department, too. I thought that seeing we'll have a crowd of women tonight, I'd whip up a few cheesecakes. The hangi'll take care of the pork and chicken and vegetables. Steve's out there in the garden now, digging the pits—"

"Pits?" Tracy wondered if she had heard correctly, and Lucie, busily beating eggs in a basin, laughed merrily at Tracy's puzzled expression.

"A hangi's just food cooked the way the Maoris used to do it long before the pakeha, the white man, arrived in this country. It's delicious! The meats and vegetables are put into a Maori flax bag, covered with a cloth and lowered down over the hot embers. Steam does the rest. When you lift out the baskets, everything's cooked to perfection. You'll be surprised!"

Tracy was surprised already. It was astonishing to discover that Lucie, who had always appeared somewhat careless regarding household matters, appeared to be completely in control of the situation when it came to catering for a gathering such as the evening's hangi-barbecue. But then, Tracy reminded herself, Lucie had lived for years on a vast station where no doubt she had often been called upon to entertain crowds of visitors. Whatever the reason, without undue effort she was calmly going on with the preparations. "Coffee mugs can go out on the table outside now," she murmured, and Tracy took the laden tray, making her way out into the sunshine and along the path to the sunken garden.

Steve was working nearby on a grassy plot, tossing spadefuls of earth from the pit he was digging in the sun-baked ground.

"Lucie tell you about the hangi idea?" he inquired.

He was friendly, Tracy realized with a surge of sheer happiness; his expression quizzical still, but the cold wary look was gone. Her heart did a queer little flip.

"I'm learning." She put down the tray on a low concrete table and came to watch him. He shoveled out a few more spadefuls of earth, then kneeling, made a fire in the bottom of the pit. "That should do it!" He placed some stones over the leaping flames in the earth oven.

"What do you put in to cook?" she inquired curiously.

"Just about everything you could want for a man-sized dinner—pork, chicken, kumera, potato, cabbage, puha—you wouldn't know that one. It's a green the Maoris like to eat. You name it, the hangi way cooks it better."

She eyed the smoking pit uncertainly. "I'll wait and see."

The day seemed to fly and Tracy was in her room that evening when she caught the echo of door chimes, then the sound of voices and laughter that faded away in the direction of the garden. She should have been ready long ago, but she couldn't decide on what to wear. Now, meeting her reflection in the long mirror, she was glad she had settled on the culotte suit. Burnished dark hair fell loosely over the green-and-gold brocaded jacket, and the soft green material swirled softly around her ankles. All she needed to complement the outfit was a piece of matching jewelery, but unfortunately she possessed nothing suitable. Wait, what about the cardboard box filled with a tangled assortment of costume jewelery that she had discovered pushed to the back of a high shelf in the wardrobe? No doubt it belonged to Alison, but there couldn't be anything of real value among it or she would have taken it with her. Wasn't there a pendant among the mass of clips and chains and pins? A dark green stone carved with strange symbols—that would be a perfect choice for her outfit. Reaching toward the high shelf, she carefully sorted the pendant from a tangle of chains and brooches and slipped the thin leather cord over her head. She was only just in time for the next moment someone knocked on the door. "Ready, Tracy?" came Stephen's deep voice. "I'll take you down if you like. There's someone arrived who knows you. I—" He stopped short as she came to stand in the opening, young and slim and vibrantly alive, a look of excitement in the sea-blue eyes.

"Someone," she dragged her gaze from that brilliant look, "wants *me*?"

"That's what they said. Diane and Lawrence—"

"You mean, one of the picking staff?"

"This is someone else. Come on, let's go— Wait!" His expression changed and Tracy's lighthearted happiness fled in the face of his dark and angry look.

"Where'd you get that?"

"What do you mean?" She stared back at him bewilderedly, lips parted and eyes wide. "Oh—" she realized his grim look was fixed on the hanging green stone "—you mean this?" *Now* what was the matter with him? It seemed there was no pleasing him. She gathered herself together, answered calmly. "It's just—it was stuffed into a cardboard box in the wardrobe. I thought Alison must have left it there when she went away." His unsmiling look was unnerving, but she forced herself to go on. "I didn't think it would matter. I mean," she faltered uneasily, hating herself for the apologetic note that had crept into her tone. "It couldn't be anything valuable or she wouldn't have left it here—"

"Take it off!"

"Oh, all right, then!" She couldn't understand the straight line of his lips, the steely expression in his eyes. What was so wrong about her having borrowed her cousin's costume jewelery for a few hours, for heaven's sake? She turned away, slipped the pendant over her head and dropped it on the bureau top where it fell with a little clatter.

Still he made no reply, no explanation even. Seething with anger, Tracy flung the pendant back in the box. "There! Does that please you?"

He ignored that. "Shall we go?"

He looked as grim and unyielding, she thought as together they moved along the passage, as if she had committed some sort of crime. He hadn't even given her an explanation of all this—but wasn't that just like him? She was always annoying him in one way or another, that expressive set jawline left no doubt about that, but how could she help it when he never explained anything, never told her anything but merely regarded her in that chilly expressionless way as he was doing at the moment?

In silence they went down the steps and out to the darkness of the tree-shadowed path, then suddenly they were in sight of a crowd of people. Colored lights were strung among the branches of the towering evergreen trees that made a backdrop for the paved courtyard, and flares flamed among the greenery of low shrubs.

"Here she is!" a girl's voice cried. Tracy pushed her resentful thoughts aside as the pixie-faced girl whom she had met on the night of the centenary celebrations in the city left a group of young people and came hurrying toward her. A tall young man strode along at her side, a thin figure in scarlet shirt and fawn slacks. As he neared her the flickering light from a high flare caught the sheen of smooth blond hair, lighted up the smiling young face. Why, she knew him. She'd met him before, quite often, but where?

"Tracy! At last! If you only knew the trouble I've had tracking you down!" A fair head was cocked to one side. "I thought you were going to phone me once you'd got settled?"

Realization returned with a rush. Of course! The voyage from England. Glenn.

"I'm sorry I didn't. Let's just say—" wildly she sought in her mind for an excuse "—that I never got around to getting settled, not really." She eyed him with a puzzled expression. "But how did you know where I was?"

"I didn't. I had to find out for myself."

"He's phoned every vineyard in Auckland looking for you," Diane put in smilingly.

Glenn threw a laughing glance toward Tracy. "'I'll be staying at a western vineyard,' she said, just like that. And there must be at least a dozen of them! Diane's and Lawrence's place was the last one on my list."

"And was he excited when he found out that we knew where you were!" Diane gave a trill of laughter. "Anyone would have thought to hear him raving on that you were the most important girl in the world!"

"How do you know she's not?" The smooth boyish face wore a delighted grin. "Come on, Tracy, hear that?" Beguiling notes of guitars throbbed through the darkness. "Don't let's waste it!"

"He's got something there!" Lawrence, fair, bearded, came to join them. Soon the group was moving toward the paved courtyard and as she turned away with the others Tracy was aware of Stephen standing silently in the shadows, smoking... and watching.

She was glad, glad, glad that Glenn had arrived here tonight. As she fell into the familiar movement of the dance her thoughts were still on that hateful Stephen Crane. She was getting very tired of being at the receiving end of his swiftly changing moods.

"Smile!" With a jerk she came back to the present, laughing up into Glenn's excited face and throwing herself into the insistent beat provided by two Maori boys with their singing guitars.

When at last the couples wandered back to form into groups, Glenn drew Tracy toward a low stone seat in a shadowed corner, slipped an arm around her shoulders. "There's a lot to catch up on. Your friends Diane and Lawrence put me in the picture about what happened over here. Must have been one heck of a shock to get here and find you weren't needed for the celebrations after all?"

"It was rather."

"Well, it worked out pretty well for me, finding you were still in Auckland." She felt relieved that he had no wish to pursue the subject of Alison and her fiancé. "I had this feeling all the time that you might have taken off on a tour of some sort and I'd never catch up with you again!"

"Oh, Glenn," she laughed mockingly, "and to think I never knew you cared!"

"Never knew myself until I thought I'd lost you!" A serious note tinged the light tones. "Seeing you again, after all this time—I kind of missed you, Tracy. Somehow I couldn't seem to get you out of my mind."

"With all those friends of yours I saw waiting on the

wharf? I bet they gave you parties, took you out, introduced you to masses of nice New Zealand girls!"

"Oh, they did! They did! But I happened to be looking for just one girl—" His voice dropped to a whisper. "And until tonight I couldn't find her. Tracy—"

"Dance?" At the cool voice Tracy glanced up to find Stephen standing at her side. How long had he been there she wondered. Then her heart lifted. Maybe he was regretting his brusque treatment of her earlier tonight. He'd come to make amends.

"See you later," she murmured to Glenn, and as if mesmerized, rose to her feet and went with Stephen along the darkened path. She realized almost at once, however, that any ideas she might have entertained about Stephen regretting his actions she could forget right now. Oh, she might have known that he was the type of man who wouldn't apologize, ever. You only had to glance at the grim line of his jaw, his mouth so set and stern, to realize that. Why then had he come to seek her out? Probably because of a simple duty toward a guest or an employee—of a sort.

In silence they moved into the lighted courtyard and immediately were swept into the foot-tapping rhythm.

"Enjoying it?"

She dropped her gaze before his sardonic look. "Of course." A nervous reflex made her add, "Glenn was on the boat with me coming out."

"So I gathered."

It wasn't the words, she thought, moving automatically to the beat, it was the way in which he said them, mocking, satirical. What could it matter to him, anyway, that Glenn had been seeking her ever since she had left the *Oriana* and was so obviously delighted at finding her again? She bet *he* wouldn't ever seek any girl so assiduously, even Alison. Alison. Her random thoughts drifted and the notion that she had pushed to the back of her mind returned so that there was no escaping it. He was in love with Alison. He must be. That was why he couldn't bear to see any other girl wearing the green pendant. Obviously it reminded him too painfully of all he had lost. If only she had never found the wretched thing! If only.... Well, she told herself hotly,

Vineyard in a Valley

glancing up at his unsmiling face as the sobbing guitars died away, he'd performed his duty dance, now he could relax!

Glenn was waiting for her and she went toward him, aware that Stephen had excused himself and gone to join a group of men standing nearby.

The next moment Tracy found herself surrounded by the party of women whom she had not seen since the abrupt ending of her ill-starred grape-picking venture.

"We never even knew you'd copped a sting that day!"

"Why didn't you let on? We'd have done something about it right away!"

"When Steve told us next morning that you'd been rushed into casualty—"

"I had a cousin once who was like that—an allergy they called it, only he died from a wasp sting. He was away in the bush at the time and he didn't know—"

"Oh, well—" she smiled around at the sympathetic, tanned faces "—it was just about the end of the picking season anyway." All at once she became aware of Glenn's mystified expression. "It was only a wasp sting I collected one day out in the vines—"

"Only!" a chorus of voices chimed in. "She's one of those unlucky folk who happens to be allergic to stings. Do you know, she almost *died*!"

"It's not true?" Glenn's fair young face was horror-struck.

"I'm quite all right now," she disclaimed laughingly, "and if it wasn't that the grapes are finished," she turned to the cluster of women, "I'd be back picking with you next week!"

"Good on you!" they chorused. "Come again next season."

But next season was a lifetime away, and where would she be this time next year? Unconsciously her gaze went to Stephen, still standing among a group of wine growers, a wavering flame illuminating the dark strong face.

"Come on." Glenn took her arm. "They're starting up the barbecue. The hangi, too. Ever been to a hangi before, Tracy?"

She shook her head, then together they joined in the crowd around a barbecue where already smoke was rising from sizzling steaks and lamb chops. There were sausages in foil. Men were opening cans of beer. Corks popped and someone handed her a stemmed glass where the tiny bubbles were rising in the palest of pink champagne. "Try Stephen's Valley Rosé," Lucie whispered. "It's the one that's making his name famous around here. Here's luck!"

Around her the air was filled with the pungent smell of smoke, laced with the clear fragrance of the bush. Wisps of steam rose from the hangi pits, flares cast their dramatic shadows over the scene. The Maori group took up their instruments, plucked at their guitars and the haunting cadence of a native chant rose on the still air. Soon a chorus of voices drowned out the fluting notes of the cicadas.

Tracy watched as the men lifted flax baskets from the steaming earth ovens, throwing back snowy napkins to reveal the succulent food wrapped in leaves and steamed to delicate perfection. Glenn handed her a portion of steamed pork and green cabbage, golden kumeras, then lifted a forkful of his own helping to his lips. "Wow! This is really something!"

Throughout the remainder of the evening he remained at her side, dancing, talking excitedly and happily, obviously delighted at being with her once again. A nice boy, she thought indifferently, yet on the *Oriana* she hadn't regarded him in that light. She had been attracted to him, just a little. Blame it on a Pacific moon! Or could it be that her changed attitude had something to do with Stephen Crane's forceful dark face that somehow made Glenn appear youthful, dull almost, by comparison?

At last the plaintive notes of a Maori chant of farewell throbbed through the clear night air and voices took up the melody. Everyone seemed familiar with the English translation of the lyric except Tracy.

> "Now is the hour
> For me to say goodbye...."

As the last notes died away in the clear night air, Glenn caught her hand in a warm clasp. "I've got to see you again! Pick you up tomorrow and we'll take in a drive. Okay?"

She hesitated. Would Lucie need her services tomorrow? But the other car wasn't yet back from the repair shop and for some reason she couldn't explain, even to herself, nothing would ever induce her to drive Alison's orange Mini. She smiled up at him. "That'll be fun."

"Time to get going, Glenn!" He was joined by Diane and Lawrence. "You can pick up your car at our place."

Reluctantly he loosened his clasp. "Why did I let them bring me? See you tomorrow, Tracy!" With a backward glance over a thin shoulder he went with the group that was converging toward the line of cars in the driveway.

Afterward she helped Lucie clear away the remains of the food while Stephen and Bill attended to the barbecue, throwing water on the embers, throwing earth in the hangi pits. All the time Tracy was conscious of a strange feeling of letdown. She couldn't understand what she had expected of the evening. Glenn had been more than pleased at finding her once again and everyone had been friendly—everyone but Stephen. Why must her thoughts always come back to that disturbing man? Incomprehensible, moody, aloof. Useless to deny that for her the evening's enjoyment had been ruined from the moment when Stephen's sternly disapproving voice had ordered her to remove Alison's pendant from her neck. All at once, like a fragment on a tape, the conversation overheard in the vineyard came back to mind.

"She was crazy about him."

"But what about Stephen?"

If only she knew the answer to it all!

CHAPTER FOUR

TRACY TOLD HERSELF she was thankful that today was the start of the weekend, when for a time at least she could escape Stephen's swiftly changing moods. Still smarting from his unpredictable reaction in connection with the wearing of a mere pendant, she would like to show him there were some men who had an idea of how a girl should be treated, instead of roughly ordering one around, not even taking the trouble to explain his motives. She only hoped, she thought vindictively, that seeing her leave the house with Glenn might cause him to regret his high-handed behavior of the previous night.

Unfortunately for her plans, however, Stephen was working in the distant vineyards, clearing away the undergrowth from between the russet-tinged vines, when Glenn arrived at the house. He was promptly on time, smooth blond hair brushed carefully over his forehead. He wore a tangerine shirt, dark brown corduroys encasing his long legs, and he chatted brightly with Lucie, who appeared delighted to meet a young man who showed such a flattering interest in her rug-making activities. Soon he was escorting Tracy out to the gleaming late-model car waiting on the driveway below.

"Anyone would think," she teased as he saw her seated, "that you were thinking of going in for furnishings instead of glassware and ornaments!"

An elbow resting on the ledge of the open window, he bent his tall height until their eyes were on a level. "And how do you know I'm not? A hand-worked rug might come in mighty useful one of these days. That is—" he sent her a significant look "—if certain little plans of mine work out!"

Tracy laughed lightly, pretending not to catch the underlying meaning in his words. They swept along the narrow, winding path leading to the road ahead and as they swung out of the vineyard entrance, Glenn said, "I thought I'd take you over to see the folks, the ones who are putting me up in Auckland. I stayed with them before I left to go overseas and they've been keen to meet you ever since they saw you that day on the wharf. What do you say?"

"Anywhere suits me." *What you really mean is,* jeered the small voice in her mind, *anywhere that takes you away from Stephen Crane's infuriating authoritative ways.* Why must she persist in thinking of him, anyway? With an effort she jerked her thoughts aside.

"After that," Glenn was saying, "our time's our own. We could take a drive up to the Waitakere ranges—there's a massive dam up there that supplies water for the city." His gaze swept the misty blue outlines of the hills around them. "Up in the vineyards you must have seen plenty of bush already. Sure you don't mind taking in a bit more on the scenic drive?"

"It's all new to me. Tell me, whereabouts do your friends live?"

"That's where I'm lucky! It's a suburb no distance from here. They're some sort of distant cousins, actually. Don't ask me how it all works out, it's beyond me, but they've sure been good to me ever since I came to live in Auckland. Frank and his wife, they're a great couple, and Pam—"

"Pam?" Tracy's sea-blue eyes glinted laughingly up at him. "Is she young?"

"Uh-huh."

"Pretty?"

"Not like you. Good-hearted, though." He sent her a wide grin. "She insists on laundering my white office shirts."

"Like that, is it? Could be it's love?"

But he only laughed, swinging from the main thoroughfare into a quiet street. Soon they were turning in at the entrance gates of a ranch-styled home set amid sweeping green lawns. Picture windows overlooked the immaculately tended flower beds and clipped green hedges.

Almost immediately Tracy felt she was being welcomed as if she were one of the family. Surrounded by smiling friendly faces, she and Glenn moved into a spacious room crowded with people and after a few moments she gave up trying to memorize the names of the various acquaintances. There were so many cousins, aunts, friends of the family, while outside children chased one another around the laden peach trees and flowering shrubs that dotted the spacious lawns.

She gathered that the chunky genial man with a lined, tanned face was Frank Rorke, the father of the family. Apparently his interests were centered in two grown sons, both leading players in the district rugby team. His wife, Eva, was silver haired and comfortably plump, with a merry smile. She appeared to be not at all put out by the stream of weekend visitors, for whom she provided mountainous piles of sandwiches and seemingly endless cups of tea and coffee.

One girl in particular captured Tracy's interest. A few years older than herself, tall and well built, she had a forthright manner and would have been attractive, Tracy mused, had it not been for having such a prominent nose. She wondered why the stranger's eyes were fixed continually on Tracy and her escort.

"Here comes Pam," Glenn said suddenly as the tall girl with cropped brown hair made her way through the throng in their direction. "She's the one I told you about. A whiz on the tennis court! She's Auckland's leading woman player and now she's going on to contest the national tennis championships." He raised his voice above the soaring notes of a radio as the girl reached his side. "This is Tracy, Pam. I've just been telling how famous you're getting to be."

"Oh, you mean tennis?" She looked toward him with laughing gray eyes. "I'd rather shine at something useful, like you."

"Me?" He looked surprised. "What have I done?"

"Don't listen to him!" she appealed to Tracy. "I think it's fabulous being chosen by your firm to go overseas and study the markets there. I bet there were swags of older men with heaps more experience they could have picked for the trip. Do you know, Glenn hadn't been with the firm for more than a few months!"

"My press agent," Glenn said lightly, and turned away as he was hailed by a young man.

"I was the first one he told about the offer to go overseas!" The shining eyes, the ring of pride in the other girl's warm tones betrayed to Tracy an unmistakable depth of feeling. "He knows me so well, you see. He stayed here at the house before he went away to England."

Perhaps, Tracy mused, he likes her a lot, too. Hadn't he hinted about making plans for a home of his own? How lucky some couples were in their love affairs, with nothing to complicate their romance but just straight going all the way!

"Got to get going, folks!" Glenn took her arm as he shepherded her through the throng. "We're off to see what the Waitakere bush looks like at close quarters."

Everyone shouted farewells, and Pam and her mother came to the car to see them off.

"We'll see you again?" There was no warmth in Pam's flat tones. "Glenn said you were only here on a visit?"

"That's right."

The other girl averted her face, but Tracy had caught the telltale color that was creeping up the tanned cheeks.

So that's it. The thoughts chased one another through her mind. *She's in love with him and desperately afraid that I'm planning to take her precious Glenn away from her. That was why her mother looked at me in that odd way when we met. She was kind and welcoming, but just the same there was a worried look in her eyes. If only she and Pam knew how ridiculous it all is! He's no more in love with me than I am with him.* If only she could come right out and tell Pam the truth, take that stricken look from her eyes—but of course one didn't do such things. Anyway, it might all be merely her imagination.

"Goodbye! Goodbye!" While the two women stood waving the children ran alongside the car for a few yards, then fell behind.

Soon they were sweeping upward toward the blue hills that dominated the landscape in this western area of the city.

"They call this the scenic drive." Glenn was taking the

ever-ascending slope where the fronds of spreading pungas leaned from either side of the smooth roadway to brush the car as they passed by. Below the road level were steps cut in steep banks leading to homes hidden in thick bush. From the winding track Tracy looked down on waving green treetops, the feathery foliage of rimu, giant kauris, totara, with always the dense tea tree and native bush, and far below the blue sheen of the sea. At intervals the furry bodies of opossums were sprawled on the highway. "They're a pest up here," Glenn explained. "They're dynamite on native bush, eat everything in sight, but it's at night that they get killed—the car lights blind them as they try to cross the roads."

They swept around a curve of the scenic road to glimpse from the mountain ridge two great harbors, one on either side of the range. Then a little farther on, looking down the steep slopes Tracy caught a fleeting glimpse of a white track through the bush. "Look! There's a track!"

Glenn followed her gaze toward the narrow path snaking down to the gully below. "Like to have a look?"

"Would I!"

"Right! We can't park here, though; there's no room." He drove for some distance until he found a wider space between the highway and the bush-covered bank. "This should do it!"

They got out of the car and strolled back until they reached the entrance to the overgrown track.

"Come on!" Tracy ran on ahead, her sneakers making no sound on the thick fallen leaves underfoot.

"Hey, wait!" She could hear Glenn hurrying behind her. "You'll come a cropper if you don't slow up."

She took no notice, running on down the steep slope. throwing a laughing glance back at him, she failed to notice a long rope of black supplejack that trailed from towering forest trees overhead and barred her path. The next moment she stumbled and would have fallen headlong had not Glenn caught her in his arms. His grip tightened around her and she felt the beating of his heart against her own. Then his lips came down on hers with swift pressure. Unresponsive and unyielding, she felt herself stiffen.

Vineyard in a Valley

He released her gently. "What's wrong, Tracy?"

"Nothing. I—" In truth she didn't know why his light caress was all at once distasteful to her.

"Okay," he grinned penitently, blue eyes twinkling. "It won't happen again, if you watch your step—and I watch mine! It was just that you—well, it's been a long time since I've been close to you. Couldn't resist the chance of making the most of it. On the ship coming over you... didn't seem to mind."

"Well," she laughed lightly and hurried on ahead, "that was on the ship!"

But her thoughts were in a turmoil. Why did she mind now? Why had she changed in her attitude toward him? In all fairness it wasn't Glenn's fault. He was the same as ever, but she.... *It's that Stephen,* she told herself angrily. *He gets me so annoyed and het up that I never get a chance to think of anyone else. He puts everything else out of my mind.* Well, this was one day when she was free of his disturbing ways, his aloofness and disapproval. Today she would forget him.

Pausing, she waited for Glenn to catch up with her on the narrow track where there was room only to walk in single file. "You wouldn't think," she marveled, "that it would be so far to the valley. You can't even see the end of the track from here."

Indeed, as they went on the track seemed to curve endlessly through the filtered green gloom. Once a bush pigeon with a flash of iridescent blue went past their faces to alight in a kauri tree high overhead, and around them flew tiny fantails darting from bush to bush, so close that once or twice Tracy put out a hand as a tiny bird flew past.

"What's that?" She paused, listening, as a chime of bell-like notes fell crystal clear on the bush-spiced air.

"A tui. See him? The black bird with the white throat up on that high branch!" He threw an arm around her shoulders, his face close to hers, but Tracy pulled herself free and went on ahead. On and on.... Still they could see no end of the winding path. Then quite suddenly they found themselves in a gully where water rippled somewhere close at hand. Going forward, they came on a stream almost hidden by overhanging tree ferns and low-growing bush. Following the tinkling sound for some time, at last they dropped down to one of the punga logs with its stringy bark, that had fallen across the leafy ground.

"Tracy! There's something—"

At the sudden note of seriousness in his tone, she got swiftly to her feet. "Come on, I want to see what's around that next bend."

Resignedly he followed her lead. "As you say."

As they moved deeper into the bush, Tracy was conscious of the utter stillness. There wasn't even a bird song. They could be alone in the world, but thank goodness, she told herself thankfully, the thick green undergrowth held no poisonous snakes or dangerous wild animals.

Suddenly Glenn caught her hand. "Had enough?"

She nodded. "We may as well turn back."

"I wonder—" he was eyeing a trail that zigzagged up the bush-clad hill above "—if we could get back that way? It would bring us out nearer to the car."

"Is that how you're feeling?" Tracy laughed.

"Well—" he studied her with appreciative eyes "—I wouldn't mind carrying you out, but—"

"Let's give it a go! We can always come back here if it doesn't end anywhere."

He took her hand and they began their upward climb, pushing their way through twining creepers and dense green undergrowth. Sometimes for a time it was easy as they cut through clearings beneath the trees, then once again they were forced to stop at intervals to disentangle themselves from hanging vines and the long trailing black ropes of supplejack.

"You know something?" Glenn paused to extricate Tracy from the thorny clutch of a trailing bush lawyer vine. "Maybe it would be an idea to turn back?"

"No use!" she laughed. "We must have passed the point of no return ages ago. We'll be in sight of the road up on top soon."

But they weren't. Indeed, it seemed to Tracy that the higher they climbed the farther away they were from any sign of civilization. At last the thought that she had been loath to acknowledge could no longer be ignored. "Glenn, you don't think we've taken a wrong turning somewhere between here and there?"

His grin was forced. "That place where the path branched off in two directions—maybe we should have gone straight ahead."

"Just as well," she laughed a little jerkily, "that we're not somewhere in a real jungle instead of just the Waitakere ranges. All the same—" Her tone sobered as she remembered Lucie telling her of various tramping parties who through the years had become lost among these hills. Parties who at least were familiar with the walking tracks, whereas with she and Glenn.... But it was too ridiculous to think they could really be lost in the bush, so near to the popular scenic drive with its passing motorists.

Glenn seemed to echo her thoughts. "If only I'd been a boy scout I might have brought a compass along with me. As it is...." His voice died away uncertainly.

"As it is, we're lost," Tracy said. She tried to smile at his worried frown. "But I guess we may as well keep going. That way we'll be pretty sure to hit the road sooner or later."

"Just what I was going to say!" She had a suspicion that Glenn was acting with more confidence than he felt. "No need to be worried."

"We'll probably be laughing about this in an hour or two—" she glanced up at the sky where lowering gray clouds, heavy with moisture, hung overhead "—or wishing we'd brought our Windbreakers with us!"

They didn't speak much after that, both busy with their own thoughts. The swift darkness was already filling the gullies, throwing a purple haze over a dense bush where even if there had been tracks, it would be difficult to distinguish them.

To add to her discomfiture, Tracy's sneaker was wearing a painful blister on her heel, and at last she could no longer disguise her limping progress.

"You should have told me!" Glenn stared down at her sympathetically. "We've been hiking for hours. That does it, we may as well face it, we're good and lost! In another few minutes it will be really dark. All we can do now is try and find some sort of shelter, even if it's only tree ferns, and wait for daylight."

"Guess you're right!" She no longer particularly cared. All she wanted to do was to rest her aching limbs, wash her hot face and hands in water, sit down for a few minutes. "At least the stream's here." For they had come once more within sound of running water in the tree-lined gully. Perhaps, Tracy thought wearily, they had described a full circle in the way she had read that travelers often did when lost in the bush. Pushing their way through the bushes and ferns, they knelt on the mossy ground, plunging hands into the cool clean water, splashing it over their heated faces.

"Couldn't we just stay here?" Tracy said.

"You've forgotten the mosquitoes!" Glenn's fair skin was already marked red with welts from the bite of insects and Tracy was aware of a maddening itching on arms and legs.

"You've got a point there," she conceded.

Under the tree branches farther up the rise they were conscious of the hum of insects, too, but at least they weren't entirely at the mercy of the mosquitoes.

As they dropped down on the rustling leaves, Glenn caught her hand. "Sorry, Tracy," he said in a low tone.

"It's all right. It was just as much my fault as yours. It was my idea to come down the track. Remember? One thing—" she glanced up toward the spreading fronds of pungas overhead "—we've got something that looks like a big green umbrella up there. If only we don't need them!"

As if in answer to her light remark a drizzling rain began to fall, softly at first but gradually increasing until, although they shifted from place to place in an effort to find shelter below the dark foliage of tall trees above, there seemed no escape from the pelting raindrops that were now slashing down in sheets of water. Huddling close together because it was the only way to keep warm, shaken by violent shivering as time went on and the rain didn't abate, it seemed to Tracy incredible that she could be so cold after the heat of

Vineyard in a Valley

the day. And the rain—it wasn't just rain but a torrential downpour.

A shaft of lightning lighted up the bush around them, illuminating Glenn's pallid, wet young face. He looked utterly miserable and in spite of her own discomfort she felt a pang of pity for him. Although she knew he was longing to do all he could to help in the situation, somehow he looked so helpless. Now if it had been Stephen Crane, he'd have done something—she didn't know what, but something to make the position more bearable. But that's not fair, she scolded herself the next moment. Stephen was accustomed to bush country, he would be well versed in bushcraft and rescue procedure in the mountains, whereas poor Glenn....

Another shaft of light played over the bush.

"Don't worry, Tracy," Glenn murmured comfortingly, "I'll look after you!"

"I'm not frightened!" In spite of her brave words she shrank closer to him as the jagged illumination of forked lightning played over the trees and zigzagged through the darkness. Hadn't she read of trees being struck by this type of lightning? The next moment there was a shattering explosion, then peal after peal of thunder crashed and reverberated around the bush with a volume of sound that Tracy had never heard in any ordinary storm.

Drenched, shaken by long shivers that shook her from head to foot, never had she felt such utter discomfort. The constant slanting rain slashing down through the punga ferns above swiftly soaked their thin summer clothing, plastering their hair close to their heads, running down their faces until Tracy thought there couldn't possibly be anything more chilling and unendurable. Only they had to endure it, get through the long night somehow, as the slow hours passed in the wind and the rain.

Toward morning she must have dozed, for when she opened her eyes sunrise, in glorious streaks of rose, apricot and gold, flooded the eastern sky. Stiff in every limb, drenched, more cold than she had ever felt in her life, she lifted her head from the soaking ferns. Blessedly the rain had ceased, though drops of moisture on the bush all around her still remained from the night's deluge.

"You awake, Tracy?"

"Heaven knows how I slept, but I must have, near morning...."

"Me, too. Thank the Lord it's over." He got to his feet, his slacks and shirt clinging damply, exposing the thinness of his shoulder blades. A racking cough shook him. "Sorry," he gasped when he could speak, "not used to this exploring lark! Thing is," he went on after a moment, "do we stay here and wait until someone comes along to collect us? The car's up on the road, so they'll guess what's happened. Or do we make our own way back, if we can?"

She glanced up into his face, thinking how deathly pale he looked. Then another fit of coughing shook him. "Maybe we'd better keep moving," Tracy suggested. "If only the sun would hurry up and get some warmth into it, but that won't be for a while yet." She bent to wring the rainwater from her soaked skirt. Chilled, shivering, they made their way through the dripping undergrowth until Glenn paused, shaken by an almost constant cough. "It's nothing. An old complaint that comes back on me sometimes—not often, though."

"Only when you're nearly drowned and worn out with exposure?"

"That's about it." He gave a twisted grin.

"Wait! Did you hear something?" They strained their ears, listening. There was no mistaking the sound of voices and it was clear that rescuers, though not in sight, were not far distant.

"Hello!" Tracy called in her clear young voice. "We're here! This way!"

"Hi!" Glenn's attempt to shout ended in another burst of distressing coughing.

A minute went by, then to her vast relief she caught the unmistakable sound of someone crashing through the undergrowth. The unseen voices were louder now, closer at hand.

"This way!" Tracy called again, wishing there were some way in which she could identify their position. She glanced swiftly around her, but could see no particular landmark, so she went on calling. At length two figures appeared, plunging through the tea trees and making their way toward them.

"Hi there!" Tracy's pleasure in being discovered was tempered with dismay as she recognized one of her rescuers. Stephen! Stupid of her to mind who it was who had found them, yet she hated him to find her in this disheveled state of mud-smeared hair and drenched clothing. She hated him even more the next moment, for there it was again, that insufferably indulgent look. Wouldn't you know he'd be gazing at her in that way, just as though she'd got lost in the bush on purpose!

Suddenly everyone was talking at once except Glenn, who was once more caught helplessly in the grip of a fit of coughing. The ranger, a sinewy-looking man with grizzled hair and an erect carriage, whipped a flask of brandy from his pack and held it toward the younger man.

"This is what you need! You, too." He handed a small glass to Tracy.

"Yerck!" She made a face. "I hate the stuff."

"Drink it!" She raised her eyes to Stephen's stern glance. A moment later she had to admit that the spirit warmed her through and through.

"We thought we knew the track," she said, "but somewhere or other we went astray."

"Then the storm broke and the rain pelted down," Glenn gasped.

"Here." The ranger threw a rug toward Glenn. He held another toward Tracy, but Stephen took it, throwing it around her shoulders. "Better put this around you, then it's back to the house for a hot bath and a rest."

The ranger went ahead with Glenn while Tracy and Stephen followed. The silly part of it all was, she mused, that the path branching off was the right one. It all seemed so easy now in the daylight that it was incredible to think she and Glenn had managed to lose themselves so close to the roadway. She tried to say as much to Stephen, but his warm clasp was putting everything else out of her mind, making the most ordinary conversation difficult. When they reached the original track he dropped back.

"You go on ahead, Tracy, and I'll keep an eye on you." The warmth that had stolen through her veins was fading and she was shivering once again. She said faintly, "How was Lucie? I hope she wasn't too worried about me last night."

"She wasn't too happy, what with the rain and the storm," came the deep tones behind her, "but I told her I'd make a search first thing in the morning and that brightened her up a bit."

Tracy's bare feet plodded on. "I don't know how we could have made such a stupid blunder—"

"Easier than you think!" For once he forbore to lecture or ridicule her. "You're not the first ones to wander off the track up in the Waitakeres, eh, Alan?"

"You can say that again!" The ranger glanced back over his shoulder. "You can be within half a mile of the main road and lose your sense of direction in a few minutes. It happens."

The journey seemed endless and although the sun's rays had a slight warmth Tracy shivered and pulled the blanket closer around her shoulders as she climbed the steep, fern-encrusted slope. Slipping in the mud, she grasped at bushes on either side of the track to steady herself. She was determined not to miss her footing and land herself, a wet and muddy bundle, in Stephen's arms. At length they reached the tree-covered summit and there was the curving road above, with cars waiting on the grass at the side of the highway. As the party emerged from the dripping bush Tracy waved a hand to Lucie, and the expression of anxiety in the young-old face changed to one of delighted relief.

Nearing a small Morris car where a girl sat at the wheel, Tracy recognized Pam, whom she had met at the house in Avondale. Could it have been only yesterday? Through a fog of fatigue, Tracy took in the set, pale face. Why, Pam looked as if she were the one who had been out all night in the hills in an electrical storm!

Glenn, too, was approaching the small car, but a fit of coughing made speech impossible, and Pam turned an angry face toward Tracy. "You've done this to him. He's never ever supposed to get chilled or wet, and now—"

"But I had no idea—"

"How could you? He wouldn't tell you that he's subject to bronchial trouble. He told *me*, though!" The low tones were hoarse with emotion. "*I* wouldn't have let it happen—" She flung a glance of such contemptuous rage toward her that Tracy stared back in astonishment. Before she could make a reply Pam leaped from the car and went hurrying toward the distraught figure standing in the roadway.

Stephen, catching up with Tracy, raised inquiring dark brows. "What was all that in aid of?"

"Nothing! Nothing! If I won't be glad to get home!" Home! She hoped he hadn't noticed the slip or that if he had done so he would put it down to her state of fatigue.

"Won't be long now!" Stephen said. "Here she is, Lucie, safe and sound."

"Oh, thank heaven you're all right, child! All night I was worried sick about you, out in that frightful storm. Steve kept telling me there was no need to get in a panic, that you'd be all right."

He would, Tracy thought ungratefully. She sank down in the back of the car, huddled in the blanket. "Goodbye!" She leaned from the window and waved back toward the ranger. "And thank you."

"That's okay, miss. All part of the job!"

She caught a glimpse of Glenn's drawn features as the other car shot past, to be lost almost at once around a curve of the winding road ahead. Then the ranger took off in his jeep in the opposite direction and Stephen headed back at speed for the western valley.

It was surprising, Tracy found, how quickly a steaming hot bath followed by a meal of sizzling bacon and eggs could make life seem so different. She rested throughout the morning, falling into a deep sleep that lasted until the sun was high in a washed blue sky. In the sunlight the chill and misery of the long night faded and she ceased to blame herself for the incident. It often happened, the ranger had told her. No blame could be attached to Glenn or herself. She wondered if her companion had suffered any serious aftereffects from damp and exposure. Glenn's racking cough sounded as though it would take more than a meal and a rest to dispel. She decided to wait until the evening before she rang through to the Rorkes' house to inquire as to his health.

When she got through to the telephone number, however, it was Pam who answered the call. Her cold, angry tone left no doubt that she was determined to foil any attempts by Tracy to speak to Glenn.

"He can't come to the phone," she said flatly. "He's feeling far too sick."

Tracy decided to ignore the other girl's ill humor. "I'm sorry to hear that. Is it... because of last night?"

"What else could it be? What else could you expect?" All at once the cold tones were red-hot with resentment. "Thanks to you, he's ill! I hope you're satisfied!" The sound of a receiver being slammed back in its cradle echoed in Tracy's ear.

Well! As she went on down the hall, Tracy's brief flare of resentment died away. She remembered Pam's warm championship of Glenn's business acumen, her anxious glance toward Tracy almost as though she were afraid of Glenn's shipboard acquaintance. Once again the thought came to her. *She's not sure how he feels about her, but she's in love with him, so crazy about him that knowing we were lost in the hills all night had driven her into all manner of wild fancies. Then today, the sight of Glenn's obvious distress made her so frantic that she had lashed out at the one person she blamed for the man's state of ill health. She's got some stupid idea,* Tracy mused, *that he's wrapped up in me. All that misery for nothing! If only I could get through to her that she's got everything all wrong.* But how could she make the other girl realize that, a girl who already regarded her as her enemy?

AFTER SO MANY LETDOWNS regarding employment at the vineyards Tracy was determined to be at her desk at the office the following morning. Now that the season's picking was over, Stephen would no doubt be making an effort to catch up with the backlog of office work, and that was one place where she felt confident of not making a mess of things as she seemed to have done so often, even if through no fault of her own, during her short stay.

A trim figure in a cool dark shift, hair caught severely back from her face, she was already sorting out a pile of receipt forms when Stephen came running down the steps and entered the dim coolness of the underground office.

"You've made a start here? Good on you!" As the hours flew by and they worked side by side at the big desk, she was conscious of a feeling of deep content. Was it because at last she felt confident in her work, her surroundings? Or just that Stephen, absorbed in the work in hand, treated her differently? The tensions between them fell away and instead there seemed born a sense of real companionship. The only thing was—she glanced toward the dark head bent over the outspread account books on the desk—it was slightly dampening to have to admit that although Stephen treated her differently in working hours, the difference seemed to consist of regarding her more in the line of office equipment. She could be a robot typist really, or just something that efficiently worked the adding machine. Whatever the reason there was no doubt that down here in the big cool room, personal feelings were shelved, and certainly the endless piles of paperwork were gradually being diminished to neat, orderly small lots; orders and correspondence now filed under their appropriate headings.

On two occasions during the week Tracy had endeavored to contact Glenn by telephone to inquire as to his health. The first ring had brought Mrs. Rorke. She at least seemed to bear no grudge toward Tracy for the night Glenn had spent in the open. He was having a week's rest in bed, the older woman told her, under doctor's orders. Maybe she'd better not bring him to the phone. Maybe next week. She would tell him Tracy had rung to inquire about him.

On the next occasion on which she rang the house, Tracy was unlucky enough to hear Pam's voice at the other end of the line. Resisting a cowardly impulse to replace the receiver, she said, "Oh, Miss Rorke—Pam—I just wondered how Glenn is getting along?"

"He's getting better, thank you." Tracy guessed that others in the house were within earshot, for the voice at the other end of the line was carefully polite. "I'll pass on your message to him. Who shall I say rang?"

"I think you know who it is!" This time it was Tracy's turn to have the last word—not that she wanted to continue with this childish verbal warfare. How ridiculously Pam was behaving, blaming her for everything, even her wild imaginings! When Glenn was up and about again everything would be straightened out and surely that would put the other girl in a more pleasant mood.

It was a further week, however, before Glenn himself contacted Tracy. Stephen took the call and held the receiver toward her. "For you." His cool contained tone held no clue as to his thoughts. "It's your friend Glenn Roberts."

"Hello! Are you all right now, Glenn?" she asked, a note of urgency in her tones.

"Of course I am! Just fed up with not seeing you all this time!" With relief she realized that his racking cough had left him. "Doctors! They give the orders and boy, does the family around here see that they're carried out! Stay in bed! Do this! Eat that! Don't get up! Don't go out! Am I glad to be my own boss again! Only good thing about it all is that it's almost the weekend again. You did say you work up there in the vineyards?"

"Oh, yes, I do." She was conscious of Stephen who could hear everything she said in the lounge close by. "I'm giving a hand with the office work, nine to four-thirty."

"Office work? I thought you said you had a driving job? Piloting Lucie around, wasn't it?"

Oh, yes, I do that, too. Stephen... lets me off for that."

"Stephen? Oh, I get it. The boss? Well, we won't need to worry about him, seeing the weekend's coming up, I've been thinking—you haven't seen Rotorua yet. Why don't we take a day trip down there? It's one of the top tourist attractions in the country—you've got to see it, and soon. What do you say?"

"I don't know." She was taken by surprise. "I'll have to see.... Look, I'll ring you back later. Okay?"

"All right, but make it 'yes.' Got to go, someone here wants the phone. Bye now."

Tracy couldn't understand why she felt this queer diffidence about asking Stephen for the weekend off duty. If Lucie didn't require her services, she would be free, so why was she hesitating? Better find out right away, then she could keep her promise and let Glenn know the outcome.

"That was Glenn," she said unnecessarily, returning to the lounge where Stephen was reading a newspaper spread out before him, and Lucie, crouched on the floor, studied a craft magazine.

"How is he?" Lucie inquired absently, still absorbed in her reading.

"Oh, he's all right. He was pretty sick after that chill he collected up in the Waitakeres, but he's over it now. He wanted me to ask you—" She jumped as a dark shape moved in the half-light of the terrace. "Whatever's that?"

Stephen glanced out to see the wrought-iron railings, where a small furry animal was poised. "That's just Blackie. He often appears about this time of the day. It's a wonder you haven't seen him before." Striding to the kitchen, he returned after a moment holding an apple, which he threw out to the darkening terrace. "There you are, mate!" Greedily the opossum pounced on the fruit, sinking sharp teeth into the crisp apple, then as silently as he had come, vanished into the night.

"You were saying?" Stephen sent her his bright inquiring look that seemed to Tracy to convey so much more than his words. Or was she merely imagining a significance where none existed?

"Oh, just that Glenn wants me to take a day trip with him to Rotorua on the weekend. That is," she added hastily, "if you don't need me to help with the driving, Lucie?"

"Oh, no, dear." Lucie emerged from the colored pages of her magazine to glance across at Tracy. "Steve will be here and he can take me anywhere I want to go. I can't think of anything special on this weekend, anyway."

"I see." Tracy couldn't understand why she wasn't more pleased, excited at the prospect of a trip to the famous volcanic wonderland. She turned away. "I promised I'd ring him back."

"Tell him he'll have to make it some other time!" Stephen's decisive tones brought her up with a jerk.

"But why?" She gazed toward him in perplexity.

"It doesn't happen to fit in with my plans...or yours."

"Mine?"

"And Lucie's." He grinned. "They're putting on a wine-growers' conference at Tauranga on the weekend—it seems a good chance to take a run down the coast, around the cape, too, and see how Cliff's getting along. Lucie's longing to show you some of the country, and the east coast beaches are her favorites."

Lucie shot up into a sitting position, her magazine sliding to the floor. "We're going down to see Cliff? But that's wonderful! All this time I've been wondering when we could take a trip down to the hospital, but you've been so busy with the picking. Now—"

"Now things are different! We'll take off from here early," Steve went on in his peremptory way, "go right around the cape, break the trip at Opotiki on the way down. We'll have a look at the gorge on the way back."

"You'll love the journey!" Lucie turned to Tracy with shining eyes.

She laughed. "All right, all right, you've convinced me." Deep in her heart she knew she was only too ready to be convinced. For somehow the thought of the trip south to Gisborne was infinitely more inviting than Glenn and Rotorua. The reason being, she assured herself, that this way she would see much more of the country, go farther afield.

It was more difficult to convince Glenn of her reason for not being able to accept his invitation. The telephone that so clearly revealed nuances of feeling told her that he was deeply disappointed in her decision.

"We can go another time," she told him, "if you like."

"But I don't like! I've been looking forward to this for days, showing you around Rotorua. Why the devil," he asked petulantly, "does *he* have to shove his oar in?"

"Stephen didn't set the date for the wine makers' conference," she argued.

"Hey, whose side are you on?"

"Yours, of course." But even as she said the words she was trying to subdue a flicker of excitement that was stirring in her. "You could go just the same. Why don't you take Pam instead?" she suggested mischievously.

"She's been there, dozens of times. She wouldn't want—"

"Are you sure? Ask her and see!"

"But don't you see, Tracy, it's *you* I want—"

"I'll see it with you another time, I promise. How's that?"

"Okay, then." He gave in with a bad grace.

"I'll see you when I get back." She seemed powerless to subdue the sheer happiness that colored her tone, no matter how much she tried to hide it.

CHAPTER FIVE

EVEN LUCIE WAS UP EARLY in readiness for the start of the journey south. When Tracy came hurrying down the steps, cool and attractive in a lotus-pink shift and cork-soled sandals, the older woman was already waiting on the pathway below, a slim and youthful-looking figure in a trim green pantsuit.

"Morning, Tracy!" Stephen's dark head was thrust from the car window as he brought the Holden to a stop beside her. Leaping from the vehicle, he reached a hand toward her modest overnight bag. "I'll take that!" Swiftly his glance ran over the young eager face, alive with anticipation, dark hair glinting in the sun and swinging around her shoulders. "You look as though you're looking forward to the trip!"

"Am I!" There was an unspoken message in his glance that sent her pulse racing, but he only said, "That goes for me, too!"

A little faintly she murmured, "Camping gear?" For in the open trunk of the car she glimpsed a folded tent and sleeping bags. A cardboard carton held a smoke-blackened billy and a fat-encrusted pan. "Will we need that on the trip?"

He was stowing Lucie's luxuriously fitted traveling case beside the rolls of sleeping bags. "Only if we happen to strike trouble somewhere in the never-never."

"We always take the camping gear with us on a long trip," Lucie explained, arranging a scarf over her carefully coiffured golden hair. She waited until Tracy seated herself, then slid into the car at her side. "The road's pretty rugged around the cape, a long way from civilization in some places. Besides, we've got oodles of room!" She laughed her tinkling laugh. "It's ages since we've had to camp on a motor trip, but still, you never know your luck!"

"Mmm." Tracy was studying the road map outspread on her knees. "According to this Gisborne seems an awful long way away, over three hundred miles if we take the route right around the cape. How far are we planning to go today?"

Stephen slammed the car door shut, then came around the side of the vehicle to drop into the driver's seat. "No hurry. We'll take our time over it, seeing—" his swift sideways grin quickened Tracy's lively feeling of anticipation "—we happen to have an overseas visitor with us! We'll put up for the night somewhere along the coast before we hit Opotiki. That way you'll be able to have a look at Ohope Beach." Slipping dark sunglasses across his eyes, he started the car.

"Oh, Steve," Lucie suggested eagerly, "let's stay at Whakatane! Remember that place right on the beach where we stayed last time? The Sea Shell, wasn't it?"

"If you like." His tone was indifferent and a little of Tracy's hidden excitement died away.

The last time, she thought with an odd little pang, would be the occasion when they had taken Alison and Cliff with them on the tour that had ended so disastrously. She jerked her thoughts aside. Why must she always remember Alison? This was *her* day, her chance to see something of an unfamiliar, unspoiled country. Distant hills rose against a pearly sky shading upward to a translucent blue, the air was diamond clear and beside her sat Stephen, his profile outlined against the blue. Tracy felt her heart rise on a surge of sheer happiness.

Bill came to the pathway to see them off. Tracy, turning back over her shoulder to wave, could see him looking after the car until a fern-lined bend hid the stocky figure from view. They swept along the shadowed bush track where long fronds of black-veined tree ferns and pungas, still damp from the heavy overnight dew, glittered in the morning sunshine. Presently they swung onto the main road and before long they had left the western districts behind and were turning into the smooth lanes of a southern motorway with its long center avenue of ornamental bamboo, pink and white flowering oleanders and bronze flax blowing in the wind. On either side of the highway rose cleared green hills where closely barbed sheep fences marched up to meet the horizon. Then all at once the motorway came to an end, merging into a road that cut through green farmlands where sheep and cattle grazed.

On and on, with always the sheep hills rising around them, but now rocky outcrops were visible on the high slopes and at the roadside the banks rose, red and copper colored, the clay raw from recent cuttings. Drifting cloud shapes broke the sun's glare and the breeze blowing through the open windows was cool and fresh.

They crossed the low-lying area of the Hauraki plains where farm boundaries consisted of giant bushes of toa-toas, their tattered plumes bent to the breezes. Occasionally small settlements, a garage, a post office, a general store, loomed into sight and were swiftly left behind. Then they entered the rocky canyon of the Karangahake gorge, where unseen waterfalls tinkled among the ferns and high sheer walls enclosed them in a somber gray world.

"All this district was a thriving gold-mining center once," Stephen told her. She followed his gaze over a swing bridge spanning the turbulent waters far below toward the ghostlike remains of an old battery rising among the tea-tree clad hills. Then they were taking the long palm-lined street leading to the old gold-mining center of Waihi.

"Now this town I like!" Tracy spoke her thoughts aloud as they sped through wide streets of the colorful city of Tauranga with its modern ranch-style homes and citrus and passionfruit plantations. There were sparkling modern stores and shopping complexes, dwellings ablaze with flowering shrubs and bright flower borders. At intervals roadside entrances bore notices: Fruit for Sale. Peaches, Passionfruit, Tamarillos. Tracy's gaze moved to the glittering waters of the harbor where vessels were moored at the wharves. "Those look like overseas cargo boats."

He nodded. "They're loading timber, mostly for Japan. It's getting to be quite an industry around here—bring your swimming gear?"

Vineyard in a Valley

She smiled up at him, sea-blue eyes alight. "What do *you* think? Somehow I got the idea I might be needing it. There must be some wonderful beaches around here."

"You haven't seen a swimming beach until you've seen the long white stretch of the Bay of Plenty," he told her. "We'll pull in there and grab some lunch, then you'll see what I mean!"

She saw what he meant a short time later when, after following the coast road for some miles, they drew up at the side of the road in the shelter of towering macrocarpa pines. "Come on," Stephen suggested, "and we'll take a look at the beach."

"But I don't see—" She gazed around her, mystified.

"You will, once we're over the sandhills!" He took from the car Lucie's picnic basket and beach umbrella, then the three crossed the strip of long dried grass and made their way over high drifts of blowing sand.

"I only hope it's worth all this effort," Tracy said laughingly, her sandals sinking into the soft sand at every step. The next moment she reached the summit of the sandhill and drew an appreciative breath. "But I guess it is at that!" For framed in the branches of giant windswept pohutukawas clinging to the shore, the long stretch of clean white sand stretched away mile after mile into the misty distance. A seemingly endless sweep of sand, lapped by white-crested waves breaking gently on the vast shoreline. She was struck by a sense of remoteness. There was nothing, no one along the whole length, only the gulls wheeling and soaring overhead, their cries mingling with the soft wash and drag of the surf. It was a blue day, she thought—blue sea, blue sky, an unforgettable day!

She became aware that Stephen was regarding her closely. He seemed to read her thoughts. "Told you! How about a dip to wash away the car travel and the dust?"

"I can scarcely wait!" Indeed the prospect of the touch of that cool bracing sea was infinitely inviting.

"Come on, then." Together they raced headlong down the high drift, gaining momentum with every step until at last they slid to a stop on the firm sand below.

Still breathless, Tracy scanned the empty shoreline.

"Changing sheds?" Stephen was thrusting the point of the gaily striped beach umbrella deep in the sand while Lucie, having caught up with them, spread a rug in the shade. "There are some farther along the beach, but what's wrong with the trees? There's no one about for miles!"

Tracy laughed. "I suppose." It was too good an opportunity to be missed, and anyway, she mused a few minutes later as she reached the shelter of thickly growing flax and tall tea tree growing beyond the sandhills, what did it matter? It took only a few moments to slip from her garments, pull over her shoulders the straps of her brief white swimsuit. She made a mental vow to take in some sun-bathing, if only to blend in that unattractive line where the apricot-tan of her low-cut shift met the other hemisphere pallor.

When she emerged from the shelter of the undergrowth he was waiting for her; strong, virile, so deeply tanned that it was difficult to distinguish between the dark swimming trunks and the mahogany-tanned skin.

"Was I long?"

He shook his head, a glint of appreciation in his eyes. "Even if you had been it would have been worth it!"

Tracy didn't ask him what he meant. She was content to make her way at his side as they climbed the slope where marram grass and tall lupins held at bay the drifting sands. Then all at once the patches of green came to an end and she winced with pain as her bare feet touched the scorching sand.

"Wow!" she gasped. "It...hurts!"

"I bet it does! You're not used to it. Well, there's only one way to fix that!" Before she could argue the matter he had picked her up in his arms and, ignoring her wild kicking and her cries of "put me down," strode purposefully over the drifts and down the other side to the beach below. Lucie, seated in the shade beneath her beach umbrella, glanced up in surprise. "For heaven's sake." She took off her sunglasses the better to observe them. "What on earth's happening?"

"Just doing a good deed!" Steve gazed back at her with blandly innocent eyes. "And getting no thanks for it! There you are, Tracy." He set her down gently. "It's cool enough here where the tide's been. Let me know if you get any more transport problems!"

"I'll be all right." Her voice was muffled, for in truth the unexpected encounter had shaken her more than she cared to admit. What was it about him that disturbed her so? To cover her confusion she said quickly, "Aren't you coming in for a swim, Lucie?"

The other woman flashed her young-old smile. "With this expensive hairdo? No, thanks, dear. It looks marvelous, though, the sea." Doubtfully, she eyed Tracy's shining dark strands. "With you it's different, and if *you* don't mind—"

Tracy smiled and shook her head. Somehow today she didn't mind about anything. It was that sort of a day, and she intended to make the most of every moment of it. Turning, she met Stephen's amused glance. "Like me to carry you down to the tide and throw you in?"

"No, thanks, but I'll beat you in!" In a flash she was off to a head start, her bare feet moving lightly over the gleaming wet sand, but long before she reached the shower of foaming spray he caught up with her. She felt the warm clasp of his hand and a tingle of excitement shot through her. The shimmering sunshine splintered into fragments, the sparkle on the tossing waves glinted, and all at once she was part of it all—the movement and color and exhilaration of the golden day.

"Come on!" They ran on, splashing through the shallows, diving into the green glass wall of a curling breaker to emerge a moment later, breathless, laughing, their hair plastered wetly around their faces.

The next moment a great wall of water surged toward them and Tracy went down in a thundering shower of spray, she got to her feet, spluttering, laughing, blinking the saltwater from her eyes. Then with one accord they struck out beyond the tossing spray toward the blue green depths beyond. Tracy could see Stephen's dark cap of hair as he moved ahead, his effortless crawl taking him swiftly through the water. Once she lost sight of him, but swimming underwater he suddenly appeared at her side. Then, turning, they gave themselves to the waves, sweeping far on the crest of the thundering green comber until it splintered on the shore in a mass of foam. Again and again they plunged their way through the tossing spray, feeling the drag of the surf beneath their feet, to come surging in on a wave, breathless and laughing, as the comber swept them into the sandy shallows.

At last, becoming aware of Lucie's beckoning hand, Tracy pushed the dripping curtains of black hair back from her face and made her way through the swirling foam-flecked water. Stephen followed her and, glancing back over her shoulder, she giggled. "With your hair plastered down like that, you look like a seal—swim like one, too!"

"And you—" His warm smiling gaze appraised her, the young attractive lines of her figure, the blue eyes with their wet dark lashes. "Well, I'll tell you another time."

She laughed on a throaty, happy note. "I'll remind you."

Silly words, meaningless words, yet she knew she would treasure them long afterward.

Against the immensity of sea and sand the beach umbrella made a gay splash of color. Tracy dropped down beside Stephen on the warm sand, letting the sun dry the saltwater on her skin, conscious of a delicious sense of relaxation. Lucie's sandwiches of smoked schnapper were delicious, or was it just that everything seemed larger than life, better than ordinary, on this most sparkling of days? They washed down the picnic meal with flask tea from picnic cups that Lucie had provided, throwing the crusts to the hovering gulls. Tracy was smoking a cigarette, idly watching the blue smoke drifting past in the sea breeze, when Stephen rose and came toward her, a towel hanging from his hand. "Better watch that sunburn—it pays to take it in small doses!" Somehow for once, just for once, she didn't resent his words. Or could it be that she was bewitched by the deep feeling of relaxation following the swim, the warm touch of the sun so that she didn't mind his advice, or the fleeting caress of his fingers as he threw a towel around her shoulders.

"One last dip?" She nodded, leaping to her feet, and together they ran down to the breakers once more, plunging into a froth of foam, conscious once again of the bracing touch of the sea.

Vineyard in a Valley

When they returned to the picnic spot, Lucie had folded up her rug. Slipping her scuffs from her feet, she held them toward Tracy. "Put these on, dear, while you go up to get dressed. They'll save your feet."

"Thanks." Gathering up her garments, Tracy made her way over the sand dunes. Soon she was dressed, running a comb through her damp unruly hair, adding a touch of gleaming pale pink to her lips. In a few minutes she made her way back to the beach, conscious of a feeling of utter content, excited yet relaxed, that was no doubt the result of sun and saltwater... and Stephen! She had got him into her blood somehow along with the tossing waves and the golden sunlight.

Back in the car the wind tossed her streaming hair behind her ears and soon the wet strands were dry again. Not that it mattered, she mused. What was wet hair compared to the incomparable delight of swimming underwater, glimpsing the white shells through the crystal-clear tide, feeling the surge and drag, the swift sensuous pleasure of being carried on that blue green wall of surging water?

They ran along the winding road in sight of the endless coastline, then all at once they were heading toward a modern town lying in the shadow of towering cliffs. As they moved into the busy shopping area Tracy eyed with amazement the great outcrop of rock rising in the heart of the business area that dominated the scene.

"I've never seen a town like this," she murmured.

"You won't see another Whakatane," Stephen told her in his deep tones. "We'd better book into a motel for the night." He was drawing up beside a block of modern apartments not far from the beach. "This do?"

Lucie nodded agreement and they went into the attractive foyer with its trailing tropical plants and greenery, where Stephen arranged for a one-night stay. Tracy realized with a sense of relief that both Lucie and Stephen had apparently forgotten their earlier intention of staying at the Sea Shell.

She found the bedroom she shared with Lucie to be surprisingly attractive, with its soft carpeting, dark gold decor and diffused lighting. Close by was a luxuriously fitted bathroom and beyond, a small model kitchen.

"But we won't be cooking here," Lucie murmured, eyeing the snowy electric range. "Steve's taking us out to dine at the Reef tonight. It's a restaurant out at the Whakatane heads."

The soft summer dusk was falling when later the party went out to the Holden, standing not far away in the well-kept grounds of the motel. Although Stephen said nothing to Tracy beyond a prosaic "hop in," his eyes said something else—there was no doubt that he approved of her appearance, and indeed she quite liked it herself. The cream dress with its gold-linked belt was simplicity itself, but it definitely did something for her. Maybe it was the sun that lent her skin this glowing look. Or could be it was just plain, old-fashioned happiness! She'd never had a holiday like this, with everything so different, unexpected. Whoever heard of a great rock in the business center of a main street? Who would have dreamed a few short weeks ago that Stephen could ever look at her... like that?

It wasn't far to the heads. Once out of the main street with its views of fishing boats and harbor, they came in sight of the headland. Sparsely settled, it consisted of sun-dried paddocks and grazing sheep and cattle. Out at the heads, on a high rock at the entrance to the river mouth, a bronze statue of a Maori girl stood poised, outlined against the gold and apricot of a blazing sunset.

"She looks," Tracy observed in her warm soft voice, "as though she's just about to dive into the water!"

"Who? Oh—" Stephen glanced toward the graceful curves of the feminine figure "—that's Wairaka. That rock she's standing on happens to be quite historic, sacred to the Maori people. They say the karaka trees that still grow in its slopes are planted from seed brought to New Zealand in the canoe that brought the first Maori settlers here when they migrated from somewhere out there in the Pacific."

"Really?" Tracy's eyes were wide with interest. "But who was she, the Maori girl?"

"That's quite a story." Lucie took up the tale. "She was the daughter of Toroa, the captain of the historic canoe. You see, when they arrived here they paddled up the river for a short distance, then they beached the canoe in a cave.

Vineyard in a Valley

When the warriors went ashore the women were left to guard the canoe and as the tide came in it began to float away. Wairaka—that was the captain's daughter—she was pretty high rank—she wouldn't ever have to paddle a canoe, but when it started to drift away she called out—I don't know Maori, but anyway it meant, 'I will acquit myself like a man,' then with the other women she paddled the canoe back to shore."

"Quite a girl," Tracy murmured. "She was really a bit ahead of her time, don't you think? A sort of early women's lib?"

"Oh, definitely," Stephen agreed. "Nowadays she looks out at the big game fishing boats putting out to sea—here comes one now!" They watched the launch with its twin outriggers, a flag fluttering at the masthead signifying the day's catch, as it shut off the engine and glided over the water. "Here's the Reef!"

They moved into a softly lighted restaurant where strains of music mingled with the dull roar of the surf. The waiter led them to a corner table where wide windows looked out to the harbor entrance and the reef beyond.

On Stephen's advice Tracy selected from the menu a truly New Zealand meal. A seafood cocktail, toheroa soup, succulent New Zealand lamb accompanied by roasted kumeras, and a luscious dessert featuring the sharp-sweet flavor of tamarillos. She didn't know why all at once she was content to take his advice instead of trading insults with him. It seemed that happiness made one disinclined for battle. It was easier tonight to drift on this lulling tide of contentment.

"One more local product—" Stephen beckoned to the wine waiter. "Have you any Valley Red?"

A few minutes later the waiter returned with a bottle of wine bearing the familiar label and Tracy raised her glass to Stephen's. "A good trip!" Fascinated, she watched the tiny diamonds rising in the goblet, marveling that from the terraced vineyards in the bush-sheltered valley had come this sparkling matured red wine with its unique blending of flavors.

"Care to dance?"

She nodded, and rising from the table went with him toward the cleared area in the center of the tables. Soon they were merging into the music and movement, and that, too, she thought dreamily, formed a part of the enchantment. Certainly they matched each other perfectly—steps, height, everything. Once again she was aware of the magnetism flowing between them, powerful as an electric current.

They were seated once more at the table watching an outsize pumpkin-colored moon climb over the sea, when two men stopped beside Steve.

"Hey, Steve! Thought it was you!" The swarthy looking man in his early thirties was accompanied by an older man so resembling him in features and coloring that Tracy took them to be father and son.

"Joseph! Take a seat!" Stephen shook hands with the strangers, then made the introductions. "Joseph Selevich junior and senior. My Aunt Lucie and—" he turned toward Tracy "—this is Miss Cadell. She's staying with us at the moment back at the valley." As the two men seated themselves at the table, Stephen said to Tracy, laughter glimmering in his eyes, "These two characters happen to be winegrowers, too. Just too bad their second-rate northern varieties don't compare with our wines from the valley!"

The short dark-haired man grinned. "What went to his head, Miss Cadell, was winning the gold medal last year for his Pinot Chardonnay at the International Wine Exhibition, top wine of the show—"

"You must admit, though, Joe," his father argued, "that we've got to hand it to Steve. We're all in on that win. It proved there's a place for the small wine maker in New Zealand as well as the big business concerns."

Joseph Junior was eyeing the wine bottle in its wicker cradle. Raising his thick black brows significantly in Tracy's direction, he said with a grin, "I see he sticks to the home product!"

"Nothing but the best!" Stephen agreed in his laconic tones.

"We'll thrash that one out later at the conference," the older man said with a chuckle. "I hear you're making a big name for yourself, Steve, with your Valley Pearl. We're trying out something along the same lines. There's no doubt it's the classical whites we've got to concentrate on in the future if we're going to put our wines on the map."

Stephen nodded. "Now you're talking!"

The older man swung around to Tracy. "Don't you agree, Miss Cadell?"

"Oh, yes, yes," she stammered, jerking herself from thoughts of Stephen and trying to hide her obvious inattention.

"What do you think of this wine business, anyway?"

She laughed. "What gets me is this sort of intense personal dedication to the vineyards. You know? And those gorgeous exotic names—Palomino, Pinot, Gamay—but of course it's all new to me."

"You're learning fast. Bet you could tell me which vines turn yellow in the autumn and which change to red?"

She wrinkled her nose at him. "Not that fast."

"Forget it," Joseph Senior said with a smile. "Anyway, you'll be able to see for yourself in a few months."

A few months. In spite of herself a deep sigh escaped her and the winegrower caught her downcast glance. "You're thinking you might not be around the valley to make a personal inspection of the vines, eh?" he teased.

Tracy shrugged slim shoulders, forced a smile. "Who can tell?"

She brought her mind back to Stephen's voice. "Sorry I've got to take off with these blokes, but someone's got to talk some sense into them at the conference. Okay if I drop you and Lucie back at the motel, Tracy?"

"Of course." Her light tone belied her feelings, for underneath she felt a stab of disappointment. A stroll along the cool sandy beach would have made the whole day complete. Just the two of them, she and Stephen. Somehow they never really managed to get things out into the open. There were so many matters that puzzled her, questions she wanted to ask him, but there never seemed to be any opportunity. For although they worked side by side in the vineyard office, there he was very much her employer. Today in the relaxed holiday atmosphere everything seemed different, and out there on the silvered sands....

Back at the motel a short while later, she watched as he turned the car and swept away. There was an odd little ache in her heart. If he had stayed, if they had been alone together, would he... would she? She turned away with a sigh. Oh, well, there would be other times, other nights.

She was still thinking of him when later she went to her room, moving silently in the darkness because Lucie was already asleep in the twin bed.

Now that she had succeeded in changing Stephen's opinion of her maybe they could start afresh. There was no doubt but that he drew her with a dangerous magnetism against which she had no defense. Trouble was, she thought, rummaging through her overnight bag in search of pajamas, that she never really knew him—disturbingly attractive to her one moment, antagonizing her the next—but always someone you couldn't forget. A thought crossed her mind and she wondered if Alison had found him so. According to the conversation overheard among the women pickers in the vineyard, her cousin had found him more than attractive, but that was mere gossip. Nothing that concerned her; how could it? She pushed the disturbing thought aside.

WHEN SHE ARRIVED at the sun-splashed breakfast table he was waiting there, looking fresh and alert, and undeniably pleased to see her, she thought with a telltale leap of the heart.

"Lucie's not coming down to breakfast; say's she'd rather sleep in today instead. How did it go, the conference?" Tracy asked, sipping a glass of pineapple juice.

"Oh, it wasn't bad, although I could think of a lot of things I'd rather have been doing last night—" For a moment their glances locked. "General opinion seemed to be," he went on his laconic tones, "the same as I think myself, and that is that the day of any old wine for New Zealand is passing. Folk are getting wine minded, more choosey. They know what they want and they expect to be able to get it in the local product. It's the classical whites that are what we'll all have to go in for. The Auckland area

Vineyard in a Valley

will never produce quality reds, that's for sure. Thing is, in Auckland we've got a white, not a red-wine climate."

Absorbed in his subject, he looked alert and clean-cut and so utterly heart stirring that Tracy's mind slipped away from the matter so near his heart to other more personal reflections. When he was like this, intent on his work, confiding to her his dreams of the future, everything else was forgotten and she could study him to her heart's great satisfaction, the dark intelligent face, the vibrant tones with their ring of vitality and purpose. Was that what stirred her so about him?

Soon they were on the road, moving through the small picturesque township, then swinging inland to the coast and the "sunshine town" of Opotiki. As they left the settlement behind a sign at the bridge bade them Farewell and Good Luck. A nice gesture, Tracy reflected, but as it happened the good luck had already come her way, for hadn't she succeeded in overcoming Stephen's initial misconception of her capabilities? And somehow all at once that seemed the most important thing in the world! As if that wasn't sufficient good fortune, here she was heading along a winding road where every bend disclosed a fresh vista of the countless bays.

As they moved along the highway Tracy reflected that the coast road was far removed from the ordered highways she had known in Auckland. Through the tangled branches of windswept pohutukawas on the cliff edge she caught glimpses of campers' tents and caravans nestled among bush at the water's edge; fishermen were surf casting on the rocks. In this rugged country, wild and remote, it was as if they had left civilization behind.

The metal roads were now steep and winding, but Steve was a competent driver, she'd give him that. Slowing to a crawl, he waited while two Maori boys mounted on the broad backs of their sturdy rock ponies, sugar sacks for saddles, thundered past on the loose metal. Around the next bend they came suddenly on a milling herd of black cattle, and Stephen pulled over to the roadside as the Maori drover and his dogs moved the stock over a narrow, one-way bridge.

Then they were climbing up, up into the clouds, it seemed to Tracy, swinging around bends over dizzying heights to drop swiftly down precipitous slopes. At length they cut inland to the rugged sheep-farming country. Blackberries grew wild in the paddocks and the dried grass at the edge of the highway was splashed with the pink and white of belladonna lilies. Tracy raised her instamatic to her eyes to snap a cluster of steers that were gathered around a drinking hole bulldozed in a paddock and ringed with cabbage trees.

The vehicles they passed now were jeeps and Land Rovers, great transporters with their long trailers tightly packed with sheep. As they swept through a small Maori settlement a group of smiling dark-eyed children trudging along the road home from school raised chubby hands in greeting. A little farther on two stockmen seated on the rails of a tea-tree corral waved their battered Kiwi hats in salutation as the Holden swept by.

Then they were once again in sight of the sea, and soon Stephen guided the car off the road and over a narrow path overgrown with fern and bracken that led toward a sandy inlet. The twisted roots of gnarled pohutukawas clung precariously to the bank and thick sand below was crisscrossed with the footprints of gulls. Tide and weather had piled heaps of driftwood high along the shoreline and the far end of the bay was hidden in a cloud of spray.

"You may as well take in a bit of the coast at firsthand," Stephen told Tracy. He was guiding the dust-covered car down a rough track bulldozed down to the sand below. Soon they were out of the car and seated on a great bleached fallen log, while Lucie poured tea into plastic cups from her ever-ready thermos.

It was heavenly, Tracy thought, to feel the fresh invigorating sea breeze tearing at her hair after the dust of the road. Afterward she and Stephen strolled along the beach beside the breaking waves and Tracy paused to pick up a strange shell.

"It's so hot and sticky." She glanced up to meet his gaze. "Could we—I mean, have we time?"

"Just what I was going to suggest! So what are we waiting for?"

Vineyard in a Valley 343

No need to put the thought into words, that shimmering sea was infinitely tempting. On this occasion Tracy had no need for instruction in the matter of changing sheds on remote New Zealand beaches. The thickly growing creepers and dense bush nearby provided a natural shelter and it took only a short time to slip from her clothing and pull on her swimsuit, still damp from yesterday's dip.

After the heat of the journey, the sharp cool touch of the crystal-clear water was a delight. Together they moved through the waves, striking out for the depths ahead, then turned to follow the long line of the shore. After a time Tracy fell far behind. A good swimmer, she knew herself to be hopelessly outdistanced by Stephen's effortless crawl and her strokes were flagging. Stephen, however, slowed his pace to her progress and at last they emerged from the water, moving toward the log where Lucie still sat in the shade of overhanging trees.

"You still won't change your mind about a swim?" Tracy asked her lightly.

Lucie pulled a face. "Ask me on the way back. I just can't let Cliff see me looking too frightful!"

Cliff. With a little shock of surprise Tracy realized that she had almost forgotten the object of the long motor journey. It's *my* holiday, she told herself, that's why I'm enjoying the trip so much! Not just because Stephen Crane is here with me—well, not altogether, honesty made her admit. Not *just* because of him!

Reluctantly she got back into the car. She thought she could never have enough to satisfy her of bathing in these crystal-clear bays with their water and sense of remoteness.

"I wish we didn't have to go." She was speaking her thoughts aloud as Stephen reached a hand toward the ignition.

"You know something, Tracy?" His repeated attempts to start the engine brought no response, merely an ominous unfamiliar whirring. "I've got an idea you might get that wish!"

"Steve!" Lucie glanced across at him in alarm. "You don't mean to say we're stranded here, miles from anywhere?"

"We are, you know!"

"But surely you can do something to get her going?"

"I'll keep trying, but if the trouble's what I think it is...."

He broke off and, getting out of the car, lifted the hood and peered inside. "Hmm—just what I was afraid of! Seems to be a wire hanging loose. It looks pretty hopeless. We'll have to have a replacement pump before we can get her moving again. Just a small job, once you get a new pump!"

A worried frown lined Lucie's forehead. "But, Steve, this place is miles from civilization. All the same, there might be a village somewhere around, some tiny settlement with a local garage...." Her voice died away uncertainly.

"A local garage mightn't have one in stock! No—" he slammed down the hood "—we'll just have to wait until someone comes along and ask them to get a message through to the nearest garage. If they don't happen to have an electric pump they'll be able to phone through and get one sent out from Gisborne."

"But it might take ages—"

He shrugged. "May be able to get it tomorrow, if we're lucky! Good thing we threw in the tent and sleeping bags." He turned toward Tracy. "Ever done any camping out?"

She shook her head. "I've never had the chance."

"Well—" something in his deep intent look sent that silly illogical happiness of yesterday surging back "—there's got to be a first time! Looks like you're about to try it out in just about the most remote place you could pick on—how's the eats department, Lucie? Anything left?"

She shook her head. "Not a crumb. But I've got some tea," she added hopefully, "and a tin of condensed milk, cigarettes. *And* that old black billy you always carry in your car will be around somewhere."

"What more could you want? Come on, Tracy, give me a hand to find a place to pitch the tent! That clearing under the trees should do it! Looks like there's a creek running alongside, too—couldn't be better!"

Soon he was hammering tent pegs into the hard ground while Tracy knelt to sort out the supports. She couldn't help thinking that although Lucie might be horrified at the delay, for herself being forced to camp out in a clearing by the sea was all part of the delight of this unexpected holiday. Why pretend to herself that her feeling of elation had nothing to do with Stephen? Why deny the growing intimacy between them? Endlessly she found herself thinking of him—that was, when she wasn't stealing secret glimpses at the dark profile at her side. Driving, swimming, sunbathing—it was all a part of this deeply satisfying content that made the days seem divorced from ordinary living, shot through with a sparkle as golden as the endless brightness of the "sunshine coast."

I'm in love with him. I love him. That's why I'm only happy when he's near me, why I love to listen to him, look at him, even just to think about him. In love with a man who regards me as a not incompetent secretary, if he thinks of me at all.

But it didn't matter. Today was hers... and tonight. In this mood of high excitement, that was enough.

CHAPTER SIX

"OH, WELL," Lucie murmured philosophically, "what I always say is that what can't be helped must be enjoyed!" Her expression lightened as she gazed along the length of the shoreline. "And these east coast bays are known as the best places ever for collecting driftwood. Look, Tracy, there's oodles of it here, piled up all along the banks!" She wandered off along the sand, pausing at intervals to pick up pieces of bleached timber, whittled by tide and weather into grotesque likenesses of birds and animals. A twisting serpent, a llama's long face, a deer's head.

All the time Tracy and Stephen swam in the clear water, splashing each other, running up to sunbathe on the warm sand where heaps of seaweed bore witness to a recent summer storm. Again and again they plunged back into the sea, cool and invigorating to skin still glowing from the rays of the sun.

They were seated on a fallen log, idly watching a cargo boat on the horizon, when a lone figure appeared around a point of the bay. As he came nearer Tracy realized the stranger was a cheerful-looking Maori fisherman, his tattered trousers rolled above copper-colored knees, a sugar sack roped over one shoulder. With a friendly grin he paused beside them. "You picked a good campsite here! Staying long?"

"That depends." Steve picked up his shirt from the log and fishing in a pocket, offered the stranger a cigarette from a crumpled packet. "We had a breakdown," he went on in his laconic tones. "Petrol pump just packed up. What we want now is to contact someone going through to the nearest garage to pick up a part. What do you think of the chances?"

"Pretty good." The dark face broke into a friendly grin.

"My brother Stan, he's going over there tonight, he'll make a call at the garage for you."

"Great. If he could just ask them to send us back a new petrol pump for a Holden, will you? If they don't have one in stock—"

"He'll have it," the Maori fisherman grinned. "I've never seen him stuck for one of those yet. My brother Stan, he'll bring it along in the morning!"

"That's darned decent of you—"

"No trouble. How about tucker? I've got a bagful of fish here. Nice and fresh, eh?"

"We wouldn't say no!"

The fisherman extracted a silver schnapper from the sugar sack, then slung the bag over his shoulder. "This fellow big enough for three of you? Better get going now. See you in the morning with the pump. You like to bet on it?"

Stephen laughed. "I'll take your word for it! Thanks a lot!"

The stranger lifted a hand to his forehead in a gesture of farewell, then moved away. They watched him disappear around a point of the bay. "He must live somewhere around here," Tracy murmured.

Lucie said, "What luck, his brother going to a garage tonight! Anyway, I don't care now about the breakdown. It's fun, isn't it, camping out in this lovely bay!"

"I'll go along with that!" Stephen's gaze lingered on Tracy, dark hair clinging wetly to her head, face and limbs touched with faint color from the sun's warmth. "How about you, Tracy?"

"Me?" She pushed aside a curtain of wet hair and smiled up at him. "It's all new country to me!" But in her heart she knew that the experience would have meant little to her, had not Stephen been here to share it with her. Especially as right at this moment his eyes held a warm message for her, a glance that if it hadn't been so fantastic, she might have interpreted as "make no mistake, I love you." Too much sun, she chided herself, it was giving her ideas. Breathtaking, impossible, *wonderful* ideas!

A little later, feeling cool and refreshed, she went with Stephen as he broke off dead branches of fragrant tea tree from tall trees growing near the creek. Heaping the firewood over crumpled sheets of newspaper thrust between two great rocks on the sand, he held a match to the paper and soon the crackling flames rose high. Fat spluttered in the smoke-blackened frying pan as he lowered into the smoking pan the filleted fish.

It was, Tracy decided a short while later, quite the most enjoyable outdoor meal she had ever tasted. The tea that Stephen made from the creek water boiled in the billy was strong, hot and, even if slightly smoked, delicious. Afterward they sat around the glowing embers, watching the last rays of the sun fade in a splendor of tangerines and reds splashed over the horizon. Soon nothing except a primrose glow remained, fading up into the blue, pricked by faint stars.

They all strolled along the darkening beach, the sand cool now to the touch of bare feet. Then as they returned to the camp fire, Lucie stifled a yawn. "I'm beat. Think I'll turn in."

"You've got the flashlight out of the car?" Stephen asked.

"Yes, thanks. How about you, though, Steve?"

He shrugged carelessly. "I'll doss down in the car."

"Well, good night, then...." She hesitated. "It's awfully quiet here, isn't it? No one around for miles. I'd feel a lot happier if you two were somewhere around. You won't wander too far away, will you? It's... kind of lonely somehow, once it gets dark."

"Don't worry," Tracy said with a smile, "we won't be far away."

Swiftly trees and bush around them were transformed into dark smudged shapes, a shower of stars was pinpointed against the soft dark violet blue of the night sky. It was very still, the only sounds the gentle murmur of the waves washing softly on the shore and the eerie cry of a native owl in the branches of a tree overhead.

Tracy dropped down by the firelight, hands clasped around her knees, and Stephen tossed a fallen branch of tea tree across the glowing embers. As the leaping flames soared upward she caught his glance fixed on her face and her heart quickened.

"Tracy!" In a few strides he had reached her, dropping down at her side. "This is something I've been wanting for

Vineyard in a Valley

a long time." Trembling, she felt herself responding to the swift and urgent pressure of his lips on her own.

Through the wild excitement racing through her veins she became aware of his deep soft tones. "You know how I feel about you, don't you?" Placing a hand beneath her rounded chin, he tilted her face until she caught the dark brilliance of his eyes. "You must have guessed?"

She raised a finger to trace the dark contours of his shadowed face. "I thought," she said very low, "that you could scarcely stand the sight of me. That day at the wharf when I first arrived here... and afterward...."

His soft laugh answered her. "If you only knew." She felt his arms tighten around her. "I've loved you right from the start, Tracy." A surge of happiness was lifting her high on a tide of elation. "I always will."

She stirred in his arms and for a moment there was a silence. The dancing flames threw into relief the strong dark face she loved—yes, *loved*. So this was love, all this time when she'd thought she'd hated him! This was what it was all about! Dreamily she stared into the firelight. "You know something?" She sent him her wide and friendly smile. "I got so mixed up about— Oh, you know, what happened before I ever arrived here. You'll laugh at this, but do you know once I had this crazy idea—I got to thinking that you and Alison—"

"Alison!" A log crashed, sending up a shower of sparks and with a sinking heart she saw the muscles tighten around his jaw. Oh, why must she spoil everything with her mention of the other girl? He wore his closed look again and when he spoke his voice was curt and clipped, almost guarded. "Look, my sweet, there's something—"

Her heart fell with a plop. But just for once she refused to let Alison spoil the radiance of the night, just as intentionally or otherwise she had so often done in the past. All that mattered tonight was that she was alone with Stephen at last. Alone and in love, in love, her heart sang.

Swiftly she put up a finger, held it against the firmly cut lips. She smiled appealingly into the stern face. "Do me a favor, will you, Steve, please? Tell me about it another time?" *Any other time,* her heart whispered.

"Maybe you're right!" The somber expression fled from

his eyes and all at once, in one of those lightning changes of mood, he was gay again. "It's too good a night to spoil with confessions, and there's always tomorrow. Right now—" As though it were the most natural thing in the world she moved back into his arms. Roughly he caught her close and the next moment his kiss, the intoxication of his nearness, blotted everything else from her mind.

The heady excitement still possessed her when, much later, she made her way to the darkened tent. Lucie's even breathing indicated that the older woman had long been asleep. Tracy wondered how anyone could waste time in sleeping on such a night. Lying in her sleeping bag, hands crossed behind her head, she lay staring into the darkness. How could she not have realized before the reason for her growing feeling of excitement, her sense of heightened perception? Stephen—she found infinite pleasure in just being near him, hearing him speak, watching the changing expressions of the dark mobile face. Even though there were times when withdrawn, distant, sardonic, he was beyond her understanding, it made no difference. She only knew she loved him, and always would. The miracle was that he loved her, too. And there was time ahead, time for love, for getting to know each other better, straightening out all those stupid misunderstandings that had bedeviled her in the past. Her thoughts went off at a tangent. How foolish of her to have worried so about Alison, to have allowed the other girl to throw a shadow over her happiness, even for a moment. She had other, more important matters to think about. Even, perhaps—her breath caught on a wave of longing—a lifetime of shared happiness.

IN THE MORNING Stephen was dashing a billy of creek water over the camp fire, douching the glowing coals to gray ash, when the Maori acquaintance of the previous night appeared around a point of the bay.

From the tent opening Tracy watched Stephen stroll along the beach to meet the other man. "Hi there." She caught the beloved deep tones. "Hope you've got some good news for me. How did you make out last night? Manage to get a message through to the garage?"

"Better than that! I've got the pump you wanted!" The stranger drew from the sack roped over a muscular shoulder an electrical replacement pump.

"Great! How much do I owe you?" As the money changed hands Tracy heard Stephen say, "How about a cuppa? I can soon get the fire going again."

"Thanks a lot, but I've just had breakfast. Gotta get going now. A good trip!" With a parting wave of his hand he strolled back the way he had come and soon the barefooted figure vanished around the rocks.

Soon Stephen had fitted the replacement part to the car, sleeping bags were rolled up, the tent folded and the camping gear stowed in the back of the car together with piles of driftwood, stones and shells that Lucie had collected during her short enforced stay at the remote bay. Before long they were on the road once again, following the dust-choked highway with its narrow bridges and sheep—threaded hills; passing vast sheep stations where homesteads were set among towering shelterbelts and the mellow red of woolsheds gleamed among tall macrocarpas.

Presently they pulled in at the entrance to a carved Maori meeting house and Stephen explained to her the symbolic meaning of the intricately carved scrolls, the significance of the crossed center poles where small squat figures gazed down at them from iridescent *paua*-shell eyes. Bemused with her newly discovered happiness, Tracy was scarcely aware of what he was telling her of ancient Maori lore. She was far more conscious of other, more important matters. The message in his eyes when he looked at her that signaled a secret "I love you." The new note of tenderness that tinged his tone. Surely Lucie must sense the feeling, strong and warm, almost tangible, that flowed between the other two. You only had to look at Stephen to know that he, too, was radiantly happy. It was there in his eyes, the timbre of his deep baritone, singing a song as he put the Holden into low gear and they climbed the hilly roads where yellow dust rose behind them in a cloud.

Soon they were speeding along in sight of the coast once more. Stephen pointed out to her the remains of an old whaling settlement, the gigantic pots still lying near the beach. At Te Puia they paused for a hotel meal and a bathe in hot mineral springs with their picturesque outlook on the Pacific.

Then as they neared Gisborne the high hills on either side of the roadway were cleared and sheep grazed on lush green pastures. Soon they were passing great plantations of tobacco, followed by undulating acres of maize crops. At length the road skirting the sea brought them to Gisborne, a colorful city with its clean wide streets and modern stores with wide attractive display windows.

"They've got a new post office now," Lucie told her. "The old one was demolished in the last quake."

Tracy nodded. She was back in her own private dream, so much in love, she admitted to herself, that she scarcely cared what Lucie was saying. It was sufficient to know that Stephen was here at her side, the center of her world. She mused that she would always think of Gisborne with pleasure. A lovely city with its masses of flowers, giant hydrangeas covered with blossoms in pinks and mauves and blues; flowering oleanders in city streets and suburban gardens. She would remember it for what the trip around the cape had brought her, the love of a lifetime!

THEY PULLED IN at the entrance to a block of modern apartment buildings with adjoining restaurant, and while Lucie and Tracy waited in the pleasant foyer Stephen went to the office to arrange the booking.

A softly spoken Maori girl led them along a carpeted corridor toward an attractive unit where dark peacock-colored furnishings contrasted with the stark white of the paintwork. In the bedroom shared by the two women Tracy crossed to the windows and, throwing them wide, stood looking out over clusters of red-roofed houses and winding rivers to the high, sheep-dotted hills beyond.

A little later, feeling delightfully refreshed after a cool shower, she slipped into a crisp lemon pantsuit and went with Lucie to the courtyard where Steve was wiping the dust-smeared windscreen of his car.

Soon they were moving through suburban streets, taking a bridge that spanned a wide river, then sweeping up a winding road that led them over sun-scorched hills where sheep were dotted as thickly as confetti and all around was the brooding stillness of the country.

All at once a low white building swept into view and they turned into the entrance gates of Cook Hospital, moving past green lawns and flower beds. A smiling young Maori nurse's aide wearing a pastel-pink smock led them through a pastel-tinted ward and out to a porch where sunshine streamed through wide glass windows over a bed. A young man lay propped on pillows, one leg extended high on a frame held with pulleys. As the party came through the opening he turned a pale face toward them, his expression of idle interest changing to one of delighted surprise as his brother strode forward.

"How are you, mate?"

"Steve! Good to see you!" He gripped the outstretched lean brown hand.

Tracy had a brief thought that even the thick drooping black mustache couldn't quite conceal the shy, vulnerable look of the young face. The eyes were a clear gray, Steve's eyes without their sardonic glint. Honest eyes. He was the sort of man, the thought came unbidden, who would fall a willing victim to Alison's glittering charm.

"Hi, Lucie!" Cliff grinned up at his aunt. "Nice of you to come all this way to see me—"

"I wouldn't have missed the chance for the world!" The soft brown eyes misted. "How are you feeling now, Cliff?"

"Pretty good. I look okay, don't I?"

"Oh, you do, you do! A bit pale, that's all. But your back?"

"Coming along fine! So is the leg. They tell me the breaks are healing up as good as gold. I'll be on crutches any day now and after that I'll be out of here in no time, thank the Lord!" His curious gaze moved to Tracy, standing quietly in the background. "Why didn't you tell me," she caught his whispered remark to Lucie, "that old Steve had fallen for—"

"Oh, sorry, Cliff," Lucie murmured apologetically. "This is Tracy. We brought her along with us on the trip. I should have told you—I did mean to write to you, but somehow I put it off and so much has happened since—" She stumbled, caught herself up and went on in a nervous rush of words. "She's staying with us at the valley for a while."

"Tracy Cadell." Stephen's tone was expressionless. "Alison's cousin."

For a moment a shadow of pain clouded Cliff's gray eyes, then he smiled. "Tick, tick, tick, it's all coming back. You were the girl who was coming out, from England—correction, the girl who *came* out here, for the wedding?"

"That's right." Tracy's voice was perfectly composed, but inwardly her heart was crying wildly, *not Alison's wedding—my wedding! Mine and Stephen's!*

"I guess—" Cliff looked away, passing a tongue over his lips "—they put you in the picture, Steve and Lucie, about what happened down here before you arrived?"

"Oh, yes." Tracy was aware of a loaded silence, then Cliff was speaking again.

"Alison—she told me about you—"

"What did she say?" Tracy inquired lightly.

He shrugged slight shoulders. "Nothing much, actually. Just that you were a funny conscientious sort of kid, always trusting everyone, believing everything you were told—"

"Tracy," Steve broke in in his vibrant tones, "is helping out with the office work at the valley. Don't know how I'd get along without her now—"

"Now that I've let you down, you mean?" Cliff's tone was low and strained.

"I didn't say that."

"No need. Talking of the office—" Cliff turned an anxious face toward Tracy "—tell me, has there been any mail for me, by any chance, from a firm called Smith & Galway?"

Before she could make an answer Stephen cut in. "It's okay. I've fixed all that!" His voice tightened. "You won't be hearing from that outfit again."

"Whee!" Cliff relaxed against the piled pillows. "That's one worry off my mind. If you only knew—"

"Forget it!" At Stephen's taut and forbidding tone, Tracy glanced up at him in astonishment. Lucie, in an obvious effort to divert the course of the conversation, delved into her flax bag and produced a wrapped fruitcake. "For you, Cliff—"

"Gee, thanks a lot, Lucie!" He placed the cake in his bedside locker. "They feed us pretty well here, but they don't exactly go in for homemade cakes, not like you make, anyhow. Oh, by the way—" his tone was carefully controlled "—there hasn't been any other mail for me, by any chance?"

"From the islands, you mean?" Tracy was aware that Steve was wearing his dark angry look again, his mouth a hard line. It seemed that today his brother was in for a share of the chilly treatment he had once handed out to her. "Were you expecting any?"

Cliff glanced aside. "No, no, just a thought—how was the trip down, Miss Cadell? Enjoy it?"

"Tracy!" she corrected him in her soft, warm tones, aware of the effort it must have cost him to repeat that particular name with all its painful associations. "Did I ever!" Her face was alight with enthusiasm. "It was just about the most exciting trip of my life. We followed the road around the cape—fabulous!"

"I know, it's breathtaking, isn't it? Those views—we did it all just a while ago...." Cliff's voice altered and a spasm of pain crossed the young face.

Lucie was once again delving in her capacious Maori bag, extending a bundle of papers. "There was some mail for you, Cliff, all these mountaineering magazines—"

He made a wry grimace as he took the packet from her hand. "Insult to injury! Thanks, anyway Lucie."

"I was going to post them on to you, but Steve said we'd be making the trip down to see you soon, so I held on to them— Oh, goodness." The soft brown eyes were anxious. "You don't mind about them? I mean—"

"I know what you mean." The boyish face relaxed in a teasing grin. "It's okay, Lucie. It's all in the luck of the draw! And I can still take an interest in climbing, you know, in my quiet way." For a moment the light tones were tinged with bitterness, but the next moment he was smiling again. "I'm not giving the game away yet, you know." At her look of disbelief he added laughingly. "Oh, not the high peaks, the record breakers. They're not for me, not now, but I've got another idea. How would it go, I asked myself, if I had a bash at writing a book on climbing? I've got plenty of stuff to use, swags of photos. Who knows? My modest experience in climbing New Zealand peaks might come in handy for some of the overseas climbers who come over here. I could give them a few pointers on mountain safety and rescue. Could be it would be interesting to them, at any rate. What do you reckon, Steve?"

His brother didn't answer for a moment. The dark intense face was lost in thought. "Should work out! It's worth giving it a go! At least the market in that line isn't too overcrowded!"

"What he really means—" Cliff turned toward Tracy "—is that to really grab the interest it would have to be a history of wine making. It's an idea, at that!"

"There's that little portable typewriter in the office," Steve suggested. "I'll send it down to you with the books and diaries."

"Great," Cliff said. "Shove it all in a box with the photographic stuff and I'll do the sorting out." He appealed to his aunt. "Lucie, you know where all my gear is?"

She nodded. "We'll see to it, Cliff. Anything else you want?"

"How about two good pins?" But he was laughing. "Apart from that, you mean? Anyhow, what's all the news of the valley? Picking all finished, I guess, or you wouldn't be here, Steve. Still got the same old bunch on the job?"

"Just about." For a second Stephen's lips lifted at the corners as he shot a swift and secret glance toward Tracy.

"How about the conference at the Bay of Plenty? You wouldn't miss that?"

"We didn't. Took it on the way here." The deep tones quickened with interest. "The change is on, that's for sure! With Auckland growers this year will be remembered as the start of something good in local wines. The rush is on to plant classicals, even a few good reds. A couple of years and New Zealand should be producing some splendid wines. One thing's for sure, the days of the cheap good New Zealand wines are over. We've got to concentrate harder, grow better grapes, forget about copying European names!"

"Funny that," Cliff murmured with a grin, "even though we plant the same vines the taste will be different."

"That's because of soil conditions."

"Listen to him!" Cliff appealed to Tracy. "Don't you get browned off with wine talk all the time? I don't know how you put up with it. He's dedicated to the vineyards, haven't you noticed?"

Tracy smiled her wide heartwarming smile. "I get that feeling, too." But her thoughts were busy. "I'm fascinated with wine growing, too. I want to learn more about it, the bottling, the selling angle, so that I can discuss it with Stephen, be a real help to him in his work." With an effort she brought her mind back to Cliff's pleasant tones.

"How do you feel about being in on the wine-making caper?"

She glanced down at him, blue eyes alight with enthusiasm. "It fascinates me! Honestly. From what I can make out it's a sort of..." she hesitated, "personal thing."

Cliff grinned back at her. "Mystique? You've got something there!"

She laughed. "Something like that. The first day I came to the vineyards the big purple grapes were simply bursting on the vines. It really got me. I think it's a wonderful idea, replacing so many of the common grapes with the classical vines. Even if it does mean waiting a while to get results, it would be worth it in a few years when—" All at once she realized that Steve was listening intently and she broke off, adding after a moment in confusion, "I get a bit carried away sometimes. I guess to me it's all so new and different. But then, of course," she laughed lightly, "I have nothing to do with the hard slog out in the hot sun among the vines. I'm down below in a nice cool office."

"Funny," Cliff teased, "I had an idea—someone told me...something about you having a bash at the picking?"

"Oh, that." Once again she was conscious of Stephen's quizzical glance. "That was ages ago, when I first came to the valley and tangled with one of your local wasps. We didn't exactly hit it off."

"So I gathered. You're like old Steve." There was a teasing light in his eyes. "Two of a kind. Wine making never did a thing for me. I reckon it's one of those things you're born to. What do the old hands in Henderson say about it? 'Anything you do with wine making should be done with love.'"

Love. Tracy averted her glance, conscious of the faint pink that was creeping up her cheeks. Cliff, however, had swung around to face his brother. "How's about that classical white you've been experimenting with at the valley? The one you talked of pioneering? Wasn't it always your big dream to switch to all classicals?"

Steve said quietly, "Changing over to classicals means a hang of a lot more equipment, expense...." He shrugged broad shoulders. "Maybe I will—one of these days."

"But you—" the younger man broke off, looking discomfited. After a moment he went on in a low tone, "You mean you can't run to it. Not after Smith & Galway! I get it! Gee, I'm sorry about that, Steve."

"I said forget it!"

"Oh, Mr. Crane...." A smiling young nurse was approaching the bedside. With her twinkling green eyes and lively smile she was the type of girl, Tracy thought irrelevantly, who one would like to have around when lying imprisoned in a remote country hospital.

"Oh, Lord," Cliff groaned. "The visitors' bell. It must have gone ages ago!"

"I thought you hadn't heard it. Or didn't you want to?"

Something in the warm intimacy of that intercepted glance that passed between them told Tracy that the injured man had found some feminine consolation for his shattered love affair. She was young, no more than eighteen probably, with cropped red hair showing beneath her pink cap, a small square freckled face—as different a girl from Alison as one could imagine. But then perhaps Cliff had had his fill of sophisticated charmers.

Amid a chorus of goodbyes, messages and good wishes the little party left the sunny porch, moving through the ward with its many smiling Maori faces and out into the upturned blue saucer of a cloudless sky.

Vineyard in a Valley

It was later, when Tracy was perched on a high stool in the bedroom brushing out the long strands of her hair, that Lucie wandered into the room and seated herself at the writing desk, a picture postcard in her hand.

"Funny," Tracy's voice was thoughtful, "about those letters that Cliff spoke of, the ones from some special firm. I thought I handled all the mail that came into the office, but I don't remember seeing any by that name."

"You wouldn't, you know!" Lucie was searching through a drawer in search of a ball-point pen. "Steve would have grabbed them before you ever set eyes on them. The moment he caught sight of the name on the envelopes he'd have ripped them open and paid the money."

"Money?" Tracy turned inquiringly toward her.

Lucie sent her an odd look. "I may as well tell you. Seeing you keep the books at the office you'd probably come across it anyway. And it's not as though you're likely to go blabbing about family affairs to anyone we know. It's just that anyone local would recognize the name Cliff mentioned as a firm of moneylenders, and he was in with them pretty deep. I wouldn't have guessed how deep except that Steve told me all about it. He was afraid I'd give Cliff money to settle them. Not that he ever asked me—trouble with him is that he's far too good-natured, he always has been. He'd give anything away and money just slips through his fingers. He got through the capital his father left him ages ago. Those overseas climbing expeditions ran into real money. But he managed along all right with wages, that is, until he met Alison."

Lucie stared past Tracy, brown eyes dreaming. "He was crazy about her, right from the beginning. I don't think he'd ever really fallen for a girl before and he fell hard! Seeing she was so much better off financially than he was he seemed to think he had to prove himself to be on an equal footing, buy her the most expensive gifts he could think of—that orange Mini was one. And some of the jewelry he gave her must have cost the earth. There was one piece, a rare greenstone pendant that had once belonged to a Maori chieftainess. I can't even imagine what he must have paid a collector to obtain it. Poor old Cliff, he really got carried away with his big ideas. Once he climbed up on the merry-go-round he just couldn't get off. He made Alison the wildest promises of what they'd do once they were married, promises he couldn't possibly have made good. Then he put a huge deposit on an expensive ranch-style house. Of course in the end he lost that, too. When Alison discovered the truth of it all she was furious. No doubt that was one of the reasons why the wedding plans were all off! It's too bad for Cliff. He won't get over it in a hurry. Awful enough to be turned down by his fiancée...." Her voice trailed away and Tracy mentally supplied the unspoken ending: But to be disillusioned in the loved one as well!

Lucie's voice blended with her musing. "It was so hard on Steve—"

"Steve?" Tracy glanced up quickly. "What do you mean?"

"Why, don't you see? He paid out big money to settle all those debts of Cliff's. It means that now he won't be able to follow up his plans of changing over to classical wines, going in for personal named wines in a big way. It would mean equipment, endless expense. With classicals he'd have to keep the wine for four years before selling—one year in oak, three in the bottle. Just imagine the storage problem, and the cost of that alone! He'll have to make the move in the end, of course; his whole future depends on what's in the bottle that carries his name. It's just too bad that he can't afford to change over right now when the other growers all around are switching."

"I suppose." But on another level she was flooded by a tremendous sense of relief. So that was the reason why Stephen had been so incensed at her wearing Alison's greenstone pendant. To him it would be a painful reminder of his brother's long list of debts, money squandered on a girl who wasn't worth such sacrifices. Far from ever having been in love with Alison, he had for her cousin only contempt. Obviously he despised her aimless existence, her selfishness, her treatment of his brother. At last she understood the bitterness that had extended even to the strange girl who bore Alison's surname.

Vineyard in a Valley

Lost in her thoughts, she was scarcely aware of Lucie's incredulous tones. "Would you believe it? It's been here all the time, in my writing case! I must have zipped it in the pocket that last day. Honestly, I was in such a tizzy at the time I scarcely knew what I was doing! It's pretty stale news now, but if you still want it—"

"Want it?" Tracy was still away in her private dream, a preview of the future where she and Stephen worked side by side in the vineyards, extending the winery; over the years winning national, perhaps even overseas recognition, for their unique personal named wines.

"Don't you understand? It's the letter! The one Alison left for you when she went away! Only I couldn't find it all this time. Here it is, anyway. I'll leave you to read it."

After Lucie had gone, Tracy still hesitated, resisting an impulse to toss the message in the basket unread. A vague presentiment of disaster urged her to destroy it. For whether by accident or intent, somehow Alison had that unhappy knack of spoiling things for her. She always had done. The next moment she told herself not to be so stupidly imaginative, and slitting open the sealed envelope, she scanned the straggling writing.

Tracy dear,
  I'm in a frightful rush, just off to the airstrip to catch a plane back to Auckland where I'm joining up with a cruise ship going to the islands. By the time you read this I'll be oceans away, but I just wanted to let you in on a few things. You see, Steve and I...

Steve and I...Tracy's heart plunged and the words danced before her distraught gaze. What could she mean? It was a moment before the writing slipped back into focus.

...thought it would be better if I went right away for a while. Heaven only knows what wild story the others will cook up between them as a cover-up for your benefit. I can't see Steve broadcasting the story that he was crazy about his brother's girl, tried to get her away from him and sent Cliff crashing into an accident. But that's what happened.

Thing is, Steve and I—well, he told me last night that ever since the day he first set eyes on me, he's been crazy about me, can't live without me, and he's never going to give up trying to make me feel the same way about him. Everything would have been okay, but his brother had to walk in right in the middle of a big love scene, and did Cliff go to town! Not that I care now what he thinks! It was all a stupid mistake, the engagement. I was going to finish with him even if Steve and I hadn't felt this way about each other. But Cliff—imagine, telling me all those lies, making out he was wealthy and all that. Once you've met a man like Steve you don't think anymore about his young brother, and believe me, he's a lot younger in his ways than he looks!

Steve says that as soon as things have blown over a bit and Cliff's up and about again he's going to send for me, wherever I happen to be, and then it will be wedding bells for us both. But don't waste time waiting around for *this* wedding, Tracy, because I've no idea how long it will be before Stephen gives me the green light to go ahead. And whatever you do, keep all this to yourself. It's top secret.

Until I hear from Steve to come back to New Zealand, I'm staying on in the Pacific islands. Not a bad place to wait around in. Sorry about the bridesmaid thing and you having to come all this way for nothing, but you'll have had the trip out of it.

Will write later when I get an address. See you sometime. Excuse scribble, but my hands are a bit shaky.

Love, Ally

Ally. The old name they had used as children. Only they weren't children any longer and Alison had just a moment since smashed her world to fragments. The color drained from her face and she was shaken by an inner chill, a sickening sense of anguish.

Vineyard in a Valley

But surely you knew all along, a tiny voice echoed from the dark corner of her mind. *It was just that you wouldn't let yourself face the truth. Ever since that first morning when you got off the ship you've known there was something wrong. You tried to tell yourself it was because Steve despised Alison, but really it was because he loved her. Well, now you know.* Oh, yes, she knew it all—too late. *Stephen, Stephen... and I trusted you so, believed you when you said you loved me. How easy it was to make me believe, already halfway in love.* She hated him, no, admit it, she still loved him, in spite of everything! She was such a fool at hiding her emotions and there was still the long motor trip back from Gisborne to be endured. She must learn to disguise her real feelings, and fast.

It couldn't happen like this, she thought numbly. Surely she must have misread the meaning of the words. Once again she read the letter, knowing all the time that there was no mistake, that the swiftly scrawled sentences would be imprinted on her mind forever.

Vaguely she was aware of Lucie hurrying into the room. "Handkerchief—I always forget one—" Swiftly Tracy put up a hand to shield her ashen face.

On her way to the door Lucie halted, glanced back. "That letter from your cousin, was there anything special in it?"

With an effort of will Tracy forced her voice to a careless note. "Not really. Just... telling me what happened... saying she was sorry to have to rush away. She said she might come back one day."

Lucie looked surprised. "Come back? Here?"

"Oh, not for a while, but... later...." Each word was fraught with pain. With relief she realized that Lucie apparently was satisfied with her explanation.

"I shouldn't think she would," she remarked in a puzzled tone. "Not after what happened."

And that just goes to show, jeered the tiny voice in her mind, *how little you really know of Alison. Why, she wouldn't care about the past, she wouldn't care about anything. If there was something she wanted, she'd come right back here and take it! Even if it happened that what she wanted was... Stephen.*

It all came rushing back, the agonizing sense of betrayal,

the heartache and, in spite of everything, the aching hopeless longing.

"I think," she muttered in a thick unnatural voice, "I'll take a rest for a while. Not feeling quite the best. Don't wait for me at dinner. I'll give it a miss tonight."

"That's too bad." Lucie was all solicitude. "I get those frightful heads myself sometimes on a trip. It's the glare, you know, looking into the sun. That's why I always carry these tablets with me. They're really marvelous!"

Tracy was scarcely aware of the sympathetic tones. Obediently she swallowed the tablets Lucie handed her, sipped a little water from a glass.

"I'll leave you to it, then," Lucie said. "Sometimes it pays to skip a meal occasionally. Pity you can't see a bit more of Gisborne while we're here, but maybe you'll be feeling better in an hour or two."

"Maybe." If only her misery could be eased so swiftly. But the bitter anguish that filled her was beyond the power of Lucie's miracle tablets, beyond her own control. *I'll just have to live through it,* she told herself despairingly. *No one can help me. It's happened and somehow, somehow, I've got to go on.*

Like an animal crawling into a dark place in its pain, she drew the blinds, dropped to the bed and pulled the covers over her. If only she could stop the tears—but it was useless. Her face would be a mess, blotched and swollen. He'd think, he'd know—but still she couldn't subdue the shuddering sobs that racked her.

Hours later she dropped into a restless sleep to dream that she was back in the firelit darkness of a quiet beach back in Stephen's arms, conscious of the ineffable strength and comfort of his nearness, looking up into the dark face. The next moment she awoke and sickening realization returned with a rush. There was no future in that dream, she thought bleakly. If only she could forget!

She must have dozed, for when she opened her eyes again the bed opposite was empty and it was clear that Lucie had already dressed and gone down to breakfast. Breakfast! But she couldn't hide here forever.

Listlessly she peered at her reflection in the mirror. What a mess she looked! Stale makeup still on her face, rumpled hair due to tossing restlessly through the hours, and her eyes—the dark circles she could camouflage, but those swollen eyelids—she'd die if he guessed the truth; knew how much the revelation of Alison's letter had cost her in pain and heartache and bitter self-recrimination. She forced herself to shower, combed the long dark hair into order, fastening it back from her face with a clip. Fresh makeup, dark glasses to hide those telltale lids. Now all she had to manage was her own undisciplined heart, and that she knew was something over which she had no control at all. Just to see him, to feel him close to her....

A knock on the door set her heart thudding, but it was only Lucie calling in her high clear tones, "How are you, Tracy? Headache all gone?"

"Just about."

"I'm going down to breakfast. Coming?"

"In a minute."

"We'll wait for you at the corner table."

She had to go through with it. There was no escape. Snatching up a pair of sunglasses from her bag, she thrust them on, thankful for the feeling of privacy they afforded.

As she moved across the sunny dining room, Stephen, grave and quiet, rose to pull out her chair. "Morning, Tracy! How are you feeling now?"

"Much better, thanks." In spite of all she knew of him the deep tones still had the power to touch her. Pain ran along her nerves. If only he *really* cared!

"But you're wearing dark glasses!" Lucie's voice pierced her fog of misery.

"Yes, they help a lot." Even to her own ears her laugh sounded stupid and nervous. "I get them sometimes," she chattered wildly on. "Sore eyes, I mean."

"It's probably because of the dust on the roads," Lucie remarked. "I remember on a trip I did once with my husband—that was around the East Cape, too. We had this old jeep and all the side curtains were flapping around...." The remainder of the story was lost on Tracy. She was aware only of Stephen's grave inquiring glance, a look that she suspected had already taken in the signs of a white night and anguish of mind.

She knew that she would have to get through at least a light breakfast, even if it choked her, were she to succeed in hiding the extent of her misery from those all-observant gray eyes. "Just coffee and toast for me, please," she murmured as Lucie passed her the menu. There were few guests at the tables this morning; most people staying at the hotel would breakfast later.

It seemed to her that the interminable meal would never come to an end, but at last Lucie got to her feet. "I'll go and get my things together—"

"Me, too!" Tracy rose from the table and was about to make her escape when Stephen's firm tones arrested her.

"Wait a minute!" A strong brown hand caught her wrist and pinned her to the spot. "Something I want you to see!" He propelled her down to her seat, then whipped a touring map from the pocket of his bronze shirt. "I wanted to fill you in on the route we're taking on the trip back, through the Waioeka Gorge this time. Makes it more interesting." His grin did things to her heart, almost made her forget everything that she must, *must* make herself remember. But he didn't unfold the touring map. Instead he caught her hand fast in his and to her horror the trembling overtook her, the betraying trembling that would tell him...tell him....

"What's wrong, Tracy?" His voice, so deep and concerned, still had the power to touch her. Oh, why couldn't he be as he seemed? And how could she ever bring herself to explain her disillusionment without giving herself away? The shame-making part of it all was that at his touch all her carefully prepared speech, every shred of common sense she'd ever had fled, leaving her wildly excited, as stupidly vulnerable as ever.

"Why have you been crying?"

So the dark glasses, too, had been a failure, at least so far as he was concerned. Oh, she might have known that she couldn't conceal anything from that penetrating gaze. It had taken only one swift glance from those keen gray eyes to correctly size up the situation.

"Oh, Steve—" Blindly she was aware of Lucie hurrying back toward their table. "I almost forgot to tell you, the luckiest thing! It was in my writing folder, the one I hadn't used since the other trip, and that's why I hadn't come across it before—"

"Hmm...." His low tone was abstracted. "Found what?"

"The letter, of course! The one I've been searching the house for ever since Tracy arrived, the one Alison left for her that morning. I knew I had it somewhere!"

There was no abstraction now in Stephen's steely tones. "You gave it to Tracy yesterday?"

"Yes, yes, she'll tell you all about it. I must go. See you in about half an hour, Steve. I won't keep you waiting, seeing you want to make an early getaway."

"So that's it!" His searching gaze blazed into her heavy-lidded eyes. "It's that letter you got from Alison, isn't it?"

She nodded, not trusting herself to speak. If only he would let go her hand perhaps she could think clearly, decide what to say. Oh, she should have anticipated this moment, but she'd been so devastated by the suddenness and shock of it all.

"Now come on." His grip on her hand tightened. "What's this all about?"

She winced with pain. "You're hurting me."

"You're hurting *me*! What did she tell you?"

She jerked herself free, tried to stop the quivering of her mouth. "She told me all about...what happened. About you—"

"And just what," his voice was very low, "did she tell you about me?"

"Just—" she raised a chalk-white face and for all her determination to keep a firm hold on herself, her mouth puckered "—the truth! What else?"

His lips were set in a grim line. "And that's why you're like this all of a sudden?"

"Yes, that's why!" All at once she forgot all about being calm and composed, not letting him suspect that her cousin's disclosure mattered to her so damnably. "Who wouldn't be different?" She was horrified at the croaking sound of her voice. "Why didn't you tell me that you were so involved in it all? That broken engagement, the row—" her voice broke "—everything!"

"If you remember," his tone was coldly impersonal, "I tried to put you in the picture about all this, but you weren't interested at the time."

It was true. Intoxicated by his nearness, she had refused to listen to him. Now she wondered if deep down she hadn't been afraid of this all along, hadn't wanted to risk spoiling the heady enchantment of the star-ridden night. "It wouldn't have made any difference when I knew."

"Wouldn't it? Look at me, Tracy!" Before she could guess at his intention he had whipped the dark glasses from her eyes. "Why have you been crying, then?"

She dropped her heavy gaze. "None of your business."

"Look here, Tracy, let me—"

"No! It's too late for all that, much too late!" She didn't trust her traitorous heart. In spite of everything she knew of him, if she stayed another minute that masculine magnetism of his would work its magic and she'd forget... forget.... Gathering together her remaining shreds of sanity, she reminded herself that wasn't that just what had betrayed her before? Remember, she told herself, he's a cheat and a liar. He betrayed his own brother! Her only refuge was in flight, and she knew it! To stay would be to put herself at the mercy of the dark spell he seemed to be able to exert over her at will. The same spell, she told herself, that had held Alison in thrall, made her forget the man she had planned to marry. *Escape, escape, Tracy! It's the only way. You can't fight him. You can't fight love!*

"I was taken in before." She sprang to her feet, trembling. "I'm not going to let it happen again! So don't bother to try to talk me out of it! It's no use!"

She caught the flicker of his eyes, almost like a man taking a physical blow, then his jaw tightened. She flung herself around and hurried away, out of reach of that insidious force that was drawing her back to him, even now when she realized the truth. Hating herself for that treacherous urge, she stumbled blindly on toward her bedroom, then once there, stood still, assailed by a sickening moment of doubt. What if she had misjudged him? What if Alison had lied to her? She remembered Cliff's welcoming attitude to his brother at the hospital yesterday, seeming to bear no malice toward Stephen. But then men hid their feelings well, especially before their womenfolk. The brief hope faded almost as swiftly as it had come. There were too many items that added up to an inescapable conclusion. Stephen's reluctance to discuss the matter of the broken engagement, his initial resentment at being forced to have her around the place. But then, she thought wistfully, she supposed she was rather a poor substitute for her glamorous cousin. Fragments of conversation overheard among the women pickers on that hot summer day in the vineyard came back to mind. No, it was all too clear, too convincing to allow any doubt.

CHAPTER SEVEN

AFTERWARD SHE COULD RECALL LITTLE of the long journey back to Auckland. She was uncaring as to where she was or what her destination.

In offering her a window seat, Lucie appeared to imagine she was granting Tracy a favor, as indeed perhaps she was, she mused bleakly. For somehow it was easier to remember that she hated him when she wasn't thrown close against him on the sharp bends of the long winding road cut through the hills. Her eyes with their dazed expression rested on the passing scenes as they swept through the gorge with its rocky outcrops. Workmen with bulldozers were clearing away the giant boulders that had slipped down the sheer rock face onto the road below. Cool green bush lined either side of the highway. Ahead a long transporter loaded with logs cut from nearby pine forests was grinding its way up the steep incline. Road signs went flashing by. *Slips. Washouts.* Later she realized dully that they were leaving the rugged grandeur of the gorge and heading back to Opotiki...and civilization. But today the sunshine city held no meaning for her. It had been an illusion, that good luck she had thought was hers for the taking. To think she had actually believed that Stephen loved her, had built all those crazy hopes and dreams on a future that would never exist, except in her own imagination. All the time it was Alison whom he loved. The old crippling feeling of inferiority, left over from childhood, once more enveloped her in its dark cloud.

Pushing aside the despairing thoughts, she tried to concentrate on Lucie's voice as the older woman indicated various landmarks in the green countryside through which they were passing. Funny that Lucie didn't suspect any special feeling between her and Stephen, but then, she thought

Vineyard in a Valley

bleakly, not so funny really, for what was there to know? A man and a girl thrown together for a night on a remote and lonely bay. A kiss, a few light words, but no promises, no strings. Nothing that couldn't be conveniently forgotten afterward. Nothing *real*, except to her! If she had any sense at all, which she hadn't, she would forget, too, just as he had. She made a determined effort to wrench her heavy thoughts aside, take an intelligent interest in Lucie's conversation. But it was no use. Her thoughts drifted back, back, and the pain started up all over again. The aching intolerable sense of loss. She would have to leave the vineyard, of course. To stay at the house any longer would merely prolong the heartache, underline the anguish and humiliation.

"I've been thinking—" as they sped between rolling farmlands she spoke her thoughts aloud to Lucie "—I'm afraid I won't be able to stay on at the Valley after all."

"Not stay?" Lucie turned to stare at her, aghast. "You can't mean that, Tracy! Why ever not?"

She sought wildly in her mind for a ready excuse, but all she could come up with was a lame "something's come along." At Steve she didn't look. What did it matter to him anyway what her movements were?

"But you can't do that! It's just that you haven't been feeling the best on the trip. Tomorrow you'll think differently about it all. Besides, there's Steve and the office—you can't let *him* down!"

Can't I, she thought with bitter anguish. *Why not? He let me down!* She jerked her heavy thoughts back to the present.

"Why," Lucie was saying, "he was just telling me the other day that he never would have believed his luck in getting anyone so knowledgeable about the work. He said he couldn't get along without you. Honestly! Didn't you, Steve?"

"That's right." His tone was expressionless.

Still she didn't glance toward him. She couldn't. A pang seemed to pierce her heart. Was that a lie, too? Perhaps not. In the comparatively remote surroundings of the vineyard, it would be difficult for him to find a suitable office helper. Probably she was a useful acquisition to him. That was all she had meant to him all along. Someone to string along, maybe to have a light affair with, if she were inclined to play along. And she had! Oh, she had needed no encouragement on that score! She'd been quite wrapped up in him, easily trapped into caring for him so deeply that now she didn't know how to bear the nagging sense of heartache, or how to get through the days ahead. She wrenched the painful thoughts aside. "All the same—"

"But, Tracy—" the small, carefully made-up face looked suddenly old "—you said—you promised...."

"I've changed my mind." Could that be her own voice, so low and despairing? She *must* pull herself together, not give him the satisfaction of knowing how deeply the wound had penetrated.

"But you *said* you'd stay until I got my driving license back." There was a note of genuine regret in the older woman's tones. "It's only another three weeks. Just stay until then, Tracy. *Please.*"

All at once it seemed less trouble to agree than to carry the argument further, especially as she was painfully aware of Stephen's disquieting presence. Though saying little no doubt he was thinking a lot. Her heavy thoughts ran on. She wouldn't have to see a great deal of him, except in the office, and there to all intents they would be merely employer and employee. That was all they had ever been, actually. She said on a sigh, "I guess I could stay on for that long."

"Thank heaven for that!" Lucie sank back on the seat at her side. "You've no idea what a joy it is to me, having you at the house. Otherwise I'm stuck there with only the men for company, and you know what that means. Men's talk, wine talk, but with you it's different. Having someone around who's so young and pretty—"

But Tracy wasn't listening. *Three weeks,* she was thinking. *Surely I could endure anything for three weeks.* She would have to do better than she had today, though, if she were not to betray her feelings. On one point her mind was made up. While at the Valley she would arrange for her air passage back to London. She had no heart now for sightseeing, even in this country of scenic wonders. Once back amid familiar surroundings maybe the nagging anguish might lessen; Steve, the vineyard in the valley, seem no more than a half-forgotten dream. Forget Stephen? Once again the small insistent voice deep in her mind made itself known. *Who do you think you're fooling?*

When they reached the house they could hear the telephone ringing inside and Lucie ran toward the instrument. She turned back to Tracy with a smile. "It's for you! Sounds like that friend of yours, Glenn."

Slowly she picked up the receiver. She had actually forgotten him and it took her a moment to drag her thoughts away from her own problems. She summoned a note of gaiety into her voice. "Hello!"

"It's you!" Excitement and pleasure rippled over the wire. "Glenn here! If I'm not glad to hear from you! Seemed as though you were never coming back. I took a chance and rang through just in case—how was the trip anyway?"

"The trip? Oh, it was fine! We've just this minute got back."

"I won't keep you, then. But I've just had a thought. How about coming out for dinner with me tonight? There's a place by the water where they turn on quite a decent meal, with a spot of entertainment thrown in. Interested?"

"I don't know." Her tone was uncertain. Then she was aware of Stephen passing near her as he carried in her travel bag. A reckless impulse made her say quickly, "All right, then, I'll be ready. What time? Eight o'clock? See you then!"

THE EVENING SET A PATTERN for the following days, for rather than be alone with her troubled thoughts, she clutched at the opportunity of escape that Glenn offered her. Anything was preferable to staying here at the house with Stephen, knowing...remembering.... It was surprising how you got through the days, she told herself drearily, as the week dragged by. Somehow you found you could carry on over shock and heartbreak, even over despair, if you had to. And she was all right—most of the time. Working duties in the vineyard office helped, for a sudden influx of orders brought a constant stream of clients to the long counter. One morning a party of Japanese visitors arrived to be taken on a tour of the city's most picturesque vineyards. And always there were the orders to be compiled, correspondence to be dealt with. Afternoons were taken up in driving Lucie to various places of interest in the city. Sometimes Tracy would leave her at a craft display, a shopping mall, an art gallery, arranging to pick her up later. But the arrangement proved unsatisfactory, at least as far as Tracy was concerned, for alone in the car her random thoughts would take over and despite all her resolutions to banish such ideas, the despairing sense of letdown, the hopeless longing would return once again to overwhelm her.

Nights were the hardest to endure, but even for that problem, she reflected wryly, there was a remedy. For it seemed that Glenn was always on the telephone, pleading to take her out. Each evening he appeared at the house promptly on time, immaculately dressed for dining or dancing, eager to escort her to a movie, a concert, a nightclub. "Wherever you'd like to go," he told her gaily. To Tracy it was all dreamlike, unreal. At times she wondered if Glenn suspected the truth. He was so gentle with her, so considerate in every way. She went with him to the various places of amusement, and if her laughter held a brittle note and she felt nothing but a blank emptiness of spirit, he apparently noticed no difference in her. Being with him helped to pass away the hours, and sometimes she even forgot, for a time.

Once or twice the idle thought crossed her mind that the one place Glenn did not suggest taking her was to the home of his friends where he was still living, but she didn't really want to return there. The girl was there, the big strongly built girl who had stared at her with an expression of baffled hatred in her eyes, jealous of her because of Glenn's attentions. If Pam only knew how little he figured in her scheme of things. In her book he was nothing more than someone to go out with, someone to help her forget.

She hadn't yet told him how soon she was leaving the country and returning to England. Somehow it seemed less trouble to let herself to be carried along on a tide of ceaseless activity. Each night when he brought her back to the vineyard she would promise herself, "I'll tell him tomorrow." Each night she postponed letting him know.

Fortunately neither Lucie nor Bill appeared to notice any difference in her relationship with Stephen. Incredible how one's life could alter in a few hours yet on the surface nothing was changed, so long as you could go on doing the everyday things, pretend that nothing had happened. But of course she had the advantage of being a stranger here. Those at Valley Vineyards had no way of knowing that she wasn't always like this, a restless creature seeking gaiety night after night in a desperate effort to forget.

If she anticipated any difficulty in the situation as regarded Stephen, she need not have concerned herself, for he was more distant and aloof than ever, speaking to her when he needed to in home or office, in a cool polite tone that only she knew hid an icy disdain. At times she wondered if she could have dreamed that scene on the firelit sands. Could he have been so different, this cold and distant stranger?

Working in the office with him proved more difficult to endure than she had anticipated. Seeing his dark head bent over the account books a short distance away from her, listening to the deep tones as he interviewed local and overseas clients, watching through the window as he guided the cultivator between the long terraced rows of vines, a lithe figure in shabby gray shorts and cotton shirt. It seemed as though she couldn't drag her thoughts away from him.

Since their return from Gisborne she had contrived to avoid any close contact with him. Not that it was difficult, she thought with bitter anguish, for his cool employer approach to her simplified the situation. If only it could erase memory, too, blot out the mind pictures of a darkening shore, promises that had proved to be as empty and meaningless as windswept sands.

One afternoon she had returned from a trip to the city with Lucie and was putting the car in the garage when a massive, dust-smeared old Chrysler drew up on the pathway below the house.

"Surprise! Surprise!" Cliff waved a crutch from the car window and a small red-haired figure in a tan pantsuit leaped from the driver's seat and came smilingly toward Tracy.

"Hi! You're Tracy, aren't you? I'm Kim."

Tracy smiled across at the square-jawed, freckled face. "I remember you! You were at the Cook Hospital in Gisborne. You were a nurse there."

"Still am! But I had a weekend's leave due and Cliff was mad to get home for a while, so I said I'd drive him up to Auckland. Dad lent us his jalopy and here we are! Cliff wouldn't let me send you a wire; he wanted to surprise you."

"Glad you did!"

"Wait a minute!" She ran back to the car, holding the crutches in readiness as Cliff lowered himself from the vehicle.

A few moments later he was negotiating the steep concrete steps leading up to the house. "Don't help me, woman! I can manage!" He waved away Kim's outstretched hand.

She shrugged good-humoredly. "You can see what I'm up against."

But Tracy had seen something else, the warm feeling of intimacy that flowed between the other two. Was it because she was so emotionally caught up herself that she felt this flash of awareness concerning the feelings of Kim and Cliff? Aloud she murmured, "Just wait until Lucie sees you both! She'll be thrilled to bits!"

"She is!" Kim turned her head to laugh over her shoulder, for already Cliff had swung himself at the open door and Lucie's arms were around him as she laughed and talked and questioned all in one breath. The next moment, realizing he wasn't alone, her gaze went to Kim.

"My private nurse," he grinned. "Kim wouldn't let me out of hospital by myself, so the only way I could make it up here was to bring her along with me. We've come for the weekend!"

"That was a wonderful thought!" While Lucie hurried toward the kitchen to plug in the coffee percolator, Cliff swung himself over the unfinished sheepskin rug on the floor and dropped down to a low chair. The next moment

Vineyard in a Valley

Stephen stood at the open doorway, and it seemed to Tracy that as usual these days he avoided her glance. Not that she minded... but somehow she did... horribly. Watching Cliff's transparently happy features she wondered again at the pleasure both men appeared to find in their meeting. How *could* Cliff forgive his brother so soon and so effortlessly? Perhaps though now that Cliff had found someone to take Alison's place... it would surely be less painful to forgive when one was happy and not the guilty party... like Steve. She brought her heavy thoughts back to the present.

"You know," Lucie was saying excitedly, "you'll be able to come back to Auckland now, Cliff. You could easily arrange a transfer to a local hospital for your therapy treatment."

"I could, but I'd rather stay down at the Cook for a while, the way things are."

Lucie's brown eyes held a puzzled look. "But why?"

"Let's just say—" Cliff's smile broadened "—that down there I'm getting a rather special kind of therapy, the kind I like!"

Tracy's gaze moved from Cliff to Kim's radiant face. "You two are engaged!"

"I thought you'd never notice!" Proudly Kim thrust forward a small, workworn hand. A simple sapphire ring gleamed from a stubby freckled finger.

But Tracy's swift glance had not missed the expression of sudden relief that lighted Steve's features. No doubt, she mused, now that his brother was obviously happy and contented with someone new, Steve need have no further worries regarding Alison... and himself. It's like a ghastly game of Happy Families, she thought bleakly. Everyone's getting paired off except me. She forced a smile to her lips, dutifully admiring the modest little ring and adding her own voice to the chorus of congratulations.

"What do you think of that for an idea?" With a start she realized Cliff was regarding her with his open, friendly smile.

"Sorry." She dragged her thoughts back to the present. "I wasn't listening, I'm afraid."

"Steve's idea! How about if we all make up a party, go

out to dinner tonight, by way of celebration? There'll be Lucie and Bill, you and Steve—"

In an unguarded moment her glance flew to his. How could his gray eyes appear so dark and shadowed? At his grave unsmiling glance she twirled her long hair beneath her chin in a nervous gesture, but there was nothing she could say, no way of escape. Anyway, what did it matter? No doubt he would find some way of avoiding contact with her as much as possible during the evening, just as she.... She became aware of Cliff's puzzled glance. "Hope I haven't spoiled anything for you two. I mean, you haven't got other plans for tonight?"

"No, no!" Tracy summoned up a smile, forced her voice to a light careless note. "Of course not! No plans at all!" Her heart underlined the words. "At least—" belatedly she remembered a date with Glenn this very night "—nothing that I can't put off."

"Good on you! Funny, you know—" Cliff's tone was thoughtful "—somehow at the hospital the other day I got the feeling that you and Steve—"

"Don't take any notice of him, Tracy!" Kim's bright voice cut in. "The trouble with Cliff is that he thinks too much. It was about time I got him up out of that hospital bed and up onto crutches!"

In the ensuing wave of good-natured laughter the dangerous moment passed and soon Cliff was recounting anecdotes of life on the remote and unspoiled east coast. It was a man's country, Tracy gathered. A place where a short plane trip could transport a hunter swiftly to the heavy bush of the outback, where the fishing was unsurpassed and race meetings were held on a long sandy stretch of a surf beach.

Tracy soon realized that Kim, young, impressionable, quick to help in any way she could, was as different a girl as one could possibly imagine from Alison. There wasn't the slightest doubt as to how Kim felt about Cliff. It was there for all the world to see, in the deepening light in the green eyes when she met his glance, the tone of her voice, the swift anticipation of his needs. Tracy wondered whether Cliff realized how fortunate he was in having met her. Unconsciously she sighed. If only he didn't allow the memory of Alison's sophisticated charm to linger on, corroding everything that was real and worthwhile in life, the way it had for her.

That evening Tracy was stroking aqua-colored shadow lightly over her eyelids when there was a knock at her bedroom door.

"Come in!"

Kim threw herself down on the bed, crossing shapely legs. "You don't mind if I wait here? I'm sharing Lucie's room and I thought I'd get ready first, then we wouldn't fight over the mirror!" She leaped to her feet. "Like me to give you a hand with that back zip?"

"Thanks."

"You'd never think you weren't a dyed-in-the-wool Kiwi." Kim flicked up the zipper over Tracy's sun-tanned back. "You must have been here for quite a while."

"Only a couple of months." In spite of herself the pain, ever waiting to pounce, attacked her out of the blue, but she pushed it aside. "It doesn't take long to get a tan here. All you need," she forced a light laugh, "is lots of valley sunshine...and your bikini!"

"For you maybe," the other girl's tone was abstracted, "but you're not a redhead—lucky you!" Dropping down to the bed, she played nervously with the pale ring on her finger. "Then you must have been here when...when...." The catch in her voice betrayed a depth of feeling. "You know...that other engagement of Cliff's?" she finished painfully.

"You mean Alison?" Tracy peered toward the mirror, avoiding the other girl's eyes. "No, I came just afterward."

No need to explain that she had arrived here with the intention of being one of the wedding party.

"It's not like you think, you know!" Kim burst out impulsively. "He just isn't marrying me on the rebound, like everyone says at the hospital!" The clear eyes raised to Tracy pleaded for understanding.

Tracy said gently, "I never thought that. I just thought how awfully lucky he was to find you, after all that happened." In spite of herself, her tone hardened. If she had been Cliff she would never have forgiven a brother who had cheated, stolen his fiancée.

"She was your cousin, wasn't she?"

At last Tracy turned to meet the other girl's frank gaze. "I still think he's lucky to have you!"

"You really do, don't you!" Pleasure and relief lighted Kim's small square face. "He loves me," she said simply, "he *really* loves me. I mean, not like it was with Alison. Down at the hospital in Gisborne he told me all about it, and you can understand when you know the truth of it—"

I *can't*. Tracy made the observation silently as she bent to slip her feet into black sling backs.

"He'd never really fallen for a girl before," the warm young tones ran on. "Can you imagine? At twenty-two? But that's the way it was with Cliff. I guess he'd been so wrapped up in mountain climbing and all that... and then he's kind of shy. So, when *she* came along—"

Tracy wanted to throw her hands over her ears, do something, anything, to stop the flow of words that were like sword points aimed straight for the heart. She began snatching up garments, hanging them in the wardrobe, turning her face aside so as not to betray her own inner distress.

"He really fell for her, but she—" Kim stopped short in confusion. "Gee, I keep forgetting that she's your cousin."

"It doesn't matter about that, but look, it's getting late, the others will be waiting...." She scarcely knew what she was saying; she only knew that at all costs she had to say something to halt Kim's confidences. Another moment and she would be telling her all about Stephen and the sorry part that he had played in the affair.

Kim got to her feet, her bright smile flashing toward Tracy. "Anyway, I don't need to tell *you*! You know all about it already."

Tracy pulled herself together. "Not really—come on, let's go and meet the others."

They had reached the balcony when Cliff came to join them. "You and Kim go on ahead," Tracy suggested smilingly. She stood watching as Cliff tap-tapped his way down the steps while Kim moved at his side.

"Hello, Tracy!" She swung around to find Stephen standing beside her and something in the way he was looking at her moved her with a poignancy she could scarcely bear.

"Suits you!" His grave appraising glance took in the slim figure in dark chiffon, the breeze ruffling the diaphanous material around her ankles; the pale composed face beneath the severely upswept hairstyle. "Black, Tracy? For an engagement party?"

For a moment her guard was down and still confused by something in his glance she heard herself say the words that sprang unbidden to her lips. "It's not *my* engagement party!" Appalled, she wondered the next moment what had made her say such a thing, and to him, of all men!

"No." To Tracy the silence seemed to last forever. Then, distractingly close, heartbreakingly good-looking, he was taking her arm. "Shall we go?"

CHAPTER EIGHT

Faint lights pricked the dark landscape around them as Stephen guided the car along fern-fringed roads and up the winding slope of a bush-clad hill. Soon they were turning down a narrow track. For a moment the arc of the headlights picked out a faded notice board half-hidden among the trees pointing the way to a dine-and-dance restaurant ahead. Then all at once they were swinging in at the side entrance, sweeping through spacious grounds where colored lights glimmered among greenery and landscape windows looked out over a setting of native bush.

The party waited while Cliff click-clacked his crutches up the curved entrance steps, then together they made their way inside the softly lighted room, and a waiter guided them to a candlelit table. The breeze drifting in through wide open windows was spiced with the clean sharp tang of the bush; soft background music echoed around them. If only everything had been different, Tracy mused, toying with the attractively served fruit cocktail. Tonight she had no appetite at all; no heart for gaiety, either, not with Stephen's dark face directly opposite. What if he was wearing his closed, aloof look again, the one he reserved especially for her? What if he was in love with someone else? It made no difference. Telling herself a dozen times each day that she hated him made no difference, either. The shame-making truth was that she loved him in all his moods. That was what love could do. Who was it who had once said, "I offer you love, not happiness"? Happiness! She had forgotten there was such a thing, yet only a few short days since....

"You're very quiet tonight, Tracy!" Cliff smiled at her across the table. "Don't look so sad. It's a celebration! Happy talk. Remember?"

"Did I look sad?" With an effort she rallied herself. "Blame it on that Maori music." She nodded toward the group of Maori guitarists. "It always seems to have that plaintive sound."

Fortunately the others in the party were in a mood to enjoy themselves and her own lack of appetite went unnoticed... or at least so she hoped. With Stephen you could never tell. He had that uncanny knack of seeming to read her thoughts.

A swaying group of Tahitian dancers were spotlighted in changing lighting effects and Tracy applauded with the rest at the table, but tonight for her everything had a dreamlike quality. Even the toasts drunk to the newly engaged couple had no reality. Vaguely she was aware of Cliff's light tones as the guitarist group broke into a soft waltz-time melody that flooded the room. "Aren't you and Steve going to dance, Tracy?"

As she hesitated, not knowing how to reply, Kim sent her a laughing glance. "If you're holding back because of Cliff and me, don't give it another thought! We love to see other folk enjoying themselves. Isn't that right, Cliff?"

"In that case—" Bill touched Lucie lightly on her arm "—care to have this one with me?" The two rose and made their way toward the small parquet area in the center of the spacious room. Tracy watched as they moved with the grace of long experience amid the other couples on the dance floor.

"Shall we?" She was aware of Stephen's gaze. You could scarcely term his expression inviting, but then he was being forced into this, just as she was. After Kim's pointed reminder what else could he do? Rising to his feet, he came to stand at her side. "How about it, Tracy?"

If only, she thought distractedly, he wouldn't say her name... like that. It brought it all back, the pain, the ecstasy, the bitter knowledge that she was leaving here so soon, while he and Alison.... Remembrance of Alison steeled her to smile up at him as together they made their way toward the cleared space amid the scattered tables.

Fortunately she had taken lessons in ballroom dancing.

What she had never learned was how to combat the sweetness and sting of being held in his arms, her chin tucked close to his white shirtfront. She was scarcely aware of movement; all she could think of was that she was near him for the last time. Damn it, why did that Maori group have to swing into a haunting melody that plucked at the heart? Oh, damn everything!

It finished at last. Couples dispersed in various directions and Stephen, unspeaking still, escorted her back to their table. It had meant nothing to him, of course, a mere duty dance that he would have no need to repeat.

As the evening wore on she was relieved to find that various cabaret entertainers filled in the time. Someone, probably Bill, informed the management of the restaurant of the special occasion dinner and an announcement was made over the microphone by a genial compere. As if by magic, a suitably iced cake was produced from the kitchen and duly presented to the newly engaged couple. Glasses clinked all around them and everyone in the room joined in the chorus of congratulations and good wishes.

It was some time after midnight when the party returned to the car, parked in the shadowy grounds. Back in the house at last Tracy was about to make her escape to the privacy of her room when Bill's voice made her pause.

"Get your mail today?"

"Why, no." She looked up at him. "Was there something?"

"One for you. I put it on the mantel in the dining room. Thought you'd have noticed it."

"Thank you, Bill." As she moved through to the other room she caught sight of a blue aerogram. It was probably from someone back in England, and somehow tonight England seemed very far away. It wasn't until she was undressed and ready for bed that she remembered the flimsy sheet of paper crushed in her evening bag. Taking it out, a little shock of apprehension ran through her as she recognized Alison's scrawling handwriting. Swiftly she scanned the words.

Vineyard in a Valley 385

Reef Hotel, Suva

Tracy dear,
Just a hurried note to let you know I'm still in the islands, Fiji at the moment, but not for long. What do you know? I ran into a guy here the other day who I knew in Auckland and he told me he'd met up with the Cranes and a girl who sounded awfully like you, when he was on the way to some wine conference thing in Tauranga. I was surprised; thought you'd have taken off ages ago on some sight-seeing tours. Can't see what you find to keep you at the winery all this time.

Anyway, I might be seeing you yet as I'm heading back to Auckland at the end of the week. Don't let Steve know I let you in on this little secret, will you? He's funny about these things.

Hope you're enjoying yourself over there.

Love, Ally

Long before she had finished reading this letter, she knew what the end would be. Hadn't this been on the cards all the time, only, idiot that she was, she hadn't been able to tear herself away, knowing that once she left the vineyards it would be forever. Now she had no choice. The letter was dated three days earlier. Why, Alison could arrive here tomorrow—*tomorrow!* To be here when that happened, to be forced to witness the happiness of the other two—no, that she couldn't, wouldn't endure. Plans began to form in her mind. She already had her plane booking for London. Maybe it could be altered to an earlier date and with a bit of luck—*luck*; tears pricked her eyelids—she'd be on the plane tomorrow, be hundreds of miles away when a radiant Alison returned to the valley vineyard... and Steve.

After a sleepless night it was a relief to get up. Swiftly she dressed in a dark blue pantsuit, automatically picked up her makeup and did things to her face. A peep between the curtains at the high window showed her that Stephen was up early, too. She caught a glimpse of him and Bill as the two men strolled toward the far vines. In the house, however, all was silent and she knew that the chances were no one else was yet awake.

In the shadowy lounge the curtains were still drawn. Carefully closing the door behind her, she went toward the telephone, dialed the air travel center and lowered her voice as someone answered. The official was polite and blessedly helpful. Yes, as it happened there was a spare seat available. A cancelation at the last moment, but it was on today's ten o'clock flight—not much time.

"That's time enough for me." Tracy thanked the airport official.

"So long as you don't mind a stopover for several hours at Fiji," he told her. "You can connect there with the night flight to London."

And that was all right with her, too. She thanked the man and hurried away. It was Sunday morning. The others in the house would probably sleep in for some hours yet and if she failed to make an appearance no one would be at all surprised. When they discovered her absence it would be too late. Feverishly she plucked garments from hangers, began stowing dresses, shorts, swimsuits haphazardly into her travel bags with trembling hands. Let them think what they liked. Only one thing mattered now and that was for her to make her escape before she was trapped here. She would be leaving in ten days' time anyway. What was ten days? And who would care whether she went or stayed? Tears blurred her vision and she dashed them away with the back of her hand. To everyone at the vineyard she was nothing more than Alison's cousin, that was all she had ever meant to them—even Steve. But she mustn't think of him, that way danger lay. Better to get it all over with quickly. Something fell from a pocket of the cotton shift she was folding and she bent to the floor to pick it up, crushing the dried twig between her fingers. At once the scent of tea tree, sharp and evocative, assailed her. A twig from manuka branches broken off for a picnic fire. Now it held for her all the essence of a lost happiness.

Don't think, Tracy—don't dream. Concentrate on the pres-

ent, that's all that matters now. Wait! She must get away from the house unseen. She would have to order a taxi. At the thought she hurried once more to the telephone and dialed the number of a city taxi rank. She gave the address of the vineyard, adding, "Could you pick me up in half an hour, please, and take me to the city airport terminal? Would you meet me at the entrance to the Valley Vineyards? You understand? Not the house but at the gates on the roadway. It's a long drive up to the house. If I'm not there, just wait, please. I won't be long!"

In spite of her fumbling haste soon everything was in readiness. Now all she had to worry about was making her escape from the house unseen. Her travel bags were heavier than she had expected them to be, but she could manage them, if she could take her time. And once beneath the shade of the overhanging trees lining the long drive she would be out of sight from those in the house. It wasn't as if she would be likely to meet anyone at this early hour on a Sunday morning. Meanwhile, she zipped up her bags, then glanced around her in search of a ball-point pen. She supposed she should leave some message for Lucie, but in this state of mind she couldn't think straight and anyway, what could she say? "I've fallen in love with Stephen"? No, let her think what she liked, anything, anything but the truth. She'd drop Lucie a note from one of the stopovers on the route; maybe by that time she would be more in control of herself. The minutes now seemed to drag, but at last a glance at her wristwatch told her it was time for her to meet the taxi. What if the driver made a mistake and called here at the house? The thought made her hurry into the shadowed hall. As she glanced through a slit between the drawn curtains in the lounge she caught a glimpse of Bill in his white coat. He was accompanied by Stephen, and the two men strolled along the pathway beneath. She held her breath as they neared the house, but they went on, to disappear down the steps leading to the wine cellars below.

Bracing herself, she picked up her bags and went swiftly down the steps, hurrying along the winding path until a bend hid her from view of those in the house above. A short pause while she recovered her breath, then she was off again, almost running between the avenue of tall trees, drops of dew brushing her face as she hastened on, a small figure with a tense white face.

She was almost in sight of the entrance gates when a black car with a taxi sign drew up at the opening. The next minute a man got out of the vehicle and came hurrying toward her. "Miss Cadell? I'll take those." With relief she surrendered the bags, thankful that he asked no questions. No doubt in his line of business he was accustomed to meeting people in strange and desperate situations. She was grateful that he made little attempt at conversation. Perhaps, she thought, catching a glimpse of herself in the small overhead mirror, he realized that she wasn't in the mood for small talk, or indeed capable of it, not with that drawn, tense face, pale beneath the tan.

She was early in arriving at the city air terminal, but before long other passengers came to join her as they waited for transportation to the airport. In the bus on the way to the Auckland International Airport, the young man seated at her side attempted to engage her interest, but almost at once he abandoned any further attempts to get through to the strange lovely girl with the curiously blank expression who seemed scarcely aware of his presence.

In the luxurious comfort of the great jet, she was fortunate in being assigned a window seat at the side of two middle-aged businessmen who were apparently deep in their own concerns and left her to her thoughts. She stared with unseeing eyes out over the endless expanse of the South Pacific. Stephen. What would his reaction be when he found her gone? None at all, probably. With Alison's arrival so imminent what would it matter to him that the other girl's cousin had taken it into her silly head to vanish without explanation? Angrily she jerked her thoughts back to the present. Why must she always think of him? Somehow, somehow, she *must* forget him!

She was scarcely aware of the passing of time until all at once groups of scattered islands loomed up over the horizon and soon the giant jet was swooping down toward Viti Levu. All around her passengers were gathering together magazines and travel bags. Women were making last-minute repairs to hair and complexion, but Tracy sat still and silent as the great plane touched down at Nandi International Airport. A sudden surge of warm air met her as she stepped down from the airport steps at the colorful airport with its tall and stately Fijians in their native skirtlike sulus, sari-clad Indians and white-shorted British officials. But to Tracy it all seemed slightly unreal, as though she were taking part in a play. Merging into the stream of passengers moving into the transit lounge, idly she eyed the groups gathered at the duty-free stores with their display of luxury goods from a dozen different cultures. Then she stood still. The tall girl standing at the crowded counter, green sunglasses pushed up on her flaming hair.... Holding up a string of pearls, the girl turned, laughing and looking up into the face of a stout middle-aged man at her side. Then over his balding head her glance met Tracy's look of wide-eyed astonishment. Even in her own turmoil of spirit she was vaguely aware of an odd expression that flashed across the lovely face—alarm? The next moment it was gone, replaced by the blank look of a stranger. It couldn't be, but it was... Alison! The other girl's initial expression was no doubt caused by the shock of seeing her here.

"Alison!" She was pushing her way through the milling throng. At length she reached the counter of the duty-free store, leaning forward to touch Alison's bare arm.

"Alison! I knew it was you!"

Once again that odd, guarded expression crossed the lovely face to change swiftly to a look of bored interest. "Oh, it's you, Tracy!"

Now that she had captured Alison's attention she didn't quite know what to say to her, especially as the other girl was eyeing her so warily, almost as though she hadn't wished to recognize her here. "Listen! I've got to speak to you! Have you got time? I take it...that you're on the way back to New Zealand?" No one would ever know what it cost her to get the words out.

"New Zealand! That's a laugh!" For the first time Tracy realized that the stout man in the impeccably tailored suit intended to accompany Alison on her flight. "We're going a lot farther than that! Isn't that so, honey? It's Los Angeles for us, then New York, and right around the States. I want to show Alison here some of my own country before we settle down for good in old Arizona. Isn't that so, honey?"

In bewilderment Tracy gazed up into the florid, smiling face.

"I'm sorry." Alison had turned away and was pushing her way through the crowd at the counter. "I haven't got a moment. I'll write...later."

"Take it easy, honey! We're not in that much of a rush!" A plump hand with a large winking ring halted Alison's impetuous progress. "You take your time. Say," his smile broadened to include Tracy, "you forgot to introduce me to your friend here—"

"I'm her cousin," Alison said urgently. "That's why—"

"Cousin, eh! Well, now, what do you know? You two girls sit right down at the table over there and catch up with the family news while I do some shopping for my best girl here. Alison, she's so surprised to see you she hasn't even told you about me. Bentley's the name. Alison—" he winked confidentially behind horn-rimmed spectacles "—she calls me Will."

Tracy smiled back into the florid friendly face, but all the time she was aware that for some reason she couldn't understand Alison was displeased and angry. She knew the signs only too well—the tightening of the lips, the hard cold glitter of the green eyes. But as she looked up at her male companion, Alison's smile was as warmly provocative as ever. "You don't need to do that, Will. Tracy won't mind if you stay."

Tracy had the strangest feeling—if she hadn't known better she would have imagined her cousin to be frightened and nervous, desperately seeking a way out of an unpleasant situation. Already, however, the short well-dressed figure had moved back to the crowded counter and there was nothing Alison could do but accompany Tracy to a nearby table.

"I've only got a moment!" Alison flung herself down on a chair. "Oh, what the heck! You may as well know!" She smiled the old reckless smile that in their younger days had presaged an admission to some misdemeanor.

"Is it true?" Tracy couldn't seem to take it in. "He said you're going to settle down...over in the States. You're getting married to him?"

Alison's laugh was nervous and high-pitched. "Trust Will to spill the whole thing! He's so besotted about me that he wants the whole world to know—but how about you?" Alison sent her a quick, inquiring look. "Where's Stephen?"

"Stephen? What makes you think he'd be here with me?"

The other girl shrugged. "You tell *me*! From the last word I got from New Zealand I gathered that you and he were getting pretty friendly...maybe a bit more than friendly?"

Tracy shook her head. She avoided that shrewdly mocking gaze. "I'm on my way back to London, just here in transit to connect with the night plane."

"Well—" Alison's brows were arched in surprise. She gave a short bitter laugh. "If I'd known that I wouldn't have bothered—" she stopped short.

"What do you mean?"

Alison answered the query with one of her own. "He told you, then, Stephen, all about what happened?"

"Oh, yes, when I first arrived—"

"That's okay, then. You wouldn't be taken in by those letters of mine?"

A shattering suspicion was taking hold in Tracy's mind, an idea that was almost too terrible to contemplate.

"You lied to me!" Her eyes were blazingly blue. "You had no intention of going back to the valley, ever! You never did have! You lied about everything. Cliff, Stephen—" *Especially Stephen,* she thought over heartbreak.

"Not really." Alison's brittle smile held no humor. "What happened with Cliff was all his own stupid fault! Pretending he was a partner in his brother's wine business, leading me on to think he had money to burn, when all the time—"

"All the time he was squandering what little he had on you!"

"And what was wrong with that? He didn't interest me one little bit! Not once I'd met his brother!"

Tracy was following the matter to its bitter conclusion. "That note you left for me, the first one, it was all lies, what you said about... about Stephen...?"

Alison took a silver cigarette case from her shoulder bag, flicked it open and held it toward Tracy. She shook her head.

"You seem awfully interested in Stephen." Alison sent her a shrewd look. "Don't tell me that you've fallen for him, too?"

Tracy dropped her gaze. "I just want to get things straight, that's all. Why did you leave that letter?"

"Oh, grow up!" Tracy, as she caught the cruel glint in the green eyes, wondered how she could ever have thought this girl beautiful. "You always were a naive little fool, just asking to be taken down. I knew I'd be quite safe, that you'd never let on to Stephen what I told you."

"But why?"

"Can't you guess? You've known me long enough to know that I don't take kindly to not getting what I want, when I want it!" Viciously she stubbed out the ash from her cigarette in the glass ashtray on the table. "I'll tell you something, Tracy! I've got an old score to settle with Stephen Crane. That's why! No man's going to turn me down and get away with it!"

"I still don't see—"

"No, you wouldn't! Wouldn't you," she cried fiercely, "invent some sort of cover-up if a man had let you down like that?"

"Let you down? How do you mean?"

Tracy had to strain to catch the muttered words. "He turned me down flat—*me!* And I was crazy about him! He made it very plain—" the low tones were laced with bitterness "—that he wanted nothing to do with me, and that was after I had thrown myself at him, practically proposed marriage. It was just bad luck that that fool of a Cliff had to wander into the room at the wrong moment! And that really did it! Hearing me make my big confession to his brother made him see red. Not that he was any loss. It wasn't *my* fault—" she met Tracy's look of wide-eyed disgust "—that he took it so badly and smashed himself up that night in a car accident. Why, it could have been me who was hurt that night, and it would have been all *his* fault, driving like a madman. As to that Stephen—I swore that night that I'd get even with him! For a start I wasn't going to take any chances on his getting too friendly with my little cousin when she arrived, so I took care to nip that in the bud. Took you in, too, didn't I?"

Tracy struggled with a wild primitive urge to administer a stinging slap to that mocking face. Then wisdom prevailed and she crushed down her anger. Why give the other girl the satisfaction of knowing how very well her plan had succeeded? She was, however, determined to get to the bottom of the affair. Not that it mattered—now. She raised her heavy glance. "And the letter I got this week?"

Alison drew on her cigarette. "You may as well have it all. A few days ago at the hotel here I happened to get talking to a guy who I used to know in Auckland, a Yugoslav winegrower. Old Joe might look a dumb sort of character, but he's right there when it comes to romance. He told me he'd run into you and Stephen when he was on the way to some wine conference thing in Tauranga, said he could almost smell the orange blossoms." Again that cruel smile. "I couldn't allow that to happen could I? Oh, well, if Joe was way out in his ideas of you two, no harm done. But if he wasn't—" The narrowed eyes, the pinched look around the nostrils, shocked Tracy. It was as if she were gazing at a woman grown suddenly old. "He deserved it."

"You did that to Stephen?"

"My!" A sneering smile lifted the corners of the curving lips. "Joe was right, then!"

Tracy realized that her transparently horrified face had betrayed her secret to the other girl. She never could hide her emotions successfully.

"That's one score I've settled! You know something? When I first caught sight of you here today it really threw me! I thought I must have made a mistake; that you wouldn't be going back to London, alone, if Joe had been right. Now I can see it was worth all the trouble. It worked—put a finish to any ideas you might have had about Stephen Crane! Don't bother to deny it! I can see it in your face! You never were any good at hiding anything from me. So now you're on your way back to London, alone!"

"Thanks to you." Flushed with anger, Tracy leaned across the low table. "Ally, how *could* you?"

"Easy! Remember, I've had lots of practice. All it takes is brains and a little bit of finesse...and knowing who you're dealing with and—"

The mocking tones were drowned by the booming sound of a loudspeaker. "Will passengers leaving on flight number one-nine-one for Los Angeles please proceed to the aircraft. Will passengers...."

Alison got to her feet, pulling the strap of her suede handbag over a slim shoulder. "That's my call! I've got to go. Here's Will—"

Tracy realized that the stout man pushing his way through the moving stream of people was making his way in their direction. For a moment Alison paused, looking down into Tracy's ashen face. "He's quite a pet, isn't he? Not like Stephen, of course, but—" she turned away, throwing a mocking smile over her shoulder "—you can't have everything, can you?"

Tracy didn't answer. Aware of nothing but a chill sense of despair, she stared blindly after the other girl. Sick at heart, she sat on as the crowd of passengers moved toward the flight of stairs leading down to the gleaming jet below.

Stephen, Stephen, what have I done? Ever since that day in Gisborne he must have wondered at her sudden change of heart, but she had given him no chance to make explanations, even had his pride allowed him to do so. Then the coolness between them had grown until there'd been no way of mending matters. She wouldn't again love a man of Stephen Crane's caliber. She had had her one big chance of happiness and had thrown it away! How could she have believed Alison's fabrications, against all she knew of Stephen. When had he ever done anything discreditable? When had he ever lied to her, even when he'd told her he loved her? And she—what must he have thought of her? She'd held a lifetime of happiness in her hands and she'd tossed it aside. Now it was too late. Too late for tears...or regrets...and that was the hardest of all to endure—the sense of regret.

CHAPTER NINE

SHE HAD NO IDEA how much time had gone by when at last, realizing the big room was almost empty, she pulled herself together and moved down the stairs and out into a blaze of sunshine. Stepping into a waiting taxi, she gave the driver the address of the hotel in Lautoka where a helpful travel agent in Auckland had already arranged her booking. At least it would be somewhere to hide away while she waited until it was time to proceed on the next stage of the long flight back to London.

It was only a short distance to the hotel. The route took her through quiet winding roads with green hills on either side. Then she was checking in at an attractive building where a smiling attendant welcomed her to the modern palm-shaded hotel. The surroundings were so beautiful, she mused, taking in the tropical palms throwing their dramatic shadows over lush green lawns, banana trees with their hanging clusters of fruit, hibiscus blossoms in flaming scarlet and rose. It was a perfect setting for love, had one been fortunate enough to qualify for that category, instead of....

Listlessly she moved along the corridor beside the smiling young Fijian girl, who led her to a clean and comfortable room. It wasn't worth unpacking her travel bags for such a short space of time, but she took a cool shower, trying to rouse herself from the depths of misery into which her meeting with Alison had plunged her.

Through the window she glimpsed tourist cars drawing up at the entrance to the building, waiting to transport sightseers on excursions to Suva and nearby islands, but Tracy turned away indifferently. What matter that this was her one day in a colorful south-sea island? Nothing mattered anymore. Perhaps if she could sleep the hours away....

She threw herself on the bed, closed her eyes, but the ceaseless whirring of the fans seemed to keep time with her thoughts. Too late...too late.... You couldn't run away from love, it seemed. It didn't matter who you were with or where you were. You couldn't escape the pictures that kept forming in your mind, banish the bitter regret. Yet later she must have fallen into a deep sleep, for when she awoke the room was in darkness and for a moment she wondered where she was. The next minute it all came flooding back—the heartache, the aching longing. But you couldn't hide here with your grief forever. She changed into a cool dark shift and went along the corridor, passing a softly lighted restaurant where diners sat at small candlelit tables. Tracy left the babble of voices behind her and wandered out into the Pacific night where the stars hung like spangles in the soft darkness above.

Slowly she crossed the grass of the spacious, sloping lawns. A sheet of water glimmered ahead and moving to the pool, she dropped down beside it, staring blindly down at the shower of stars reflected in its depths. Gradually the shadows around her deepened, the night air, fresh and cool after the tropical warmth of the day, caressed her face. Still in a daze of misery she thought she had imagined a voice, deep and vibrant, calling her name, but of course it was all a part of her imagining...and longing.

"Tracy!" There was nothing dreamlike about the determined way in which Stephen came striding toward her, the purposeful note in his voice.

"What...are you doing here?" she gulped.

"I've come to take you home." He dropped down at her side and as she caught the glint in his eyes the old magic took over and she scarcely knew what she was saying.

"But I'm going—"

"You're not, you know. You're going to do some explaining, young Tracy, and so am I! For a start—"

"But my plane for London! It's leaving in an hour."

"Let it go! We have other plans."

"We?" Her heart was beating suffocatingly. "What do you mean?"

"I mean that Lucie gave me a letter to read, the one from

your cousin Alison that sent you rushing away from the Valley this morning! And that—" his voice was grim "—explained a lot. No doubt," he went on, still in the same ruthless tone, "the one she wrote when she left the country was in the same vein?"

This was the other Stephen again, his voice sharp and crackling, shooting questions at her like rifle bullets, his eyes icy, demanding an answer, a clearing up of all the misunderstandings that had clouded the way between them.

She nodded, said very low, "And I believed her... then."

"You mean you don't now?"

"No. You see, she'd twisted the whole thing around—"

"How do you know?"

"She told me!"

"Told you!" His tone was incredulous. "Alison—"

"It's true." She might as well tell him of the encounter and all she had learned from it. It didn't matter now anyway. "I ran into her at the airport today. She was getting a plane for L.A. and she let me in on what had really happened at the Valley. I guess—" she glanced uncertainly up into the strong dark face "—that I shouldn't have needed her to put me right. I should have known—"

"*Why* should you have known, Tracy?"

He wasn't making it any easier, but she was past caring now. One thing about having lost everything you valued in life, nothing seemed to matter anymore. "Well—" she raised heavy eyes to his intent gaze "—you see, I knew *you*," she said simply.

"Yet you believed those lies of Alison's?"

"I've always believed her, until I found her out. And you see, I'd always known she had that terrific attraction for men—"

"Not for me."

In the starshine she caught a look in his eyes that sent her heart singing. All at once she was aware of a feeling of freedom. What Alison said or did would never matter to her ever again. She was herself, Tracy Cadell, not just Alison's cousin, and by the way Stephen was regarding her at this moment that was how he thought of her.

"It was pretty hard for her to take," Tracy murmured. "I mean, for her to throw herself at any man was something new in Alison's life. And then for you to turn her down. No wonder it made her mad enough to do anything."

"She was jealous of you, Tracy."

Alison, jealous of *her*! It was a novel and oddly satisfying thought.

"Forget her." She brought her mind back to Steve's vibrant voice. "She doesn't matter anymore."

"I know. I know. How stupid it all seems now—"

"That's a mild way of putting it. Especially as I happen to have been in love with you since the first day I saw you at the wharf—"

She couldn't believe her ears. "*What* did you say?"

"Love, Tracy. That's what I've been trying to tell you for weeks, only things got in the way." He gathered her into his arms, tear-stained face and all. "When you changed toward me so suddenly," he murmured against her hair, "I got the idea something was wrong, that Alison had managed to snarl things up some way, and after that—"

"I wouldn't let you explain—"

"And everything seemed to go haywire! Then when I found you'd gone and in the rush left Alison's letter behind you, things began to come clear. I took a chance that you'd come back with me—"

"But how did you know?"

"I didn't! Had the dickens of a job tracing you, but I finally found your name on the airport passenger list. After that I had to get moving... and fast! To get myself over here, get your name on the flight for the trip back to New Zealand tonight—there's a plane taking off from here in a couple of hours."

Tracy smiled up into his face. "You seemed awfully sure of yourself—"

"Oh, I am! I am! It's *you* I wasn't sure about—" He broke off as a couple came strolling from the lighted courtyard in their direction. "Hell! This place is getting too crowded for my liking. Let's get out of here!" Gently but firmly he drew her to her feet, leading her toward a narrow path that gleamed faintly among the palm trees. Soon there was nothing but the darkness, and far below, the sheen of

Vineyard in a Valley

the sea. Where the shadows were deepest, he paused, and once again, drew her close.

"Why didn't I listen?" she whispered.

"Why didn't I make you?"

They spoke together, then Stephen's seeking lips found hers. Tracy didn't know whether the low-hanging stars really were so close or whether it just seemed that way because of the heady excitement that was sweeping her away into a new and unknown world.

"I love you, Tracy." His lips brushed hers. "I'd better warn you what you're coming back to. Bill, Lucie—"

"Lucie!" She straightened in his arms. "I didn't even leave a message for her! She'll be in a tizzy, wondering what's happened—"

His look was unfathomable as his arms pinned her close. "She's got a good idea."

"What do you mean?" Tracy inquired faintly.

"Well, the last I saw of her she was down in the cellars with Bill, sorting out the last bottle of vintage champagne."

"Whatever," Tracy asked innocently, "would she be doing that for?"

"Can't you guess?"

She could scarcely think for the thud-thud of her heart and the wild happiness surging through her.

"If she'll say yes, I mean?"

Then once again his lips sought hers and her senses went flying into ecstasy.

"We'll get married right away—"

"Just as soon as you like—"

"That's what I hoped you'd say." His soft triumphant laugh sent her trembling.

They had returned to retrace their steps along the winding path beneath overhanging palms when Tracy paused. "Heavens, I've just remembered! Glenn! I should have told him I was leaving, but I forgot all about him."

"He didn't forget you, unfortunately. He's kept the phone busy at the house ever since you left, ringing every hour on the hour."

Tracy giggled. "He'll be all right with Pam. She's madly in love with him."

"But does he—"

"Not yet, but he will! All Pam needs is time and a clear field."

"I'm doing my best for her in that direction! There's something I've remembered, too. The house in the valley. We'll have to make some improvements to the place. It was okay for a couple of bachelors, but—" he carried her fingers to his lips "—when it comes to Mrs. Stephen Crane—"

"Forget about the house!" She smiled up at him, blue eyes alight. "Do you know what would please me a lot more? I'd like you to get started on switching over to those new classical whites in the vineyard!"

"Hey!" He eyed her with delight. "You really mean it, don't you?" Once again he took her in his arms and the urgency of his kiss swept everything else from her mind. At length he released her, then cupped her face in his hands. "I hope you know what you're letting yourself in for. A house in the bush, Lucie, Bill. You're not just taking on a husband, you're taking on a vineyard as well. You know that, don't you?" Gently he brushed her lips with his own.

"Oh, I do! I do! Ever since the beginning I've known how you felt about it. All that tradition—"

"It's a bit more than that," he said softly. "A sort of father-and-son thing."

"I know," Tracy agreed happily, relaxing in his arms. After a moment she murmured contentedly, "Myself, I'm a great believer in families. Only children often are, you know. Besides," she whispered, "isn't there a saying in the valley that anything you do with wine should be done with love?"

"That," said Stephen, "is what I've been trying to tell you." And this time his kiss was far from gentle.

THE FROST AND THE FIRE

The Frost and the Fire

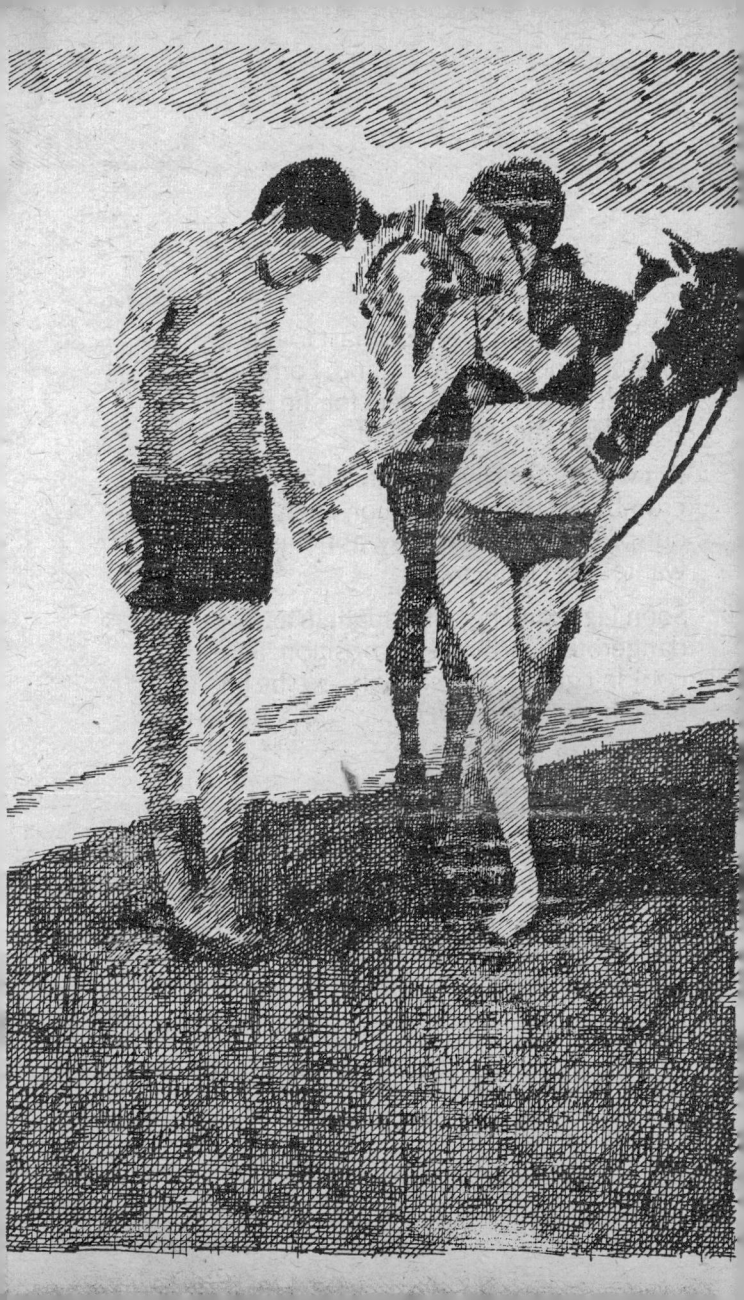

Liz had made up her mind fast to buy the property for sale in Auckland. Forty acres including ponies—perfect for the riding school she meant to set up!

But when she arrived she felt her dreams crumble. Her new neighbor, the handsome outspoken Peter Farraday, announced he'd wanted that land, too.

Soon Liz found herself caught in a dangerous heartbreaking position. She couldn't give up the school—so she had to fight the man she loved....

CHAPTER ONE

THE GIRL SEATED AT THE WHEEL of the big old car raised an anxious glance toward the rearview mirror as the creaking horse float behind her lurched around yet another fern-encrusted bend on the road cut through glistening New Zealand bush.

The brief glimpse of the chestnut's flowing mane assured her that her mount was as steadily balanced as ever. Liz had endured a few uneasy moments on the journey on his account. The float was awfully old, almost falling apart really, and if anything should go wrong on this lonely bush track with its steep grades and winding bends.... But of course Red was accustomed to traveling in the float and, despite his coloring, wasn't a temperamental type. After all, he was no longer a skittish two-year-old.

Liz concentrated her attention on the red clay and rough metal of the road ahead, swerving sharply in order to avoid a washout left from winter rains, where the road edge crumbled away to the edge of tea-tree-covered slopes dropping hundreds of feet to a gully below.

A fragment of metal thrown up from the roadway struck the undercarriage of the vehicle with a dull thud. Tattered toa-toas leaning at drunken angles along the highway tossed their feathery plumes in the breeze as the old car whined around a hairpin bend. She was fast becoming accustomed to the sheer drops on either side, the red clay banks where tall pungas raised their tightly curled fronds against the blue. She would just *have* to get used to the road now that she had committed herself to a stay in this unknown area, where the dusty winding bush track would be her main link with the outside world.

A bank of billowing gunmetal-colored clouds drifted over the sun; ahead of her stretched an undeviating length of highway. Liz relaxed against the tattered upholstery of the sagging seat and reviewed the situation. It seemed an ideal time for her to make a change from city living, now that her friend and flatmate, Mary, had left the district to be married to a farmer in another part of the country. And after her own break with Leon.... Unconsciously she sighed. Well, she wasn't the first girl to be let down by someone she'd trusted, to find she had been stupid enough to fall in love with a man who preferred someone else. If only he had told her when it all happened, instead of letting her go on blithely hoping, planning, dreaming. Oh, she should have guessed right from the beginning that a sophisticate such as Leon would choose as his wife a girl more his own type. Someone like Elaine, a fashion model with flair and finesse. Not a girl who was nuts about the country and whose tastes ran to shows and hunts and gymkhanas—things like that. Or was that merely an excuse she had dreamed up to ease the sense of bewilderment and letdown? Once again she found herself back on the dreary treadmill of her thoughts. *It's over,* she reminded herself sternly. *It was over six months ago. You're over it, too.* Why, there were times now when Leon didn't enter her thoughts for days at a time. Her soft curving lips tightened. One thing was for sure—if that was all love was about, misery and disillusionment and heartache, she was done with it! As from today she would concentrate on other things, seek new interests. For a start, this new venture that she was entering into—thanks to Uncle Harry! She sent up a tiny silent prayer of thanks to the relative whose legacy had made it possible for her to make a dream come true. Well, not quite—not yet—but she intended to give it a darned good help along the way!

Funny to think that the first tiny advertisement under the heading Property for Sale she had found in the local newspaper had proved to be the single one that she could afford to even consider purchasing. Forty acres, it said, with cottage, outbuildings, ponies, suitable riding school. Liz had felt excited merely by reading about it. At the incredibly low price at which the property was valued she would have sufficient funds left over from Uncle Harry's money— somehow she always thought of it that way—to cover the necessary expenses in getting her venture off the ground and allow for her modest living costs. By being very economical she wouldn't require a lot of new frocks and slacks out there in the bush and she had plenty of riding gear. She should be able to run the place as she wanted to for a year. If at the end of that period it proved to be successful, chances were that someone else would be willing to carry on with the work, once the riding school had been proved a workable proposition. If only the property weren't too far distant from town for her purposes. Rangiwahia.... The soft Maori syllables sounded so remote. When, however, she put through a telephone call to the solicitor who was handling the property sale, the place transpired to be not so far away from town after all, a small farming area on Auckland's wild and rugged west coast. The previous tenant, the dry legal tones informed her, had intended using the property as a riding school, so if that was what Miss Kennedy had in mind....

"Oh, it is! It is!" she assured him in her husky eager tones.

In that case she would need to make up her mind immediately, as another client was anxious to purchase the land, but she had made the first inquiry, so if she were interested....

Miss Kennedy was more than interested. She made up her mind at that moment to acquire the place that promised to be ideal for her purposes and that happened, wonder of wonders, to be available at a price she could afford.

On the following day the legal agreement was duly drawn up, signed and witnessed, and Liz found herself in possession of forty acres of land, cottage, various outbuildings, two ponies. Before taking up residence on the property, however, there were matters in town that must be attended to. She would need to hand in her notice to the director of the Crippled Children's Institute, where she worked with small cerebral palsy patients. There was her hunter, Red, to be shod and the flat to be vacated. Her few pieces of furniture would have to be transported to the cottage at Rangiwahia.

When later in the day Liz put through a phone call to her

older sister, Helen, living in a town a hundred miles south, she found the telephone connection disappointingly bad. "Look—" she caught Helen's clear precise tones "—I can't hear a word you're saying, but I gather you're thinking of making a change. Don't do anything until we've had a chat about it. I've got to come to Auckland sometime soon. Alan wants me to do some business in town for him, so I'll catch the afternoon plane."

She was as good as her word, arriving at the flat as Liz finished laying the small table for two. On being informed of the projected venture, Helen was anything but enthusiastic.

"I think you're mad," she announced with sisterly candor. "Rushing off to the back of beyond without even stopping to think! It's Uncle Harry's legacy that's given you these wild ideas! I bet he'd never have left you a cent if he'd guessed what you planned to do with the money!"

"He would, you know! He often told me that if anyone wanted to invest his capital in this country he couldn't ever go wrong by putting it into property."

"Not if the property happens to be in the outback with a name that no one's ever even heard of. What did you say it was called?"

"Rangiwahia. And what do you think it means in the Maori language? You'd never believe it! 'An invalid getting better' or 'sunshine breaking through a rift in the clouds!' Anyway, it's just the place for me." She laughed. "What I mean is, that's the whole idea of the riding center. To give the handicapped kids a chance—let them have, just for once, a place in the sun!"

Helen smiled her superior elder-sister smile. "Long on sunshine, short on everything else—that's what it'll be like. You'll see. There'll be no shops, no amenities, nothing—remote as can be."

"Not really," Liz pointed out reasonably. "It's not all that many miles out of town."

"On those winding west-coast roads," Helen retorted grimly, "a few miles can mean quite a step!" Her calm blue eyes were fixed on Liz's animated face. "What gets me is why you're taking on all this?"

"Why?" The great dark eyes were thoughtful. "I guess it's just something I've always wanted to do, ever since I started work with the disabled kids. It's been at the back of my mind for ages, but I never mentioned it to anyone before. There didn't seem much point when I couldn't do anything about it. Then when old Uncle Harry, bless his kind heart, left us equal shares of his money, wow! That did it!"

"Disabled kids?" Helen's thin face with its chiseled features wore a puzzled expression. "But I thought you were planning to set up a riding school out there on the coast. What on earth are you talking about?"

Liz sighed impatiently. "I keep telling and *telling* you! It's this idea of mine! I know, I just *know*, that if some of the spastic children could be got up on a horse, have a chance of being taught to ride, it would work miracles for them. They'd feel they could do something that ordinary kids could do. It would build up their confidence in a way nothing else could. Once they got to riding without any fear, were really relaxed, then they'd be willing to have a go at other things—maybe get themselves up on crutches, try out something else that they never dreamed they could manage to do. It would be terrific for them in other ways, too— exercise out in the open air, mobility, a complete change out in the country. It's something I've been longing to do for so long, but now I've got it all worked out," the warm husky tones ran on. "I've got permission from the doctors to have the children brought out to the horses. It'll be quite a thing, really—involve ambulances, drivers, therapists, as well as the medical men at the beginning to make sure there'll be no danger. I'm planning to have a special timber railing put up, where the children can be lifted up onto the backs of the ponies—"

"A crippled child wouldn't be able to balance himself on a pony—"

"He would if he had someone to lead the pony and a helper on each side of him to keep him steady by holding on to a special safety belt—"

"What helpers?" It seemed that Helen was bent on being discouraging.

Liz waved a careless hand. "Friends, relatives, anyone who I can get to come along for a day and lend a hand! If I can't find helpers any other way I'll put an ad in the city newspapers, make an announcement asking for them over television and radio. Some of the helpers could bring the children out from town in their private cars and that would help, too."

Helen's mind, however, appeared to be working along entirely different lines. "It's a crazy scheme! You never stop to think what could happen—"

"I know." Liz flashed her quick smile. "That's half the fun of things, not knowing. Anyway—" she lifted a small square chin "—who said it was crazy? The doctors and therapists I spoke to about it think it's a tremendous idea. They said it's something well worth trying out, that it could make all the difference in the world to these handicapped kids. And that would be just the start! If it's a success—and I *know* it will be—it could be extended later to include lots of other disabled children. Blind, deaf—they'd all require different types of treatment, of course, but they could all benefit by it. Just imagine it, Helen—" the dark eyes glowed "—a full-time riding center for the disabled!"

"You must get it from dad," Helen murmured morosely. "You were too young to remember him much, but he was like you, always dreaming up some grand scheme or other, wanting to sell up everything to finance a harebrained idea, a mythical oil well or something. It was lucky he had mum to keep his feet firmly on the ground. If only," she wailed, "you had asked Alan about it first. He would never have let you rush into a thing like this blindfolded."

"I know he wouldn't," Liz grinned cheerfully. "That's why I wanted to do it this way. Oh, I know Alan would have known about all the financial angles," she added quickly, for Helen's face had fallen. Liz was well aware that in her sister's opinion there was no one who could match her husband in the matter of business acumen. "It was just that I wanted to handle it myself."

"You don't mean to tell me...." Helen's small mouth had dropped open. "You haven't actually paid over the money?"

Liz nodded. "So it's too late to worry about it. For me it had to be Rangiwahia—or nowhere at all. I knew I'd never get a chance of any other block of land that distance from town at the price, not in a hundred years!"

"If you got forty acres of land for the money Uncle Harry left you there must be something wrong with it."

"Less—"

"Then there *is* a catch in it! Liz, how *could* you be such an utter idiot?"

"You're wrong, you know. The solicitor rang me at work and told me all about it. The place is all in grass and there's a cottage I can live in. A caretaker and his wife have it at the moment, but there are three bedrooms, so it must be fairly roomy. And what do you know? There was someone else trying to buy it, too, on the same day! I had to make up my mind right away. It'll be all right—honestly," for Helen's smooth brow was furrowed. "The previous owners intended using the place as a riding school. The barns and outbuildings are already there. There are even a couple of ponies and a certain amount of riding gear, so the solicitor told me."

"Solicitors don't always tell all."

"Oh, well, if there were anything terribly wrong I could always sell again. You can't lose out on land, especially at this low figure."

"Don't be too sure. There's a catch in it, you'll see." Liz could almost see her sister's mind turning over. "It seems to me that this project you're so carried away with is some sort of charity work. How can you possibly expect to make a living out of that?"

"Oh, I don't!"

"Now I know you're mad! Just how do you intend to live?"

Liz, however, had an answer to that one, too. "I can manage for a year. I've thought it all out." Her eyes were shining, excited. "I've enough money saved from my wages at the institute to keep me going for twelve months. If things get tough I might even think about taking a few ordinary children for rides at the weekends. Adults, too, as long as they'd be happy with a ride in the country. I won't be geared for instruction. It would be better for the ponies, keep them trim." Ignoring Helen's tightly compressed lips, she swept happily on. "It'll be great for Red, too. Just think, no more being tossed out of grazing paddocks every few weeks. He'll have swags of gorgeous green grass, fresh country air for a change, swims in the surf. He just won't know himself—"

"I wasn't thinking about Red," Helen cut in impatiently, her voice sharp with disapproval. "When did you say you intended going to this peculiar setup?"

"Next week."

"Next week!" Helen's voice was a horrified squeak. "Isn't that just like you! Impulsive to the point of idiocy! Oh, I don't mean it isn't a good idea for the spastic children," she added quickly. "I guess it would give them confidence and get them out in the open air and all that, but why can't someone else do it, some charitable organization with loads of funds?"

Liz shook her dark head. "There is no one else. If I don't carry it through the scheme won't ever get started. This is my chance to give it a go."

"Bet you haven't even been out to see the place?"

"There hasn't been time, and anyway, I don't need to. If it's suitable for a riding place and there are some ponies and somewhere to live, that's good enough for me."

Helen's blue eyes rose ceilingward. "'Don't need to,' she says! Why, it could be anything! That's you all over, burning your bridges behind you, not giving yourself time to think, tossing away a good job to rush off on some wild scheme just because you're sorry for the children. I'm sorry for spastic children, too. So is everyone else, but—" She broke off and added after a moment, "You just don't care about the things that really matter."

"Such as?" Liz got up to help herself to an apple from the sideboard and perching herself on the edge of the table, swung a slim tanned leg.

"If only," sighed Helen, "you'd think about getting married."

"Oh, that...." Liz turned her head aside before her sister, with her uncanny knack of guessing her secrets, could catch the shadow that had clouded her eyes. Thank heaven Helen had no inkling of how many times all through last year she had dreamed of marriage. It was Leon, she mused bleakly, who hadn't given the subject a thought, at least not as far as she was concerned.

Helen's thoughtful gaze rested on her young sister: petite and dark with enormous brown eyes that mirrored every change of expression. A clean jawline and that small, delightfully curved mouth. Long dark hair caught carelessly back from a center parting by a rubber band. An impeccably neat person herself, conscientious over the slightest detail of her appearance, Helen sighed exasperatedly as she took in the clear skin, innocent of makeup, the schoolgirlish white cotton blouse open at the throat, faded blue hipster jeans, rubber thongs on bare tanned feet.

"It's not as if men aren't attracted to you," she admitted reluctantly. "They are, somehow. Must have something to do with that wide-eyed stare of yours. Makes you look about seventeen, instead of twenty-two."

For answer Liz opened her brown eyes wider, wrinkling her short straight nose in derision.

"If only you'd meet some nice man. It's not as though you don't have opportunities."

Liz nibbled a long strand of dark hair in an unconscious gesture. "But I do—"

"Once or twice maybe, and that's it! The trouble with you is that you just don't *try*! Take Neville, next door to me," Helen swept on as Liz opened her mouth in protest. "Ever since that holiday you spent with us he's been quite wrapped up in you. He's everlastingly ringing me up, hinting that I write and ask you down for a weekend. All the time you were in the room he couldn't seem to take his eyes from you. You *must* have noticed!"

Liz grinned unrepentantly. "Oh, I noticed all right! That's why I haven't been down to stay lately."

"No, you wouldn't! You never ever do the right thing for yourself." You could tell by her tone, Liz thought, that she knew she was beaten, but still Helen pressed doggedly on. "If you'd only be sensible, play your cards right, you could have a well-paid nursing job in town, Neville, a nice house in the suburbs. Why don't you think about it?"

Briefly Liz thought about Neville, his neatly parted auburn hair and the suburban life that he was no doubt planning to offer her in his neat accountant's mind; then dismissed him from her thoughts.

"I told you before," Helen said, "you're just not interested."

"And the trouble with you," retorted Liz, laughing, "is that you've got this thing about marriage. Just because you've got a nice man like Alan for yourself you're always trying to con everyone else into getting married, too. But heavens to Betsy—Neville!"

"He'd make any girl a wonderful husband."

"Any other girl, maybe!" Liz laughed her warm husky laugh and slipped down from the table.

"I just can't understand you," her sister burst out. "You'll never meet anyone out there on that wild coast," she prophesied gloomily. "There's no one out there to meet. I went for a drive to the coast once and believe me, it's just about the end of the world. Nothing but high cliffs, breakers pounding in on miles of black sand, thick bush—"

"Lovely quiet roads for the kids to ride on," Liz reminded her happily.

She was accustomed to Helen's dire warnings of disaster and forgot them immediately they were uttered, in much the same way that as a child she had become used to her elder sister's protective attitude. She supposed it stemmed from both girls having lost their parents when they were so young; Helen a child of ten, Liz only a baby. But golly, to hear her talk, anyone would think Helen was her mother! Neville, indeed!

No matter what Helen said on the subject, or anyone else for that matter, she intended to take a chance on the opportunity that fate had sent her way. Even if monetary rewards were nonexistent, at least it would be work that would be satisfying and worthwhile. On the coast, and in the country, too! She could almost smell the salty tang of the sea, the fragrance of wild flowers and grass. It would be a fresh start for her, doing work she enjoyed with children to whom life had given a raw deal. In a way, it would be a sort of holiday, and even if things didn't turn out quite as well as she hoped, well, she'd have given it a go, and a year wasn't for ever.

The next moment she swung around a bend and forgot everything else in the scene that met her gaze.

A haze of spray veiled towering black sandhills, and in the sweep of bay with its wide expanse of dark sand, sunlight pinpointed myriad sequins in the glittering iron sands. From the beach a narrow jagged pinnacle soared high against a backdrop of high flax-covered hills, and beyond gleamed the misty blue of the Tasman. All at once she was struck by a sense of remoteness. There was nothing but the wind tracing patterns in drifting sand, waves thundering in a shower of spray on a wide expanse of black sand, the endless dull boom of the surf.

As she ran the car down a narrow path and turned into a patch of lush green grass in the shade of giant, gnarled pohutukawa trees, Liz decided to break her journey and take a swim in this lonely bay. Now that she had reached the coast she couldn't be far from her destination, and a dip in the cool blueness was just what she needed to dispel the heat and dust of the winding bush roads.

A swift search through her shabby travel bag made her realize that she had forgotten to include in her luggage a swimsuit or bikini. No matter, they would arrive later with the furniture in the transporter. Meantime she would go in the water in the drip-dry shirt and shorts she was wearing. The hot sunshine would dry out her garments in time for her to arrive at the property looking fairly presentable. Not, of course, the way in which Helen would reach a new destination, but still....

A check of the horse in the float assured her that the chestnut had suffered no ill effects from the journey. "Won't be long, feller!" With a friendly pat on the sturdy neck she turned away and made her way over drifts of burning black sand, cooling her feet in a fresh-water stream flowing down from the high, flax-covered hills above. Then, plowing her way over the sandhills where marram grass retained its precarious hold, she moved toward the stretch of sand, where checkered red-and-yellow flags fluttered their message, indicating an area of the beach that was safe for swimmers.

At last her feet touched cool wet sand, still flecked with fragments of foam left from the last breaker. Liz ran into a cloud of spray, enjoying the crisp tang of the water as a wave carried her away from the shore. It was invigorating, exhilarating, altogether a delight. She felt she never wished to leave this world of tossing waves, burnished sunlight and clean wet sand. But at last she flung herself toward a great wall of glassy green, letting the surging comber sweep her into the shallows. Then she splashed along the wet sand at the edge of the breakers, her dripping shirt and shorts clinging wetly around her. In the stiff sea breeze a brisk stroll to the end of the bay and around the point and she'd be dry again—at least she hoped so. She could imagine her sister's horrified expression. "Liz! You didn't arrive there looking like a drowned rat!"

A shadow fell across the water, and she realized she wasn't alone on the beach. She swung around, startled, and a deeply bronzed young man threw her a swift appraising grin as he splashed past in the shallows. Watching the tall figure in bright orange shirt and faded shorts as he moved swiftly ahead of her in the direction of a rocky point, she noticed he was carrying a kon tiki, a diminutive fishing craft with a tiny sail and short baited lines. She could see no vehicle in sight other than her own, and concluded he had come down on foot from the hills rising sheer from the black sand of the beach. A local farmer probably, judging by the mahogany tint of his skin so early in the summer season.

Funny how in that one instant the dark intelligent face had become so clearly imprinted on her mind. Strong features, soft dark hair.... But it was his expression that stayed with her: contained yet vital, pulsing with life. If it hadn't been that she was finished with that sort of electric attraction she would have been alerted to this instant awareness of a stranger, run up a danger flag in her mind! As it was, of course, she was immune; what she felt about him was a matter of mere idle curiosity. Understandable really when you considered how few residents there were in this isolated coastal area. You couldn't help but take notice of anyone you met. Especially, an unexpected thought intruded, when the stranger chanced to be so undeniably attractive!

When she reached a rocky outcrop at the point of the bay, where waves were dashing high in a cloud of spray in a gap between the rocks, she caught sight of him again. In a sheltered bay beyond the point, he stood in the foaming surf at the water's edge, waiting as the breakers, aided by an offshore wind, carried the frail craft past the line of breaking surf and out toward the depths beyond. Two farm dogs waited on the sand.

Liz stood watching him launch his little kon tiki raft. For some reason the stranger continued to hold her attention. Broad-shouldered, very erect, he was definitely worth looking at. Or was it merely the effect of a bronzed profile and vividly colored orange shirt against a blue sea? At that moment he caught sight of her and lifted a hand to his forehead in a careless gesture of salute. Liz felt a shade of embarrassment in being caught out in staring so openly. She gave a hasty wave in return and turning aside, began to seek a foothold in the spray-swept rocks, from which she could leap across the gap to the opposite side.

"Don't jump!" The strong sea breeze whipped the words away, but she caught his shout faintly and paused, balancing herself with her back pressed against a high rock as she glanced toward him.

"Wait for me!" Abandoning his line, he hurried toward her with long purposeful strides. He was nearer to her now and she caught his words clearly. "It's tricky crossing just there. There's a better place. Hold on, I'll show you!"

"It's okay!" she called back above the thunder of an oncoming breaker surging toward her. She waited until the spray dashed over her and the wave ebbed away.

"Don't try it!"

Liz decided to ignore him. If this were a method of scraping up an acquaintance it was a new approach. If he were all that anxious not to lose sight of her all he need do was wait on the rocks on the opposite side. As for there being any possible danger in the jump across, the windswept gap was certainly not a narrow one, but it wasn't too far for her to span in a leap from the cleft in the rocks where she stood. A wild sea was surging in through the opening, but if she chose the right moment to leap across....

He had almost reached her when she braced herself, watching a wave ebbing away, dragging seaweed and sand in its wake. Now! For a moment she stood poised, then leaped toward a ledge in the rocks on the other side. Somehow, though, she missed her footing and all at once she was slipping, clutching wildly at the smooth surface, her fingernails scraping along the wet rocks, finding nothing to which to cling. Then she was falling to the jagged rocky surface below, conscious of a blow to her head. At the same moment a great wall of water thundered toward her to splinter in a shower of foam high above. She was tossed over and over, helpless as a rag doll, carried away by its force and submerged in a swirling sea. Frantically she tried to fight against the waves, to make her way to the surface. At last, gasping for air, she surfaced, but another comber swept in, dragging her with it, tossing her over and over, sucking her down, down.... She was conscious of pain, of exploding red flashes, and after that she didn't have the strength to struggle any longer. It was easier to let herself slide helplessly into a tunnel of darkness that loomed ahead and toward which she felt herself being carried, faster, faster. Then there was utter blackness, nothingness....

She came back to consciousness slowly, vaguely aware of being in some shadowy place. Somewhere near at hand she could hear water dripping and around her rose the damp, fern-encrusted walls of a cave. A cave? But how could that be? And who was the man who was kneeling at her side? Even in this soft diffused light she was aware that he was watching her closely, appearing intensely relieved as she opened her eyes and fixed her glassy stare on his face. With wide dilated eyes she took in the strong features. "What happened?"

Somehow his grin was infinitely reassuring. "You slipped on the rocks over at the point, took a dive into the water when that king-size wave swept you off the rocks and out to sea. I thought I was never going to catch up with you!"

"Oh." For a moment she was content, wrapped in a sense

of strength and security. In her dreamy state of mind she was satisfied to take his word for what had happened and why she was here, but another part of her mind insisted stubbornly on sorting things out. If only it wasn't all so hazy. She tried to raise herself to a sitting position, but his face wavered out of focus and she sank back into his arms.

"Take it easy."

Bewildered, she put a hand to her forehead, conscious of soreness there, but swiftly he jerked her arm aside. "Hey! Don't touch that! You don't want to start it up bleeding all over again!"

Mystification deepened in her mind. Don't touch what? A bandage, by the feel of it. Slowly, painstakingly, she was piecing the pieces together. When she'd last seen him, she told herself carefully, he had been wearing an orange shirt. Now the shirt was hanging open, one side roughly torn away, exposing a bare bronzed chest. So *she* was wearing *his* shirt, or a part of it. It was all very puzzling. Her head was beginning to ache and it was difficult to concentrate. "I don't get it."

"Don't try! You collected a gash on the head when you zoomed down on the rocks. Not much of a cut, but it bled a fair bit. There's always a strong rip out there at the gap. The rocks are slippery as hell, and if you miss your footing when one of the big fellows comes surging in over the rocks it can really put you in the drink! It's a risky jump at the best of times, worse from where you took off! That extra big wave swept you way out of my reach for a while—thought I'd never catch up with you. I yelled out, tried to warn you not to take it on, but you—" his grin took the sting from the rebuke "—weren't having any. Guess you didn't hear me hollering with the wind blowing the other way."

For once in her life Liz forbore to blurt out the truth, admit that she had imagined he had merely wished to scrape up an acquaintance with a girl on the beach. She was too intent on her thoughts.

"Feeling okay now?"

"Oh, yes...yes!" To prove her words she jerked herself to a sitting position and found herself staring directly into the face of the man still kneeling at her side. For a moment she was struck by his eyes. A lively hazel, they seemed to be full of light. All at once unaccountably confused, she glanced away, said quickly, "I remember now! That huge wave! I couldn't do a thing. It just sucked me down with it. Then you," she finished thoughtfully, "must have swum out and grabbed me. I...."

He waved aside her proffered thanks, and getting to his feet stood looking down at her. "Just happened that I was the one who chanced to be on the spot at the right time. Lucky really—" He broke off, a serious note tinging the vibrant tones. Liz remembered the expanse of wildly tossing sea and shivered. It had been a near thing, a brush with death, no matter how lightly he pretended to regard the sea rescue.

He misinterpreted her silence. "I brought you in here to get away from the hot sun outside. You had a spot of concussion, but you weren't out for long after I caught up with you—five minutes or so."

He had lost no time in coming to her rescue, she reflected. She owed him her life, yet somehow she couldn't seem to find the right words with which to thank him. She would make one more attempt, but this time she wouldn't look at him. There was something in his vital alive gaze that seemed to put everything else out of her mind. "I guess I owe you—"

"Forget it!" His cheerful grin dispensed with the words that trembled on her lips. "You could call it good practice! Out here on the coast we have plenty of surf rescues in the season, but it's a bit early in the summer yet. You happen to be the first!"

She had a dim recollection of having passed a small building rising from a pile of rocks on her way along the beach. It must have been the Surf Lifesaving Clubhouse. To think she had been careful to swim only between the flags, and then to slip on those treacherous rocks! He was evidently a member of the local surf rescue team, a fact that no doubt explained his athletic appearance. He would need to be a powerful swimmer to battle against these rough seas. She brought her mind back to the deep tones. "Is that your car and float over there on the grass under the trees?"

She nodded.

"Think you can make it that far?"

"But of course! I can easily walk back. I'm quite all right now, honestly!" She leaped to her feet, but immediately the rock walls around her tilted alarmingly, and she put out a hand to steady herself on the damp mossy surface.

"Okay, you've made your point." She was aware of his searching glance. "That does it. You'll have to travel the easy way. Quicker anyhow, and safer. I can't have you flaking out again."

Before she realized what was happening he had stooped over her and she felt herself gathered, wet garments and all, in strong arms. Liz was so surprised she was speechless. Not that it would have made any difference, for what would be the use of arguing the matter with a man who was already carrying her toward the cave entrance and who obviously hadn't the slightest intention of doing anything else, no matter what she said to the contrary. He was infinitely gentle, holding her as effortlessly as though she were a child, his long easy strides taking them swiftly through the soft green gloom of the cave and out into a sudden blaze of sunshine. There was something disturbing yet oddly comforting in being held close against the suntanned chest. As he moved along the sands she stole an upward glance at the strong dark face. He didn't *look* as though she were any great burden to him. Indeed, on the contrary he appeared to be enjoying all this. Suddenly he caught her glance and the firmly cut lips twitched at the corners. "What do I call you?"

"Me?" Hurriedly she collected her thoughts. "Oh, I'm Elizabeth." A glimmer of laughter lighted her eyes. "But I usually answer to Liz."

"Right, Liz. I'm Peter—Peter Farraday. Just over the sandbanks now and we'll be there."

They passed the Surf Lifesaving Clubhouse, its high lookout affording an extensive view of the wide expanse of tossing sea and below, the stretch of beach where flags fluttered from tall poles. Then he was striding up the burning black sands of the sandhills and down the other side. Apparently the heated surface made no impression on his bare tanned feet, but no doubt, Liz mused, he was accustomed to the glittering iron sands.

When they reached the car he put her gently down on the long green grass beneath the trees. "I'll be fine now," she said quickly. "Thanks for everything. Poor Red," she glanced toward the chestnut, who was eyeing them inquiringly from the float, his long pale mane flying in the wind. "He must have thought I was never coming back." *Never coming back.* She shivered as she realized how very close to the truth were the carelessly spoken words. "Well—" she turned aside "—I'd better be on my way."

"Hold on." He placed a hand firmly beneath her elbow, and she glanced up to meet those bright hazel eyes. There it was again, that intent look she found so difficult to meet. "Travel bags, a horse and float. Planning to go much farther today... Liz?"

"Not really."

"You're in no shape to drive a car, you know. Better let me run you up to the house. You can get into some dry gear, slap a bandage on that cut of yours. You're not in a mad rush to press on? There's no one you want to let know you'll be a bit late in arriving?"

She shook her head.

"Right! You're coming up to the house with me!"

All at once it seemed too much bother to argue the matter, and besides he was already holding open the passenger door of the old car, settling her inside. A minute later he closed the door with a bang and slung his long tanned legs into the driver's seat. The two dogs suddenly appeared and came to join them, scrambling joyously into the rear seat among a jumble of cartons, boxes and horse gear.

She watched him in a bemused way as he put the car in gear, and swinging across the grassy patch ran along a short stretch of sandy roadway, then took a steeply winding road curving up into bush-clad hills. A battered jalopy with twin fins of surfboards rising from a roof rack swept past them on the narrow road, and as the dust cleared, Liz realized they were moving along a well-worn track. Overhanging punga fronds and dust-coated spears of tall flax brushed the car as they went on. Tall tree ferns clustering around a wide

The Frost and the Fire

entrance gate all but obscured a faded notice board: Arundel Station. Beneath was a more recent notice: No Shooting.

Her companion got out to fling the gate wide, then returned to close it behind the car. Liz smiled gaily up at him. "I always thought that was the passenger's job, opening and closing the gate?"

"You're excused today."

They were taking a winding road that cut around the side of a cleared hill. Arum lilies grew wild on the grassy slopes, and sheep scattered in mad panic at their approach. Presently there were two farther gates to be opened and closed behind them, two more notice boards nailed to tree trunks: No fires. No trespassing. Private road. Liz raised inquiring dark eyes. "Your property?"

"That's right."

"You've put up an awful lot of notices, made your message loud and clear. Away out here in the country it's so quiet I shouldn't think—I mean, do you need them?"

"I need them." At the sudden tightening of his jaw Liz did not pursue the subject. Glancing upward toward a green-roofed timber house that sprawled against a backdrop of tall blue gums, she murmured lightly, "You must be able to see for miles from up there on the hilltop!"

This time her remark evoked an entirely different reaction. The lean brown face was alight. "It's one of the best views around. Up here we take in the whole sweep of the bay, can see right away down to the heads."

They rattled over a cattlestop and took a curving driveway that led them past a loading ramp, the mellow red of shearing sheds and stock-pens. Then they were sweeping past garages, taking a winding path bordered with drifts of pink, lilac and blue of massive flowering hydrangea bushes.

"Right, we're here!" He braked at the foot of a flight of worn timber steps leading up to a creeper-shaded veranda running the full width of the old colonial-style house. For a moment he sat motionless, well-shaped hands resting on the steering wheel, and Liz followed his gaze to the scene outspread below. She caught her breath. "I can see what you mean by the view!" Far below was the incredible violet blue of the Tasman, breakers creaming in wave after wave on a dark shore. A succession of bush-fringed bays fell away into the misty distance.

The next moment he was out of the car and the two dogs leaped down at his side. He reached for Liz's travel bag, then holding open the passenger door, eyed her closely. "Feeling all right?"

"Oh, yes, of course I am!" It was annoying and dismaying to realize she still suffered from the stupid dizziness. Not that she would admit such a thing to him! She had a dreadful suspicion that at the slightest sign of weakness he would scoop her up bodily once again, just as though she were a sheep or something, and carry her up the steps. Fortunately the wave of weakness passed, and pulling herself together she went up the steps at his side, hurrying to keep pace with his long easy strides.

They moved down a long passage until he threw open a door at the side, ushering her into a large airy lounge room with its worn carpet of indeterminate coloring, deep comfortable chairs and an old kauri table from an earlier era. Someone had covered the massive old settee with floral linen in cool shades of muted greens and turquoise, and a massed flower arrangement standing on a low table gave evidence of a woman's touch. Liz couldn't understand her absurd sense of disappointment. She didn't know why she had taken it for granted he was unmarried simply because he had chanced to be alone when they met.

Crossing the big room, he leaned from a wide-open window and called to someone outside, "Hey, Kate, are you around?"

"No use." Withdrawing a dark head from the opening, he turned toward Liz with a philosophical shrug. "I may as well give up trying to get her. She's got this thing about gardening, and now she's started on the vegetable plot down in the valley she can't keep away from it. Won't be back for hours! Anyway, this is what you need...." Moving toward a cocktail cabinet in a corner of the room, he poured a small glass of brandy and held it toward her. "For you!"

"Must I?" She pulled a face but did as he asked—or rather ordered, she reflected ruefully. Nevertheless she had to admit that his suggestion had been a good one, for soon a warmth was stealing through her veins, banishing the last lingering remnants of weakness.

She reached up to place the empty goblet on the mantel, then stood transfixed as she caught sight of her reflection in the long-framed mirror overhead. What a mess she looked! A wet, bloodstained orange bandage around her head, scratched arms, torn fingernails, damp clothing encrusted with black sand. She only hoped the unseen Kate wouldn't make an appearance before Liz could escape from the house.

He seemed to read her thoughts. "Your bag's over there in the room opposite." He jerked his head toward an opening on the other side of the passage. "Shower's down at the end," he went on matter-of-factly. "Why don't you dive in? It'll freshen you up, loosen that bandage, too. You won't know yourself afterward."

"Well...." Liz hesitated, aware of her grotesque appearance: clinging dark sand all over her, smudged clown face with its orange headgear and dark bruising on her cheek. It would be heavenly to take a shower, but....

He sent her a direct glance from alert hazel eyes. "Kate would never forgive me if I let you go on without doing something about it."

Kate. All at once she made up her mind. "All right, then." In the spacious, simply furnished bedroom with its heavy old-fashioned chest and twin beds, Liz took undergarments, shirt and jeans from her travel bag. The garments were worn and faded but blessedly sand free and dry. Then, making her way along the passage to the bathroom, she was soon reveling in the cool shower that washed away sand from her hair and skin and loosened the bloodstained bandage from her forehead. It was only a small cut after all, she realized now.

Presently she made her way back to the lounge room: a small slim girl with enormous brown eyes in a face pale beneath the tan; damp dark hair combed and hanging free; a cool cream silk shirt falling loosely over faded blue jeans.

The man waiting by the window spun around to face her as she came into the room and Liz smiled up at him. "Is this better?"

"Better? It's quite...." He broke off, a glint of amusement in his appreciative glance.

"A transformation?" Liz put in. "Yes, I know." No doubt she did look rather different from the disheveled spectacle she had presented a short while ago.

"There's just one thing...." Swiftly he crossed the room and reached toward a small box on the mantel. With deft tanned fingers he placed a small square of adhesive plaster over the cut on her forehead. He was very close, but surely, Liz told herself confusedly, that was no excuse for her intense awareness of him. Blame it on those brief moments of concussion.

"I've made coffee." She turned away, realizing there were two steaming pottery beakers standing on the big table. "How do you like it? Black or white?"

"Black, please."

"Good! That's how it is!"

She took the beaker he was extending toward her and went to perch on a low seat by the window. She couldn't help but wonder at the reaction of the absent, garden-loving Kate were she to return at this moment and find her husband entertaining a strange girl. Perhaps, though, folk who lived in this coastal area with its wild and dangerous surf beaches were accustomed to unexpected guests and sea rescues. Aloud she murmured, "From up here you can see right down to the bay. There's a Surf Lifesaving Club lookout on the top of the rocks."

He came to stand at her side, his gaze roving the windswept sandhills and tossing sea far below. "It's a terrific spot! Great for fishing, too."

"Fishing!" All at once she remembered the tiny kon tiki raft he had been in the act of launching when she had reached the gap in the rocks. "I hope I didn't spoil things for you today?"

"Not to worry. I usually leave the line out for a few hours. Later on I'll go down to the beach and see what the tide's brought in. Going far?"

Liz realized that as yet she had given him no explanation as to where she was bound for or how she chanced to be swimming alone in a remote bay, while nearby her chestnut

The Frost and the Fire

waited in his float. All at once her face brightened; her husky voice was warm with enthusiasm as she glanced toward him. "You'd never guess."

"Tell me!"

"I've bought some property! It can't be far from here, and what do you know? I'm starting up a riding school for kids!"

"Riding? Not the old Rangiwahia block?" he cut in sharply.

"That's it! I'm the new owner."

He didn't look at all impressed. On the contrary he appeared taken aback, wary all of a sudden. "*Bought it*, you said?"

"Why, yes," she faltered. "What's wrong with a riding school anyway?"

He raised sardonic black brows. "Nothing—yet."

Liz decided to ignore his disagreeable attitude. After all, what she did with her money was no concern of his.

"I couldn't believe it," she said warmly, hands cupped around the pottery beaker, eyes dreaming. "You see, I'd been longing to go in for something like this for ages, but I simply didn't have the capital and the properties were all so expensive—way beyond anything I could ever afford. Then the most wonderful thing happened. I was left some money—not a great deal, but enough. I knew as soon as I saw this ad in the paper that it was just what I'd been looking for. Forty acres, it said, all in grass, with cottage. That means I'll have somewhere to live. Outbuildings—somewhere to keep the saddlery and all the rest of the gear I'll need. There's even a couple of ponies and some riding gear. That'll be a start anyway. 'Suitable for riding school,' the ad said."

She glanced toward him, but he appeared more disapproving than ever. "And you haven't seen the place before buying it?"

It wasn't so much what he said as the sardonic expression in his eyes that was so infuriating. All at once she couldn't endure his discouraging attitude one moment longer. "No, I haven't!" She set down her empty beaker with a little clatter. "You're just as bad as Helen!"

"Am I now?" He was merely amused by her outburst. "And who's Helen?"

"My sister." Liz's voice was taut. "She's always raving on like that, too, making difficulties, spoiling everything! Anyone would think," she swept on hotly, "that starting up a riding center for kids was just about the most impossible thing anyone ever heard of. But I can manage it, and if Rangiwahia turns out to be anything like what I'm hoping it will...."

Peter Farraday sent her an unfathomable look, but merely murmured quietly, "Well, you'll be able to see it for yourself pretty soon. Cigarette?"

She shook her head. "Not just now, thanks. I must get on. I just can't wait to see it!"

"Mind if I smoke?"

"Of course not."

He flicked a lighter, held it to his cigarette and replaced the lighter in the pocket of the crisp white shirt. "I'll run you over there."

"Oh, no, *please*. I'm quite well again now. There's no need—"

"Just the same, I'll take you. You've taken one knock already today." What he meant by that remark she couldn't imagine, although something about his wry grin was faintly disquieting. The protest she had been about to make died on her lips. Instead she asked, "Is it far from here, the place?"

"No distance." He waved his cigarette in the direction of the window and the sheep-dotted hills rising so near the house. "Just over the hill. Bang next door to here, actually."

"Really?" So he would be her nearest neighbor, this unpredictable man who in some strange manner managed both to annoy and attract her at the same time. She got to her feet, thankful to find that there was no longer any unsteadiness in her limbs. "Do you think we could get along now?" Somehow she didn't want his wife to return and find her here. There would be endless explanations to be made and she had a growing conviction that the accident had been due to her own carelessness. Besides, she wanted to see her own land—and soon!

"Right. Let's go!" He crushed out his cigarette in a green glass ashtray. Liz hesitated, glancing back over her shoulder toward the glasses and stained beakers. "How about those? Shall I...."

He waved a careless hand. "Don't give them a thought. Kate'll fix them when she gets back."

As they went down the veranda steps together Liz couldn't help but feel a sense of relief that she hadn't been forced into a meeting with the absent Kate. She might not.... She knew if *she* were his wife she wouldn't welcome.... She brought herself up with a jerk, aghast at the direction in which her thoughts were leading her.

"But how will you get back?" she asked as he tossed her travel bag in the rear seat of the car and settled his long length in the driver's seat.

"It's no distance over the paddocks when you know the short cuts!" He swung the car and float around in the driveway, and presently they were retracing the route leading back to the main road.

"Do you run all sheep here?" she asked.

"At Arundel?" He nodded. "That's right. I was brought up on a station; my folks are still over in the old homestead farther up the coast. It was rough going when I first took the place over, covered in bush, overrun with gorse and blackberry, but I'm breaking it in gradually. Cleared away the bush for a start, except in the dips between the hills." Liz's gaze moved to the patches of burnished green running up the gullies. Clusters of tall forest trees: kauri, tawa, rimu, rose above thickly growing pungas and lacy tree ferns. She brought her mind back to the deep vibrant tones. "Helicopters do a tremendous job when it comes to spraying gorse and blackberry, and you can't beat the top-dressing boys with their light aircraft when it comes to ringing in the hill country."

"You work it on your own?"

"I've got a couple of lads with me. They help out and get a line on how to do the job at the same time. There goes one of them now!" In the distance Liz discerned a motorcycle hurtling at a precipitous angle down a grassy hillside, followed by two sheep dogs. "Wayne likes his 'mountain goat' to chase around the boundary fences, but Tim, he's like me. He prefers the horse every time for hilly country. I guess that's something you'd understand." He lifted his gaze to the small mirror overhead with its reflection of the horse float behind them. "Is he a show jumper?"

"Is he ever!" As always when she spoke of Red, Liz's small face was alive with interest. "Red's won oodles of ribbons. Do you know once, just once, at a big country show, he won the purple ribbon for champion hack! I've never felt so proud! Only—" the eager tones fell a little "—I haven't shown him or hunted him for the last two seasons. It was so difficult living in town and grazing Red miles away in an outer suburb, and what with working at the hospital and having odd hours...." Her voice trailed away. It wasn't true. It was because of Leon that she had given up the outdoor activities she loved. He had had no time for horses or riding. And where had all the sacrifices got her? Just nowhere at all! Catch her ever again putting aside her own interests merely to please a man! Aloud she said, "I'm just longing to get Red settled in alongside where I'm living instead of having him twenty miles away!"

As the last gate was closed behind them she realized they had left Arundel Station behind them and were taking a winding, bush-fringed road. It seemed only a short distance and they were turning off the main highway, running in toward an opening in a long boundary fence of macrocarpa pines.

Liz turned a surprised face toward him. "But this isn't... Rangiwahia?"

"It is, you know." He was skirting a taranaki gate of barbed wire and light batons lying in the long grass at the entrance.

"It can't be—I mean, I didn't expect it to be like this!"

CHAPTER TWO

PETER FARRADAY MADE NO ANSWER, and as they bumped over the rutted ground Liz gazed in growing consternation at the rough paddocks over which they were traveling. Ahead she could see a red-roofed timber cottage, clearly in dire need of painting and repair. As they turned in at an open gateway and sped down an overgrown pathway between trailing roses and giant overhanging shrubs, the picture became even less prepossessing. The area of lawn surrounding the buildings had been recently trimmed, but the cottage was a dismal-looking dwelling with flaking white paintwork and rotting front steps. A short distance down the broken pathway stood a huge empty shed, doors swinging open and sagging on their hinges. Could that derelict-looking place be the barn mentioned in the advertisement, she wondered wildly as the car slid to a stop.

"The view—" Liz clutched at the single aspect of the property that appeared to match up to her glowing expectations "—is really fantastic! Almost the same as the one you have from your home—" She stopped short. Imagine comparing *his* well-stocked thousand-acre station with *her* rough paddocks! Ignoring his lack of response, she struggled determinedly on. "One thing, there's oodles of grass everywhere. Long grass, too."

It seemed, however, that he had no intention of letting her off one thing. "Always is at this time of the year."

Suddenly a question sprang into her mind, something she should have considered first of all instead of now, when it was probably too late. "Fences?" Her gaze swept the flat green paddocks around her. "I wonder...."

His shrug was ironic. "What fences?"

It was, she realized all too true. A few short lengths of boundary fences remained intact, but the greater part consisted of sagging posts and rusted trailing wires. There were gaps where stock had pushed its way through—or broken through more likely, for what was there to prevent them? Now she realized why the taranaki gate at the entrance to the property had been left lying in the grass. Open or shut, what difference did it make? She made a final effort to rally her swiftly fading hopes. "The horses. I caught a glimpse of them just now. They were grazing at the back of the big shed down there. Perhaps...."

He shot her one of those swift sardonic glances, and she found herself regretting having allowed him to bring her here. If only she could have faced her moment of truth alone! In a flash she leaped from the car and slammed the door behind her. Then she was hurrying down the overgrown pathway, pushing aside long sprays of pink rambler roses that clutched at her with their thorny tendrils. Uninvited, unwelcome, he caught up with her and strolled along at her side, but she no longer cared. All she knew was that she might as well find out the worst and get it over with. Passing the derelict shed, she glanced inside, but the dim recess appeared to be empty, except for a few cracked and rotting bridles hanging from a peg on the rough wall, a bulging sack standing in a corner.

When she reached the back of the building the two ponies grazing nearby raised their heads to gaze at her with lackluster eyes. They were both quite old, she realized at once. One, a piebald, evidently accustomed to being fed bread or carrots, moved toward her with an expectant air and limping gait. Liz stooped over to lift a small hoof, placing an exploratory hand over a hard swelling on the fetlock.

"It's no use trying to do anything about it," Peter told her. "It's a permanent injury."

He was right, of course, damnably, horribly right—as usual! Unconsciously she sighed and turned toward the bay pony, who came trotting toward her. He had, she realized, a definite swayback, and it was clear that neither pony would be of the slightest use to her. Absently she stroked two soft muzzles.

The perceptive hazel eyes that seemed to see so much more than she would like were fixed on her despondent face. "Not quite what you expected, hmm?"

"Not quite." She tried to keep her voice steady.

"I did try to warn you."

Liz didn't answer. He seemed to make a habit of warning her, she reflected crossly, and all to no purpose. First of all the rocks, then Rangiwahia. Not that it made the slightest difference—she made an effort to control her trembling lips—for today she seemed bent on collecting trouble for herself.

"It sure could do with a spot of doing up. Well—" he spun around on his heel "—I'll go and get your chestnut out of the float. He must be about browned off with it by this time. All right if I put him down here with the ponies?"

"Yes, of course." What did it matter, she thought wildly as he left her to stride toward the car. What did anything matter today?

When the horse had been let loose to explore his new surroundings, Liz gazed toward a large closed shed not far from the cottage. "I wonder what's in there? We might as well go and take a look." Together they moved up the broken pathway.

As Peter flung open the double doors a large rectangular area sprang to view. The big, high-ceilinged room was dim and shadowy in contrast with the bright sunlight outside, but as her eyes became accustomed to the gloom Liz discerned a long table beneath a window. A telephone stood on the table and she moved toward it. It wasn't surprising to find the line wasn't connected. At least, though, the barnlike place appeared to have been recently built and was of more solid construction than the ramshackle old shed down the yard. Her gaze slid around the unlined walls, the emptiness. "Whatever could it have been meant for originally?"

"The first owners of the place ran a poultry farm. They had this built for use as a broody shed," he told her.

A broody shed! She had a wild impulse toward hysteria.

"Hello, there! I didn't hear the car arrive or I'd have been out there to welcome you!" A tall angular woman of middle age wearing a sleeveless floral frock stood in the open doorway, her short wiry gray hair outlined in a nimbus of light. "You'll be Miss Kennedy, the new owner?" The tanned face broke into a pleasant smile. "We were wondering, Stan and I, whether you'd get here before dark."

Liz nodded. "That's me, and you're...."

Another wide and friendly smile. "We're the Gallaghers, Evelyn and Stan. We heard the cottage was empty and moved in last month. But there's plenty of room," she added quickly. "Come along, inside. Stan's somewhere around. I'll go and find him."

There was no need, for at that moment a stockily built man in his early sixties with muscular shoulders and grizzled gray hair strolled toward them. He extended a toil-roughened hand toward Liz.

"Stan's been a bushman most of his life," his wife explained, "but he's given it up now, and we thought we'd take a holiday for a few months while we look around for something easier he can do. Meantime—" even in the midst of her crushing sense of disappointment Liz was aware of the anxious note in the clear tones, the silent appeal in the gray eyes "—would it suit you if we stayed on for a while? We'd pay the usual rent for the cottage, of course."

"Evvie's a first-rate cook," her husband offered with a shy grin.

"And he's ever so handy at fixing things around the place," his wife put in, laughing.

"I don't see why not." Somehow Liz couldn't seem to think straight. Everything she had found here had turned out to be so different from the perfect riding-school setup she had envisaged. "You're both welcome to stay meantime. Afterward...." She sighed. "Well, I'm not sure yet what my plans are."

"That's good enough for us," Evelyn said on a note of relief. "Now come inside and I'll show you around the place. We've only been here a short while ourselves, but if we stay on we could do the rooms up a bit. Stan's a dab hand when it comes to painting and paperhanging, and the cottage is simply crying out for some work to be done on it." She turned toward the tall man standing silently in the background. "How about you, Peter? Are you coming along to the cottage, too?"

"Thanks, Mrs. Gallagher, but I won't join you this time. I've got to get cracking." His gaze lingered on Liz's wan face with its dark bruising on the cheekbone, and a hint of concern colored his tones. "Have an early night Liz. Time enough to worry about things in the morning."

"I suppose so." She turned dispiritedly away, a sick feeling of disappointment welling up within her. She had been so certain that everything here would match up to her dream picture, and now.... Oh, for those shining white fences, prancing ponies, the well-stocked barn with its saddles and bridles neatly arranged on their brackets! The dilapidated old shed was large enough for use as a barn, goodness knows. Large—and empty. Bare of saddlery, feed, gear, of everything she had hoped to find there. The inner fences on the property were practically useless as they stood, or rather didn't stand, she told herself ruefully. And as to the horses....

Peter's vibrant tones broke in on her despairing thoughts. "Think about it tomorrow. And look, if you get the slightest sign of anything wrong, headache, blackout, anything, just give me a ring at Arundel and I'll be over right away with the doc." He turned toward the other two. "Liz took a fall out on the rocks today over at the gap. Collected a spot of concussion."

"Oh, that's too bad. But don't worry," Evelyn Gallagher said in her deep quiet tones, "we'll keep an eye on her."

"Right! I'll get back. See you!" A lift of a bronzed hand and he had turned away to vault a low fence and go striding away across the paddocks.

"Wait!" Liz was out of breath when she finally caught up with the waiting figure. "I just wanted to say.... Well, thanks for everything! And will you tell your wife," she rushed on in her soft husky voice, "that I'm awfully sorry about all that sand I left on the carpet—"

"My...wife?" For a moment he eyed her with a puzzled stare, then his expression cleared. "You mean Kate? She's not quite in my age group. Aunts never are, do you think?" The lively hazel eyes glinted with a teasing light. "I'll tell you something, though, Liz." He threw a backward grin over his shoulder. "When I find my own special kind of girl, you'll be the first to know!"

Liz went back over the paddock in a turmoil of emotion.

She didn't know what to make of him. That boob she'd made mistaking him for a married man—anyone could have made the same blunder. There was no need for him to make such a thing of it! Maddening to remember how deeply she was indebted to him. She owed him her life, no use trying to get around it. She had been knocked unconscious by a blow to the head—thoughtfully she fingered the swelling on her forehead—and but for his swift action she would have drowned out there on the sun-lit beach.

"I couldn't help hearing what you said." She became aware of Evelyn strolling toward her. "That Kate, she's a relative of Peter Farraday who housekeeps for him and the two boys working on the station. Not that they'll be needing her there much longer, from what folks are saying around here." They climbed through the sagging fence and approached the cottage. "Stan and I used to live in this district a few years ago, and at that time Peter was in love with a local girl; Beryl Manning her name is now. Her parents were alive then. They owned a huge sheep station not far away. Then quite suddenly there was some sort of quarrel. No one knew what had really happened, but Beryl rushed away to Queensland, and after a while we heard she'd married a grazier there, a widower with a young son. Darryl his name is, and they say she dotes on him just as though he were her own. Beryl only came back here for a visit, but they tell me she's been here for months now, staying with Darryl and her Aunt Olga up at the old homestead. And now that Beryl's free..."

"Free?" Liz was well aware she was encouraging a gossip session, but she couldn't seem to help herself.

"Oh, didn't I tell you? Her husband died just a few months ago. He was years older than she was and he took a sudden heart attack. One thing, she'll have no financial worries. They say her husband was awfully wealthy, and she was well off even before she married him. No property problems, either. The manager who had been looking after the station since her parents died left a month ago, but she sent to Australia for a new man, and he's living now in the farm cottage on the property. Beryl's come back looking

The Frost and the Fire

lovelier than ever, though I simply can't imagine how that could be! I always thought of her as the most beautiful girl I ever saw. I caught sight of her again just the other day and she's exactly the same—Oh, she's not young anymore," she ran on in answer to the surprised expression in Liz's dark eyes. "But she *looks* young, and that's all that matters. Not the sort of girl a man could forget in a hurry. Heaven only knows what brought her back to this little corner of the world, a girl like that who could live in any capital of Europe if she wanted to. Or what keeps her here now," she added significantly. "She always said she hated living in the country. She made no secret of it, yet now she doesn't seem to think of leaving."

"Maybe she has friends in the district?"

Evelyn shook her cropped gray hair back from her face. "Beryl was never one for girl friends, and all the men she used to know around here are married now—except Peter. Oh, well, she's the sort who always manages to get her own way in the end. Good luck to her." Reflectively she chewed a long blade of grass. "He looks you so straight in the eye it's hard to believe what happened a while ago between Peter and the last owner of this place, but from what Lance Pritchard's parents told us—"

"Come into the cottage and have a look around!" Stan had come to join them, and the three went up the rickety steps together. Soon they were moving through a tiny dark hall into a sparsely furnished living room. "The picture from the windows makes up for a lot!" Stan jerked aside the long faded velvet curtains, and a vista of sea and bush-clad hills and far bays sprang to view. Somehow, though, Liz was having difficulty in concentrating on anything in the cottage. Her thoughts kept reverting to that disturbing Peter Farraday. Not married yet, apparently, but it wouldn't be long. So he had already found "his own special kind of girl," although why it should matter so much to her was something she failed to understand. Something else, too, nagged below the surface of her mind. What had Evelyn Gallagher meant by her reference to some sort of disagreement between Peter Farraday and the previous owner of the property?

"There's a nice big kitchen." She became aware of Evelyn's friendly tones as the three moved into another room. "And the electric range cooks well, even if it is an old model. Stan says if we're staying here for a while he'll put in a stainless-steel sink bench. He's got one stashed away in the shed— These are the bedrooms." The rooms were spacious and airy, the floors covered in worn cheap linoleum. Dressing chests and beds were in need of a fresh coat of paint. In the front bedroom her worn travel bag lay on the tidily made bed. On the bureau a glass vase held a single shot-silk rosebud.

Evelyn thrust aside a hanging curtain in a corner, exposing a line of hooks and hangers in a makeshift wardrobe. "It looks a lot worse from the outside than it really is. There's nothing really wrong with the place."

"No." But there was a lot wrong with her own private little world—so much so that she could see no way out of her difficulties. Later, seated with the Gallaghers at the small round table covered in gay floral cloth, Liz picked listlessly at the tastefully prepared meal of salad and cold meats as her mind went over and over the situation. She wouldn't give up right at the outset. There *must* be a way of surmounting the unexpected financial hurdle, if only she could think of it.

"How much would it cost to replace the fencing?" she inquired suddenly.

"How much?" Stan put down his knife and fork while he considered the matter. "Well, now, you'd have to get a contractor to do the job. Mind you," the rich thoughtful tones flowed on, "the boundary ones are good enough for a year or two yet, and a lot of the others could be patched up to last a long time. Were you thinking of running stock on the place?"

Liz nodded. "I thought ponies—about fifteen. A sort of riding school was what I had in mind."

"I see. Well, horses would take a lot less wiring to keep them in than sheep would. Guess you could count on a thousand dollars at the very least."

A thousand dollars! For all the difference it would make to her state of finances it might just as well be ten thousand.

She realized the other two were eyeing her curiously. Stan said, "You planning to get the place fixed up right away?"

"No." Liz's head was bent, dark curtains of hair falling around her face as she absently traced a pattern with her fork on the tablecloth. "Just thinking." After a moment she glanced up. "You know, I got the idea from the solicitor when I bought the property here that the last owner had ideas along the same lines, but he couldn't have done much about it. There's no gear about the place—well, none that's any good at all. No horses except those two pathetic old ponies down in the yard. No proper fencing inside the boundaries. What happened? Did he change his mind?"

"He had it changed for him," Evelyn said. "He would have stayed longer but—"

Her husband sent her a warning glance. "He wasn't the type for country life. We only met him once, just as he was moving out, but anyone could see he wouldn't be interested in that sort of setup. Seems his father set him up here, hoping Lance would give it a go as a riding place, but it was all just a waste of money as far as he was concerned. He had a holiday here and so did his friends from town, but as to making a living out of the place—" he threw up weathered palms "—I believe at the beginning he did have a small amount of riding gear, a few hacks and a couple of decent ponies—his parents saw to that—but that was as far as it went. He didn't even take the trouble to fix up the fencing. Guess he'd never tackled that sort of work, a city bloke like him...."

"Or any sort of work, either, if you ask me!" Evelyn's husband silenced her with a significant glance that wasn't lost on Liz.

When the tea things had been cleared away she arranged her clothing in the bureau drawers that jammed each time she opened them. With her radiogram and records standing in a corner of the living room, her personal belongings scattered around the bedroom, the cottage took on a slightly more homey air. The Gallaghers, after assuring her they would be on hand if she needed them, retired early, and soon Liz, too, prepared for an early night. Not, she told herself, because *he* had suggested it, but merely because there seemed little else to do.

Picking up a novel, she settled herself comfortably against the pillows and attempted to read, but the printed letters danced beneath the light from the naked bulb overhead as more pressing matters clamored for her attention. "Leave it till morning," Peter Farraday told her. Sound advice, if she could follow it. Switching off the light she closed her eyes, but she felt too strung up to sleep. She lay listening to the unfamiliar sounds breaking the intense stillness of the country; the mournful "more-pork" of a native owl somewhere in the bush-filled gully below, the dull roar of the surf. Yet she must have drifted off into slumber, for some time later she found herself hazily wondering where she was. Recollection came rushing back, and at the same moment she became aware of a sound that alerted her to instant attention, the soft pad-pad of footsteps passing on the path below her window.

Slipping from bed, she went to the window, and parting the draperies, peered outside. Could that be a man's shadow moving toward the barn at the end of the path? Not that it would do him any good if burglary was his aim, she thought wryly. Perhaps she had imagined the moving shadow, but just to make certain.... Throwing a filmy brunch coat over her shorty pajamas, she caught up a torch, and moving down the dark little hall let herself quietly out the door and into the moon-silvered night. As she hurried down the path she collided with a tall figure emerging from the cave of blackness that was the open shed, and without stopping to think she pressed the switch of her flashlight. Immediately a man's startled face sprang to view, a thin young face with a shock of tousled blond hair and a fair beard, eyes wide with apprehension.

"You scared the wits out of me! Put that thing out, will you?"

"You scared *me*!" Liz realized the gangling figure wore dark jersey and slacks, rubber-soled shoes. A sack dangled from his hand. "What have you got in there?" she cried sharply.

"Hold on!" He put the sack down on the pathway between them. "I can guess what's on your mind, but you've got it all wrong! I just nipped back for something I left behind in the barn the other day when I lit out— Hey!" The flashlight that Liz held in her hand wavered over the narrow features. "Now I get it! You're the girl who bought me out!"

"That's right." Liz was feeling more and more bewildered. "Now I'm going to ask *you* something! Why all the secrecy? You could have come back here any time. I'd have given you whatever it is you want—" All at once a thought flashed through her mind. She had been told by the solicitor that there had been a certain amount of gear left at the cottage and included in the sale of the property. Was he...?

"Saw the lights were all out. Didn't want to wake anyone up," he muttered. "It was just some personal stuff—clothing and all that," he went on evasively. "What was the idea of buying this place anyhow? Thinking of an investment?"

"I haven't decided... yet."

"Well, take my advice and don't ever go in for running a riding school. Believe me, I know what I'm talking about! It doesn't work out—not with Farraday living bang over the hill. He's forced me out of the place and he'll do the same to you if you try anything in that line."

"You did start a riding school, then?"

"I had a crack at it. Half a dozen nags, a bit of gear—that was about it. I was going to go in for more horses, more gear, but hell, what was the use? The fences were in a mess, and Farraday went crazy if stock got into his territory. In the end I decided to call it a day, thanks to Farraday. I got rid of the lot. He wasn't satisfied until he'd spoiled my chances, sent me packing."

"But he couldn't *force* you to go."

"You reckon? I'll tell you what he can do! He can make life so damned unpleasant for you that it isn't worth the effort trying to make a go of it! Do you know what happens if one of your nags happens to stray over the boundary into his precious hillsides? He threatens you with legal action! Once he pointed a gun, scared all hell out of me! How was I to know I'd made a mistake and was on his land instead of my own? Take it from me, you'll never get anywhere with him around. He's forced me to opt out and he'll do the same for you!" An ugly sneer twisted the slack lips. "But I got my own back on him! I kept my mouth shut about getting out of here, waited until he was well out of the way down south. Then I shoved a For Sale ad in the city papers. I knew he'd never see it. The next week I got a sale for the place, thanks to you!"

She switched off the flashlight. "But I don't understand. Are you trying to tell me that this little property could possibly mean a thing to a big landowner like Peter Farraday?"

"It could mean a lot! I happen to know that he's mad keen to get hold of it."

"With all the acres he owns?" They were speaking in whispers. "I can't believe it. Why would he—"

"Can't you guess? This place happens to have easy access down to the beach. All it needs is a track bulldozed through the bush. Besides, there's something else that's a lot more important in these hot dry summers, and that's a good water supply from the creek down there in the gully—" He stopped short, staring down at her, and all at once his voice was hoarse, ingratiating. "Hey, you look mighty appealing in that getup. Can't think why I didn't notice before." He took a step toward her. "What are we doing wasting time?" Before she could guess at his intention he had caught her in lean arms and was crushing her roughly against his chest. Liz struggled violently, pushing against him with both hands.

"Get out!" Her muffled cry cut through the silence of the night, and at the same moment a shadow, darker than the rest, advanced swiftly toward them. A businesslike fist shot out to land squarely on a bearded chin, and the youth crumpled and fell to the ground. The next minute he was on his feet, shaking with fury. "What's the big idea? I wasn't doing any harm!"

"What were you hanging around here for, then?" Even in the dim light Liz could see Peter's threatening expression.

"Nothing, nothing!" The youth fingered a bruised jaw. "Can't a guy come back to collect his own property?"

"So that's it!" In a swift movement Peter bent, spilling the contents of the sack out onto the pathway: a gleaming saddle, obviously new; a jingling bridle; a silver-mounted whip. "*Your* property!" Peter's voice was cutting. "You knew these went with the sale of the place. Thought you'd get away with it, just as you did with the rest of the gear! It's not your stuff and you know it!"

"Give me...." The whining tones died into silence as Peter took a menacing step toward him.

"Get out of here, Pritchard, *fast*, or I'll see that you do!"

"My dad's whip—it's got his name on it...."

"Take it—" Peter flung the whip after the cringing figure "—and get moving! If ever I catch you hanging around here again you'll be sorry. Get it?"

"Okay, okay, I'm going!" Mumbling something under his breath he scuttled away, and in a few moments the sound of a motor revving up came clearly to the two standing on the driveway.

"I thought he was up to something." Peter's expression remained grim. "I happened to be passing and saw his bus standing at the gate."

Liz knew she owed him some thanks for his timely intervention, yet somehow the words stuck in her throat. Illogically she felt angry with him. In some queer way she *had* to be angry with him, otherwise.... "You needn't have hurt him!"

"He deserved a lot more than that! Sneaking back here, making off with your property, making a nuisance of himself. One thing, you have no need to worry about Lance Pritchard. He won't be back."

"No." She wasn't particularly concerned with the previous owner of the place. It was the man at her side who mattered. The thoughts tumbled wildly through her brain. Come to think of it, she had good reason for any antipathy she felt toward him. The other prospective buyer for the property—could it have been one Peter Farraday? If so, if he still coveted Rangiwahia, how gratified he must be at her obvious disenchantment with her purchase. Was that the reason he had insisted on escorting her here today, in order to witness her disillusionment? He had only to play a waiting game, and before long she would be pleased to pass the property on to him. Was that what he was counting on?

"Why didn't you tell me about what happened to the last owner here when he had ideas of starting up a riding school, instead of letting me rave on about it? All the time—" her husky tones rose indignantly "—you must have been laughing at me!"

"Just what did he tell you about me?" His voice was dangerously quiet.

"He said you threw him out of the place—"

"That's not true. He—"

"Well, as good as." She shrugged slim shoulders. "He said you made things so darned unpleasant for him he was forced to go. He told me—"

"And did he tell you—" his tone was low, contained "—that he and his mates from the city had a merry old time shooting wild duck and pheasant out of season, over my land? That gates were always left open, valuable stock killed on the road by fast cars, ewes frightened, fences broken? One night I happened to see some tractor lights over in the paddocks. Caught Pritchard and his gang out there with guns and magnetic torches. I sent them on their way in a hurry! It wasn't until morning that I came across my stallion." His voice deepened. "A great horse, one of the best. He'd been so badly injured with a rifle shot that I had no choice but to finish the job. *He* said they'd been shooting possums in the trees, that it was an accident."

"No," Liz whispered, "he didn't tell me all that."

"I thought not. Now look, Liz—" his tone lightened "—I didn't let you in on all this before because I didn't think for one moment that you'd give the idea a thought, not once you got a line on what the place is really like. That is, not unless you've got a heck of a lot of cash stashed away to spend on doing it up!" He sent her a keen look. "Have you?"

"No," she whispered despondently.

"Pity. It would help."

"I bet that pleases you a lot!" She couldn't seem to stem the words that came tumbling from her lips. "The solicitor told me there was someone else interested in the place, and

The Frost and the Fire

Lance Pritchard said that because of the creek you wanted the property here for yourself."

"That's right." His tone was deceptively casual. "I'm still in the market. Interested?"

It took a moment for the significance of what he had said to register. "You mean, will I hand it over to you?"

"Well, will you?" He spoke so quietly, yet she had an impression that he was waiting expectantly. "You won't get any other bids if you put it back on the market, and you won't lose by my offer, I promise you."

Liz knew she should consider the opportunity to rid herself of a purchase that promised her nothing but worry and frustration. Maybe if the offer had come from anyone else she might have decided right then to call it a day, but to hand it over to the owner of Arundel Station, the stranger who one way and another had already become all too involved in her affairs....

"No!" She drew a deep breath, contrived a shaky smile. "I guess I'm a bad loser. I'm just not giving up without a struggle. I'll think of something," she added wildly, not knowing how the miracle was to be achieved. "I'm not sure what yet, but something!"

"Just as you say. It's up to you, and don't forget that if you change your mind the offer still stands."

Forget. She only wished she could. Trouble was, there was something about *him* she couldn't put out of her mind. Tall, tanned, vibrantly alive, already he seemed a part of her life. Liz pulled her thoughts together and attempted to sound businesslike.

"Now say I manage to get the place fixed up." Her attempt at nonchalance fled before his mocking look, and she glanced away. "Just say I do. Well, you won't need to worry about the ponies being any trouble to you. I mean, they'll have to be quiet and not too young for crippled kids to be safe on them—"

"What's *that* you said?" He was staring down at her incredulously.

"Spasitc children," she explained patiently. "Oh, didn't I tell you?" She went on to describe in detail the project that meant so much to her. "But I've just had an idea." She lifted thoughtful dark eyes. "I've got a little capital left, and if I could get a couple of paddocks fenced off then I could look around for some ponies and secondhand gear. It would be a start, even if it meant taking a few children at a time. Is there a contractor around these parts? Someone who would do the job in a hurry?"

If he was disappointed at losing his chance of acquiring the land with its plentiful water supply, he concealed it well. "Sure there is. I'll get in touch with Charlie first thing tomorrow. He'll get on to it right away."

"Thank you. Ask him to send the account to me, please."

"I'll tell you something," Peter said. "There's a horse sale coming up at Omera, a few miles from here, next Friday. I'm hoping to pick up a stallion there so if you'd care to come along just to have a look...."

It was scarcely a warmly extended invitation, but then they hadn't been exactly friendly during the last few minutes. Anyway, what did it matter? The thing was to get her project launched as quickly as possible.

"All right, then." She tried to match his cool tone. "Who knows? I may even come back with a few ponies myself!"

"Pick you up around nine, then."

There was a little silence. A round fat moon overhead emerged from a blanket of cloud and flooded the lawns with silver, softening the outlines of the ramshackle buildings. The cool night wind that was whipping Liz's garments around her slender body tossed a strand of dark hair across the man's face. Swiftly she jerked her head aside. She glanced up, and meeting that dark and brilliant gaze, she wondered for a heart-stopping moment if he was about to kiss her.

"'Night, Liz." Abruptly he turned and moved into the shadows of the driveway. Liz stood where he had left her. She felt almost disappointed, until she remembered about "his own special kind of girl" and took a firm hold of her runaway thoughts. And only just in time, she told herself a moment later, as a feminine laugh echoed out of the darkness. Somehow it hadn't occurred to her that Peter might not have been alone when he stopped at her gate. "But, honey—" a voice childishly high and sweet, with an unchildlike note of intimacy, reached her clearly "—what kept you so long? I thought you were never coming back." Slowly Liz moved back toward the cottage. There was no reason why he shouldn't be with Beryl. Beryl, who had everything.

Back in bed once again she went over the events of the long day, and suddenly the old tempestuous spirit rose in her. All she needed to make a success of her venture was some spirit, a little organization—and a lot of luck! What if there were fences to be renewed, horses to be bought? She'd manage, just, if she started in a small way. It would of course mean a short-term venture—six months instead of a year. But once she got the scheme under way and could prove it to be a success, others might be interested and willing to carry on. And she *would* get it started, for this wasn't just in her own interests. This was something involving a lot of kids who otherwise night never know the exhilaration of riding in the open air. They would enjoy a place in the sun! It was her one chance, and she refused to allow anything to beat her, right at the outset. A challenge, but—all at once she came face to face with the truth—was her interest entirely selfless? Could it be that her stubborn determination to stay and make a go of things had a lot to do with proving herself to that strangely disturbing Peter Farraday?

CHAPTER THREE

ON THE FOLLOWING MORNING a truck piled with fencing materials drew up in the driveway, and a middle-aged man with a bare tanned chest and shabby khaki shorts asked to see the owner of the cottage. If his eyes betrayed surprise at Liz's youthful appearance he said nothing of his thought, but swiftly got down to business. Soon they were strolling over the paddocks, discussing the cost of labor and materials.

By the end of the day the work was completed, and as the dust-coated truck moved away Liz was formulating plans. If she bought three ponies and a few secondhand saddles and bridles at the horse sale, at least it would be a beginning.

During the following few days she found herself kept frantically busy, owing to the continuous ringing of the telephone at the cottage. It all began when Stan inquired of a farmer friend in the district who happened to have two saddles for sale at a low price. On learning the purpose for which the saddles were intended, however, he refused to make any charge, throwing in a number of used bridles for good measure. In the manner of news in country districts, word traveled swiftly on the grapevine regarding Liz's needs, and soon other farmers were following the example. Cars, trucks and Land Rovers pulled up on the broken driveway, and soon a mounting pile of saddles and bridles, horse covers and gear littered the floor of the old shed.

One evening Liz answered the telephone to a male voice, who told her he was speaking from a farmhouse a few miles distant. Stafford was the name. He'd just heard of Liz's worthwhile venture for the handicapped kids, and if she could make use of a couple of ponies that his own lads had outgrown...? He could guarantee them to be sound, quiet, good-natured, and if she'd care to take them both he'd send

The Frost and the Fire

them over in the morning with one of the boys. Liz was delighted with the offer and thanked him warmly.

The "boy," when he appeared the following morning at the wheel of a big cattle truck, was a dark-eyed young man, very tall and thin, with a slow manner of speaking and a pleasant smile. As Liz went to meet him he was unloading a black-and-white pony from the truck, and for a moment he seemed to have difficulty in wrenching his gaze from her excited face. "But they're just what I want," she cried delightedly. "What are their names?"

"He's Silver...."

"I could have guessed that."

"And this fellow's called Little Joe."

"And you're...?"

"Malcolm." A dull brick color was creeping under the tan of his cheeks. Liz thought, he's shy of girls. He's more at home with horses. To help him out she moved toward the truck, picked up a fleecy white sheepskin. "Don't tell me you're giving these away, too, and the saddles, and all the gear?"

He nodded. "Dad threw it all in." He eyed the ponies, standing docilely at his side. "They're pretty overweight—could do with some exercise. If you like," he offered eagerly, "we could take them for a run down to the beach and see how they go?"

"I'd like that. Come on, we'll saddle them up and try them out!" Liz stooped to pick up a bridle and fitted it in the mouth of the small white pony, then threw a sheepskin over his back. As stirrup leathers were lengthened and harnesses adjusted she reflected that both mounts appeared quiet enough to be trusted to stand perfectly still while small disabled riders were lifted up onto saddles.

"You know something?" She turned a laughing face back toward Malcolm as they set off on a narrow path that led down to the gully below. "I haven't even been down this track to the beach yet!" Her own mount had a jerky action, but she couldn't help thinking that Malcolm appeared even more uncomfortable as he bumped along behind her, his long legs hanging incongruously at the sides of the black pony.

Presently they moved into the filtered green light of native bush. Branches of great evergreen trees met high overhead, and the ponies had to step over fallen punga logs lying on the damp leaf mold underfoot. A peal of bell-like notes broke the intense silence, and looking upward Liz discerned, high on a branch of towering puriri tree, a tui's white throat and black plumage. At her side she caught the sheen of water among overhanging bush and thickly growing ferns. The creek, however, made her mind revert to Peter Farraday, whom she had already allowed to intrude far too much into her life and her imaginings. Swiftly she wrenched her thoughts aside.

Quite suddenly they emerged into the sunshine. Pulling up her mount, Liz looked down the steep bush-covered hillside to the wide expanse of diamond-bright black sands below. She was forced to cling to a coarse white mane as the pony's short steps took her down the twisting crumbling cliff path dropping sheerly to the beach. They reached the sand at last and their mounts sluggishly responded as they were urged into a trot, then an uneven canter, the hoofs leaving a line of small indentations on gleaming wet sand.

All at once a helicopter came into view, dropping low over the sea as it followed a line of tossing breakers. Someone waved from above, and the two riders on the beach pulled rein. Malcolm's gaze went to the ponies, already breathless, their shaggy coats wet with sweat. "They need exercise, these two, that's for sure!"

But Liz's eyes were raised to the helicopter cruising above the white surf. "He waved to us," she said in surprise.

"Who? Oh—" Malcolm squinted up into the sun "—that would be Peter Farraday."

"For goodness' sake!" Liz continued to eye the copter in wonderment. "What would he be doing up there?"

"It's a safety patrol chopper." Malcolm's voice was careless. "Just part of the Surf Lifesaving program. Peter's quite a guy in that line. Got his lifesaving bronze medal, captain of the local club, and was in a team competing for the world championships a year or so ago. He's well known around these parts as a champion swimmer."

"Yes, I know." How she came to know of Peter's lifesaving technique she didn't explain. Somehow she didn't want to remember all that she owed him, how very much in his debt she happened to be.

She pulled on Silver's bridle. "Race you back to the track!" Now there was no reluctance on the part of the ponies to hasten their pace. They cantered along the beach, flew up the dry sand and were soon scrambling up the crumbling cliff path.

When they arrived back at the cottage Liz slipped from the saddle. As they rubbed down their sweating mounts Malcolm turned on her an inquiring dark-eyed gaze. "Well, what do you think of them, Miss Kennedy?"

"It's Liz—" she smiled across at him "—and they'll do me just fine! They're both exactly the type of ponies I've been thinking of for the children. A bit sluggish, maybe, but exercise will soon put that right. What I like about them is that they stop and start obediently, and they don't jump at an unexpected sound. A pony that leaps at something that zooms up out of the blue wouldn't be any use at all. I was so pleased when the helicopter skimmed over just above them. All that noise, yet neither Silver nor Little Joe turned a hair."

"Good." He was still regarding her with a puzzled stare. "But if the kids are handicapped, with their legs no use to them, won't you have to fix up the gear a bit to suit?"

"Oh, I've got lots of ideas about that! I've been working on it for ages! This isn't something I've dreamed up in a minute, you know! I've got it all figured out. Safety stirrups are a must, and the same goes for neck straps to help the children learn to balance on the horse's back. But the main thing is a belt with leather handles. It goes around the rider's waist and means the helper can hold on and keep him steady. Know the sort of thing I mean? Wait, I'll show you!" She went to the big open shed and after a moment returned and extended toward him a special safety belt.

"Tremendous!" Malcolm inspected the belt, then eyed her with a grin. "You really are wrapped up in this project of yours, aren't you?"

She laughed. "I really am." Then her voice sobered.

"You would be, too, if ever you'd worked among kids like that."

"I guess. Look, could you use any help? I mean, anything at all?"

"Could I ever! I've got oodles of things waiting to be fixed up before the children come out for a ride next week. Stan's awfully good. He's over there now sorting out timber to make a wheelchair ramp, and when that's done he's promised to put up a long railing we can hitch the ponies to. But if you could give me a hand to fix up the gear.... There's such a lot to be done." She hesitated. "But can you spare the time? I mean, how about your own work on the farm?"

He grinned. "I'm a tiger for good works! Especially when it happens to be over in this direction! And it's not like you think. I'm anything but indispensable over home. My brother, Philip—he's the one who's crazy about farming and country life, but it's not for me. Engineering's more in my line. I'm off to university in town at the start of the new term. Meantime I'm a sort of dogsbody around the place. At least, at home that seems to be the general idea. My time's my own—" he grinned cheerfully "—and yours! I'm all for project Liz Kennedy!"

They spent the afternoon seated on the grass outside the cottage, sorting out piles of neck straps, safety belts and riding caps. "I've got the special irons made for the stirrups," Liz told him, "but they'll all have to be changed over. Not that I'll be able to take many children for a start, but we can get the gear fixed up, even if there are only half a dozen riders at the beginning. Then maybe, after a while...." Her eyes were wistful, her hands idle on the leather stirrup she was unbuckling as she stared unseeingly over the unkempt grounds.

"Gee, it's really something, what you're taking on." She brought her mind back to Malcolm's heartfelt tones. "I bet there aren't many girls as pretty as—"

Liz laughed and wrinkled her nose. "There aren't many girls who have a chance to work with handicapped kids, getting to know them...."

"But to go to all this trouble and expense...."

"No trouble! I'm enjoying it." In spite of herself she

sighed. "It's just.... Well, I'm a bit short of funds at the moment."

The young boyish face wore a puzzled frown. "But you can't mean you're trying to do this all off your own bat? Isn't there something—anyone else to help, financially I mean?"

Liz shrugged and tightened a rusted buckle on a leather strap. "There's a fund being set up whereby the public can send donations for special equipment, improvements to the grounds and all that, but so far it hasn't really got going." Her usual buoyant spirits asserted themselves. "But once I can get some advertising started, when people really get to know what I'm trying to do...." She tested a rusted buckle. "Everything just has to be *safe*, that's the thing! It's all been done before, you know. I've read about it, but not so far in this country. I want the children to have proper lessons," the warm eager tones ran on, "learn to ride as well as they can with the special gear, play ordinary gymkhana games, egg and spoon races, bending—all on horseback."

"I get it," Malcolm said. "Treat 'em the same as if they were ordinary kids learning to ride."

"That's the idea. Well, I'm on my way, and with a bit of luck...."

Luck, it seemed, was already heading her way, for the following morning when she went out to the mailbox nailed to the rickety front gate, she found a typewritten letter awaiting her. What was even more important, it contained a check. Her eyes widened as she stared down at the slip of paper. It was unbelievable; it was too good to be true, but it was! A check for one thousand dollars! An accompanying letter from the fund-raising committee of the Riding School for the Disabled informed her that the donation had come from an Auckland firm of solicitors whose client preferred to remain anonymous. The donation was for the purpose of purchasing ponies, or buying special equipment needed for the school or making improvements to the existing grounds.

She ran down the path, waving the check toward Stan, who was busy with hammer and nails as he worked on the timber ramp he was constructing. Malcolm, who had appeared early in the day, was helping the older man in his task.

"Look! It's just arrived in the mail! And guess what? It's a thousand dollars! A donation! Now we can get the whole place fenced into paddocks. I can buy more ponies, really get going...."

"And I thought," Malcolm groaned, "that I was finished with sorting out horse gear and mending halters."

"How about me?" complained Stan. "This means I'll have to get cracking on making a corral as soon as I've finished the timber ramp." His creased, weather-roughened face, however, betrayed an expression of satisfaction that matched Liz's look of excitement.

"Not to worry," Malcolm told him. "Just call on me any old time at all and I'll give you a hand!"

They were both so kind, Liz reflected gratefully. Indeed, everyone in the district had been helpful—except Peter Farraday! Apart from his offhanded offer to escort her to the horse sale—and he intended going there himself in any event—he had made no offer of assistance toward her project. But then—how could she have forgotten—it was scarcely in his interests to further her schemes, harebrained and impracticable as he no doubt thought them. She could scarcely wait to tell him her news! The thought of her victory over him made her sing happily to herself as she moved toward the barn, now converted into a recreation room for the small riders. A dresser held cold drinks and glasses, and a coffee percolator and beakers were arranged on a table beside an electric point, for the convenience of helpers and parents. The children could eat their lunches while seated at the big table, and on a wet day the barn would prove ideal for wheelchairs. Evelyn had discovered some long forms for seating, and Malcolm had driven up one morning with an old honky-tonk piano, which he and Stan had lifted down from the cattle truck and placed in one corner of the big room. A door at the end of the barn led, surprisingly, to a small washroom, and now that the place had been cleaned and dusted it was a definite asset. The telephone connection had been renewed, and that, too, was an excellent arrangement. Liz went inside and dialed the home number of the fencing contractor, who by a lucky chance was there. Yes, he would come back right away; he could get the job finished by the end of next week. Liz was feeling so pleased at the unexpected stroke of good fortune that she rang the Crippled Children's Institute then and there.

How was she making out at Rangiwahia, the superintendent inquired with interest.

"Oh, everything is going along fine!" Liz's husky tones rang with enthusiasm. She could be ready for the children's first lesson by the end of next week, so if arrangements could be made for them to be transported by ambulances to the riding school...? By organizing two separate parties, one to ride in the morning, one in the afternoon, she could accommodate quite a few riders. She'd expect them with the doctors and therapists on Friday, then?

Her mind was running ahead excitedly. She'd get more ponies tomorrow and then, glory be! In a few days she'd be away! Wonderful to think that tomorrow, when Peter arrived to take her to the horse sale, she would go there not as a mere onlooker, as he anticipated, but as a definite buyer! She had the money, now that she had no need to spend her entire capital on fencing the place. And won't *that* make your black eyebrows rise, Mr. Peter Farraday!

THE CLUSTER OF DUST-COATED VEHICLES on the country road left no doubt in Liz's mind that they were nearing the saleyards. The next moment pens and stockyard swept into view against a backdrop of fenced green paddocks. Peter maneuvered the big cattle truck in a space between a stock truck and trailer and a late-model car, and soon they were making their way through the crowd of young and old who had come to look and perhaps to buy. Liz was aware of a blending of smells compounded of horse, dried grasses and hay as they moved toward the pens.

"Hey, boss!" Peter swung around as two youths of about seventeen years pushed their way through the throng in her direction. Wearing light shirts and faded blue hipster jeans, they were deeply tanned and obviously worked out-of-doors. The short youth with freckles and red hair and the slight dark one were both eyeing Liz, neat and trim in her white shorts and sleeveless striped tan-and-white shirt, tan sneakers on her feet.

"Liz Kennedy, this is Wayne... Tim. Liz is here on business."

Two sinewy young arms shot out as the boys continued to gaze appreciatively at Liz, who was smiling and animated, her great brown eyes glimmering with her own secret triumph.

"That's right." She giggled. "I'm playing the stock market—just for today! We're on our way to have a look at the ponies."

"But...." Wayne's round freckled face expressed bewilderment. "Not the one who's running the new riding outfit over at Rangiwahia? You can't be," he finished slowly.

Liz laughed. "I am, you know. Why, what did you expect me to look like?"

"*He* said—" Wayne swung hotly toward his mate "—why did you say she was fiftyish if she was a day? Horsey type, you told me, and bossy as they come!"

"Aw, gee," the slim youth squirmed uncomfortably. "I was only having you on," he muttered. "How was I to know she'd look like that— Sorry, gotta go!" He turned abruptly and escaped among the milling crowd.

"Well, anyway—" Liz couldn't help but be amused at Wayne's obvious embarrassment "—why don't you come on over and see what the place is like for yourself? I'm hoping to get the school really started on Friday."

"Thanks, Miss Kennedy, and if there's anything we can do to help, just sing out."

"I'll do that."

She threw a smile over her shoulder as Peter, an arm placed beneath her elbow, swept her away and they made their way through the groups. The women and girls looked cool and attractive in their gay cotton shifts. The men wore shorts and shirts featuring vivid flower and sea motifs of the neighboring Pacific islands. All wore rubber thongs on bare brown feet.

Peter appeared to know the greater portion of the farmers who had come to the horse sale, but he merely lifted a hand in salutation as other men hailed him or sent a friendly grin

The Frost and the Fire

toward an acquaintance. Liz was unaware of heads turning to glance at the tall, broad-shouldered young station owner and the slim dark girl whose head barely reached his shoulder.

Presently they neared the pens where the horses waited, each stamped with a number. Liz's gaze ran along the pens where the sun gleamed on the shining chestnut and gray black coats of hunters and hacks. A half-broken colt with rolling eyes restlessly circled his pen. Liz paused beside an enclosure, where three foals stood close together, far from the mothers they would never see again. "If only...." she sighed. "Today I've got to keep my mind on ponies. What I need is something over five years, yet not too old or unsound. You know?"

"You've made up your mind to get a couple today, then?" His tone was quite offhand, as though the subject scarcely interested him. But he'd be interested enough in a minute, Liz mused with secret glee, when she told him.... Deliberately she dropped her gaze, fearful he might surprise the triumph that danced in her eyes. She made her voice match his careless tones. "I thought maybe if the right sort turned up, I'd pick up half a dozen or so while we're here."

"Wow!" His low whistle of surprise was infinitely gratifying. "Just as well I brought you along today!"

"Oh, well—" she caressed a wooly-coated foal who was pushing against the pen "—it makes a difference having the place fully fenced. It means I can get going with the classes sooner than I thought I could. Next week, actually."

"Good for you, Liz!" Glancing up, she didn't quite know what to make of the quizzical expression in his hazel eyes—or the silence. She wouldn't be surprised if he weren't deliberately withholding the question she had been angling for. In the end she was forced to enlighten him. "I suppose you're wondering what happened to make me change my mind since I saw you at the cottage that day?"

"What did make it happen, Liz?" His voice was unexpectedly gentle. "Another legacy? Some of that luck you wanted land on you after all?"

"Oh, yes, yes!" Her face was alight with excitement. "Something fantastic happened! You see, this check from the solicitor arrived in the mailbox. Someone in town had made a donation to the fund. The moment it arrived I knew I could carry on with getting the fencing done. The contractor has promised me he'll have it finished by next week. And since I've seen you, a farmer around here, a Mr. Stafford, gave me two ponies his family had grown out of, and that meant I could buy half a dozen more with the cash I had in hand," she ran on a trifle incoherently. "So—" she smiled gaily up at him "—here I am."

"I see. Well, after that—" he took her arm and began to pilot her through the throng "—we'd better check on the ponies." It was at that moment that something happened to Liz, something entirely unexpected. A wild excitement fluttered along her nerves, and she was flooded with a sort of in-depth happiness. The green and gold day? Fulfillment of a dream? Which dream? The riding school for the disabled? Or this man at her side, his bronzed hand resting on her bare arm? *Why do you feel that you could go on forever like this, just the two of you, alone amid the crowd? What makes you wish the day would never end?*

They had paused beside the pens housing their shaggy ponies. "Which one of these takes your fancy, Liz?" Peter's matter-of-fact tones, his inquiring sideways glance, jerked her back to reality.

Still fighting that bemusing sense of happiness, she gestured toward the pony nearest to her, a small plump piebald. "He doesn't look too young or inexperienced.... Doesn't seem as though he'd have any bad habits. What would you say... Peter?" The name came strangely to her lips. Absurd to feel this sudden self-consciousness about a name, merely because it was *his*.

"Not that fellow, Liz! Not in a hundred years!"

"He looks okay to me."

"Maybe, if you don't happen to know him! That chap's got a nasty little habit of kicking up his heels at the slightest excuse. He'd toss a kid off his back in no time at all!"

"This one, then? He looks quiet enough." She moved toward a small bay pony who stood with half-closed eyes, drowsing in the sunshine.

Peter shook his head. "I know her, too. They can't keep

her weight down, and she founders quite a lot. For my money—" he ran his eyes along the line of ponies "—this one is a good buy, and this bloke and the one at the end of the row. The little black mare, too. I'd say they're a sound enough bunch," he pronounced a few moments later when they had inspected the selected ones.

"What I like about them," Liz said thoughtfully, "is that they're so quiet. I mean, if they can take all this hullabaloo without getting excited...."

"You've got something there." He was writing numbers down on the back of a cigarette packet, and she came to peer over his shoulder. "Number eleven?" She was surprised. "You don't mean that skinny little gray with the dull coat and the don't-care look about him? He looked to me as though there was something wrong with him."

He grinned. "Nothing that a few good feeds won't put right. I happen to know where he comes from—" his tone hardened "—and it's an outfit that shouldn't be allowed the care of animals. You can take it from me, Liz, he's a great littly pony—just the ticket for those special kids of yours. You won't ever be sorry about having Cobber as one of the gang."

"Cobber! That's a nice friendly little name."

"He's a nice friendly little bloke! Nothing of the odd-bod about him, believe me."

"I believe you." She smiled toward him and as their glance met and held, Liz felt herself shaken once again by that surge of wild sweet happiness. Almost like... love. With an effort she brought her mind back to the matter in hand. "I'll... take him."

All at once a thought occurred to her. "How about the stallion you were thinking of buying?"

He shook his head. "There's nothing outstanding here. Not one to match the one I lost. Looks like things are moving. Let's get up on the stand, shall we?"

They climbed up on a bench on the makeshift stand and took a seat between a family party and two brawny Maori farm workers.

In a high box the auctioneer overlooked the crowd, and as a broadly smiling Maori man led in a black-and-white cattle dog the auctioneer launched into an amusing patter. The cattle dog went to a young farmer, and a wirehaired terrier was led into the yard.

"I'd love to buy him," Liz whispered. "He keeps looking right at me and he's awfully hard to resist, but I've got a dog already. At least, Evelyn's promised to get one from a friend of hers. What I really need is a goat, a nice tame one I can christen McGinty." At his glance of surprise she ran on. "I have to have lots of smaller animals than the horses, ones the children can play with while they're waiting for their turn to take a ride. They'll be useful, too, so the ponies won't be startled or frightened of strange noises or sudden movements—" She broke off, staring down into the yard below. "He's going to sell some gear. This I must see!"

Bidding eagerly in her soft voice, Liz presently found herself the owner of a dozen used bridles and a number of worn but well-cared-for saddles, still in sound condition.

The assistant rushed around the yard as the first horse entered the enclosure, a bucking stallion ridden by a Maori youth in a gay pink shirt and denim jeans. There was the crack of a stock whip, a wild "Yahoo" as horse and rider approached the jump and sailed over the rails. The hunters were brought in next, followed by the yearlings. Then a man came into the yard leading a sturdy stock pony, and Liz leaned over to consult the numbers Peter had jotted down on his cigarette packet. "Will you do the bidding? The auctioneer can hear you a lot better than me, and you know what I'm wanting."

"Leave it to me." It seemed that for the first time in their brief acquaintance they were in complete agreement. Certainly she had confidence in his judgment. He had helped her to choose the ponies, he understood the type of temperaments she wanted in the mounts and she felt he would offer a fair price, but no more than they were worth.

The bids came slowly for the ponies, and one after another was knocked down to the couple on the center stand. Presently the auctioneer blew his whistle, and the sixth pony was disposed of to the same bidder. "Knocked down to the man in the top row and his lady!" the auctioneer told the crowd, and all eyes moved toward Peter and

The Frost and the Fire

Liz. She wanted to cry out and tell them all that, of course, she wasn't "his lady." They were here together on a mere matter of business. *Are you sure?* Deep down a tiny voice plucked at her mind. *Are you certain that's all there is to it?*

They waited a little longer, watched the transfer of the wooly foals and high-spirited yearlings, then Peter turned toward her inquiringly. "Had enough? Shall we make a move now?"

She nodded. "If you like." She was feeling so happy and excited she didn't much care what they did, as long as they were together. That, she scolded herself the next moment, was what success did to her. Went to her head and made her feel quite light-headed.

Peter arranged with the officials that he would pick up the ponies in an hour's time. Then they were strolling along the dusty path toward the waiting vehicles. She was so lucky, she mused, in Peter having brought a big cattle truck to the sale, even though he had probably expected to take back only a stallion, maybe a pony on her behalf.

"Where are we going?" she asked as the truck moved off along the quiet country road.

"Just to get a spot of lunch, if you're interested?"

"Oh, I am! I'm so thirsty! All that heat and dust...."

"And bidding!"

"You did most of that!"

He sent her a swift glance, deep and intent. "Happy, Liz?"

"Am I!" She laughed her throaty laugh on one note, gazing out of the window at the sweeping green paddocks with their grazing beef cattle. "I should be," she added contentedly. "I'm really on my way now. The ambulances are bringing the children out next week for their first riding lesson."

"It's not going to be a matter of kids just having a bit of fun, then?"

"It is not! They're going to get a new look at life, those kids—complete mobility, and they're going to be taught to ride the right way." She laughed up at him. "Weekly riding lessons with all the thrills but not the spills! You wouldn't believe—" all at once her enthusiastic tones were touched with feeling "—the mental anguish of kids who can just never get around except in wheelchairs or on crutches. It'll mean a lot more to them, the lessons on horseback, than just strengthening muscles." Her eyes were thoughtful.

"You mean, the psychological benefit?"

She nodded eagerly. "You wouldn't believe what it's going to do for them. Many children are able to get around indoors by slithering, fishlike, across the floor. And while this affords them greater mobility, I like to think this one thing, this one step, will spur them on to others! It's funny, but riding seems to relax the muscles that react so violently to any other ways of making them respond—" She broke off, adding after a moment of silence. "I guess I get carried away sometimes, but it means such a lot. It's more than just giving them a sense of achievement—"

"A new dimension in life?"

"That's it! I'm even hoping..." Her voice died away. It seemed such an ambitious scheme for one person to hope to achieve.

"What are you hoping, Liz?"

"Oh, just that some day in the future it could be turned into a national center of riding for the disabled. A place where helpers and instructors all over the country could gather for classes and courses. You know?"

"Why not?" He appeared unsurprised at her grand schemes, or maybe he was merely not interested. "You don't mind all the work?"

She shook her head. "When it's giving the kids so much pleasure I get a lot out of it, too. Sounds corny, I guess, but that's the way it is."

"And you're planning to do all this on your own?" Nothing could be more casual than his careless inquiry.

"Oh, yes. You see there's only me."

"No male friends around to give you a hand with things?"

"Well, there'll be the ambulance drivers. They're marvelous really. Some of the doctors who work along the same lines are interested, and I'm hoping a few of the fathers will care enough to come along as helpers."

"That," he said dryly, "wasn't quite what I had in mind."

"Oh, you mean boyfriends? I haven't any," Liz said

The Frost and the Fire

cheerfully. With a little shock of surprise she realized that Leon had scarcely entered her mind since her arrival at Rangiwahia. It must have been because there had been so many other matters to fill her thoughts.

They swung around a corner and entered a street, where a handful of old-fashioned shops were scattered along the main road. A sign outside a small timber building said, Teas. Lunches. Peter pulled up beneath a shady tree growing by the footpath and escorted Liz through the open doorway and toward a table under a wide-open window, where the wind blew refreshingly cool and fresh on their hot faces. Lunch was a simple affair consisting of freshly cut sandwiches and cups of steaming hot coffee. Afterward Peter lighted her cigarette and one for himself, and they sat talking, the blue smoke rising companionably between them.

"So you're all set to go next week, Liz?"

She nodded and ran on in her impetuous way. "I can hardly wait to try out these new ponies we got today! I'll have to start thinking of names for them. How does—" She stopped short, staring in surprise toward the tall, quite startlingly beautiful blond girl who had entered the room. Liz was so astonished at the sight of anyone so incredibly lovely, wearing such eye-catching fashion garments in this tiny tearoom at the back of beyond that it took her a moment to realize the girl was threading her way between the tables in their direction. Her walk was the unhurried stroll of one who takes attention as her due.

All at once Liz had no need to ask who the stranger was. Who could it be but Beryl? The happiness that had colored the day faded like a rainbow in the mist. In that one brief glance she had taken in flawless features, short-cropped silver gilt hair. Cool and poised, fresh as a shower of summer rain, the other girl made Liz miserably conscious of her own dust-smeared hands and grubby white shorts.

"Peter!" The vision paused beside them, laid a proprietorial hand on the man's tanned arm.

He rose to his long length. "Hello! You two girls had better get to know each other. Beryl, this is Liz."

For a fraction of a second pale frozen blue eyes moved toward Liz. "Oh, yes, I heard you were living in the old cottage down the road." She made it sound, Liz thought indignantly, as though she had taken up residence in a slum.

"I thought you'd taken off for the weekend," Peter was saying.

"Oh, come on." Pink iridescent lips pouted teasingly. "Can't a girl change her mind once in a while?"

Liz was struck by the high, little-girl tone, which contrasted so sharply with the older girl's sophisticated appearance. The same voice, she realized now, that had reached her out of the darkness a few nights previously. She brought her mind back to the light tones.

"Sandy thought we might pick up something at the sale for Darryl. He's got this thing about wanting to ride horses all of a sudden. Goodness knows why, unless it's through watching too many cowboy serials on television. Anyway, I thought a pony might be a better idea to start him off with, so we came over to the saleyards today to have a look. Trouble was we struck car trouble—Sandy's down at the garage now having the car checked by a mechanic—and by the time we got to the sale all the ponies had gone. We saw your truck parked outside. I should have let you know I was going." Her tone implied that had Peter known Beryl was attending the sale, too, he would, of course, have dropped all such trifling matters as Liz Kennedy and her schemes for a riding center and taken Beryl instead. "Did you pick up a stallion?" She contrived to entirely exclude Liz from the conversation.

"No." Peter crushed out his cigarette in the ashtray on the table. "Actually Liz was the one who was doing all the bidding at the sale."

"So I heard." With one flick of her sweeping lashes the other girl dismissed all Liz's grand schemes. She felt as though she weren't there at all, but the next moment she told herself that she refused to allow herself to be relegated to nothingness.

"That's right," she said brightly. "I bought six ponies! Now I'm longing to get them home to see how they turn out. They're for the children—"

"Oh," Beryl murmured contemptuously, "kids."

Evelyn had been right about this girl, Liz mused hotly.

She was certainly accustomed to having things all her own way. If this was all that eye-catching loveliness did for one.... Jealousy, jealousy, she chided herself.

"Here comes Sandy now," Beryl said, and Liz turned to see a fair-haired stocky man in his late thirties advancing toward them. As she smiled up into Sandy McPhail's rugged features Liz found herself taking an immediate liking to this open-faced man with the honest gray eyes and firm handclasp.

"I've been hearing things about you, Miss Kennedy." There was a suggestion of a Scottish burr in the forceful tones. "That's a great effort you're putting on over at Rangiwahia."

"Thank you." Liz felt a warmth stealing around her heart. "But I'm really just beginning—"

"Sorry, Pete," the high imperious tones cut across Liz's husky voice, "but we can't stay. Sandy's got this appointment back at the house with a stock agent."

The manager of her property, however, appeared in no hurry to leave. "Let him wait!"

"No, we'd better go!" Beryl flashed her brilliant smile in Peter's direction. There was an intimate note in her voice. "See you tonight, Pete."

Liz's gaze moved to the tall figure, but his gaze was inscrutable. "Bye. See you Sandy!"

A vague nod in the direction of Liz's flushed face and Beryl had turned aside, leaving behind her a faint fragrance of Blue Grass perfume, and as far as Liz was concerned, a definite sense of deflation.

Mingling with her tumultuous feelings was a wave of sympathy toward the station manager. Imagine being in the employ of Beryl Manning! How could a strong, self-reliant type of man such as Sandy McPhail appeared to be ever have put himself in such an invidious position? Especially since he had known Beryl before coming to the district and must be well aware of her demanding ways. There would be no lack of employment for a man of his capabilities and experience. It was difficult to understand why he stayed, unless.... Was he, too, under the spell of that cool blue gaze? She wouldn't wonder. Peter and Sandy! It wasn't *fair*.

Her thoughts went off at a tangent. Odd, the haunting sense of familiarity she felt about the other girl. It was unlikely they had ever met. That was another thing that Evelyn had correctly assessed, she reflected wryly. The blond elegance of the other girl was something one simply couldn't forget!

"We'll have to be getting back, too." All at once the shining sunshiny day had lost a little of its peculiar magic. It was only a shabby little tearoom, after all—dull painted walls, fly-speckled pictures, and it *was* growing late. She gathered up her suede shoulder bag, got to her feet. "Shall we go?"

While Peter paid at the counter she strolled out to the truck, and soon they were driving back in the direction of the saleyards.

When they reached the yards the crowd was dispersing, and the Land Rovers, trucks and trailers jammed the narrow road. Liz waited in the cab while Peter went to fetch the ponies and load them into the truck. The sun had slid behind a billowing mass of gunmetal cloud, and the breeze was whipping up little puffs of dust in the roadway. All at once she was in a hurry to get away from here and back to the cottage. There was so much to be done in preparation for the opening of the riding school next week. Besides, keeping herself busy prevented her from thinking too much about ridiculous things like she and Peter Farraday becoming friends in spite of the turbulent beginnings of their acquaintance. Just for a while, back there on the sand she'd had a warm contented feeling—found herself liking him... quite a lot. Somehow she'd got the impression that he felt the same way about her, but of course it was only an illusion.

Soon they had left the tangle of vehicles behind and were sweeping between vast grazing paddocks and out toward the bush-clad hills of the coast.

Liz couldn't understand why she felt so dispirited, as if the day hadn't been so successful, after all. Just the usual country horse sale. Nothing special about it. In spite of her purchase of the ponies, somehow she could think of nothing but Beryl, cool and poised, perfectly in control of the situation. *"See you tonight, Pete"*!

CHAPTER FOUR

LIZ WAS UP VERY EARLY on the day she expected the disabled children, accompanied by medical experts and therapists, to arrive from the city. She was strolling over the long grass, her bare feet brushed with heavy drops of dew, when she became aware that someone else had arrived here still earlier. A moment later she recognized the two station hands from Arundel. Wayne's red head was bent, as with a hoofpick he probed the lifted hoof of a piebald, and Tim was busy brushing the shaggy coat of a bay pony. Both youths glanced up as Liz hurried over the grass toward them. "It's awfully good of you to come over here, but you shouldn't have bothered."

"No bother, Miss Kennedy!" Tim paused, brush in hand. "We like it over here. Can't think why, though. Can you, Wayne?"

She smiled up at two sun-darkened young faces. "It's Liz, you know."

"He'll feel a whole lot more comfortable with those stones out of the way." Wayne put down the pony's small hoof. "We knew you'd be flat out this morning getting ready for that wheelchair invasion of yours. The boss said to tell you—"

"Never mind that." Impatiently she brushed aside Peter's anticipated advice as to how she should run her venture. This was *her* day, and she was quite capable of seeing it through without his instructions or interference in her plans. "Tell me," she went on quickly, "what do you think of the ponies?"

"Seem sound enough from what we can see of them." Apparently Tim, the slight dark youth, did the talking for both. "They'd be a pretty dumb bunch for ordinary riders, I guess. But for the sort of setup you've got in mind you need them as quiet as they come."

"That's the idea," she agreed. "Just so long as they're good-tempered and can be depended on to stand still while we get the children mounted. That's the main thing— Hey! Wait your turn!" For ponies were converging on her from all directions, crowding around her, as with tossing heads and seeking muzzles they competed for the carrots she was taking from a scarlet plastic bucket.

"How many kids are you expecting today?" asked Tim.

"Twenty-seven—that is, if they all turn up."

"Good on you! Just tell us what you want done and we'll get stuck in!"

"Everything's under control, I think— No, wait!" A hand flew guiltily to her mouth. "I meant to get one of the drinking troughs shifted up near the ramp. Never mind, there's an old washing-machine bowl up there and a tap, and if we could run a piece of plastic hosing into it for water...."

"Leave it to us, Liz. It's as good as done! Operation Kennedy!" The two lads, with their farming backgrounds, appeared to know exactly what was needed. Ponies were caught and led into the tea-tree corral; gates opened in readiness for the ambulances to pass through.

"They'll have the doctors and physiotherapists with them this first day," Liz told them, "so that the experts can get an idea how the children will go, if it's safe—all that sort of thing. It's a sort of tryout, really. Heavens—" she glanced down at her wristwatch "—I'll have to fly! They'll be here before I know where I am!" She hesitated. "Would you boys like to come in and have some breakfast with us?"

"We'd like it a lot, Liz." Once again it was Tim who answered. "But we've got to get back. So if you're sure there's nothing else we can do for you...."

"I'm sure, and thank you." They strolled back toward the cottage together. Then the boys got into their battered jalopy, waving a cheerful goodbye as the vehicle, belching clouds of smoke from the exhaust, turned out of the driveway.

It had been a thoughtful gesture on the part of the boys, Liz mused, appearing at the cottage to help her this morning. Not like "the boss," who hadn't even troubled to give her a ring on the phone to wish her luck today. Not that she expected any word from him, of course, but it would have been... well... neighborly. She wished— Liz took herself sternly in hand, and shaking the traitorous thought away went inside to a breakfast that after all, she found herself too strung up to eat.

When she returned to the yard she found a gleaming scarlet sports car standing in the driveway, and Malcolm leaped out. "Hi, Liz! Thought you might be glad of some help, seeing it's your big day?"

"Oh, I am! I am!" She was delighted to see him. "If you could saddle up a few ponies, tie them to the hitching rail all ready for when the children arrive...."

"Say no more!" He grinned cheerfully. "It's as good as done! Just what I was going to start on anyway!" He went whistling down the path, and a few moments later emerged from the open shed, bridles jingling over a bare brown arm.

Thank heaven for Malcolm, Liz thought as she went to the shed and began to sort out riding caps and print names on slips of white paper. By now he understood the intricacies of the special safety gear and knew exactly what had to be done.

Even Evelyn and Stan appeared to be affected by the general air of excitement this morning. When the first ambulance nosed its way into the driveway, Evelyn called to Liz, busy in the paddock below. But Liz, too, had caught sight of the vehicles and already she was hurrying back up the path. Presently private cars and a second ambulance were grouped on the grass, and Liz found herself the center of a cluster of doctors, therapists and ambulance drivers.

With swift efficiency wheelchairs were lifted down from vehicles, and boys and girls were carried from cars. Some mounted their crutches. Others, unable to stand, were helped to their wheelchairs. There was no doubt as to the happiness of the atmosphere. Laughing, excited children's faces, the cheerful ambulance drivers, all out in the clear sunshiny air. It'll work, Liz told herself. I know it will! Aloud she set out to explain to the doctors the quiet temperament of the ponies she had chosen for the special riders, the neck straps and safety stirrups, the webbing belts with their sturdy handles at the back of the rider. "So you see," she finished, "I don't see how anything can go wrong."

"Nor I." The leader of the medical team, an older man with an international reputation for his success in the field of children's diseases, sent her an appreciative glance. "I can't see anything but good coming of it, Miss Kennedy," he told her in his quiet tones. "A great scheme. Why not give each child a ride on the ponies?" He was counting heads. "You have sufficient mounts?"

Liz nodded eagerly. "I can take them all for a ride today—that is, if you can spare the time to wait? It would be a pity if anyone had to miss out—from your point of view as well as theirs," she explained in her soft husky tones.

"That's what I'm here for!" An expression of interest and approval lighted the wise lined face. "Let's give them all a tryout and see, shall we? We'll soon pick out which ones could benefit most from the exercise."

All at once everyone was busily engaged in pushing wheelchairs toward the ramp, arranging which children would be in the first section to try out the new venture. Malcolm stood alongside the tea-tree railing, ready to free the ponies when the small riders were mounted.

"Miss Kennedy! Miss Kennedy!" The radiant face of a small fair-haired girl was turned toward Liz. "It's Julie!" The childish tones rang with sheer happiness. "You're *here*! You went away, and I thought I was never going to see you again, ever, ever, ever! Miss Kennedy, am I going to ride? *Really* ride?"

"You are, darling!" Liz dropped a kiss on the blond curls, gave the child a warm hug. "Look, Julie, I've got a little pony specially for you! He's called Pinocchio. Remember how you used to ask me to read you the story?"

"Pinocchio! I'm going to ride Pinocchio!" Blue eyes sparkled with excitement as she swung around. "Daddy! This is the nurse I told you about—the one I like!"

For the first time Liz became aware of a man standing behind the child's wheelchair. Slim and small boned, wear-

The Frost and the Fire

ing dark sunglasses and immaculately dressed in a lightweight summer suit, he appeared to be in his early forties. "So you're Julie's father?" Liz smiled across at him. "At the hospital Julie was always telling me about you, too!"

He laughed, and said in cultured tones, "It's a splendid job you're doing here with these kids, Miss Kennedy!"

"Oh, I get a lot of fun out of it!" She was adjusting a riding cap over the silky fair curls. Then, pinning a slip of paper with JULIE written in large letters to the small girl's blouse, she turned to him. "If you'll give me a hand, Mr. Ridgway, we'll lift Julie up onto the saddle." The mount was one of the ponies she had purchased at the recent sale, and Liz was pleased to find that the black pony stood perfectly still as the small burden was settled on the broad back.

With deft movements the man slipped the child's feet into stirrup cups while Liz adjusted the length of the leathers. She threw the reins over the pony's sturdy head, and Julie, laughing, wild with excitement, clasped the reins in small hands. Liz passed the halter rope to the man standing beside her. "If you'll just hold Pinocchio while I go and see how the others are getting along?"

"He doesn't look to me as though he's got any ideas of making a run for it. Looks more as though he's thinking of taking a morning siesta."

"I know," Liz laughed lightly. "That's how we like them!" She moved on toward the next pony waiting at the railing.

"Danny!" A loose-limbed boy, tall for his fourteen years, glanced up from his wheelchair and smiled nervously. Pale eyes in a thin unchildlike face slid toward the overweight palomino. "Miss Kennedy—" only too well she recognized the hesitant speech, the apprehensive note in the weak tones "—he...looks so big...doesn't he?"

"He only seems like that from down here," she said gently. "Once you're up on his back you'll feel differently about him. Just think, Danny, up there you'll be higher than I am, higher than anyone on the ground!"

"Will I?" He swallowed nervously, and Liz saw the fear glimmering in his eyes.

"Come along, Danny." The physiotherapist, a cheerful motherly-looking woman whom Liz remembered from her work at the institute, came to stand beside the boy's wheelchair. She slipped a riding cap on his head and adjusted the strap beneath his chin. "You're next!"

"No." He drew back, nervous and afraid. "I can't! I can't!" he whispered.

"We'll help you," Liz told him reassuringly. "There'll be someone at each side of the pony to hold you on every minute. You couldn't fall off, even if you wanted to, and I'll lead the pony along. Just a little way—no farther than the gate, unless you want to go on. You might, you know. Well, Danny, what do you say?"

"I...I...want to...but I can't...."

"Just this once—for me?" Liz pleaded in her soft husky tones.

"All right, then, I'll...try." Terror shone in the pale eyes as with infinite gentleness Liz, assisted by an ambulance driver and a therapist, lifted the trembling lad from the wheelchair and threw the hanging legs over the saddle.

Clutching the reins in a convulsive grip, Danny sat rigid with fear. Liz reached up to lay an encouraging hand on his thin arm. "It's not so bad, is it? My goodness, you are high up!" After a few moments she felt a slight relaxation in the tense muscles. A nervous smile flickered across the pale face.

"You'll stay with me, Miss Kennedy, won't you?"

"Every single minute. That's a promise!"

A swift glance around her assured her that there were ample helpers, doctors, therapists, ambulance men to lift the remaining children up onto their mounts. So she remained at the boy's side. She didn't want to risk losing her small victory, for it was a victory! Danny, who appeared to be so tall, so nearly grown up, and yet at heart was such a helpless small boy, afraid of attempting anything new, afraid of almost everything! Liz had never become reconciled to the sight of the weak, loose-limbed figure slithering along the floor of the institute. Perhaps she felt specially concerned for him because she was aware of the doctors' verdict that it was the boy's nervousness that prevented him from making any progress in his condition. His fears stood in the way of his making any effort to be taught to walk on crutches or to help himself in any way. Danny, she knew, was one of the chief factors in her determination to start a riding school for such children. If only she could succeed in gaining his confidence—just get him to sit on a pony—he would have taken a terrific step forward. Before long he might even gain sufficient confidence to learn to use crutches, maybe progress sufficiently to try and make himself walk, even if it were in an odd awkward manner. It was a special dream she had cherished for a long time. Now the sight of Danny fighting his terror and actually seated on his mount brought an unexpected moisture to her eyes.

"Look at me! I'm a cowboy! Getty up there!" A small Maori boy gave his mount a resounding slap. Fortunately the somnolent pony was too lazy to respond to the gesture. Somehow Liz couldn't find it in her heart to reprimand Taiere—not today when he was finding a new mobility, even if only temporarily. White teeth gleamed in a wide and happy grin. "What's his name, Miss Kennedy?" Before she could think of a suitable reply, for the pony was one she had purchased recently at the sale and was as yet unnamed, the high childish treble ran on. "Betcha he's got a real cowboy name! A neat horse like him! Betcha he could go real fast, catch injuns and everything! I gotta call him *something*!"

Hurriedly Liz searched her mind for a dashing name for the plump pony, now blinking sleepily in the hot sunshine.

"Pancho!" she cried at last.

Taiere's broad grin widened. "I *knew* he was a real cowboy horse!" The bloodcurdling yell he let out might have been that of one of his ancestors, a century earlier, as he rushed into battle with an enemy tribe. "Yahoo! I'm a cowboy! Look out, you kids, here I come!"

He was utterly content, and Liz knew that while he waited astride a rough ungainly little pony, all the time Taiere was in another, more exciting world, speeding over the sagebrush, rounding up a bunch of broncos, galloping at high speed after a steer, lasso in hand.

Her glance moved down the lines of mounts to where a girl, taller and older than the rest, was being lifted from her wheelchair. Showing a slight nervousness but happy and excited, too, Gillian allowed herself to be put astride Red's back. Good old Red. She had known he wouldn't let her down. How patiently he was standing, almost as though he understood what was required of him with this new type of rider. Liz watched as the girl was settled in the saddle, the reins placed in nervous hands.

Before long, helpful kindly hands had lifted the first lot of children up on their mounts. On this first occasion Liz planned that there would be no lessons given. Later on, when the riders had learned to feel the movement, they would be taught how to make the ponies stop and go, even to rise to a trot. But today was a time for the medical experts to decide which children would benefit most from the exercise.

When all the riders had had a chance to accustom themselves to their new positions, they set off. Liz was a little apprehensive about Danny. Would he lose his newly gained confidence and again fall a victim to his fears, once he felt himself in motion? She kept a firm hold on the safety belt as they moved away from the ramp, but although rigid with anxiety, he made no protest. Perhaps, she thought, he was endeavoring to hide his terror from his small companions.

The medical men joined the party of riders and helpers, and it was a happy group that set off across the dried grass of the paddock. Glancing back over her shoulder, Liz waved to Evelyn and Stan, watching from the yard. Nearby, the children awaiting their turn to ride looked happily occupied as they played with kittens, dog and bantams. Liz was glad now that she had had the forethought to provide something the children could amuse themselves with while they were awaiting their turn to try out their new mobility.

"We're away!" Julie's father was smiling toward her. "My rider's in a sort of seventh heaven of delight. How's yours?"

"He's coming along—aren't you, Danny?"

The boy nodded, obviously too strung up and tense to make a reply.

One of the medical team, a serious-eyed young man with a pleasant smile, came to join Liz. "Don't you believe it!

Danny's doing fine!" He dropped his voice to a lower note. "I'll tell you something, Miss Kennedy. I've got great hopes for this venture of yours."

"Thank you." Liz guided the pony away from the spreading branches of a peach tree high overhead.

He strolled along at her side over the grass.

"If you get this one used to the motion, get the better of that fear complex of his, then I'd say the battle was half won. Could be he'd be inspired to take another step, and another. It would spur him on to greater efforts in other directions."

Liz threw him a brief sideways glance. "You mean," she whispered, "he might have a go at crutches?"

"That's what I'm getting at. Who knows? Later on he might even have a crack at getting himself mobile."

"That's what I'm hoping, too. Do you think there's a chance?"

"After this—" the doctor jerked his head toward the silent rider, gave a significant smile "—I'll believe anything can happen! You're doing a fine job, Miss Kennedy! Keep it up!"

Liz didn't quite know what to say. "I haven't proved a thing yet. But I will! I know I will!"

"You're working along the right lines. You know—" they were matching their gait to the pony's short jerky steps "—as far as I can tell there isn't one of these disabled kids who wouldn't benefit from this open air and exercise, maybe far more than we can imagine—as long as the lessons are held under medical supervision, of course. Funny thing—" he was speaking as if to himself "—how riding seems to relax the muscles of these cases of spastic diplegia and typical scissor gait. Yet the same muscles react violently to any other sort of effort to make them respond."

"That's what I thought, too," Liz said eagerly. "Oh, I know, of course, that they'll all benefit from the exercise, but I'm counting on something else, as well...."

"I know what you're getting at! The psychological angle, the feeling of achievement that riding gives these crippled kids—from a therapeutic angle, I mean, not just for pleasure. You know as well as I do, I expect, that one of the problems we have in the school for these cases is exercise in trying to get their legs apart. Sitting on a horse, they do it automatically." His voice was thoughtful as he gazed around the happy faces. "A new dimension for them, and boy, do they need one!"

Liz nodded. "Far enough, do you think?"

"I would say so, for the first time!"

Liz turned the pony's head, and the procession moved back over the grassy paddock. She realized that Danny's tenseness had lessened, though he still held a convulsive grip on the reins. Not like Taiere, who was calling and laughing, urging his pony on with wild calls, his small dark face still split in a huge happy grin.

When they got back to the ramp once again the ponies stood quietly waiting patiently while the riders were lifted carefully down from the saddles and reseated in wheelchairs. Presently the other group of children took their turn in being settled on the ponies. It was difficult to determine, Liz mused, which were the happier or more excited, the section who had already had their ride or the group now starting on their new mobility.

This time Liz helped Sandra up onto a pony. A pretty girl of twelve years, she was lovely to look at, cheerful and smiling. Lewis Ridgway steadied the girl from the opposite side, and Liz found herself thinking that he was the type of man who would always be found where he could be of help— quietly, efficiently there! How alike they were, he and Julie. The man with his dark clever face, and the bright child with her impish smile and alert mind. A tragedy for a parent, and yet who could feel sadness for a child who was so transparently happy—especially today! She glanced back to where Julie, cuddling a kitten on her lap, chatted brightly from her wheelchair.

There was an atmosphere of happiness and excitement in the barn as the children returned, and with appetites sharpened by unaccustomed outdoor exercise, began to open the packed lunches they had brought with them.

Malcolm volunteered to make coffee for the guests, while Stan wielded a massive enamel teapot and Liz poured orange cordial into glasses and passed them along the table.

A moment later Evelyn entered the barn, bearing a huge platter of steaming-hot scones.

A little later Liz's small figure was almost concealed by the group of medical men and physiotherapists surrounding her, all talking eagerly. There was no doubt but that the experiment had proved a success, and given a chance, promised to be all she hoped it would be. At last she managed to put the query that was uppermost in her mind. "I was wondering—" she turned toward a doctor standing at her side, an elderly man with a kindly face and a slow deliberate manner of speech "—how many of the children would benefit by the exercise?"

He balanced his beaker of coffee thoughtfully, a twinkle in the gray eyes. "My dear girl, the whole damn lot, and I'm confident I'm speaking for everyone here when I say it!"

"Of course!" There was a chorus of agreement. "No question about that!"

"Take young Danny," a younger doctor put in. "All that's holding him back from making any progress at all is sheer nervousness. But give him a few lessons here...." He turned inquiringly toward Liz. "How many did you intend giving to make up the course?"

"Ten," she answered promptly, adding after a moment, "but, of course, if anyone wanted to keep on after that they'd be welcome to do so."

All at once everyone was talking simultaneously, but the discussion was short and unanimous. The medical experts agreed that provided the school was run under medical supervision with therapists in attendance at all times, every child there would benefit. That apart from the therapeutic value of the riding in strengthening muscle and helping coordination, the psychological benefit to the children would be considerable.

The picnic meal was almost over when Liz caught the sound of feminine voices outside the barn. Threading her way through groups of wheelchairs, she made her way to the doorway. Two women stood framed in the opening, and Liz found herself meeting icy blue eyes. Beryl! What had brought her here? Curiosity, perhaps, to find out how the new girl was getting along with her crazy scheme? Or was she being uncharitable, for the other girl was smiling. "Oh, Miss Kennedy, I do hope we're not interrupting anything? This is my Aunt Olga." The tall slight woman with silvery hair gave a gentle smile. "We wondered if you were hiring out horses to ordinary riders. Actually it's for my son, Darryl, that I'm inquiring."

"Of course you're not interrupting anything. Come inside." Liz led the way into the barn. The two women followed her, and at the long table where doctors and therapists were grouped, Liz made the introductions. "Coffee?" she inquired. "Malcolm will bring you a fresh cup."

"Coffee coming up!" Already he was moving toward the bubbling percolator on an electric hot plate.

"How old is Darryl?" Liz inquired politely.

"Oh, he's thirteen," Beryl answered. "I thought it would be a splendid chance for him to learn to ride while we're staying in the country."

"But—" Liz's mind went to the large sheep station over the hills "—haven't you any horses on your own property?"

"Haven't had for years. Sandy's in charge there now, but he prefers to use a tractor and Land Rover, so.... Thing is, Darryl thinks he can ride, but actually he's never been up on a horse in his life."

"We couldn't risk anything happening to him," the slim gray-haired woman put in in her hesitant tones. "That's why Beryl wants a proper riding school where he could be taught. You know how it is...an only child...."

"Well, nothing's going to happen to him here," her niece cut in impatiently. "Not with the old nags Miss Kennedy's got around the place! And don't forget that she's trained to look after kids. It's her job."

She made it sound, Liz thought with tightened lips, as though children were some sort of household pets. "Actually," Liz said, "I don't hire out horses. Maybe you could find someone in the district who does?"

"Not a chance." Beryl shrugged, her attitude giving the impression that one stupid woman running a riding school in the district was quite sufficient, thank you.

"Please take him, Miss Kennedy," pleaded the older woman. "If you only knew how much he's set his heart on it."

Liz couldn't help thinking that young Darryl Manning had all the indications of being a rebellious and indulged youngster. But the timid older woman seemed genuinely friendly, even if somewhat under the dominance of her stronger-minded niece. Chances were, she told herself hopefully, that the boy would soon tire of his new activity under supervision.

"All right, then." She was aware of the doctors waiting to make their farewells. "Shall we say Wednesday afternoon? If you'll excuse me.... It looks as though the drivers are in a hurry to get back to town."

Liz moved toward Julie and began to guide the wheelchair toward the opening. "Did you enjoy it?"

"Oh, it was super! Miss Kennedy, can I come every week? My pony, he'll know me again when he sees me, won't he?"

"Of course, darling."

"I know why he's called Pinocchio. It's beacause he's so little. That's right, isn't it, daddy?"

Liz became aware of the slight dark-haired man who had come to join them. "Here, let me do that...." He took hold of the wheelchair, and for a second his hand rested on Liz's fingers. She drew back with a laugh. "If you insist!" She blinked, all at once aware of the depth of feeling in Lewis Ridgway's glance.

"I'll be in the first lot to have a turn at riding next time, won't I, Miss Kennedy?" The child's face was radiant with happiness.

"I'll have Pinocchio all ready for you," Liz promised. "He'll be tied up and waiting at the rail."

Out in the yard Julie was carried by her father into the waiting car. He said goodbye to Liz, then paused, a hand resting on the starter. "Don't forget, if you need any more helpers out here on riding days, I'm always available. Call on me anytime at all!"

"*Do* I need helpers?" She laughed lightly. "I want all I can get! I'm planning to put some articles about the riding center in the city papers—get a feature included in the news section on television too, if I can. I thought it might all help to attract some publicity, get me some new helpers so we can run on a sort of roster system. Of course, I wouldn't say no if someone offered a nice fat donation to the fund! If you could fit it in to come out with Julie each week it would be wonderful, but...." She hesitated. Hadn't she once heard that Lewis Ridgway held an important position in the city? "That is, if you can spare the time?"

"Nothing else is important enough to stop me from coming out here." His voice held an oddly significant note.

Julie waved back to Liz as the opulent-looking car joined the line of vehicles moving up the driveway. When Liz turned back she was surprised to find Beryl at her side, and something in the other girl's speculative glance made Liz rush wildly into speech. "His wife died some years ago. That's why Julie lives at the Crippled Children's Institute. I guess he'd do just about anything for her, even if it means coming way out here to the riding center each week."

"Just for Julie?"

Liz was annoyed to feel the pink creeping up her cheeks. Then she was even more annoyed to notice the light shrug of the other woman's shoulders, the mocking lift of her lips. If it weren't so utterly absurd she would argue the matter, but that would serve merely to lend the ridiculous assumption an air of truth. As if Julie's father had the slightest feeling for her personally!

She couldn't understand the other woman's ill will. Jealousy? But that, too, was surely beyond the bounds of possibility, for how could anyone so wildly beautiful grudge another girl so trifling a thing as a stranger's glance of approval? Could it be her harmless friendship with Peter Farraday that sparked off Beryl's deliberate hostility? *Who's jealous now?* Liz wrenched the random thoughts aside and turned to make her farewells to the waiting group of doctors.

"Goodbye! Goodbye! See you next week!" In a matter of minutes the ambulance drivers had loaded their vehicles with passengers and wheelchairs and were driving away. They were followed by Beryl and her aunt, the gleaming car glinting in the afternoon sunshine.

As she strolled back to the barn Liz puzzled once again as to the reason why Beryl's flawless features seemed so hauntingly familiar. She couldn't possibly have met her before, and yet....

The barn, when she reached it, seemed curiously empty and silent, with only Evelyn moving around the tables collecting ashtrays and Stan wielding a massive broom as he swept up crumbs and lunch papers. Liz was stacking cups and beakers on a wicker tray when Malcolm thrust his head in at the doorway. "I've brushed down the ponies, put them all back in the paddocks. Pretty lucky bunch, that lot! A few strolls up the paddock and they're off duty for a week. How about if I put a couple of them in the corral for tonight? Might get a bit of weight off them."

Liz nodded. "That's an idea! I was getting around to suggesting you do that."

"Oh, I've got lots of ideas! Here's another. I've got a spare radiogram kicking around the place at home. We could shove it into the barn here—"

Liz said, "That would be marvelous for the children. I could get some special records."

"I wasn't," Malcolm said with a grin, "thinking of the children, but I'll bring it down just the same."

"Thank you."

"My pleasure. It's all for the cause— Look, Liz, they're putting on a dance down in the local hall tonight. Funds are in aid of young Riki Manu, and just about everyone in the place is going along."

"Not the young Maori boy who's making such a name for himself with his singing?"

"That's him! He comes from around this district, and the locals are raising funds to help get him started on a career overseas. But it's not just to give Riki a helping hand that I'd like to go. If I could take you along.... What do you say? I mean—" he was suddenly overcome with embarrassment "—if you're not doing anything special...."

"Love to go!" She felt so elated she was in the mood for celebrating, and it was a long time since she'd attended a country "do," with its warmth and family atmosphere and informality.

"I know I'll be sorry about this," Malcolm muttered morosely. "It's always the same at these country hops—swags more guys than girls. I won't even get a look-in!"

"Don't worry." Liz was gathering crockery and stacking it in piles on the tray. "I'll save you the first dance."

"That's more like it! See you tonight, then." She was scarcely aware he had gone, she was so delighted with the way things had turned out. It would have spoiled her satisfaction in the day had any of the children been forced to miss out in the matter of future rides. But now each one was included in the project. It was all working out just as she'd dreamed. Lots of difficulties ahead, of course, but she felt confident now of coping with them. Malcolm's invitation to the local gathering had set the seal on the day's sense of achievement, and with or without music Liz could have danced around the barn in sheer joy. Everyone would be at the hall tonight, Malcolm had said, so surely Peter.... She couldn't *wait* to let him know of their success!

CHAPTER FIVE

WHEN MALCOLM ARRIVED to escort Liz to the dance that evening, a cool breeze was stirring the grass of the paddocks, and the pines on the hilltop were a serrated black outline against the lemon afterglow of sunset.

She closed the door of the darkened cottage behind her and ran down the steps, aware all the time that Malcolm seemed to have difficulty in wrenching his gaze away.

"Gee, Liz, I hardly knew you!" She had drawn her long hair high in a topknot, revealing a piquant profile. The big eyes were accented with turquoise shadow, and the long skirt swirling around her ankles lent her small figure a youthful and appealing dignity.

She laughed mockingly as they went down the path together. "It's me, all right!" Nevertheless she felt a moment's pleasure in the sincerity of the compliment, even if it only came from young Malcolm, who in this isolated area would scarcely meet a new girl from one month to the next. She was glad now that at the last minute before leaving town she had crammed into her bulging travel bag a filmy long-sleeved blouse, caught at the wrists, as well as the flowing skirt with its gay patchwork of colors.

"I never knew you could look like that!" The boyish gaze still lingered on Liz as they paused beside the scarlet sports car.

"That," said Liz, seating herself in the passenger seat, "is because you're so used to seeing me in ancient jodhpurs, with the odd streak of mud on my face and smelling of horse. You know?"

"Not tonight! And that's not what I meant." He sniffed appreciatively. "What is it, Liz—that perfume you're using?"

"White ginger, and it's the real thing. A girl friend

brought it back for me from a holiday in Hawaii. Like it?"

"Do I? How you expect me to keep my mind on driving...." He thumbed the starter and they shot backward up the drive. Tires scrunched on loose metal as the car swung around in the roadway. Then they went hurtling down the shadowed path in a direction that was new to Liz. Stones rattled against the undercarriage of the vehicle as dark bush flashed past on either side. Presently they shot up a straight stretch of the highway, screamed around a fern-concealed bend and came in sight of a long timber building, where light streamed out through doors open to the summer night. Swinging in at the entrance, they bumped over the rough ground to merge into a cluster of cars, trucks and Land Rovers parked on the grassy space.

As they strolled toward the hall, strains of music drifted toward them. Once inside, it seemed to Liz, pushing her way through groups milling around the doorway, that everyone living within miles of the hall must have converged here tonight. Seated on long forms set around the edge of the dance floor were girls in vividly patterned frocks and men wearing shirts, shorts, sandals. There was a sprinkling of older folk, middle-aged farmers and their wives, and children skated excitedly at the fringe of the polished floorboards. For Liz, progress was slow, since Malcolm apparently knew everyone here. On all sides he was greeted by calls and teasing remarks. To her, however, the only familiar faces were those of Stan and Evelyn. They had left the house before her and were now waving and smiling toward her from the opposite side of the hall. At that moment she caught sight of Tim and Wayne, and her heart gave an unexpected lurch. If the two station hands from Arundel were here tonight, then perhaps Peter too.... Her swift glance raked the crowd, but obviously he wasn't here.

Presently the insistent beat of pop music surged around them, and she and Malcolm moved into the crowd milling around the glassy floor. High above, colored streamers and balloons hung from the rafters, and electric lamp bulbs sheathed in pink crepe paper shed their soft glow over the shifting scene.

From the moment Liz first set foot on the floor she

found herself sought after by various partners, dancing, dancing to the tempo provided by three Maori youths who played banjo, piano and guitar. All the time she moved to the foot-tapping rhythm she found herself stealing glances toward the entrance doors, wondering if Peter would put in an appearance. Not that she cared, one way or the other. It was all the same to her. Even if he did come here he would be with Beryl. Not that she minded about that, either! All she was concerned about was a little matter of letting him know that in spite of his initial lack of encouragement, she had proved herself capable of carrying out a task that she suspected he considered beyond her powers. As the evening wore on, however, she ceased to glance toward the open doorway. She might as well face the fact that he wasn't coming. A pity, for what satisfaction in a victory where one's opponent wasn't even aware of his defeat? In a pause between dances she realized the evening's compere was making an announcement from the stage. "Will you take your partners for the supper waltz, please?"

The Maori group of musicians swung into the familiar, heart-catching rhythm of "Some Day, My Love" and Tim, who had partnered her through the last intoxicating pop tune, hesitated, wiping his hot face with a handkerchief. "Sorry," he murmured uncomfortably, "but I'm not too good at waltzing. Never got the hang of it somehow. How about you?"

They were standing together on the fringe of the dance floor. "I learned ballroom when—" She never finished the sentence, for glancing up at that moment she found Peter at her side, tall and bronzed and vibrantly good-looking. All at once the evening seemed to come alive. Meeting his grin, she was filled with an electric excitement.

"Shall we?" Without giving her time to reply he swept her away. Liz's patchwork skirt whirled around her ankles in a swirling kaleidoscope of color as they swept the length of the hall, watched by the onlookers seated and standing at the edge of the floor. Liz took pride in her ballroom dancing, although she had had few opportunities to practice it. But never had she had a partner such as this. It was as if they were molded together, steps and rhythm merging perfectly. She was unaware of the ring of watchers, the sudden hush that had fallen over the crowded gathering. Even when applause rang around them it scarcely touched her. Presently other couples rose to join what had become an exhibition dance. Confetti showered around them; paper streamers flew through the air and twirled among the dancers. Someone cut the strings of clustered balloons, and the colored shapes drifted down from the rafters high above to mingle with the blue smoke of the hall. Still Liz and Peter danced on in silence.

At length the music drew to a close, and for a moment they stood motionless. He drew a long pink paper streamer from her topknot, and Liz raised a flushed face to meet his enigmatical smile. "You're almost one of us already, Liz!"

"Yes, aren't I? Malcolm brought me along—it seems ages ago now. I thought you were never coming!"

The moment the words were out she would have given anything to recall them. No use hoping he would let her off, pretend he hadn't noticed that last betraying phrase. He didn't.

"So you missed me?" He was laughing at her.

"No, no, of course not! It was just," she floundered unhappily on, "that Malcolm said everyone would be here tonight and I...." She was saved by the group on the stage, as once again they broke into a waltz rhythm. And in the joy of movement with this man who was the partner every girl dreamed of, everything else, even her hopelessly incurable habit of blurting out whatever happened to enter her mind at that particular moment, was forgotten.

As the waltz came to an end, masculine hands carried from a back room of the hall long trestle tables heaped with a profusion of home-baked cakes, lavishly spread with fresh cream, sandwiches and seafood savories. The last notes faded into silence and Peter guided her toward the tables, then left her to join a group at the opposite end of the hall. Oh, she might have known—she had known all along, only she wouldn't allow herself to admit it—that he wouldn't come here alone. Why, then, should she feel this sickening sense of letdown at the sight of Beryl? Tonight the older girl appeared more attention worthy than ever in a deceptively simple black frock, setting off to advantage her silver gilt hair and fair skin. Just as Peter, tall and dark and distinguished, provided a perfect foil for Beryl's blond beauty. She wouldn't allow herself to think of either of them! Determinedly she flashed a smile toward Malcolm who at the moment was plying her with an outsize sausage roll and a thick china cup of steaming tea. Thank heaven for Malcolm, young and naive, anxious only to serve her. He would never know how much he was helping her in merely being here with her tonight, bless him. Almost without her own volition her gaze strayed back to the knot of people standing opposite. Beryl was chatting vivaciously, with Sandy on one side of her and Peter on the other. At that moment, catching Liz's glance, she sent her a nod of a pale gold head, a gesture clearly meant to indicate that Liz was worth no more than a careless nod of recognition. Beryl's Aunt Olga flashed Liz a warm and friendly smile before Liz's glance moved to the boy standing at the edge of the group. He appeared to be small for his age, with lanky fair hair and a sulky expression. She couldn't help thinking that Darryl, in his high-fashion jacket and tailored slacks, appeared oddly out of place among the casually attired boys of his own age who were here tonight.

When supper was over the compere mounted the stage and gave a short address on the object of the night's entertainment, the proceeds from which were to go toward financing the studies of the popular young entertainer and composer, their own local boy, Riki Manu. "And just to let you know how much he appreciates what you people of his hometown are doing for him, he's made a special trip up from the South Island to be with us tonight. I give you—Riki Manu, who's going to favor us with one of his own compositions!"

The compere's voice was drowned in a thunder of applause as a smiling young Maori youth took the stage. Well-built, beautifully spoken, and endowed with a relaxed charm and ease of manner, he plucked at the guitar slung over his shoulder. The notes fell into a pool of silence; then the singer's voice with its rich cadence took up the melody.

A deafening clapping echoed throughout the building as

the song came to an end. Again and again the young entertainer was recalled by the crowd to sing still more of his compositions, until at last he bowed himself off the stage and the group moved back to their instruments.

Trestle tables were carried away to the rear of the hall, and once again the beat of a popular hit tune pulsated through the smoke-filled air. Liz was aware of Peter standing with a group of young farmers, apparently deep in conversation. Out of the corner of her eye she noticed Beryl, her laughing face upturned toward Sandy as he guided her onto the dance floor. Liz waited... and waited, making various excuses to hopeful partners as the minutes ticked away. Would he, or wouldn't he, approach her again? All at once she realized that far from acquainting him with the news of her success, so far she had barely spoken two words to him, and what she had said had been quite disastrous. Would fate send her a second chance in order to even the score?

It seemed, however, that she had lost her opportunity, at least as far as tonight was concerned. For as dance followed dance and Liz was eagerly sought after by various partners, Peter did not again seek her out. Maybe he wasn't interested in ballroom dancing. But the next minute, as she moved to the beat of the latest hit tune, she caught sight of him and Beryl taking the floor. For a few seconds they were obscured from her view. Then through a gap on the crowded floor she glimpsed them once again. How relaxed and carefree they appeared, like old friends... or lovers reunited. Beryl was chatting with gay animation. She wouldn't ever say the wrong thing at the worst possible time! And he? Unconsciously she sighed. With Peter you never could tell. But he looked happy enough, no doubt about that.

For the remainder of the evening it seemed to Liz that Beryl was on the dance floor as continuously as she herself, sharing her dances between Peter and her manager. Liz found herself wondering what it would feel like to find oneself as confident, as lovely and sought after as the other woman. To have two men competing anxiously for her favors. Not that Liz had any lack of partners. Inevitably she was on the dance floor from the moment the Maori group of musicians struck up the first notes of the pop music, but it wasn't quite the same thing.

The Frost and the Fire

It was long after midnight when the final dance of the evening was announced. When Malcolm approached her she went with him toward the dance floor without a backward glance. Not that she need have concerned herself, she thought a little later, for Peter was nowhere to be seen. She was surprised therefore, when the dance ended, to realize he was striding purposefully toward them, and even more astonished to realize it was Malcolm whom he was seeking out.

"I've got a message to pass on to you, mate," he told the younger man. "Happened to be outside just now having a smoke, and old Toby went past in his car. Stopped for a minute to tell me that he was in the devil of a hurry to push on. His wife's not well and he had to get back as soon as he could. Said to get the word to you that your brother, Philip, has struck trouble on the road a few miles back. No danger. He's run into a ditch and wants you to come and pull him back on the road, give him a hand to get mobile again."

Malcolm's young face fell. "He *would* choose tonight to get himself in the ditch! He's a rotten driver—I'm always telling him. I've half a mind to leave him there to sweat it out till morning. Teach him a lesson!" He gave a rueful grin, then said on a note of resignation, "But I guess I'll have to go into the big rescue act. Where exactly is he?"

"On the side road just opposite Maybury's farm! Get it?"

"I wish I didn't! I'll kill that brother of mine one of these days!" He drew a palm across his throat in a sinister gesture, then turned to Liz, a note of regret in his voice. "I'm sorry about this. You do understand...?"

"Don't worry." Peter's even tones gave nothing away. "I'll see Liz back to the cottage."

"That's okay, then."

"Thanks for bringing me tonight." She smiled appealingly up at the downcast boyish face.

"Pleasure. Well, see you." He threw a rueful grin over his shoulder, then turned reluctantly away. A moment later he was lost among the crowd surging toward the open doorway.

No one, thought Liz, had taken the trouble to inquire of her if she minded being taken care of like a parcel by Peter and faithfully delivered back to her destination. She wasn't sure that she wanted to be escorted back there by him. There was something about him, something male and masterful and definitely disturbing. She had a suspicion that alone with him in the darkness and intimacy of the car it might be difficult to make herself remember that he belonged to someone else—well, near enough to make no difference! All at once she wanted to escape the drive home with Peter. Peter, who had danced practically all evening with Beryl. Wildly she said, "It's okay. I can go home with Stan and Evelyn."

"You can't, you know. They've just left!"

"We could catch them up."

"No." He shook a dark head.

"Why not?"

"Just that I prefer it this way."

"Oh!" Liz thought over what he had said. She didn't quite know what to make of it. Besides, there was something in his voice that was affecting her oddly. He couldn't mean, he must mean.... She hesitated, then made one last effort. "But what about...Beryl?"

It wasn't her night, she told herself the next moment, for saying the right thing. For he was regarding her with a hard stare. "Beryl?"

As if he didn't know what she meant! "I thought," she faltered in the face of his cool inquiring look, "that you'd come with a party tonight. You know, Beryl, her aunt, Sandy McPhail."

"That's right." Ice tinkled in his tones.

"I wouldn't want to put you to any trouble..."

"No trouble." Coolly he took her arm. "Let's get out of this mob, shall we?" He was guiding her through the throng and out into the clear night air, where the stars of the Southern Cross hung like spangles against a backdrop of pulsing purple blue.

In silence he guided the car out of the cluster of moving vehicles that were bumping along the rutted ground. Then they swung into the tree-shadowed road, and still Liz could find nothing to say. There was a compelling attraction in the dark profile outlined by the dim light of the dashboard. She couldn't seem to wrench her gaze away.

Around them the bush-clad hills rose dark and mysterious, smudged shapes against the clear night sky. A native owl flew past the windscreen and was lost in the darkness and on an empty stretch ahead a possum, dazzled by the gleam of headlights, crouched motionless in the roadway. Then within a second of death, the furry creature scampered away among the dust-coated ferns at the side of the highway.

"How'd you make out today?"

With an effort she brought her mind back to the matter at hand. This was the question she'd waited for, she reminded herself. Maybe if she didn't look at him it might be easier to think of... important things—like the answers she had rehearsed in her mind to tell him.

"Today?" She was well aware he was referring to the start of her venture, but she was determined to take her time, make the most of her victory. "You mean...."

"You know what I mean, Liz." He threw her a smiling glance, and suddenly she felt her spirits soar into such a state of high excitement that all the cool confident phrases she had so carefully practiced fled from her mind.

Instead she heard herself say warmly, "Oh, it was fabulous! A real success! Each one of the children had a ride, so that the medical men could form an opinion as to whether it would really help them—and what do you know? I've got the green light to go right ahead with the riding school! I'm going to make it a course of ten lessons," she ran on excitedly. "Then if they're getting real benefit from the riding—and I know they will—they can keep on coming out each week if they want to. The doctors and therapists were awfully enthusiastic about the idea!"

"Good for you!" His eyes were on a fern-concealed bend in the darkness ahead. "How many kids turned up in the end?"

"Everyone came, just as I was hoping! Twenty-seven altogether, and each one of the children is to keep on with the course. I was so glad that no one was left out."

"And you're planning on helping the whole bunch of them?"

Once again the special smile he seemed to keep for Liz Kennedy and her idiosycrasies was having an effect on her, piercing her defenses. She was having trouble keeping her mind on her venture—or on anything else for that matter. She wished she could keep on looking at him forever.

"Twenty-seven miracles! Isn't that rather a tall order, even for you?"

"I...wouldn't say so." Something in the atmosphere, maybe the deep softening of his tone, was doing things to her, making it awfully difficult to think of anything else, even the children.

"You sure must believe in miracles, Liz!"

"Oh, I do! I do!"

"Make them happen, hmm?"

"If I can," she said faintly. A crazy impossible longing was tumbling wildly through her brain. If only she could order one more miracle, the biggest, most important one of all—that he should fall in love with her instead of Beryl.

"So now—" with an effort she brought her mind back to his voice "—with the place more or less in order...."

She pulled her thoughts back to some sort of order, said quickly, "And with the ponies you helped me to get at the sale, I can go right ahead. The big fat check I got in the mail from nice Mr. X made all the difference."

"Mr. X, the unknown?"

"That's him. Only I always think of him as Mr. Executive. I've got this mental picture of him...."

"Such as?"

All at once it was easy to confide her hopes and dreams to Peter, even to let him in on her silly imaginings regarding her unknown donor. "I've got him all figured out. City guy, not too young. He's big and stout and just a bit pompous, and he's got so much money stashed away he doesn't know what to do with it all. He even feels the tiniest bit guilty about having so much when others are hard up for cash. Then one day he happens to hear about a girl who's starting up a riding center out in the country, one specially to help crippled children. It rings a bell. Maybe a long time ago he had some physical disability himself. But it's my bet that it takes him right back to the days when he was a barefoot country boy, riding to a little school in the back blocks."

"That was before he had any ideas of becoming a business tycoon?"

"Oh, definitely! He's a self-made character, a rough diamond. At least, that's how I imagine him. I think he wants to be in on helping the center along. But you see, in spite of being such a business success, he's shy about giving things. He likes to do his good works in secret."

"Maybe his wife doesn't approve."

"Oh, no, he's not married. Not Mr. X!"

"You seem awfully sure about it."

"Oh, I am!"

"Tempted?"

She laughed, the soft throaty laugh with a catch in it. "No, I'll keep him just the way he is, bless his kind heart! But I've been so lucky. I've had so much help from folks around here. You've no idea how good everyone's been. Malcolm's father sent around a couple of ponies, and they're ideal. No bad habits. The right age, too. A bit overweight, but that's only because of lack of exercise—"

The deep tones broke across her excited tones. "So now you're away! No more problems!"

"You've got to be joking! Problems—they're just endless!" Her voice sobered. "And the biggest one of the lot is financial. Now I've got things started I've just got to keep the school running. It's my big chance. I make a small charge to each child of ten dollars for the course of lessons. Then if they wish they can keep on afterward when the course is finished. I have to charge something to keep going, and of course if a child's parents can't afford the money I would take him just the same. I'm hoping that a lot of children will be sponsored by a private person or a firm."

"I get it. Any ideas about fund raising?"

"Have I ever!" Liz stared ahead at the curve of lighted roadway unfolding ahead in the arc of the headlights. Around them the trees were a dark mass, the only sound the whirring of tires on the rough metal, the call of a night bird in the bush. She had been speaking faster than usual in her low husky tones, in an effort to counteract the distracting intimacy of this small enclosed space cut off from the dark world outside. All the time she was aware of a disturbing masculine magnetism against which she had struggled from the first moment of their meeting. *Remember he's in love with someone else, and has been for years!* The thought gave her a moment of calmness, and she pulled her flyaway thoughts back to sanity, forced herself to speak more slowly. "I thought... some publicity would help a lot. You know—radio, newspapers, TV. Once folk get to know about what's happening up here they might get interested and feel like helping things along a bit. If not with money then maybe they'd offer their time or services. It's worth a try, wouldn't you say?"

He nodded carelessly. "It might work at that!"

They swept into sight of the cottage. Evelyn had left a porch lantern burning, but everywhere else the place was in darkness.

"Hey, where are we going?" Liz turned a surprised face toward him as they sped past the long driveway and continued along the winding road. Her eyes were fixed on the lighted portion of highway ahead. "Just for a ride. I thought you might care to take a look at the view from the cliff when the moon's rising over the water?"

"From your place, you mean?"

"Not so far away as that. There's a spot up on the cliffs, about halfway between. You'll see in a minute...."

Swiftly he took the bush-shadowed roads, and presently they were lurching up a rough track threaded with tree roots. Now Liz could hear the crash and thunder of waves pounding in on a rugged coast far below. It wasn't until she got out of the car, however, and he guided her along a narrow path at the cliff edge that she caught her first view of the sea: moon-silvered waves washing in against a dramatic backdrop of dark hills, heavy with bush. Up here on the heights there was a salty tang in the air, and the strong wind from the sea swirled her long skirt around her, tearing at her topknot until the dark tendrils loosened and blew against her face. She turned toward him, laughing. "You're right... Peter." Odd how she felt this absurd hesitation about saying this one name and no other. "It's really worth coming up here for."

"*This* is what I came for!" He took a step toward her, and some panicky impulse, an urge toward flight, impelled her to take a quick step backward, dislodging small stones that went bouncing and tumbling down hundreds of feet to the sands far below. In a second he was at her side, clasping her firmly, guiding her away from the dangerous edge, and at his touch... his touch....

"Trembling, Liz?"

"I... got a fright," she said huskily. "Heights give me a funny feeling. I've no head for them, I guess." He was still holding her, and she knew that the sensation affecting her wasn't due to heights at all but to something else, something that was really a lot more dangerous. The next moment she felt his arms tighten around her, drawing her close, and a wild sweet happiness quivered along her nerves. She heard his deep soft laugh. Then the waves of a great sea rose around her, drowning out everything else in the world but excitement and ecstasy.

At last he released her, and immediately came the thought that spoilt it all. Liz Kennedy, a funny kid, something amusing with her odd schemes and dreams, someone to kiss—when Beryl wasn't around to see! Trembling still, she flung herself away, hating him, hating herself. Oh, damn everything, she thought furiously. Wrenching herself from his outstretched hand, she stumbled back toward the car. "I'd better get back," she said breathlessly. "Evelyn will be wondering where I am."

When she glanced back he hadn't moved, but stood motionless by the cliff edge, looking after her.

"Does it matter?"

Liz pretended she hadn't heard him as she opened the car door and slipped inside.

He took his time to join her. Then without a word he put the vehicle in gear and they took the rough path back to the main road. It seemed to Liz no time at all until they were turning in at the entrance to the cottage. The moon was rising now, softening the outlines of the shabby house, flooding the grass with silver. At the foot of the steps he cut the engine, and leaning back in his seat studied her reflectively.

"I've got to hand it to you, Liz. You're doing fine. Keep it up!"

The deep intentness of his look, the timbre of his voice, as if somehow he really cared, almost betrayed her. If she

didn't know how things were between him and Beryl....
Clutching wildly at her flying senses, Liz said the first thing that came into her mind. "You don't care, then, about my being here, starting up a school on the property?"

"Care?" He stared at her in surprise. "Why should I?"

"Oh, I don't know." Liz nibbled a long strand of hair that had escaped from her topknot in the sea breeze. "Just that I got the idea," she stammered, avoiding that bright inquiring gaze, "that you wanted the place for yourself—you know, for water supply and beach access and all that."

"And you imagined I'd stand in your way simply because of that trouble I had with the guy who had the place before you came? You thought *that*?"

"Well...." She wanted to remind him that he hadn't been exactly helpful, apart from offering her a ride to the saleyards. Nor had he exhibited any special enthusiasm on learning of her plans for the center. But the words stuck in her throat. It was difficult to think clearly when he was so close to her and the singing excitement was back in the summer night.

"Liz, look at me!" A hand cupped beneath her small square chin forced her to meet his gaze. Only for a second. Then the firm lips were seeking her mouth, and once again she was submerged in a high tide of heady excitement. At last she drew herself away. What was this? Madness to feel this way about a man who belonged to someone else! "It's late," she murmured unsteadily. "Thanks for bringing me home."

"But Liz...."

Avoiding his detaining hand she slipped away, and it wasn't until much later, as she turned restlessly from side to side in bed, that she realized she had won no victory over him, after all. On the contrary, there had been moments tonight when she had been perilously close to giving him a victory over her! She had been in real danger of falling in love with a man who no doubt regarded her as someone new and different in this girl-scarce district. Impulsive, outspoken, fun to be with... for a time. But when it came to love.... Beryl's flawless features rose in her mind, and it seemed to her that the pale eyes mocked her.

CHAPTER SIX

IN THE DAYS that followed Liz was kept occupied with a variety of tasks. There were saddles to be cleaned and oiled, ponies to be inspected daily, and she really must get around to patching the torn canvas horse covers on the old sewing machine Evelyn had put at her disposal. An empty box in the shed was still waiting to be stocked with supplies of oils and leather dressings, Stockholm tar, embrocation and various disinfectants.

One evening she was seated at the desk in the barn, endeavoring to compose an article dealing with the riding center for submission to the editor of a national women's magazine. Half an hour later, after endless crossings out and rewriting, she sat nibbling her pen. Who would have thought that the putting together of a few hundred words on a subject that was of such deep interest to her could present such difficulties? Yet somehow she must find the words to let the public know of her urgent need for funds with which to carry on her venture—explain how urgently she needed helpers who would give their time and services on regular visits to the riding center. She had completed only one sheet of writing when she realized she had no photographs of ponies or grounds with which to illustrate her account of the disabled children and the benefits they would receive from their hitherto unknown mobility. Well, the article would simply have to wait until she could snap some pictures with her instamatic of the children's next visit. She rose, stretching, then stood motionless, listening to the peal of the doorbell that was shrilling through the cottage. It might be Peter! Why did her thoughts fly instantly to him? Why was he in her mind practically all the day and half the night? Since the night of the dance, when he had taken her to the clifftop, she hadn't seen him, but ever since she found herself listening for his step, the sound of his voice. How could a kiss make everything so different?

The doorbell rang again. Evidently Evelyn and Stan were watching television in the house and hadn't heard the summons, for the next minute she caught the sound of approaching footsteps.

"Miss Kennedy!" Lewis Ridgway, immaculate in his lightweight summer suit, stood at the entrance. "May I?" He smiled and moved toward her, his shoes ringing on the bare floorboards.

"Hello!" Liz was still feeling surprised to see him here, surprised... and disappointed.

"I should have rung you and let you know I was on the way." He swung himself up on a high stool facing her. "The only excuse I've got is that I had a lot on my mind at the office today, and anyway—" he smiled again "—I was fairly certain I'd be lucky enough to find you in."

"That's right. I'm usually around the place." All at once her tone sharpened. "Julie? There's nothing wrong, is there?"

"Good grief, no! She's her old happy self! You know Julie. Right now she's busy counting the days until the next riding day comes up."

"Thank goodness!" Liz breathed out a sigh of relief. "For one awful moment I wondered.... Would you care for some coffee? It's on the perk. It's a long drive out here from town on the winding roads in the dark."

"Wonderful!"

While she busied herself with the percolator he glanced idly down at the desk, his gaze resting on the sheet of paper with its crossed-out paragraphs. "What's this?"

"Oh, just an article I was trying to put together." She was reaching down two beakers from the hooks above the table. "If you could call it an article! Would you believe that those few paragraphs have taken me ages to think up, and it still doesn't read like anything that's worth a second glance."

"You won't mind if I run an eye over it?"

"Mind? I'd be delighted!"

Taking the steaming beaker of coffee she was extending toward him, he scanned the sheet of handwriting.

"It's okay," he pronounced at last. "I'd better admit right away that this is just what I had in mind when I came up here to see you tonight. Had a thought that all this is more in my line of country than yours, seeing that running an advertising outfit happens to be my game! If it's all right with you we could draft something out for the newspapers. One or two of the local magazines run this type of article, too. I'll get my secretary to run them off in the morning. What do you say?"

"Oh, *would* you?" Liz felt almost as pleased as though the unknown Mr. X had sent her a second thousand-dollar check in the mail for the benefit of the fund.

"Leave it to me. If you don't mind, I'll work from this page of yours. It gives all the data, fills in on the main points, the general idea of the riding center." His gray eyes were thoughtful, abstracted. "Now, about the newspapers. I know the editors of the two main city papers. I'll give them a ring in the morning, and they can send out reporters to get the story. They could cover the riding lesson next week. Okay?"

She nodded eagerly, hands clasped around her beaker of coffee. "Oh, that would be fabulous! You've no idea what a relief it is to have the whole thing taken out of my hands! It's awfully good of you to go to all this trouble...."

"I'd like to do a lot more than that, for *you*." She barely caught the low words, and at her puzzled glance he made a gesture with outspread well-shaped hands. "Forget it—just a long-term project of mine." All at once his tone was once again businesslike, impersonal. "Now about advertising the place, getting yourself known. Radio reaches a lot more folk than you'd think, actually. Just happens that I'm in touch with the chief of the main station, so there won't be any problems there. We should get results almost right away."

At the clipped confident tones Liz eyed him in amazement. "You do seem to know an awful lot of influential people."

He nodded carelessly. "It helps, especially when you want to get something off the ground in a hurry! Saves all the messing about and wasting time." His tone was that of a man accustomed to organizing, to giving orders to subordinates. "I'll get cracking on this first thing tomorrow. Three magazine articles.... That means you'll need some pictures to send along with them to grab public interest."

Liz's face fell. "If only I'd thought to take some snaps of the children when they were on the ponies. I could have had them processed by now. We could have got the articles ready for submission to the magazines right away. Some of them only publish once a month."

"Not to worry. I took a few snaps myself that day," Lewis said modestly. Taking a folder from his breast pocket he spread out on the desk a number of black-and-white prints. "They're small, but they can be blown up easily enough."

"Look, there's Julie!" Liz pounced on a picture of a radiant fair-haired girl. "Did you ever see such a wonderful smile?"

"I know. With Julie, happiness is a pony! She's a bright kid anytime, but out here with you and the horses— Here's one of Taiere. Only a truly happy boy could produce a monstrous grin like that! No fear there—he's enjoying every moment of it. He's getting the devil of a kick out of it. He looks as proud as though he were riding in the Melbourne Cup."

Liz laughed. "He probably was, and winning the race, too. In between being a dashing cowboy, that is!" Her face sobered as she picked up another picture. "Poor Danny. He's simply terrified, but he's brave, too. He *made* himself get up there and take that ride."

"Next time it won't come so hard, or the next."

"I know, I know."

"They'll do for a start." He shuffled the pictures back into the folder. "Oh, something else, too, that nearly slipped my mind. I took a chance and contacted the TV boys about your project. They're sending out a camera team in two weeks' time. Seem to think the riding school would make a good news feature, so I'm hoping it may whip up a lot of public interest and a bit of financial support, as well. One thing, at least you'll get some helpers out of it. By the way, the TV team is doing a riding commercial for some cosmetics outfit, helping along a new brand of makeup they're putting on the market. It goes under the name of Today's Girl."

"I've never heard of it."

"You will! Seems they're on the lookout for a riding background, somewhere not too far away. Wanted to know if they could come up here and shoot some outdoor scenes. They told me to ask you if you'd be willing to do them a favor and let them film some shots of you on your chestnut."

"But—" she stared across at him incredulously "—they wouldn't want *me!*"

"Why wouldn't they? Ever done any TV work? Announcing, fashion modeling, advertising? That sort of stuff?"

She shook her head. "Heavens, no. I'm not the type."

"How do you know you're not? I'll tell you something, Miss Kennedy." His voice was warm, enthusiastic. "From what the TV boys told me I got the impression that you happen to be just the sort of girl they've got in mind for the particular commercial they want to film."

Liz was scarcely listening. Fashion modeling? At last she knew the reason for the vague sense of familiarity Beryl had for her. It must be some years ago that the even features and superb figure had flashed across the tiny screen. Beryl holding a modern stance, displaying the latest in sports gear, race-meeting fashions, glittering theater gowns. All at once she realized Lewis had stopped short and was eyeing her curiously. "What's the matter?"

"Nothing, nothing." She switched her mind back to the present, and noticed with some surprise the sudden softening of his gaze.

"Thing is they're looking for a girl who's an outdoor type. Nothing fussy or glamorous, just a barefoot girl—hair blowing in the wind, out riding for the fun of it!"

Liz sent him a teasing smile. "When you put it that way it does sound a bit like me."

"That's what I'm trying to get through to you! Well, Miss Kennedy, what do you say?"

She hesitated, nibbling a long strand of dark hair in an unconscious gesture. "I suppose... if it's not a close-up...."

"I wouldn't imagine so. What they're after is a country-background shot of a girl taking a horse over a hurdle. 'Give life a whirl with Today's Girl!' That sort of thing!"

"I've only got Red," she murmured doubtfully, "and he's a chestnut. Would he be all right—his color, I mean—for photography?"

"Sure! They said anything except a white horse would suit them fine. Told me to tell you to bleach his mane and tail; it's more effective to get some contrast into the picture." Once again his tone softened. "From what they said I got the idea that you'd be just about made to order for the part."

"For goodness' sake!" She stared up at him.

"It's not *my* idea!" He smiled at her. "You need the money, don't you? Think how it would help the fund!"

"Oh, yes, the fund! I'd forgotten all about that." Suddenly her mind was made up. "All right, then, I'll do it!"

"You will? Great! I'd better warn you, though, that it's a rush job. Could you make it tomorrow, two o'clock?"

"You seem," she said suspiciously, "to have it all arranged for me already."

"All but your say-so, Miss Kennedy!"

The slightly formal tone amused her, and she said lightly, "Isn't it about time you called me Liz, like everyone else?"

"If you'll make it Lewis...."

"It's a deal!"

"Let's shake on it!" The thin dark face was faintly flushed with pleasure as he caught her hand in his. "I'm beginning to see why young Julie thinks the sun rises and sets in you!" Liz wondered if he had forgotten to release her small brown hand. The next moment some instinct of being observed drew her glance toward the doorway, where a tall shadowy figure stood silhouetted against the opening. He was motionless, the tip of a lighted cigarette a scarlet glow against the darkness outside.

"Hi, Liz!" Did she imagine an ironical note in the deep, well-remembered tones? And how long had he been standing there, taking in the little scene of the two seated at the desk, hands in a lingering clasp?

"Peter!" Wrenching her hand away, she leaped to her feet. "Did you want to see me?"

But he was already turning away. "Sorry, can't stay. I just brought you something—left it with Stan." As she continued to stare after him bewilderedly, he threw over his shoulder, "Something you said you wanted. You'll see."

She made a wild guess. "It's not—you didn't bring McGinty?" she cried delightedly.

"He's a bit on the small side for McGinty. Better make it Mac. Sorry, I've got to get cracking. See you around."

She moved back into the lighted room, all her previous enthusiasm in the matter of arranging publicity for the riding school forgotten. If only she hadn't been involved here tonight with Lewis Ridgway! If only Peter had chosen to come another night—any other night. All at once she became aware of Lewis's intent glance. "Friend of yours?" he inquired sharply.

"No, no." She sank back on the stool, endeavoring to gather together her whirling thoughts. "Just a neighbor. Now where were we?"

"Just about packed up for tonight, I'd say." He was collecting papers, putting them into a leather folder. A few moments later, after thanking her with old-fashioned courtesy for the coffee, he left her to drive away.

Even before the twin red taillights of the opulent-looking car had been swallowed up on the winding road, Liz was running down the broken pathway toward a pale blur in the darkness of the paddock, which she just knew would be McGinty. Sure enough, as she came nearer she made out a kid with soft long hair and a stubby tail. "McGinty! Mac! Come here!" As if already familiar with his name the tiny creature moved toward her, and Liz cradled him in her arms. What a pet he would be for the children, and how they would revel in the feel of his silky coat. If only she'd been free tonight to thank Peter for bringing him to her.

"Will he do?" Her pulses leaped as Peter, accompanied by Stan, strolled around a corner of the shed. While the older man went back to the cottage Peter moved toward her.

"Oh, he's just a darling!" She put the kid down on the dew-wet grass and turned to face him. "I...I thought you'd gone," she heard herself say inanely.

"I should have." He leaned an elbow on the sliprails. "But Stan wanted some advice on a building project he's working on for the boss."

"Oh, that would be the new ramp he's going to make for me."

"You've certainly got things under control around here, Liz." His laconic tone sharpened. "What did Ridgway want?"

"Lewis? Do you know him?"

He shrugged. "Only by sight. I've seen his picture in the papers often enough. I gather he's the brain of the country's leading advertising outfit. The sort of guy who could help you a whole lot in that direction if he wanted to. *Does* he want to?"

In the starshine she couldn't glimpse his expression, but there was no mistaking the satirical tone. She wished he wouldn't shoot questions at her in this peremptory way, questions that seemed to hint at a lot more than the mere words conveyed.

"I scarcely know him, really. He's just interested in the riding school because of his daughter."

"I didn't say he wasn't! You *are* touchy tonight, Liz!"

"I am not!" How had she got herself involved in this absurd argument? "It was just...the way you said it." She glanced down at McGinty, who had apparently attached herself to the enemy and said defensively, "He's been awfully good about arranging publicity for the center. He's really going to get it known about." She paused, and in the silence she was sure he was mocking her. "He's getting reporters to come out and feature the place in the local newspapers," she ran wildly on. "And he's arranging for shots to be taken for a TV program."

"Good for you, Liz!" The ironic tone made her wonder. Was he laughing at her once again? She wished she knew. Confusion made her add, for something to say to break the silence, "He told me the producers are looking for a riding-school background and a girl to match. Seems it's a commercial they want to make—something to do with a product called Today's Girl. They're sending a camera team up here tomorrow," she ran on breathlessly. "Isn't it ridiculous? Me!"

"I wouldn't think so." Now she was glad of the soft darkness, certain that at this moment he was regarding her with a mocking glint in those lively hazel eyes. "I think you'd feature quite well under that heading."

"It's not a heading," Liz protested unhappily, confusedly. Why must he discuss her as though she were a commodity, or a feature, or something of the sort? "It's advertising for a line of cosmetics. Silly, isn't it, when I scarcely ever use any."

"That's why you'd be just the one for it!"

To get him away from the subject of herself, she heard her own voice saying, "Have you ever watched a TV commercial being made? They'll be here at two tomorrow afternoon...." Oh, heavens, now he would think she was building herself up, boasting. "If you'd care to come along?"

"I can hardly wait."

Now she knew he was mocking her. "Well, anyway," she said awkwardly, "thanks for bringing Mac over. He'll be a real favorite with the children and he'll be great for the ponies, too. Get them used to other animals and sudden movements—all that sort of thing."

"Glad he's what you wanted." He spoke offhandedly. "See you tomorrow—Today's Girl!" He swung around and moved toward the car standing in the driveway, leaving Liz with a niggling sense of unease. What had caused his sudden change of attitude toward her since the night of the dance? The two suppositions that flashed through her mind were each too utterly ridiculous to consider seriously. For how could Peter be jealous of Lewis Ridgway, jealous because of *her*? And for that matter, how could a kiss matter to him, a man already in love with another girl?

If only she hadn't blurted out the matter of the TV commercial. Now he would feel himself duty bound to come out here tomorrow whether he really wanted to or not. And the answer was probably the latter. How humiliating to remember that any day now Peter would give Beryl a token of their love in the form of a glittering engagement ring. For Liz Kennedy he brought McGinty! Somehow it wasn't even funny. She sighed and moved slowly toward the lighted cottage.

IN ANTICIPATION of her afternnon engagement with the TV cameramen, Liz took unusual care with her dressing, pressing crumpled blue jeans and mending the torn buttonholes in her white cotton blouse. Seeing that there had been mention of a barefoot rider her lack of respectable jodhpur boots wouldn't matter. It wouldn't be strictly a riding photograph, of course—not strictly anything—but still.... She washed her hair and seated herself on the top step at the back door of the cottage, while the hot sunshine sparked reddish lights in the black strands. All at once she paused, gazing down toward the house paddock. This morning McGinty had been there, safe and sound. Now he was nowhere to be seen. A swift search of the area confirmed her suspicions. Small and agile, he had pushed beneath a loose wire of the fence and made his escape. Liz couldn't understand why she felt suddenly so bereft. All at once it seemed awfully important that she find McGinty before Peter arrived here today. The trouble was, she realized almost right away, that a small white animal was difficult to distinguish.

She searched for an hour without success. There were so many paddocks and small patches of bush where McGinty could be hidden from sight. At last she went up the path, searching among the overhanging shrubs on either side and calling his name. When she reached the road she went scuffling along in the dust at the side of the rough metal, glancing around her as she went on. She must have moved a hundred yards or so, when a flash of white among a tangle of flax and fern not far from the roadside alerted her. McGinty was reaching up to nibble at a blackberry bush above his head. She tried to creep silently up behind him and take him by surprise, but the snap of a small twig betrayed her, and jerked to sudden awareness, the kid leaped ahead. Liz leaped, too, landing on her stomach among the blackberries. But she scarcely felt the prickles, for she was clasping McGinty triumphantly by a leg and hauling him through the undergrowth. At last she jerked the struggling animal into her arms, and pushing her way through closely growing fern and tea tree, she emerged in sight of the road. A familiar car was approaching, and Beryl waved from the driver's seat, then braked to a stop. The other girl gazed toward Liz's flushed face. "What on earth...?"

"It was McGinty." Her voice died away beneath the cool amused stare from the pale eyes. Faced with Beryl's flawless perfection, Liz was suddenly discomfitingly aware of her own disheveled appearance. Swiftly she recovered herself and floundered on. "He got out of his paddock, and I had such a time finding him. But I caught him in the end!"

"Hop in!" Sandy flung open a rear door, and Liz, still clinging firmly to a struggling McGinty, squeezed in the back seat between the silver-haired woman and the lad she had already seen at the local dance. The small sulky face was turned to Liz in obvious amusement. "You look funny. You've got grass in your hair!"

"So would you if you'd chased a kid all through the bush!" Liz felt hot and sticky with paspalum grass, and she had just noticed that purple berries she had fallen on during her wild dash after McGinty had squashed down the front of her one presentable blouse, with disastrous results. A further dismaying thought struck her. "You weren't on your way here for a riding lesson today, were you, Darryl?"

"That's right. Did you forget? Only it's not a lesson; it's a ride." He sent her a contemptuous glance from beneath heavy lids. "I don't have lessons. That's kid stuff!"

Liz brushed back long hair from a heated forehead. "Don't you believe it!" she said with asperity. "You'd be surprised at the number of grown men who take riding lessons, even though they may have been riding for years."

Sandy turned a backward glance toward Liz. "Just what I've been trying to get through to him all week."

"Me, I'm all for children having confidence in themselves," Beryl was swinging the car in at the opening of the driveway. "The way I see it, it's far more important for Darryl to have faith in his own ability to ride a horse than being taught a lot of stuff that doesn't matter a scrap!"

"Aren't you forgetting something?" Sandy argued as they moved down the drive. "A little matter of self-preservation? If he's going to get on a horse at all he should be taught the fundamentals of how to handle his mount. That is, if he isn't going to take a header onto the ground one of these days."

"Oh, Sandy!" Beryl braked and turned toward him, the beautifully curving lips parted in a mocking smile. "On these ancient nags? You've got to be joking!"

"I'm not, you know," he persisted in his quiet serious tones. "Even a quiet-tempered pony can get a fright at something that looms up on the roadway and take off, bolt with the rider when he least expects it—"

Soft pink lips pouted. "You're so hard, Sandy! You don't seem to understand Darryl at all."

His mouth was a stern line. "We've had all this out before. It's only for his own good that I'm telling you. I know what I'd do if he were my lad...."

"Well, he's not, is he?" She gave a short angry laugh. "Or likely to be!"

Sandy was silent.

"I'm not riding any crummy old pony!" Darryl cried rebelliously. "You wouldn't have got me to come here at all if I'd known I had to get up on one of those dopes!" Imperiously he pointed toward Red, standing quietly within the tea-tree bars of the corral. "I'll have the chestnut! That one over there!"

"Sorry—" Liz was polite but firm "—but he happens to be Red, my show jumper. He's only suitable for experienced riders." She added smilingly, "You don't want to have to bail out in a hurry, do you?"

"I wouldn't do that!" The boastful tones rang with self-confidence. "I could handle him easy!"

Liz, however, was accustomed to dealing with difficult children. "Later on when you've had a few lessons, maybe I'll think about letting you have Red, *maybe*. But for a start everyone has to have a quiet mount." She reached a hand toward the door handle. "You can take Cobber."

"Thank you for nothing!" The boy's mouth was set in a sulky curve. "I'm not riding any stupid little pony. Beryl," he appealed to his stepmother, "you said I could have a decent horse if I came here!"

"I'll go and put McGinty back in his paddock." Calmly disregarding the whining tones, Liz got out of the door Sandy was holding open for her. At that moment Stan came to join them. He smiled toward the group, and taking the kid from Liz said, "So you found him! I'll attend to him for you."

"Thanks, Stan. Darryl's come for a ride. If you'll just wait here," she called over her shoulder to the group, "I'll go and fetch Cobber. Won't be long!"

Together she and Stan went down the path, and in a few minutes Liz returned leading a thin gray pony, while Stan went to the shed to collect sheepskin and saddle.

Ignoring Darryl's petulant expression, Liz led the pony forward.

"Here he is," she said cheerfully, throwing the white fluffy sheepskin over the pony's back. She fitted the saddle and bent to fasten the girth. "He's the biggest of the ponies we have here."

"Ha, ha!" The lad tossed back lank fair hair in an insolent gesture. "If that old nag's the biggest you've got on the place.... Look at him! You can see his bones! Don't you feed your horses around here?"

At the contemptuous curl of the boy's lips Liz controlled her rising anger with an effort. In a brief flashback she had a sudden vision of another lad of much the same age, who had taken his first ride on one of these ponies, too—a ride that had called for every ounce of determination Danny had possessed. That had meant a battle against almost insurmountable obstacles. Crushing down her rising indignation and the disgust that filled her, she forced herself to say calmly, "Come here. I'll give you a leg up."

A little awed by the unmistakable note of authority in the soft tones, Darryl swaggered toward her.

"The other side when you mount a horse, please, Darryl!"

"Aw, I know." With an attempt at bravado, he hitched his hipster belt with its great chased-silver buckle, and after many awkward attempts at last managed to haul himself up into the saddle.

"Now, remember," Liz told him firmly, "you hold the

reins so—no, not like that! This is the way. Don't hold on to Cobber's mane; you're not to rely on that. Knees in, close to the pony's sides. Back straight—straighter than that! Now I'll lead you up to the gate and back."

"I'm not gonna be led, like a baby. Everyone'll see me!"

Disregarding the whining tones, Liz set off up the path. "It's the same for everyone. Later on, when you get more used to riding, you can take Cobber along the road by yourself, but not today."

"Aw, heck...."

For an instant, as she led the pony past the watching group, Liz met the glance of Sandy McPhail. Taking in the angry expression in the strong face, the tightened lips, she guessed that he, too, was having difficulty in restraining his feelings. But what was the use? He had no authority over the boy. Darryl was in Beryl's care, and she seemed bent on indulging him in every way possible, regardless of the damage being done to his character.

Liz led the pony to the front entrance and back to the car. "You can take Cobber into the paddock by the house now," she told the boy. "Remember you're not to take him out of a walk. Now turn...."

With a cruel jerk of the reins he pulled the pony toward a small gate. Liz waited there to open it and closed it after him. "You understand, Darryl? You're not to ride anywhere but in the paddock!"

"Okay, okay, you told me."

As she went back to join the others she reflected that it was useless to attempt to teach the boy anything of the principles of riding correctly. He had already made up his mind that he knew it all, and to cause an open argument wouldn't help anyone. It was a cheering thought, she reflected, that after this one experience of riding she probably wouldn't be troubled with him again.

"You don't have to *watch* me!" called the rebellious voice from the paddock. But, of course they did, eyeing Darryl as he urged the pony around and around in continuous circles on the grass, until Liz thought that Cobber must surely be feeling giddy. At length she strolled toward the boy. "Had enough riding yet?"

The Frost and the Fire

"Call this riding?" he scoffed. "If you'd let me go out on the road I'd show you. I'd zoom along...whee! Nothing to it!" The bragging voice followed Liz as she went to open the gate. "Back in Queensland where I come from there are ranches that would make this dump look like nothing at all."

"Right, that'll do for today. I've got another appointment in a few minutes."

"Another one?" Darryl eyed her in surprise. "Is there someone else coming for a lesson?"

"Not exactly. I'm the rider this time." Liz spoke without thinking. "It's a TV camera team, actually." She glanced up toward the empty road winding over the hills.

"Gee!" Darryl's voice held a new respectful note.

Beryl, who had strolled across the grass to meet them, was also eyeing Liz with interest. For once she appeared to have abandoned her customary superciliousness attitude toward her and was saying eagerly, "Did I hear you say that a TV team is coming here today to do some filming?"

"Uh-huh." Liz was helping Darryl to dismount. "Seems they want a riding background for a commercial they're producing. Some cosmetics thing. Heavens—" she glanced down at her wristwatch "—I'll have to fly! They'll be here in a moment and my blouse.... I'll simply have to change!"

She turned to find Sandy at her side. "Let me put the pony back in the paddock." Already he was taking the reins from her hands. "You zip inside and freshen up." He smiled toward her and added in his steady tones, "Don't worry, Miss Kennedy, we'll hold them at bay until you get back."

"Oh, we'll do more than that!" All at once Beryl was gay and animated. "Isn't it the luckiest thing," she cried in her high tones, "my just happening to be here today! To think I only came because of Darryl's pestering me to have a ride...."

"You mean," inquired her aunt in her hesitant way, "because of your TV experience?"

"What else? You see," she explained to Liz with unaccustomed friendliness, "I've had oodles of experience in television acting." She raised an exquisitely manicured hand to touch a cloud of silver gilt hair. "I've been told a hundred times that natural blond coloring like mine is perfect for photography. So if they're wanting a girl to feature in the commercial, well...." The smile she flashed around the group spelled the message out clearly. Beauty, talent, experience—what more could anyone want in a television advertisement?

Olga said, "Here they come now."

Liz, too, had caught the sound of an approaching station wagon. Hurrying to her room, she rummaged wildly through her bureau drawers in search of a clean blouse. She found one at last. It was hopelessly crumpled, but there was no time to use the iron, for already voices reached her from outside the window. Liz was aware of one voice in particular—feminine, high, argumentative. She dragged the blouse over her head, popping off a button in the process. No matter, she would just have to hope no one would notice. She flew out of the door.

Despite her haste she saw at once that the cameraman was already adjusting his equipment. She hurried toward him and the director. "Sorry I'm late!" She was still breathless as she gestured toward the small knot of onlookers. "Do you all know each other?"

"Now we do!" A tall thin young man with a drooping brown mustache eyed her consideringly. "You're Miss Kennedy?"

She nodded smilingly, and his fellow worker, an older man with a pleasant freckled face, moved toward her. "Hope you can oblige us with some pictures today, Miss Kennedy?"

Liz said doubtfully, "Yes, of course...if you still want me?"

The keen eyes of the young cameraman raked her hesitant face. "What's all this about not wanting you? Is there something wrong? We only want a few shots—won't keep you long."

"No, no, it's not that. It's just that I thought you might prefer to have someone more...well, professional. You see, Mrs. Manning has had a lot of experience before the cameras. You might remember her work on TV?"

"Before my time, I'm afraid," the man with the brown mustache replied carelessly. All at once Liz realized that Beryl was pale, her lips pressed firmly together. Clearly the other woman was very, very angry.

"I've met Mrs. Manning somewhere—" the director's tone was smooth and conciliatory "—but can't think where. Wait, I've got it! Wasn't it at a fashion show that was televised on an overseas liner in port at the time, in Auckland, a few years ago?"

"Yes." Beryl appeared to have some difficulty in getting the word out. Liz couldn't help thinking that the blue eyes appeared to be paler than ever, as though the color were washed out of them—or was that just because of the bleakness of Beryl's expression?

"Too bad we couldn't make use of you today." The freckled-faced man was squinting into the lens, testing camera angles with his colleague. But you see how it is. We have to consider the sponsors, seeing they're the ones who are footing the bill, and with a makeup with a tag like Today's Girl...."

"What do you mean?" Beryl's voice was ominously quiet. "Are you telling me that I'm not—"

"Oh, don't get me wrong, Mrs. Manning. You'd be fine for the usual type of commercial." The director obviously enmeshed in a delicate situation, was feeling his way with care. Liz thought he could scarcely have escaped the impact of Beryl's icy stare. "But it just happens that for this commercial we're looking for a certain type. Just a girl with a happy smile...free...high-spirited...*young*. I guess Ridgway was right when he told us that the girl he'd found had no need to play the part; she was ready-made!" All at once his face cleared, and on an inspiration he added, "Of course, what we're looking for is a girl who can ride like the wind, sail over a high jump, take a farm fence in her stride!"

"Oh, that's different, then!" It was obvious to everyone that Beryl was grasping eagerly at the proffered opportunity to escape from an intolerably humiliating situation. It must surely be the single occasion in the other woman's life, Liz thought, when Beryl had been denied something she really wanted. "Of course, if that's the way it is, I really couldn't consider the part."

"That's what I thought," the director answered smoothly. "Now, if you'll just move out of the way?" He turned toward Liz. "Ready, Miss Kennedy?"

"I haven't any proper riding gear...."

"Who the devil cares about that?" he answered warmly. "Today's Girl doesn't, and that's for sure." So he wasn't particularly concerned about her crumpled denim blouse, Liz thought with relief. She brought her mind back to the quick tones. "What if she doesn't wear conventional gear for riding? She couldn't care less about that sort of thing. She's got an air of living every moment to the full. She lets her hair blow loose in the wind, and when she takes her mount over a high jump she enjoys it as much as he does! Get the picture?"

She laughed. "As long as you're happy about it." At least, she reflected, Red was carefully groomed, for she had brushed the chestnut coat to a silky gleam, combed the long pale mane and tail.

While the men made final adjustments to the cameras Stan went to the paddock to fetch Red. But when the chestnut appeared, coat gleaming in the sunlight, mane and tail newly bleached to a pale cream shade, someone else was leading him. Liz felt her heart plunge. For Peter was leading the mount toward her, and as she met the special smile he seemed to keep for her, the scene around her suddenly became dazzlingly clear and sharp, a moment she knew that would be forever etched in her memory.

He helped her to mount. "Good luck, Liz!" For a moment he held her gaze. Then with an effort of will she wrenched her glance aside.

"Thanks, Peter."

As she guided Red toward the gate opening into a wide paddock, Darryl cried, "Wait a minute! She hasn't got a saddle! And that jump looks hangofa high!"

The young cameraman grinned toward him. "Leave that to us, son. Miss Kennedy doesn't look too worried, and if she's happy seated on an old sugar sack.... Okay with you,

The Frost and the Fire

Miss Kennedy, if we have the jump raised a bit? The higher the better for the picture, if you get us?"

She nodded and turned to Peter. "Will you...?"

He raised the red-and-white pole which Stan had erected in the side paddock for the occasion. "Right! You're away!"

Liz urged Red forward, and he moved off with his long easy canter. Liz's hair streamed behind her. Then the jump loomed up, and she felt Red gather himself for the leap. Crouching forward, she felt the big chestnut stretch himself out over the rails, clearing the high bar with inches to spare.

"Fine!" The freckled-faced director sounded pleased. "Now for another!" Once again she set her mount to jump, and Red flew effortlessly over the bars.

"Was it all right?" she called.

"Tremendous!" The cameraman shot her a swift inquiring glance. "How would you feel about one more shot, with the jump raised higher still?"

She was giving the chestnut an appreciative pat. "No trouble to Red."

"Right!" Once again Peter raised the bar.

"Here we go!" She touched the horse's side with a bare foot, gripping with her knees as Red cantered toward the painted rail. She was aware of the strong muscles beneath her flexing, and as always at this moment when Red took off the ground, excitement gripped her. Blue sky and green paddocks rocketed together; then all too soon it was over. Liz circled the paddock. Flushed and smiling, she pulled up at the side of the watching group.

"Will that do? Have you enough pictures now?"

"Thanks, yes, Miss Kennedy. We took plenty of shots. Just what we were looking for, eh, Alec?" The director appealed to his coworker. "The right girl in the right setup! With this bright sunshine I reckon we've got some sharp pictures." All at once he appeared to remember Beryl, standing silently a short distance away. "We might be calling on you one of these days, Mrs. Manning—if you're still interested in TV work?"

For a second a gleam flickered in the frozen blue eyes. "Anytime. You'll find my telephone number in the book."

"Right! We'll be in touch."

As the team turned away, Beryl glanced toward Liz with such unmistakable malice that Liz knew she had unwittingly made an enemy. Previously she had sensed in the other woman an attitude of careless contempt, but now jealousy and dislike flared in her glance.

"We'll be out next week to get some shots of the handicapped kids on their ponies...." Liz became aware of the cameraman's voice. "That is, if it's okay with you, Miss Kennedy?"

"Yes, of course."

"We're always looking for good news items, and this riding outfit of yours for the disabled kids sounds like something that would catch the public interest. Right now we've got to get back to the studio. Bye! His cheerful wave included the group of watchers standing in the paddock.

From a corner of her eye Liz realized that Peter, too, was leaving. For a moment he paused beside her, and she was at once agonizingly conscious of his nearness. There was no doubt of the pleased expression in his eyes. "Congratulations, Liz. I'll be watching out for you on the screen!" With a parting grin he turned away. The next minute Beryl was running after him, calling in her high carrying tones, "Pete! You'll be over for cocktails tonight? You promised...."

"Sure." Liz watched him get into his car, and as the vehicle shot up the drive the excitement of the afternoon somehow faded. Was it because of Beryl's timely reminder that as far as Liz was concerned, Peter Farraday was merely a slightly interested neighbor, nothing more, that she felt this sudden sense of letdown?

While Stan led the chestnut away Liz moved in the direction of the cottage. She hadn't realized that others, too, had made their way there, until feminine voices echoed from the open window of the kitchen.

"Thanks, Beryl, dear." Olga's slightly apologetic tones floated through the clear air. "I was dying for a drink of water," the wistful voice ran on, "but I just couldn't bear to tear myself away. I was fascinated watching that girl taking those high jumps, and looking so carefree and happy about it. I do think it's marvelous what Miss Kennedy's doing for all those handicapped children. I mean, it must

The Frost and the Fire

be costing her the earth, and she gets nothing out of it!"

"Oh, Olga, don't be so naive!" Beryl's forceful tones came clearly to the girl strolling up the path. "You don't really think she's doing it all just for the sake of the kids?"

"Well, isn't she?"

Liz found herself pausing, listening in spite of herself.

"For heaven's sake, be your age! She's already got Lewis Ridgway eating out of her hand. A widower, one of the wealthiest and most influential men in the city—great work, if you can get it! Oh, don't look at me like that! It's only what everyone will be saying pretty soon! And how about all those interesting doctors and specialists who are always around on the days the kids come out to get a ride?" The high tones were tinged with malice. "Wonderful, Miss Kennedy! Keep up the good work, Miss Kennedy! We couldn't do without you, Miss Kennedy! It makes me *sick*! For a girl who's husband hunting she can take her pick—if she plays her cards the right way! Why, even Peter...." Liz was holding her breath. "Make no mistake, she'd even get hold of him if she could!"

Liz felt a stab of almost physical pain. She didn't care what Beryl said about the others, but Peter.... That hurt, that *really* hurt, made her realize all over again how utterly hopeless it was for her to imagine she could mean anything in his life—ever. She became aware once more of the venomous tones. "Anyone else would see what her game is in a minute—anyone but a silly sentimentalist like you!"

"I don't care what you say." Olga's tones quivered but she stuck to her guns. "I still think you're all wrong about her, Beryl!"

A laugh—short, bitter, without amusement. "You would! You're as soft as butter! But you'll come around to my way of thinking one of these days. She's got Lewis Ridgway just where she wants him and if she can do that in one meeting— well, you'll see that I'm right—and before too long, either!"

"I don't believe that's all she's doing it for."

Liz didn't wait to hear any more. She turned away and went blindly toward the barn. She scarcely knew or cared where she was. She only knew she couldn't, wouldn't meet Beryl Manning face-to-face at this moment. With a faint sense of surprise she noticed that her suntanned hand was visibly shaking. So this was the other woman's revenge for being overlooked by the TV team in favor of barefoot Liz Kennedy in her shabby denim shirt and jeans. How *could* she!

But a jealous woman would say anything against a rival, especially one so indulged and pampered as Beryl. No doubt she would take pleasure in spreading those cruel lies around the district, lies that Liz would find difficulty in refuting. Could it be, the thought came unbidden, that Beryl had yet another reason for her black jealousy? Was it because, out there in the sunshine a few minutes ago, Peter had looked at her with such pride and pleasure?

Only Olga had defended her. Liz could imagine the older woman's earnest wistful face. She knew a moment's pity for her. Imagine having to live with that lovely spiteful creature who was so utterly different in outlook from herself! Perhaps Olga was a poor relative, offered a holiday in the country in exchange for light household duties. But to be forced to be at the receiving end of Beryl's changing moods.... She sighed, thinking that if Peter were in love with her she'd be so happy she wouldn't ever say a cruel word to anyone. But of course Beryl was accustomed to having adulation; it was nothing to her. A woman like that would take it as her due. As to herself, she would do better to put her mind to other matters instead of dreaming the impossible dream.

Peter.... She stared unseeingly through a high window and for a moment the scene outside shimmered in a mist because of the moisture that clouded her eyes. It hurt, what Beryl had said about her and Peter, because it was the truth. She'd give anything for him to love her as she loved him. There! She'd come right out with it. So... one could love again—only this time it was real. The other had been a brief physical attraction, a jolt to her pride, and that was all. But this.... And he belonged to Beryl. Even though she knew it was too late, even though nothing could ever come of it, she would go on loving him just the same, wanting him with this hopeless longing because she couldn't help herself. There was just nothing she could do about it.

CHAPTER SEVEN

On Tuesday when the first ambulance nosed in the driveway, Liz was glad she had got up early. With Stan and Malcolm's help she had the ponies saddled and tied to the hitching rail in readiness for the children's arrival. Almost immediately a second ambulance appeared, followed by private cars, and soon smiling St. John Ambulance drivers were placing wheelchairs on the grass. Children were carried toward them and crutches handed to those who could use them. In a matter of minutes the area was alive with sudden activity, and an atmosphere of happiness and excitement pervaded the air.

"Miss Kennedy! Miss Kennedy!" Liz, talking with a young woman therapist, glanced around as a gleaming car pulled up at her side and a child's fair head appeared at the window. She met Julie's infectious smile and laughing eyes.

"Here you are!" Liz pushed forward an empty wheelchair, and Lewis lifted the small girl from the car and placed her in the chair. Wildly excited, Julie's small face was one smile of delight as Liz helped Lewis to lift the child up to the back of a small black pony. "Pinocchio knows me!" she cried as Liz guided her legs into special safety stirrups. "He winked at me! What'll I do now, Miss Kennedy? This is my *real* lesson, isn't it?"

Lewis sent Liz a quizzical look, then shrugged his shoulders. "She's wild with excitement! Suppose in a way you can't blame the kid!"

"It's something to be excited about, getting mobile all of a sudden!" Liz was fitting a riding cap over the blond curls. "Now first of all, Julie, you've got to learn how to balance on Pinocchio."

"What's balance?"

"Sitting up straight, feeling comfortable."

"But I am!"

"So you are! You're wonderful!" For the child, relaxed and happy, showed no sign of apprehension. "But there are a few things you must learn if you're going to be a good rider. Back straight...." She placed the reins in the small hands. "Hold on to these, not the pony's mane. Do you understand?"

Julie nodded eagerly. "Look, daddy, I'm riding!" A look of unbelievable pleasure and surprise crossed the small face. "I'm higher than you!"

"It's not fair," her father complained, but a secret look passed between him and Liz—on her part a glance of satisfaction, on his an expression of delight that deepened to something warmer. Or was she imagining a special significance in his smile? Today he wore dark rectangular sunglasses, and his expression could be deceiving.

"After that," she told Julie, "we're going out into the paddock, and I'm going to teach you how to make Pinocchio stop and go when you want him to."

Leaving Lewis holding the black pony, she turned away. All around her was a scene of activity. Ponies were being led out of the corral, and ambulance drivers were helping to lift children up onto mounts already saddled. Liz moved toward a group of women whom she took to be the mothers of handicapped children, together with helpers. She thanked them for their interest and gave one of the helpers the task of pinning a cardboard name disc to each child's shirt or sweater.

At the railing a doctor and a therapist were lifting a tall gangling figure onto the back of an overweight sleepy pony. Danny was clinging desperately to the pony's white mane. A spasm of sheer terror crossed his pale face. "I'll fall!" he gasped. "Let me get down! I don't feel well!"

"Hold the reins, Danny." Liz's voice was gentle as she placed the reins in the thin hands. His hunched shoulders and tense features betrayed his agitation. "Just try, Danny... for me. You were all right before, remember? You did so well last time and I was so proud of you. We all were. Look, there's someone standing at each side to hold you steady, and I'll be leading Silver. Nothing can happen to you, Danny. You believe me, don't you? You know I wouldn't let anything hurt you!"

"Don't leave me!"

"I won't, not even for a minute!" If he could remain seated on the pony for a little time she felt sure he would overcome the nameless terror that had him in its grip, the fear that had for so long barred his way toward making any progress. It was a fear, she realized now, that was beyond all her powers to reason away. The only weapons she possessed were patience... and love. Perhaps if she could encourage him to look on the pony as a friend rather than a terrifying hazard.... "Look at him, Danny. He likes you."

But the rigid figure remained motionless.

"Did you hear what his name is?"

There was no response beyond a quick nervous shake of the head.

"He's called Silver, and do you know why he's so fat and lazy? Because he's been put out in a paddock for years and years. The children who used to ride him went away and forgot all about him."

"I like that!" Malcolm paused beside Liz, a halter swinging from his hand. "Us kids couldn't help growing up, not with all that good healthy farm milk and cream and stuff! And how could you forget a piggy animal who stuck his head in at the kitchen window, wanting scraps of bread whenever he caught sight of you? It's his own fault he's so disgustingly overweight."

Liz ignored him. "So he was given to me for the riding school, and now he's feeling ever so happy because he can be with children again—not horrible big boys who grow into horrible big men," she hissed at Malcolm, who showed every indication of making further comments regarding his childhood mount.

Tentatively Danny ventured to put a hand on the shaggy gray neck. "Would he... like me?"

"*Would* he? He'd be so pleased at being taken out in the paddocks for a ride, you've no idea! How would you like to be cooped up—" Just in time she realized she was on dangerous ground and hurriedly changed what she had been about to say. "In a corral all day, waiting for someone to come along and ride you? It's lucky for him that this is the day you're going to take off. Remember?"

He shrank back nervously. "Do I *have* to?"

"Of course not, if you don't want to, but poor old Silver'll be disappointed. He's been waiting all week to get out over the paddock. I bet he could hardly wait for today to come!"

"What an exaggeration!" Malcolm hissed in her ear, his gaze on the sturdy plump pony, half-asleep in the hot morning sunshine. "But who could guess at a pony's deep-down wishes anyway?"

Danny, too, was gazing at his mount, and for a moment surprise overcame fear as he peered down at the pony's muzzle. "Look, he's got a sore nose. It's all red!"

Liz followed the boy's gaze. "Oh, that. I meant to do something about it this morning, but in all the rush I forgot."

"What's wrong with him?"

Liz laughed. "You'd never believe it—he's sunburned! White horses get their muzzles burned sometimes."

"Sunburn?" The pale face expressed only interest and concern. "Does it hurt?"

"A little. Tell you what, I'll go and get something to put on it from the medicine box." She turned away, and hurrying to the shed, found a jar of coconut oil. When she got back to the gray pony Danny was eyeing her excitedly. "Can I put it on? *Please*, Miss Kennedy?"

"Why not?" She handed the jar up to him, and he leaned forward. The thin fingers, awkward and slow, smeared oil on the pony's pink muzzle.

"He didn't mind! He let me put it on the sore place!"

"Why should he mind? He knows you're his friend, his mate."

"That's right." The boy's beaming smile tore at Liz's heart. "We're mates, aren't we? Can I take him out now? Me and Silver, we're going out to the paddock."

Trying not to show her surprise, Liz called to two of the helpers and together they set off, the older women clinging to each side of the safety-belt handle while Liz took the lead rope. Although Danny stiffened as he moved over the grass, the weak back muscles relaxed almost immediately, and it was clear that his thoughts were still on his mount. "He feels better now, doesn't he?"

Ahead of them Liz could see Julie, her blond curls bobbing in the sunshine, with Lewis walking on one side of her and a therapist on the other, while Malcolm led the black pony.

She threw a swift backward glance toward the children awaiting their turn on the ponies. Excited voices and snatches of laughter reached her. Taiere, the small Maori boy, was playing with the white kid, while the black cat and kittens were being fondled by other children seated in wheelchairs. Stan's black-and-white terrier, excited at finding himself such a center of attention, barked wildly among the group.

The cavalcade moved on over the long grass, skirting overhanging branches of trees that could pose such a dangerous hazard to an unsteady rider. Presently Liz halted the riders, giving them a brief period of instruction on the control of the ponies. Danny alone sat quiet and unresponsive, but she made no attempt to force him to take part in the exercise. Already he had made progress enough for one day.

A little later, as she was helping a second section of riders to mount, Liz caught sight of the young cameraman who had visited the riding center a week previously. Heavens, until this moment she had all but forgotten the TV team, who were to come here today for the purpose of recording a program featuring her venture with the disabled children. As she hurried toward the tall young man she realized that the well-built fair girl standing at his side was one of the television team.

"Miss Kennedy, this is Ann."

"Don't worry about us just now." The smiling young interviewer turned friendly blue eyes toward Liz. "We can see you're right in the thick of things, and that's how we like it, being where the action is! Alec's getting some good on-the-spot pictures of the ponies and riders, and I can pick up the main points of the scheme later when you're through with the children. This seems to be their day. Okay?"

"Nice of you." Liz's smile included both members of the team. "If you wouldn't mind waiting until this lot take their turn? The children have their lunch then, before they're taken back to town, and I'll be free to tell you all about it."

The young cameraman smiled. "Of course. Ann and I'll get busy on some notes and shots of the ponies."

A short while later children were helped down from their mounts, and helpers wheeled them to the rough forms that Malcolm had set up in the barn. While he and Stan attended to the ponies, Liz was kept busy filling glasses with fruit cordial and passing them around to the children seated at the long trestle tables. Already they were opening lunch boxes and enjoying the sandwiches they had brought with them.

At last everyone appeared to be taken care of, and Liz brought beakers of coffee to the cameraman and the reporter. The fair girl took it thankfully. "That was delicious," she said a few moments later. "Now—" she took a notebook from the bag slung over her shoulder and poised her ball-point "—if you could fill me in on a few details. I think I've got most of it right." Eagerly Liz told her of the aims of the riding school, and soon the story was captured in squiggles and loops that later would feature as a news item during a program entitled "This Day."

"Thanks very much, Miss Kennedy." She put away her notebook. "Now we're off back to town. Looks as though everyone here is, too." For lunches were being packed away and children carried into waiting cars and ambulances.

"Oh, by the way," the cameraman said to Liz, "the sponsors are delighted with their commercial for Today's Girl. They said it was the girl who made the whole thing come alive. We're pretty proud of it ourselves." He grinned. "You'll be seeing it for yourself at the beginning of the month, and you'll get a check in the mail before that. Just thought you'd like to know how you made out. Bye for now, Miss Kennedy!"

"Goodbye, and thanks." The fair girl threw a smile over her shoulder as she turned away.

"Quite a success, Liz, that commercial of yours!" She

hadn't realized that Lewis was at her side, quiet and unobtrusive as ever.

She nodded carelessly. "Just as well, seeing as it will probably be my one and only appearance on TV. Anyway, it was as much Red's picture as mine. It's today that really mattered, though. It *was* a success, wasn't it, Lewis?"

He nodded gravely. "Absolutely. I'd say you're really going to make out on this idea of yours, Liz. And the rest of us are with you all the way. With the publicity you'll be getting soon—"

"Thanks to you."

"My pleasure, Liz." He stooped to pick up Julie from her wheelchair and stood with her in his arms. "When can I see you again?"

"I don't know. Next lesson, I guess." Her attention was fixed on the children being settled in a waiting ambulance.

"Far too long. I'll ring you before then. Maybe come out one night to see how things are going."

Liz was scarcely listening. "Goodbye, Julie! See you next week!"

The child pouted. "I wish *you* were my mother. Then I could stay with you all the time." The blue eyes danced with excitement. She plucked at her father's sleeve. "Ask her, daddy! Ask her if she will!"

"Don't be so silly, Julie!" Liz said lightly. But the child was not to be put off.

"*Why* can't you, Miss Kennedy?"

"Why...well, because...." Liz wished Lewis would come to her aid, but instead the silence deepened.

Over the curly blond head he was eyeing her with a glance she had failed to interpret. To cover her sudden feeling of confusion she said quickly, "Next week, then," and moved away to help Taiere from his wheelchair. Soon crutches and wheelchairs were whisked away. Vehicles moved up the drive, and as suddenly as it had come the procession vanished.

In the barn Evelyn was gathering up glasses. Liz helped her and afterward went outside to Malcolm, who was sorting bridles and gear into piles belonging to separate ponies. He looked up with a grin. "Happy about today, Liz?"

She bent to help him. "Am I ever. If you only knew how many times I've pictured it all happening, and then to find it all really coming true...."

"Funny how only one father seems to come out here with the kids," Malcolm murmured thoughtfully as he untangled a stirrup leather from its mate.

"You mean Lewis Ridgway? Oh, well, I guess Julie's all he's got. What with having lost his wife years ago and Julie being—"

"Tough luck. But this Lewis guy, he seems pretty interested in what goes on here at the riding center. He's got swags of dough. Could finance the whole show if he were keen enough—" He broke off, for obviously Liz wasn't listening. "Penny for them?"

"Oh, I was just thinking about Danny. Did you notice how different he was today? He actually wanted to go over the paddock with Silver."

Malcolm's dark eyes glimmered with a teasing light. "Thanks to your cruel slander. Mean to horses, she said. Forgetful.... Animal hater!"

Liz laughed and helped him to untangle a halter rope. She had already forgotten Malcolm. She was wondering how long it would be before she would see Peter again. She was longing to tell him of her success, and how the children had reacted to their first riding lesson. After all—her busy fingers paused and she stared unseeingly out over the fenced paddocks—even a man who happened to be in love with someone else could be interested in her project. And he *was* interested, she was certain of it!

Almost as though he had tuned in on her wavelength, at that moment the telephone shrilled in the barn, and hurrying back to pick up the receiver she caught the well-remembered tones. "That you, Liz? How did things go today?"

"Tremendous! I just couldn't tell you—"

"You could, you know! Tomorrow. I've just had a ring from a bloke I know. He's got a job as ranger over in the state forest. Those pine plantations are a great place for a ride. I thought you might like to come along with me. It's a fair distance, but we could truck the horses out there. Don't forget to bring your swimming togs; we could take the horses for a swim in the tide on the way back. What do you say, Liz?"

"Oh, I'd love that!" When would she ever learn to curb her natural enthusiasm? The way she sounded, he'd think... he'd think....

"What time shall I be ready?"

"We'll make an early start. Nine too early for you?"

"No, it'll be fine." It's never too early to see *you*, her heart was saying.

"See you, then. Bye."

Why was it, she wondered, replacing the receiver in its cradle, that just the sound of his voice could make life all at once so different? Exciting, unexpected, wonderful!

The feeling was still with her when she awoke on the following morning. Absurd, this happiness that was flooding her simply because Peter was taking her riding in the pine plantations today. Deep down a small voice warned her that such happiness couldn't last. She thrust it away. What matter? Why not enjoy the unexpected outing? He was in love with someone else, she knew, so there was no need to make a big production of it. A day away from the riding center, a ride through the forests—it was nothing. Why, then, did she have this feeling of exhilaration, as though she were riding high? Riding for a fall, Liz? Once again she smothered the small niggle in her mind and went out to the paddock to find Red. How dreadful if he had chanced to cast a shoe or developed a return of the old injury to his leg, today of all days. At that moment he whinnied and came cantering toward her. Even the sight of the bridle she carried failed to curb his enthusiasm. Clearly the chestnut, too, welcomed an opportunity to be out and away from the fenced paddocks that had so recently become his home.

When a long gray car towing a double horse float appeared in the drive, Liz was waiting, her saddle, bridle and sheepskin rug lying in a heap on the grass, her brief black bikini rolled in a towel alongside. She had told herself that today she would think of nothing but the ride. Yet the moment she caught sight of him striding toward her, her pulses fluttered and the sunshiny day, the breathless blue sky merged into a heady wave of excitement.

"Hi, Liz." His gaze rested on the girl standing near the corral. "It's about time you had a chance of a ride yourself."

"I'm looking forward to it." She led the chestnut toward the float, where a big gray horse already stood, his hoofs beating an impatient tattoo on the timber floor.

"Me, too." His look was warm and intent. The pounding of hooves increased in volume as he led the chestnut forward and fastened down the flap of the float. "It's not every day of the week I get a chance to take out a girl like you." The expression in the hazel eyes conveyed more than the words. "And one who can ride, too!"

Her soaring spirits fell with a plop. Of course, Beryl was no rider. It was the single advantage she held over the other girl—if one could term such a trifling accomplishment an advantage.

"Hop in!" She slipped into the passenger seat, glancing back over her shoulder at the two horses' heads with their flowing manes, one gray, one chestnut, in the float behind.

"Goodbye! Goodbye!" Evelyn had come to the porch to see them off. "Have a good day!"

Liz smiled and lifted a hand in farewell. Then they were moving away, swinging into the quiet road, which was sharply perfumed with the pungent smell of tall white daisies that raised their long stems from the fern. Unbidden, the sense of wild happiness came surging back. Was it because of the bronzed man at her side?

"I had a word with the ranger," he was saying, "about riding over the tracks in the plantation. Just a matter of getting permission, but it's okay."

"Isn't it always allowed?"

He shook his dark head. "Not if the timber experts happen to be zooming through the plantations on that particular day. Or if it's too dry no one can get near the place on account of the fire risk. But today—" he swung around and sent a happy grin in her direction "—everything's just fine."

They sped past clay banks cut into the tea-tree-covered hills around them, and presently through a gap in the hills

Liz caught a glimpse of the sea: intensely blue, violet shadowed, with breakers rolling in on an expanse of black sand. Then they were taking a twisting track that led upward toward a fringe of tree ferns silhouetted against the skyline. She realized that he was driving with care, avoiding potholes and rough patches, making the journey as smooth as possible for the horses in the swaying float behind them. On and on.... Now they were swinging down a steep slope edged with fern and tightly curled fronds of lacy pungas. It seemed to Liz that there was nothing in the world but the endless range of hills, tea-tree-covered, the dark green bushes starred with their myriad tiny white blossoms.

"How'd things go yesterday with the kids?" he asked suddenly.

So he had remembered about the riding lesson. "Oh, it was a real success! You've no idea! I just wished you could have been there to see it all—" She checked herself, aghast. There she went again! She might just as well be saying, "I love you. I want you... all the time. Without you nothing is worthwhile."

"I will be—next time!"

"The ponies," she said faintly, making an effort to choose her words with more care, "the ones we got at the sale—they all behaved perfectly. Stood as still as could be while the children got mounted, just as if they knew what it was all about."

He nodded, his eyes on a curve of road ahead. "They looked a quiet bunch."

"And the most marvelous thing happened! One child, a boy called Danny... he's most dreadfully nervous. Frightened of just about everything, and especially horses. But today he forgot all about being scared, and I'm hoping that next time...."

"Rewarding, eh?"

"That's not the word for it! It would be just fantastic to have every single one of them relaxed and happy on the ponies! With Danny it would mean a lot more than just getting over his fear of riding. It would lead on to his acceptance of other things, as well—things he's simply terrified of now, like learning to use crutches."

He nodded. "I get it. How about the others?"

"Oh, they were so happy! Just to see their faces! Young Julie, she sat up on Pinocchio just as though she'd been there on his back a dozen times. We had such a lot of helpers turn up, too—I couldn't believe it. And then—"

"How about Ridgway?" he cut in. "Did he turn up?" There was a note of urgency in his tone that puzzled her.

"Lewis? Oh, yes. He's planning to come out for every lesson. He seems to have the time to spare, and of course, he thinks the world of Julie. It must be dreadful for her—I mean, to have no mother as well as being born spastic. Yet she's the brightest, happiest child I've ever met. Malcolm's terrific help," she ran on. "He comes over almost every day. I'm going to miss him a lot when he starts varsity in town next year."

He didn't appear to be listening. "Lewis comes out every week?"

"Why, yes." She wondered again at his interest in a man he scarcely knew. "He's got a fast car and the inclination."

"That's right."

She couldn't fathom him in this odd satirical mood. To change the subject she said brightly, "And what do you think? The TV camera team turned up, too, so that means there should be some good publicity pretty soon. It might even bring in some funds to help along with all the things we need. New equipment, a decent concrete ramp— Oh, oodles of improvements."

"Lewis again?" He threw her a swift look, raised black brows.

She nodded. "He offered to help out in that line. Seems he has a lot to do with advertising in his work, and, of course, having Julie at the riding school, he's interested—"

"Oh, he's interested all right. I've noticed."

Liz, darting a glance toward the closed face, was nonplussed. She couldn't understand him in this strange mocking mood.

"He's certainly a man of ideas, I'll give you that!" His tone was quietly controlled. "I take it that Today's Girl was his idea, too?"

"Yes... it was." There seemed no pleasing him in this

sudden dark humor. "I thought," she ventured in the growing silence, "that when it's such a help toward the funds and everything, you'd be...pleased."

"*Pleased?* About having Ridgway hanging around all the time, shoving his oar into things?" Liz found herself regretting ever having introduced Lewis's name into the conversation, though for the life of her she could see no reason for his annoyance. If such a thought hadn't been so utterly fantastic, if things had been different between them, she might almost have imagined him to be filled with unreasoning jealousy. Yet he hadn't objected to Malcolm's helping her at the center. She simply couldn't make him out. She decided to ignore his odd attitude.

"McGinty," she said, "is a pet. He was a great success when the children came yesterday. I don't think any of them had ever been able to handle a kid before. And did he enjoy all the attention! He was the star of the show, believe me!"

"Good."

Determinedly she struggled on. She'd make him lose that dark abstracted look that had come with the mention of Lewis's name. Poor Lewis, who was only trying to help her, after all. Anyone would think, looking at Peter's glowering expression, that he was in love with her himself. Anyone who didn't know him, that was.

"Darryl came for a riding lesson when the children had left."

"He did?" At last she appeared to have captured his attention. The stern features relaxed a little.

"I'm afraid he wasn't too happy about being forced to ride a shaggy little pony. Seems his ideas run more to racehorses and flighty thoroughbreds."

"But you made him take the pony?"

She laughed. "I had to. He knows nothing about riding—not a thing! I don't believe he's ever been up in the saddle before!"

"He didn't try to put one over you? Take off up the road and away?"

"He didn't have much chance! Cobber always comes to a dead halt when he gets as far as the front gate. If I'd allowed him to take Red as he wanted to, goodness knows what would have happened! He tells me he's coming back for more lessons, so I suppose it will be a battle with him every time!"

She wondered at his interest in the boy's riding progress. Was he planning to change matters when he became Darryl's stepfather? After he and Beryl— Oh, why did she keep forgetting about Beryl? She sighed and glanced ahead to the hills, clothed in dense pine trees, their outlines sharp and spiky against the intense blue bowl of the sky.

Like the somber forests of an old German fairy tale, row after row of dark green pines stretched away into the distance, broken by long corridors of firebreaks. Soon they were swinging in at the entrance to the vast plantations, where the air was spiced with the clean sharp tang of the pines and the wind sighed overhead with the sound of distant surf.

"We'll leave the float here and take the horses." Peter was pulling in close to the nearest line of trees, and soon he was leading both horses out onto the grass.

Liz gazed up at the powerful gray. "He's a big fellow. What do you call him?"

"He's Troy. Reliable type. Takes a bit of handling, but he's got a good action. Hold him for me, will you, Liz, while I saddle Red?"

"Troy." Lightly she stroked the big gray muzzle. "I like that name. It's perfect for a big fellow like this. He'd be—" thoughtfully she studied the muscular frame "—how old?"

"I reared him from a foal ten years ago. Don't take any notice of him," he added, for the massive head was moving from side to side. "You can't believe a word he says!"

Liz laughed. He helped her to mount, then swung himself up on Troy. She couldn't help but think how well the big gray suited the man who sat him with such careless ease. She would like to have snapped a picture of Peter on Troy against this background of undulating sea of pines. She had brought her instamatic with her, but how could she snap a picture without having him gain an entirely false impression. He'd think.... What would he think? That she was fast becoming to care for him, quite a lot. That try as she would she couldn't seem to wrench her gaze from his strong features.

Presently both horses were flying at a gallop down the long grassy lane of a firebreak. Liz leaned forward, urging Red on, and soon their mounts were racing neck and neck. At length Peter pulled his horse to a walk, and Red fell in beside Troy. Long dark hair streaming behind her ears, face flushed, Liz was enjoying every moment of the ride.

After a time they turned off into a narrow path winding among a plantation of young pines. Now they were forced to ride in single file and soon they came in sight of a hut deep in the green depths of the forest. The ranger, surrounded by his dogs, appeared in the doorway, a lean brown young man whose startled gaze changed to one of delight.

"Peter! You're just in time for lunch. Come on in—billy's on the boil inside."

They tethered the horses, then entered the small timber hut, austere and spotlessly clean. Soon they were seated at a table in a tiny kitchen, drinking cups of tea and helping themselves to thick slices of bread; spreading them with butter, honey or jam. The two men discussed the ever present need for fire prevention in the pine forests through the dry summer months ahead. Liz gathered that a radio was being installed at the headquarters camp with an extension in the ranger's truck and two portables for the working gangs. The workmen were proud of their recently acquired fire engine, and soon they were getting a lookout tower, to be manned by a watcher on duty through the day and night for fire danger. Liz was content to listen and gaze toward Peter. She didn't get many opportunities to gaze at him without anyone being aware of her interest. At that moment he turned toward her, and hastily she picked up the thick white china cup, brought her mind back to what the ranger was saying.

"It's fairly lonely up here in the plantation, but I'm determined to stick it out for a year or two. It's the best way I know of getting some money saved up. No distractions, no outings, nothing to spend it on." He grinned. "Dull, but worthwhile. At least it is when you happen to have something worth saving for—and believe me, Lois comes right at the top of that category. I'd do a lot more than that if it meant getting a home together quicker for us."

He passed around cigarettes and leaned forward to hold a lighter toward Liz. "Lois has had a raw deal all the way. Looked after a mob of brothers and sisters for years after her parents died. And now, just when she could be free, she's taken on caring for an ailing elderly uncle. Trust her to be there when something or someone has to be looked after and no one else in the family will take on the job! That's why I want to make it all up to her, if I can. How about you, Peter? Still single?" He grinned toward Liz. "Can't you do something about it, Miss Kennedy?"

If only she could! Liz summoned up a shaky smile and tried to sound nonchalant. "Don't look at me! I scarcely know the man!"

The ranger's appreciative glance swept over Liz, taking in her heightened color and downcast lashes. "What's wrong with Peter anyhow? And what the heck's time got to do with it?"

What, indeed? How long had she known him? A few weeks? A lifetime? A swift glance in his direction told her nothing, for his eyes had a curiously veiled expression. Avoiding a cloud of cigarette smoke perhaps—or an awkward question? But trust him, she thought ruefully the next moment, to have the situation well in hand. "Liz has other... things on her mind."

Has she, indeed? And what would you know about that? It's you, Peter, who are on my mind every day, every night, all the time! Even if I live to be a hundred I'll never forget today, just because we're together. To you, I know, it means nothing, but that makes no difference. I know something else, too. Danger flags are flying in all directions. There's nothing ahead but pain and disappointment, but that doesn't make any difference, either!

She turned away to crush the ash from her cigarette, fearful of betraying the secret that the ranger had all but stumbled on. What was Peter saying now? Something about handicapped children. Liz had got her idea off the ground and now she was well away. There'd be no stopping her now she'd got started. At any other time she would have been roused to instant enthusiasm over the fulfillment of her scheme. Today she had to force herself to explain to the ranger the aims and objects of the riding center.

They chatted for a while over cigarettes, then in spite of the pleas of the lonely man in the hut to stay a little longer, they took their leave.

"Why not go and have a look through the state forest park that bounds the pine plantations?" the ranger suggested as he came to see them off. "There are fifty-five thousand acres of it, with lots of native bush."

Peter turned to Liz. "What do you say? Like to take a look through the bush?"

"Love to!"

"Right! We'll be on our way!" Goodbyes were said, and soon they were once more galloping along an endless corridor, where tall dark trees enclosed them on either side and the air was sharp and spicy with the pungent scent of pines. As the end of the firebreak came into view, they slowed the horses to a trot. Now they were in sight of the great natural giants of the bush: tawa, kauri, rewa-rewa, their leafy branches piercing the blue far overhead, while beneath low-growing ferns and bushes made a filtered shade. They found a track and moved deeper into the bush. Here the horses' hooves made no sound against the layers of moss and dried leaves on the narrow path, and the bell-like notes of a tui sounded clearly on the still air.

After some time they passed two trampers, packs on their backs, and a little farther on they caught the sound of something crashing through the undergrowth. Swiftly Peter put a hand on Red's bridle as both horses paused, ears pricked and eyes alert. The next moment a wild pig emerged from the bushes, to vanish among the dense undergrowth at the side of the track.

"He's safe enough." Peter indicated a notice nailed to a tree trunk: No Fires. No Shooting. "See those old ruins of buildings through the trees? They're the relics of an old sawmilling industry. They used to cut a lot of kauri here in the days of the first settlers."

"Awful thought, cutting down those forest giants!" Her gaze traveled far upward to where the boles of giant kauri trees rose undeviating for more than a hundred feet. "Some of these trees must have been growing here long before the white man ever came to New Zealand."

"Or the Maori. They were in great demand in the early days for making spars for the sailing ships. No need to worry about their fate now, though. These big fellows in the state forest park are protected, and a good thing, too!"

Liz pulled on her rein, listening. "Can you hear water running somewhere? Come on, let's go and see!" She urged her mount forward, and together she and Peter swept over a fern-covered rise. Below them, almost concealed by thickly growing bush, they caught the faint sheen of water. As they came nearer they caught sight of a man moving along beside the banks, and farther on a party of women were collecting stones from the edge of the stream.

When they reached the water Liz dropped lightly down from the saddle. It was at once clear as to the reason why "rock hounds" had taken the trouble to come to this remote spot, for among the shallows gleamed smooth stones shading from tones of milky white to pink, topaz, and jade. Bridles looped over their arms, they moved along the banks, and Peter suddenly bent to pick up a smooth violet-colored pebble. "Like it?"

"Thank you. It happens to be my lucky color." She added, at his glance of surprise, "I'm a February bod and I love mauve!"

"Thanks for telling me! A bit of information like that might come in useful one of these days!" Once again he was laughing at her. Liz fingered the cool stone that was so pleasant to the touch.

They followed the stream around the next bend, where they came in sight of another party of trampers. Then once again they got on their mounts. As they rode on over the track she sniffed the air appreciatively. "Funny...I keep getting drifts of the most heavenly perfume, yet I can't think what it could be!" She was glancing around her toward the tangled tree ferns, clustered green five-finger and tall spears of flax. Nothing there to produce the delightful scent.

"It's the flowers of the cabbage tree," Peter told her.

The Frost and the Fire

"Sometimes it drifts for miles on the breeze, and once you've caught it, it's unforgettable."

Liz thought that today everything was unforgettable. Just being alone with him, the sight of the strong bronzed face, the hazel eyes with their swiftly changing expressions. It all added up to a feeling of completeness, of happiness and content.

They were progressing now at a walking pace, for the track twisted among thorny climbers and often their way was barred by long ropes of trailing supplejack. At other times the horses were forced to pick their way over stringy black punga logs lying across the path, or the leafy branches of a tall forest giant that had come crashing to the ground during a winter storm.

He pulled on the reins. "Let's turn back, shall we?"

She felt she could have gone on forever under the sun-burnished sky, with the green bush all around them, and Peter.... It all came back to him. Surprisinly, she realized now, the sun was lower in the sky than she had noticed. She sighed. "Okay." There was still the ride back to the pine plantations, she comforted herself.

But it was over all too soon, and a little later she found herself seated once more in the car, waiting at the edge of the line of trees. Then she remembered that they planned to swim the horses in the surf on the way back, and she felt happier.

It seemed such a little time before they came in sight of the white-flecked sea, and presently they left the car at the top of the cliff. Once again in the saddle, Liz guided Red down a winding path, where loose rubble and small stones dislodged by the horses' hooves went tumbling down the steep slopes. When they dropped down onto the beach breakers were pounding in on a limitless expanse of black sand. Liz took her bikini from her saddlebag. "Be with you in a minute!" On the shore, thickly edged with tall, densely growing flax, she changed swiftly. But when she ran down the sand the saddles were lying in a heap and Peter was waiting for her, lean and brown and muscular in swimming trunks. He placed his hand beneath her foot, helping her to spring up onto the back of the chestnut. She pressed Red's side with her heel, and both horses moved over the wet sand and plunged into a shower of spray.

Once over the line of breakers the horses swam out into the deep, only their heads visible as they moved out with the tide. Liz, clinging with her knees to the wet sides of her mount, hair drenched and face beaded with drops of sea water, sent a laughing glance back over her shoulder.

"Now!" Peter called, as an oncoming white-crested comber came surging toward them. They turned, and the next second horses and riders were swept inshore on the force of the wave. Liz felt a delightful sense of exhilaration in the surge of the sea, the relaxing yet invigorating force of the breakers. It was sheer joy to search for Peter's dark head amid a shower of spray, before they both turned and once again urged their mounts toward an expanse of glittering sea.

At last the horses scrambled out onto the sand at a point a distance along the shore from where they had entered the water. Soon Liz and Peter were urging their mounts to a canter as they moved along the tideline, the flying hooves leaving indentations in the wet sand behind them. When they reached the saddles, Liz dismounted. Cool and refreshed, conscious of a delicious sense of relaxation engendered by sun and sea, she flung back her wet hair and gazed around her. Against a backdrop of sun-flecked sea, a mirage danced over the dazzling iron sands, pricked with a thousand diamonds in the afternoon sunlight. All at once she met Peter's glance and felt her heart contract. How vibrantly alive he looked! The sort of man who would look after a girl. What would it be like to be loved by such a man? With an effort of will she turned away, and picking up her towel began to dry her hair. But all the time the crazy thoughts went spinning through her mind. If she didn't look directly toward him he mightn't suspect that she was in love. Love! Once before she had imagined herself to be in love, but how could she know the difference until she had met a man like Peter? *I'm in love with him,* she marveled, *just like that! I have been ever since that first day we met here at the beach.*

"Hey, Liz, you're miles away!" He had flung himself down on the hot sand, and leaning on an elbow gazed up at her, laughter glimmering in his eyes. "Come back! No, come on down here with me!" A swift tug at her hand and he had pulled her down on the sand at his side. "You looked awfully sad all of a sudden. Come on now, what's wrong?"

The intent glance that so often seemed to probe her innermost thoughts raked her face. She picked up a handful of sand, watched it sift through her fingers. Like time, she thought, like days with him, running out. "That first day on the beach," she murmured inconsequently, "you had on an orange-colored shirt...."

He was grinning. "*Had* is right!"

"I know. It was all my fault. I'll get you another one when I go to town next time, to make up."

He didn't answer. Very gently he put a hand against her hot cheek, and she didn't know whether it was the dazzle of the sun or the dazzle in her heart that was sending waves of excitement through her. She only knew that if he kissed her again, she'd forget everything else, even Beryl. Being with him was like being under a spell—nothing else mattered. Surely she could snatch one day from fate, enjoy the deep enchantment of being in love. There would be so many days in the future when she would be far away from him, a whole lifetime of them! Sun, sea and the salty relaxation of the surf all conspired against her, and as he drew her close she was swept by an aching longing to feel his lips on her own.

When he released her she was still caught in the poignant happiness of his kiss, and for a moment she failed to realize that they were no longer alone on the beach.

"I could swim farther out in the surf than either of you!" The moment of magic splintered into fragments as, startled, she glanced up into Darryl's small sulky face. He was standing facing them, hands thrust into the pocket of his jeans.

"You reckon?" Peter lay back on the sand, hands crossed behind his head. His glance slid to a car standing on the grass beneath spreading pohutukawa trees not far distant. "Where did you spring from anyway? Did your mum bring you down here?"

"I don't need *her*! I can drive! Didn't you know? I can

ride a horse, too," the light bragging tones went on. "It wouldn't matter to me how high-spirited or wild it was!" He swung an accusing face toward Liz. "If only you'd give me something to ride, Miss Kennedy, instead of a corny old pony, I'd show you what I could do. I bet I could go out a lot farther in the surf than either of you! No trouble!"

"I wouldn't advise it, mate," Peter's voice was crisp. "Beryl know you're taking the car out by yourself?"

"She knows." Darryl gave a childish grin, half fearful, half swaggering. He kicked at the shells lying on scintillating sand. "Well, anyhow, she will soon when I get back." His bravado faltered in the face of the man's direct look. "She's not *my* mother," he muttered half under his breath.

"Near enough."

For answer the boy pulled a face. Then, turning, he made his way over the sand, wading through the clear stream on the way back to the grassy patch beneath the trees. When he reached the car he got inside, slammed the door and started the motor. A moment or two later he went hurtling up the road, to be lost to sight around a bend of the track winding up the steep bush-clad hill.

Peter's mouth was grim. "He needs a man around the place to straighten him up a bit! The way he's going it looks like his mother's heading for a whole heap of trouble one of these days!"

"I guess you're right." But to herself Liz was thinking, did Beryl need a man too, one man in particular whom she had never ceased to love, in spite of an earlier marriage, followed by a new life in another country? "Perhaps," she said in a thick unnatural voice, "he'll be getting one... before long."

He threw her a swift surprised glance. "Now just how did you drop on to that? It's supposed to be a dead secret. You don't miss much, do you, Liz? You must be well up on the subject of love to catch on so quickly." He grinned and made to take her hand, but swiftly she moved away.

"Not really." The bitter pain that was flooding her made normal speech difficult. Could that be her own voice so low and charged with emotion? Springing to her feet, she turned aside to hide her trembling lips. "I'm off to get

The Frost and the Fire

changed." Picking up her bundle of clothing, she stumbled blindly away over the sand.

So it was true, the suspicion she'd had all along that he was merely filling in time with her. Only a stupid nit like herself would have read anything more into his friendship. Her idea of providing a riding school for the handicapped had intrigued him, just as she herself had amused him, for a time. But it was Beryl who was his real life. The pain in her heart was as sharp as a physical wound. Once he had told her lightly, teasingly, prophetically as things had turned out. "When I find my own special kind of girl, you'll be the first to know!"

Behind the thick wall of densely growing flax bushes she paused, and with unsteady fingers slipped from her bikini. It was easier to bear the pain now she was out of range of the disturbing masculine magnetism that seemed so hard to combat. The shaking of her hands made her movements slow and awkward, but at last she was ready. She ran a comb through damp, windblown hair, rolled her bikini in the towel. Well, she'd have to face him sometime. Her lips were still a little out of control and there was a stinging moisture behind her eyes, but she supposed that to everyone else—and why not admit that by "everyone" she meant one man whom she happened to love?—she would appear to be perfectly normal. Heartbreak need not show if you were careful to avoid looking directly into perceptive hazel eyes.

And anyway, she reflected as she pushed through flax spears and made her way over the sun-flecked iron sands, the day was almost at an end. Her last day alone with Peter, for after this she would make certain not to run the risk of putting herself in this dangerous heartbreaking position. She slowed her steps, reluctant to face him, afraid that he would guess how deeply she cared. She was such a fool at concealing her emotions, especially where he was concerned! All this time at the back of her mind there had been a crazy hope that somehow a miracle would happen. Well, now she knew. There wasn't the slightest chance in the wide world of his ever returning the feeling she had for him.

But she couldn't dawdle along the sand forever, and when at last her dragging footsteps brought her back to him she told herself that, after all, she need not have worried. For he looked relaxed and cheerful. He had changed back into shirt and shorts, his dark hair springing back in damp waves from a bronzed forehead.

"You should have told me."

Her heart flipped. "Told you?" Why was he regarding her in that speculative concerned manner? Her glance was evasive.

"You've gone all white under that brand-new tan of yours! Stayed in the water a bit long, by the look of things. I'd better make up for it by getting you home right away!" To her relief he began to saddle the horses.

He brought Red to her side, and she placed a bare brown foot on the strong tanned hand he extended and leaped up into the saddle. For a moment he stood motionless, smiling up at her. Just as though, she thought wildly, there were nothing to keep them apart... no Beryl. "I forget sometimes that a girl might not be used to being in the surf for hours at a time. Not like me, in training all the year round with the surf club. I won't let it happen again, Liz."

Her smile was tremulous. "Not your fault," she said huskily. No, the fault lay with herself and her own stupid vulnerable heart. For her own sake she knew there would never be a next time. That way lay danger.

CHAPTER EIGHT

Torn by her inner conflicts, in the following week Liz threw herself more than ever into her duties. Once she had imagined that to realize her dream of helping the handicapped would be to gain for herself perfect contentment—that it would be all she would ever ask of life. But that was before she had met Peter, and things hadn't worked out that way. Not that she wasn't pleased with her progress at the riding center. The work itself was deeply satisfying, as far as it went. If only there weren't always the dreary hopeless longing to see Peter again. The sense of desolation, the despair that swept over her at moments when her guard was down, all pinpointed what life could have meant with him. How could she have known that outside love's magic circle even success in one's chosen field failed to satisfy? That nothing could take the place of being loved by the one man in the world to whom you had been foolish enough to have lost your heart?

She supposed she should feel grateful for interests that demanded all her time and attention, she told herself forlornly when the telephone rang for the sixth time since breakfast. The speaker was a woman, a reader of one of the magazines that had recently featured an article dealing with the riding center at Rangiwahia. Liz thanked the inquirer for her offered donation and told her, yes, they were always glad of extra helpers on the weekly visits of the handicapped children. Liz would add the newcomer's name to the roster of helpers. She went on to detail the route by motorway from the city to the riding school. It was a pattern to which she was fast becoming accustomed, for the recent publicity afforded to her venture by magazines and newspaper articles had sparked an immediate interest in a sympathetic public.

She had been pleasantly surprised, too, at the response to the TV feature with its pictures of children riding their ponies, together with interviews with medical superintendents and therapists. Screened at news time on an early-evening session, the feature had captured viewers' imagination, and from that night onward donations, offers of help and gifts of ponies and gear had continued to pour in. It seemed she had actually launched her venture successfully at last and from now on things should run fairly smoothly. She should be so happy, and yet....

Even her sister, Helen, had written that for once in her life she had to admit to being proved in the wrong. Liz's crazy scheme looked like turning into something worthwhile, after all. Although, Helen had pointed out with sisterly candor, she couldn't help thinking that in spite of the rewarding nature of Liz's work, when you came right down to it there was really nothing to match marriage with the right man. Had Liz met up with any eligible young farmers yet? There must surely be one or two stashed away up there in the bush!

One was sufficient, Liz reflected bleakly, when the man in question happened to be Peter! She drew in a short sharp breath. There she went again, thinking of *him*! In a spurt of anger she tore the letter into fragments, scattering the pieces into the wastepaper basket beneath the desk.

The fact that Danny was at last making definite progress was the one gleam of light in the darkness of spirit that caused her to sleep fitfully and to pick listlessly at Evelyn's wholesome, well-cooked meals. Danny was now much more relaxed, and when she was with him Liz forgot, for a little time, her own heartache. No longer did he flinch and hold back nervously on being lifted up onto Silver's broad back. What she had scarcely dared to hope for had happened. His newfound affection toward the shaggy white pony had pushed fear into the back of his mind. On the last riding day he had even responded to instruction, and his pride and excitement as the weak hands pulled on the rein and turned the pony in another direction was, to Liz, well worth all her patient weeks of gentle perseverance. If only she could tell Peter of her victory with Danny. The traitorous thought sneaked into her mind and was as swiftly thrust aside.

Peter. The only way in which she could carry on with her life here was to try to make her mind a blank. But how to do that when you froze to instant awareness at each peal of the telephone when your thoughts flew into a turmoil at the mere appearance of a long gray car in the driveway? Or the sight of a tall masculine figure approaching the cottage? A figure that might be him, only, of course, it never was!

She knew that he had been away for a week, buying sheep in the South Island, but he would soon be returning to Arundel and then.... If he should contact her once again, somehow she would have to steel herself, make him understand she had no intention of seeing him again—ever. It was possible to continue with her life as usual, almost, but if she came face to face with him even for a minute she had a frightening suspicion that all her good resolutions would vanish like manuka smoke in the wind, and she would be at the mercy of her own vulnerable heart and his mocking smile.

Once again the telephone shrilled through the big room, and abstractedly she lifted the receiver.

"Peter here."

"Peter!" Her heart gave a great leap, then just in time she remembered what she had schooled herself to do. If only he didn't make it too difficult.

"Just thought I'd check up," came the deep, friendly, heart-catching tones. "I've been away for a while, down south. Had you noticed?"

Had she noticed! "Yes, no—I mean I heard...."

"You're stalling, Liz, but I'll forgive you if you let me take you out tonight!" He sounded as confident as ever. "Seeing you on TV isn't the same, Liz, but it was something! That program on the riding school was darn good viewing—let everyone in to what's going on up here at Rangiwahia. Happy with it?"

"Oh, yes, I was!" Nervousness made her add, "Did you happen to see the commercial, too?"

"It was tremendous! Great of you, and old Red gave a good account of himself! You know something, Liz?" She caught the teasing note in his voice. "You'll be famous around the place pretty soon. Everyone'll know Today's Girl with the old-fashioned sweetness in her smile!" As usual, she thought with a pang, he was laughing at her. "I thought we'd celebrate your success?"

"Celebrate?"

"Why not? It doesn't take long to zip into town, and I've booked a table for two at the Matador. What do you say?"

The temptation to go with him was so strong she had to force the longing aside. She mustn't give in to herself. "I'm sorry." She hoped he would lay the blame on the connection for the unevenness of her husky tones. "But I'm afraid I can't make it tonight. Some of the heads of the hospital in town are making a special trip up here to see me—at least, I think they are...."

"Tomorrow night, then?"

"No, no..."

"More conferences?" How gay and confident he sounded, just as though there were nothing to keep them apart. Why not. He already had Beryl and marriage plans in mind. Who was to know if once in a while he took out another girl for a night's entertainment in the city?

"The same ones," she managed breathlessly. "You see, I'm not quite sure which night they're coming and I have to be here, just in case."

"How about next week, then?"

"I'm sorry." If only he wasn't making it so difficult, and it didn't hurt so much to say the words.

"*You're* sorry! Well, tough luck!" She caught an odd inflection in his tone...bewilderment, surprise, disappointment? "But we'll make it one of these days. Some other time, then. Be seeing you, Liz."

"Bye, Peter." The words lingered in her mind like the tolling of a distant bell. Goodbye. Goodbye. He wasn't the type of man to plead with her to change her mind. There'd be no need to spell it out. It was her own wayward heart that was proving so difficult to discipline. Yet somehow, no matter how painful, she must cut the ties that over the past few weeks had strengthened to ever tightening bonds, at least as far as she was concerned. Short of flight, and circumstances put that out of the question, this was the only way. Let him think what he pleased of her seemingly puzzling behavior.

Nor did her decision grow any easier to maintain as the slow days crept by and there was no further word from him. But life went on and outwardly everything proceeded much as usual. One morning the mail brought another generous check from the unknown donor, whom Liz still thought of as "Mr. X," for the benefit of the riding school. Now she could at last afford to have the drive from the gate to the cottage concreted—an urgent need. Her first impulse was to rush to the telephone. She must tell Peter of her good fortune! Then she remembered, and the pain came back.

Tuesdays were the best days when, involved with the children and ponies, her own conflicts slipped into the background and the pain eased for a time. Malcolm had fallen into a habit of coming to the cottage almost daily, and was at hand to help with the ponies and the endless tasks concerned with their care. In the evenings and at weekends Lewis had become a frequent visitor. Tonight he had brought account books with him. As he sat opposite Liz at the desk in the barn, the hanging electric light bulb illuminated his bent head and carefully tended black hair. As he opened the lined pages of a cashbook Liz sighed and made a face. "Must we?"

He smiled across at her. "This won't take long, and it's important to know how you're going along. But if you'd rather leave it until another night, just say the word."

"No, no. I've got everything ready for you. Here are the checks, and this pile is all the cash donations. Receipts are on the file, and I've kept all the accounts together for payment." As he totaled up the money, Liz found herself thinking what a good friend Lewis had proved himself to be. All this bookkeeping.... It was a chore, as well as something of which she had very little knowledge. Now she came to consider the matter, she really owed a lot of the success of her venture to Lewis's business acumen and expert assistance. He was friendly, yet always so correct. She could have smiled to think how ridiculous was Peter's obvious jealousy on Lewis's account. But she mustn't think of Peter.

They worked steadily for an hour. Then they were interrupted by a telephone ring. Liz picked up the receiver. "Yes?"

"Oh, Liz, this is Beryl." The other woman seemed so excited and happy that for once she had forgotten to treat Liz with her usual brand of condescension and disdain. "Is Peter there with you by any chance? He said something about calling around to see you about something."

"No."

"Well, listen, if he does come, tell him to hurry back here, will you? I've got some important news to give him. You can let him know that I've made the big decision at last!"

"I'll tell him if he comes." Funny how perfectly ordinary she sounded, as though it were nothing whatever to do with her, which was indeed the truth. All at once the import of the message struck her. Peter! Coming here tonight! That she couldn't endure.

Thoughtfully she replaced the receiver in its cradle. A momentous decision made between a man and a woman who were on the verge of starting a new life together? Maybe they had quarreled and Beryl wanted to put things right between them without further delay. Or more likely the other girl had set a date on which to announce the engagement. Perhaps even a wedding day, for what need was there to wait? No wonder Beryl had sounded so happy!

"What's wrong, Liz?" She became aware of Lewis who was eyeing her with concern.

She stared blindly back at him, unaware of her sudden pallor or of the pain shadowing her dark eyes. "Nothing... just a message I had to give...someone."

"Sure?" His tone softened. "You can tell *me*, you know. You look as though you've taken a shock. Not bad news?"

She felt an urge toward hysterical laughter, but instead she stilled her trembling lips, said huskily, "It was just a call. Nothing...important."

"I see." He was still regarding her thoughtfully. "Look, you're tired tonight. All this stuff—" he glanced down at the account books and papers outspread over the desk "—it's not urgent. But something else is. Let's take a run

The Frost and the Fire

out—that is, if you're not expecting anyone to call here tonight?"

Although the night was warm she felt a shiver pass through her. "No, no, nothing like that!" All at once she felt she had to escape. She couldn't wait here to endure the bittersweet misery of meeting Peter again. "A run out in the car?" The words came jerkily. "That would suit fine. It's one of those evenings!" Feverishly she sprang to her feet, in her haste sending a sheaf of papers fluttering to the floor. Lewis bent to pick them up, and when he straightened she noted in some other part of her mind that his hands were unsteady. And something else struck her too. He was looking animated, almost... elated. But he only said quietly, "Come on, then, let's go before you change your mind!"

Change her mind! If he only knew what a fever of impatience possessed her to be away from the barn as soon as possible. If Peter came here tonight she couldn't face him. She wouldn't! It seemed an age as she waited while Lewis gathered up account books and files. Her ears alerted to every sound on the driveway outside, she wanted to cry, "Hurry! Hurry!" as with maddening precision Lewis continued to place folders in his briefcase. At last, however, he snapped the catch and they went out into the cool freshness of evening. Not until she was seated in the car did Liz's taut nerves relax a little. As Lewis thumbed the starter she leaned forward anxiously, fearful that at any moment she might catch the gleam of car headlights shining in at the entrance.

"You're very quiet tonight." Lewis swung through the opening and they turned into the shadowed road.

She had been peering through the window, her gaze alerted to car lights on the hill ahead, and she came back to the present with a start. "Was I? I was just thinking...."

"Don't! Just relax. Enjoy yourself for a change. Not that you can see much at the moment, but still...." He flung her a smile. "You certainly picked a scenic spot for your riding center when you settled for Rangiwahia—whatever it means."

"I know the translation from Maori," she answered

dully. "It means 'A Shimmering Sky,' a sort of breakthrough in the clouds."

"Sounds great."

"Yes." She was speaking her thoughts aloud. "It paints a picture. Rift in a clouded sky. Things looking up...."

"Maybe for me it's a lucky omen!" She had no idea what he meant, nor did she particularly care, for at that moment a car swept around a bush-shadowed bend. As it scraped past on the narrow road she caught a fleeting glimpse of Peter's dark head. He was heading in the direction from which they had come, so evidently she had made her escape only just in time! Had he recognized Lewis's car, she wondered. Not that it mattered one way or the other. It was no concern of his where she went or whom she chanced to be with. She sank back in her seat. "That's more like it," said Lewis. "Now tell me, where would you like to go tonight?"

"It doesn't matter." The next moment, realizing how clearly her listless tone betrayed her heaviness of spirit, she roused herself to add hastily, "I mean, it's all the same. There's no moon... yet."

"Right! We'll head for the coast!"

If only, she thought wildly, he didn't take the path leading to the cliff overlooking the sea, where she had gone with Peter. But already they were swinging into another track that led through dark bush. Presently they emerged in a clearing, and Lewis ran the car to the end of a grassy headland, where the roar of the surf was loud in their ears. Farther up the coastline a scattering of lights indicated a township, and below, the headlights picked up the dark, wind-tossed waves.

He switched off the engine, leaving only a small bulb on the dashboard alight, then swung around to face her. All at once his tone was deep, hoarse with emotion, so un-Lewis-like that she stared at him in surprise.

"You don't know how much I've wanted this!" His arm slipped around her shoulders, and before she could pull away she felt his mouth on hers. Her own lips were unresponsive, utterly without feeling.

"I love you, Liz. I have right from the beginning! Oh, I

told myself I'd wait until I was a bit more sure of how you felt about me. But hell, Liz, I'm not a boy anymore. A man can't wait forever, not when he's as crazy over someone as I am about you! Look," he said softly, "why don't you let me take care of you—for good, I mean? Now, don't say anything," for she had opened her mouth to protest. "I didn't mean to come right out with it for months yet. Courting's an old-fashioned word these days, I guess, but that's what I had in mind. But seeing you tonight, watching you trying to cope with problems and finances as well as giving the kids their riding lessons...." Softly he caressed her hair. "We *need* each other, Liz, whether you realize it or not!" His smile was very tender, and she found herself wondering why she hadn't guessed at his feelings long ago.

Aloud she said the first thing that came into her mind. "But you scarcely know me."

"I know you well enough, Liz. And I don't think you'd find me such a bad sort of guy to get along with. No bachelor habits, no particular vices. I've only got one obsession, and that's... loving you!"

"I know, I know, Lewis. It isn't anything like that!"

His tone sharpened. "There's someone else."

"No." Her tone was infinitely sad. "There's no one."

"Well—" he let out a long sigh of relief "—that's something. I can take it from here. I know it's a bit underhand to mention it, but don't forget, there's Julie. Together we could make a decent life for the kid, a real home. Think of it that way, Liz. Oh, I know," he went on, very low, "that you mightn't be all that wrapped up in me. But give me time. We'll make out. Together we'd make a great team. You'll see. Just give it a chance! Marry me, Liz," he urged, "and we'll set up a riding center for the whole of the country—one that'll cater for every sort of disability you can think of. If you like we'll move somewhere else, start afresh. You'll never have another financial worry."

"Silver stirrups, Lewis?" Her sad little smile didn't reach her eyes.

"Why not? Gold-plated if you like, every single one of them! All you have to do is just say the word. For my wife, Liz, nothing is too good."

"You're very good to me. If only...."

Swiftly he placed a finger against her lips. "Don't say it—the 'if.' 'When,' Liz, that's the operative word. *When* you're my wife. How does that sound to you?"

She didn't answer. It was no use. She simply had no feeling for him, or if she had it wasn't the sort on which one could plan marriage. If only he wasn't so certain that he could persuade her to change her mind.

He lowered his head, and as she felt the touch of his lips on her brown hand she had an odd sensation that all this was happening to someone else. Illogically, with another part of her mind, she noticed the thinning patch on the bent dark head. Poor Lewis, he had already taken so many unexpected blows from fate: a tragically brief marriage, an adored only child born a victim of cerebral palsy. Why did he have to fall in love with her when there must be so many other women he knew who would appreciate his kindness and reserved charm?

He looked up into her eyes. "You'd never be sorry, you know. I'd love you all my life! Think, Liz, we'd have shared interests, a happy life together with enough funds to do the things you want to for the handicapped youngsters. If you like we'd go overseas—take a look over at the other side of the world, see how your setup here compares with what's being done along the same lines there. Not such a bad life, would you say? I mean, what more could one ask for?"

"Just...love." She scarcely realized she had spoken her thoughts aloud until he caught her up sharply.

"But I love you, Liz, truly I do. I always will. You know that."

"Yes, I know, but...."

"I could teach you to love me, Liz...like this." The next moment his lips were pressed to her mouth in a tender caress. And still she felt no emotion of any sort.

"Not so bad, was it?" Lewis was saying as he gently released her. But he must have guessed how she *really* felt about him, Liz thought, for without giving her time to reply he was running on, eagerly, persuasively. "Why waste your life waiting for something that may never come along? Could be it's all an illusion. We'll have something a lot more lasting to build on. Trust me. Marry me, Liz." His voice dropped to a low pleading note. "You'll never regret it, I promise you."

She hesitated. A glance at his set face made her realize that his calm exterior hid a depth of feeling. He really cared, although up to now he had kept his emotions well under control, given nothing away. She flinched from the thought of having to inflict on him the nagging heartache she herself was suffering right now. The shame-making misery of being hopelessly helplessly in love with no hope of one's affection ever being returned. At this moment, no doubt, the thought came unbidden, Peter and Beryl were happily arranging the details of their approaching wedding, while she....

All at once her mood of despair faded and a desperate recklessness took over. Why not consider Lewis's offer? What did she have to lose? All that she had left now, all she would ever have, were the children. If she could make life more bearable for these unfortunate ones, wouldn't that be something worthwhile? By joining her life with Lewis she would be in a position to help them all, and especially one small motherless girl whose smile tugged at her heart. In her mind a child's voice echoed with wistful longing, "I wish *you* were my mother."

The thoughts went rushing wildly through her mind, and she nibbled a long strand of hair in indecision. It wasn't as if she didn't like him—as a person, that was. And there wasn't the slightest question of his deep affection for her. So why not make him happy, too, as well as the children? The only one who wouldn't share in the general felicity, she mused with bitter anguish, was Liz Kennedy herself. But wasn't that all her own fault? Falling in love with a man to whom she meant nothing, a man who had been in love with another girl long before she had ever met him. Because he'd smiled at her, teased her, she loved him without rhyme or reason or hope or anything else. But love, it seemed, wasn't enough. It happened and there was nothing you could do about it. Or was there?

All at once everything became plain—too plain. Either she went on living here, watching Peter and Beryl enjoying their new life together, or she made Lewis happy, and with him widened the scope of her chosen work somewhere else. Why not prove to Peter that even if he regarded her as merely a girl with an unusual goal, someone else cared enough for Liz Kennedy to ask her to marry him? Yes, that would show him! If only she could feel some pleasure in the prospect, in place of this frozen feeling of detachment. On a note of recklessness she heard herself say, "Maybe I'll think about it, one of these days!"

"You will? Liz, my darling, that's the best news I've had in all my life! But why wait? Tell me now!" He was so incredulously delighted that she knew a moment of misgiving.

"I've got to think it over. Give me a little time." Wildly she searched her mind for a reasonable excuse. "I'm putting on a Christmas party for the children next week and I'll be awfully tied up for a while, but after that...."

"I'll be waiting on the doorstep, and the moment you're finished with the kids...." He caught her close, and once again his kiss registered exactly nothing with her. Was it because of Peter—but she mustn't think of him. She realized Lewis was gazing down at her, an unreadable expression in his voice. "You'll feel differently about me one of these days!"

So her lack of response hadn't gone unnoticed. What if he guessed the truth? The thought made her say hastily, "You're quite sure about me?"

"Never been so sure of anything! We'll have so much to talk about...plans and arrangements—" He broke off, said pleadingly, "You will make it 'yes'?" He carried her fingers to his lips. "Can't you just see Julie's face light up when she hears this news!"

"No!" Alarm sharpened her tone. "Please, Lewis," she begged, "don't say anything about us. There's nothing to tell...yet."

"Okay, then." His indulgent smile was the nearest thing to a caress. "If you say so, but just until I bring the ring down next week. That sounds a bit off, I know, darling—not giving you a chance to choose it yourself—but it happens to be a family tradition in our family that the bride-to-be wears the heirloom ring. It was my mother's."

"And Edith's, I expect." She was scarcely aware of what she was saying, but the next moment she realized that Lewis had taken her idle remark as a jealous reference to his first wife.

"It's up to you, Liz," he said eagerly. "I'll bring it out after the Christmas do, and you can see what you think of it. Actually it's rather a lovely thing, a big emerald square surrounded by diamonds. But if you don't care for it you don't need to have it. Just say the word, and we'll take off into town and you can choose something you like better."

"I'd like it, of course I would, if I—" She stopped short, for how to explain that she had so little interest in the matter that one precious stone was as good as another.

"It's going to be a long week," Lewis was saying softly.

"It'll soon go."

"Worth it if you give me the answer I want."

He seemed not to notice her silence. "We'll have to make some plans for a house. I'll get an architect to draw up some designs, and you can see what you think of them."

"A house?" she echoed bewilderedly.

"Why not? We could build right here by the riding school if that's what you'd like. I could run into town to the office every day from here."

"All that way? It would mean changing your whole way of life."

He kissed her fingers. "That's what I'm hoping for, my sweet. If I had you do you think I'd care about anything but this...?" Once again she felt his swift caress as his mouth came down on her cold unresponsive lips.

When they got back to the cottage it was late and Evelyn and Stan had long since gone to bed. But Lewis, in his present mood of elation, seemed reluctant to leave. His arm was thrown around her shoulders. "With a bit of luck, soon there won't be any more goodbyes for us."

"No."

Tenderly he put his hands on each side of her face. "You know something? It's just about time someone started taking care of you. Lately you've been looking...I don't know...different from when you first came here. Sort of wan-looking. You're running yourself ragged over this project of yours!"

She laughed away his concern. "Don't be silly! I told you before, I love it."

"Don't waste it all on the kids!"

She watched him get into the car, waving as he drove away, knowing all the time that the moment he disappeared into the night he would have passed from her mind. If only she could feel the same way about Peter! All at once she wondered if she were being fair to herself or Lewis in considering this marriage. But there was still a little time left. The children's Christmas party was a whole week away, and in that time anything could happen. Perhaps even...one more miracle!

Peter's vibrant tones echoed in her mind. "Twenty-seven miracles! Isn't that rather a lot to ask of fate?" Yet here she was, praying for one more, the most impossible one of all, and with a time limit at that! She stumbled blindly to her room and fell into bed. But hour after hour sleep eluded her as the thoughts milled endlessly through her brain. Maybe if she and Lewis went away, if they moved the riding center to another part of the country, somewhere where there would be no danger of her running into Peter, she would be able to forget, to start afresh. But a wave of longing washed over her, and she knew she couldn't tear herself away, not while he remained here. *Peter, Peter, you're in my blood, part of me, and somehow... somehow I've got to stop loving you!*

CHAPTER NINE

IT SEEMED TO LIZ now that time was rushing inexorably by. So short a time before Lewis would be here for his answer. She *must* make up her mind. A dozen times a day she told herself that the marriage would work out, of course it would. If only she could rid herself of this feeling of a cage door about to close, shutting her away from life, from happiness, from Peter, forever. Putting aside her own problems, she tried to concentrate on the party she planned to give the children at the close of the next riding lesson, the last one before the intervention of the long summer school holidays. It wasn't the children's fault that she was in no mood for festivities. And they well deserved a treat, for each one had progressed even beyond her hopes. Julie and Taiere were now able to ride without the aid of helpers, and in common with other small riders, had learned to rise to the trot. In the next term they would be taught to play mounted games such as bending around poles, lifting a cap off each and dropping it back in a can. They would enjoy their games on horseback in the New Year.

New Year.... As had happened so often during the past few days she fell into a daydream, telling herself that Lewis was kind and intelligent, and dependable. He had a personal interest in the riding center as well—and besides all that there was Julie. Who could help falling a willing victim to that gay laughing little face, the bright smile that made one forget her disability, the wheelchair waiting by the railing? Oh, yes, she and Lewis certainly had a lot in common. Unconsciously she sighed. If only there were love too—or was it all an illusion as he had said? If only she could persuade herself that her deep involvement with Peter didn't matter. But in her heart she knew it did matter—terribly. Even after not seeing him since their day in the pine plantations, in the face of having as good as told him that she never wished to set eyes on him again, still she found herself waiting and hoping for some word from him. But, of course, nothing could be more unlikely. Whatever there had been between them—and looking back there really hadn't been much to remember—it was over. It was high time she stopped herself from jumping each time the telephone pealed. Anyway—she made an effort to will away the dreary thoughts—just because she was desolate and unhappy, was that any reason why she shouldn't do her utmost to give the children an end-of-the-year celebration?

On hearing of the Christmas party, Evelyn was enthusiastic and Stan offered his help. To prove his point he disappeared soon after breakfast, returning later and carrying in his arms a fresh young pine tree. He arranged it in a corner of the barn, where its spicy aromatic tang filled the air.

Malcolm, strolling in at that moment, recollected that there were boxes of yuletide decorations stowed away in the attic of his home. Evelyn produced a length of plastic tablecloth patterned in a gay design of reindeer and Christmas angels.

Swiftly Liz's mind was running ahead, planning the program of festivities. One thing was for sure. There must be a gift for each child among the parcels heaped beneath the Christmas tree. But where to purchase the presents? She remembered the small township to which Peter had taken her on the day of the horse sale. How long ago it all seemed now, and how happy she'd been. Would she ever again know that wild happiness that had throbbed tthrough her that day? *Don't think, don't remember. Concentrate on the township.* There had been a general store, but the choice there would be strictly limited, and these partygoers wouldn't be ordinary children. For her small riders she wanted gifts that would be treasured, appreciated, special. She had a swift mental picture of Taiere, the small Maori boy with the outsize grin. A wide cowboy sombrero, a silver metal holster to wear at his belt, would enable him to feel more than ever a rider of the Wild West such as he envisaged himself to be while high in the saddle. A small price to pay for a child's world of enjoyment!

And Julie... darling, mischievous, heart-catching Julie, who had once said with all the candor and truth and longing of a six-year-old, "I wish *you* were my mother!" On a sigh she reflected, *I might even be able to hand you that particular wish, little one, and as an extra, how would you settle for a thin gold chain with a locket engraved in the shape of a pony?* Or maybe a tiny silver locket containing a snapshot of her beloved Pinocchio?

And how about Danny, whose courage brought a mist to her eyes? Maybe a book on the training and care of ponies would please him. Thoughts of the children dispelled for a time her own sense of desolation and heartache. In the end she decided to write to Helen, who for all her maddening habit of handing out unasked-for advice, had a soft heart where children were concerned—and an eye for a bargain! In the modern city stores she would be able to find the right gifts. Perched on a corner of the desk in the barn, Liz picked up pad and ball-point and scribbled a note to her sister, telling her of her plans for a children's Christmas party and enclosing a list of suggested purchases. In addition Liz would be glad of party favors, novelties, tinsel streamers. The important thing was for the parcel to arrive at Rangiwahia by the end of the week. Helen, practical minded and thrifty, could be depended upon to get good value for the limited amount of money Liz had to spare, and she knew she could depend on her sister to have the parcel sent in good time.

Sure enough the huge box arrived by mail van with a day to spare, and Evelyn and Liz lifted it onto the kitchen table and drew out the contents.

It was at once evident that Helen had performed her commission faithfully. She had even included odd decorations from her own store of Christmas novelties together with sheets of sparkling colored cellophane wrapping paper and name cards. As to the gifts for the children.... "You have to hand it to Helen," Liz murmured to Evelyn, "she's a wizard when it comes to shopping! Just look at this!" She snapped open a small silver locket suspended from a slender chain. "I can put Pinocchio's picture in here. I'll cut it out from one of the snapshots Lewis gave me and fit it in for her."

Evelyn, busily counting Christmas crackers included in the parcel, nodded. "It'll be the first time in his life that old pony's been in on such a fuss! But I guess Julie would rather have a picture of him than anything else you could give her."

Liz thought she couldn't have chosen better had she herself been able to purchase the gifts. Taiere's cowboy sombrero was even wider and more dashing than she had anticipated. The holster was complete with a gleaming sharp-shooter. There was even a sparkling sheriff's badge included in the outfit.

For the girls there was an exciting assortment, varying from books featuring stories of ponies and their care to boxes of handkerchiefs printed with riding motifs and scarves stamped with pony designs. For the boys there were tooled leather belts, cowboy shirts, pistols and rifles. Helen had even baked a Christmas cake and sent it along with the other articles. Rich and dark, it was complete with snowy icing and decorated with sprigs of artificial holly. Suddenly Liz glanced up. "Heavens, we've forgotten something, party hats!"

"Not to worry," Evelyn said in her calm tones. "I've got swags of crepe paper put away. I'll run them up on the sewing machine in no time!"

But she did much more than that. Soon the big refrigerator was packed with jellies, attractive desserts and fruit drinks, while the tins in the dresser were filled with small iced cakes and miniature meat pies. Stan picked the first strawberries from his garden to serve with Evelyn's home-made ice cream.

That evening Liz decorated the tree, and soon it glittered with tinsel balls and colored streamers. Malcolm brought long branches of greenery and arranged them around the walls. He blew up balloons and anchored the clusters of floating spheres high on the rafters. Afterward they all helped to parcel up the gifts and arrange them around the base of the small pine.

The next morning everything was in readiness. Liz planned to give only a short riding lesson today, just down the slope and over the back paddock. Then, instead of being loaded back into ambulances on their return, the children would be taken in wheelchairs to the barn.

Following the ambulances came Lewis's car. Liz could see Julie waving from the window. Smilingly Liz waved back. Then her gaze slid to Lewis, and unconsciously she sighed. He looked so happy, so hopeful, and still she couldn't bring herself to make a decision.

At that moment a party of medical experts approached her, and she recognized among the group the lined kindly face of a specialist well-known in his own country and overseas for his achievements in the treatment of children's diseases. Introductions were made, then the great man took Liz's brown hand in a friendly clasp. "Could I have a word with you later, Miss Kennedy, when you're free?"

"Of course," she promised, and moved toward the wheelchairs being assembled at the side of the railing, where the ponies that Malcolm had already saddled stood waiting.

Immediately she was conscious of a babel of happy voices, and before long she was setting off across the paddock with the others, leading a small shaggy pony while Danny held the reins. There had been times during the past few weeks when she had despaired of his ever breaking through the barrier of fear that had grown with him through the years. Yet today for the first time he was riding without the aid of helpers on either side. He really was making astonishing progress.

"Looking forward to the party, Danny?" She smiled up over her shoulder toward the thin figure in the saddle.

He nodded. "I've been marking the days off on my calendar, and do you know what, Miss Kennedy?" The hesitant tones had taken on a new note of confidence. "I've got a surprise for you!"

Liz led the pony toward a group of riders ahead, some of whom were urging their mounts into a trot. "Good for you! What is it, Danny? A Christmas gift?"

"Sort of." The sweetness of his smile never failed to give Liz a pang. "I think you'll like it."

"I'm sure I will." She was reflecting that a month ago he would never have chatted away in this fashion. He would have been far too tense and nervous to think of anything else.

As always on lesson days, the time flew by on wings. Liz had forgotten the important visitor who wished to interview her until, as the second section of children were returned to their wheelchairs and Malcolm began to lead the ponies away, the distinguished man approached her.

"Congratulations, Miss Kennedy! I've been watching the children riding their ponies, and to my mind—" the gentle lined face broke into a smile "—your center presents a perfect example of what can be achieved with this particular form of outdoor exercise. Before coming here today I spent some time in going over the medical records of these children, and it's noticeable that in every case there's been a distinct improvement, physically from the exercise and psychologically from the feeling of achievement that riding gives them. In my book—" to Liz the warmly appreciative glance was akin to being handed a bouquet of fragrant roses "—you deserve a vote of thanks from us all for what you've done in helping these handicapped children."

"I'm glad if what I've done helps a little." She felt a trifle overawed at the compliments of this brilliant man, whose work in the treatment of cerebral palsy had brought him fame all over the world.

"A little! Believe me, Miss Kennedy, your riding exercise for cases like these is more in the nature of a breakthrough! You know what we're up against in the treatment of spastic diplegia? The typical spastic scissor gait, the difficulty in getting the legs apart that often reacts violently to any effort to make the muscles respond? The boy Danny is an example—nervous strain, tense muscles. As far as mobility goes, his improvement from now on is practically a certainty—thanks to your help. You must feel very gratified, Miss Kennedy, at the success of all this!" He waved a hand toward the scene of happy activity where children and animals mingled in an atmosphere of gaiety and relaxation.

"Thank you, but it's really just a beginning. You see...." She hesitated. It seemed presumptuous of her to rave on about her wider vision to this eminent visitor.

"Yes, Miss Kennedy?" The lined intelligent face was bent attentively toward her.

"I thought, in the future, if everything goes along well, maybe the center could be improved a lot. One thing I'd like to do would be to have a covered riding area made where the lessons could be taken even in bad weather."

"An excellent suggestion."

Encouraged by his interest, she hurried on. "This is just a long-term project, but I've always hoped that some day when the center is firmly established, wouldn't it be fabulous if it could be extended to include lots of other types of disabled? Deaf, blind, all sorts—a national center for the disabled. Of course," she finished breathlessly, "it's all just an idea."

"Why not?" The great man appeared to share her enthusiasm. "It's been done before in England, so why not here? You've made great progress already, Miss Kennedy. I want to thank you. Don't ever forget that we in the medical profession are with you all the way."

The glow of gratification lasted all the while a group of medical experts joined their distinguished colleague in congratulating Liz on her work with the handicapped, and for a short while afterward. But as the medical team strolled away the momentary excitement went, too. It seemed that even the satisfaction of making a dream come true wasn't enough. It failed to ease the pain in her heart or to fill the sense of incompleteness that had been with her ever since she had learned the truth concerning Peter... and Beryl. She had come a long way toward achievement of a life's ambition, but on another level— If only Peter could have been here with her today. In spite of everything, you would think he would come to see her at Christmastime, if only to wish her well. With a sigh she turned away and moved toward the cottage.

To give a more festive air to the occasion and to make the small guests feel more "Christmassy," she changed into a long frock. The soft sea-island cotton with its high bodice and full long sleeves fell softly around her ankles, lending her a deceptive air of fragility.

When she reached the barn the children were already settled on the long forms beside the table, and Malcolm, seated at the old piano, was banging out "Silent Night" on the yellowed keys. Excited shouts filled the air. "Look, there's a Christmas tree!"

"I know—I can see my name on a parcel!"

"So can I!"

"Where's mine?" The children were unfolding crepe paper hats, pulling them over their heads with comical effects as Liz pushed her way through the throng of helpers, a huge plate of potato chips in her hand.

"Wait!" The quietly authoritative tones of a woman therapist cut across the rising buzz of voices, gaining instant attention. "No one's to start yet. There's someone who isn't here. Can you guess who it is?"

"It's Danny! Where's Danny?" Childish voices rose in chorus.

"Here I am, Miss Kennedy!" The high tremulous tones came from the doorway, and Liz felt a lump in her throat. Danny, on crutches! He was moving over the floor toward her, slowly, carefully—but moving! Could this be the boy whose only way of moving had been to slither around the floor like a fish, and who for so long had resisted all efforts to help him achieve some degree of mobility? Liz didn't know whether to laugh or cry, then found she was doing both at once. In the silence, as Danny tap-tapped his way slowly and painstakingly toward the table, Liz hoped and prayed that he would come to no mishap. At last he reached the long form, and eager hands took the crutches from him, helped him to his seat. Liz let out her breath on a sigh of relief.

"That's marvelous, Danny!" She flew to him, hugged him tight. "That was the best surprise I ever had! You did it, Danny! You really learned to use crutches!"

Suddenly overcome by so much attention, he hung his head, but Liz had caught the expression of pleasure and pride in the pale eyes. "Oh, Danny, I'm so proud of you!"

At that moment Malcolm broke into the rhythm of Christmas carols, and the children, appetites sharpened after their ride, needed no encouragement to eat with enjoyment and gusto. At last, when most of the plates on the table were emptied, Liz heard the pop of a champagne cork, and looking up, realized that Lewis was pouring the sparkling liquid into chipped cups, for they had run out of glasses. He handed them around until medical officers, therapists, drivers and helpers each held a cup. "To Liz and her riding school! May she have many more successes!"

"To Liz!"

Across the room her glance met his look of pride, and something warmer, for his eyes signaled a secret message. Her glance slid away. At this moment only one name filled her thoughts. If only Peter were here to share it all with her! Time enough when the children had gone to force her reluctant thoughts back to Lewis, and the answer to his proposal that she *must* give him today. The rousing strains of "For She's a Jolly Good Fellow" cut across her thoughts, and she realized that all eyes were turned in her direction. Laughingly she disclaimed the applause. "Not just me, you know! Everyone else was in it, too. Don't forget all the helpers, the therapists, the medical people—and of course, the ambulance drivers. You've all been wonderful—" smilingly her gaze moved toward Malcolm "—and that goes for the pianist, too!"

Soon she was helping to push wheelchairs toward the Christmas tree, watching as, with shrieks of delight, the children opened up their gifts.

Suddenly, above the din rose a child's scream. "Look, everybody! It's Father Christmas!"

"Jingle Bells! Jingle Bells!" thundered Malcolm from his seat at the piano. Liz, gazing in astonishment, recognized Wayne and Tim. Wearing paper party hats pulled over suntanned faces and lustily blowing tin whistles, they were running across the room pulling behind them a sled, wherein sat a smiling, red-cloaked Santa Claus. The sled paused beside Liz, and she found herself meeting hazel eyes with a familiar glint.

"It's *you*!" she whispered.

"It's me, all right, and it's damned hot behind these whiskers," came a sibilant whisper from the bearded face. "Don't blame me for all this...." He threw a glance toward the bulging sack behind him. "We got wind on the grapevine of your show today, and Beryl wanted to help, so.... I'll tell you this much," came the low mutter from lips almost hidden by the flowing white beard, "I wouldn't have done it for any other girl!" He meant Beryl, of course. His tone rose to a jovial shout. "Right, kids!" Stepping from the sled, Peter moved among the cluster of wheelchairs, handing each child a gift taken from the giant sack. "Boy, girl...boy, girl..." Riotous cheers and calls all but drowned his voice. But what expensive gifts, Liz thought, taking in the china tea sets, huge lifelike dolls and battery-driven toys, which the children were taking from professionally wrapped parcels. They must have cost the earth. All at once the carefully selected gifts that had been heaped beneath the sturdy little pine seemed awfully cheap and ordinary.

"Look!" As all eyes turned toward the open doorway Liz glanced at the resplendent fairylike figure standing poised in the opening. Even without the golden curls of a blond wig, she would have recognized those palest of blue eyes.

"Meet the Puppet Girl," the red-cloaked figure was saying. "She's come along here today to entertain you—show you what her animal puppets can do!"

Liz was forced to admit that the other girl manipulated the puppets with amazing dexterity, and the childishly high tones added to the illusion. She remembered hearing that when Beryl had lived in the district previously she had taken the lead in amateur theatricals that had been held in the nearest township. But why must she come and take the lead *here*, Liz thought uncharitably, for in some indefinable way the other woman appeared to have taken over, usurping Liz's place at the celebration, spoiling the children's pleasure in their simple gifts.

At length, amid thunderous applause, Beryl completed the show and returned the glove puppets to their box. "And now—surprise! Surprise!" From a carton she lifted a great three-tiered Christmas cake, intricately iced, and set it on the table.

As Liz caught the "Ohs" and "Ahs" of delight, she told herself she should be glad her small guests were so pleased. She would be too, if only the great iced confection hadn't the effect of making Helen's homemade cake look so small, almost pathetic. Oh, damn, what was the matter with her that she was allowing Beryl's well-meant efforts to get under her skin? In her heart she knew that had the donor been anyone else but Beryl she wouldn't feel this bitter resentment.

There was no time for personal feelings, however, for voices were crying impatiently, "When are you going to cut the cake, the *big* cake?"

"Shall I?" Nothing could be more sweetly deferring than Beryl's honeyed tones as she stood at the table, knife poised.

"Go ahead." Liz was feeling cross and mean, and hating herself for it.

"Wait! Wait!" shrilled Julie's high piercing tones. "Don't forget the mistletoe!"

"Where? Where?" The children peered upward.

"There! Up high, on the middle rafter. I threw it up there among the tree branches, and that means you have to kiss someone underneath it, Miss Kennedy!"

"Hear, hear!" called the ambulance drivers.

Liz was aware of Lewis, hurrying across the room toward her. But before he could reach her side his way was blocked by a tall figure. Peter was standing facing her. He had shed his crimson robes, and the way he was looking at her....

"A kiss under the mistletoe, Miss Kennedy!" The chorus of childish voices blurred, and she was aware of nothing but his dark and brilliant gaze.

"You heard?" Before she could make her escape he had caught her close. Then his arms tightened around her and she felt his lips on hers. Pulses leaping, she was seized by a trembling excitement, and for all she knew to the contrary Malcolm's honky-tonk tune could have been the singing of a thousand violins. A moment, a minute—she had no idea of how long she stayed in his embrace before he gently released her. She was aware only of ecstasy and longing and anguish.

A peal of childish laughter splintered the moment to fragments. "It wasn't *really* mistletoe!" Julie's high tones shrilled above the babel of voices. "It was just old pohutukawa from the tree outside tied with one of my old red hair ribbons, but daddy said it would do!"

In the ensuing burst of good-natured merriment she was aware of Peter's intent glance. "Too late." She never could guess what he was thinking. Her cheeks were burning while he appeared as cool and collected as ever. Why not? Just a Christmas kiss. If only he hadn't noticed her wild response to his nearness, he would put down her heightened color to the heat of the crowded room.

Breathlessly she turned away, to surprise an angry gleam in Beryl's pale eyes. The momentary expression was gone in a flash, and now the lovely face was smiling. "My goodness! I can see I'll have to keep an eye on you, Peter, from now on!"

Vaguely Liz was aware that Malcolm's touch had faltered on the piano keys, and like everyone else in the room he was watching her.

"Don't worry," said Liz, and bit back the words that trembled on her lips. "You've nothing to fear from me." All at once a wave of angry frustration swept her, and the hot tears stung her eyelids. Why should Beryl have everything? Why did Peter mock her with his lovemaking, which to him meant nothing but a moment's amusement, a funthing?

"Too bad I missed out!" In her blind misery she was scarcely aware of Lewis, or of the deep disappointment in his gray eyes. It seemed that he was fated to be always at hand when she needed him, ready to pick up the pieces!

Automatically she began to catch the balloons that Malcolm had released from the ceiling beams, and which were now drifting down to the floor. She handed them to the children to take back to town with them, but all the time she was aware of Peter. He was standing at Beryl's side, her golden curls brushing his shoulder, and they were laughing together at some shared secret joke. Well, let them laugh! She didn't care! A bitter recklessness surged through her. She didn't care about anything! Let Beryl smile her cruel smile; Peter play his meaningless game of love! She would make a life of her own in spite of them! They'd be a family, she and Lewis, she thought wildly. Funny to think of being

The Frost and the Fire

a family all at once. She was trying desperately to convince herself, arguing away the flicker of doubt that she didn't want to acknowledge, not with Peter's kiss still burning on her lips.

"Looks like it's all over." Lewis's tone was low and intimate. Together they watched as children, each clutching a paper hat, a balloon and various gifts, were wheeled away. He caught her fingers in a swift and urgent pressure. "Liz, you haven't forgotten...."

"Later." At that moment, to her relief, she found herself surrounded by groups of children and adults, all calling farewells and extending thanks for the end-of-term celebration.

Tim and Wayne, the two station hands from Arundel, thrust out work-grained hands. "Great to see you again, Liz!" Both suntanned faces were grinning engagingly.

"Almost worth yanking the boss around the place in that flipping sled," Wayne put in.

"We'll see you in the New Year!"

They moved aside, and she found herself looking directly into Beryl's smiling features. Liz heard herself murmuring the conventional phrases. "Thanks for your help. The children enjoyed the puppet show." She scarcely listened to Beryl's words. What was she saying? Something concerning Darryl.

"Thought he might have arrived here by now. He said something about coming over for a ride after the party. Something must have come up and made him change his mind."

If only she'd go, Liz thought. She felt she never wanted to see Beryl again.

At length everyone appeared to have departed, the private cars forming a long line behind the two ambulances that were moving up the winding road. Now only one vehicle remained on the grass—Peter's long gray car. In spite of herself her heart plunged as he came toward her.

"That was a great show you put on today, and did those kids enjoy it!"

"Thanks for coming," she whispered, "and for being such a good Father Christmas."

"It was darned hot, that outfit, but I guess it was worth it to see the look on those kids' faces when we made the big entrance scene."

Not as pleased as I was to see you, Peter, but you'll never know about that. Aloud she heard herself say in a cool, polite, uncaring tone, "Was it...your idea?"

He nodded, his eyes never leaving her face. "I found the fancy-dress outfit and the white whiskers in one of the rooms at the house. The boys knocked the sled together, shoved a coat of red paint on it and we were in business. When can I see you again, Liz?"

She hesitated. How easy it would be to fall into the old trap! "I don't know," she murmured vaguely. "Sometime."

"What's wrong with tonight?"

"No, sorry. Lewis is coming over."

The gaiety died out of his face in an instant, leaving the hazel eyes as cold as river pebbles. The look he slanted her was cutting. "I get it. Well, so long, Liz. Be seeing you."

But he wouldn't, she thought. It was the last time he would ever ask her out. From now on there would always be Lewis... and Beryl.

"Bye." She turned away before he could glimpse the bleakness that must surely show in her face, for all her efforts to hide her anguish.

He didn't glance back. Why should he? She watched him sea himself in the car, the pain in her heart like a knife. At first the barking of the dogs failed to register in her mind. Then she realized that the wild clamor must mean something was wrong. The next moment she caught the sound of galloping hooves on the road approaching the cottage, and even as she glanced toward the entrance a riderless horse swerved in at the opening, swept past the car in the driveway and came to an abrupt halt at her side.

"Red!" He was flecked with foam and wet with sea water. A broken bridle trailed in the dust. She glanced up to meet Peter's inquiring look. His voice was sharp. "Did you know someone had him out today?"

"No, but...."

"Are you thinking what I'm thinking? Young Darryl...."

"Peter! You don't think he could...." Her eyes widened as the frightening supposition flashed into her mind.

"Don't worry. He's probably bailed out on the way home! Come on, jump into the car!" She sensed the urgency in his tone. "We'll go take a look and see if we can pick him up."

She paused only to call over her shoulder to Stan, who had strolled into sight at that moment and was staring in surprise at the horse's wet coat. "Someone had him out. We think it may have been Darryl. Will you give Beryl a ring? Tell her we'll bring him back as soon as we find him." Even as she spoke the vehicle was leaping ahead and in a moment had swung onto the main highway. A swift glance along the ferny verges of the road showed no sign of anyone lying there, nor was there any sign of life along the lonely, bush-fringed road ahead.

"We'll take a look down at the beach!" Peter told her. They were traveling at high speed, and Liz knew that the same terrifying possibility filled both their minds. If the boy had been tossed into the wild surf below....

"At least he can swim," she voiced her thoughts. "He always wanted to take Red down into the tide, and Beryl told me today that she was expecting him to come over this afternoon for a ride. He must have taken a chance on helping himself to Red when we were all busy down in the barn with the party."

"He's taken a bigger chance than that if he's out in the surf today." Peter's tone was grim. "I put a broadcast over the air this morning to swimmers, warning them of danger. A heck of a lot of deep holes appeared during the night, and now with this strong rip.... He couldn't have chosen a worse time for his dip!"

They lurched into a winding overgrown track leading down the cliff to the beach below. Tree-branches scraped the car roof as they swept on beneath overhanging tea-tree, and stones flew up from the undercarriage. At last they jolted down onto black sand, and leaping from the car Peter scanned the tossing sea.

"There he is!"

Peering over his shoulder, Liz could at first see only a

turbulent sea. Then in a trough in the waves she glimpsed a fair head. She caught her breath. "He's an awfully long way out."

"Come on!" They were in the car and speeding over the sand in the direction of the clubhouse. Even before they reached the small building perched on the rocks they caught the chop-chop of a helicopter overhead.

As Peter ran toward the building a bronzed young man appeared on the lookout platform. "It's all right! We've phoned for a chopper. Here he comes now."

"Right! I'll go up with him!" Already Peter was peeling off outer garments, and as the machine swooped low on the sand he swung himself aboard.

"How long is it since you noticed Darryl out there?" Liz spoke to the young lifesaver without taking her eyes from the machine that was moving so swiftly toward the bobbing head out among the waves.

"Darryl? Is that who it is? I saw a hand raised in the signal for help about ten minutes ago." The gaze of the man was fixed too, on the hovering machine. "But he wasn't so far out at sea then. I could see right away that it was going to be a tough rescue. The rip would carry him out in no time, so I rang right away for the copter."

"He took one of my horses and went into the surf."

"Is that what he was up to? I didn't see the horse. It must have taken off for home by then, but I can make a good guess at what happened. The horse must have stumbled into one of the deep holes in the sand and tossed him off. After that, with the tide against him and this dangerous rip, he'd be lucky if he ever made the shore again! Now it's up to Peter, and he'll soon have him aboard the copter. There he goes! He's put in a lot of practice this season jumping into the sea from one of those!"

Liz didn't answer. She was holding her breath as a figure dropped down, down into the tossing waves beneath. It seemed to her an age before rescuer and rescued, clinging to a lifeline beneath the machine, were dragged from the sea.

Then the copter was heading toward the beach, and only then did she realize that others had come, too, to wait beside her on the sand. Beryl, still wearing her wig of golden curls, was clinging to Sandy's arm, and near at hand stood Evelyn and Stan. It was a silent group. All were eyeing the machine now dropping down to the beach. As it touched the sand Sandy hurried forward, and soon he was carrying Darryl toward the waiting car.

"How is he, Peter?" Liz had never seen Beryl like this, ashen faced, white lipped. "Will he...."

"He'll be okay. He's under the weather a bit at the moment from shock and exposure, but a day or two's rest will soon fix that."

"You're all right, Darryl!" She burst into tears and ran to fling her arms around the boy.

"Aw, mum, I'm okay," he mumbled. "If old Red hadn't gone into a hole...."

"Take him home," Peter said. "A hot drink is what he needs right now. Some dry clothes. Keep him warm; make him rest."

"Oh, I will! I will!" Beryl turned to Sandy, and Liz caught the tremulous tones. "Will you drive, please, Sandy? I don't feel up to it today." Release from tension appeared to have rendered the other woman vulnerable to emotion, for she was laughing and crying as she clung to Sandy's arm. "Darling, darling, you were right all the time!" Darling.... Liz could scarcely believe her ears. "I knew you were, but I just wouldn't let myself come right out and admit it. He *does* need a firm hand! He needs you, Sandy, and so do I!" The tears ran unchecked down her cheeks. "You know what it is I'm trying to say, don't you?"

"I know, honey." His deep tones conveyed an intimacy that Liz failed to understand.

He had tucked a rug around the boy lying on the back seat of the car and now he climbed in behind the steering wheel. But still Beryl's high tones ran on. She seemed determined to make everything clear between them, regardless of who overheard her confidences. "It's going to be all different from now on." The words spilled from her trembling lips as she seated herself beside Sandy. "No more pretending I'm crazy about Peter and he about me just to try to make you feel jealous! He knows as well as I do that all that was finished years ago! From now on it's you, Sandy. You're the boss!"

"Let's go home, honey." Sandy laid a hand on her fingers for a moment, then started the engine. As the car moved up the cliff path it was followed by Evelyn and Stan in their battered Holden. When the copter had taken off again, Peter said to Liz, "Wait for me, will you, while I change in the clubhouse?" He was back in a few minutes, wearing a dry shirt and shorts, his thick dark hair curling wetly against the back of his neck. There wasn't anyone to compare with him, Liz was thinking, not in all the world! Not for her anyway! Yet she still couldn't really believe....

"I'll see you home," he was saying.

"But aren't you going up to the house... with them?"

He tossed back damp hair. "Good grief, no! They don't want me around, especially just now! Didn't you hear what Beryl was telling Sandy?"

A wild hope sang in her heart, and she could scarcely catch his words for the excitement that was surging through her.

"It mightn't be a bad thing at that, young Darryl getting himself half-drowned. Might teach him a lesson that he can't go throwing his weight around all the time and get away with it! It just needed something like this to fix things for those two! Beryl and Sandy will be great for each other, but I guess it took a real shock to make her see reason, get her to finally make up her mind."

"About what?"

"Teaming up with Sandy, of course. What else?" It was his turn to look mystified. "I got the idea that you'd caught on to that ages ago."

"No...."

"Every time Sandy tried to use a bit of discipline with Darryl, Beryl flew into a state and all the marriage plans were off. I should know! Only the other day I got an urgent message to rush over to her place. Big decision. Would I act as best man at the wedding? Next week they were arguing over Darryl again, and everything was back to square one. He just couldn't get it through to Beryl that she was making the mistake of her life in giving in to the boy on every count. The kid needs a father, and a strong one at that. That's what she was getting at just now when she told Sandy that he'd been on the right track all along. So it's happy endings for them, thanks to a near accident."

Liz continued to stare up at him, amazement and an almost unbelievable happiness surging through her. Vaguely she was aware that everyone, even the bronzed young lifesaver, had gone. The long black stretch of sand was left to the wheeling gulls, and there was only Peter, regarding her with a sudden bleak expression in his hazel eyes. "You... and Lewis—"

"But I thought—" being Liz she had to blurt out the thoughts that were clamoring in her mind "—that you and Beryl... that it was *you*—"

He gripped her arm so fiercely that she could feel the pain, or would have had she not been so filled with a soaring excitement that she was unaware of anything else.

"Tell me, Liz—" his voice was ragged with emotion, so low she was forced to strain to catch the words "—would it have made any difference, if you'd known? They tell me that you and Lewis are getting engaged any day...."

"Not now! Not ever!"

"*What!* He was the Peter she had known at first, alive, vibrant, hers! "I love you so much...." She didn't hear any more because her senses were drowned in his kiss.

Lost in the intoxication of the moment, neither was aware of the car that had drawn to a stop on the path directly above them. Nor did they notice a grim-faced man who stood silently observing them from the cliff. Only for a moment, then sunlight caught the flash of jewels as the ring he had held in his hands went hurtling through the shimmering air to vanish in a trough in the waves among the blue depths below. Turning on his heel, Lewis got back into his car and drove away.

But Liz heard only Peter's deep tones. "You couldn't marry anyone else, Liz. You belonged to me from the first moment we met, and you know it!"

She murmured from the ineffable comfort of his arms. "A drowned rat...."

"An adorable drowned rat! But I'm not going to take any

chances of letting you go out of my life again, ever. Marry me, Liz. Stay here with me!"

She stirred in his embrace, smiling up into his eyes. "You have to take the kids, too, and the horses, and probably Evelyn and Stan as well."

"What of it? The kids are your department, sweet." Lightly he caressed her dark hair. "With a little help from me, of course." He kissed her again. "You can come over the hills from Arundel any old time to see how things are running. Stan and Evelyn can keep an eye on the place when you're not there. It'll work out. You'll see!"

She sighed contentedly. "Wonderful! I couldn't give up the riding center—not now. But to have someone to share it with, someone who understands. You know, Mr. X. won't ever know that he's not the most important man in my life anymore."

"Don't bet on it!"

As she caught his teasing grin a number of puzzling matters suddenly sorted themselves out and clicked neatly into place. Drawing herself free, she stared up at him accusingly. "It was *you* all the time."

"Do you mind?" His low exultant laugh as once again he sought her lips put everything else from her mind. A little later she gazed into his glinting eyes. "I might have known! So that was why the checks always came through a solicitor, and I never got a personal letter back in reply to my thank-you notes. I didn't ever think," she marveled, "that you were all that interested."

"I was always interested." His tone was deep and soft and infinitely caressing. "It was all part of the girl I love."

Love. Liz's heart was a wild tumult of emotion. It was coming home after a long, long time. It was setting out on the biggest adventure of all—but not alone, not alone ever again. Always they'd be together, she and Peter!